THE ADVENTURES OF

FAIDIT AND CERCAMON

ARTHUR GILCHRIST BRODEUR

THE ADVENTURES OF
FAIDIT AND CERCAMON

ARTHUR GILCHRIST BRODEUR

INTRODUCTION BY
SAI SHANKAR

ALTUS PRESS • 2014

EDITED AND DESIGNED BY
Matthew Moring

PUBLISHING HISTORY
"Introduction" copyright 2014 by Sai Shankar.
"Fisherman's Luck" originally appeared in the November 10, 1921 issue of *Adventure* magazine.
"Before Midnight" originally appeared in the December 10, 1921 issue of *Adventure* magazine.
"The Sword of the Prophet" originally appeared in the January 10, 1922 issue of *Adventure* magazine.
"Faithful" originally appeared in the February 10, 1922 issue of *Adventure* magazine.
"Red Night" originally appeared in the March 10, 1922 issue of *Adventure* magazine.
"For the Crown" originally appeared in the May 10, 1922 issue of *Adventure* magazine.
"With Song and Sword" originally appeared in the January 10, 1923 issue of *Adventure* magazine. Copyright 1923 by Popular Publications, Inc. Copyright renewed 1950 and assigned to Adventure Pulp LLC. All Rights Reserved.
"The King's Choice" originally appeared in the February 10, 1923 issue of *Adventure* magazine. Copyright 1923 by Popular Publications, Inc. Copyright renewed 1950 and assigned to Adventure Pulp LLC. All Rights Reserved.
"Judgement by Steel" originally appeared in the March 20, 1923 issue of *Adventure* magazine. Copyright 1923 by Popular Publications, Inc. Copyright renewed 1950 and assigned to Adventure Pulp LLC. All Rights Reserved.
"The Black Thief" originally appeared in the May 10, 1925 issue of *Adventure* magazine. Copyright 1925 by Popular Publications, Inc. Copyright renewed 1952 and assigned to Adventure Pulp LLC. All Rights Reserved.
"Brothers-in-Arms" originally appeared in the December 30, 1925 issue of *Adventure* magazine. Copyright 1925 by Popular Publications, Inc. Copyright renewed 1953 and assigned to Adventure Pulp LLC. All Rights Reserved.

THANKS TO
Doug Ellis, Joel Frieman, Everard P. Digges LaTouche, Gerd Pircher, Rob Preston and Sai Shankar

TABLE OF CONTENTS

Introduction by Sai Shankar i

Fisherman's Luck 1

Before Midnight 35

The Sword of the Prophet 73

Faithful 112

Red Night 143

For the Crown 191

With Song and Sword 242

The King's Choice 271

Judgement by Steel 333

The Black Thief 417

Brothers-in-Arms 486

Correspondence 552

A RTHUR GILCHRIST BRODEUR was born on September 18, 1888 in Franklin, Massachusetts. He was the son of Clarence Arthur Brodeur and Mary Cornelia (Latta) Brodeur. His father was then the principal of the State Normal School, Westfield, Massachusetts and had graduated from Harvard.

Arthur grew up in Westfield and went to Harvard, where he met Farnham Bishop, who was to be his best friend and writing partner. He completed his education at Harvard, getting his A.B. degree in 1909, and his M.A. (English Philology) in 1911. After this, he worked for some time as an English teacher at the Volkmann School, Boston.

Bishop introduced Brodeur to his wife, Ophelia Maude Noland, a Radcliffe student, to whom he got married on September 3, 1912. She listed her profession as stenographer on their marriage record. Arthur went back to Harvard and completed his Ph.D. in 1916. His thesis was "The Grateful Lion from Henry of Brunswick to Guy of Warwick."

In 1915, he published his translation of the Norwegian poem, "The Edda." This was an attempt to popularize the poem with a rigorous, scholarly basis for the translation. I think he succeeded, I wanted to go and read the rest after I read this:

> Night 'tis called among men,
> And among the Gods Mist-Time;
> Hooded Hour the Holy Powers know it;

Sorrowless the giants,
And elves name it Sleep-Joy;
The dwarves call it Dream-Weaver.

1916 was also the year when his writing partnership with Farnham Bishop started, with their first serial, "In the Grip of the Minotaur," being published in *Adventure*. He came to the University of California, Berkeley as instructor in English and Germanic philology.

His lectures were enjoyed by his students, who liked the way he treated the characters in the old sagas as human beings, not mythical characters. In his view, they had human problems, were shaped by the society they lived in and their actions were governed by their heroic code.

This also reflects in his stories. The Fulvia series (jointly authored with Farnham Bishop) was centered on a Sicilian princess, the only child of her aging father. It deals with her opposition to men who want to conquer her and their realm. It was the same with his tales inspired by the Scandinavian sagas; a good example is "The Honor of a King" in the September 20, 1923 issue of *Adventure*.

In 1921, he received a stipend of a thousand dollars (now worth about forty thousand dollars) to study language and literature in Uppsala University, Sweden. He became a professor in 1930. On 23 Nov 1944, his wife passed away. In 1946, he became the founding chairman of the newly created department of Scandinavian studies.

He remained as its chairman until 1951. He received the Royal Order of Vasa, First Class, from the government of Sweden for his services to Scandinavian culture. He continued teaching until his retirement in 1955.

He said that he had three ambitions "all divergent and improbable—a quiet country life, eminence as an archaeologist, and some modest reputation as a writer of fiction". He managed to accomplish the last two, for in addition to his writing, he did considerable field research into Californian Indian life in the past.

Arthur was a member of the Adventure Camp-Fire Club, a group of men who met at irregular intervals to talk about adventure. He also liked to entertain his students. He died on September 9, 1971. He was survived by his brother, Clarence, and his second wife, Josephine Thompson Brodeur.

FISHERMAN'S LUCK

MANY MEN called Pierre Faidit's success pure luck; but Pierre thought it the finger of Providence. It can not be denied that luck gave him his opportunity, but does not luck do as much for many men? Does not Pierre's history show that he had the brain to use his luck to best advantage, and to turn bad luck to good, as well as good to better?

When he was born, the midwife—who felt obliged to maintain her fame as a wise woman—said to his father, Jehan the Fisherman:

"Never was a finer lad born in the county, good man. Let me tell you something: his luck will be the spear."

Jehan Faidit, being fond of his calling, and loving well the salt reek of the lagoon, thought she meant a fish-spear, and was well pleased. He nodded soberly, as if to say:

"Why not? It is a good trade, and brings food." So he had the boy christened after the great apostle who fished for men; and the parish register of Cap Estang bears, under the year 1119, the name and birth-notice of him who was to be its greatest son.

IN THE Spring of 1133, when he had just passed his fourteenth birthday, Pierre happened to catch the greatest turbot ever seen on the coast of the Languedoc. This was not the beginning of his luck; for he was blessed already with the healthiest and biggest of bodies, and a handsome, clear-cut face of the Roman type, that a duke's son might have been proud of. Half-grown as he was, his strength already was as that of a young Mars, with muscles that played smoothly under a clear skin.

But it was the turbot that gave his luck a wrestling-hold on the world: for his father Jehan determined that such a prince of fishes must be sent as a gift to their master, the feudal lord of Cap Estang, and of much country besides. This was Roger, Vicomte of Béziers and Carcassonne. Now it chanced that Pierre's turbot reached the Vicomte's table just in time to be served to a greater than he.

Alphonse-Jourdain the Magnificent, Count of Toulouse, whose vassal Roger was, as Pierre was vassal to Roger, rode into Béziers with a strong company of men-at-arms, to pay a visit of friendship and supervision. Roger felt that the turbot was just the delicacy to prove, subtly but clearly, how he appreciated the unexpected honor of the Count's visit.

Alphonse, a stern soldier in time of stress, was in his easier hours a most responsive companion and good fellow. Pleased with the turbot, he declared his intention of conferring his personal thanks on the skilled fisherman who had caught it. It pleased his humor to be thus gracious; moreover, it endeared one to one's subjects.

"But Cap Estang is a filthy hole on a sour-smelling lagoon!" the vicomte protested. "Let me show you Carcassonne first! You have not seen that splendid city since your return from Jerusalem, two months since. Béziers and its country is well enough, but Carcassonne—"

Alphonse of Toulouse shook his head. "Carcassonne will wait; my thanks will not. I must see this Pierre in the morning, before I forget him and his catch."

So the two noblemen rode south the next day, with an escort of six spearmen. It was a sun-drenched morning, with just the hint of a tang in the air—the best that the south can give in weather. This was well for the count's humor. Vicomte Roger also was pleased, for it occurred to him that a master who took

such delight in an eight-mile jaunt to a dirty fishing-village would be much impressed with the richness of the land and its prosperity under his vassal's rule. Likewise Alphonse would see Carcassonne last of all—and for the first time in years—and that jewel of Roger's domain would richly crown his guest's entertainment.

As they rode out under the vaulted arch in the strong walls of Béziers, Count Alphonse gazed about him with fierce approval. Already, in his thirtieth year, the most distinguished soldier in France, he liked his vassals to fortify and man their cities well. His bold hawk-features relaxed in a thin smile as the cavalcade clattered over the Pont de l'Orb; the wind blowing over the turreted town brought an acrid smell of wine-lees to his nostrils. Then the guard at the bridge grounded their lances with a brave clang; and high good humor beamed in his snapping gray eyes.

"By St. Guirand!" he swore. "I am glad to see this land in such good hands, Roger! A stout castle, a loyal garrison, and—good wine! Ha! Vineyards yonder, at the foot of the slope!"

"You shall ride through six miles of them," the Vicomte promised; and they did.

Alphonse-Jourdain was still dreaming of good fighting and good wine, when the distant breath of Cap Estang smote his nostrils. The fishing-village huddled on the inward side of a salt lagoon which the river tried in vain to freshen. No sooner did the count sniff the sea than he rose in his stirrups, shouting with delight:

"Salt water! Death of my life! Now for the snarer of our turbot!"

An hour before noon the village was in sight, with the gray glimmer of the lagoon beyond it. Now Alphonse clapped a hand to his nose; for the breath of Cap Estang was very bad at close quarters. The smell of the water was enough; but over it rose the stench of rotting fish, enough to turn even a soldier's stomach. He grimaced and rode on, trying to use his eyes without opening his nostrils.

The horses plodded fetlock-deep in the stinking dust of the village street; the houses that lined both sides and straddled the river were mean little things of ill-laid stone. But beyond, the lagoon lay still and smooth, reflecting the gleam of red and green and blue sails against the sand-dunes that divided lagoon from bay; and the sight was richly lovely.

Into the unglazed windows of the nearest houses, the bright sun of the Midi flashed the gleam of mail; and women's heads bobbed out to wonder at the martial sight. A few ragged children ran up, staring. No men were to be seen, for all were out on the lagoon, or the bay beyond, at the day's work.

As Alphonse gazed down the village street to the yellow beach, he laughed suddenly.

"Look there! A race!" he cried. Three boats were pulling swiftly in, one a little in advance of the others.

"A day's catch so soon!" the Count approved. "Your subjects are industrious, Roger."

The vicomte shook his head. "The second and third are empty, my lord; only the first is deep-laden. That is Pierre Faidit's boat; and it is he whom we came to see."

The first boat grounded. Its occupant—a magnificent figure of a lad, with bare, brawny arms and stout legs crusted with salt—leaped out and hauled up his cumbrous craft with one mighty tug. He saw nothing of the horsemen, who had halted under the overhanging eaves of a cottage.

Then, with a swish of water, the other two boats beached by the first, and two sturdy boys sprang from each. Without a sign or a word, the four paused not to draw up their empty skiffs, but hurled themselves on the lad Pierre.

Taken by surprize, Pierre went down, but was up in a flash, laughing and shaking his adversaries from him. A heavy fist crashed against his mouth, wiping his laughter away. Vicomte Roger raised a hand in signal to one of his spearmen; but Alphonse waved the soldier back.

"Wait!" he commanded softly. "The big lad holds his own. I would not have a good fight spoiled."

PIERRE FAIDIT held his own indeed. Though the four against him were all big fellows, and quite as old as he, he overtopped them by a head. Far broader of shoulder than they, he used his powerful hands with force and skill. Two he knocked reeling with successive blows before the second pair came to close grips; then, one arm about each of these, he strained them to him till they gasped for pain and breathlessness. Bringing their heads together with a smart crack, he let them drop.

One of those who had first fallen staggered up again; but seeing Pierre make for him, he backed rapidly toward his own boat. There he turned quickly, and snatched up an oar.

"Hold fast! No murder!" shouted Count Alphonse. He urged his horse toward the boat as the beaten fisher-lad whirled his ugly weapon. Pierre dropped to the ground to avoid it, and the broad ash blade swished within a foot of the count's nose. Instantly the nobleman was out of the saddle, and his strong fingers fast in the offender's collar.

"Is it not enough," he roared, "that you must four of you fall on one, without trying to butcher him? Fair play, you cowards!"

The startled boy strove to wriggle away; then, as his slow wits took in the rich chain mail and velvet of his captor, he stiffened, gray under his sea-tan. *"Oy Deus!"* he whimpered. "Pardon, my good lord!"

Fast in the grip of the spearmen, the other three were dragged to the count's feet. One soldier laid an officious hand on Pierre's arm. Smiling again, the son of Jehan Faidit took the hand in his own fingers, squeezed it till the soldier's nails trickled blood, and threw it scornfully aside. Vicomte Roger drew up, his face black as a thundercloud. He would have spoken; but Count Alphonse silenced him with a gesture. "Let me deal with them, Roger," he commanded. "Now, Pierre, what is this quarrel that moves your companions to set on you so villainously?"

Pierre shrugged, but neither knelt nor bowed; his native grace seemed somehow to acquit him of discourtesy. His great dark eyes twinkled merrily in his handsome face; his cheeks were ruddy under their southern olive. He carried the weight of his splendidly muscled body with lithe ease; the poise of his curly head on its sculptured neck had all the dignity of a Caesar's.

"I sought no quarrel, my lord count," he answered.

Alphonse looked searchingly at him. "How know you who I am?" he questioned.

The boy bowed to Roger of Béziers. "I know my master, the vicomte," he replied. "There is but one man whom he would allow to take even so small an affair out of his hands. You are the Count of Toulouse, *monseigneur!*"

Alphonse laughed.

"This lad has wits as well as fists!" he cried; and then, turning to the four frightened captives:

"Explain, you rascals, if ye would not be whipped!"

The four stole scared glances at one another, till one, more dogged, spoke out with averted eyes:

"If it please your lordship, this Pierre Faidit is a sorcerer. Every day he lures our catch from our nets to his! We go out at morning, and at sunset we return empty-handed, or near it. He comes back before the day is half done, with such a haul as your grace sees there! It is black magic, by which he takes our living from us! For this reason we pulled back after him today, to beat the magic out of him!"

Suddenly grave, Count Alphonse looked askance from his captive to Pierre.

"Is this true?" he asked, crossing himself. "Do you practise the black art?"

Roger of Béziers was shuddering.

"If he does, then, turbot or no turbot, he shall hang!" he swore.

Pierre's eyes swept proudly from his master to the greater baron.

"It is fisherman's luck," he answered. "Providence is good to me. I have no dealing with evil powers. Father, Son, and Holy Ghost be my witness!"

The count's brow cleared. Seeing no fiends rise in blue smoke to seize the boy, he was satisfied. The names of the Trinity must infallibly disclose a wizard.

"Free the prisoners!" Alphonse commanded. "The lad is innocent, and his assailants fools. If they fight on such unfair terms again, whip the skin from their bones!"

The cowed bullies fell to their knees, babbling their thanks. But Count Alphonse, turning his back squarely on them, ran admiring eyes over the massive shoulders of Pierre Faidit.

"I came hither to thank you for the rarest turbot that ever passed my lips," he said. "But I think you would make a better soldier than fisherman. Will you go to Toulouse with me, and serve under my banner? I will buy your services of the vicomte."

The boy's eyes shone with sudden joy. "I have dreamed and prayed," he cried, "that I should some day wear a sword! If my lord vicomte will but consent—"

Roger nodded. Snatching up the count's hand, the fisherboy kissed it in an abandon of devotion.

"Give me but time to say farewell to my mother!" he begged. "I will come back instantly!"

And so, by fisherman's luck, Pierre became a soldier.

ALL THIS was sheer good fortune; but from now on, for eight years of drilling, fighting, and guard duty, luck let Pierre alone. Henceforth his rise resulted from his own efforts; nor did any one speak of Pierre's luck again till it revisited him, just for a moment, in a strange form: the death of his friend Guilhem. It was the rough voice of old Simon, the Master of the Garrison, that brought him the first news.

"Pierre, you lucky devil! The count sends for you!"

With a gasp of surprize, the big soldier leaped to his feet. A hone, he had held on one knee, slithered to the floor. Alone in his own stall in the armory, he had not heard Simon's approach. His eyes roved furtively from the keen, perfectly kept sword in the crook of his arm to the rugged face of his superior; his cheeks flushed guiltily.

The officer laughed harshly.

"Never blush, lad!" he commended. "A man may spend his time worse than in polishing his sword. Many a time I have stolen up on you, and have seen you, as now, crooning over that blade of yours as a mother croons over her child! I think the better of you for it. You keep your armor spotless, you handle your men smoothly, you do each duty with a prompt, glad perfection that brings joy to my tough old heart—I can say these things to you now, for you are no more a mere sergeant. You are to be promoted!"

Pierre Faidit flushed redder than before; but his eyes were happy.

"Promoted!" he echoed. "But that is impossible, Simon! Four years a man-at-arms, four more a sergeant! What more remains for me, the son of a humble fisherman?"

The Master of the Garrison laughed boisterously.

"What more, eh? That is good! But come, away with you to the count!"

They crossed the great armory, an enormous, stone-flagged rectangle in the heart of the castle of Toulouse: high-vaulted, and ill-lit by the straggling sunlight that filtered through the tall and narrow arrow-slots, and gleamed dully on stacked arms and on mail hanging from pegs and antlers.

Pushing open a heavy oaken door, old Simon led the way into the inner bailey, where soldiers off duty sprawled in the warm sun, helmets off and mail unbraced, shaking dice with noisy oaths. Then, passing along a gloomy cloister with fine wreathed capitals, the two mounted a dark, winding stair to the apartments of the count and his household.

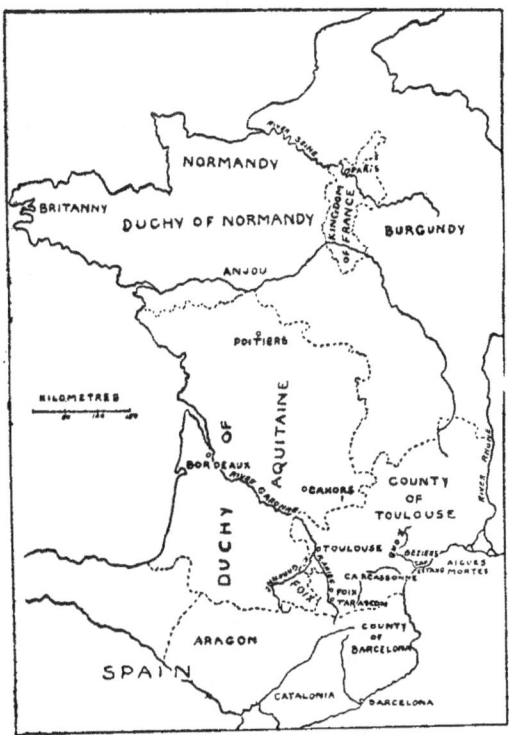

The stair-head opened directly into a vast hall, splendidly lofty, whispering with cross-drafts from the narrow windows. The rich tapestries on the walls bellied out in the Summer breeze, so that the knights and ladies embroidered on them moved as in life. Slender columns, in rows like forest-aisles, supported the minstrels' balcony above the canopied dais; long tables, massive and carven, bore vessels of copper and chased silver. Two men-at-arms stepped aside from an inner door.

"This way!" Simon muttered; and Pierre, who had never before penetrated the lordly region above-stairs, followed wondering. From the hall they came into a series of chambers, the last of which was small and bare, but far a bench and secretary's table set with pens, parchment, and oak-gall ink. The secretary, a lean youth in black, rose as they entered, but seated himself as he recognized the Master of the Garrison.

"The count will see you presently," he announced; and they waited.

Soon the mellow sound of a gong rang from a room beyond; the sentries at the door stood aside, and the door opened. At the secretary's nod, Simon pushed Pierre within the count's own chamber.

Alphonse-Jourdain sat in a great oaken chair cushioned with leather. He was unarmed and in his leather *gipoun,* a close-fitting tunic, and hose stained with the marks of his mail. Opposite him stood Roger of Béziers, gloomy and thoughtful.

For a long moment the Count of Toulouse, looking more fiercely hawklike than usual, fastened his eyes on Pierre. The young man bore his gaze well, neither afraid nor ill at ease. At last Alphonse spoke, a sudden smile flitting over his thin lips:

"Pierre Faidit, Simon reminds me that eight years have passed since you followed me from Cap Estang. I have scarce set eyes on you since then, but I have heard much of you. Your officers have often praised your obedience, your high spirit, your soldierly qualities. Most of all they praise you as a swordsman. In the border raids, and the few small wars that have disturbed our peace, you have shown not only courage, but resource and skill as well." He paused, then asked abruptly:

"You know Guilhem, whom men called the Swordsman, because of his marvelous mastery of his weapon?" Pierre bowed.

"I know him, my lord. He is captain of the South Gate.

Though I am not under his command, he has been most kind to me, and has taught me how to use my sword."

"Even so. You may thank Simon for that. Your first year of service convinced him that you would make a rare soldier; and he begged me to put you under his care and that of Guilhem, that your strength and skill might be developed as they deserved. You have fenced with Guilhem every day, Simon says; every day that leisure afforded, for seven years. How does your skill compare with his?"

Pierre hesitated, then answered:

"For the last month, my lord, I have held my own with Guilhem."

Here Simon broke in bluntly:

"Held thine own, dolt? Nay, thou hast fairly beaten Guilhem every bout for two months past!"

The count turned to Roger of Béziers, who raised his brows as if to say:

"It is your affair, not mine." Then Alphonse said:

"Pierre Faidit, you are to replace Guilhem as captain of the South Tower. Your appointment begins now. Guilhem died of a broken neck this morning, having fallen from his horse. Do you know the responsibilities of your office?"

THE YOUNG soldier choked, half with surprize, and half with the sudden shock of his friend's death. But his grief would wait; his master must have a reply. But a captaincy! Why, many a good soldier lived and died without the hope of it. And Guilhem dead! Guilhem, his master in the trade of war; Guilhem, the strong man! With an effort at composure, he replied:

"It is my duty to hold my tower and my gate against any odds, against steel, starvation, treason; ay, against death itself! I am responsible for the safety of castle and city, for the honor of Toulouse!" The last words rang clear and proud; and as he heard them Alphonse straightened, and smiled.

"You have spoken well. Go to your post. One word with you, Simon!"

After Pierre had gone, the count addressed the Master of the Garrison:

"It was your advice that persuaded me to this, Simon; and I think it good advice. This lad was born to be a soldier. He is two and twenty now, you said? The best age, nowadays, for both brain and brawn. Eight years of your sharp training, and Guilhem's, ought indeed to produce a warrior. Books you know not, but you can read men. I pray, and believe, that your confidence in Pierre is not misplaced, for much depends upon it. We are at war!"

Simon's eyes gleamed.

"At war, my lord? With Aquitaine?"

"With Aquitaine—and with France! Hark you, Simon. Will the men take kindly to Pierre's promotion? He has deserved it, but few of his birth rise to a captaincy. Will the men follow him!"

"Follow him?" Simon's pride was touched. "Would I have commended him else? He is no mere fencer of the *place d'armes!* He has shown himself a champion in battle, a true swordsman, who plays for love of the game! Why, there are hardbitten veterans, gray in your service, who would follow him to the death! They feel for him that mixture of fear and admiration that gives the soldier confidence in his officer. I would follow him myself! He will make a captain of captains!"

So luck smiled on Pierre again, and passed on; and as he had always done, Pierre made the most of what she had left him. But neither Simon, as he left his master's presence, nor that master himself, guessed how much Pierre would make out of it.

Alphonse-Jourdain handed a letter to his vassal Roger. "There you have it, as I told you," he said.

The vicomte read, slowly, anger mounting to his cheeks.

"What devil," he cried, "possesses the king of France, that he treats his truest friends so shamefully?"

Alphonse strode to the narrow window. The chamber was in the western tower, which looked straight toward the border of Aquitaine. He pointed across the open fields beyond the ramparts.

"There dwells the devil that masters the king!" he retorted. "You have felt that devil's malice yourself, Roger. It was William of Aquitaine who forced you out of your fair city of Carcassonne, and held it, till my armies chased him back to his own marches. Now it is his daughter—more wicked even than she is beautiful—who stirs up the king against me, his ally and friend! It was an ill day for Toulouse, aye, and for France, when Aliénor of Aquitaine became queen!"

"Why, then," Roger hazarded, "we shall have to face a threefold enemy: Paris and the North, Aquitaine, and Guienne!"

"Of course. King Louis would never have threatened me had not Aliénor urged him on. His wife's beauty sways his soul; her ambition and savage greed drive him to his ruin. She has hated me and mine since I saved you from her father's power; and now, with three-fourths of France behind her, she strikes through the king's mad love for her. Roger, I am sick when I think of the good French blood that must be shed through one evil woman!"

Roger pondered. Then:

"The King bids you, in this letter, to surrender all your lands save this city alone, the walls of which you must dismantle. If you refuse, he will attack you; if you assent, then we are both ruined, ripe for the stroke of the first turbulent baron who wins the queen's favor. Dare you refuse, my lord?"

The war-scarred face of Alphonse flushed; his fists clenched.

"I am no subject of the King of France!" he cried. "His borders stop at Avignon. I am a free prince, ruling in my own right. Louis has no more title to Toulouse than I to Paris! Resist! Aye! I will resist till no two stones of this city hold together! I will sell my liberty so dear that every house in France shall curse the name of Louis the Tyrant, Louis the Wife-ridden!"

He sat down, breathless, plucking at his beard. Then, scowling, he spoke again:

"Roger, bid my seneschal place the city in a state of defense. Have Simon call out the Municipal Guard, see to the gates and the equipping of the towers; let the engineers prepare the catapults! Send riders to Béziers and Carcassonne! Gather in all the supplies to be bought or seized throughout the countryside! We will give Louis of France a savage welcome!"

THE HOSTS of King Louis compassed the city on every side, a circle of steel that crossed the Garonne above and below, and swept, a forest of bristling points, up the southern and eastern heights. All day their wagon-trains crawled in, gray with dust, from Bordeaux, from Périgueux, from Cahors, from Poitiers; all day their ambulance-trains, a slow, sad procession of jolting, red-stained carts, wound back over the rutted roads.

The fair vineyards were trampled into the earth that the king's horses had fouled; the stately church-spires of Toulouse looked down on the glow of a thousand camp-fires, and stifled in the reek of burning villages. A ceaseless storm of arrows, javelins, and stones beat upon the towered walls; an answering rain of missiles poured down among the daring riders of the North.

Full-armed in ring-mail to the knees, his proud young features hidden behind the nasal and cheek-guards of a peaked helmet, Pierre Faidit measured his untried strength against one sector of the most splendid army in Europe. Looking down from the South Tower upon that portion of the king's host that confronted him, his heart swelled to think that to him had been given the task of holding them at bay. He noted the proportion of horse to foot, counted the catapults ranged against him, figured their range carefully, and ordered his own engines so as to hold the advantage without undue waste of missiles. Untried he was, but he had both courage and judgment and succeeded well.

The royal camp was indeed vast, its forces outnumbering the garrison of Toulouse at least two to one. From the north had come the king's army, well-armed and disciplined veterans of the Norman wars; from the west the gorgeous feudal hosts of Aquitaine flooded down the Bordeaux and Bayonne highways: men of short stature, but sturdy and inured to warfare. These were the men of Aliénor, the queen, who fought for revenge.

As much as he outmanned his enemy, so much also King Louis surpassed him in number and weight of siege engines. But the walls were staunch and high, so that, to inflict any damage, the royal engineers and their cavalry supports must come dangerously close. The result was that Louis lost two men and two catapults to every one he put out of action.

Twelve days the siege dragged on, with no general engagement; so far, the advantage lay with the garrison. But Alphonse the Great, hurrying from tower to tower, saw how soon the tide must turn against him. Louis had swept down on Toulouse within ten days after his letter, proving that he had counted in advance on war.

Thus, before the count had been able to draw on the stored grain and the flocks of his domain for sufficient provision, the king had cut him off from his own fertile plains, and now Louis had all the countryside to feed his troops, without counting the inexhaustible supplies of Aquitaine. Meantime, Alphonse must feed not only his garrison, but the sixty thousand non-combatants of his civilian population. Unless the king lost heart within a fortnight, Toulouse must come down to half-rations. And Louis was notorious for dogged courage.

On the fourteenth morning, Pierre looked down from the battlements of his tower, to see unwonted bustle in the lines opposing his position. Here lay the host of Aquitaine and Guienne, their camp like a crescent moon, with horns that extended far around to east and west, their center supported by two companies of Burgundian engineers.

It was the Burgundians Pierre dreaded most, with their long-armed catapults that ceaselessly drove his little garrison to cover behind the merlons. Now, those thick-set men of the East, clad in half-mail, had dragged into position an extra battery of heavy engines, and toiled like ants to roll up the heavy stones that served for ammunition. Behind the Burgundians, and out of range, the Aquitanian cavalry was forming as if for an assault.

Swiftly Pierre despatched a messenger to the count, and on his own responsibility ordered such men as he could spare to extend the battlements with balks of timber. The thrill of approaching battle hummed in his veins; it would be his to resist the first shock of the assault. Proudly he measured the depth of the forming lines across the moat; they were the chosen heroes of the South, who had won glory from Syria to Spain, of whose dauntless valor troubadours had sung. And he, Pierre, would bear the brunt of their resistless shock!

But the orders that came back from Alphonse-Jourdain cooled his ardor.

"It is only a feint," the messenger reported back, "to hold your men-at-arms and engines where they are. The attack will center on the North Gate, where the king's catapults have made a wide breach. Send half your engines to the North Tower at once!" Pierre had no choice but to obey.

Yet all day long the Aquitanian cavalry massed over against Pierre's post; and all day long the king concentrated his energies in widening the northern breach, without ordering the assault. Nevertheless the garrison maintained a feverish vigilance well into the night, certain that the attack must come.

And come it did, shortly after midnight. The watchers on the walls were first aware of the soft *clink-clink* of muffled mail, and the grating of feet on pebbles; then a trumpet in the north tore the night with its blare. Instantly the walls of Toulouse were starred with the light of torches; great flares of pitch and pine-twigs were thrown out from the battlements; and against their glare the defenders on the northern wall saw a host of dismounted men-at-arms gathered close for the assault. Alphonse had read the royal plan unerringly.

Every third catapult on the wall rained down fresh-kindled flares, while the rest hurled their jagged missiles full into the massed assailants. With one wild yell of triumph, the royal host dashed toward the breach. As they came on, light-armed engineers sprang ahead, throwing bundles of fagots into the moat to form a bridge.

IT WAS war between masses of men and masses of rock. The count had called in all the catapults that could be spared from the east, west, and south walls to repel this stroke; and in the glare of light that shone red on the breasts of the assailants, three hundred engines hurled a ceaseless tempest of stone into the ranks of France. Yet on they came, across the moat under the curtain-wall, and surged up to the jagged twelve-foot hole that yawned in the face of the North Tower.

From the South Tower, Pierre sent messenger after messenger to inquire concerning the progress of the battle. Nothing could be seen across that great expanse of night-wrapped city save the distant flare of torches and pitch-balls; and the mingled uproar of clashing steel, of many-throated cries of pain and rage, and the clanging impact of stone on armor, reached him only as a faint, confused echo that told him no more than he knew.

He could do nothing; though the success of that fierce attack on the other side of the town would mean defeat, rapine, and ruin to Toulouse, he must stand helpless at his post until the count should call on him for reenforcement. The fight was still indecisive when his last messenger returned.

For, while he raged with disappointment, Pierre kept constantly in mind that his duty demanded vigilance as well as patience. Unceasingly he maintained his watch, going the rounds to see that his sentries were at their posts and alert, and such engines as remained to him ready. It was in the dark hour before dawn that his own keen ears caught some stealthy sound in the night; and then one of his sentries gave the alarm. Instantly Pierre ordered his depleted force of engineers to hurl flares over the wall. They obeyed; and Pierre saw, in the swift crimson light, a dense mass of men at the foot of his own tower!

Scarcely had he seen to the pointing of the catapults when messengers ran up breathless to announce that the men of Guienne had closed in on the east and west, narrowing the circle about the city and squeezing in the defense, to distract the count's forces from the main attack on the North Tower. Now Pierre understood: while the Parisian troops forced the assault, the queen's southerners were to attack the South; on east and west the men of Guienne merely waited, to reenforce whichever attack first succeeded, and prevent that part of the garrison which they confronted from sending any help.

Then Pierre struck, without waiting for orders which might not come. At his command, the buzz of two hundred taut gut cables ripped the air; and from the whole length of tower and curtain-wall stones, beams, and pikes crashed into the ranks of Aquitaine. The howl that followed was drowned by the crash of a hundred missiles against the battlements; and Pierre knew that the king's engines had been moved silently up, behind the Aquitanians, under cover of the dark.

The first volley had been too low to break over the wall; but the second would be better aimed. Instantly Pierre ordered his men under cover of the merlons, and waited for the escalade. Any other course would cost too much in life. While he waited, peering down between two merlons, a hand touched his shoulder. It was the Vicomte of Béziers.

"The count has sent me to take command," Roger announced. Under other conditions Pierre would have resented this seeming evidence of mistrust; now he welcomed it as an indication that the North Tower still held its own.

For a quarter of an hour the Burgundians kept up a steady hail of stones against the south battlements; then, suddenly, they ceased. Roger sprang to the ramparts with a cheer, the

Tower garrison closing in about him. Trembling with excitement, Pierre knew the escalade was on; the king's engines had ceased only because the Aquitanians must have climbed so high that further volleys would have struck them down.

Roger of Béziers, hot-headed for all his campaigns, heeded only the imminent attack; and Pierre was forced to attend to that which Roger had forgotten. Detaching a score of men, he ordered the catapults tilted straight down, and poured a dense volley into the gleaming mass that his flares showed clinging just below the battlements.

The rain of rocks and timbers smashed down the whole crest of the climbing horde; they collapsed, the ladders breaking beneath them and sweeping away as many more. But a dozen ladders held; and up these, before Pierre could reload, the ardent Southern infantry scaled the wall.

Even as they swarmed over the battlements, the garrison charged to meet them. Pierre waited only to kindle the two great cressets that lighted the curtain-wall, and then threw himself into the fight. It was a weird battle in the air, armor and steel blades darting crimson flashes and ringing like a thousand forges. The advantage of position lay with the garrison; but numbers were with the enemy, who could scarce have been less than three thousand against the six hundred of the vicomte.

Bellowing swift commands, Roger of Béziers marshaled his men in the very teeth of the attack; then, sword flashing, he closed in. His fiery courage spurred his men on to heroism; but the pressure was great. Step by step the garrison gave ground across the wall. Crying them on, Roger bored deep into the hostile tide; spears swirled about him, and still striking, he fell. His overthrow was hardly noticed, so close-pressed were his outnumbered followers. On flooded the assault, bearing them back toward the inner wall, against whose face they must soon be crushed in red ruin.

Pierre, fighting desperately in the center, knew now what

war meant. His great body was a river of sweat under his armor; the blows that rang on his helmet deafened him. All the skill that Guilhem the Swordsman had taught him flowed invincibly from his brain-centers to his mighty arms; but the throng of foes was so dense that he could not parry every thrust. His great stature and terrible strokes attracted blows; for the fiery Aquitanians sought glory in death.

Then the boy suddenly became aware that Roger of Béziers was no longer in the battle. It dawned upon him that Roger must be slain, and he, Pierre, in command once more. His voice rang high in a rallying shout; he threw himself against the massed rank before him like a thunder-bolt. Redoubling his strokes, by sheer skill and force he carved a gap in the opposing line, and cried his men on to widen it.

THE DEFENSE stiffened; the battle began to sway, back and forth along the wall. Thrilling with triumph, Pierre wielded his sword with all the vigor he could summon. His example fired his men with new courage; on either side of him the Toulousans formed a narrow, dense phalanx, and bending their backs, charged into the gap. His great blade dripping, his shield hacked to splinters, Pierre fought like one inspired.

"At them!" he roared. "St. Sernin for Toulouse!" Wielded more swiftly and deftly than shield could parry, his sword bit deep into flesh and mail and bone. His eyes seemed to burn in their sockets; his head reeled with his efforts. But his spirit spread like flame through his men; the lines swayed farther and farther; deadly swirls opened in the press, with vicious thrusts and knife-strokes. Then, with slowly gathering momentum, the men of Toulouse pushed their enemies back toward the merlons.

The slight advance gave more room for weapon-play, and they of Aquitaine were torn into disarray. Now Pierre ordered a second rush, and led it with a burst of swift strokes. Triumph raising their hearts, the garrison quickly formed shoulder to shoulder, and swept on in a terrible wave.

Then, before Pierre's eyes, the Aquitanians seemed to melt

away; they were mysteriously caught up in a stream of men that poured from the curtain-walls on either hand and drove them like sheep over the battlements. In one frightful avalanche, they rolled over the edge and dropped to destruction far below. A few moments more of scattered fighting, and the men of Aquitaine, save for a handful of prisoners, had ceased to live.

Leaning on his sword, Pierre drew breath in great gulps. He felt himself seized and shaken joyously. Alphonse-Jourdain himself clutched his hand and wrung it.

"Well done, Pierre Faidit!" he cried. "You had them beaten even before we came to the rescue from the North Wall! Never have I seen better sword-play!"

Pierre stared at him.

"Then—" he gasped.

"Aye, we drove them back from the breach, just in time to reenforce you. But Louis has still enough men to starve us out, if he is prudent enough to waste no more of them—Saints have mercy!"

Hastening to a pile of dead and wounded by the merlons, he raised a bleeding body in his arms. It was Roger of Béziers.

Pierre stooped over the wounded man, took off his helmet, and unlaced his mail. The vicomte's lips parted slightly; his eyes quivered open.

"Thank God!" the count exclaimed. "See, his head is gashed, his shoulder pierced by a lance; but he will live, I trust."

"Aye, he will live," Pierre muttered. "But he will fight no more while this siege lasts."

"THE COUNT has transferred me to the South Wall," Simon explained. "Nay, I shall not disturb your authority; you are captain here. But now that fresh reenforcements have joined the king, and the breach in the North Tower is repaired, our lord foresees a strong attack here."

Pierre nodded.

"Aye," he said. "The king believes this gate weakened by the

Aquitanian assault. Moreover, this is a hard position to defend. See how the river borders the road, protecting any advance from such sallies as we might make from the Western wall!"

The master of the garrison smiled.

"Your head has more wit than a duke's! Such is doubtless the king's plan; and he is a fool if he acts otherwise. He has three thousand fresh men from Paris, while our bellies are pinched with hunger. If he lets us starve a week more, he can safely trust all his hopes to one grand stroke."

"Do you fear?"

"I never fear till I am beaten, and then fear is useless," the veteran answered. "Has not the count the cunning of a Cæsar? And has he not discovered a Hector in you?"

Pierre laughed.

"I have heard the tale of Messire Hector from the chaplain. Was he not killed by King Achilles? And shall I fare better, who am but a sorry Hector, with the reek of fish-bait still on my fingers?"

BUT EIGHT days passed, and the expected attack did not come. Made prudent by their losses, the royal hosts camped sullenly about the city, and let hunger fight for them. Their engineers continually beat upon the walls with their missiles, hopeful of a second breach, and certain that their activities prevented the damages they made from being repaired. The cavalry performed stately evolutions up and down the plain, but kept out of range; bodies of footmen drilled ankle-deep in the dust. But as the days passed with no assault, Alphonse began to feel the prick of fear.

He could not hold out much longer: the miserable half-rations Simon served out were cut down once more. The citizens fared worse than the soldiers; reduced to the flesh of dogs and the scraping of cheese-rinds, they deafened the provost's ears with their lamentations. A little more, and they might flock to the castle, demanding that the count surrender rather than starve them further.

Something of this sort Simon remarked to Pierre, laboring over the snarled ends of a broken catapult-cable. He was gloomy enough, now that his lord had lost confidence. Pierre, who had said nothing for some time, now interrupted him in the midst of his grumbling.

"How many stones have we hurled from this tower in the last two days?" he asked abruptly.

"How do I know? Close to three a minute, and we are running short! Out of food, out of—"

"Have you begun digging up the cobblestones?"

Simon snorted.

"Cobble-stones? They have not weight enough, baby!"

Pierre hummed a snatch of song.

"True," he said lightly. "All the more reason for shooting them into the king's camp!"

Straightening up, Simon darted a keen glance at him.

"What devil's scheme do you hatch behind that angel's face?" he asked.

Pierre became serious.

"Why, this," he answered. "If the king delays his attack much longer, we shall be too weak to fight. Our only hope lies in the faint chance that he may attack soon, while we have strength left to resist. Why not trick Louis into thinking us weaker than we are, so that he will strike at once?"

"Trick a cat into eating hay!" Simon scoffed. "Why, it was only last night that the count said to me: 'Simon, it is all up. The king has gone back to his old method. Rash at first, he becomes cautious with defeat. He will starve us out without the need for a blow!'"

Pierre shook his curly head.

"I have netted cunning fish ere now," he said. "Let the bait be luscious enough, and the fish hungry, and—you have him! Look you, Simon: rip up the cobbles from the streets around this gate, and use them only from the catapults on this Tower.

As you say, they are too light to do much harm; but all the better. Louis will think us out of weightier missiles. Also, discharge many cobbles this morning, fewer between noon and dark, a very few tomorrow morn, and—none tomorrow afternoon! And now, take me to the count!"

An hour later Pierre and the master of the garrison stood in the count's presence. He had just finished checking off the latest list of their dwindling supplies, and his face was clouded.

"Well?" he asked, dismissing his clerk. "Ha! Pierre!"

Pierre approached somewhat timidly, grown suddenly fearful lest his cunning plan seem absurd to the count. But it was Simon who spoke:

"My lord," he began, in tones that held an eager curiosity beneath their gruffness, "our brave young cockerel has a scheme for forcing Louis to attack."

The count smiled bitterly.

"It will not do, Pierre. I know Louis Capet; nothing will drive him to rashness again, once he has suffered loss. He is a lion at the beginning of a campaign, a mule at the end."

"My lord!" Pierre implored. "Will you but hear me?"

The count assented; and for five minutes Pierre spoke uninterrupted. When he had finished, the despair had left his master's features.

"How know you that the royal forces are discontent and losing discipline?" he asked. "I have seen nothing of it."

"I have watched," Pierre replied quickly, "hour by hour, day by day! Twice a day his cavalry has approached almost within range, of my catapults, to see what damage their own have done the Tower. Each successive time, a longer space passed between the call for the retreat and the withdrawal of the horsemen. Yesterday, they withdrew slowly and irregularly; in the afternoon, the trumpet had to recall them twice. That means that the king's troops are impatient for battle. Their anger at their first repulse, and their knowledge that we grow weaker with hunger every day, make them so eager for revenge that they can

scarce be held back. Moreover, I have seen officers in fine armor
as slow to withdraw as their men. The high pride that burns in
the blood of the northern barons, their love of open fight, causes
them to chafe at delay. Let them once be persuaded that our
catapults are out of munitions, and the king will not be able to
withhold them from the attack. If he refuses to order the assault,
their own impatience will force his hand. They will compel him
to assail us!"

Alphonse nodded.

"I did not see that, being overbusy with hurrying from tower
to tower, from storehouse to provost's office. But you, Simon,
an old soldier, have been eight days with Pierre on the Tower,
and have not seen what he has seen?"

"Why, if you will take me from patrolling the ramparts, and
set me to pointing catapults," the veteran retorted, "how can
you expect me to watch horsemen? I was too busy smashing
Burgundian engines."

Alphonse ignored him.

"And the rest, Pierre?" he asked.

When Pierre had finished his reply—which was uttered not
only with all the eloquence of his lips, but with a multitude of
eager gestures as well, the count summoned his clerk.

"Pen, ink, and my seal!" he demanded. "You shall have all you
ask, Pierre! St. Sernin! What a net you have spread for the king,
fisherman's son!"

AT NOON of the next day, Pierre's trap was in readiness.
It involved certain operations within the South Gate, at which
a thousand civilian laborers toiled under Pierre's orders. Also,
a series of ditches was dug from the river, converging on the
gateway. Meanwhile, Simon carried out Pierre's program of a
dwindling rain of cobbles from the wall above; and by noon
every catapult on the South Tower was idle. Between tall buildings, in every street near the gate, the gleam of mail indicated
the presence of many men-at-arms.

On the north, east, and west walls the volleys from the

engines had likewise diminished, but only slightly. Everything gave the impression that the South Tower having quite exhausted its missiles, the other batteries, though still too well supplied to be safely attacked, were unable to assist the South. Yet very quietly, under cover of the merlons, Simon's engineers had been gathering a secret store of big stones. Just before noon, four hundred archers took up their position on the Tower, but took care not to show themselves between the merlons.

Pierre cast a satisfied glance from his work to the teeming southern plain. Already the royal forces were nibbling at the bait. Late on the previous afternoon, when the Tower's reply to the Burgundian catapults had grown preceptibly feebler, small movements of horse and foot toward the walls betrayed the growing eagerness and curiosity of the enemy.

Well after dark, a stealthy reconnaissance by the king's infantry roused Pierre first to startled vigilance, then to stifled laughter. In the morning, the royal camp had pushed out a great, gleaming arm of steel-clad horsemen almost within stone-range; then, as the engines on the battlements withdrew entirely from action, parties of light-armed cavalry darted forward to explore, as best they might, the condition of the defense.

They saw no heads exposed between the crenelations, no movement of the great engine-arms, that now pointed, empty and harmless, to the blue sky. Only an occasional javelin, ill-aimed and barely tossed into the moat, told the false message that Pierre wished to convey: that famine had too far enfeebled the garrison for even effective hand-to-hand fighting.

Two hours after noon. The long arm of cavalry pushed out slowly, steadily, till its tip was well within range. But the Tower was silent, apparently deserted. A single troop, under the king's banner, dashed up to the very lip of the moat, so close that the fall of a single timber might have crushed half a dozen at once. But still, seeming cowed and beaten, the garrison hid behind its bulwarks.

A trumpet shrilled behind the king's lines; and as if launched by the sound, a swift torrent of horsemen, from east; and west and north, galloped toward the south, with a thunder of hoofs that fairly shook the plain. It was then that Pierre laughed aloud; for the king, convinced that the South Tower was without missiles and weak with starvation, was concentrating his whole force upon it for one final attack!

It seemed an eternity to Pierre before the royal host was at length marshaled in column for the assault; and the sight, for a moment, filled him with surprize. Then, fathoming the reason, he nodded to himself. The royal forces were arrayed as if to charge, *on horseback,* against the stout walls of the Tower! But the purpose was clear, and—if the king had been acting on fact instead of belief—sound enough.

The French host knew no reason to fear those lifeless, apparently harmless walls; so they planned to spare themselves the oppression of an approach on foot, weighed down with heavy armor, under the hot sun. They expected to ride in unchecked and in comfort, batter down the gate, and sweep into the helpless city. Such opposition as they must face would doubtless be massed inside the gate; from horseback they would have the advantage of height and power in their sword-strokes. A cavalry assault on a walled city was unusual, but doubtless seemed wisest against a city whose walls were defenseless.

When at last the trumpets blew the charge, Pierre's soul was uplifted as on wings; for the sight was wonderful. Spurring forward briskly, the vanguard came on first, while the rest reined in their impatient chargers till they should have room. Rank by rank, the vast body of horsemen rippled forward, their long mail flashing back the sun that kissed their helmets. Now they were trotting; now—to impress the starving garrison—they broke into the maddening gallop of the charge!

Their spears, useless till they reached the gate, were carried in rest; but they rode with tossing plumes and flowing manes, each man hunched behind his great round-shouldered shield. The air roared with the crackle of three thousand wind-tormented pennons. First came the King's Own, the knights of

Paris; then the big-shouldered men of Champagne; last of all they of Guienne and the remnants of the Aquitanians, battered but dauntless. The banners of ten provinces waved above the proud barons who captained them.

A hand touched Pierre's shoulder; it was the count.

"It works, lad!" he whispered eagerly. "Ah, we should thank God that the king did not suspect our trick!"

"I counted on his suspecting," Pierre answered; "but I held it certain that his barons and the army would not suspect. They are impatient, warlike men, hungry for revenge as we are for food. France is too young a kingdom for a king to hold them from the throat of a shaken foe. They have forced Louis to choose between attack and the loss of their support." He broke off, and pointed.

The advance was in full career, a rushing river of steel, tossing spears as a spring flood tosses straw and drifting wood. Their columns seemed interminable, irresistible; yet still the walls of Toulouse were unstirred. Now the first rank splashed into the moat, the horses—which were themselves unarmored—swimming gallantly. The water frothed and creamed with the churning mass of them, till its banks overflowed.

Then at last Pierre ordered the men-at-arms crouched behind the merlons to cast spears; but feebly, and few at a time. Here and there, by sheer gravity, a point found its way into mail and flesh; here and there a horse went under, a rider pitched into the water. But the damage was too slight for more than ridicule. A mighty roar of laughter rose from the dense ranks of the North.

Even as they laughed, their first four ranks had crossed the moat, and advanced in three bounds to the base of the tower. Lance-butts hammered on the gate; a thousand throats yelled themselves hoarse with triumph, while still the moat boiled with those that came behind. At the rear of the cavalry pelted the engineers, with beams and crossties to make a bridge for the infantry. Last of all the pike-bearing footmen ran in irregular bursts of speed, trailing their weapons to save strength for the fight.

Pierre's eyes danced.

"Now!" he shouted to his engineers; and sent a messenger scurrying to the Southeast Gate, to the troops who, in accordance with his plan, had been concentrated there.

Alphonse-Jourdain swung to the door. He was armed, helmeted, and girt with his long sword. Pierre caught his arm.

"You lead, my lord?" he asked. The count nodded curtly.

"Then let me ride with the spearmen! Simon can hold the Tower!"

Alphonse found time to chuckle.

"Your horse is waiting at the Southeast Gate. Go, young fisher after men, and St. Pierre speed thy sword this day better than he sped his own!"

Pierre ran from the Tower at his master's heels.

THE SOUTH Gate quivered under a rain of blows; a dozen dismounted horsemen battered upon it fiercely with a green pine log, while the dense column behind them waited with thirsty swords. The moat, now bridged by Louis' engineers, gleamed with the mail of close-packed horse and foot; behind, the long column had deployed, to be nearer the doomed city.

Crash! One massive oaken plank, torn from the spikes that held it, fell shattered under the archway. The blows redoubled, till the whole great surface parted at every joint. Then, all at once, the gate burst in. Like the sea smashing through a broken dike, the royal army poured in.

As they broke through the breach, a trumpet pealed from the wall. The battlements of the Tower, and of the adjoining curtain-walls, leaped to terrible life. The twang of engines shrieked above the clang of armor and the shouts of the assault. An avalanche of stone streamed from the Tower's catapults into the rear of the king's great host, driving the rearguard forward. Forward: for no man cared to retreat when the city lay open to conquest and pillage. As they came on, four hundred archers riddled them with three-foot shafts.

The surge was irresistible. Beginning in a swift rush at the van, it spread more and more slowly down the line, and ended in a dogged push at the rear. The king's army flooded over the fallen gate; while from the walls stones, spears, and arrows drove upon them pitilessly.

The onrush of spurred and stumbling horses not only could not be stopped; it could not stop itself. Sheer weight and momentum made it an irresponsible force, mad with passion to kill, blinded, each rank, by the mass of steel backs in front. The mighty column, crowding the archway to the walls, burst through—to destruction.

For beyond the gate, where the open street should be, Pierre's thousand workmen had dug a terrible abyss, deep, with shelving sides, filled with water led by channels from the Garonne. Into this vast pit the whole vanguard shot, rank after rank, driven by those behind. The fall tumbled riders from their horses; weighted down by their heavy mail, kicked and trampled by their struggling horses, barons; captains and men-at-arms hurtled splashing to a hopeless death. The cries of the trapped were drowned by the din of hoofs to the rear; all warning was lost in that headlong charge for victory. Rank by rank and troop by troop, that tide of glorious cavalry tumbled in unending ruin into the net of Pierre the Fisherman. Nor could the main host see beyond the shadowy reentrant angle of the gateway; so that none guessed the death ahead till he was engulfed.

But the end must come, for the horrible trap was filling fast; and soon the rearguard would ride in over a human causeway. Now, therefore, Alphonse-Jourdain sounded the advance. The Southeast Gate was flung open: a bridge of beams and planking was thrown across the moat; and four thousand men-at-arms—who had massed there under Pierre's directions—sallied out beyond the wall.

There they deployed, and swept on in line of battle. Only the royal rear could see their charge, for they were hidden by the south wall from the main army, which still poured into the death-trap of the South Gate.

Now the riders of Toulouse broke into the gallop. One hundred yards—fifty—ten. They smote the hostile rear a smashing flanking blow, whose impetus bore them deep into the crowded ranks. The weight of their horses, the swift strokes of their swords, wrought ruin. Seized with consternation, the men of Guienne fled first, foot and horse. After them pelted all who could tear themselves from the destruction of the pit.

As they ran, the archers and engineers on the battlements tore and battered them, while the count's cavalry wrought, in pursuit, worse havoc than in the first charge. At last Alphonse, weary of slaughter, gave the order to retire. All that remained of the king's army was a scattered, panic-stricken rout, and captives too many to count upon the field. Proudly, with heads erect, the garrison turned back to the city they had saved. Yet a thousand men sped to harry the abandoned royal camp, that Toulouse might eat.

But Pierre turned not back. His ardor, and the terror inspired by his sword, had carried him too deep among the fugitives to hear the trumpet. Followed close by his own men, he harried hard on the heels of the retreat for a full two leagues. The fleeing horde was strung out in a pitiful, ragged chain that trailed away toward the Aquitanian border. Along their flank Pierre raged, physical hunger forgotten in that greater hunger for glory which is the pride of France. Nor did he stop to strike the gasping soldiers that raised wretched hands toward the blow, but spurred on, seeking nobler prey.

He found it at last. Followed rather than guarded by a score of splendid spearmen whom his finer horse outstripped, a tall man in magnificent armor rode full career for Aquitaine and safety. At sight of him, Pierre raised the view-halloo, for here was surely a baron at least. With a shout to his men, Pierre drove the spurs home in fleet pursuit.

The men of the South Tower responded with a splendid burst of speed. Well they knew their captain's purpose, and well they fulfilled it. As the fugitive nobleman roweled his swift barb, widening the space between himself and those who should have guarded him, Pierre's troop caught them up, shot past, wheeled, and flung themselves between. In a flurry of sword-strokes, king's men and Toulousans clashed together.

The matchless horse which had separated the French baron from his men was in a fair way to bear him safely out of Pierre's reach, though the latter urged his own heavier mount to its utmost. Already the fugitive was so far ahead that his very dust dispersed before Pierre could overtake it. But suddenly the barb stumbled and went down; his tall rider rolled free, and strove to resume his flight on foot. He went not far, for his mail was heavy. Hearing hoofbeats close behind, he faced about and drew his sword. With a shout, Pierre, was upon him.

"Yield!" he cried; but the other smiled sourly.

"If thou—" he used the "thou" of contemptuous address—"if thou wert unhorsed as I am, I would kill thee for thy insolence. Thy charger gives thee the advantage!"

Instantly Pierre dismounted. The first touch of steel told him his enemy was no common swordsman. The Northerner's supple wrist and skilful play for a moment held his younger foe fiercely at distance. But Pierre's giant strength, backed by a skill scarce less, drove him back and back. The older man grew weaker; yet he fought on, with a set and dogged smile, till Pierre beat his weapon from his hand.

"Now yield!" he commanded.

"Not to thee!" the noble cried angrily. "I would die rather than give up my sword to a common man-at-arms!" And he threw himself sullenly down in the road. Sheathing his sword, Pierre picked him up bodily, and flung him into his own saddle. The result set him to gasping.

"Hands off!" his prisoner cried in a blaze of fury. "Fool! Dog! I am the King of France!"

But Pierre only held him tighter. Behind him the *mêlée* died down in a final clatter of steel, a shout of triumph; and Louis of France rode back toward Toulouse a prisoner, behind his captive bodyguard.

"WHO WAS he who took me?" the king asked wearily. Alphonse stood by the side of his own chair of state, in which he had made the king sit, like a victor rather than a captive.

"He is called Pierre Faidit," the count replied. "Your ransom is his; I will send for him."

So Pierre stood in the presence of King Louis, and bowed low—not to the king, but to the unhappy prisoner. Now Louis was a proud man, but a thrifty one; and some years as monarch of a bankrupt kingdom had taught him to bargain without shame, where the treasury of France was involved. Likewise he knew Alphonse-Jourdain for the pattern of generous chivalry. Thus his first words now to Pierre were:

"You are to set my ransom, having captured me. Being a commoner, you will not ask overmuch?"

"I am a fisherman's son," Pierre answered. "I know little of ransoms. Let my lord set the price."

Louis had judged Alphonse correctly. His magnanimity, and his desire for peace with France, had to contend only with his sense of what was due Pierre. Moreover, he wished to comfort his captive, and so essayed a feeble jest.

"I shall not demand much," he said. "It was not our power that captured your majesty; it was fisherman's luck!"

"Not so, my lord!" Pierre broke in. "It was God's Providence!"

Though niggardly, Louis was the most pious man in France, and loved piety in another.

"Well said!" he approved. "Be ever humble, young man, and grateful to God for your success!"

Straightway Alphonse, seeing the king for a moment in a better mood, spoke that which was burning in his mind:

"Will your majesty concede our independence? Will you make peace? If so, the ransom will be small!"

Louis laughed, a little bitterly.

"Make peace with you? Ay! Being ill-counseled, I have treated you shamefully! I will give the boy a thousand crowns, make peace on your terms, and—God grant it may bring joy to our poor France!"

"Amen!" said Alphonse; and "Amen!" said Pierre Faidit, who had fished for an army, and caught a king in his net.

BEFORE MIDNIGHT

PIERRE OBEYED his master's summons with a little quickening of the heart, which he could not explain. Certainly there was nothing to provoke excitement in the mere fact that the Count of Toulouse had sent for him; Pierre was frequently the count's companion. Nor did he know of anything that had happened to disturb the monotonous luxury of his life in the castle. Very little had happened for many months, and Pierre was weary of hunting and hawking, of reading romances to the countess, of the hours of catapult practise and cavalry evolutions that kept the garrison ready for an imaginary enemy. It was the year of grace 1145; a peaceful year, and therefore a dull one to men bred to the sword. It was very dull to Pierre, who was just turned twenty-six, and hungry for glory.

He found Count Alphonse on the new terrace, which had been constructed just outside the postern of the citadel, and presented vivid proof of that peace which Pierre found so wearisome. Even in its many wars, Toulouse had not seen an enemy inside the outer fortifications; and now the entire absence of trouble had induced Alphonse-Jourdain to build this terrace for his countess. It was a wide, gently rolling lawn of velvet grass, on the very brow of the hill which the castle crowned with a coronet of stone. A fountain, which kept the grass lush and thick, also watered a hedge of roses, still faintly fragrant with a few belated blooms, and an arbor of grapes that would soon be purple.

Below, its lights starring the soft southern night, lay the great city of Toulouse, silver-girdled by the Garonne, armored with towered ramparts and steel-clad men-at-arms. From the terrace one could see the gray loom of the walls where lurid torchlight struck down upon them from tower and turret; beyond, the high-gabled dwellings of the prosperous city lay hiding in the dark, through which their lights peeked like a thousand jeweled eyes. Then, far down the river southward, a dark line athwart the moonlight, a looming blur—the foothills of the far-off Pyrenees.

Count Alphonse rose as his favorite captain approached, and took the young man's hand.

"Welcome, Pierre Faidit!" he cried, the anxious undertone to his voice revealing the strain under which he labored. "Welcome! Will you undertake a perilous errand for me?"

The quickening at Pierre's heart seemed to mount to his brain; his pulses pounded.

"Is it war, my lord?" he cried.

Alphonse-Jourdain smiled at his ardor. The count was very fond of his handsome young officer, who had indeed deserved it. Pierre Faidit was a lithe young giant, a very marvel with the sword, and endowed with a keen brain inside a curly head that had the stern, aquiline beauty of a Cæsar's.

"It may well be war," the count answered, "unless you can

avert it. If you fail, the blood of seventy murdered men will be lost in the blood of half my people, as this tiny fountain would be lost in the great waters of yonder river!" He pointed to the Garonne, rippling silver under the moon.

Pierre waited, his breath coming quick, for the news behind the count's outburst.

"You have heard of Red Hugo?"

Pierre nodded.

"The Norman adventurer who seized the castle of Tarascon three years ago?"

"The same," Alphonse confirmed. "You know Tarascon lies on the Ariège, in the southern part of the county of Foix; and the Count of Foix is my vassal. When this Norman, Hugo, took Tarascon, I sent an order to the Count of Foix, commanding him to throw the intruder out, and punish him for violating my territory. But Roger of Foix replied that Red Hugo paid his taxes as honestly as if he had come by Tarascon by peaceful means, and acknowledged my sovereignty.

"So, seeing that the count had no complaint to make against the man who had seized one of his strongholds, and consider-ing it more the business of Foix than of Toulouse, I dropped the matter. After all, I thought, it is Count Roger, not I, who must have this Norman for a neighbor, and so long as they live together in peace—"

Alphonse paused a moment, then resumed:

"But this Red Hugo is not a peaceful man. I have been hearing, from time to time, of many petty outrages between Tarascon and Foix, and have referred all complaints to Count Roger. It is not my affair until he proves incapable of dealing with it. But now—the message reached me not an hour ago—Red Hugo has done a deed which places him under my direct jurisdiction. He has slain seventy pilgrims, who were on their way from Arles-sur-Tech with gifts for the shrine of St. Sernin, here in Toulouse!"

Pierre Faidit cried out with horror. "Pilgrims! But they are sacrosanct, inviolate, by the order of Holy Church!"

"Even so. The Prior of St. Serain, as you know, is my cousin; and all his years of prayer and fasting have not purged the fiery spirit from his blood. He was here but now, clamoring for vengeance. I have promised he shall have it, and resolved to put the affair in your hands. Will you go?"

"You know I will go!" the young man answered. "Ah, my lord! What is there that I would not do for you? You found me a humble fisher-lad; without hope or power ever to make more of myself—with nothing but dreams that could not come true! You made those dreams come true! In your service I have won honor and rich rewards; you made me captain of your South Tower. Nay, more, you have treated me like a son, have brought me up, these last four years, in your own household, teaching me to read, as if I had been nobly born! Ah, what do I not owe to you?"

"Ah, *zut!*" the count protested. "What did you do for me, four years ago, eh? You saved Toulouse and my honor. It was your sword-arm and the cunning of your brain that sent King Louis' army reeling back across the border, and made the king himself my prisoner. And three years hence did you not win back Aigues-Mortes from the Moors? And last year, when, as my ambassador, you negotiated peace with Thibault of Champagne, on terms that Thibault still mourns over!—Well, you will go. I can spare you but nine hundred men, but I will give you credentials to the Count of Foix."

"Nine hundred should be enough," Pierre reflected. "No, not enough, by themselves, to take so strong a fortalice as Tarascon; but enough with such forces as Roger of Foix will lend me."

Alphonse-Jourdain's smile was bleak. "I will command him to lend you all the men he has available; but he may not consent."

For a moment Pierre was nonplused.

"Not consent? But, my lord! He is your vassal, sworn to aid

you against your enemies. Is not Red Hugo your enemy? How can the Count of Foix refuse? Would he make himself a traitor?"

"I—think—not," Alphonse hesitated. "I have always held Roger of Foix a brave soldier and gallant gentleman. But—there is something strange in his unwillingness to get rid of this Hugo himself. The complaints, these three years past, have been enough to spur him to action. And—you know—the Count of Barcelona has always disputed my right to the overlordship of Foix."

"But you do not mean—"

"I mean," Count Alphonse interrupted, "that Count Raymond-Bérenger of Barcelona, Red Hugo of Tarascon, and Roger of Foix may have common interests—interests which threaten mine. Ho, there!"

"My lord?"

The answer came from an angle of the wall where the terrace joined the rampart; and a soldier strode toward them up the slope, his long mail hauberk rippling white in the moonlight.

"A torch!" the count commanded.

The man-at-arms was off at a run, his mail jingling musically through the half-dark. A pale red splotch heralded his return with the light, which he set in a socket in the arm of the marble bench whereon Alphonse had seated himself.

"Read this!" the count commanded; and Pierre took a letter from his hand.

It bore the seal and awkward scrawl of Roger of Foix; and though it opened and closed with assurances of devoted loyalty, Pierre scowled as he read it. It had arrived too soon to touch upon the murder of the pilgrims, of which Alphonse himself had just heard; but replying to an earlier request that Roger expel Red Hugo from Tarascon, the letter confessed its writer's inability to obey.

I have received strict warning (wrote the Count of Foix) from Bérenger of Barcelona that the first blow I strike against Red Hugo will be counted a declaration of war against Barcelona itself. Raymond-Bérenger claims that this Hugo is a subject of his, and thus under his protection. He asserts also that my own failure to attack Tarascon during the last three years is an admission of Hugo's right to keep it. If I march on Tarascon now, Bérenger will attack me for infringing the privileges of his vassal. He denies that Hugo ever swore allegiance to me and to Toulouse. Do not ask me, my lord, to court my own destruction!

"You see now," Alphonse broke in, "why the murder of these pilgrims may mean war—war between Toulouse and Barcelona. And Raymond-Bérenger has five men to every three of mine! The only way to avoid a war which we could not win is to take Tarascon by a swift coup. Of course Bérenger had nothing to do with the slaughter of the pilgrims; but as soon as he hears of it he will concentrate his armies on the southern border of Foix. I can not let those murders go unpunished, and Bérenger will know it. We must take Tarascon; and hold it, before his troops can reach it.

"It is strong enough to defy siege for a month, if fully garrisoned; and by that time I could buy help from the King of France. But if we attack Tarascon and fail to capture it, Bérenger will use this pretext that Hugo is his vassal to occupy it himself. In that event he can overawe Foix into submission, and take the whole county from me.

"Thus all hangs on your ability to persuade Roger of Foix to lend you his troops. With them, and your nine hundred, you may be able to take Tarascon by storm; without them, your nine hundred will be too few. I can not spare you more, for my spies report that Aquitaine is meditating another invasion of Toulouse.

"If Roger will not help you, or if you can not overcome Red Hugo by direct assault, do not attempt a siege. It would take too long, and the hosts of Barcelona would get time to come up and overwhelm you. Your task, then, is to win Roger's support. Remind him of his allegiance to me, promise him any rewards; aye, even threaten him, if need be!"

"Nine hundred men," Pierre pondered. "Give me eight hundred mounted men-at-arms, my lord, and five-score archers. If they can be in readiness to march at dawn? Good, my lord!"

OLD SIMON, master of the garrison of Toulouse, had the privilege of a bed in the armory. On this bed he was enjoying a glorious dream of some fierce battle of his youth, when something shot through the dream and stung him broad awake. Pierre Faidit, torch in hand, was bending over him.

"Well?" the veteran growled.

Though he loved Pierre, he never felt obliged to be polite to him. Twelve years ago Pierre, a boy with the muscle and resource of a man, had been a common soldier under Simon's handling; and the old man could not quite escape the feeling that most of the young captain's distinction had been somehow due to that handling.

So he patronized Pierre, though ready always to admit Pierre's greater abilities. Simon was an admirable officer, knowing every corner of the fortifications, every face in his garrison, and full of resource in the proper use of both; but none knew better than he that Pierre was his master in strategy, if not in tactics.

"You are to go with me to Foix," Pierre announced; and the old man struggled up, blinking.

"Foix? What next? Why?"

"We march to turn Red Hugo out of Tarascon," the other explained. "Nine hundred strong. It is so delicate a task that, after pondering it, I asked the count to send you as my lieutenant."

"Your lieutenant!" Simon jeered. "Why, you undubbed cockerel! But for the count's favor I should still be giving you orders, and you taking them with a bow and an 'As you command, good Simon!' Well, I will go with you. There will be good fighting, I hope; and you have a head on your shoulders!"

So the gray dawn saw the south gate of Toulouse pour out a stream of horsemen and brown-jerkined archers; and sunrise flashed on the armor of eager men that advanced down the vineyard-bordered road with the briskness of soldiers who go forth from hateful idleness to long-desired action.

Pierre rode in the van, deep in talk with old Simon, but ever casting a watchful eye down the white highway.

The road ran roughly south from Toulouse, following the Garonne and its tributary, the Ariège. Rutted and deep-worn at best, it had been badly washed out by the floods of the Spring before, so that the horses found it heavy going. The advance was slow, determined not only by the state of the road, but even more by the plodding archers that marched, in three divisions, before, behind, and between the two troops of cavalry.

Thirty miles above Toulouse, finding himself in territory where burned and ravaged villages bore witness to Red Hugo's raids, Pierre sent forward a dozen riders to act as scouts.

Ten miles farther, the high hills near Foix rose in wild loveliness; but Pierre saw it with a soldier's eye. The terrane was perfect for ambuscade: the road hugged the Ariège in all its windings, often between overhanging banks dense with shrubbery. So Pierre took no chances, and maintained ceaseless vigilance; though Red Hugo would scarce dare attack nine hundred men.

At Varilhes, fifty miles out of Toulouse, he ordered a halt. Here road and river plunged into a deep, rugged mountain defile, and night was coming on. When his scouts returned to report all clear, Pierre gave Simon his final orders.

"We can bring the host no nearer to Foix," he said, "until I have spoken with Count Roger. The garrison will already have seen our approach from the walls. Roger of Foix, who seems to have a bad conscience already, would think we were marching to attack him, and would refuse to let us enter or pass.

"Therefore I must ride ahead to Foix, to present my credentials. I will take ten men-at-arms with me; you must remain behind with the troops. My first task is to learn whether Count

Roger will help us against Red Hugo; and if not, whether he is in league with Barcelona, or merely afraid of its power.

"At dawn I will send a man to tell you what I have learned. If Roger will help us, this man will carry you my orders to advance and enter Foix, where the Count's men will join us. But if Roger refuses help, I shall ride on to Tarascon with the few men I have, and send you a messenger to instruct you when to advance."

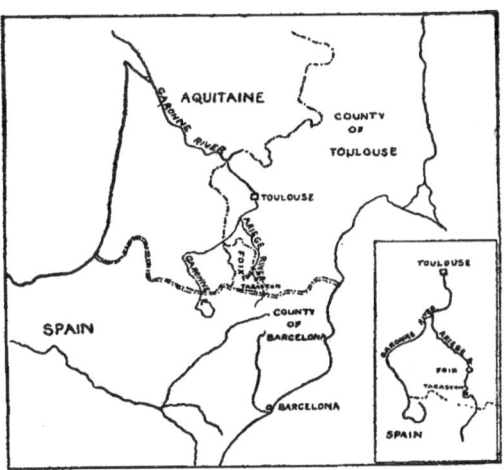

"Death and the devil!" swore Simon. "You would ride with a mere handful to Tarascon? You would be gobbled up by Red Hugo's riders before you have gone a league; or once inside its walls, you will never come out alive! You will need every man of us!"

"Nay, old thick-wit!" laughed Pierre. "Unless Foix joins us, can nine hundred take Tarascon? Or would Red Hugo open his gates to so many? He would stand us all off till help reached him from Barcelona. My only chance of capturing Hugo is to get inside his walls; and the only chance of that is to go with so few men that he will neither suspect nor fear us."

"But once in Tarascon, what can ten men do?" the veteran grumbled.

"Leave that to me. If I can not match this bandit's wits with mine, and find some trick to lure him to his ruin, I will fling away my sword and be a fisherman again!—But there may be no need of that; Roger may join us. If not, then my credentials will persuade him to let me pass through the city; and he will certainly let you follow. He can not stop an armed company of his lord's men without declaring open war on Toulouse. In that case, as soon as my messenger reaches you, make the best speed you can."

ROGER OF FOIX was a big man, strong-limbed and strong-featured; but his restless eyes had something furtive in them. This he seemed to know, for he would not meet Pierre's gaze. He reread the letters Pierre had handed him, scowling and plucking at his thick black beard.

"You know what your master writes?" he asked, looking past the young man rather than at him.

"I have my lord's full trust," Pierre answered.

The Count of Foix looked him over with more interest. He saw a clear-eyed young giant, in splendid armor such as only men of noble blood were wont to wear. It was the gift of Alphonse-Jourdain; but to Roger of Foix it implied rank and wealth. Therefore, not knowing the young man's humble birth, he spoke as to one but little his inferior.

"I do not remember you among the knights of Toulouse," he said. "Your name and title?"

"I am Pierre Faidit, captain of the south tower."

Roger of Foix opened his sly eyes wide. There were few in France who had not heard of Pierre Faidit, whose deeds of arms and brilliant strategy had for four years helped to make Toulouse great. He remembered that Alphonse-Jourdain was said to prize Pierre more highly than any of the proud knights that fought under his banner. For a single instant Roger's gaze met Pierre's fairly; and Pierre did not like its expression.

"What is your answer?" the Toulousan asked bluntly.

The Count of Foix sighed heavily.

"I can not help you," he replied, "though I would if I had the power. Heaven knows I have been faithful to Toulouse! But Alphonse-Jourdain can not ask me to cut my own throat."

Contempt edged Pierre's voice as he retorted:

"Is the great Count of Foix afraid of a mere brigand? Does he not dare to reclaim his own land, stolen from him by an outlaw?"

"*Cap de Deus!*" swore Roger. "Afraid? I? No, not if it were man against man! Does Alphonse know that Bérenger of Barcelona would crush me if I raised a hand against Red Hugo? Does he reflect that my towers are but five days' march from Barcelona itself?"

"I understand," Pierre spoke slowly. "Then I must finish the matter myself. You will of course grant me and my forces free passage through to Tarascon?"

Roger smiled queerly.

"With pleasure," he replied.

BEFORE SUNRISE Pierre passed with nine men-at-arms between the guards at the southern gate of Foix. Half an hour before, he had dispatched a single rider north to Simon's camp, with this message:

> Foix refused. Follow me to Tarascon. If a second messenger does not meet you by one hour past noon, reporting that I am in Tarascon and have found a way to open the gates to you, you may know that I have failed. In that case, press on with all speed; be at Tarascon at midnight; lay siege to the walls, but do not force the fighting at once. Make more noise than trouble!

Pierre and his little band had a scant ten miles to Tarascon; which lay on a crag girt half-round by a bend in the Ariège, and much higher than the citadel of Foix. But the way was rough and steep, and the going slow. The horses had been climbing half an hour when Pierre looked back at the gray ramparts of Foix, rising, one line of defense above and within another, in impregnable pride above its hills. The first rays of the sun bathed it in soft pink as he gazed, his eyes troubled.

"There is mischief somewhere," he mused. "Roger was too willing to let me through. I do not trust him."

Rough as the road was, Pierre made far better time with his nine than Simon's larger company could hope to do. Even when Tarascon was clear in view, he could see no trace of them behind. This did not trouble him; his message to Simon had said "midnight" for a purpose.

The Ariège flowed turbulently now, for the rise was steep and rocky. Sparse undergrowth half-concealed the flashing water till a sudden twist in the mountain trail brought the riders abruptly to the edge of a ford. The farther bank was lower, and thickly shaded with willow.

"On the alert!" warned Pierre; and his men drew as close together as the boulder-strewn ford would allow.

Each loosed his sword as he splashed into the icy stream, which deepened in mid-current. The horses were over their knees, and stumbling on hidden stones, when a horseman loomed up in the path beyond.

"Who goes?" the stranger challenged.

Before Pierre could answer, arrows flickered from the cover of the willows. One of the men-at-arms screamed, and slid from his horse.

Pierre's sword flashed.

"Over, and at them!" he shouted.

The Toulousans, disregarding the tricky footing of the ford, drove their spurs deep, till their mounts, snorting and scenting blood, had plunged up the farther bank and through the willows. They charged full into a second arrow-flight, which swept two more men down at close range. Then they were through, driving four archers into flight. But the skirmish was only begun.

Beyond the willows, which had given the archers cover, the land lay flat and bare, a rocky plateau below the crag of Tarascon. A dozen horsemen in mid-road covered the bowmen's flight.

Plainly the archers had orders to take position again at the end of the plateau, behind the riders, and loose their shafts a third time.

But Pierre gave them no chance. Outnumbered as he was, he led his handful of veterans in a smashing charge full on the hostile cavalry. The enemy's struggles to hold their mounts in line proved them bandits rather than drilled soldiers. The heavy horses of Toulouse, trained to war, knew their duty as well as their riders; they bore down straight and true, recoiled when their impact had thrown the ill-mounted bandits into confusion, and half-wheeled to let the Toulousan lances, already dripping, plunge in a second time.

Borne back by the first assault, the bandits were forced to cast down their spears and draw sword. Three were already unhorsed, with lance-wounds in throat or breast, and two more were thrown by their wounded horses. Helped up by their companions, these strove to exchange strokes with Pierre's mounted men, but at a disadvantage all the greater for the skill with which the Toulousan horses rode them down or bowled them flat with shoulder-thrusts. And wo to him who fell, with the sword poised above his head!

"Make an end!" Pierre cried, spurring straight for him who urged the bandits on.

This was more to the enemy's liking, for they knew sword-play, and their lighter horses did not wince from close combat as from the thunder of a charge. But their rally lasted not long; for a few swift sword-strokes ended in their captain's fall, Pierre's blade cleaving him to the chin. Wheeling their horses briskly, the brigands broke into full flight for Tarascon, their archers scampering behind.

The Toulousans would have pursued, furious at the treachery of the attack and the slaughter of their comrades; but Pierre held them sternly in check.

"We have wrought enough harm," he observed grimly. "It will be hard for us to get peaceful entrance into Tarascon now.

We have taken five lives to pay for three; turn to now and bury our fellows. Leave these sons of dogs to the ravens!"

The slain were laid in a common grave, and rocks were piled above the fresh-turned earth. As the party mounted again, one asked:

"Those were Red Hugo's men? Giles, posted on the rock there, saw them enter Tarascon."

Pierre nodded.

"We may look for trouble, lads. We were expected, or we should not have been attacked. Red Hugo must have had word of our coming. But how?"

Nor, cudgel his brains as he would, could he find a satisfactory answer. Could the Count of Foix have warned the enemy? He could have had no motive. It would have been treason, and what profit was there in it?

His lips compressed in an angry line, Pierre led his six riders straight for the crag of Tarascon. Within the quarter of an hour they were close enough to see the glinting helmets of sentinels three-fourths concealed behind its walls; half an hour, and Pierre was sure that the battlements boasted no siege-engines. He might be wrong; but catapults hot in use show their presence by the sky-pointing wooden arms above the merlons. Anyhow, so small a stronghold would scarcely be equipped with engines.

For small Tarascon was, though very strong. The north wall measured scarcely sixty feet; and Pierre guessed the whole less than eighty feet on east and west. It consisted of a tower surrounded by a wall of masonry, built on the solid rock of a high crag around which the Ariège nestled protectingly.

It would be necessary for Pierre to cross the river again just south of the castle, and—so he guessed—climb the southern face of the cliff by a winding way. It would go ill with any force that tried that escalade; for, as the Toulousans forded the stream and gained the narrow road that led to the outer gate, they saw how every foot of the approach was commanded by the grim walls above.

"Deus!" the soldier Giles exclaimed. "This place can not be undermined. Shovels can not dig through rock. Nor can it be taken by storm. Unless we can open the gates, good captain, old Simon will have a desperate time trying to win through!"

This was bad enough; but worse thoughts vexed Pierre. He was surprized that they had been allowed to come so far without a second attack; and now he and all with him felt the hair prickle on their necks with the expectation that at any moment a mass of rock or a dozen javelins hurled from the ramparts above might tear their lives from them.

Indeed, Pierre wondered why that hail of destruction did not come, since the garrison must know of the fight on the plateau by the ford.

Now rough laughter drifted down from the walls, but no finger was raised against them. When his horse breasted the last foot of the slope, Pierre could not keep back a great sigh of relief. Yet his perils were truly just beginning. Within that castle Red Hugo waited, doubtless infuriated by the defeat of his ambuscade.

Pierre had hoped to enter Tarascon not as a confessed enemy, but as the bearer of orders from Toulouse. His plan had been to appear before Hugo with Alphonse-Jourdain's command to get his bandits out and across the border. Of course, Hugo would have laughed such an order to scorn; but Pierre, as an envoy, would at least have been safe, and would have had until midnight to work out some scheme to open the gates to Simon's troops. Such things had been done, over and over again; and though the plan could not be definitely worked out till Pierre could observe the construction and plan of the castle, he trusted the keenness of his own brain.

But now he must enter—if he could get in at all—as a confessed enemy, with the blood of Hugo's retainers still on his sword. He would not be allowed the freedom of the castle; he might be thrown into the dungeons, or slain outright before the gate.

He made the resolve, then, that he would enter or perish. A second, more desperate plan shaped itself in his mind, to be used if he lived to come before Red Hugo's presence.

Tarascon had no moat, nor needed any, the approach being so perilous. The stout gate, flanked by projecting demi-turrets, was open as if to receive its visitors. A number of men-at-arms, rough fellows in coarse mail, stood about armed to the teeth; while others peered down from the battlements. A pair of them swaggered up to meet Pierre, grinning insolently; and one spoke:

"Welcome to Tarascon, noble sir! Our master expects you, and prays you to enter!"

More disturbed than pleased by this ambiguous greeting, Pierre rode under the arch of the gate, his men at his back. But here, in the bailey between tower and outer wall, his guide waved back the Toulousan men-at-arms.

"Nay!" he said, abandoning all pretense of courtesy. "Your men must bide here. They will be well cared for!"

Giles clapped a hand to his sword, but Pierre rebuked him. Violence could avail nothing now. He had come to match wits with Red Hugo; and wits alone must save or ruin him. But he was very glad he had compelled Simon to hold the main force back.

A direct attack on that castle would have brought his men full under a death-dealing hail from those walls, all along the steep and winding way. It would have meant ruin. Moreover, he saw now that a slow siege would accomplish no more than assault. A great stone cistern, plainly fed by springs in the crag itself, provided an inexhaustible water-supply even though a mighty army, with powerful siege-engines, should so dominate the walls that the garrison could not lower buckets to the river.

So on Pierre went, following his guide across the bailey to the tower, or keep. As he went, he stole swift glances to right and left, noting the stables, and soldier's quarters built against, and even in, the thick walls.

"You are well garrisoned," he remarked with forced amiability. "I see many men in yonder barracks."

The guide nodded curtly.

THE GROUND-FLOOR of the tower was a guard-room, from which a stair led to the living-apartments, and still higher to the battlements above. The tower as a whole was a fortress within a fortress, the refuge of the garrison in case the outer wall should be stormed. Yet it seemed to Pierre's roving eyes that two hundred men might easily hold this keep against seven times as many.

As he set foot on the stair, he heard the noise of gusty merriment roll down to meet him, swelling to a loud hum as he reached the top; and at last a very riot of talk, laughter, and shouted oaths.

The guide thrust aside the heavy hangings of the hall doorway, revealing a revel truly barbaric. The great room was crowded with men, sturdy rascals all, feasting at two long tables, sprawling on benches and gnawing gobbets of greasy meat, or drinking without restraint. Others, armed and mailed, stood along the walls, and lined the approach to a dais at the opposite end from the doorway.

This dais was a wide, low platform, with its own table for the lord of the castle, his highest officers, and noble guests. Now there were three men at this table: one in the high seat of the master, and one on each side of him.

The din was so loud and the merriment so high that for a moment Pierre and his guide stood unnoticed within the doorway; and Pierre had time for a swift glance at the three men on the dais. His eyes first sought out him who sat in the midmost seat, the lord of the castle; whose appearance bore out the worst reports of his bloodthirstiness. For this was Red Hugo.

Hugo, with massive limbs awkwardly asprawl; hair, brows, and beard one tangled mane of red; evil eyes in which danced the twin devils of cruelty and drink; a hooked, scarred nose and hard lips—this was he on whose soul lay the murder of seventy unarmed pilgrims.

To one entering the hall as Pierre had done, his fierce figure was framed as in a picture, so that the eye was drawn to him at once. Pierre's quick brain guessed the picture prearranged for his benefit, and despised the trick.

Yet Hugo held his gaze, as a thing superlatively evil must, till Pierre's shrewd scrutiny saw the man's smallness under his ferocious aspect. It takes more than ferocity and low cunning to make a strong man; and Red Hugo was not so strong but that he could serve as the tool of Barcelona.

The man on Hugo's right was a tall, thin soldier, with the fine features of the aristocrat, and frank, soldierly bearing. He on the bandit's left drew Pierre's gaze last, and held it longest. He was younger than the others, and shorter, though very strongly made, with big shoulders. Pierre noted the splendor of his attire; his long robe of azure silk was of the new fashion, with wide sleeves to the wrist, richly embroidered in heavy gold thread, and bound at the waist with a narrow girdle of gold plates.

But it was not his brave array, nor the long, fine black hair that reached his shoulders, nor his bold, beautiful features; it was his eyes that commanded Pierre's admiration. They were wide, sea-blue eyes, with just a tinge of green; they fascinated like jewels, and gleamed like steel.

But as Pierre's eyes clung to them, a harsh voice blared through the din, silencing it instantly:

"Hail, Pierre Faidit! We have waited for your coming. Will Alphonse-Jourdain have my head on a silver trencher, as Salome had St. John's? Or shall I wait for your nine hundred varlets to come and fetch me? Speak, that I may serve you!"

All Pierre's native poise could not hide his astonished dismay. Though he had not hoped, since the fight at the ford, for more than a desperate chance, he had not dreamed that Red Hugo would know his name or the nature of his errand. Indeed, he had counted on the brigand's ignorance of these things for that gambler's chance that alone could afford him some means of eluding vigilance long enough to throw the castle open for Simon.

Now there was no chance; somehow Red Hugo had learned all, and had not only numbers and position, but even the final advantage of playing with his own dice. In his sudden hopelessness, his mind grasped at the wild thought that had come to him as he had clambered up the perilous way to the gate—

"Leap upon him now, slay him, and go down fighting!"

But even this was denied. A knot of armed men stood between him and the dais, watching his every move.

As he hesitated he saw a smile of derision flit over Red Hugo's thin lips. He must say something, something which should uphold the dignity of Toulouse. So he answered, coolly enough:

"As you say, Sir Hugo, I am the envoy of Toulouse; though I know not how you learned of me. I need not your head, having one of my own. If I had wanted it, should I not have brought all my nine hundred men-at-arms with me?"

The bandit's head wagged with mirth.

"Well lied!" he shouted. "See, good youth, how the jest pleases my companions!"

And indeed the men-at-arms that thronged the hall echoed Hugo's laughter uproariously.

"But I will answer your riddle for you. Last night, while you slept at Foix, Count Roger sent me a secret message warning me of your errand."

He paused; then seeming suddenly to fly into a fury, he cried out:

"Laugh, you fool! You would have laughed had you tricked me to my death; can you not laugh when the shoe is on the other foot? Is not the joke merrier when he who would bite is bitten?"

His anger died as swiftly as it had risen, and he added silkily:

"There is a dungeon beneath this tower, cold and damp enough to chill even your ardor. There you shall lie until Alphonse-Jourdain buys your freedom on my terms. Would you hear those terms? Your master—if he would see you alive—must grant me full amnesty for all deeds with which I am charged; confirm my title to Tarascon, and pay a ransom of ten thousand marks. Five thousand will go to me; the rest to Roger of Foix, who recognized the high price you would fetch as soon as you told him your name!"

Now Pierre understood indeed. He knew Alphonse-Jourdain well enough to be sure he would pay this price, vast as it was—aye, though it cost him Foix—rather than let his favorite captain perish in the foul dungeons of Tarascon. The Count of Toulouse held his men's loyalty because he was first of all loyal to them. But Pierre wished not for life on such terms. His humiliation was almost more than he could bear.

But Hugo was speaking again, his insolent voice heaping up fresh taunts.

"Look you," he triumphed, "your master can not claim that I have wantonly molested an envoy; for I shall say that you slew five of my men, without provocation, on my own soil. Ha, you see the purpose of that ambush now?"

Bitterly Pierre admitted to himself how entirely he had been outwitted. All France would have risen in arms—except for the worst enemies of Toulouse—against the man who dared vitiate the immunity of an envoy. But now he had been put hopelessly in the wrong. Who would believe his word that Red Hugo's men, not Pierre's, had been the aggressors at the ford?

He could see, from the faces of the two men at Hugo's side, that they accepted the bandit's statement. And in a little while Pierre and his men would be in a dungeon, where they could not testify. It was this thought that unloosed his tongue. He would testify now!

"Dog, and son of a dog!" he cried. "You know well your men attacked mine! You charge me with murder; I hurl the charge back in your teeth, before these men of yours! If you dare defend your lie, draw sword and fight me! I claim trial by combat. God will show the right!"

Straightway Red Hugo's men-at-arms closed in, fingering their weapons. Knowing himself safe, the bandit laughed in scorn.

"Fight you? Nay, why should I? Are you not in my power? Seize him, guards!"

Pierre's sword flashed out; he sprang forward to cut a path to his enemy. But swiftly as he moved, another moved more swiftly. A lithe form broke through the soldiers between Hugo and Pierre, and struck up his sword.

It was the richly appareled officer who had sat on the bandit's left. He had drawn and leaped with incredible swiftness. Now he faced Pierre, his point, however, playing in menacing little flashes toward Hugo's men-at-arms, who would else have fallen on the Toulousan.

"Nay, Sir Hugo, you must fight!" he interposed. "Has he not given you the lie? Have you not accused him of murder, and he flung back the charge? No French gentleman can refuse a challenge! Am I not right, my lord of Armagnac?"

The last words startled Pierre more than the aid so unexpectedly lent him. Armagnac? There was but one lord of Armagnac; that was Bertrand, Seneschal of Aquitaine! And the Duchess of Aquitaine, even more than Bérenger of Barcelona, was the bitter enemy of Toulouse! Bérenger desired no more than a rich slice of Alphonse-Jourdain's territory; but Aliénor of Aquitaine would give her evil soul to see him dead, and Toulouse in ruins. But she had married the King of France, who was bound by treaty with Toulouse to keep peace with Alphonse. As Duchess of Aquitaine, Aliénor could declare war in her own right, but she could not involve the Kingdom of France.

But before Pierre could make out what this meant, the third man on the dais spoke out quietly:

"Cercamon is right, Hugo. You are in honor bound to fight!"

The garrison howled its disapproval, and Hugo bellowed furiously:

"I will not fight him! Am I not in my own house? Let him be thrown into the dungeon!"

But Cercamon of the rich robes interfered again; his fine eyes blazing.

"If you will not fight him, let me!" he urged. "I will take your quarrel on my shoulders. Rather would I die than see a soldier condemned without his right to appeal to arms. You must let me fight him; and if he slays me, you must let him and his go free!"

The name Cercamon cleared away Pierre's bewilderment. It was one of the most famous names in France; the name of a man preeminent for his poetic skill, and no less for his mastery of the sword. All the world knew Cercamon, first of troubadours, pattern of chivalry, and—trusted servant of Raymond-Bérenger!

Pierre saw now that Cercamon must be here to close the bargain between Red Hugo and Barcelona, the bargain by which all of Foix was to be torn from Toulouse and given to Bérenger. And Bertrand of Armagnac presence meant either that Queen Aliénor was helping Bérenger, or that Aquitaine—without the King's authority, but quite within its legal privileges—was bidding against Barcelona for the same prize! Pierre remembered that it was fear of invasion from Aquitaine which had prevented Alphonse-Jourdain from marching on Tarascon himself.

Cercamon's readiness to fight Pierre in Hugo's quarrel was now also clear. The troubadour's honor would have been stained had he connived at Hugo's treachery; moreover, the famous swordsman must have felt confident that he could kill even so formidable an antagonist as Pierre, and thus defeat Alphonse-Jourdain's one chance of saving Foix. By killing Pierre in fair fight Cercamon could both save his honor and serve his lord.

Red Hugo must suddenly have perceived some advantage to

himself in Cercamon's offer, for his eyes lighted with an unholy gleam.

"So be it!" he agreed. "Fight him, then! Stand back all, and give them room!"

All obeyed; and Pierre, seeing his opponent unarmored, stripped off his own hauberk. The troubadour advanced with catlike grace, and the two blades clashed. The play of point and edge that followed was so fast, so clean, so beautifully matched, that none could see advantage on either side. Again and again Pierre's point flickered in, only to be turned by the other's skilful guard.

Over and over the troubadour struck, to meet a parry as perfect as his own. Blue eyes and black burned into each other, watching for the gleam that foretold the stroke; and never did either misjudge by a hair. The bandits massed about, neither spoke nor moved, watching with quick-taken breaths and little sighs of excitement.

For several minutes neither gave ground; then Pierre's weight and muscle began to tell. But they gained him no real advantage; for Cercamon, instead of giving ground before his onset, danced around him with lithe nimbleness, ducking now to right, now to left; and always his point played on the very quick of Pierre's guard, as Pierre's played close to his.

It was a wondrous duel, such as none there had ever witnessed. Both antagonists were breathing short, striking with shorter, quicker thrusts and little, dangerous side-cuts, when, catching the eye of one of his blackguards, Red Hugo raised his hand.

Pierre heard a sudden cry of rage from the Count of Armagnac; but he was poised for a blow, and dared not look aside. Even as he struck, something beat him down from behind. He fell prone and senseless. Instantly the troubadour leaped over, his body, struck out like a tiger, and buried his blade in the skull of the coward whose mace-handle had felled Pierre.

AS A SWIMMER who has been under water too long

comes up through an agonizing darkness that weighs on breast and brain, so Pierre struggled up through a sea of painful night into slow consciousness. One by one his faculties awoke from a clinging dream, till he sat up with a start, and felt sick with sudden pain. Wondering, he strove to rise, but something that clung to his right ankle flung him back. The hand with which he fumbled felt an iron shackle locked about his bare leg.

He touched his breast, his arms, his thighs. He was naked, and fettered. His finger followed the chain that bound him. It was no more than four feet long, and ended in a massive staple in the stone floor. Rising cautiously, he peered into the gloom all about him, till, high above his head, and some distance to the right, he saw a single star. Craning his neck to look at it, he felt a numbness at the back of his head; his exploring fingers touched something wet and sticky.

Then memory came back; the fight in the hall, the troubadour's darting blade, the—but he could recall no more. Now he was a prisoner, in a stone cell, stripped of arms and clothing, chained to the floor. And it was night!

Night? But what time? Was it midnight yet? God forbid, or the next moment might bring Simon and his host, with no one to open the gates to them—to attempt a forlorn assault upon walls impregnable; walls manned by a garrison, warned and alert.

And he, Pierre, was helpless even to shout a word of caution! He had ruined his own enterprise; made certain the destruction of his own men; flung away his master's one chance of saving Foix! Too vain of his own shrewdness, he had let himself be played with like the dull-witted peasant he was!

Yet he did not despair. Once more his brain set itself to solve the impossible problem, to rebuild the temple of success from the ruins of defeat. Back and forth his thoughts fluttered, alighting nowhere on solid hope, but searching ever for some support, however frail. He knew not how long he lay on the cold stone, husbanding his strength and unraveling the tangled skein of thought; yet at last an end came.

Somewhere back of him iron bolts slid back with a rusty screech; a blaze of light seared his eyes. Voices; then a steel-clad form stood before him, sharp against the red glare of a torch. The face was hidden, but the voice that greeted him was Cercamon's—

"You are badly hurt?"

Pierre shook his head, but would not speak. His thoughts of this man were black; for he had no way of knowing that the troubadour had not connived at the foul blow that had struck him down. He knew only that in the midst of fight he had been smitten treacherously from behind, and now was in a plight to which no honest enemy would have consented. But Cercamon's next words set him right:

"I have done what I could to save you, Pierre Faidit. He who struck you lies dead under my sword. I prayed Hugo to confine you in a chamber above, rather than here; but he refused. More I can not do without imperiling my master's affairs, which are already in bad plight."

It is hard for a naked man in chains to preserve his dignity before one mailed and free; but Pierre achieved the feat. Gravely he thanked the troubadour; and for Toulouse's sake asked further—

"Can you not find some way to help me to escape?"

Cercamon laughed shortly.

"Not I! You serve Toulouse; I serve Barcelona. I bribed the jailer to let me speak with you; but if I did more, you might yet find some way to defeat my master's purpose. Already Bertrand of Armagnac has bought Hugo's support away from Bérenger to Aliénor; the bandit has agreed to deliver Tarascon not to me, but to Bertrand. Within four and twenty hours troops from Aquitaine will be here, with catapults and provisions, to take over the castle.

"With Tarascon safe in the Count of Armagnac's hands, Aquitaine can send an army against Foix with no danger of an attack from its rival, Barcelona; Foix will fall, and then Aliénor's forces can strike at Toulouse from south and north at once. The King of France will not interfere; for his treaty with Alphonse binds him only not to make war on Toulouse himself."

Pierre groaned; and Cercamon continued:

"The only escape for Toulouse from this double danger lies in Raymond-Bérenger's getting possession of Tarascon before tomorrow night. Having learned from my spies in Aquitaine that Armagnac's host would follow him here, I came myself to buy back Red Hugo's allegiance. I foresaw that Armagnac might outbid me again, and therefore had two thousand men from Barcelona hidden in the mountain passes south of here. I ride forth now to lead them against the castle. When Armagnac's troops come, they will be too late!"

"Why has not Red Hugo thrust you in prison, as he has me?" Pierre interposed; and the troubadour laughed.

"Because he has no pretext, and he fears Barcelona more than he fears Toulouse. Has not Bertrand of Armagnac convinced him that Aquitaine is about to crush Toulouse?"

Now Pierre's thoughts had indeed found something to light on. Though Tarascon in Bérenger's hands would cost Toulouse only the county of Foix, and not its own destruction, it would mean as much shame to Pierre as would Aquitaine's success. But—how if there were a way to outwit both Bérenger and Aquitaine at once? Craftily he shifted the subject:

"I owe you much gratitude for your kindness; but it will avail me little. Sooner or later Red Hugo will learn that my master will not pay one copper to ransom me!"

"But you are a great soldier!" the troubadour protested. "You are the prince of swordsmen. Surely Alphonse-Jourdain would go deep into his treasury to free such a man!"

Now it hurt Pierre to deal uncandidly with one to whom he owed at least generous treatment; but there was no help for it. Barcelona was unjustly attempting to seize Toulousan territory. It was war between them; and strategy is fair in war. All that counted for Pierre was his new, faint hope that he might yet save Foix. So he answered with well-feigned gloom:

"I am but an ass masquerading in a lion's skin. My father was a fisherman; no pride of rank will urge my master to save me. Moreover, I have failed; and Alphonse-Jourdain never pardons failure. He will leave me in Red Hugo's hands!"

Now that which had put it into Pierre's head to say this was no more than the glimmer of the troubadour's jeweled dagger-haft in the torchlight.

But Cercamon's distress was deep.

"But Red Hugo has sworn to torture you," he cried, "if you are not ransomed!"

"Can any hear us?" Pierre whispered.

"Not a soul. The jailer who unlocked yonder door for me waits outside; but the wood is six inches thick. Would I else have told you what I have?"

"When do you depart?"

"At once!" the troubadour answered.

"And the time now?"

"Three hours after sunset."

Pierre stifled his gasp of relief. At that season four hours more must pass before midnight and Simon's coming. There was still time, if only—

"One thing you may do, troubadour, to save me from the torture. When you go, leave your dagger with me. Put it in my hand, for the chain that binds my ankle gives me no great reach."

Cercamon started back.

"You would take your own life?"

"Why not?" Pierre asked grimly. "Would Heaven hold the deed against a man who slays himself only to escape a more horrible death?"

"You are right. A Frenchman should die so, rather than by the hands of merciless thieves."

Stooping, the troubadour gripped Pierre's hand in farewell, then drew his dagger and placed it in the captive's fingers.

"May God strengthen you, and the Virgin intercede for you!" he prayed, and turned away.

Once more the door screamed on its hinges, a gruff voice spoke, and the light was blotted out.

Pierre's one hope lay in his knowledge that, since he was to be held for ransom, he would be fed, and—Heaven willing—before midnight. Nor was he wrong. On the heels of Cercamon's departure Pierre made ready for the jailer's coming; and within ten minutes the key turned in the lock again.

The staple that held the captive's short chain was so placed that he who fed him had no need to fear attack. Still, it was with caution that the jailer, torch in one hand and a hamper in the other, paused just within the cell to shove bread and wine to a point where Pierre could barely have reached it.

But in doing so he raised his torch to make certain of Pierre's position; and as the light fell on the prisoner, he fell back with an oath. For Pierre lay prone, sprawled out ominously; he moved not, though the jailer edged in and prodded him. There were blood-drops on the floor; a bloodstained dagger lay beside him.

Snatching up the knife, the jailer held it under the torch.

"Body of the devil!" he swore. "The Barcelonan! What hate he must have held against this man, to stab him in helplessness! Why, it was fair fight between them, and no cause for rancor!"

Tossing the knife toward the open door, he bent over Pierre, to turn him over and examine the wound.

But it was no corpse that clutched him by the throat, choking back the cry that would else have burst from him. In an unhappy moment the struggling jailer snatched from his girdle his massive bundle of keys, and brought them down blindly on his assailant's shoulder. The act cost him his life. Pierre's convulsive forward thrust with both clenched hands broke the fellow's neck. It had all happened without a sound that could have been heard ten feet outside the door.

Calmly Pierre picked up the spluttering torch and swung it

till it blazed. It was perilous, for if the light should be seen through the open door by any passer-by—But no one passed.

Swiftly he examined the jailer's keys, and soon found one that undid the steel ring about his ankle. Being free of his chain, he could now close the door. His next act was to bind up, with a strip from the dead man's none too clean gown, the raw cut in his arm which had supplied the blood to deceive the jailer.

Then, to gain strength to carry out the plan that was taking shape in his mind, he munched the loaf and drank the thin wine that had been brought for him. When this was done, he put on the dead man's long gown of fustian; hid Cercamon's dagger in its sleeve, and left the cell, locking the door behind him.

Still, as ever since he had left Toulouse, his plan was incomplete, elastic, dependent on such contingencies as might lie in wait at any of the dangerous stages ahead. But the next step was clear; he must find his six comrades, if they still lived. Probably, like himself, they had been disarmed and imprisoned. Since in every small castle the dungeon cells lay close together he need search only in the vicinity of his own.

The first risk lay straight ahead. He was in the vaults under the tower; a square stone crypt, damp with water that seeped between the courses. Doors opened in the wall along which he advanced; but not twelve yards ahead, two men-at-arms leaned on their arms about a fire that glowed in a brazier. The gloom of the place hid his face from them; his body, wrapped in the jailer's garments, appeared to them but a flitting shadow whose shape and function they knew well. They neither challenged nor spoke. The door next his own cell lay close to his hand. Its key would be one of the three great fretted bars on the bundle at his belt. His choice lay between two, since he already knew the one for his own cell. In a moment he had the door open. His heart thumped violently as he stole a glance at the two guards; but to them he was a familiar figure on its accustomed round.

The cell was empty, save for something white in the ring of a fetter. Shuddering, Pierre bolted the door again, and moved toward the third cell. This brought him nearer the guards, wherefore he held his torch away from his face. Once more he swung open a massive door, and thrust the light within. Then he slipped inside, and closed the door tight. Six men lay on the damp floor; two chained as he had been; four, for whom there were no fetters, bound hand and foot and dumped together like sacks.

He whispered: "Be still! It is I, Pierre."

Then his knife severed their bonds; the fetters opened to his keys; and his comrades, stretching their cramped limbs, fell on their knees to thank him. But he silenced them abruptly:

"No words! Bide here till I fetch you arms. We have but three hours before Simon comes. Nay, you can not help. Lie still, till I come."

Then he was gone, bolting them in, lest the guards look in upon them.

Beyond the fire and the two armed knaves lay the stair to the guard-room. As he passed the two on duty one greeted him sleepily:

"Ho, Arnolt! Bring us wine. It is damp here, and our very bones freeze. 'Twill be long ere we are relieved, and then only to perch on the cold battlements watching for the men of Toulouse."

Pierre knew the danger of speaking; yet he felt he must know whether the bulk of the garrison had yet mounted to the ramparts to repel Simon's expected assault. Therefore he asked; hoping his voice might resemble that of the jailer for whom they took, him. He forgot that he was a man of Languedoc, speaking a dialect distinguishable from their Norman.

The words no sooner left his lips than he who had asked for wine straightened up, eying Pierre sharply. The first glance assured him this stalwart giant was not Arnolt; but the second's time for that glance was enough for Pierre.

Before either guard could raise a pike or draw sword, he was on them. His right fist smashed the thirsty one senseless to the stones; the dagger leaped from his sleeve into his strong fingers, and found its sheath in the second man's throat. He stooped over the first, muttering anxiously:

"A brave clatter his mail made. A wax candle to St. Sernin if none hears!"

He waited a little, but there was no stir above stairs. Dragging the corpse and its unconscious companion to the cell that had been his own, he thrust them inside, bound and gagged him who lived, and bolted the door. The blood about the fire must remain; but he carefully scattered the coals in the grate to dull their glow, and extinguished the torch. Groping along the wall, he found the stair, and mounted softly.

The guard-room also, had its fire; but only three men lay about it. At this, Pierre's heart bounded. It meant that the impending approach of Simon's host had forced Red Hugo to draw away almost all his garrison to the ramparts. From the shadow of the stair Pierre watched the three, pondering how he should come at them without rousing the garrison. He must have their armor for his own men; but he must get it without noise.

The men-at-arms could not see him in the gloom outside the firelight, and he took care they should hear nothing, holding his very breath. They were talking in low tones, ever and anon laughing derisively. Though he could not distinguish the words, he guessed they spoke of the attack to come, and the ease with which they would repel it. He knew not how long he waited for some diversion that might offer a chance for action. It seemed eternity. At length one of the three rose yawning; then another.

"Time to relieve Gaucelm and Fermelin!" the first spoke. "*Peste!* It will be cold down there!"

He moved toward the stair, followed by the second who had risen. That only one man should be left on duty in the guard-room was natural; with the prisoners supposedly secured, and no enemy within the walls, no more were needed. And the expectation of Simon's attack made it advisable to spare no more men from the walls.

Pierre shrank back into the dark stair-mouth, to let the two men pass him. The first brushed his face with his cloak. Then the second was near, .feeling for the first few steps and cursing the darkness. His voice guided Pierre's hand to the fellow's mouth, whose astounded gasp was muffled by strong fingers. Pierre's other hand found the soldier's waist and lifted him high in air. Before he could cry out, he was hurled down the stair-well with terrific force. A choking curse and the crash of mail on stone!

With all of Pierre's strength to speed his fall, the second man-at-arms had struck the first at the turn of the stair, and both hurtled against the stone with terrific force. Pierre was after them as they landed; one lay still, the other groaned. But in a moment, the latter, his first agony subsiding, started to cry out; and Pierre's fist struck the life from his body, barely in time to make the cry incoherent.

Even so, the third man came running down from the guard-room. His failure to give the alarm showed how far he was from suspecting more than an accident. Pierre thrust out a foot as he passed, and he too fell headlong. But his fall was softened by the bodies of his comrades; and it was plain that he knew he had been tripped, for he came up full of fight.

Pierre heard the swish of a sword leaving its scabbard; and, fearing a shout that would alarm the garrison, leaped upon him with his knife. He felt the hot scratch of the sword on his cheek as his dagger plunged. Then, descending, he dragged the three corpses away, and locked them too in the cell that had been his.

"Two more will serve!" thought Pierre, with an eye to armor for all his little company.

He wondered, however, as he returned to the empty guard-room, how he should find two victims more, without perhaps

finding too many. But he had no need to find others. He discovered chests of arms in the guard-room, and helped himself
to both mail and swords. His only trouble was to find a hauberk
that would fit his mighty shoulders; fortunately there was one
that would slip on him, though it gave his arms something less
than full play. A helmet he must do without for the present. So
he descended the stairs, his booty in his arms.

The cramps had now left the limbs of his fellows, and their
hearts were glad enough to see him, still safe, and armed.
Quickly he drew them into the cell where his captives lay, with
their armor waiting but to be stripped off. In brief space the
Toulousans were armed and equipped.

"Now follow me," Pierre ordered. "Make no noise."

Softly they stole up through the guardroom, mounted the
stairs above, and stood on the landing before the entrance to
the great hall.

"Five of you have helmets, and may hold this stair," Pierre
instructed them. "If any pass you, ye will be taken in the dark
for men of the garrison, and perhaps ordered to the ramparts.
If so, obey. Ye will not be recognized in the night. But at the
least alarm or uproar, run down to the gate, and wait there for
me. Giles and I, who have no helmets, will set to work in the
hall."

Now began the nerve-racking part of Pierre's vigil. He had
important work to do, but must time it to tally with an event
he could not closely time—Simon's arrival with the Toulousan
host. As nearly as he could compute, it still lacked an hour and
a half to midnight. He knew old Simon well enough to count
on his arrival at the precise hour set.

Quietly he thrust aside the hanging and entered the hall. It
was empty; but some quick ear detected his approach, for a face
was thrust through a door that Pierre guessed led to the kitchens. At sight of an armored man—whose features were indis-
tinct in the light of a few scattered torches—the head withdrew.
Pierre smiled, knowing that to a servant he must seem—since
he was armed—one of the garrison.

He sat down, Giles beside him, and deliberately let the greater part of an hour pass. His men he was sure would avoid discovery, since if seen they would merely be sent to the walls; his only fear was that some officer might come down to the hall. But there was little chance of this either, the whole garrison being certainly on the ramparts.

When he judged it time, he strode to the kitchen door, and tapped, stepping back quickly where the light would not fall on his face. When a servant appeared, he commanded—this time careful to imitate the guttural Norman dialect:

"Bring fagots. Our lord commands a fire."

In a few minutes the kitchen knaves staggered in with logs, shavings, and light-wood; and one applied a torch. Till they had gone, Pierre kept his face turned away.

In a little while the fire was leaping merrily. A glance toward the closed kitchen door reassured him; but for a little while he continued to watch. Then with a quick command to Giles he swiftly lifted one bench after another to the fire, measuring the distance to the dim ceiling as close as he could guess. Understanding, Giles set to work busily; and the two men lost no time in making above the flames a pyramid of benches and boards from the loose-topped tables.

When the bonfire towered as high as Pierre could reach, he flung dry rushes from the floor upon it. These caught greedily. In a moment the fire was a menacing mass of upward-shooting flame, a pillar of destruction in the center of the hall. Even now it licked the dry beams of the ceiling. The arrow-slots on the two long sides of the room gave excellent draft. The beams began to char odorously, then give off sparks and glow. It crackled fiercely now; soon it would roar so loud that the servants in the kitchens would know it was something greater than a mere hearth-fire.

Pierre slipped out to the stairway. His five men waited still.

"No one has come," one whispered.

Pierre blessed his luck, though indeed it would have been

strange if any had left the ramparts when an assault was expected.

"Two of you go to the ramparts," Pierre ordered. "Mingle with the garrison, but do not speak. When first ye hear or see Simon's approach, steal down and tell me."

Two glided away; but before they could reach the stair, the bray of a trumpet reached them through the arrow-slots. A clash of iron followed, and the shouting of near a thousand men.

"Bide here," Pierre cautioned. "Simon has come. Good man! He obeys my order to make a noise and keep aloof at first. Wait a little till yonder beams blaze beyond quenching."

For perhaps five minutes they waited, while the fire swelled in volume, and the acrid smoke stung in their nostrils. The roar of the blaze now rose high. The servants, roused at last, poured in from the kitchen; but the sight of armed men sent them back, yelling their alarm.

"None will hear them," Pierre chuckled. "Simon makes too much din. One moment more, and we succeed!"

He burst out coughing, in a billow of enveloping smoke.

"Now!" he wheezed. "You, Giles, up that stair and to the battlements! Cry, 'Fire!' In the alarm that follows, none will think to examine your face. Take care to be first in the rush down the stair, and get to the gate as fast as you may. We shall be there before you."

A TONGUE of flame, sucked out by the draft from the stair-well, reached out at Pierre's heels as he fled down the stairs. He and his companions had scarce crossed the bailey when a cry of wild alarm told them that Giles had fulfilled his errand. From the courtyard Pierre looked back, to see black smoke outlined by lurid flames pouring out of the arrow-slots, and heard the yells and the running feet of men in terror.

He reached the great gate just as a surging mass of men, with all the momentum of their descent from the tower behind them, piled up in the guard-room gate. Their struggles to get out were frightful; their mail grated as their bodies jammed together, and their shrieks proved how close the flames were to the unlucky ones in the rear. But they soon won through for the gate was none so narrow, and erupted into the courtyard.

Their alarm set the men on the bailey walls into like panic. Until the first wild cry burst forth, these had had eyes only for the noisy host of Simon that clamored at the base of the cliff, just out of spear and arrow-shot. But when the tumult from the burning tower readied their ears, they turned to see flames shooting out of the arrow-slots, and curling up to lick the stones.

Then their own terror drove them from the walls. They ran down into the court at top speed, their shouts swelling the din. There was much pitch and oil stored in drums in the tower, for use in siege; and well the bandits knew that, once the conflagration reached the inflammable stuff, the explosion would hurl the tower walls outward in an avalanche of stone that would crush all it struck; and flying brands would kindle all the combustibles stored in the casernes.

The pandemonium within the outer walls was horrible. The entire garrison, quite two hundred strong, swirled about the gate, or struggled to get nearer to it. What armies could not have done to demolish their morale, the cry of "Fire!" had done at once. Pierre had enlisted on his side the one invincible ally. With no means of fighting flames but water borne all the way from the cistern, bucket by bucket; with no escape save through the main gate in the outer wall, and a small sally-port in its rear, the garrison had to choose between the flames and the possible mercies of Simon and his host outside.

The choice was quietly taken. The first to reach the great gate—even had it been Red Hugo himself—would have thrown it open rather than wait to be burned inside. But the first there was Pierre, who had planned for this moment. His strong arms wrestled with the great bars, threw them aside, and, backed by the weight of his six companions, flung it wide.

A wild shout from the foot of the cliff bore witness to the

savage joy with which the Toulousan host saw the flames and the flight of the garrison. A wild clamor filled the night, made up of the cries of the terrified bandits, the roaring joy of the assailants, and the clang of nine hundred mail hauberks as their wearers rushed up the undefended slope that led to the gate.

But just outside that gate Pierre waited, his keen eyes flickering over every man that fled the flames. The foremost of the Toulousan advance was almost up the hill when that which he waited for came—Red Hugo helmetless, but still clutching his sword; fiery mane flashing in the greater fire of the burning castle.

Pierre's hand seized him as he burst through, swung him off his feet, and set him down against the wall.

"On guard!" Pierre cried. "I have longed for this!"

A moment Hugo stared, bewildered; then he struck out with a savage oath. As Pierre's blade met his a voice bellowed:

"Ha! Pierre! Well done!"

But Pierre neither turned nor answered. His eyes were on Red Hugo, his sword flashing about Red Hugo's head. Twice he struck, three times; and the fourth blow shore the bandit's head from his shoulders.

Scarce a drop of blood, save Hugo's, was shed in the brief flurry that followed. The garrison had but one thought; escape from the flames. That escape was granted them by the opening of the gate. Little they cared then that they ran into the hands of a host too great for them to fight in the open.

As Pierre wiped his blade dry, his own men-at-arms were binding the captives, who had no more will to resist than so many sheep. Then, as he looked on with a smile of triumph, Old Simon thumped him on the back.

But Pierre pointed north.

"Come away before the brands fly," he commanded. "Who is that you have there, Simon? Why, 'tis Bertramd of Armagnac! Unbind him; he is a knight. Sound the trumpet!"

As the long column swung down the hill, Pierre looked back

toward burning Tarascon. Even as he gazed, the tower fell in with a sounding crash and a great heavenward spout of flame. He turned to Simon.

"Before this time tomorrow," he said with laughter in his voice, "the troops of Aquitaine and of Barcelona will finish their race to occupy yonder castle. They will march home again with mournful faces; for they can not defend a heap of charred stones. Without the walls of Tarascon, they can not threaten Foix; without Foix, they dare not march on Toulouse. Well, we are weary, lads, but tomorrow we rest in Foix! Count Roger will be glad to purchase pardon by giving us free entry, and pardon he must have, unless my lord can find one better than he to hold his lands."

Bertrand of Armagnac, mounted between Simon and Pierre on a horse lent by a man-at-arms, spoke up sheepishly.

"Would that I might see Cercamon's face," he said. "For if, as you say, Barcelona sends a host to head ours off, it will certainly be Cercamon who leads it."

Then he smiled to himself, adding—

"But if Cercamon could see me now!"

"Ah me!" sighed Pierre. "I am sorry for Cercamon!"

THE SWORD OF THE PROPHET

A LOYAL HEART, a keen brain, and a stout sword-arm—these make a great captain. When all three are found in one man, *messires,* that man acquires fame and his lord's love, and is on the road to greatness

Such a man was my captain, Pierre Faidit. Me? Bah! I am a spearman, and, as you see, something of a minstrel. Jehan the Big, men call me. But I was talking of Pierre. Let me strum a few notes as I talk, *messires.* I am not like the strolling vagabonds who sing lying tales. I saw the deeds of which I tell; aye, and had a hand in them.

Pierre was as much bigger than I as I am than yonder kitchen-knave; and you see I am of great stature. Ah, the breadth of his shoulders! The great chest of him, made for endurance! His arms, that could crack my ribs in one squeeze! And he was as handsome as he was strong. I have seen a face like his, with its broad brow and hooked nose, on a coin that the Romans minted.

His eyes were dark and piercing; his white teeth showed in a merry smile that won the heart; his cheeks, dark like mine, had the rose of a woman's under their sun-browned olive. He could talk like a priest—aye, and read like one, *pardieu!* For our master, Count Alphonse-Jourdain the Great of Toulouse, had him taught letters. And, St. Michael the Champion! How Pierre could fight! God help the man who crossed swords with him!

It was in 1133 that Count Alphonse found him, a mere fisher lad, in a dirty hole of a coast village, called Cap Estang. He was

73

a fine boy, though but fourteen, with the promise of mighty strength. We came upon him fighting four lads, each as old as he; and the count's eyes gleamed at the sight of his great shoulders and smooth muscles. My lord took him and made a soldier of him.

Well did he repay the count's favor. For eight years he labored, drilled, and toiled to learn the trade of the sword. Yes, he learned more—the art of the sword; for he became the first swordsman of the South. Those great eyes of his were always open, always questioning; storing knowledge which he was one day to use to save our master, and Toulouse itself.

Eight years after, he was appointed captain of the south gate. It was then that his skill with his weapon, and his great wisdom, first won his fame. By a cunning stratagem he drove off King Louis VII and the French army from our gates, and took the King with his own hand.

Not a year went by without some great deed from his hand; and in all these, my masters, I had some small share. For I was stationed at Pierre's gate, and bore its banner. In 1145 he captured the impregnable castle of Tarascon, though he was a prisoner in its dungeons. In that castle he first met his dearest friend, Cercamon the troubadour.

If any man in the South could rival Pierre Faidit, whether with the sword or in the cunning of his brain, it was Cercamon. Every court in France knew Cercamon, whose voice could lure the very angels of heaven to listen, whose weapon pierced every guard, whose guile was deep as the sea. When he first met my captain, they fought, yet neither triumphed. For Pierre was struck down from behind by a dog of a spearman; and that same night Cercamon was forced to leave Tarascon. For almost a year he knew not that Pierre still lived. But the memory of that fight made them friends.

Pierre lived, and triumphed. He seized Tarascon from its bandit ruler by a ruse; and by that deed he outwitted Cercamon's plans for getting Tarascon for his own master, Raymond-Bérenger IV, Count of Barcelona. Now this Bérenger was my lord Alphonse's enemy. A fair foe, not like the she wolf of Aquitaine, the wicked Queen of France.

When Pierre next met Cercamon—and it is of this, *messires,* that I would tell you—their meeting was fraught with fate. By then Pierre was as well known as Cercamon, having wrought so many noble strokes with sword and brain that he was spoken of even in Italy. The lords who envied my master would have paid any price for his services; but he was not to be bought. He loved Alphonse-Jourdain, who also loved him.

Now I saw not all these things of which I speak, for I am but a sergeant. Some I saw, some I had from hearsay, and the rest from René the Clerk, the count's secretary. René was close-mouthed most of the time; but he loved the dice, and owed so much to me that he dared not hide from me that which I wished to know. He knew he could count on my secrecy, for I too loved my master. It will do no hurt to tell it now, for Alphonse the Great, alas! is dead; and Pierre is in England. When shall I see him more?

It was in May of 1146. Ah, where is May sweeter than on the vine-clad hills of Toulouse? The land was bright with sunshine and the fresh, new green, the songs of the birds were echoed by the voices of men-at-arms chanting on the battlements. Winter was gone, and all men rejoiced in the sun. Hopes rose with the sap, and budded with the flowers.

In this season Alphonse-Jourdain held court on the terrace outside the postern, where the grass grew thick and green, with the first roses breaking into bloom, and the castle heights ran down to the rolling slopes and the plains of the broad, blue Garonne.

My lord sat, that day, at a table beside the fountain, with the three he trusted most. You have seen the count—you remember his great, well-knit body, still agile for all his three-and-forty Winters. You recall his bold hawk-features, his fierce gray eyes. Though at an age when most men are in life's Winter, he was as lean and strong as in that stormy youth which saw his first successes on the fields of Palestine.

On one side of him sat—for he made companions of these men, though they were his vassals—René the Clerk, a lean youth in black, whose white fingers played with a roll of parchment marked with neat figures and notations in a fair round hand. On his other hand was old Simon, master of the garrison, a straight-backed veteran with a rough, scarred face. Opposite the count, you may be sure, sat Pierre Faidit, my captain; for him Alphonse trusted most. Nor was his confidence ever deceived.

Pierre—so René has told me—was speaking with an eloquence that kept hands, shoulders, and eyebrows moving. He was of the Languedoc, with all the liveliness of that fair land. His years were seven-and-twenty, and he was merry as a child when no one crossed him. But he was not merry now.

The count listened to every word he said, as men did when Pierre spoke. Aye, Alphonse listened, nodding at every sentence, with pursed lips and glinting eyes. When he finished, the count said:

"You convince, Pierre; but so do René's figures. Look at them again!"

Taking the scroll from the clerk's hand, he passed it across the table to Pierre; who, perusing it swiftly, tossed it back to the clerk with an air of contempt. His brows knitted; he sprang up, his dark eyes flaming.

"My lord," he cried, "I have heard that at each man's side stand two angels, one from heaven, the other in the devil's livery. These note all his deeds. When he chooses the right course, the white angel smiles, and makes a mark to his credit in God's judgment book; when he chooses the path of shame, the black angel exults, and adds another check to the long tally of the man's sins.

"Those angels stand at your shoulder now, waiting breathless for your decision. If you let René's figures sway you, there will be joy tonight in the bottomless pit!"

My lord's eyes held Pierre's steadily.

"You use hard words," he said.

My captain answered the look rather than the speech. "You do well to rebuke me, *seignior.* It was no way to speak to one so high, and I but a peasant who owe everything to your favor. None the less my words are true. René's accounts show that your coffers are nearly empty with the expense of maintaining a great garrison, and you can not diminish your forces without inviting attack from your enemies in Barcelona or Aquitaine.

"But if you replenish your wealth from the King's bounty, on the terms he exacts, you will lose that which is more precious than gold or life—your honor! And you will do more; you will bring the wrath of the Church, and its curse, upon this devoted land of Toulouse!"

"What think you, Simon?"

Alphonse turned to the master of the garrison.

The veteran grunted.

"I hold with Pierre," he answered bluntly. "All your life you have kept your honor stainless, and it would be an ill thing to sully it now."

"And you, René?"

The clerk looked down at his pointed shoes.

"I have but cast the reckoning as you bade me, my lord. I am no soldier, and know little of honor; but I fear the Church!"

Alphonse-Jourdain rose, and the others rose with him.

"So be it!" he smiled. "I would have said the same myself; but I owed it to you to ask your counsel. None of you has received his pay for three months."

"—— take the pay!" cried Simon. "We serve you from choice!"

Pierre said no word, but he seized Simon's hand; and René, who feared the Church indeed, gave a gasp of relief.

Now all this stir, *messires*, was caused by King Louis' quarrel with the Pope. Louis VII had it in his mind to make himself both temporal and spiritual ruler of France, and rashly defied his Holiness, Eugenius III. The blessed Bernard of Clairvaux, by urgent and humble intercession, for a time succeeded in holding off the ban of excommunication from France; but it would come as soon as Louis made an open move. All France lived in fear.

The King, purposing to meet the ban with force of arms, sent to each of his nobles an appeal to defend the Crown; and to our lord of Toulouse he offered ten thousand marks, if Alphonse would join his banner. This sum would have made the count rich once more; but as you have seen, he and his most trusted men preferred honor and their souls' salvation to money.

Now, the matter being settled, the count turned away; but before he could leave the terrace, two men came through the postern gate, between the steel-clad men-at-arms who stood guard there. One of the new-comers was a man of the garrison; the other a strange priest in cowl and gown. He was a dark-faced, lithe fellow, whose features had none of the humility which should grace God's servants. He bore a roll of parchment in his hand.

For a moment he stared from one to another of the group by the table, his gaze lingering a moment on the proud young face of Pierre; then his eyes shifted to the count. Bowing low, he placed his scroll in the great man's fingers.

ALPHONSE BROKE the seal and began to read, scowling as he ran down the lines. Though he could read—having realized, from his youth, the value of that learning which most nobles scorn—he did not boast a clerk's proficiency. The priest, meantime, stood by silent and motionless, as if waiting for the count to finish. Suddenly Alphonse cried out in anger. He stepped aside from the others, and half-turned his back, to get better light on the manuscript, which had been darkened by the frowning shadow of the wall.

Even as he turned away, the priest sprang, a knife glittering in his uplifted hand. The blade descended—it gleamed at the count's neck. In that instant a second flash leaped above it; the knife dropped harmlessly, and the priest screamed. Straightway the guardsmen hurled themselves upon him and held him, though he struggled furiously. Blood spurted from the stump of his right wrist. His knife, clutched in the fingers of his severed hand, lay at the count's feet. There was blood spattered in drops over the scroll that Alphonse still held. Seeing the wretch powerless, Pierre Faidit wiped his streaming sword on a fold of the priest's gown, and crossed himself.

Recovering from his surprize, Alphonse flung the half-read scroll to René.

"Once more I owe you a debt greater than I can pay, Pierre," he said. "Jacques and Arnolt, bind up this fellow's wound and throw him into the dungeon! Send for the Prior of St. Sernin. When he comes, put the priest to the question!"

The soldiers hustled their prisoner away; and as they dragged him through the postern, he cast back upon Alphonse a look of bitter hate.

"Now read me this scroll, René!" the count commanded.

The clerk obeyed, while the others listened. Signed by Raymond-Bérenger of Barcelona, whose jealousy had long menaced Toulouse, its message was an insolent demand that Alphonse surrender to Bérenger his province of Foix.

"This is shameless!" the count burst out. "Has he not already intrigued against me with my own vassal, Roger of Foix? Dares he think that I will give up that county which is the very barbican of Toulouse, for fear of him?"

Pierre's strong fingers played with the hilt of his great sword.

"The time is ripe for such a stroke," he said. "Bérenger wants Foix. He knows of the King's quarrel with the Pope; knows, too, that you—like all the other nobles—must join with King or Pope. Soon all France will be ablaze with war between Church and Crown. Bérenger waits only to see which side you will help. When he learns that you uphold the Church, he will join the King, and send his armies against Toulouse. His father-in-law, the King of Aragon, will aid him; and to punish you, King Louis of France will lend him money or troops."

"But Louis has sworn never to take up arms against me again!" Alphonse protested.

"He will be forced to break his oath, to prevent your eight thousand veterans from swelling the armies of the Church. Only a miracle can save France from civil war now. We shall be ground to pieces between Bérenger and the King."

Alphonse held up one hand.

"Then why," he asked, "if Bérenger is so sure of destroying me in the honest warfare, does he send this cutthroat priest to murder me?"

Here René's soft voice broke in. He was studying the priest's manuscript.

"I am not sure," he observed hesitatingly, "that this is the true seal of Barcelona!"

"What!" cried the count. "I would have sworn—Fetch me his letter of ten months gone, René!"

While the secretary was away, Alphonse strode up and down the terrace; his heel tearing the soft turf at each turn. When René came back, the count seized the two parchments, and eagerly compared the seals.

"I can see no difference," he said at last.

"I said not that they were not the same," René replied. "I said

I was not sure. They are very like; but there is a blur in the impression here. Nay, I am not sure."

"It is not like Bérenger to hire assassins," Alphonse mused. "Yet he hates me enough. Well, Pierre?"

"If my lord will send me to Barcelona—" Pierre began; but the count cut him short.

"To ask whether he sent a priest to stab me? Bérenger would take it as an insult—the more so if he is guilty—and throw you into his dungeon, or hang you!"

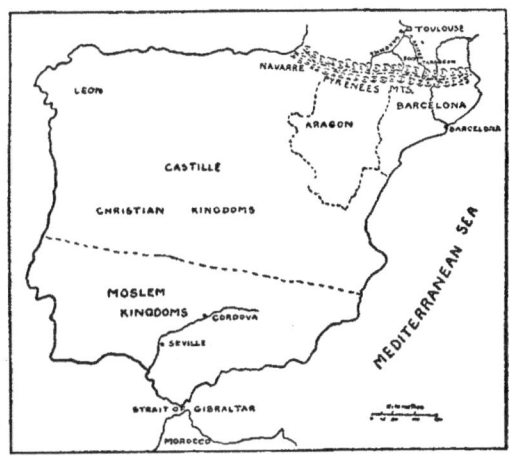

"Nay," Pierre smiled. "That were an insult indeed, and he would do well to hang me. But if you send me to him with an accusation and a challenge, thus:

" 'I, Alphonse, Count of Toulouse, overlord of Béziers, of Carcassonne, of Nimes, of Languedoc, and of Foix, do accuse thee, Raymond-Bérenger, of Barcelona, of the foul crime of attempted murder upon our person; and I do challenge thee to defend thyself against this charge in single combat with me, to the hazard of both our bodies, to the utterance!' What then? The bearer of a challenge has a herald's immunity. He would not dare decline a challenge on such a charge, lest all men hold him in scorn!"

Alphonse smiled broadly.

"Well thought!" he answered. "He and I should be well matched; and it is better for Toulouse that we settle all our quarrels at once, man to man, than that he should bring the King against us! René, draw up the challenge, and you, Pierre, be ready to ride. If the priest's confession bears out our suspicions—Ha, cousin!"

A tall, big-framed man strode through the postern, held up one hand in blessing, and shook the count's hand. It was the Prior of St. Sernin, our lord's kinsman. Some of you, *messires,* have seen him. You know how strangely his imperious face, his haughty eyes, his soldierly bearing, clash with the coarse sackcloth he wears—the garb of a poor monk, for all his princely blood. Count Alphonse greeted him with deep affection, calling him by his baptismal name:

"Thrice welcome, Robert! It is a shame that you come not to me save when I send for you! The memory of our boyhood together is very dear to me!"

"To me also, in so far as it was innocent," the prior answered. "But you live in the world, I in the spirit; and those two are strangers, Alphonse. But before you ask anything of me, I have a question for you. On whose side are you—the King's, or God's?"

"I stand by the Church. It seems that I must pay for it dearly, if the King and Bérenger unite against me."

" 'Blessed are they that are persecuted for righteousness' sake,'" the prior quoted. "You have made my heart glad, cousin. God will defend His champions. Now what is your will with me?"

Briefly the count told him of the priest's attempt, and the message he bore from Barcelona. He told, too, of René's doubt concerning the seal, and his own purpose to put the priest to the question.

"I sent for you," he concluded, "because I dared not torture or condemn an ordained priest without the sanction of one high in the Church. Will you grant me authorization?"

Now my lord count was a merciful man. I have rarely known him to use the torture. But this affair justified the rack. All men know it is but justice to wring confession from a proven murderer, or would-be murderer. The prior hesitated not a whit.

"Lead me to the dungeon!" he replied. "I will myself take down for you his confession as a criminal; his confession as a penitent will be between himself and God!"

So the company descended to the dungeon.

The prisoner suffered neither much nor long. Before the third turn of the thumbscrew, he shrieked like a coward, and the words tumbled from his lips in his haste to escape the pain.

"Who incited you against the count's life?" the prior demanded.

"Mercy, good father! Mercy, lord count! It was—my lord of Barcelona!"

This was enough; and the rest was of small import. When he had said all, the prior sent the others from the room; for the wretch was to be hanged, and must make his peace with God. But half an hour later the prior came again to the terrace, his cheeks crimson with rage.

"The dog!" he cried. "The heretic hound!"

"He refused absolution?" the count asked.

"Nay; he shrived himself and received absolution with all humility. But after he received the wafer, and when he thought my eyes turned aside, he spat under cover of his hand! Aye, he spat at the sacred wafer!"

All who listened shuddered, and crossed themselves. Ah, *messires,* what a sacrilege! But Pierre Faidit, bowing to the holy prior and to the count, begged leave to withdraw.

"Before I prepare to depart," he said, "I would fain see the rascal hanged."

Nor did any ask what was in his mind, though it was a strange thing for Pierre to do, who loved not to see men die in cold blood. He came back after a while, with something in his hand. It was a round, red box, no bigger than a cherry. Opening this before the company, he drew forth a bit of silk, with strange characters upon it.

"I used my authority to get a place by the prisoner," he explained. "When the cart moved from beneath his feet, and the rope choked him, he coughed this from his throat. I suppose he had tried to swallow it, but was too late."

All gazed on the box and the cloth, but none could understand the characters, which were in a writing such as they had never seen.

"Well?" the count asked, his eyes on Pierre.

"If my lord pleases," my captain answered, "I wish twenty spearmen to ride with me to Barcelona, as a guard through the mountains. I would fain take this cloth with me; I may learn something from it, with God's help."

The next day Pierre set forth, bearing the challenge to Raymond-Bérenger; and as always, *messires,* I bore the banner.

WE RODE fast, being few and well-mounted; moreover, my captain was eager to reach Barcelona and the danger that he loved. For danger there was in bearding that grim warrior-noble, Bérenger, even for one who bore a formal challenge. The Count of Barcelona, son-in-law to Ramiro the Lion of Aragon, looked upon himself as a king in all save the name, and loved not to be opposed.

The sun sank as we reached the crag of Tarascon, where lay the black ruins of the proud tower where once Red Hugo defied Toulouse. Pierre smiled as he drew rein on the bank of the river girdling it. He himself had burned that wicked place, to free our lord from its menace, and to prevent Bérenger or the Queen's men from occupying it. Here we camped till dawn.

We mounted again as the morning sun burned on the snow-caps of the Pyrenees, that lay ahead like sullen giants across our path. The mountain trails were none too good. Our captain bade us ride as close as the road allowed, and be silent and watchful. This was needful, *messires;* for the wild Basques inhabit those frontier solitudes, and they heed not the sacredness of an ambassador. Yet we saw none of them.

Now it must be remembered that neither Pierre, nor the count, nor any of us was sure that Bérenger had sent my lord that insolent letter, or hired the priest to murder him. We believed it, yes; but we were not certain. Nobles as good as he had done such deeds; but there was René's doubt about the seal. No great matter, but the least doubt will cling in a man's mind on such an errand. Moreover, there was the strange behavior of the priest, who had spat at the sacrament.

Bear these things in mind, *messires*, before you accuse my captain of violating his orders. He was deep in the count's trust; and that trust was so great that the understanding between them went beyond words. All Alphonse-Jourdain demanded was that Pierre accomplish what the count wished done; Pierre might settle details for himself. In this affair, the count wished, first, to find whether Bérenger had done those base things of which we believed him guilty; and next, to punish him in single combat if he were guilty, so that their enmity might be settled without a war. Pierre chose to accomplish those things in his own way; and I think he was right.

By noon we were in a deep mountain gorge, through which a snow-fed torrent boiled with savage fury. We had crossed a stone bridge a little while before, and now came to a sharp bend in the stream-bed. The walls of the gorge, and the stream, turned here as if twisted violently by the Creator's hand. One of the men, Red André, cursed aloud as his horse stumbled; and Pierre glared at him. Then, even as André muttered excuses, he held up his hand, and we halted, listening. Somewhere beyond the bend came a sound that all soldiers know well—the jangle of mail!

At a gesture from Pierre, we retreated, and straightway our three scouts rode back upon us in haste, reporting that a body of horse was advancing upon us. As quickly as we could without making noise, we made our way back to the bridge, and there drew up in column—the way was too narrow for battle-line—

at the head of the bridge. It was very old, of solid Roman work, with a coping not more than a foot high. We felt safe now. In that position we could hold at bay ten times our number; and we remembered, proudly, how great a soldier our captain had proved himself before, against odds such as we should certainly not need to face that day.

It was a wonderful setting for a fight, *messires*. All about us the tremendous mountain-walls, the mighty white peaks, seamed with ice and veiled in waterfalls; the road behind us as clear as the blue sky above; the ancient bridge at our feet—with heaven knows what clinging memories of long-past wars—and the singing river below. Then—the drumming of many hoofs, the clanking jangle of mailed men riding in careless confidence—and they were around the bend and upon us.

Ah, what a flurry when they sighted us! A shout from him who led them, and they pulled up short, their lances bobbing as they halted. Never have I seen men look so astonished; for look you, this was their own territory. Short, massive Catalans they were, splendidly armored, arrogant of eye. It was plain to us all that these were no mere men-at-arms, but gentlemen all; and their commander the greatest gentleman of the troop.

He was a man well-made and strong, on a clean-limbed Spanish barb that must have cost him more than his gold-washed mail. In his peaked helmet he wore a single crimson plume; his shield was gold-bossed, and bore a black eagle on a silver field. Of his face we could see nothing save his proud eyes, and the thin lips between his steel nasal and mail gorget.

Beside him another, full as gay as he, sat a dainty ambling Arab horse, black as coal. This man could scarce be an officer; for he carried himself with an indifferent air, and glanced at us as if we were no concern of his. Yet suddenly I saw his eyes narrow, and marked that he stared with keen interest at our captain. So I watched him, and found him worthy of all my interest.

He was young; perhaps five and twenty. Though under the

common height, he had massive shoulders and a broad, deep chest. His arms were very long, and somewhat loosely hung. These, and the quick, blue-green eyes of him, told me he would be both strong and swift in action. His helmet hung at his saddle-bow, so that his face, which was as beautiful as a woman's, was quite unhidden; the length of his loose locks, and his rich attire, marked him for a troubadour. His robe was of blue silk, its collar showing above his mail; a scarlet cloak, belted with a narrow girdle of gold plates, lay open about his bright hauberk. I observed him well, and set him down for a man to love and fear.

For a long moment the whole cavalcade glared at us, as if their haughty eyes could drive us from our strong position. Then, seeing we neither budged nor spoke, their leader rode slowly toward us, calling for a parley. Bowing, Pierre Faidit advanced to meet him.

"What do ye here on the march of Barcelona, ye dogs of Toulouse?" the officer cried; for he had seen our banner in my hand.

Pierre stiffened in his saddle.

"Dogs are we not!" he answered. "It is a hard name for men with whom your lord is at peace. We come on a message to the noble Count Raymond-Bérenger, and crave leave to accomplish it without hindrance or insult."

He of the crimson plume laughed harshly.

"This is insolence indeed!" he sneered. "Having failed to murder our lord, ye send an embassy to him!"

Now it was Pierre's turn to stare.

"I know not what ye mean," he replied slowly; and the wrath rose in his voice as he went on: "Murder? Who has attempted murder but Bérenger? Your master hires knives against Toulouse, and then seeks to hide his guilt behind a false charge against us! Nay, sir—" for his adversary was about to speak—"I am no nobleman, but my sword is as keen as yours, and is at your service if you speak more villainy of Toulouse!"

I raised a cheer, and the men behind me joined their voices to mine. But Crimson-Plume claps hand to hilt, and cries:

"No noble? Who are you then, who dare to challenge a knight of Barcelona?"

"I am a soldier, called Pierre Faidit, whose title is vested in his sword!"

Before the Barcelonan could retort, the unhelmeted troubadour spurred forward, his black hair flying above his scarlet cloak. No deference had he for rank or office, but rode even between his officer and Pierre, and seized our captain's hand.

"Nay then, Pierre Faidit, it is you indeed!" he cried; and his smile would have won the heart of man or woman. "I thought I should know those shoulders; but I believed you dead in the ashes of Tarascon! How escaped you?"

Pierre smiled back joyously.

"Let Tarascon wait till a better time, Cercamon," he answered. "Glad am I to see you once more; but if you have any liking for me, I pray you persuade your companion to file his rough tongue to courtesy. He has spoken words that require much explanation from us both."

So Cercamon—for, *messires,* it was none other than that most illustrious of troubadours—spoke to his officer; and not gently, nor with the humility due to rank, but as a master speaks to a servant. And though the nobleman's eyes flashed, his tones were mild enough when he spoke again. That which he said set us all to gasping.

On the very day—if he spoke truth, and of that Cercamon assured us—on that very day when the villainous priest strove to stab Count Alphonse, another priest had driven a dagger into the heart of a courtier whom he mistook for the Count of Barcelona! Before he could be seized, the miscreant had stabbed himself, and perished. Nothing was found on him but—a letter sealed with the arms of Toulouse, and containing a defiance to Bérenger.

Thereupon Pierre, marveling, told of the attempt upon our

own lord's life, and of the letter borne by the priest, with the seal of Bérenger. Great was the astonishment on both sides, and for a little the Barcelonan officer would not believe Pierre, swearing he had but fashioned his tale upon that he had just heard. But Pierre's fierce snatch at his sword, and Cercamon's ready oath that he would vouch for Pierre's word upon his life, convinced him.

Nay, Cercamon's own hand was on his hilt, and his greenish eyes burned into the officer's, as he gave this assurance. For that troubadour was so high in Bérenger's favor, and so terrible a swordsman, that no man south of the Pyrenees dared gainsay him.

FOR AN hour the three talked before us all, weighing this strange matter. It was clear now, of course, that both letters had been forged, both to conceal the true murderer and to stir up Barcelona and Toulouse against each other. But how, or by whom, the deed was plotted, was a mystery: Crimson-Plume declared the plotter a fool, to risk a trick which must be found out as soon as the emissaries of both lords met; but Pierre answered him well:

"If this bridge had not been here, or if I had not fallen back upon it, would ye not have ridden us down without stopping to question? It was that on which he who plotted murder counted, if both his assassins failed. If one or both succeeded, he knew that war would break out at once between Barcelona and Toulouse. If both failed, then he counted shrewdly on a clash between such troops as would be sent out from our masters to seek redress; and the spilling of blood here in the mountains would have been but the beginning of a war that would have reddened all the South."

"Aye!" quoth Cercamon. "And now we must seek out him who planned the deed, if we have to look for him in ——! Both the murderers priests! Has Count Alphonse joined the King against the Church? I'll wager he has, and some great prelate has taken this means to deprive Louis of his help! Raymond-

Bérenger, as you know, has always denied the Pope's authority in Barcelona."

Pierre shook his head.

"Both priests," he answered; "but I can not believe the Church had a hand in this. Count Alphonse has always been in the Pope's favor, and has but now determined—"

Here he stopped, lest he reveal the count's secrets. But Cercamon interrupted:

"He has determined to help the Pope? Why, and so has Bérenger! Having heard rumors that the Moors meditate war, he dares not risk his life against them without the Pope's blessing. But he has not yet announced his resolve; and an overzealous prelate, remembering his old antagonism—"

"It is not likely," Pierre broke in. "Did I not tell you the priest spat at the sacrament? There is something wrong in this business; a zealous priest would not do such a sin. I will give you admission for admission; my lord has joined the Pope. No prelate would strike against our masters until he was sure they would oppose the Church."

"Why, then," the troubadour said, "with two such great lords against him, the King will not dare carry the struggle further. He will submit to the Pope!"

Which later turned out to be true, *messires;* but that is not the tale.

Pierre drew from his neck a little bag on a cord, and from it took a tiny red box, the shape and size of a cherry—the same he had taken from the hanged priest. Opening it, he showed the silken cloth, with its strange characters, to Cercamon and Crimson-Plume.

"What make ye of this?" he asked; and the two eyed it.

"Why, it is Arabic!" cried Crimson-Plume. "I can not read it, but I have seen such characters often in Saragossa."

"Arabic indeed," said Cercamon. "I speak the tongue, but know not its letters."

"Then it is in my mind," Pierre remarked, "that the two murderous priests were no priests at all, but Moors disguised. You speak of a Moorish war. We must look to the paynims of Andalusia for the solving of this mystery."

But Cercamon shook his head.

"The Moors are our foes, it is true," he admitted. "They would like well to stir up strife between Barcelona and Toulouse, so that they might attack Aragon and win back Saragossa. But the Moor is no murderer, Pierre. I have sung in their courts, and crossed swords with them in their lists; and I have ever found them knightly gentlemen. We Christians may use the knife and the poison-bowl against our enemies; but I have never known a Moor who would not rather die than stain his knightly honor so!"

Every Catalan in the troop bore witness that this was true; nor would they believe that the Arabic writing found on the priest was aught but a blind.

"For the pink of chivalry," swore Crimson-Plume, "commend me to the Moors! Paynims though they be, though they will fight to the death against hopeless odds, they scorn to win advantage by treachery!"

So we were no wiser than before; and none of us knew what to do, seeing that to bear our challenge to Bérenger now would be folly. Crimson-Plume gnawed his nails, for he had been on his way to Toulouse on a like errand. It was Cercamon who settled the matter.

"Why, there is a rare adventure in this!" he cried. "An adventure made for you and me, Pierre! Send your men home; I will persuade Count Urgel here to take his troop back to Barcelona; and we two shall set forth on a quest to unravel the mystery!"

Pierre thought, and at last agreed.

"But I want my men," he answered. "Do you return to Barcelona, Sir Count, with your gentlemen. Cercamon and we of Toulouse will undertake the quest."

Count Crimson-Plume had no wish to let us of Toulouse seek a glory denied to his Catalans; but Cercamon persuaded him. He himself, being of a romantic soul, was displeased at Pierre's insistence that we troopers come; but he could not shake Pierre's resolution.

When Count Urgel and his men were half an hour on their way homeward, Pierre bade us wheel about.

"But whither?" urged the troubadour. "Not to Toulouse?"

Pierre laughed.

"To Narbonne!" he answered; and his friend stared.

"Why to Narbonne?" he cried.

"Narbonne has a harbor."

"A harbor? What, in the fiend's name, do we want with a harbor?"

"Ships!" Pierre replied. "Look you, Cercamon: your report of Moorish chivalry has so stirred me that I can not rest till I have seen these paynim knights for myself. The way overland is too rough, and dangerous for so few men. Therefore we will go by sea."

Cercamon seized Pierre's rein.

"But I tell you no Moor would murder! You will not find your arch-villain in Spain!"

"Where shall I find him?" Pierre retorted; and he was serious enough now. "We have undertaken to find and punish him, whoever and wherever he may be. It is like shooting an arrow in the dark, my friend. One place is as likely as another. We may as well go anywhere; and so, since I am anxious to see the Moorish courts, let us go there first!"

"You have some scheme!" the troubadour hazarded. "Since you could come alive out of the cells of Tarascon, and leave the place in ashes, I am willing to trust your wits for anything. Well, to what Moorish court will you go?"

"Which is the greatest?"

It was Cercamon's turn to laugh.

"You inland Frenchmen know nothing of Spain! There is but one Moslem court of much importance—Cordova. Ah, Pierre!

It is a fair and great city, the center of Moorish grandeur from Segovia to Gibraltar! It is—"

"It is our goal!"

So we turned our horses' heads northeast; and on the second day we took ship from Narbonne.

OF THE voyage, *messires,* I say nothing; save that it lasted eleven days, during which all of us save Pierre—a fisherman by birth—were sick. Of our flight from a Berber corsair—

But that is not in the tale. The last day we were under the escort of a Moorish galley from Seville, one of a squadron that patrolled the Straits against the Berbers.

Its captain gave us a gallant welcome when Pierre told him we were men of France come to win martial glory in the lists at Cordova. We knew then that Cercamon had spoken truth about the Moorish love of feats of chivalry.

Past the tidal marshes of the Guadalquivir this galley bore us company, and through a most fertile region to the great city of Seville. Here we were obliged to quit our ship, which was held till our return by command of the emir of the city, Ibn-Wezir.

By his order also our escort dropped us, for this galley was his. He was lord of the West of Spain; but east of Seville all the land was ruled by Ibn-Hamdin, Caliph of Cordova. So we continued up the river in a lateen-rigged river-boat, manned by naked blackamoors, with a guard of a dozen spearmen.

Their officer was a gaily bedizened Moslem, and as courtly a gentleman as ever I saw. His name was Ibn-Abdallah. He knew French; and we needed not to rely on Cercamon's bad Arabic. Nor in all that land did we ever see a noble who knew not some French; and many, as Cercamon said, knew Latin. The Moors cherish learning as much as we, *messires,* despise it.

All the way to Cordova the river-banks were green with fair gardens and ablaze with flowers. The roses nestled even about the great tower which we presently sighted at the head of a huge stone bridge spanning the river. Armed guards lined the parapets of tower and bridge; and, landing, we proceeded to the tower-gate, where we were questioned—though most courteously—before we could go farther. When Pierre and the troubadour gave their names, the paynim soldiers clashed their weapons together as a mark of honor to two such famous soldiers.

Those Moors were lean, sinewy fellows, with the mark of the drilled cavalier. Their chain-mail was so fine of mesh that it could be rolled up in a small packet, and their surcoats were striped with bright colors. Their turbans also were gay, and were wrapped around their spiked and inlaid helmets; their weapons were slender javelins, long lances, bows, and simitars. Some, however, wore the famous straight blades of Murcia, made on the pattern of our own cross-hilted swords.

It was high noon before the messenger sent to the palace returned to bid us enter the city. By the caliph's order Ibn-Abdallah was commanded to bring us to the royal presence. Many were the compliments the caliph heaped upon us in that gracious message; for Cercamon he knew already, and Pierre's fame as a swordsman had long since reached Spain. It was like their Moorish chivalry to judge men by deeds instead of rank.

Ibn-Abdallah led us by a roundabout way, that we might see more of Cordova. Ah, *messires,* never was a city so beautiful! Crossing the bridge, we found ourselves before the chief gate of a massive crenellated wall, beyond which lay a great square, paved with large mosaic stones as flat as a table.

All about us were splendid buildings with arches of fretted stone and plaster, delicate as lace. Above them in the distance rose a score of dainty minarets. Walls and columns gleamed with marble, bronze, and alabaster; fountains were everywhere, and flowers.

Once, passing down a narrow street, we reached a lovely gate set under a horseshoe arch, carved in an intricate design of such beauty that we stopped to marvel. Ibn-Abdallah frowned, and hurried us on; but not till the door opened, to reveal a vista of slender columns and many-colored arches all agleam with gold in the glow of bronze lamps. It was a Moslem church, *messires*—their chief mosque.

Our eyes were sated with beauty, weary with gazing at the brilliantly garbed people, before we reached the palace. It was a city in itself—a city of marble, gold and jewels, with a population of its own. Nobles in silks and gems bowed to us; soldiers in fine armor swaggered past; scholars flitted through forests of sculptured pillars, with books in their hands. We walked long through its courts before we reached the throne-room; and there, at the end of a double row of guardsmen, we saw a flashing throne on a dais. Upon that throne sat a man in middle age, robed in white, white-turbaned. It was Ibn-Hamdin, the caliph.

Unbelievable is Moorish hospitality! Here were we, Frenchmen, enemies both by blood and by creed to him who sat enthroned above us. Yet he received us as friends—nay, as kinsmen—for the sake of our leaders' names. Cercamon, who had sung in his presence the year before, the caliph kissed on both cheeks.

When Pierre told him we were come to try our valor with his champions in the tournament, he smiled upon us, graciously saying that on the fourth day thereafter there was to be a festival at which we might meet the foremost swords of Spain. In the mean time we must rest, and taste the pleasures of his palace.

And so we did. We reveled in hot and cold baths, dined on foods more exquisite than any we ever tasted, drank the finest wines—for the Moors, as you know, cared little for their prophet's injunction against wine. We were lodged in the east wing of the palace, overlooking the river and the town. In the courtyard there was ample space for the martial exercises which our captain would not let us neglect. Every day Pierre and Cercamon fenced before us all; and, oh, *messires!* Never had I seen such sword-play. They were as nearly matched as men can be, and each was a master.

During these three days Cercamon often questioned Pierre, but our captain put his questions by with a smile. The troubadour still believed that some unscrupulous ecclesiastic had hired his underlings to attempt the murder of our lords, though he could give no sound reason. It was the priest's garb that influenced him. Pierre insisted that the Church had nothing to do with it; yet he agreed that, if all Moors were like the caliph and his nobles, the guilt could hardly lie with them.

He had every chance to test their character. Each day the Moors flocked in to do us honor: the nobles of the diwan, the chief officers of the palace guard and the army, the councilors— all visited us, squatting at our feet and praising us in courtly phrases. The least of them was a soldier and a man of learning. Most of them greeted Cercamon as an old and valued acquaintance, and he often sang for them. Yet, I could see, Pierre's strong features and mighty limbs won their esteem as much as did the troubadour's sweet songs.

AMONG THOSE who paid us honor was a very great man, the Syrian Emir of Edessa, who was on a visit of state to the caliph. This Arab was the biggest man I have ever seen— taller even than Pierre, and well nigh as broad. His face was swarthy even for a Moor, with great black eyes that rolled fiercely, a jutting jaw, and the hooked beak of a bird of prey. Cercamon liked him little, for all his fine ways; but I marked that Pierre seemed to hold him in high esteem.

Now Pierre did a strange thing. During all these three days before the tournament, he wore upon his breast the silken cloth with Arabic characters which he had taken from the hanged priest. Every Moor who visited us saw it; every one, as his eyes rested upon it, started and frowned.

As he noted their astonishment, Pierre questioned them concerning it; but he got little satisfaction. They answered that it was an accursed thing, and begged him to destroy it; but they would not tell him what the characters meant. His eyes grew bright with excitement, for he felt that somehow, if he could but find a man who would interpret the writing, he would find the key to the strange plot against Barcelona and Toulouse.

Only one man failed to show confusion at sight of the cloth; and that was the Syrian emir, whose name was Mulai abu-Hassan el-Ussari. He smiled, but would no more explain it than the others, beyond saying that all good Moslems abhorred the words written upon it. When he left us, Pierre gazed after him curiously, but said nothing.

On the day of the tournament we rose at dawn. Pierre and Cercamon armed each other; and when they stood full-mailed, Pierre bound the cloth to his helmet. We breakfasted frugally, taking no wine. Our mail and arms were spotless, our weapons ground to the utmost keenness.

As we waited for our summons a marvelous thing happened. We had not been able to bring our horses. Had we come by land, they would have been worn out, and we could not easily take them by sea. Our captain and Cercamon had determined to fight on foot, in the sword-combats. We men-at-arms were to stand by, for the tournament is not for such as we. But even as Ibn-Abdallah came to lead us forth, there approached one whose gorgeous dress and gold-washed armor proclaimed him a noble of great estate, who bowed low before us, saying:

"*Effendim,* the officers of the caliph's guard have the honor to place their best horses at your disposal. Slaves will have the chargers in readiness at the lists; and you will find them trained to bear you in the tournament. The Emir of Edessa himself begs that Faidit *Effendi* will accept his Barbary stallion!"

The courtliness with which Pierre thanked him matched his own. But as Pierre bowed, the Moor caught sight of the cloth in his helmet, and cried out:

"Whence got you that, *effendi?* Know you what it means?"

Pierre's eyes gleamed; but he answered calmly:

"I had it from a priest of my faith. I know not its meaning. Do you?"

And he watched the man narrowly.

The Moor replied:

"I do; but a Christian would not understand. There is a curse upon it!"

Pierre would have asked more, but at that moment the trumpets blew and the naquirs clashed; the Moor bowed, and went away in haste. As Pierre made to follow, Ibn-Abdallah pulled him back, saying:

"Peace! To one side! The caliph comes!"

We waited in an angle of the great gate fronting the lists to take our place behind the caliph. A gorgeous sight lay beyond the open archway. On the wide plain between the river and the *sierra*, a wooden enclosure of great space had been set up, gaily painted and hung with streamers of rainbow silk. The road between it and the palace was lined with archers and spearmen.

On both sides a multitude had gathered, waiting, like ourselves, for the caliph to pass. Outside the lists and beyond the throng, horsemen in full armor galloped up and down, throwing blunted javelins or going through mock tilts in preparation for the stern encounters to come. They made gallant figures, and their mounts were superb.

Heralded by the clang of harsh music, and preceded by the household guards, Ibn-Hamdin rode down between his troops. The multitude fell on their faces; none stood upright save the soldiers and we Christians, who prostrate ourselves only to God. But as the caliph drew alongside us, we knelt, and he noticed us. His eyes rested upon the cloth in Pierre's helmet; and I would have sworn he turned pale.

"Whence came that, Frank?" he cried; and Pierre answered him as he had answered the noble.

The caliph turned his eyes away, and rode on. Yet Pierre would not remove the cloth. He was a stubborn man; and now he knew that it held the key not only to our mystery, but to something hidden that these Moors feared and hated.

When he had passed, Ibn-Abdallah led us to a great pavilion that was set up for us on one side of the lists. Our horses were there; but though they had been given us, our captain would not permit us to take part in the tournament. Therefore we were stationed, mounted and armed, on one side of the lists within the great enclosure, opposite the caliph's guards; and Pierre and the troubadour led their horses within the pavilion.

I know not what they said or did till they came out to fight. But I heeded not at the time, for my eyes were on the gorgeous throng about the caliph. Though the lists were long they were of no great width. We could almost count the jewels on the caliph's turban; and faces we could see plainly.

For some while, lesser combats preceded the great tilts. Splendid enough they were, with feats of horsemanship to delight the eye, and marvelous skill in casting of the dart. We saw, too, encounters such as we love in France, one warrior hurling another from the saddle, or splintering his spear with honor. The Moors had learned this kind of combat from the Christians of Leon and Aragon. But at last all these were over, and the trumpet sounded for the great combats between champions.

An officer of the royal household rode out as challenger—a big man on a roan stallion. He rode thrice around the lists, bowing to the caliph, and uttered his challenge in loud tones. I looked to see my captain or Cercamon come out against him; but the curtain of their pavilion was still drawn.

A second Moor spurred into the ring. Their combat was glorious. The challenger unhorsed his man at the third course, slew a second with a thrust through the throat, and dismounted a third.

Still Pierre came not forth, nor the troubadour. An Andalusian knight overthrew the challenger, and took his place. The crowd stared with impatient wonder at our pavilion, but they stared in vain. The encounters followed one another, a Christian Spaniard from Burgos winning high honors, so that I blushed that he, and not a Frenchman, upheld the Cross against the Crescent.

THEN THE caliph commanded that the contenders fight six pairs at once; and now Pierre Faidit and Cercamon dashed into the ring. For an hour the warriors strove together, each man who fell replaced by another who hoped to unhorse the victor, and always twelve champions clashing in six courses at a time. Four men constantly overthrew their opponents: the Spaniard, a dashing Cordovan emir, and our two Frenchmen. At last no more came out; and these four wheeled to meet one another.

But the caliph gave order that Pierre and the troubadour might not face the other pair yet, for these had fought in more combats than our men, and were wearier. Yet when Pierre and Cercamon cried out for men to fight them, none dared answer. So the caliph ordered a rest of an hour, that the wearier men might regain their strength. Only when this period was over did the trumpets sound for renewed conflict.

Swiftly the four, who had retired to their tents, trotted back to their places in the arena; Pierre and Cercamon at one end, their antagonists at the other. Cercamon faced the emir; Pierre, the Spaniard. The spectators could not keep their seats. This was the decisive moment of the greatest tournament in Spain. If the Frenchmen could overthrow those proved champions, they would win both the prize and the prestige of conquering the first lances south of the Pyrenees.

Some strange instinct moved me to turn my eyes from them for a moment. I looked toward the caliph's seat. There beside him, leaning far over the rail in his excitement, was that huge Syrian, Mulai el-Ussari of Edessa. His eyes gleamed with cruel light; an evil smile twitched on his lips.

The contestants met in a cloud of dust, with a shock that set their armor clanging. Then rose a cry from ten thousand throats, for the Moor and the Spaniard were down! Slowly our captain and Cercamon trotted back to their places, and our French hearts swelled with pride. We had won the day over the chivalry of Spain! But even as I clapped my hands, I stole a glance at the Syrian. His face was savage as a thundercloud; then it changed, his eyes lighting with fierce resolution.

Now Pierre cried his challenge. He defied the chivalry of Andalusia; but none replied. The caliph rose to ask the two victors to ride against each other. Courteously, but with resolution, they refused.

Suddenly the Syrian, Mulai el-Ussari, vaulted the rail into the arena. In his white burnoose he stood there, his gesture commanding silence. His eyes on Pierre, he shouted so that all could hear:

"Give not the prize to these, O Caliph, Prince of the Age! Before the Crescent shall bow to the Cross, I myself will ride against them. Let the tall Frank face me first!"

As the caliph hesitated, he spoke again:

"The *effendi*, Faidit, and I will ride three courses with the spear. If neither is unhorsed we will fight with the sword till one of us be overcome. If I prevail, then I will fight the troubadour!"

The caliph protested. Though blood had been shed in the earlier courses, it had been by the hazards incident to the tournament, not with evil intent. This challenge of Mulai's was a deliberate defiance to mortal combat, from which death could be the only outcome, since surrender would mean disgrace. But Mulai insisted on his right to challenge in the lists, on any terms his antagonist would accept; and I thought there was more than the mere joy of combat in Pierre's acceptance. So our two men trotted gently up and down the ring, lest their horses grow stiff, while the Syrian went to arm himself.

He rode into the ring at a thundering gallop; and I trembled for Pierre, great soldier though he was. On horseback and in mail the Arab looked much bigger than before; his charger was a big black beast that caracoled with the energy of boundless strength. The two antagonists drew back for the charge.

They came together with a crashing shock that forced both horses to their hind legs. When they recovered, it was seen that the great weight of men and beasts had caused both lances to shiver at the butts, and both shields were pierced. Yet neither man seemed hurt.

The attendants brought fresh lances, and again they met. This time Pierre swayed in his saddle. Then we Frenchmen groaned indeed; yet he held his seat. The third time, just before they came together, a shrill whistle sounded; and a terrible thing happened. I saw the Syrian sink his lance so that he aimed not at Pierre's shield, but strangely low; and instantly our captain's horse fell flat.

A thousand throats raised a wild shout, all the spectators crying out one word. Later I learned that the word was "Treachery!" These gallant Moors, who loved a fair fight, were cursing their own champion for his villainous trick.

There was no doubt of Mulai's guilt. A horse may indeed stumble by accident; but the horse Pierre had ridden had been given by Mulai himself. The whistle was a signal, at which the beast was trained to fall. What put this past all doubt was Mulai's action after Pierre had fallen.

His soldier's instinct saved Pierre; else the Syrian's spear would have torn through the mail at his throat. As you know, *messires,* the armor coming into fashion now, with its burden of plate above mail, cumbers a man's movements; but Pierre wore only chain-mail, under the lesser weight of which a man can move freely, unless he be weak. As his charger fell, our captain threw himself from the saddle, lighted on his feet, and raised his shield to ward his head. Mulai struck it fair, the momentum of his charge flinging Pierre headlong. As he fell, he rolled, barely escaping the trampling hoofs of Mulai's horse.

The caliph, standing on his seat, shouted to his guards to stop the fight; and they, whose duty it was to see fair play, hurried forward to separate the combatants. But before they could act, Pierre was up, his sword out, and ordered them to stand bark and let him settle his own quarrels. The rules of the tourney, with the Moors as with us, gave him the right to do this. Treachery had been practised against him; he had the privilege of demanding that the victory be awarded to him by forfeit, or of fighting out the battle without interference.

Choosing the second course, he was free thenceforth to fight as he would. His adversary's foul play gave Pierre the right to win—if he could—by taking advantage of any means that came to him. No rules bound him now; but his treacherous opponent was put in the wrong. If Mulai won, his life would be forfeit to the caliph, for his offense; if he lost—death at Pierre's hands.

Understanding this, the Syrian brought his horse about, and spurred down on his dismounted enemy. Pierre awaited him grimly, ready to leap aside from the point of that menacing lance. But there was one in the arena who cared more for his friend's life than for an angry man's desire to take personal vengeance.

As the Syrian bore down, I set my lance in rest; but I reined in when I saw Cercamon spur to met him. The troubadour's lance pierced Mulai's horse through the breast; and as the beast dropped, Cercamon drew off, crying:

"Now, Pierre! Sword against sword is fair play!"

The massed crowd broke into wild cheers of applause. Their chivalrous love of a fair field took Mulai's treachery as a stain on their honor and their religion; Cercamon's swift stroke, though a breach of strict rules, had only restored the balance of the fight. As he had said, sword against sword was fair play. By his sudden change of aim to a point lower than would profit in an honest tilt, and his readiness to attack a dismounted man from the vantage-ground of his own saddle, the Syrian had justified any act that took this unfair vantage from him.

Now it was taken from him indeed. His own horse slain, he was barely prepared for Pierre's furious onrush, and for a little while he gave ground rapidly. Cercamon kept his horse abreast of the fight, watching against further foul play; and the guards, though withdrawn in order not to impede the combatants, were ready to spur forward at need.

Finding his stance at last, the Syrian covered up with his round shield and took the offensive. His sword was straight and long, like a Christian's or a Berber's; as he struck, it drove home with a weight and a ring that showed its temper and its owner's. Both men were so powerful that their shields could not stand the blows, and, hacked to splinters after a few strokes, were cast aside. Then it was sword to sword, skill against skill. By our Lady, they were closely matched! It needed all Pierre's cunning to fend that terrible blade from face and breast and thighs; yet again and again he snatched a stolen second to strike back shrewdly.

Of a sudden the Syrian leaped back. Before Pierre could close on him, he whirled up his weapon, made one stride forward, and smote down with all his might. Pierre flung up his own blade to ward the stroke; but Mulai's steel cut through the fine French sword as if it were lath, and struck Pierre's helmet from his head. Cercamon threw Pierre his sword; but our captain, ignoring it, flung his own shattered stump in the Syrian's face. It stuck in the space between and below the cheek-bones, where no mail protected. I saw blood burst from Mulai's lips.

His dagger drawn, Pierre sprang for the Moslem, who waited in murderous rage. I looked to see Pierre split like a herring by that awful sword; but as Mulai raised it, Pierre's dagger flew from his hand. It pierced the mail above the Syrian's upper arm, and buried itself in the flesh. Unable to wield his sword, Mulai dropped it and fled from the field. Pierre sped after him; the guards closed in to seize the fugitive; Cercamon set spurs to his horse.

Even as the guards drew about him, one of them, reaching forward as if to seize him, urged his horse between Mulai and the others. But instead of leaning over his horse's neck to catch the Syrian's mantle, the guard leaped from the saddle, quickly helped Mulai to mount in his place, and faced about to impede the other guards. Astounded, they let a precious moment slip; and in that moment Cercamon bounded up. His horse had given him a start of Pierre, who was running forward at full career.

But Cercamon, in his haste, had neglected to pick up his sword. As he closed in, the false guard launched a furious blow at him. Cercamon swerved; the blow missed him, but cut deep into his horse's thigh. Then the traitor fell, pierced by three swords at once. The faithful guards left him lying, and spurred off after the Syrian.

Mulai el-Ussari was riding down the arena at a frantic gallop, his spurs plowing up and down his charger's flanks. After him streamed the guards; a second detachment pelted up from the gate of the lists to head him off. Before they could reach him, a dozen Arabs sprang from among the yelling crowd and threw themselves between. From under their burnooses they drew short swords; they charged full at the advancing guardsmen, and fell to hacking and stabbing. Their unexpected assault threw the horsemen into disorder for a moment; and in that moment Mulai shot past them unscathed, through the gate, and beyond our sight.

The lists were in an uproar, the crowd pouring down to assail the Arabs who had enabled Mulai to escape. As I shouted to our twenty Frenchmen, I heard the caliph cry upon his soldiers to overtake the Syrian and drag him back to death. Then I was in the road, our men behind me. Back of us as we galloped, we heard the gathering thunder of the Cordovan pursuit; and I judged the strange Arabs overpowered or slain.

Ahead, almost at the palace gate, the rascal Mulai was urging his horse at a tremendous pace. Through the gate he bounded, into the courtyard beyond; and, remembering that there were guards there, I thought we had him. But to those guards in the palace, who had not seen the fight, he seemed no villain, but an honored foreign prince. When we reached the gate, he was out of sight.

There was not a doorway, not an arch, in that palace that a man could not ride through. We separated in the great court, some taking one way, some another; and on horseback we hunted through the grand palace of Cordova. Behind us followed the Moors, and as eager to run him down as we. We combed that palace through and through, but found him not. There was not even a drop of blood to show which turn he had taken; the torn padding under his armor must have stopped the rent in his mail, and let the blood flow down under his armor. The multitude of courts and corridors so confused us that we may well have missed him by a few yards a score of times. It was long ere we gave up the search within the walls to seek him through the city.

When I and a few others came out by the gate that faced the city, a troop of the caliph's horse was clattering down the broad street toward the heart of town and the bridge. We followed, thinking of nothing save the chance to lay hands on the Syrian. Straight for the bridge rode the Moors, and we after them, passing at every cross-street, square, and by-lane other soldiers searching the city for the caitiff. The town was seething with the caliph's soldiery; I saw them enter house after house, ransack the market-booths, peering under rolls of matting and behind bales of goods; nay, they searched the very mosques.

We pelted over the bridge to the tower at its end. The guard at the bridgehead turned out at sight of the troopers ahead of us; and as we rode up an officer questioned the guard. Aye, they had seen the Emir of Edessa; he had come across the bridge but a little before us, riding like a *djinn* on the wings of the wind.

A swift boat, one of the caliph's pleasure-craft, had been moored at the water's edge. Into it he had leaped, crying that he went on the caliph's business; and knowing him the caliph's honored guest, the guard had let him go. Hoisting the lateen, he was off down-river with a following wind. See! Yonder his sail!

A score of Moors leaped into three boats and made after him. Knowing ourselves of little use, we rode back, slowly and in weary disgust, to the palace.

OUR CAPTAIN and Cercamon awaited us in our quarters. The troubadour was still cursing, but swore that the false guards and those who had impeded pursuit were no true Moors. We reported our useless pursuit, and Pierre smiled.

"Now that it is too late, I have learned something," he said.

He sat on a cushion on the floor—for the Moors use not chairs as we do—and across his knees was that great sword which Mulai had let fall when the dagger pierced his shoulder. It was a masterpiece of the smith's art: gray-blue Damascus steel, heavy, but of such perfect temper that Pierre, exerting all his great strength, could bend it double. As he let its point go, it straightened with a deep hum and a flash like lightning. The cross-hilt was plated heavily with gold; a large ruby gleamed in its pommel; and from guard to point it was richly chased in gold.

Holding the blade so that the light caught fairly, he pointed to the midmost of its designs, and then drew forth the silken cloth he had worn on his helmet. The characters on the blade were tiny—so tiny that it must be held close to read them—but though I am no scholar, *messires,* even I could see that, line for line and dot for dot, the writing on the cloth matched the inlaid figures on the sword!

"We have found our man and lost him again," laughed Pierre; and Cercamon cursed again, his blue-green eyes like the sea when a storm is making.

Toward dark we were summoned to the caliph. Aye, all of us; for this noble monarch so valued his honor that he must justify it in the eyes of even the lowest spearman of us all. We found him in a small, bare chamber, reading by a cluster of bronze lamps.

Motioning Pierre and the troubadour to sit, "He has escaped," he said. "He had confederates; not only the spy he had among my guards, and the swordsmen among the spectators, but others outside the city. When the pursuing boats pressed him hard, and my horsemen followed him down both banks of the river, a column of smoke rose from a hill on the left bank, and a galley bore up-stream and picked him up. I have sent couriers to Seville, to pray Ibn-Wezir that swift galleys be sent in pursuit; but the dog has a long start."

"I thank your Majesty," Pierre answered. "I would give much to have him caught. May I show your Majesty this?"

Into the caliph's hand he put the silken cloth, and showed the sword, with its writing in gold.

"The characters are the same," he said.

The caliph nodded.

"I might have guessed. If I had known this morning what I know now, he who called himself Mulai Abu-Hassan would have been thrown headless into the Guadalquivir. But tell me now, *effendi*—" and his eyes grew stern—"your real reason for coming to Cordova! The last few hours have shown that your possession of this cloth has some secret meaning."

Pierre hesitated.

"I can tell your Majesty only on the condition that you will not use what I say against France."

"Or against Barcelona!" put in Cercamon.

The caliph touched his hand to brow, lips and heart.

"By the faith of a Moslem," he swore, "I will never again raise a hand against any Christian state! It is an easy promise, since all my strength will be needed to defend Cordova. Speak, *effendi.*"

So Pierre, with interruptions now and then from the troubadour, told him all I have told you here, from the attempts upon the lives of Bérenger and Count Alphonse to our arrival in Cordova. He listened intently, with a bitter smile.

When Pierre had finished—

"Let me read you these!" the caliph said. From the folds of his burnoose he drew a number of parchment rolls. "These, *effendim,* were found by my men in Mulai's apartments. As Emir of Edessa, he enjoyed the hospitality of my palace. He fled too fast to visit his lodging, for he knew well how I would punish such treachery as he practised against you. Listen!"

As he read the scrolls, one after another, the hairs lifted on my head. The first was a minute account of the strength of Cordova: its walls, its towers, the garrison and arms of each. The second was a like description of Barcelona; and by Cercamon's outcry I judged it was exact. The third contained a list of all the strongholds of Aragon, the condition of the roads across the Pyrenees, the revenues of every district under Bérenger's rule. And the fourth, *messires,* numbered accurately the garrisons of Foix, Nimes, Carcassonne, Béziers, Aigues-Mortes, aye, and of Toulouse itself! Having finished, the caliph handed this parchment to Pierre. Drawn with an engineer's skill, the plan of city and castle of Toulouse!

"That man is the devil!" cried Pierre.

"Nay, but the chief of the devil's servants," the caliph answered. "He it was, *effendim,* who tried to procure the murder of your lords. His spies are everywhere, from Syria to Spain. Learning from his agents of the quarrel between your King and your Pope, he recognized that the chance he has long waited and prayed and intrigued for had come."

"But who is he?" Pierre and the troubadour gasped together.

"He is Abd-el-Mumin, false prophet of the heretical Moslem sect of the Almohades, the foes of all true Moslems! Having lured the Berbers from the true faith of Islam, he had made himself master of North Africa. Now his eyes are on Spain, and beyond Spain, on—France!"

"But how did he deceive you?" cried Cercamon.

"I welcomed him for what he claimed to be—the Emir of Edessa in Syria. He had credentials—forged, as he forged the letters received by your lords. For a skilled hand such a thing is easy. Do not all rulers set up, in the market-places, proclamations signed with their seals, for all to see? Only the tardy discovery of his records showed me—"

He paused, and then resumed sadly:

"I must make a confession, *effendim.* I have long dreamed of the day when my troops should overwhelm Aragon, Catalonia and Barcelona, and bear the green banner of the prophet into France. Yet I knew that this was but a dream, that all the swords in Cordova would not suffice for such a conquest. Then came this false devil, calling himself Emir of Edessa, which the Syrian Moslems have recently won from the Franks.

"He promised me, if I would proclaim a holy war against the Christians, that all Syria would pour out its multitudes to help me. When I hesitated, he told me of this impending strife between your King and your Pope, and that soon all France, aye, and Barcelona, would be at civil war. Then I swore I would attack you, as soon as that war should break out. It was to force the war that he abused my hospitality to plot murder against your lords. If I had but known, had but guessed, who he was!

"The writing on his sword, and on the cloth you bore on your helmet, is the Almohade creed: 'Allah, God One and Indivisible! To the Moslem who worships saints, to the Christian, death and the fires of Eblis!' The priest who struck at the Count of Toulouse, like him who failed to slay Bérenger, was an Almohade, the fanatical servant of Abd-el-Mumin. The cloth, in its box, was an amulet to ward off the damnation that wearing Christian garb would otherwise have cost his soul.

"Seeing that cloth in your hands, Faidit *Effendi*, Abd-el-Mumin must have feared that you had guessed his plans, perhaps his identity. It was necessary, therefore, that you die. He hoped that you would be slain in the tournament. When you emerged victorious, he felt compelled to kill you himself. Your skill forced him to resort to treachery, which he hoped in vain to accomplish without detection. But how did you know, *effendim*, that the man you sought was in Cordova?"

"We did not know," Pierre answered. "But I had seen that any other chance was impossible. I set out to punish Bérenger for what I thought his crime. The attempt on his life proved he had no hand in the assault on my master. No Christian prelate would have had sufficient reason for such a deed; therefore, I knew that the priestly garb was a disguise. The guilty man must be one to whose interest it was that Toulouse and Barcelona should destroy each other.

"She who is Duchess of Aquitaine and Queen of France had such an interest; but now, when the King, her husband, is bidding for the support of all his nobles, she would not dare. The only other power to profit by war between these provinces was Moslem Spain; and Cordova is the heart of Moslem Spain. Therefore, and guided by the Arabic written on this cloth, I came. God forgive me, I thought your Majesty guilty, though Cercamon told me I was wrong. Your pardon!"

The caliph bowed.

"Wrong though you were, your wisdom has saved France. For Barcelona is the gateway of France; and if war had broken out between your lords, my armies would have poured through that unguarded gateway. You may well have saved Cordova also. These writings show that the 'Syrian' troops that would have come to my aid would have been the savage Berber hordes of the Almohades, who hate true Moslems as bitterly as they hate Christians. And they would have been led by the false Mulai, the evil prophet, Abd-el-Mumin. He has left my land now; doubtless he has fled from Spain, since I have warned Seville. But one day he will return, *effendim;* and then—may Allah help Andalusia!"

He prophesied truly, *messires:* as you know, two years later the Almohades made Cordova a waste of blood and ashes.

"You will stay with me a while?" the caliph resumed.

Kneeling, Pierre kissed his hand.

"Your Majesty must give us leave," he answered. "We must go home. Our thanks be with you, and the blessing of God!"

The caliph pointed to Abd-el-Mumin's sword.

"And that?" he asked.

"I shall take it with me," Pierre replied. "It shall be blessed by the Prior of St. Sernin; and one day, if God lets me live, I will plunge it into Abd-el-Mumin's heart!"

From that day, *messires,* he was rarely spoken of as Pierre Faidit. Men called him *Pierre de l'Espée*—"Pierre of the Sword."

FAITHFUL

I MUST SPEAK the truth. For two years I have kept silence. Not for myself; but for the king, and because a man of honor must conceal stinging truths about a woman. So much that is evil, however, has ensued from my silence that it forces me to speak out at last.

For many months ignorant and malicious voices have been raised against the king himself; even in his court men who have profited most from his munificence are whispering behind his back, accusing him—him, the soul of piety and honor—of the foul sin of murder. These lies are believed; they have cost him the support of his strongest vassals. Even the Church lends credence and threatens the king with its terrible curse for a crime of which he is innocent.

Unless the truth is known he will lose his grip on France, and our land will break up again into the dozen bickering baronies from which he formed a kingdom. The tyranny of the nobles will once more crush down the people; there will be strife and burning everywhere. So I must tell the truth, cost me what it may—for the king will not tell.

It is part of my great debt to my beloved, murdered master, Alphonse-Jourdain, Count of Toulouse, that I possess the knowledge of writing, without which these words could never spread through France. Alphonse, who found me a poor fisher-lad and made me his trusted captain and counselor, taught me also the craft of letters. All thanks to him, and praise to God that I can use this craft to prove before the world the innocence of my king.

This declaration of mine, copied many times by the holy Prior of St. Sernin, will go to every court and abbey in France; aye, and to his Holiness the Pope, that the truth may be known to all men. And if any dare to doubt my word, let him meet me with sword or lance, afoot or in the saddle, that I may write the truth on his body in letters of blood.

Three years ago, in the Summer of 1147, King Louis of France marched from Metz with the greatest French army that had ever crossed the Rhine. Yet we marched not against the Germans, with whom we were at peace. With the Cross on our breasts, and our hearts overflowing with divine zeal, we set forth for Palestine. The blessing of the holy Bernard of Clairvaux still rang in our ears. To us was entrusted the pious task of rescuing from the Turk the hard-pressed Christian principalities of the Holy Land. The Pope had hallowed our banners, prophesying the most brilliant victories.

I was gay, for I was young—seven and twenty—and had traveled just enough to make me the more anxious to see the wonders of the East. And to see them in such a service! To dedicate my poor sword to the deliverance of the Sepulcher! There was only one sorrow in my heart: I left my dear master behind.

For Alphonse-Jourdain could not go. At the last Council, when the route was laid out, King Louis' summoned my lord of Toulouse and bade him strip the Cross from his breast. For when the king left France some one must remain behind to rule in his stead, and hold our turbulent kingdom together. In all the land there was but one noble whom the king dared trust with this mighty task—my lord, Alphonse of Toulouse.

Before all his barons Louis clasped his scarlet royal mantle about my master's shoulders, and commanded that all France obey him while the king was absent on the great Crusade. Aye, though the king had once been my lord's enemy and tried to

take Toulouse by storm, he knew how Alphonse-Jourdain loved
France.

My lord count was moved to tears, and he remembered that
it was the queen whose wicked counsel had first stirred up the
enmity between Toulouse and the crown. For the king loved
her well; and she, who had been born Duchess of Aquitaine,
hated my master because of the old feud between him and her
greedy father.

Now to most of our French nobles France was but a vast
treasure-house to ravish and plunder; but to my lord Alphonse,
and to the king, she was the motherland, sacred as religion,
loved as one loves her who gave him birth.

But my master accepted that great offer on one condition;
that the king would acknowledge him a vassal of the crown.
Many of the most powerful French nobles, among them my
lord, ruled their fiefs as sovereign princes, independent of the
king. Alphonse of Toulouse was greatest of these free princes,
and next to Bérenger of Barcelona, the most powerful.

Fearing that his appointment as regent in the king's absence
would make them rise in rebellion—for they were all jealous
of his power—he gave up to the king all his cities and estates—
Toulouse, Nimes, Béziers, Carcassonne, Aigues-Mortes and
Foix—gave up his titles and his independence that the barons
might know he cherished no desire to be great at their expense.

The other nobles cried out in astonishment. King Louis cast both arms about my lord's neck, and kissed his cheeks.

"Alphonse!" he cried. "How you have rewarded me! Once, guided by evil councils, I fought you, and would have taken your lands by force. Now, when I forbid you the Crusade, depriving you of the glory you might win in Palestine, you give up your sovereign liberty to serve France and me!"

Alphonse of Toulouse answered with a proud light in his eyes:

"I have added to France all the land between the Garonne and the Mediterranean; I have doubled the kingdom your father left you. I have by doing this, helped you to make France one people, one nation!"

Yet the exaltation of his surrender was touched with sadness. Born in Palestine, by the Jordan's bank, he longed to pour out his blood that the Holy Places might be safe from the defilement of the infidel.

Now all this time I, who had attended my master to the Council, stood sore at heart that he must give up the Holy War, and that I must give it up also. How could I go when my master stayed at home? I was his man, bound to him by oath, by love, by all the many kindnesses I had received from him. Yet again the king was speaking, his eyes resting on me:

"Is not that the young officer who took me prisoner when I warred against you, Alphonse? Is he not that Pierre Faidit—he whom men call Pierre of the Sword?"

"It is he, your Majesty."

"Then I must place myself still deeper in your debt. Many dangers will beset me in the Holy Land. I must have a squire who will serve and defend me with unswerving loyalty; and one who has grown up in your service, Alphonse, must have learned more loyalty than others."

My heart thumped.

"He is yours, my king," the count replied. "But I am loath to let him go."

Then to me:

"Be faithful unto death, Pierre," he said in a low voice. "In serving the king, you serve Toulouse, France and Christ!"

So, as I have said, we marched from Metz, going through Germany to Hungary and Thrace. We marched singing; our hymns of praise arose when we were footsore, hungry, and in rags. What was hardship to us? If we suffered wounds, each drop of blood shed in Christ's cause would wipe out ten years of purgatory; if we died by the way, or in battle against the Turks, we should go, as Christian warriors, straight to the throne of God and the joys of Paradise. This had been promised us by the Holy Father.

All men know the fate of that second Crusade, launched to rescue the Frankish kingdoms founded in Syria by the heroes of the First Crusade. Disease, famine, the treachery of our Greek guides, the arrows and simitars of the Turks—these wove for us a crown of martyrdom. I shall not tell of that; it is bitter.

One thing I must record. The Greek Emperor, who had received us with flattering hospitality and false promises, bribed our guides to betray us to the Moslem. Yet we should have escaped the net woven for us but for the folly of the queen, Aliénor of Aquitaine, whom the king had been reckless enough to take with him.

Riding out with her women, in the very heart of the Turkish country, she drew down on us the whole advance guard of Noureddin, the Turkish governor. To save her, we were forced to throw ourselves into the very ambush the Turks had laid for us. The fifth part of our host was destroyed, though we beat off the enemy.

Ah, would to God Aliénor of Aquitaine had died beneath the simitar!

The Crusade was doomed. We knew it, every man; yet we still cherished a faint, sullen hope. Somehow, by a miracle, God would preserve us; and through us would drive the infidels from Palestine. So, when our wounds were healed, we marched grimly forward. In February of 1148 we reached Antioch, weary and broken.

We were met at the gates by the Prince of Antioch, Raimund of Poitou. He leaped from his splendid white Arabian charger to kiss the king's hand; but the queen he kissed on both cheeks, for she was his niece.

We were greeted as deliverers. For that purpose we had indeed come. Our enfeebled host alone stood between Eastern Christianity and the engulfing tide of Moslem invasion.

The first week passed in wild rejoicing and feasts that lasted from sunset to dawn. The king, the queen, and our foremost nobles were the guests of the prince himself; and I, whom the king kept constantly about his person, had my first sight of a civilization as lovely as it was degenerate.

In that beautiful city nestled between the Orontes and the mountains, the adventurous French of fifty years before had begun their swift conquest of the Holy Places from the Arabs. Now, while the Turks who had mastered the Arabs threatened the children of the French conquerors, we lived in idle luxury instead of attempting that rescue for which we had come.

Grievous was the change in our king. If his faith had weakened, it would have been better for him and for France. But even in the depths of his despair, he still believed himself ordained by God to drive the Moslems out of Syria. The bitterness of disappointment drove him to folly, but shook neither his courage nor his stubborn faith.

Prince Raimund lodged him in a splendid villa across the city from his own palace, and near the river. There, every day, came the chiefs of the Eastern Franks to consult with him. Partly in honor to Alphonse-Jourdain, partly in gratitude for my services in the battle with the Turks, the king admitted me to the Council.

The Council meetings were disgraced by bitter wranglings. Three divergent opinions were offered. Thibault of Champagne, who commanded our rear-guard, had come to realize that we had small hope left of conquering the Turks and winning loot; therefore he urged our return to France. This angered the king, whose devotion to Christ's cause was as great as his hatred of avarice.

Arnaut of Tripolis, an envoy of Baldwin III, the boy King of Jerusalem, prayed Louis to leave Antioch with all his hosts and hasten to the Holy City, which, he declared, was caught in a trap between the Seljuks of Asia Minor, the Turks of Bagdad, and the Moslems of Damascus. In the Spring Noureddin would doubtless set his armies in motion from all three regions, and the Holy City would be doomed.

Each time Baldwin's envoy spoke, Raimund of Antioch cried out upon him with jealous bitterness, charging that he concealed the truth. To go to Jerusalem now, he maintained, would be to leave not merely Antioch but all Christian Syria at Noureddin's mercy. Antioch was the bulwark of Jerusalem itself. The only effective blow that we French could strike against Noureddin must be struck from the north, above Antioch.

I said nothing till I was asked; the word of a simple soldier weighs little against the prestige of princes. But at length Louis required my opinion, and there was but one thing to say. As a soldier, I agreed with Raimund of Antioch. He was concerned with his own ends, but his judgment was right.

Baldwin's envoy would have had Louis help Christian Jerusalem break its alliance with Moslem Damascus, only to gain for the boy king a city whose very possession would extend our lines too thin for defense, and leave them menaced by Asia Minor in front and Bagdad in the rear. By concentrating in the north, above Antioch, we might drive a wedge between the two centers of Turkish dominion.

As I said these words, I saw that the king liked them little. His zeal mastered his reason; to his priest-like soul Antioch meant little and Jerusalem much. Moreover he was fighting a battle with himself; a battle in which love wrestled with jealousy. His queen was his evil genius now as she had ever been.

Not content with causing the loss of thousands of his bravest soldiers, she was even now preparing the crowning crime of her wicked life.

Well-nigh every day she left the royal villa by the Orontes to go through the city in her litter, guarded only by two knights of her household, men of Poitou. I know not where she went, but report whispered that she visited Raimund of Antioch in his palace. Nor could the king offer any valid reason to restrain her if this were so, seeing she was Raimund's niece. But there were ugly rumors that the queen, for all Raimund was her uncle, cherished a guilty love for him.

These rumors had reached King Louis, and because Aliénor urged him to follow Raimund's counsels and defend Antioch, the king in his jealousy grew more embittered against him and despised his advice. The matter was bound to end ill.

One day the king summoned me to his closet, where he was wont to spend long hours upon his knees, praying for guidance. His eyes, red with sleeplessness, were ablaze with resolve. He shut the door as I entered, and spoke in low, sharp words:

"I have sent a messenger to Paris," he said, "by a swift galley. I have bidden Alphonse-Jourdain surrender his regency to the

Abbot Suger, and come at once to Antioch with as many troops as he can quickly assemble. I go to Jerusalem!"

I was staggered, thinking he had yielded to the counsels of Baldwin's envoy and to his bitterness against Raimund.

"With the army?" I gasped.

Louis shook his head impatiently.

"Alone!" he answered. "I am sick of selfish counsels, sick of men who advise me to do that which benefits them. Save you, Pierre, I trust but two beings—Alphonse of Toulouse and my God. Therefore I must have Alphonse with me. And I go to the Holy Sepulcher to seek God's guidance.

"Perhaps there—" his eyes glowed with pious fervor— "perhaps there, where He was buried and whence He rose, Christ will deign to reveal His purpose to me." He paused, and then resumed in a changed voice:

"Watch over the queen while I am away! She is a woman, and beautiful—therefore the devil lays his snares in her eyes. Pierre—" his fingers bit deep into my arm—"do not let her leave this roof unwatched. Follow her! Aye, though she go to Raimund's palace, follow her. Here is my seal, which will pass you anywhere. If she has one chance to see or speak with him alone God knows what harm may rise!"

Now I was aghast indeed. What sort of task was this, to spy upon the queen? With what countenance should I follow her; how dare intrude upon the Prince of Antioch?

That afternoon the king departed for Jerusalem. Acting on my orders, I stationed myself at the door of the queen's apartments, armed with the royal seal. But I wore also my sword and hauberk, knowing that he who angered Aliénor of Aquitaine must be prepared against more than her tongue.

I had resolved on a course of action—it would be impossible to shadow the queen through that great city, impracticable to force myself on her company within Raimund's palace; therefore I had determined not to let the queen leave her quarters during the king's absence. If Raimund came to her, I could forbid him to see her alone. Whoever resisted me in the royal villa would be resisting France.

The king had not been gone an hour when the queen's door opened. A waiting-woman came out. At sight of me she started.

"What do you here?" she cried. "The queen has not sent for you."

I showed her the royal seal, saying that the king's orders bound me to attendance on her majesty.

"But the queen would go out!" she protested.

"Tell her Majesty that she must bide in her quarters till the king's return," I answered.

The woman stared at me open-mouthed, then turned on her heel and went back to the queen.

"Now for the storm!" I thought.

And I was right. The queen came forth from her chamber and stood before me with a swirl of silk and the gleam of angry eyes.

"I am a prisoner then?" she asked haughtily. "You are my jailor, sir? A pretty fellow, truly, to lay commands on a queen! Withdraw, peasant!"

Never had I seen Aliénor of Aquitaine close to, though often at a distance since I had been squire to the king. Now, enraged though she was, I thought her the most beautiful creature on earth. She was tall, slender, with the lithe carriage of healthy youth; her eyes were large and blue; her golden hair, finer than the finest silk, hung over, her bosom in two great braids that fell to her knees.

But it was not hair nor eyes nor figure that made her more glorious than other women, nor the rose tints of her perfect skin, which did not spot beneath the eyes when she was angry, but glowed with an even, lustrous beauty. It was something within her, that seemed to transfuse her whole being. Her voice, even in its fury, thrilled with deep-toned music.

Never had I felt the compulsion of a presence as I felt the

compulsion of hers. My resolution sank, my very feet seemed
to impel me away at her command. Yet I stood my ground.

"I am not your jailor, madame," I replied respectfully. "It is
the king who commands; I but carry out his orders."

She stamped her tiny foot, "The king! The king imprisons
me! Why?"

"I have not the skill nor the right to argue with your Majesty,"
I answered. "I know only that my duty will not permit me to
let you depart."

Instantly she perceived that I was no mere spearman to
tremble at her anger. Fury fell from her like a dropped veil. She
smiled, and her beauty increased, if that were possible. Her fine
eyes were those of an angel. Nor did they counterfeit innocence;
her loveliness was neutral—neither hiding nor revealing anything.

She seemed now to see me clearly for the first time; to look
upon me with gracious favor.

"Who are you, sir?" she asked gently. "Who are you, who
find it so easy to deny my will?"

God knows I did not find it easy. I was disturbed as I had
never been before. Before I could answer, she spoke again.

"I know you," she said. "You are Pierre Faidit, the king's
squire. You are the famous swordsman whom men call the first
champion of France."

Her smile was radiant, bathing me in an admiration which
stirred me, though I knew it to be false. Treacherous and hyp-
ocritical, it was perilously sweet.

As I stood there like a fool, knowing not what to say, she
edged past me, slipped by like a soft breeze in Spring, that
passes almost before it is felt; but her purpose had gleamed one
tiny instant in her eyes, and I roused myself. I reached out
quickly and seized her hand, drawing back on it.

"Your Majesty can not pass!" I exclaimed.

"Why—so I can not!" she breathed softly.

I had looked for a torrent of regal rage; but her fingers relaxed in mine, seeming to caress my rough hand, and she smiled.

"You are very strong, Pierre," she continued in beautiful, heart-softening tones. "Let me go from here. I smother between these gloomy walls. I wish but to be rowed out on the river, to feel the warm sun, to breathe in the air from the mountains.

"Nay," very prettily, "if you do not let me go, I shall grow sick with this dull air, and my cheeks will wither."

She had melted to the appealingness of a child, her concern being now, as ever, the end she sought, not the mode she employed to gain it.

Praying for firmness, summoning to my aid the remembrance of all the wrongs she had done Toulouse, and the needless slaughter of our soldiers caused by her recklessness, I forced her back through the door. "Forced," I say, but indeed I was most gentle with her. Realizing that her wiles had failed, she began to storm in earnest. But the way was barred, and she within. I set my back against the door, and that was the end.

But my vigil was just begun. Having felt the magic of her beauty, I dared not trust any other man to share or relieve my watch. So I shouted for a servant, impressed him with my authority, and ordered food and wine to be brought at fixed hours each day, for the queen, her household, and myself. All day long I would stand guard. At night I would lie down at the threshold, trusting my soldier's sense to waken me if any touched the door from within, or approached me from without.

But the queen must have foreseen that the king's departure would involve some such precaution against her, and had left certain orders with her own knights. Two hours after she had spoken with me two Poitevin gentlemen came up from their quarters outside the villa. They demanded access to the queen; I refused, showing the king's seal. It would be neither convenient nor safe for me to be constantly passing her gentlemen in and out. If I permitted it, sooner or later the queen would escape.

The Poitevins stole angry glances at each other, but they

dared not resist royal authority. A little later came one harder
to refuse; a tall, thin man of middle age, whose fine features
were known throughout France. It was Bertrand d'Armagnac,
who had been seneschal of the queen's duchy of Aquitaine till
he gave up that office to follow her on the Crusade. We had
met before.

"Is it true that the queen is a prisoner by the king's order?"
he asked. "May none see her, Pierre?"

It were idle to split hairs with such a man.

"Even as you have said, my lord," I answered bluntly.

"You will let me see her for a moment?" he asked. "I pledge
my word not to come again, nor in any way to make your task
harder."

Knowing him for an honorable gentleman, I assented. It
occurred to me that the Count d'Armagnac might even make
my task easier.

"I will pass you this once, my lord," I said, "if you will try to
persuade her Majesty to be content with her position."

He bowed, and I made way for him. Within ten minutes he
came out again, and left with a compliment for me.

"I will give orders," he said, "that none of the queen's men
disturb you. Her Majesty seems resigned. I go now to the Prince
of Antioch. It will be better for you, and easier for the queen,
that he should not expect her Majesty's visits during the king's
absence. If he instead came here, you would have to forbid his
entrance; therefore I shall tell Prince Raimund that the queen
wishes him not to come to her, and not to make inquiries."

Though d'Armagnac had truly done this only to save the
queen from the scandal of a quarrel between Raimund and
myself, I thanked him deeply. The Prince of Antioch must have
taken his advice, for he did not come to the villa.

WHAT FOLLY in me to think Aliénor of Aquitaine so
easily managed! A few days later I was to learn how resolute
she was. Two servants brought her food. As they passed out
one day with the empty dishes, one of them spoke to me.

Just as I was turning toward him I caught the too-quick gleam of steel in the hand of the other and whirled barely in time to ward the dagger from my throat. I felled the would-be assassin with a plunge of my fist, and drew my sword to cut down the other; but he had fled. When his fellow regained his senses I bade him leave the royal roof on pain of death.

Eighteen more days went by. On the nineteenth, as I raised to my lips the cup of wine brought with my dinner, I smelled a sharp fragrance that the wine of Lesbos should not have. Calling the servant back, I bade him drink it off. He backed away with a white, scared face.

"Go back to the kitchen," I commanded, my voice trembling with anger. "Bid another bring my food henceforth, and do you flee for your life!"

When his successor brought my supper, I told him it would be part of his duty to taste each viand before it touched my lips.

It was the next day, as I stood at my post, that a sturdy man-at-arms ran down the corridor toward me. Knowing not what to expect, I half-drew my sword; but the man called my name joyfully. A tide of gladness flooded my heart, for this was Big Jehan, a man-at-arms of Toulouse, who had borne the count's banner at the south gate when I commanded there. His presence in Antioch could mean but one thing: Alphonse-Jourdain, my dear lord, had come!

It was true. Jehan reported that the Count of Toulouse had set sail as soon as he received the king's message, leaving France in the hands of Abbot Suger, the chancellor. With thirty galleys and eight thousand men he had reached Acre, the great port of Palestine, five days before. It had been his purpose to set out at once for Antioch, but in Acre he had come down with a fever.

I was dismayed, but Big Jehan hastened to reassure me. Our master was not very sick; he would be in armor again within three days.

Four days after, the king returned, gloomy, but inwardly

glowing with that holy ardor which the thought of the Crusade always kindled in him. He received my report of the queen's imprisonment with satisfaction. I did not tell him of her appeals to me, nor of the two attempts upon my life; but I assured him she had not seen the Prince of Antioch.

He was much rejoiced to hear that Alphonse-Jourdain had landed. A messenger was sent to Acre at once, to inquire after the count's health.

My lord returned with the messenger. I was thankful to see him alive, but I could scarce hold back the tears at sight of his meager, wasted features. The fever had dealt more harshly with him than had been expected. He came in a litter. Yet his eyes held their old sparkle, and it was plain he would get well.

Despite his weariness, the king insisted on taking counsel with him the morning after his arrival. I, who was now released from my watch over the queen, attended my lord, by the king's graciousness. Raimund of Antioch was not present, for Louis would not have him any longer in his councils. This troubled me greatly, for such an offense to the prince whose guests we were would stir up bad blood.

The king awaited us in his antechamber, a small room with bare marble walls, and with no door other than a thick hanging. An officer was stationed beyond the curtain, with orders to admit no one.

Hastily, without prelude, Louis plunged into the matter of the conference. At Jerusalem, he said, he had seen the young king and his mother Mélisande, Regent of Jerusalem. They had shown him how desperately the city was threatened by Damascus, a treacherous ally which might at any hour join the Turkish forces of Noureddin and overwhelm the feeble Christian kingdom.

He had resolved, after praying at each of the Holy Places, to lead the entire French army south and attack Damascus. Damascus taken, its Emir would be helpless to combine with Noureddin, who might be overwhelmed later by a joint Christian attack.

My lord lay back feebly on a couch, his head supported by silken cushions. His brow was clouded with anxious thought.

"It is not a good plan, your Majesty," he hazarded bluntly. "Jerusalem has lied to you. The friendship of Damascus is true. Even if its Emir were not the honorable prince he is, his great fear of Noureddin would hold him to his alliance with Jerusalem."

"St. Denis!" the king swore angrily. "How can you know these things, Alphonse? You who have but just landed!"

"Your Majesty asked my opinion. Is it your will that I give it?"

Louis bit his lips and nodded.

"New-come though I am, and sick, I know Syrian politics," Alphonse resumed. "Your Majesty forgets that I have spent half my life in Palestine.

"And now for France. I left there at your Majesty's command, but most unwillingly. There all my skill was needed—and needed constantly—to break up conspiracies among those nobles who did not follow you to the Crusade. Great man though the Abbot Suger is, he lacks the prestige of a soldier. I fear your Majesty will have no kingdom left unless you return to France at once."

Louis bowed his head in unhappy thought. The count's words had shaken him; yet when he raised his face again it was set in stubborn resolution.

"Ask me not, Alphonse, to leave this land till I have struck one blow for Christ!" he cried. "Have I borne the Cross for nothing? Have French lives been spilled and the enthusiasm of French hearts been freely poured out to no purpose? No! I can not believe that God will let us fail, if we but have faith in Him, and strike once more for His Sepulcher."

"Then why did you send for me, if you meant not to heed my advice?"

The count's sickness had left him neither the patience nor the strength to bear with his headstrong monarch.

Louis made a gesture of despair.

"Because I wanted one honest noble at my side," he sighed. "Because, right or wrong, you are devoted to me and to France. Because—I need more men to take Damascus!"

"Then you already purposed this attack before you sent for me?"

The king's temper broke.

"Body of my life, no! I was in doubt whether to fight Damascus in the cause of Jerusalem, or to advance north to cover Antioch. But I do not trust Raimund, and I saw the fear in men's eyes in Jerusalem. What, Alphonse! Are you a stone, that you feel no concern for the city of Christ's death?"

Alphonse struggled to sit up, and I caught him in my arms. As he sank back against me his voice came clear and loud, impelled by the last shreds of his strength:

"Louis of France," he exclaimed, "go back to your own land! I have proved my faith to you and my country by giving over my sovereignty into your hands. You must believe what I tell you. If you would save your kingdom from the gluttonous barons that threaten to devour it, go back! Unless you would lose crown, life, and—honor—go back!"

Right athwart his last words came the command of the officer on guard outside the door:

"Back! Your Majesty may not enter."

Then the curtain was flung aside, and, ablaze with fury, the queen burst into the antechamber.

"You, Alphonse of Toulouse!" she flared. "You, who were ever the enemy of my house! You bid the king return to France—do you?—abandon the Cross, desert Antioch in the face of its peril! Your spite against Aquitaine never sleeps. You would not give such counsel if the Prince of Antioch were not my kinsman!"

Amid the shocked silence she stormed on:

"Honor! You bid the king return to save his honor! Who threatens it? Do you accuse me?"

"Aliénor!"

The king was on his feet, his face stern with anger against her rude intrusion.

"None here accuses you; beware lest your own conduct accuse you! Go!"

Even she dared not outface his resentment; but as she passed through the door, her eyes rested a moment on Alphonse of Toulouse with an ugly hate.

"In truth," my lord protested, "I meant nothing against the queen. I meant only that this Damascus campaign will bring you shame and disaster, and encourage your enemies at home."

Louis strode up and down the chamber.

"Alphonse," he said at last, "you will stay in Antioch while I besiege Damascus. You are not fit to wear armor, nor will be for weeks. I must find quarters for you outside my villa. I am sorry; but to keep you under this roof would be a needless offense to the queen, and no pleasure to you."

My lord nodded assent.

"I thank your Majesty," he said. "I have taken the old palace of Bohemund in the Norman quarter. Let me but recover from this fever, and I will hasten to join you. May I have Pierre?"

"Nay, Alphonse. Pierre must resume his guard over the queen. Do you hear, Pierre? I have had enough of her frivolities with that villainous uncle of hers. Do not let them see each other!"

My lord had been gone an hour when Louis overcame his ill-humor enough to send for his queen. I truly believe it was his purpose to soothe her anger, but he was too late. The servant who carried his summons returned stammering with fright, and the king's wrath kindled at his words:

"My lord—your Majesty! The queen—is gone!"

"Gone? Whither?"

"None knows, Sire."

Louis darted from the room. I saw no more of him till the torches were lit, when I was called again to his presence. His face was white, and so terrible that I feared him. He himself would not be seated, but forced me into a great chair of Lebanon cedar and talked down at me.

"Pierre!"

His utterance was choked.

"Pierre! The queen is faithless to me!"

I leaped from my seat.

"No, your Majesty!" I cried.

"I fear she is," he insisted, his eyes heavy with tragedy. "Yet I should not have said so to you. You will forget."

"I have forgotten, sire."

"The queen," he amended with a forced calmness meant to wipe out the effect of his first uncontrolled outburst, "has but now gone on a visit to Raimund of Antioch, her uncle. She goes to tell him that I would not defend Antioch against the Turks. I believe this, Pierre. Raimund has a right to know. But, Pierre! As you love me, as you love France—do not let her leave this house while I am gone!"

"On my honor, your Majesty. I will not!" I swore.

Nor did I dream how soon I was to break my oath, or what evils were to come of my perjury.

FOR TEN long days I maintained my watch outside the queen's chamber, as I had done before. On the tenth day Jehan came with a grave face, reporting the count not so well, though he could sit up. Jehan, however, at his master's will, had just called in an Arab physician from Sicily, who promised a cure within the week.

But an hour after nightfall came another messenger, a man-at-arms whom I knew not, but who wore the badge of Toulouse. Jehan, he reported, was down with the fever himself.

"And the count?" I demanded.

The man gulped back his tears.

"Worse, much worse," he said. "Oh, Pierre! He is dying, and sends for you, to give you his last words."

He wept without shame. My master was beloved by all his men.

For a moment the life seemed to stop in my own veins; then:

"Take my place here!" I commanded the messenger. "Stand guard till I return! Do not budge from this spot, and let no one come or go. On your life, do not let the queen pass through this door. Swear it!"

The messenger touched the badge on his arm.

"By my love for Alphonse-Jourdain," he swore, "I will stand guard faithfully!"

I know not how I reached the outbuildings and found my way to the stables. I remember nothing of my wild ride through the crooked, narrow streets till I reached the mouth of one that opened into a deserted square. As I galloped into the open space, in mid-stride my horse dropped to the ground.

I flung myself from the saddle barely in time to keep from being crushed beneath him, and brought up on my feet reeling. I seized the bridle, only to drop it again, and clap a hand to my left shoulder, that burned with sudden pain. My fingers touched the shaft of an arrow!

I had no time to hunt down my enemy, no time to fight. My lord was dying! Knowing now that my horse had been slain by the mate to the shaft in my shoulder, I paused not to draw sword, but ran through the night-black streets toward the Norman quarter.

On I sped, my breath laboring, till a gloomy arch bulked in the street ahead. Through that I must go. But in its very shadow three figures in steel leaped upon me. The foremost knocked my helmet from my head.

My sword flashed out. I fought because I must get past these obstacles, but within my breast my heart was mad. That madness lent fury to my strokes. At the first blow I clove to the neck him who had struck me; my second disarmed one of his comrades, whom I pierced through the heart before I turned to the third man.

But he could fight; he knew his sword, and he had the advantage of shield and helmet, which I lacked. A big man, with a quick wrist, he kept me engaged so long that I was in an agony of fear lest my lord die before I could reach him. As I redoubled my strokes, I was thrown flat by a heavy blow from behind, and a horse bearing my fourth assailant dashed through the arch in the direction of the Norman quarter.

Into the gutter I rolled, and my antagonist strode over me to finish me while I lay, as he thought, helpless. But helpless I was not, though the foul stroke from the galloping horseman had lamed my left shoulder, already wounded, and left my head numb. Thinking me half-dead, the man who bestrode me left his breast unguarded. I stabbed up with my point, and felt the Damascus blade deep in his heart. A warm gush of blood sprinkled my face.

Staggering to my feet, I reeled through the arch. My shoulder bled steadily, and felt crushed. I remember now that I felt these things. It was a long way to the Norman quarter, to the old palace of Bohemund, and I was growing weak.

Somehow, I reached the house after wandering long through the city in my dazed confusion. I beat upon the door, but no answer came. Frightened, I flung myself against the cypress panels. The door flew open. I was in a corridor of marble, lighted with a single torch. No servant was there to ask my errand, an odd circumstance; odder still, no man-at-arms was there to bar my passage.

Frenzied with grief and fear, I ran into a courtyard, dimly lighted, empty. As I plunged between its rows of heavy-scented flowers, steps rang on the stones of a colonnade beyond. A mailed soldier came to meet me. It was Big Jehan—sound and hale!

I wondered at this, but now was not the time for explanations. All my cry was:

"My lord! Where is my lord?"

"Pierre! Wounded! Glory of ——!"

Jehan's big arms went round me, but I thrust him off.

"Take me to my lord!" I commanded. "Is he—he is not—dead?"

"Dead?" repeated the spearman. "Blessed saints, no! The Arab is healing him apace!"

Good Jehan's words staggered me, bewildered me, and while they relieved me too, they seemed to lessen my resistance to the weakness my wounds were working in me. The main thing was still to see my lord while yet I could hold myself together.

"Take me to the count," I gasped. "Quick, good Jehan!"

"I know not," Jehan hesitated, "if the woman has left him yet. He bade us leave her with him undisturbed."

"Take me to him!" I insisted so passionately in my ebbing strength that Jehan took fright and parleyed the matter no more.

The big spearman supported me in his arms. I saw nothing of the way we took or the rooms we passed, till Jehan, holding me in one arm, knocked at the door of my lord's apartments.

No answer. Again Jehan knocked, and again. Then Jehan, alarmed at receiving no answer, forced open the door.

A torch burned in a cresset on one wall, casting its rays on a polished table on which sat two silver cups and a flagon. We saw neither man nor woman.

"The woman is gone," Jehan muttered. "My lord must be in the inner room."

Mechanically I stepped forward; one step, two, three—till I reached the head of the table. Another step—I recoiled. My foot had struck something bulky and yielding. What soldier does not know how it feels to stumble on a corpse?

I staggered to the light, snatched it from the cresset and bent over the body. Then, moaning the worst he ever heard, Jehan says, I fell across the dead bosom of my lord.

When the shock of cold water in my face brought me to myself again I was prone on the floor, beside what had once been the man I loved best of all the world. Jehan the Big was on its other side; his arms were round my lord's shoulders, and he shook with sobs.

"Drink!" said a voice.

Liquor flowed between my lips. I sat up, and saw an Arab bending over me.

"Much loss of blood," he said in a strange accent. "But little danger. You can walk if you try, but you are not to try."

He lifted me and supported me to a couch, where he attempted to make me lie down. I shook him off.

"Put bandages on my wounds," I entreated, "and give me something that will renew my strength."

After a moment of studying me, the Arab physician decided to do as I desired him, and found a flask of some stinging liquor that brought back my energy in fiery waves.

"It will flood your veins with vigor for three hours," he said. "But you had best be near your bed when its effects pass from you."

Having done what he could for me, he bent over my lord's body. I watched, my brain tingling with purpose and the unnatural stimulation of the drug.

The Arab held Alphonse-Jourdain's head on his knee so that we could see his face, which was set in the rigid beauty of unfelt death. The Arab lifted the count's eyelids far back; gazed into the dead eyes; placed his nostrils close to the unbreathing lips. Then he reached out for the silver cups—first one, then the other; and last, the flagon.

He touched Jehan's shoulder.

"You say a woman has been here? Who was she?"

The big soldier, his voice broken with sobbing, turned his wet eyes from the one to the other of us.

"I know her not," he answered.

Then he told this tale:

An hour or more ago a woman, wrapped from head to foot in a dark velvet mantle, had demanded to see the count. She would not tell her name or errand, nor show her face. The man-at-arms on duty at the gate would not admit her till a servant, whom he sent to the count, came back with his master. Nor would she reveal herself then, except to the count alone.

So my lord had dismissed his attendants and sent for Jehan. Jehan found his master in this room with the veiled woman; he received the order that they were not to be disturbed, and that guards and servants be removed from the gate. There was no danger, he assured Jehan; it was only that his visitor feared to be recognized as she left. Then I came and forced Jehan to take me to the count.

"Your master has been poisoned!"

The Arab's voice cut in on Jehan's last words like a stab.

"He drank with the woman?"

"There was wine on the table when I came to my lord," Jehan replied. "But it was our wine."

"In that wine he drank the essence of the bitter almond, which kills swiftly, without pain. The smell of it is on his lips and in his cup; but not in the other cup, nor in the flagon. Therefore this woman conveyed the poison to his cup cunningly when his eyes were not on her.

"Your lord's death would readily have been laid to a recurring attack of his fever. The poison is not well known, and the odor it leaves behind is very faint. Truly the mystery of the woman's visit would raise suspicion, but who knows who she is?"

"I know her!" I broke in.

My words came of themselves—I did not will them.

Nor do I know whether I did wittingly what followed, or not. To myself I seemed another than I was; grief and the drug subdued me to some power that I could feel, but neither resist nor understand. To that power I abandoned myself.

"How long since I entered this room?" I asked, not knowing indeed how long I had been unconscious before Jehan summoned the Arab.

"Under a half-hour," Jehan answered.

"Get me a swift horse, Jehan!" I commanded. "Another for yourself. Ride to the king's villa and await me there."

Jehan obeyed, moving fast, but like one dream-bound.

I made my way through the court and corridor to the gate, mounted the horse Jehan brought me, and drove the spurs home. Eastward I rode, straight across the city, but away from the direction of the royal villa. The narrow streets flew behind me, till I shot out into a plain covered with olive orchards that raised their black, twisted branches into the dark.

I galloped on until I entered a garden—a boundless garden, where graceful trees and flowering shrubs formed avenues set with the ghostly figures of marble statues, and fountains played gray-white in the gloom.

I knew that garden; I had been here before with the king, when he first came to taste the hospitality of Raimund of Antioch. My horse bore me on swiftly; yet I seemed to ride for a thousand years before I drew rein at the gate of a huge, gray palace, and dismounting, knocked softly.

The gate swung open on well-oiled hinges.

"On the king's business!" I mumbled, showing the royal seal.

The soldiers on guard stood by, staring, to let me pass. As I strode down a passageway, my steps muffled in deep Oriental carpets, a servant met me. I spoke softly, but in a tone of command:

"Take me to the prince. On the king's errand!"

No servitor in that palace would refuse me; I was known for the king's squire. Only Raimund's direct order could have shut me out. That, it appeared, had not been given.

Through dainty Syrian arches I passed, through cloistered courts, up a marble stairway. Stopping at a door of thick cypress, the servant would have knocked; but I thrust him aside, and bade him see that my horse waited at the gate.

Then with infinite care I softly drew back the door, to find a heavy, embroidered curtain before my face. I was about to thrust it aside, when a voice spoke close by. My hand dropped. Unseen, I listened.

"You were mad to come tonight, Aliénor!"

It was the prince's voice, deep and vibrant.

"It was reckless folly to lure that Toulousan away and leave the villa. When Louis returns—"

A ringing laugh cut him short, a woman's laugh, filled with thrilling music.

"My uncle," she mocked, "do you indeed fear the king? Nay, let him come! I have disobeyed him, yes; but I have disobeyed my pious husband many times. Ah, how he raves!"

And again the laugh.

"You will drive him past endurance. There is danger in Louis when he is roused. Already he suspects far worse of us than we have done. Has he not refused to help Antioch against the Turks? Has he not gone to take Damascus for Jerusalem?

"Had you been prudent, scandal would never have raised its false breath against us. Your rashness has cost me his support. Do not anger him too much, lest he turn his army against me."

"You reproach me," the queen cried, "because the plots I have woven to help you have failed. Ah, you have little cause to blame my rashness—you—whose prudence has done but little for our house. While you sat here idle, Raimund, I have done that which will make the race of Aquitaine great. And in doing it I have taken a sweet vengeance for wrongs long borne."

"What have you done?" the man asked, though he seemed to fear her answer.

"Listen, Raimund, and praise me. Alphonse-Jourdain has dealt his last stroke against Aquitaine! When I hastened to you after the last Council, did I not tell you how he prayed the king to leave Antioch, to go back to France? Did he not bid the king protect his honor? You know his meaning—the old lie that you and I love each other.

"He will plot against us no more. Tonight, having bribed a Toulousan man-at-arms through one of my servants, I wiled that lout Faidit away, as I told you. My knights had warning, at a signal the same servant would convey them, to lay an ambush for Pierre on a street that he must pass to reach the count's dwelling.

"Waiting only till I knew he had ridden off, I mounted. I saw him, Raimund, fighting with my ambuscade! He had almost triumphed when I rode past him, so I smote him down with a light mace I carried. The last I saw was Guirand's sword-point at his throat. He will never hold me prisoner again!"

I heard a cry from the prince. The woman resumed:

"I rode veiled to the count's palace. I told him I had knowledge of a plot against the king. I think he did not believe me, but he took me to his apartment, sent away the servants, and heard me speak. He gave me wine, and drank himself. Into his drink I poured—"

"Aliénor!"

The word broke from Raimund's throat in a cry thick with horror.

"Not poison! You have not murdered him!"

"Murdered? Has he not always been our enemy—mine, my father's, yours? I have but removed him from our way. Did I not well?"

For a long moment there was silence; then the woman spoke gaspingly:

"Raimund! Look not so on me! Say I did well! I have taken vengeance for us both!"

"Vengeance!"

Raimund spoke furiously, brutally.

"Alphonse-Jourdain had naught to do with the king's resolve to abandon Antioch for Jerusalem. It was your rashness in coming here, and the rumors against us spread by your visits, that made Louis leave my city defenseless against the Turks."

After a bitter pause:

"You have acted evilly, Aliénor. And what is worse, you have been a fool."

I waited for no more. Swiftly and in silence I ran down those accursed stairs, across the courts, and out. Vaulting to the saddle, I made all haste to the king's villa. What I had heard—though it was what I had come to hear—snatched the strange veil from my senses. But the power of the drug was slowly dying from my veins, and I was near collapse.

Jehan awaited me in my quarters. I could not speak to him. My wounds had opened, staining my bandages. My head swam as I hunted pen, ink and parchment; but I forced it to clear while I wrote the message for Jehan to carry:

> To Louis the King, from Pierre Faidit: Come quickly, and clear the honor of France! The blood of Toulouse cries for justice!

SIX DAYS later the king came to my bedside. My message had reached him at the moment when, deceived and betrayed by the cowardly troops of Jerusalem, his army was beginning its inglorious retreat from Damascus. He bore the misery of that terrible defeat graven in his features.

"What—Pierre! You are wounded? Speak, man! What fresh terror must I hear?"

"That I have betrayed your trust, my liege. That I let the queen escape, and she has murdered Alphonse of Toulouse."

I thought he would fling himself upon me and kill me; but he mastered himself. Thrice he tried to speak; at last he must needs make a sign with his hand. So I told him, sparing nothing. All the time the devil was tempting me to conceal my knowledge that the queen, murderess though she was, was innocent of the infidelity of which he suspected her.

But I told the whole truth, honestly hoping the king might find some comfort, amid the horror of her crime, in that there was one sin she had not committed; but even the worst of sins against himself was less to Louis than the murder of his one faithful vassal.

"She shall pay!" he swore. "Would to —— she might pay as she deserves!"

"How else, sire?" I asked. "Has she not done murder?"

The king gazed sorrowfully down at me.

"Is it worse," he asked, "to murder one man, or to murder a nation?"

Not understanding what was in his mind, I only looked at hat.

"Look you, Pierre," he went on, "do not think that I would spare the queen because she is my wife. I loved her. But it is not that dead love that saves her from the death penalty. She is exempt from the law of France."

I started up. With his own hands my king laid me back among the soft cushions I hated.

"The queen, my Pierre," he continued, "rules half of France in her own right as a reigning sovereign; Poitou, Gascony, Aquitaine are hers by inheritance. If she had never been queen they would still be hers. She makes her own laws. The crown has no jurisdiction over her.

"Those lands are devoted to her, and if I put her on trial for murder all the west and half the south will revolt. France would tear itself to pieces over her. For her, the nation I have labored to build would be drowned in blood."

"But she brought all her inherited lands to you as dowry," I protested. "Now they are yours. You can deprive her of them. Is she to go unpunished? Can a queen stab and poison unrebuked?"

The king took my hands in his.

"She shall be punished," he answered, "as much as I can punish her. I will put her from me, divorce her, take away the crown I gave her. She shall be queen no more. And though she deserves to lose land and life, she shall lose neither. To save France from ruin I must let her live, to save my honor I must give her back her lands. It is the law of France and the Church that a man divorcing his wife must return the dowry she brought him."

"There is no law to punish her for murder," I agreed grimly, "but there is a law to make you return her inheritance."

Louis stood erect.

"Pierre Faidit," he said, "if a king break the least of his laws, can he ask his subjects to obey the greatest of them? There must be but one law for king and peasant alike. I shall give the queen her lands with her bill of divorce, in order that what remains of France will be under my law and obey it.

"Nay, more, it would stir up strife to publish the true cause for the divorce. I shall offer, not the accusation of murder, but the fact that she and I are within the bounds of relationship forbidden by the Church. To save war I shall hide her crime."

"But—"

"Pierre! Will it bring back the life to the cold veins of your master to murder a woman's reputation? Even the reputation of such as she? Will it help Alphonse to set France aflame with scandal? I forbid you ever to speak of this."

"Oh, my lord!" I answered. "Be it as you will, if I may but serve you all my life—loyally, as my master served you."

The king granted my prayer, but God denied it.

TWO OTHER men knew the truth of the manner in which my lord died—Big Jehan and the Arab. Not knowing that the veiled woman was the queen, one or both of them spoke out. During the two years since our return to France the report that Alphonse-Jourdain died, not of fever, but of poison has grown and grown, till it fills the land. Toulouse is ready to revolt; Auvergne and Champagne murmur against the king. For it has been spread abroad by the king's enemies that he hired the hand that poisoned the count's cup. The Pope has heard, and threatens Louis with his ban.

So, against the command of my king, I publish all the truth, and thereby serve him better, I think, than by obedience.

In this strange, dear land of ours, where it is a worse crime to make known a fair woman's sin than to commit the crime itself, I shall be scorned and hated. So be it, if but France and the king's honor be saved.

For him who challenges my faith, my glove in his face and my sword in his throat!

RED NIGHT

PIERRE FAIDIT rode alertly through the forest, his quick dark eyes noting every rustling bough, every quivering leaf. This was strange country—wild country—and therefore dangerous. A trained soldier, he let his glances rove ceaselessly while his brain occupied itself with his own troubled thoughts. His great hand caressed the shaft of his lance.

The most famous swordsman in France, he was—for the first time in seventeen years—masterless and homeless, uncertain for the future, and unhappy for the past. A great reputation had come to him early. Under that greatest prince of the South, Alphonse-Jourdain of Toulouse, he had proved himself a mighty soldier and a crafty leader of men. For this Count Alphonse, Lord of the Languedoc, Pierre had felt that great love which will take a man gladly into danger and death. Under Alphonse he had acquired all his skill, learning equal to an abbot's, and much glory. Now Alphonse was dead, poisoned by a wicked woman to satisfy an unfounded grudge.

The great service Pierre rendered King Louis on the Second Crusade had found him a captaincy of household troops after the death of Alphonse. He had not been happy in his work; for it was the queen, Aliénor of Aquitaine, who had murdered Count Alphonse. But Pierre was that rarest of things in the twelfth century—a French patriot; and he served King Louis from love of country.

Then he had committed a great offense with open eyes, and

because he conceived the highest loyalty demanded it. He had been born a poor fisher-lad, had never learned the ways of the courtier and did not know how to lie for favor. He had told an unpleasant truth, and King Louis banished him. Now he must seek another master. Any noble in France would have paid highly for such a follower, but Pierre would follow none of them. Alphonse-Jourdain had taught him to love his country; and the French barons loved themselves more than France.

Therefore he had come to Normandy, which did not belong to the French king in the year 1150, being ruled by its own independent duke, Henry Plantagenet. Henry was a master whom any man might serve with pride. Rumor said he planned a war with England. Against England a French soldier could fight willingly, without rancor, and with high hope of honor. Stephen was king in England—a good man by his lights, but selfish and foolish, who had dared seize the throne that belonged rightfully to this young Henry, the great-grandson of William the Conqueror.

So Pierre had taken his horse aboard a flatboat and floated down the Seine to Evreux, to find the duke. But Henry had already departed for his hunting-seat at Col Rouge, and Pierre

followed him across-country. It was now mid-afternoon, and
he had ridden all day.

It was a ride to make a man merry, and most men would
have been merry in Pierre's shoes. He was young—but one-
and-thirty; his huge body pulsed with the strength of hard,
smooth muscles and perfect health. He was graceful as a faun,
and as handsome, with big dark eyes, a falcon nose and cheeks
that glowed red under tanned olive. The firm lips, the strong
chin, gave evidence of a life free from weakness.

His magnificent white charger bore his heavy weight and
that of his splendid chain armor easily; the ruby-pommeled
sword at his side would have graced a king's belt. A dozen
campaigns and a thousand raids and roadside adventures, had
made him illustrious. Above all, the jewel of his honor was
untarnished. All this, and to ride free through the Norman
forest with a soft breeze in his face and the scant golden sunshine filtering down through the warm green tops of ancient
beech and sturdy oak!

A little river, the Avre, flowed down from the Norman hills
into the rolling forest. It ran swiftly, for the forest floor undu-
lated in great waves. All about Pierre's path the land rose from
eight hundred to a thousand feet, heavily timbered with the
virgin trunks that choke out all undergrowth, leaving long,
leaf-carpeted aisles where a good horse finds fair going. The
chattering of the river took Pierre's thoughts from his troubles,
for its sound might mask other noises portending danger.

SUDDENLY THE white charger snorted and increased
his pace. Pierre's hand tightened on his lance. Far away, hidden
by the mighty trees, something swift and violent was happen-
ing. A cry, distance-dimmed, rang out, and the clang of metal.
Then all was still.

Pierre's spurs pricked deep. With a splendid surge the great
horse gathered himself for the gallop. His hoofs kicked up thick
lumps of damp soil. As the forest-aisles receded, Pierre's ears
caught the jingle of mail and the nickering of horses. These

guided him on through the wood, where eyes were of small use for any distance. The sunlight, which had lain in tiny spots and shafts, grew rapidly brighter. A little ahead, a square of green-ish light marked the opening of a glade.

Now Pierre shifted his shield from shoulder to left arm, and, taking care to keep his long lance clear of the branches, swung the point forward. Reining in, he closed on the forest-opening cautiously, both to avoid ambush and to accustom his eyes to the increasing glare. At last he was under the trees which bordered the opening. A swift glance, and he understood. His lance-point sank to the horizontal, catching the sun in a sparkle of fire. He moved in the saddle, to get that knee-grip that holds the seat firm so the point can be guided well home.

In the middle of the glade, beside a spring-fed-pool bordered with saplings, sat a young man, bound and gagged. His body was trussed tight to a young oak; his legs dangled into the pool. Close by, five ill-looking fellows sat their horses jeering at him. They were well-armed, and their mounts were beautiful beasts; but they bore the stamp of broken men on their evil faces.

At the farther edge of the clearing four sturdy fellows were dragging two more captives with sacks over their heads, toward a circle of six horses, nose to nose, whose bridles were held by a scared groom. A bundle of weapons and mail was trussed to one saddle, and a jeweled horn dangled from the cantle.

Pierre knew the prisoners must have been attacked suddenly as they sat at their ease. There had been time for one wild sword-stroke—no more. Then they had been disarmed, plundered and tied. The groom, whose white face showed to which party he belonged, had had no time to mount and ride for help.

The two sacked captives were to be carried off, perhaps for ransom. He by the spring would doubtless be slain, Pierre thought, judging him an under-officer who would fetch small ransom. His surcoat had been torn off, so that there was no badge of family or service on him for the beholder to interpret. But his flat velvet cap bore a sprig of yellow broom—the emblem of the House of Plantagenet. Duke Henry, whose servant the youth must be, was the head of that house.

This, and his sympathy for the weaker party, determined Pierre's course. As he drove home the spurs one of the ruffians saw the sun flash on his armor and shouted an alarm. Flinging the groom aside, the rascals by the horses hastened to mount, while those at the pool turned to meet the newcomer.

"Take him alive!" one shouted. "He wears rich mail. A fat ransom!"

The speaker, a big man with a lance cut down to serve as javelin, rode straight for Pierre. One instant only the fellow hesitated whether to cast his weapon at horse or man. Then, at close range, it whirred for Pierre's face. But long service had taught Pierre to read the unwritten book of a foe's eyes, the movement of the weapon-arm, the elevation of the point. His three-cornered shield caught the javelin slantwise and dashed it aside. His lance bored in, through mail, breast and back. Then four more were upon him at once.

There was no time to tug the point free. Casting lance aside, Pierre drew his sword. It was his chosen weapon, and he the first fencer in France. These thieves were forest-men, fortunately who favored short weapons that would not catch in overhanging boughs. Blade to blade—Pierre's game!

Nor were the odds so heavy as they appeared. Better mail, better steel, a finer mount and greater skill—all these Pierre had to set against the greater number of his foes.

They rode at him in two waves: First, the four nearest, who had been by the pool; then, losing precious time in mounting and crossing the glade, the four who had been engaged with the prisoners. Their leader slain, they thought no more of capture, but flailed in to kill; while the man bound by the water chewed madly at his gag and glared his hate.

Circling him round, the first four crowded in on Pierre who met them with loose rein and flickering weapon. His horse he left to guide itself. He could trust its instinct; it had been trained in the shock of battle. As the foremost assailant struck, the white charger flung itself against his horse's shoulder like a stone from a catapult. Bandit and beast went down in a heap.

Two men lashed at Pierre from opposite flanks; one hand worked behind him. His feint drew one man's guard; his lunge pierced the throat. He turned to the man on his left just as an ill-timed back-stroke from the rear cut through the cantle of his saddle, glanced and bit into the white charger's flesh. The great horse flung out its heels in a frenzy, smashing the jaw of the beast behind. But the sudden plunge threw Pierre against the pommel, lowered his guard and exposed him to a blow that dented his helmet and filled his eyes with sparks.

Now came the second wave of attack, desperation and murder in every ruffian's eye. Two of their comrades were still in the battle. One, mounted, was exchanging blows with Pierre; while the second, in the rear, let his injured horse run shrieking into the wood and crept up on foot behind the Frenchman, watching his chance.

The four came swiftly, but reined in, as they drew close to avoid their comrades' error. They would take their time, careful not to block one another's assaults. Their enemy's sword-play was such as they had never seen. They knew themselves for mere butchers, broken men-at-arms.

As Pierre's edge swept the head from a comrade's shoulders they closed in; two in front, one on each flank.

He that was unhorsed thrust from behind, but Pierre turned on him, struck, and faced round again swiftly. His blow had fallen short; he had but cut away his foe's nasal. He engaged two at once, the blows that passed his shield turning on his practised guard.

"Watch your rear!" came a shout from the glade.

The captive by the pool was free, and running for the horse at whose saddle his captured weapons were lashed. The groom, released by the fight, had taken heart of grace to cut his companion's bonds.

Pierre guarded his rear by advancing. His spurs shot home and the white horse leaped forward, just as the fellow who lurked on foot slashed at its belly. The leap saved horse and rider, and bore Pierre hurtling against the two in front. Three lightning thrusts, a whirling shoulder-stroke, and Pierre's sword clove an adversary through skull and chin.

But the second man, thrusting even as Pierre's arm rose, drew blood from his armpit. Before the fellow could strike again, Pierre feinted for his throat, turned swiftly and cut down the ruffian on his right. In that instant, overjoyed at the opening granted him, the rascal still before Pierre whirled up his weapon—and toppled from his horse, six inches of steel in his back.

With a wild cry of dismay the two surviving ruffians made for the woods. He who was horsed vanished in three bounds; the other leaped to the saddle of a stricken comrade's mount and followed, fumbling to loosen a cased bow by his saddle. Scorning pursuit of beaten men, Pierre grinned down at the young man whose release had saved him from a dangerous plight, and drew deep breaths into his laboring lungs.

"Your groom—did his work—well!" he panted, pointing across the glade.

The servant was even now drawing the sacks off the two who still lay bound where the bandits had flung them. But the young man—who was indeed a mere boy—paid no heed to his words. He was striving to lift up the bandit who had been thrown by the white charger's first impact, and who still huddled, half-crushed, under his beast. Even as he got the fellow partly free and raised him by the shoulders, a loud twang bit the still air. An arrow bored through the bandit's breast.

The boy shook his fists at the sky.

"It is always thus!" he roared in anger. "Shall I never take one of these swine alive?"

"Nay, what need?" Pierre asked. "They are better dead. You are in luck, young sir. That arrow was meant for you."

"Not for me, dolt!" the lad retorted. "If your wits were greater, your tongue would clack less. Ride after him who shot, and drag him here by the heels!"

The unmerited insult whipped the blood to Pierre's cheeks; but he obeyed for the reason that if a hostile bowman lurked in the forest it was wise to catch him before he did more harm. For twenty minutes he scoured the neighboring forest finding nothing. At last he returned to the glade, remembering the cut on his charger's rump which must be cared for. As he rode into the clearing, the youth raised his recovered horn to his lips and blew a long blast. Faint and far, a second horn returned the signal.

ALL THREE of the rescued were now unbound. They were all men of striking presence—the boy as much as the others, for all his scant eighteen years. He was of middle height but of Herculean frame with rough red hair and hot hazel eyes. By his side stood a tall, thick-set man of Pierre's own age, big jawed, with dark hair and a smart hawk-like face. His square shoulders and sure poise marked him a soldier, as his thick, twanging accent proved him as Englishman.

But the sight of the third drew from Pierre a cry of joy.

"By St. Sernin!" he shouted. "Cercamon!"

The man turned in a flash. His eyes gleamed with happy recognition. He was short, with amazing breadth of shoulder, a smooth face fair as a woman's, and sharp, blue-green eyes. Long, loose locks hung down over his silken collar, which was half-torn from his white neck.

"Pierre!" he exclaimed. "Pierre Faidit! What do you in Normandy, old war-wolf?"

Pierre's face glowed. He had found once more the friend whom, next to his dead master, he most loved. Cercamon the troubadour, gallant soldier, noble poet and trusted favorite of Count Raymond-Bérenger of Barcelona, had crossed Pierre's path but twice; yet their hearts had gone out to each other.

Once the troubadour had saved Pierre from death by a treacherous hand; the second meeting had brought them to Spain together as comrades in arms. A perilous venture, they had shared both danger and renown.

It was four years since then. Pierre had heard that after Count Raymond's death Cercamon had sought another patron; but he had not known where.

They clasped hands warmly, then Pierre slipped from his saddle to examine his horse's hurt. He gave no notice to the boy, turning his back full on him. Thus he failed to see the dark scowl on that youngster's face. The boy hailed him gruffly; but Pierre, still smarting from his earlier insult, paid no heed. His horse was his comrade; this hot-tempered young man with the Plantagenet badge had no claim on him.

"Steel spurs—not gold!" the boy growled at Pierre's heels. "A soldier then, or a squire—no knight. Ha, fellow! Give ear when your betters speak!"

Pierre faced about, twin points of fire glittering under knit brows.

"My betters?" he repeated softly. "Am I, who serve no man, worse than you, who serve Plantagenet? You, who need my help to cope with a handful of varlets? Let me see to my beast, who is perchance a better man than you!"

"Pierre! Blood of Heaven!" cried the troubadour in tones of horror. "Be careful, man! You speak to the Duke of Normandy!"

In hot confusion Pierre fell on one knee.

"Your pardon, lord!" he implored with all due earnestness. "But indeed my horse is hurt and needs care."

The young duke glared at him. Though Pierre was greatly disturbed at his rudeness to one so high—the one, indeed, whom he had come to serve—he met the angry eyes fairly.

"Étienne will see to the beast," the duke answered coldly. "He is a master-leech. Now, fellow, if your name is indeed Pierre Faidit and you are a masterless man, how come you to be lolloping through my forest without leave?"

Pierre rose, and gazed at the wrathful lad. He seemed a spoiled child, this young duke whose exploits had filled France with his fame. His hazel eyes flashed the storm-signals of an ungovernable temper.

Pierre remembered the saying that Henry of Normandy rushed into deeds which his father, cunning Geoffrey of Anjou, prudently avoided; and that his victories owed more to reckless dash and brute force than to strategy. The age was one in which greatness depended more on brawn than on wit.

The man with English voice and face laid a hand on the duke's shoulder. The lad, touchy as he seemed, did not resent this man's familiarity.

"Give thanks to God," the Englishman said, "that the stranger came to our help, my lord. And give some thanks to him."

"So I would, Thomas," Henry muttered, "had he spoken me fairly. If he came to our aid, I also came to his when he was within an inch of purgatory."

"It is so, my lord," Pierre confessed. "I pray you pardon my rough tongue."

Henry turned square away from him and for some minutes maintained a glowering silence, hanging his head and tearing at his nails. At length he swung about, a smile struggling through his clouded features. He reached out a hand to Pierre, who would have kissed it; but the duke crushed his fingers in a grip of iron. Pride moved the Frenchman to put his own strength into the hand-clasp, and soon Henry's fingers went limp.

"Before ——!" the Norman roared. "Had I a clutch like yours I would squeeze the world dry in my fingers! Who are you? Are you truly Pierre Faidit, with whose skill in war France rings?"

Pierre bowed.

"Whom men call Pierre de l'Espée—Pierre of the Sword? Aye? Then you are masterless no longer, if you will follow my banner. But guard your speech hereafter, for—*gloire de Dieu!*— no man shall bandy words or glances with me as you have done. How say you? Will you take my wage?"

"Gladly, lord duke. For that purpose I came to Normandy."

Though he guarded his dignity with jealous wrath, Henry could fling it away like the boy he was. He clapped Pierre on the shoulder and grinned wide.

"Then you shall see rare deeds of arms. My fortune is young, but it mounts—it mounts! I am count and duke now, thanks to my sword, and my father's indolence, who thinks to do with my right hand what he dares not do with his own. Before I am your age I shall wear a crown!"

"England's crown waits for you, sire," Thomas spoke with warm feeling. "You have but to wrench it from the usurper Stephen."

"Nay, but I will have France too!" the duke boasted. "You shall help me take it, you lads."

Pierre shook his head.

"Not I, gracious lord," he answered. "I am Frenchman born, and never will I serve against the land that nourished me. Against England, aye—against all the world! Never against France!"

Henry Plantagenet flew into rage once more.

"Why, here is a riddle! This fellow will serve me, and he will not! He will make conditions, forsooth! If all my men served me so, how should I prosper? I will take you on my own terms, or not at all! Will you march with me against France, or go your way with the curse of twenty devils?"

Turning on his heel, Pierre strode to his horse, which stood quiet under the tender ministrations of the groom.

"I thank you," he said gently. "The beast will do well enough now, till I can reach the first town beyond the Norman border."

Cercamon was at Henry's feet.

"My lord, my lord!" he implored. "Send him not away! Let him stay on his own terms! He has the strength of five men, the wisdom of twenty clerks, the loyalty of an angel! He can handle a troop of hardbitten riders better than any captain west of the Rhine. If you let him go, you lose what gold can not buy! Bethink you, lest he take service under your enemies!"

The Englishman also was pleading with the stubborn boy, but more calmly:

"Your life is worth more than your anger, Henry, and this man has saved your life. Your temper will cost you a kingdom some day!"

"It will cost you your life some day, Thomas Becket!" the duke flared.

But in that flare his anger seemed to die. Pierre's foot had slipped into the stirrup when Henry called to him:

"Ha, Faidit! Will you make a bargain with me?"

The Frenchman mounted before he answered—

"What sort of bargain, your Grace?"

"I need good men-at-arms too sorely to turn away such as you. I will give you a troop, and promise never to use you against France—if you will prove your worth by undertaking a dangerous enterprise for me."

Gravely Pierre dismounted.

"Anything, my lord!" he said.

The sound of many hoofs and voices broke in upon their speech. A score of riders burst into the glade, pulled up at sight of the dead men and cried out in consternation.

The foremost hastened forward with a white face. He was a richly dressed, swaggering knight whose scarlet cloak fluttered above fine mail. His brow was low and broad, his pale features arrogantly handsome. His hands glittered with jeweled rings.

"You are safe, my lord?" he gasped.

"Safe enough, Odo. You were far away when my horn summoned you."

"Your Grace bade us leave you in the glade," the knight answered. "We could only obey."

Henry nodded curtly.

"So I did. I wished to speak privately with Thomas and Cercamon. See yonder dead dogs! The old story!"

The horsemen—tall, lean men, haughty of eye and scarred with service—stared in astonishment at the dead bandits.

Henry pointed to Pierre.

"His work. He is Pierre of the Sword. Up all, and home!"

THE DUKE'S hunting-seat was an old, square-towered castle on the Col Rouge, the highest of all the rolling hills that formed the district of Perche. Col Castle was scarred and ugly, but large enough to house the thirty knights, four-and-twenty ladies and three hundred men-at-arms that formed the holiday court. Henry was still prone to pass the hot weather in sport, being still young enough to think that crowns may be won and held by the sword alone, and not by constant travail of mind.

The torches were lit in the great hall, and cressets filled with pine-knots flared in the open court. Along the bailey walls in long rows of wood huts that lined the inner face of the court, ate and slept and diced and bickered the soldiers of the garrison. At supper now, their rude jests and laughter rose noisily above the reek of stew-pots and drifted in gusts into the great hall where their betters dined more decorously.

The under-officers and the castle servants, all but the kitch-en-knaves and waiting-varlets, had a long, low table on trestles within the hall. Above this on a raised dais dined the ducal household—knights, ladies, Henry, the duke and his mother, the Empress Mathilde.

Thomas the Englishman and Cercamon were there. Thomas was the duke's friend, now on a mission to him from the Archbishop of Canterbury, whom Thomas served as secretary. As for Cercamon, the troubadour may always claim equality with princes. Art, when it is great, levels all barriers.

But Pierre was not so honored. He sat at the lower table with other captains, a minstrel or two and the steward. He was at home among them and friendly to their station, not forgetting the time he himself had served as a common man-at-arms. Though his renown had won him companionship and some favors from the great, yet he did not disdain to mingle with men whose daily toils and daily pleasures, whose few ambitions and rough needs, were as familiar to him as the garments he wore.

As he sat there, however, he remembered—could not help remembering—that Alphonse-Jourdain, his old master, would have invited him up to the dais, to eat with the household. The Count of Toulouse had valued Pierre's devotion and counsel more than the fripperies of rank. But new service, new manners. Pierre was not cast down.

Cercamon sent many a quick troubled look at his friend, and at last had the hardihood to speak his thoughts to the duke.

"What?" boomed Henry. "With us? A man of no rank?"

"Aye," Cercamon insisted. "Or I go down to him. He is my friend, and worthier to sit here than I."

He shot a glance at Pierre, whose rising color showed he had heard the duke's haughty protest.

So it came to pass that by a friend's love Pierre was translated to a seat at the duke's own table. Now he was indeed uncomfortable, knowing he was but half-wanted. The sewer waved him to his new place in scandalized silence. Here were rich food and luscious wines instead of the cold mutton and ale set before the soldiers. He ate in silence, glad that these proud folk had little to say to him, anxious for the meal's end.

But in a little while he was forced into the talk, and then felt more at ease. He had eaten at princes' tables before. Henry, more gracious with the wine, drew him out on a point of fortification.

"What think you of my engines, Pierre?" he asked. "Those Sir Odo showed you on the battlements?"

"The catapults have been badly cared for, lord duke," he answered. "The sinews should have been oiled, not greased. I fear they will be too slack."

"I will speak of it to Odo," Henry remarked carelessly. "There has been no war here in my time. I look after my spears better, for I need them all the time."

The Empress Mathilde looked up from the trencher of dry bread that served her for a plate.

"It was lack of care for our engines that lost us Oxford," she said. "I have told you that often, my son."

Pierre stole a respectful glance at this formidable lady. She was a stern, bitter woman of fifty, dark-featured, with the remains of a youthful beauty that had been famous. To her first husband, the German Emperor, she had borne no children; Henry was her one child by her second husband, Geoffrey of Anjou, overlord of Britanny and Normandy.

All Europe had heard of her brave ventures in England. Daughter of King Henry I, she had herself led a Norman army against King Stephen eleven years before. For a while victorious, she had at last been penned in Oxford by Stephen's barons and forced to flee by stealth for her life. Yet for nine years she had held half of England, and held it bravely.

In her turn she stared at Pierre, but openly and bluntly, as if to learn what manner of man this was who had slain six outlaws in the forest with his single hand and saved her son from captivity—perhaps from death. It was for this son that she had risked that daring invasion of England, when he was still too young to fight for the crown she coveted for him.

Question after question the duke hurled at his new follower, seeking to probe the extent of his military knowledge, yet only revealing his own inexperience. Henry was still only a hand-fighter; he had not, as had Pierre, served in half the provinces of France, or in the Holy Land. And when the last of nine courses had been nibbled—for the Normans were a temperate folk—the empress' eyes were sparkling.

"Here is a man who knows war!" she said to her son. "It is in my mind, Henry, that you should trust him and heed his word. He has served with men whose brains are worth more than both your arms."

"We shall see," the duke replied. "Much will depend on the outcome of a task I set him. Guillaume the Faceless—"

The old woman clapped a bony hand over the duke's mouth.

"Not a word of that!" she warned him. "I have told you that there are men of your own court in league with Guillaume. If it were not so he would never guess your orders as he does. The less said of him the better!"

"My men are as faithful as most," Henry grumbled impatiently; but his mother only smiled a bitter smile.

"When you are as old as I am," she said, "you will know that few men are faithful. Gold will buy honor six days out of the seven. No more of this matter, Henry.

"But this Pierre's eyes are honest, and his lips clean-lined. Watch men's lips, Henry. What think you, Thomas?"

The Englishman ran his slow gaze over Pierre's face.

"I trust him," he answered.

"And I," cried Cercamon, "will vouch for his honor with my life!"

"Vouch for your own!" snapped Mathilde. "Pierre, I see, does not eye the pretty women as you do. Gold will not buy you, troubadour; but I would not trust you far with a lovely face—Here are the water and towels, Henry."

One by one the company washed lips and fingers at the ewers passed by servants; then all rose.

"HOW LIKE you the duke's tongue?"

Pierre smiled at the Englishman's question.

"Very little. In my province every man is courteous till he draws sword."

He sat on his cot in a chamber high in the square tower. The torches gleamed in the wall-brackets, but the moonlight flooding in through an arrow-slot made them pale. Beside him sat Cercamon, newcome from singing before the empress; Thomas Becket lay stretched out on a chest of arms.

Thomas laughed.

"Henry speaks out whatever is in his mind. Half his words he rues bitterly as soon as said; the other half he will make good in the face of —— itself. Henry is a boy, but he is also the bravest man I have ever seen. Stupid he is; but it is the mere slowness of growing youth. When his frame has reached its fulness his brain will grow to match it. Not for nothing is he the son of Geoffrey the Fox and Mathilde the Lioness. He has gleams of wit even now."

"Thanks for your praise!" boomed a voice in the doorway.

Pierre and Cercamon leaped to their feet in dismay. Becket, knowing the duke's moods better, merely swung his feet to the floor and calmly regarded him. Henry roared his amusement.

"You judge me truly, Thomas. But now get out, you and Cercamon. I would speak with Pierre alone."

It seemed to the troubadour, as he backed from the duke's presence, that there was a touch of malice on the boy's lips. He caught Becket's eye; and the Englishman nodded as the hanging fell behind him.

"Sit, Faidit!"

The duke's eyes scrutinized Pierre's searchingly; then he said without preface:

"You are to rid all this district of outlaws. I have tried, and my hand is heavy; yet I have failed."

Pierre showed his astonishment. The master of Normandy, Anjou, and Britanny, powerful beyond all princes of the North, was unable to keep order within his own borders! It was incredible. Henry's men-at-arms were the best in the world. How could a horde of thieves defy him?

"The Perche Forest," Henry resumed, "lies in the heart of Normandy. Within it are fifty villages and two market-towns; in the plains to the south and east are rich monasteries, churches and prosperous cities. All that rich country pays tribute to a nest of outlaws that lurk somewhere in the wild forest. I can not crush them, for I can not learn their rendezvous. Without that knowledge I am powerless."

"Captives?" Pierre suggested.

"Aye, captives! If we could take prisoners and keep them alive long enough to question them, we could lay our hands on their nest. But they will not stand up to us in pitched battle; they show clean heels. They can buy or steal swifter horses than I can afford. My moneys are low, what with my wars and the expense of my court; and the thieves are swollen with the loot of all my countryside."

"But you must have captured a few?"

"Few indeed," the duke growled. "Seven in the last year. Until a month ago I left the affair to Odo de Montvoisin, my seneschal, whose business it is to put down strong thieves within my marches. But his raids are useless. In the whole year he has taken but three men. They guess his movements before he stirs, and strike back when our guard is relaxed.

"Not a prisoner has lived long enough to confess. One was slain as was the fellow in the wood today—shot from ambush; another was poisoned in his cell; the third was stabbed even as his guards led him—it was by night—within the castle gate. They let no one escape to betray them.

"At last I myself rode out in pursuit of them, with my own

household troops. They had just sacked an abbey near Evreux. One of the monks escaped unseen, and brought the news to me. I had my men in full chase five minutes after the monk gasped out his story. I came upon the thieves in the open plain, forty of them, laden with booty. I slew fourteen, took four, and put the rest to flight.

"But as we returned with our prisoners we passed close by the forest where a dozen peasants were mending the road. These fled as we drew nigh, as peasants always flee before armed men. A moment after, a volley of arrows tore through the skirt of the wood, and down fell all four of our captives, riddled with shafts. It is always so—either we take no prisoners, or those we take are slain before they can be forced to betray their fellows."

"And today they attacked you," Pierre mused. "They have secret knowledge of your movements, and you can not learn theirs. I should think every village, every honest peasant, would play the spy for you. One swift-footed refugee could bring you word of their position shortly after the bandits attacked his village."

"Think you I have not questioned the peasants?"

Henry's cheeks flushed with impatience.

"If the country folk would report the outlaws' raids, I could hunt them down; or, by mapping the region with the towns most plundered, could find the center from which they conduct their inroads. But I can trace no common center, nor will the peasants complain of them.

"The thieves have put so strong a fear on the countryside that no man dares speak of them. I have ridden into a village bloodstained and charred, where the poor folk stood with glaring eyes, cursing the bandits till I questioned them. Then they swore there were no bandits, and that the blood and corpses were caused by a brawl among themselves.

"There is a legend that the bandit leader is a devil, who will tear to pieces any who inform on him. He is called Guillaume the Faceless. This is folly. Against devils I can hire priests. It shows only that he is cunning enough to be a master rascal, and merciless, enough to inspire greater terror than I can."

"Some man in your confidence," Pierre pondered, "some one of your household, must be in their pay. Otherwise they could not know your plans."

"So my mother says. They guess our movements with the fiend's own cunning. You yourself saw, this day, how a handful of them laid hands on my own person. Never before have I strayed so far from my men; yet they knew where and when to find me unescorted. They fell on the three of us while we sat by the spring and talked."

"They would have slain you," Pierre mused, "and been free from pursuit forever."

"They are not such fools! They would have carried off Thomas and Cercamon—whom of all men I value most—for ransom, and made me pay for their release. Slay me, ha? They want me to live. Me, with my hard hand and stupid brain—for Thomas speaks truly of me—me they can outwit and befool. If they harmed me or held me captive, my father would once more take over the ducal throne. These outlaws fear the brain of shrewd old Geoffrey more than the hand of his son. While I live and reign, they think themselves free to plunder safely."

"What is needed," Pierre spoke, "is a man they do not know—who is not known to hold your commission, but who holds authority."

Henry laughed.

"That is it! You have come in the very moment of time! I will give you authority, such men as you need, and all the time you ask. But no man must know that you are in this business."

"It is already known that I am with you," Pierre objected, "and tonight at table you spoke of Guillaume the Faceless. You should give orders that will seem to send me out of the district, and let me come back secretly, to ride against the outlaws."

The duke nodded.

"So be it. From now on I shall say no more of the matter.

You shall have all you ask, when you ask it. But—on your success depends all your future with me!"

"Give me a week here with the court," Pierre requested. "If at any time I disappear, say you have sent me on an embassy to Paris."

THE SUMMER night was breathlessly hot, the woods sultry. Black darkness hid the dust, but Pierre could smell it and taste it on his tongue. It rose in choking clouds about his horse's flanks. The lining of his armor was sticky on his back.

Eight days ago he had left Col Rouge, after a week's apparent idleness there. He had slid down from the battlements on a rope while Becket held the sentinel in talk. Pierre was not wearing his own armor, for he was certain that the hidden traitor in the court had already sent his description to the outlaw chief. Cercamon had procured him coarse mail, such as any man-at-arms in a poor service might wear, and a sword that though plain was of good steel.

It was the troubadour also who had by some devious means found him a tattered old cloak, and seen that an uncouth, sturdy nag was tethered at the edge of the forest. Pierre felt sure of his disguise: any one would have taken him for a broken soldier ready for any service—the more desperate the better. To foster this illusion he let his beard grow, and went as unwashed as his fastidious soul would allow.

Eight days he had wandered through the forest, following a map furnished by the duke, taking care not to keep too direct a route. From village to village, town to town he had gone, in and about the forest, his eyes and ears open for the slightest hint of unrest. He did not believe he would find the bandit headquarters in the wood itself, but rather that the forest furnished an easy means of baffling the duke's pursuit.

Their den must offer a secure hiding-place for men, horses and plunder—and there must be much of all three. The forest with its isolated, helpless villages seemed to him the spider's web rather than its hole. With the duke's rangers riding through it, the duke's court hunting its coverts for deer, heron and pheasant, the forest could not conceal so large a hiding-place as the bandits needed.

It was likelier that they would make their quarters in a town. There they could lie snug, lodging one by one in many houses, and hide their booty in some dwelling hired under the cloak of honest tenancy. Pierre remembered the thieves of Toul, who had quartered themselves among the burghers, at safely scattered intervals. By day they passed as artisans or apprentices; by night they met in an old house rented by their leader, who was esteemed a mercer. Then there was the band of Evry-le-Chanoun, in league with the townsmen, so that Evry waxed disreputably prosperous. When they were broken up, thirty townsmen had been hanged for complicity.

So Pierre rode through the thick forest perfunctorily, but he examined the villages with a watchful eye. He had already made a circle through the infested district town by town, scrutinizing the faces and dress of the people, but talking little with them. Any village which had dealings with the robbers would be less tolerant of strangers, more suspicious and prosperous, than honest folk.

He haunted the taverns, using lips less than eyes. Yet he bought drink, sipping it slowly in a corner, straining his ears for any suspicious words dropped by farmers, stray soldiers, or common idlers. He had been at pains to talk much with parish priests. These eyed him askance, for he looked like a ruffian in his disguise. Yet sooner or later they talked, for he had a persuasive tongue, and a lonely priest hungers to gossip.

But in all this time he had learned nothing. He had seen a few ugly characters, heard a few casual words that might mean much or nothing; but he had no evidence—not a sign that thieves dwelt anywhere about. Now and then a countryman would bemoan the loss of cattle or goods—but always guardedly, with a fear that proved his honesty.

The circle he had been drawing about the Perche was almost

closed. He was confident nothing had escaped him, and he held
high hopes that the last arc of the circle would yield results. On
this ninth night, therefore, he rode along a rutted forest way
toward the next village—the straggling hamlet of Maison
Morte. Even now he could see its first lights twinkling among
the trees.

It was getting late; the lights would be extinguished soon.
His horse, scenting food, quickened its pace. Pierre rode out of
the wood, caught the wind-blown scent of hay and let his beast
carry him down the one long street to the inn.

In the dark at least he saw no signs that Maison Morte had
suffered from bandit raids. Daylight might show more; but in
three other villages there had been no mark of violence. The
robbers had indeed a canny leader, who left no sign to show he
favored one place more than all others.

The inn at Maison Morte was a wretched hovel—a single
room, with walls of wattle and daub, its hot thatch dripping
dirt. A single spitting torch fitfully revealed the filth of the reeds
that strewed the dirt floor. Benches ran along two walls and
cumbered the floor-space; a single table was cluttered with odds
and ends of a mean meal. Wine-skins and jars lay heaped in
one corner, over which the greasy host—a fat man of middle
age, with one sullen eye—kept surly watch.

Three guests were drinking, seated close together on one of
the benches. Pierre took another, feeling all eyes focus on his
face. He met them with a menacing glare, in character with his
disguise. One after another, the drinkers dropped their eyes and
looked away.

They were ordinary country folk, in rough slip-overs and
galligaskins. Apart from their brutal faces, nothing about them
merited a second glance. The French peasant, in the hard old
feudal age, must needs be hard and rough to live. For an hour
Pierre watched them covertly, till one by one they rose and
departed. A little longer he stayed, sipping the vile ale that
furnished his sole pretext for lingering.

"A bed for the night?" he questioned.

The innkeeper measured him with a long look, and pointed to the rushes in the corner. Pierre shook his head.

"It is better in the wood," he said.

"As good as you have slept there," the host retorted. "It is but two sols, with one for your horse's bed and fodder, and one for the drink."

Pierre tossed him two coppers to pay for the ale and his beast's hay.

"I sleep in the wood," he answered. "I have no more money."

This was not true, but he wished to pass for a penniless, desperate man. He cherished a hope that the outlaws might hear of his presence, take him for what he seemed, and approach him with offers to make him one of them.

Riding slowly back to the forest, Pierre paused at the end of the last mowed field. The nearest house was close by the forest. He rode on in the dark till the murmuring of a woodland stream guided him to his night's quarters. Letting the horse drink, he knelt down, washed the nasty taste of the ale from his throat and tethered the beast. In a moment he was wrapped in the soldier's sleep, that sound slumber from which a man wakes at the softest step.

IT WAS dawn when he woke. Leading his horse to the last fringe of trees, Pierre looked out upon Maison Morte by day. It bore no sign of pillage, and indeed looked too poor to tempt violence. Nothing he could see gave the faintest trace of what he sought. It was a mere hamlet of scattered, tumble-down hovels, with fields retrieved from the forest. A few lean cattle cropped the mown stubble; a few starveling chickens scavenged the road.

On the left, nearing the wood, the houses ran in a crazy line toward a great hill, some nine hundred feet high, which on the town side was broken by a sheer precipice. The house closest to the forest, which was the one solid structure, was built against the face of the cliff. It was larger than the rest—perhaps the dwelling of the local money-lender, the parasite that leached from the peasants all that their overlords spared.

A woman came out with a reed broom, and began sweeping away the dust that lay thick on the threshold. Pierre noticed that the house was built on a flat, rocky outcrop that made a natural platform running out quite thirty feet from the road. It was this platform that the woman's vigorous strokes were cleaning.

Maison Morte had not even a village church. It was the meanest, most hopeless spot Pierre had found in what was otherwise a fairly rich country. He was sore it held nothing for him. A breakfast of smoked meat and an early apple from his lean saddle-bags raised his spirits a little, and he rode away for the next village.

The morning was fresh; but after four mile of dusty wood-road Pierre found its glory tarnished. All about him towered huge trunks that had never felt the ax; the birds chattered as if man had never disturbed them.

It was neither sight nor sound that warned him of the stranger's approach. He heard nothing till a jay flew screaming overhead. Another moment, and a mailed man rode toward him around a bend. This was curious: deep in dust as the road was, there were stones enough for shod hoofs to clink on. Yet here was the man, and his mount ambled on noiselessly.

He was a big man, hulking and ugly-looking. A bow was slung behind him and a great sword hung by his side. He pulled up, looked Pierre over out of evil eyes and grinned.

"Your last service paid you ill," he remarked, noting Pierre's tattered cloak and unkempt mount.

Pierre nodded, affecting surliness.

"My last service paid me blows and a thankless discharge," he growled.

The stranger grinned again.

"Duke Henry is a generous master," he suggested.

Pierre cursed, and spat.

"Generous with hard names," he said; and this was true. "How can a broken soldier get service with the like of him, with no good conduct to show?"

He watched the stranger's face from the corners of his eyes. Pierre knew well that no mailed man who wore no badge of service could be a follower of Henry's. This man might not be an outlaw, but Pierre thought the chances were against his being honest. He was at least an armed vagabond, or a discharged soldier; therefore Pierre assumed the same rôle.

"Have you money?" the stranger countered.

Pierre snarled at him.

"I would twist your neck for a copper! I am hungry, and my beast too."

Once more the man's eyes ran him over from head to foot, noting the two weeks' beard, the desperate look, the power of arm and breadth of shoulder.

"You are a pretty fellow," the stranger said at length. "I serve one who needs such as you. You need never want for food, drink, raiment, pleasure, or—gold. Much gold!"

He paused, and his wicked little eyes leered at Pierre.

Pierre's heart leaped. It was for this that he played the rôle of cast soldier. This master of masterless men could be none other than his quarry, the outlaw chief.

"Take me to this prince of masters!" he cried.

"That must march slowly," the bandit answered with a cunning look. "We show no man where we nest till we are sure of him. Ride on with me, and I will tell you what you must do to enter our fellowship."

Wheeling his horse, Pierre followed the man down the road for the greater part of a mile. The bandit spoke little, and that little was the repetition of promises of the great fortune Pierre would make by throwing in his lot with the unknown master. By and by the man drew off into a clump of undergrowth where the great trees receded.

"Follow!" he commanded. "The path is hidden."

Hidden it was. The shrubbery concealed its entrance well. Once within, they were utterly shut off from the road. Pierre was disappointed, for this could be no everyday route of the outlaws. The passage of many men would have broken down the masking bushes, and tramped the damp path deep in mud. There were but few hoof-prints, and those blurred in some way that Pierre did not at first understand. Shod hoofs would have bitten deep into the mud, leaving clear outlines; nor were these the prints of unshod hoofs either.

The path ran through the second growth for a time, marking what must once have been a road, and opened out into a little clearing. At the farther end there was a moss-grown shrine. The stranger halted.

"We trust no man untested," he said. "Mark yonder shrine. You must be here one hour before sunset tomorrow, ready to ride on a venture that will show us your pith. Say nothing to any man, or—big as you are—you will not see another sun!"

"But how," Pierre retorted, "am I to eat meanwhile?"

"Here is money."

The stranger tossed him a gold-piece.

"Bite on that! It is an earnest of your future wage."

Pierre tried to counterfeit greedy rapture; then, with a cunning thought, he laid a hand on his sword, crying—

"Give me more, or I take it!"

"You must fight for it then!"

The fellow drew sword, his mean lips curled in a smile of confidence. But Pierre dismounted, for he knew not the quality of his horse in a fight. The other also sprang from the saddle, as if less minded to kill Pierre than to try his sword-play.

From the first clash Pierre knew himself the man's master, but he recognized also that his antagonist was a better swordsman than most men-at-arms. Therefore he dissembled his own great skill, swinging wide and lunging short, parrying coarsely, barely holding the vantage. But it was enough; within five minutes the other sprang back, crying for quarter.

"You will get a thousand times more gold by joining us than by robbing me!" he gasped.

Pierre sheathed his weapon.

"You had done better to say so in the beginning!"

"I thought myself a better man than you," the rascal replied. "Fire of the pit! Our captain will give a brave welcome to such a swordsman—tomorrow, before sundown!"

While he yet spoke he mounted, gave his horse the spurs and vanished in the undergrowth. Pierre did not try to follow. The first bounds of the stranger's beast proved it a marvel of horse-flesh.

"Thank God!" Pierre muttered. "I am on the right road!"

Retracing the path to the highway, he jogged along for an hour toward the next village, then—after scanning the road in both directions—turned into the forest and put his beast to the gallop between the rows of great trees. His head was turned for Col Rouge. Every detail of the clearing was etched into his memory.

CERCAMON COULD indulge his whims unquestioned. He was a soldier, the duke's friend and a Southerner. Every North Frenchman expects a Southerner to do strange things. So it caused little talk when Cercamon won Henry's permission to relieve the sentry on the east wall of the tower, and to stand watch there from the second hour after dark till the third, every night of Pierre's absence. Under his cloak the troubadour carried a coiled rope, stout, and knotted at short intervals.

On the tenth night after Pierre's departure Cercamon heard a shrill whistle and saw the rope pulled out taut from the merlon to which he had made it fast. For safety's sake, he drew sword, and waited. But he sheathed the blade when Pierre crawled over the battlements.

"You have succeeded?" he whispered.

"I know not," Pierre answered softly. "I must see the duke."

Cercamon unfastened the rope, wound it round his waist and draped his cloak over it.

"Crouch in the gloom of the wall," he cautioned. "Wait here till I return."

It would be hard to smuggle Pierre past the men on guard at the stair-head—one of whom might be in the bandits' pay. Much better to bring the duke to him. So Pierre kept in the dark of the merlons till steps sounded on the flags, and Cercamon returned with Henry. As Pierre rose up like a ghost the duke started back.

"You!" he gasped. "How did you get within the walls?"

"Over them," Pierre answered.

Swiftly, in guarded whispers, he told of his long, close search for traces of the outlaws, and of his rendezvous with the stranger for the following evening.

"It is our chance to find their nest," he concluded. "Give me twenty archers and twoscore men-at-arms on good horses. Let them be called now, with no hint of the work before them, to the gate. I will wait well outside, where I can watch them as they come; Cercamon shall bring up the rear. Thus, if any are spies of Guillaume the Faceless, none of them can escape to warn him. We must march in half an hour!"

"I will go too!" Henry whispered eagerly.

"With your indulgence, my lord, it can not be," Pierre insisted. "When the huntsman has sighted the quarry, shall another frighten it away before he can shoot?"

The young duke drew Pierre to him, seeking his eyes in the darkness.

"I am taking great chances with you!" he warned. "Play me fair, or by God's justice, it will go ill with you!"

"If I fail my neck is yours," Pierre answered grimly.

Lest any of his officers, unknown to him, should be in league with the outlaws and so betray him, Henry himself picked the men for the ambuscade. All from his own body-guard, Normans and Angevins of massive frame and long service, they were routed out singly and sent to the gate. One by one he caught them on guard, or in their beds, laid a stern hand on the shoulder of each, bade him arm and drove him forth.

Then to the stables where the startled grooms leaped up sleepy-eyed to water threescore and two horses, saddle them and lead them out. A challenge rang from the tower and Henry's own voice thundered back:

"Duke's service! Uprising in Caen! Mind your posts!"

For by Pierre's counsel he furnished a pretext that would set Guillaume's spies working in the wrong direction. Caen lies northwest of Col Rouge; Pierre was to ride south and east. The wondering men-at-arms mounted their beasts, staring at the dark figure by Henry's side.

"Ye take orders from Pierre Faidit," the duke rumbled. "If any of you disobey him, ye shall boil in pitch when I catch you!"

They knew he would be as good as his word.

Cercamon rode up from the rear, and handed Pierre a sword.

"Your own weapon will sit best in your hand," he said. "I fetched it from your chamber, with a cover to hide the jeweled hilt. When time comes to strike, you can snatch off the cover and know a friend is in your fingers."

"And a friend by my side this night!" Pierre answered, clasping the troubadour's hand.

Direct through the forest, it was but half a night's ride to the shrine of the rendezvous. Each man carried provisions in his saddle-bags. They rode on slowly in the dark, each following the loom of his shoulders who rode before, close, to avoid straggling. Cercamon was again in the rear. No secret traitor would get past him; but Pierre ran the chance of a lateral dash into the dark forest-aisles. So, lest a spy in mid-column get away to give the alarm, he gave orders that any man who left his place be struck down by those nearest him.

AFTER SOME hours they came out on the road midway between Maison Morte and Queraille. Here Pierre halted them, and bade them camp, fireless, just within trees. If any midnight rider came down that road, they must seize him.

But no one came, the night through. At dawn the men were ordered to efface their tracks where they had ridden into the road, by dragging the dust with broken fronds, and then to hide the fronds. Meantime he searched diligently for the hidden opening that gave on the path to the shrine; while Cercamon kept a wary eye on the troopers. When Pierre returned the troubadour reported exultantly:

"All here! There are no traitors in Henry's body-guard!"

After finding the path Pierre skirted the wood on either side till he discovered—where the old clearing ceased and the great forest growth resumed—a way that would take them around the clearing. The troopers followed him into the wood, all but six archers and fifteen men-at-arms whom he placed in ambush among the trees across the road from the entrance to the path.

He had now laid a trap where such outlaws as came to the rendezvous with him must enter; it remained to surround the clearing. This he did, throwing out a thin screen of archers just within the bush all around, and posting double their number of men-at-arms behind. The archers had their bows ready and their quivers hitched to the front.

One by one he let his men lead their horses to drink, and slake their own thirst. The sun rose just before the last returned with his beast from the brook and took up his position.

Now began the long wait. It had been unnecessary perhaps to reach the spot so early. The evil-faced stranger had set the time for the meeting at an hour before sundown. But it had been most needful to bring up his men and post them earlier than any bandit scouts could be stirring; and the men were comfortable enough here.

The stranger might come with a company; more probably he would come alone, to guide Pierre to the bandit headquarters. But others might come with him; and Pierre was determined to take prisoner as many as might come, to force them to betray their fellows and to ride at once against the main outlaw force with his captives as guides.

It was a pretty ambuscade, but it had one necessary weakness: Pierre could post by the entrance to the path only as many men as the trees by the road would hide. Yet there was small chance that enough bandits would come to force a way out through the score he had posted there.

The long hours passed; the men began to grow restless. Their horses were tethered just behind them. Each man had orders, when they should hear the approach of horses, to pinch the nostrils of their own beasts, lest their neighing betray the trap. The signal for attack would be a blast from Pierre's horn, which he wore under his tattered cloak.

AT LAST the sun sank so low that the trees shut it from sight. A general tension spread over the hidden watchers. A slight haze rose among the trees; then, as Pierre rode out to the moss-grown shrine, a horseman appeared opposite him at the mouth of the clearing.

It was the man he had come to meet. He had come noiseless, with no sound of hoofs. Then—too late—Pierre recalled that the bandit's horse had made no noise at their first meeting. He waved an arm; the stranger made to ride toward him. In that moment—without warning, since there had been no sound of hoofs—a horse nickered behind the trees. Another, and another. One horse began to stamp.

The bandit reined in, suspicious. Then as certainty and rage dawned upon him an overzealous archer thrust out his steel headpiece from the foliage and raised his bow. The bandit wheeled with a cry of fury, dashed out of sight in the undergrowth and raised a wild shout:

"Flee! Flee! We are betrayed!"

Other shouts echoed his own. Pierre's trumpet rang out. His troopers, mounting in haste, galloped after him down the little path to the road. As they pursued they heard a fierce tumult, the yells of fighting men, the clash of steel. They then burst out into the road to find a heap of writhing men at the edge of the farther woods, and their own comrades cursing and pointing through the forest beyond. Six men were down—two bandits and four soldiers. The bandits were dead, as was one man-at-arms; all had been badly trampled by the hoofs of many horses.

"They rode us down!" cried a trooper, pointing back of him through the wood. "Twoscore of them! We waited for your horn. Even as it sounded and we came forth, a torrent of horsemen swept through us. We did what we could, but there was no time! No time, and they were many!"

"After them!" shrieked another. "Their blood for ours!"

But Pierre shook his head. His one promising chance had failed. He had not foreseen that the outlaws would be cunning enough to send a large force to meet him. There was no possibility the bandits did not foresee. Now, though his force outnumbered theirs three to two, they were safe in the forest, darkness coming on; and their horses were fleeter than his.

"There is but one hope," he said. "If they nest in a town they may swing back to the road, after they think us thrown off the scent, and strike back for Maison Morte or Queraille. Look for tracks that will show which way they came hither."

The tracks were soon found, though they were none too clear in the deep dust. They came up the road from Maison Morte, and down the road from Queraille! They had come from both directions!

"They will not divide now," Pierre decided. "It is well enough to come in two details; but to divide under pursuit would be to court destruction. With us after them they will be likely to seek their holes. Pray God they ride back to the road, instead of keeping to the forest!"

For a few moments he pondered the situation, not knowing which town to strike for. His men waited in the saddle, hot with impatience and rage. It would go hard with the bandits if they were caught.

"Cercamon, take twelve men and ride toward Queraille!" he ordered. "I will take twelve and spur for Maison Morte. The rest will bide here, where we may fall back on them in case of need. The first to sight traces of them will blow his trumpet; the other will return here, and join him with the host."

"What if neither of us finds a trace?"

"Then they keep to the forest, and we fail," Pierre replied. "It grows dark—be off with you!"

Pierre and his twelve rode north toward Maison Morte, watching the road for signs. But there were no dust-clouds down the road, so far as they could judge in the failing light; no hoof-prints that could be positively identified, in the thick dust of the road, as leading north. And well this might be, seeing that the outlaws might have ridden through the wood past this point before taking to the road.

For two miles Pierre's men cantered on; then, when they had given up hope, Cercamon's trumpet pealed thin in the distance. With a joyous cry the troopers wheeled and galloped back.

Picking up the main company, they spurred fast to the south, till they came up with Cercamon's detachment. The troubadour proudly held up something in one hand. It was getting dark, but Pierre, coming close and taking the object from him, saw that it was an iron horseshoe.

"A cast shoe!" Cercamon cried. "Pointing south!"

"Fires of purgatory!" swore Pierre. "We have lost time! Back, for Maison Morte!"

"But the shoe! They have made for Queraille!"

"A blind!" Pierre cut him off. "Forty riders came up on our ambush unheard. Could they do that, think you, if their horses had been iron-shod? The track I saw in the damp mold of the wood-path was blurred. They wear leather shoes to muffle their approach. This is a trick. They have turned in the forest, sent a man this way to drop the shoe and mislead us and dashed for Maison Morte or some village on the north road."

He set spurs to his horse and galloped furiously northward. Unbelieving, halfhearted, the troopers followed. Looking back, Pierre saw how they lagged and sent out a brazen-lunged shout—

"Forward, ye fools, or feel the duke's wrath!"

Their spurs tore into their horses' flanks, and they pelted down the road into the darkening night. Meeting nothing, slacking rein for nothing, they rode into Maison Morte by the feel of the road under their feet and the black loom of the trees on either side.

"Patrol the street!" Pierre ordered. "Search every house!"

Most of the houses still showed rushlight through the holes in the walls that served for windows. The baffled troopers stopped not to knock, but burst in with oaths and threats, demanding to see every inmate.

Men and women were roused from early bed or late supper; children were frightened into wails of terror. Mad with the sight of their own dead, thirsty for blood, the soldiers would scarce listen to protests of innocence. Shrieks rending the darkness sent Pierre to teach his men gentleness; but nowhere did they find sight or trace of the enemy. At last, in sheer despair, Pierre called his men off and withdrew to the wood.

"We bide here till dawn," he said. "Mayhap they will think us gone, if indeed they are here at all. We shall search again in the morning, then ride to the next town."

They camped well within the wood, far enough so that the stamping and nickering of their horses could not be heard in the village. After a cold, dry meal the men lay down to sleep under the stars, grumbling. They would be very dry by daybreak, and they knew, from the grim tone of their leader's commands, that the search would go on.

BUT PIERRE did not sleep. When the snores of the troopers rumbled in even chorus he rose and crawled stealthily to the edge of the wood. He pinned his faith to the testimony of that iron horseshoe. Country horses were unshed; the bandits used leather. Therefore the iron must be a blind. In the probable chance that the outlaws had ridden into or through Maison Morte—instead of scattering in the forest—lay his sole hope.

If he failed now he would never get another chance; the bandits knew him now for an enemy, and the duke's man.

Hidden behind a giant beech, the last outpost of the wood, he watched the lights flicker out in the hamlet. He was weary, but he kept his vigil, his eyes roving through the darkness that hid the one street from him. For an hour, two hours, he lay motionless. Then as he gave up hope he heard a sound that set his pulse tingling.

A faint, a very faint metallic chink-chink tinkled in his ears, far down the forest-road that met the village street at right angles. No, it was not far! A silent-footed horse loomed out of the dark almost before his face. He looked for the gleam of starlight on steel, but saw none. Yet here was a ridden horse, passing at a walk that barely set the rider's armor tinkling. It turned at the village street, passed down, then turned again almost at once. Then came the rasp of mailed feet as the rider dismounted on stone.

On stone! Pierre ran forward, making for the nearest house. Suddenly he fell flat in the darkness, his eyes fixed on the door of that house which two nights before he had observed from almost this same spot. He was within a few yards of it, concealed in the angle it formed with the sheer cliff. He recalled the woman who swept its wide stone base. The door creaked open. A faint light, half-shaded by a hand, fell on the threshold and flashed on a steel helmet; then the door closed.

Pierre gasped. Not only had the rider entered the house; he had led his horse in after him! Pierre sprang forward, cautiously removed his helmet, and peered in at the one window. Three people sat round the dying supper-fire: an old, bent man, an aged woman and a girl. Of horse and rider, who had entered but a moment before, there was no trace! Pierre's eyes searched the one-roomed interior in vain.

The strange rider had vanished.

The flesh crawled on Pierre's back. No freer than other men from the superstition of his day, he felt certain that the powers of evil were in this mystery. His hair rose with the half-formed fear that the bent old man might suddenly grow hoofs, horns and tail, and come straight for his hiding-place. The old woman was surely a witch.

His lips moved in silent prayer. He had a duty, from which neither men nor devils should turn him. The two old folk were talking in low, excited tones while the girl threw in an occasional word in a scornful voice. Yet he could not understand them, for they were at the other end of the house from him, and spoke in the broadest Norman dialect.

For an hour more Pierre lurked at the window, till he was satisfied that the powers of evil had indeed spirited the unknown rider away. He crawled back to the edge of the wood.

He had scarcely reached the trees when the door of the house flew quietly open. The light gleamed once more on the helm of the rider, who mounted on the wide stone threshold, flung a subdued but excited word over his shoulder and spurred his horse. Down the few yards of street he galloped, turned the corner at full speed, coming nearer and nearer Pierre's hiding-place.

Pierre had made his decision as the rider mounted. Crouching on one knee, he leaped out and grabbed the man as the horse swung past him, dragged him from the saddle and flung him violently on the ground. Bearing him, unconscious from his fall, into the forest, Pierre tied his feet and hands with strips of his cloak, and roused his men. When all were gathered about him, Pierre struck flint and steel, and lighted a pine torch, trusting to the trees to hide its glow from the village.

The stranger's fall, and the human solidity of his flesh, sent a thrill of relief to Pierre's heart, which had pounded with panic when he seized the man. As the light of his torch fell on the prisoner's face he uttered a cry of astonishment.

THE PRISONER soon returned to consciousness. Whipping out a dagger, Pierre set the point at the helpless throat, saying sternly:

"I have seen you at Col Rouge. Tell me the secret of that house or you die!"

The captive groaned, but held his tongue. Pierre thrust the dagger just beneath the skin.

"I know nothing!" the man cried.

Pierre sheathed his blade.

"I can not torture you," he said, "but the duke will unless you speak!"

He felt the fellow tremble under his hands, and knew how great must be his fear of that mercilessness which the outlaws showed to such of their fellows as were so unlucky as to be captured. Fear of a horrible death and hope of life will win speech from almost any man.

"If I tell," the captive faltered, "will my life be spared?"

"I will ask the duke to show you mercy and will swear that you will not suffer torture," Pierre answered.

"Untie my feet then, and I will show you. I have followed you from Col Rouge. My master feared your expedition might be against Guillaume."

Shuddering with his own fears, the prisoner paused; then resumed:

"I was on my way back from him, with word of your attack in the forest, when you seized me. The outlaws are—"

"Are in that house, or have passed through it!" Pierre broke in.

He understood now; his prisoner's confession, and disappearance in the house, made the situation clear. The man had seen Guillaume the Faceless *after* entering the mysterious house, and went from it with a message from the bandit leader—and the house was empty, save for a handful of villagers!

"The rear wall is false!" Pierre guessed with assurance.

"Aye, my lord," the captive confirmed, "and your way lies through it."

Slashing the bonds from the man's ankles, Pierre whistled

to his men. Leaving their horses tethered, the troopers followed him toward the door of that strange house. Their feet rang on the stone platform. A cry from within gave the alarm. Pierre seized the latch, but the door held. He heard the chock of bars flung hastily home.

Thrice he hurled himself at the heavy oak in vain. Then at his order a burly trooper ranged alongside him. Eight others, four behind each of them, formed in a tail of men, each clasping the shoulders of the man in front.

Pierre raised his voice in an old sea-chantey of his boyhood. To the measured cadence the ten flung all their weight forward, even as he thrust his own great shoulders against the wood. It withstood three concerted heaves; at the fourth it gave. A fifth, and a bar crashed; three more, and other bars burst with the rending noise of dry timber. At the tenth onfall the door flew open, precipitating the whole line within.

The old couple crouched in a corner; the girl backed against the rear wall in apparent terror. Her arms were spread, her face white in the light of a single torch. This torch Pierre snatched from its socket. His captive caught his arm.

"The midmost eight planks!" he cried.

"You, and you!" Pierre shouted to two troopers. "Bide with this man, hide him and see that no harm comes to him!"

He advanced to the rear wall and counted off the planks. This wall of the house was against the side of the cliff, apparently in contact with the solid rock. The planks were vertical, foot-wide and very thick. Pounding on them, Pierre heard them ring hollow. They must be hinged on the other side.

"Tear those planks down, or burst them open!" he ordered.

Half a dozen troopers advanced; one laid a hand on the girl's shoulder, to pull her out of the way. As he touched her, she sprang at him, a knife gleaming in her hand. The soldier met her attack swiftly, wrenching the knife from her at the cost of three slashed fingers. He flung her in a corner, where she crouched, sobbing. His fellows were already at work on the stout planks; but these held. The shouts of startled men behind the wall impelled them to greater efforts.

"Axes!" shouted Pierre.

Men ran up with battle-axes, crying for room to swing. Their broad blades bit deep into the wood, sending splinters flying. Plank after plank crashed down. Then came a humming whistle, and two men dropped with arrows in their breasts. At a word from Pierre his own archers lined the gaps, pouring in a steel hail till the volleys beyond the wall ceased.

Seizing an ax from a fallen soldier, Pierre threw all his huge strength into his blows. Others joined his assault. The wall was down at last. With a roar of triumph the troopers dashed into the opening.

There was no need of their torch; the space that opened before them was ablaze with many glowing cressets. It was a great cavern in the rocky hill—not a natural cave, but a straight tunnel, faced with cut, squared stones.

Half-way down it gathered the outlaws—fifty or more, sturdy ruffians armed to the eyes. At their head towered a burly giant whose mail was topped with a masked helmet hiding all but his glowing eyes—Giullaume the Faceless.

PIERRE HAD planned his assault while his ax yet thundered on the wall. The arrows of his archers had forced the bandits far back from the barricade; now at his shouted order renewed volleys held them at bay while his troopers formed. Thus the enemy lost the advantage of position; the gap was forced, and the soldiers arrayed for the bitter last fight.

Nor, though the bandits strove to return arrow for arrow, could they gain the mastery. Pierre's attack had been so swift that it caught them with half their bows unstrung. As fast as an outlaw wasted a precious moment to string his bowstaff— thus necessarily casting aside his shield and leaving his side exposed—Pierre's marksmen dropped him. The ruffians had but one recourse—to close at once, and by the pressure of counter-attack to smother the Norman arrow-flights.

Snarling with rage, Guillaume the Faceless cried his men on to the assault. They came—so thick and fast that the Norman archers had to drop their bows and draw blade. His eyes singling out Pierre, Guillaume leaped to meet him, shield up, sword flailing. Pierre met him with left foot out and point ready. With all the skill of his long service, with the genius for his weapon born in him and trained by Guilhem, the great swordsman of Toulouse, Pierre outfaced the bandit's fierce cuts and circling slashes.

His own blade was weapon and shield in one—which was well, for Guillaume was as strong as he. With terrific force the outlaw hammered Pierre's blade and struggled to break down his guard; nor could Pierre, with the shield-wall of his own men advancing behind him, give back. He thrust swiftly, with short-ened blade. Three times his point slid in under Guillaume's guard till it was reddened thrice. Then the bandit, mad with his wounds, abandoned defense to lash in with a mighty back-stroke. As he raised his blade, Pierre's edge drove through the base of his neck.

Drawing clear of his dead foe, Pierre found Cercamon at his side. The troubadour's point was dripping; two dead men lay at Pierre's left. Exchanging glances, the friends laughed and threw themselves into the *mêlée*.

The death of their leader left the bandits without command; the one authority which had been their strength was gone, and their habit of dependence on it was now their weakness. Knowing they must fight their way to freedom over the bodies of the soldiers or perish, they fought with wild courage; but they fought as individuals, without leadership. They did not wait for the battle to be brought to them.

Pierre's men, trained to formation and discipline, were in an irregular column five deep, their ranks extending across the cavern. Their orderly, inexorable advance, their impenetrable wall of shields, flung their enemies before them like spray from a crag, and threw the outlaws into confusion.

Now and again, their lines rippled as they stumbled over bales, sacks and piles of plunder that lay where the bandits had flung them; but always the array closed again and came mercilessly on. Held together by Pierre's shouted orders and the cries of their sergeants, they went at the butchery with veteran precision. The outlaws hurled themselves again and again on those terrible serried points, knowing that whoso survived the sword must die by the rope, unless they could tear their way through to freedom.

But they faced the impossible. As they recoiled, two of the Norman ranks formed into the point of a wedge, led on by Pierre and Cercamon. At the word of command the wedge dashed forward, hurling the bandits back. The two matchless swordsmen in the van found a mark with almost every thrust; no stroke, however fierce, could pass their guard. The bandits gave way before them, drawing back farther and farther toward a wooden partition in the rear of the tunnel, whence came the reek of a stable.

Seven of the soldiers were down and many wounded. But the spilled blood only drove them on, inspired with the passion to avenge their dead. When one was smitten, a comrade in the rank behind would hurl him back and take his place.

The implacable solidity of those ranks, lapping from wall to wall, ever surging forward, terrified the outlaws. Bleeding and broken, they reeled back and back. Their breath came in weary, gulping sobs; yet ever they lashed out at their foes as they retreated. But they were shrinking fast.

And as their number shrank, the bandits found their enemy's flanks trickling round and enfolding their own. Then they were hewn down by ones and twos, hemmed in, with still other soldiers fighting for a chance to slip in behind them. At that for the back of the tunnel, where they might get their shoulders against the partition and prolong the death-struggle. This gave Pierre the opportunity to bring his bows into play again.

As they broke he sounded his horn. Three times he blew

before his blood-mad followers would heed the order; then at last they drew off, glaring at their beaten enemy. Under cover of the men-at-arms, his archers withdrew to pick up their bows, rejoined the ranks and shot swiftly into the thick of the outlaws. Pierre, watching for a sign of surrender, saw a door in the partition open behind the enemy.

"Strike them down!" he cried. "Quick, before they loose the horses!

The smell from the farther enclosure was enough to reveal what lay beyond. He knew there could be no means of escape from the stable into and through the mountain, or the bandits would have tried it long since; but it might be perilous for spirited horses to be loosed upon his ranks in that tunnel. The smell of blood would drive them mad; there would be trampling and kicking, amid which the surviving bandits might make a bold attempt at freedom.

At his command the whole troop closed on the outlaws, striking with sword and ax, snatching them back from the stable, cutting them down without mercy. Then the survivors, seized with panic, cast down their weapons and made submission.

Swiftly the soldiers bound them. Only nine were left alive to be made captive, and of these but two were unwounded. Other troopers, with rough surgery, were looking after their own wounded and gathering their dead together.

N O W   T H E victors spread out through the tunnel, examining the place with curiosity. Pierre found it a great marvel. Though he knew it not, the workmanship of those walls was Roman—part of some ancient work which those mighty engineers of the past had builded. The walls were crudely scrawled with designs made by the smoke of torches; and here and there a mason's mark, with a rough Latin inscription, was cut into the stone.

But it was the floor which interested him and all his company, most of all. Here were piles and bales of rich goods, silks and velvets looted from the merchants who traversed France and

Italy with wares; heaps of gold and silver candlesticks, altar-cloths, jeweled reliquaries, and—in chests and bags full to bursting—coins pillaged from all the countryside. The soldiers were plunging greedy hands into the loot; but Pierre bade them leave it alone.

"This will wait!" he said. "The duke will reward you all for this night's work; but do ye not dare to rob him!"

Then, calling Cercamon, he bade his friend take half his force and stand guard over cave and village.

"Quarter the wounded in the best houses," he ordered. "I will bring back a leech to tend their hurts. Seize any man who moves from his own house, any stranger, any horseman!"

Still dripping with the sweat of the fight, he made his way back to the cave-mouth and through the house, followed by four and twenty of his men and the nine captives. The two on guard in the house, ill pleased with missing the fight, clung to the captive guide and the three peasants with grim bitterness.

"What part have these played?" Pierre asked the man he had captured in the road.

"The girl is Guillaume's sister and my masters sweetheart," the man answered. "These are her people."

"Let them go!" Pierre commanded. "It will be punishment enough to drive them from the village where they have passed their lives."

The soldiers nodded, knowing indeed that hopeless peasants would be hard put to it to find bread to fill their mouths.

Leaving the horses of the conquered for Cercamon's detachment to bring on later with the wounded and the spoil, Pierre led his men back to the wood. Helping the prisoners into the saddle, the soldiers bound their feet under the horses' bellies and fettered each man by the neck to the man ahead at intervals of twenty feet. Thus roped, and guarded by the soldiers, they would make the journey back to Col Rouge with no chance for escape.

"To the castle!" Pierre cried; and conquerors and conquered rode in a long column through the dawn-gray woods.

"YOU HAVE done a red night's work!" Duke Henry approved.

He spoke plain truth; Pierre's mailed sleeves were red to the elbows, and his over-tunic spattered with blood. His dinted helmet had been knocked half-over one eye.

Pierre gave his report fully and simply, praising his soldiers for their valor and Cercamon for his leadership.

"What of yourself?" Henry asked. "Your wit and your sword have rid my realm of a pest that long preyed upon it; yet you say little of your own work."

"I have done that which you bade me," Pierre replied.

"There is more yet."

The duke's tone was grim.

"I will do the rest. This fellow you have brought"—he jerked a blunt thumb at the cowering captive who had guided Pierre to the cavern—"is one I know—Ho, there!"

A servant came running to his call.

"Fetch me the seneschal!" Henry ordered.

In a little while the fellow returned, bowing in Odo de Montvoisin. A gesture from Henry dismissed the servant, while his eyes never left Odo.

The triumphal procession had brought its captives to the postern, where Pierre had ordered the guard to lead them straight to the duke. They had passed up the stair of the after-court, to the vast astonishment of the half-dozen men-at-arms on duty there. The duke had come so swiftly that few in the castle guessed what had really happened.

Odo de Montvoisin, as he entered the room, took in the scene with a sweeping glance—the blood-stained soldiers, the bloodier captives, and the bound, shame-faced guide whose eyes would not meet his own. Odo blenched, but recovered his poise swiftly.

"You know this dog?" Henry pointed to the frightened guide.

"He—he is my man, your Grace."

Licking his dry lips, Odo told the truth, knowing that Henry knew it already.

"What is—who are all these?"

"Stand at the door, Pierre."

Henry's eyes had already flashed a quick warning. Pierre reached the door just in time to seize Odo as the seneschal turned to run, and dragged him back by the velvet collar of his splendid surcoat.

"Speak, you!"

The duke's angry command set the prisoner to babbling a terrified confession.

"My lord—mercy! Sir Odo—"

Odo, wrenching himself free by a sudden twist, sprang for the prisoner with unsheathed dagger. But Pierre caught his elbow, and the duke struck the weapon from his hand. The prisoner finished his confession in peace; and before he had done, Odo's face was as white as new parchment.

The man's confession made it convincingly clear why the duke's movements were always known to the bandits in time for escape or counter-stroke; why Odo himself had never taken prisoners or kept them alive to be questioned. Nay, more; Odo, knowing when the duke would hunt in the forest and that he had given orders to be left alone in the glade to confer with Thomas and the troubadour, himself sent information to the outlaws.

Guillaume the Faceless, the dreaded, unknown bandit chief, was but a tool of Odo's. Odo's had been the imagination for Guillaume's bold raids; to Odo Guillaume had sent, by night convoy, the half of all his plunder; Odo was to reap half the ransom which Guillaume was to collect from the daring attempt to carry off the duke's two most trusted counselors. And Pierre's captive, who stammered out the startling confession, was Odo's own squire! It was he who had served as messenger and go-between from the false seneschal to the outlaws.

"Did you guess any of this?" the duke asked Pierre.

"I suspected much," Pierre answered. "In the week that I tarried in the castle I learned that Sir Odo came of an impoverished house, yet had always money to play for high stakes, to dress richly, to buy that which he desired. That, and his failure to hunt down the bandits, made me guess that he might be the hidden traitor. But no accusation could be brought against a knight without proof."

"There is proof enough now!" Henry growled. "Ho, one of you! Fetch *Tranche-tête!* Bid him come for duty!"

Odo shivered like a poplar-leaf in Pierre's hands.

"Not that, my lord!" he pleaded. "Not for me! I am a noble!"

And Pierre seconded his appeal, crying earnestly:

"Not the executioner, my lord! This is a knight, entitled to put his guilt or innocence to trial by combat. I will myself take the burden of proving his treachery."

Henry laughed unpleasantly.

"Look you, Pierre. If this is a knight, then you, a mere captain, can not meet him in trial by combat save by my sanction—and I will not give that sanction. If he is a traitor—and we know he is—then to cross swords with him would put a stain on your honor.

"Trial by combat is foolery. I have known an honest man's sword to play him false or his armor to give way at an unknown defect, and a foul rascal to save his own life by that means. Do you think God always gives triumph to the right? I know better than that—and Thomas says I am stupid!"

Pierre's piety was shocked, but he could say no more. A squat, heavy-featured man, clad in closefitting red, came in at the door.

"*Tranche-tête!*" cried Henry.

"Aye, lord!" the red one answered.

A huge ax, which he had held behind his back, swung up in ponderous salute.

"Take this whipped hound"—the duke pointed to Odo—"to the battlements. Strike off his golden spurs. Then—Nay, not the ax. The rope!"

Odo fell at his lord's knees, clutching miserably at Henry's robe. But the duke kicked him away, and he was borne to death between a soldier and the red executioner.

"Tranche-tête!" Henry bellowed.

"Aye, lord?" shouted the headsman over his shoulder.

"When you have done with him come back for these."

He who had confessed wailed for mercy; and Pierre spoke up in quick concern:

"My lord, I promised to plead for him. He guided us—"

"Enough! He shall be whipped from my gates, and turned loose to shift for himself. I have shown mercy enough—ask me no more!"

Pierre turned to go; but Henry called him back.

"You have done well, Pierre," he said more gently now. "You are fitter to be a knight than many who wear gold spurs. From now on you shall be my own squire. God send the day when your further deeds win you the touch of my sword on your shoulder, the spurs and the golden belt of knighthood!"

FOR THE CROWN

"**Y**ONDER SHIP sails three lengths to our two! If there is not treachery brewing, I have lost my power to read its signs!"

The speaker thrust out one mailed arm from his heavy woolen cloak, and pointed over the starboard rail. His companion followed his pointing finger for a moment, laughed, and turned away.

"You have a seaman's eyes, Pierre Faidit, and a soldier's ears—and both alike mistrustful. Last night, as we rode to the harbor, you heard hoofs in the dark behind us. I heard no hoofs, and I am not hard of hearing. But what have we to do with other horses or other sails than our own?"

Pierre Faidit turned somber eyes upon his friend.

"How many ships, Thomas Becket, sail from Normandy to England these days?"

"Why, few that are honest, that is true," Becket conceded; and his voice was now a little uneasy. "Eustace and his freebooters have swept Duke Henry's merchantmen from the seas. But you do not think—"

"This is the year of our Lord 1151, and mid-Winter at that," the soldier interrupted. "Norman shipmen are bold to face the Winter sea, but not the Winter sea and Count Eustace's rovers together. I think that no ship drives from Normandy to England these days without a mighty errand—and the mightiest errand I know is that on which we sail.

"Mark well: If we land at Winchelsea tomorrow night, yonder swift-winged craft will make port a good five hours before us. Hoofs behind us in the dark; sails behind that leap ahead; and our business is one that craves secrecy. So much hangs on our success that we but do our duty in suspecting, with or without proof, the least trifle that can not be innocently explained!"

Both men were silent for a space; but gloom gathered deeper on the handsome features of Pierre, and he resumed thoughtfully—

"Your man Loriot has a bad eye; I will wager he was born to be hanged."

"What? Arnolt Loriot! He is true as steel."

Becket's voice quivered with indignation.

"Yet you never saw him till he came to Caen a fortnight past?"

"He bore the archbishop's letters to me—enough in itself to prove him honest. The holy Theobald employs no man whom he has not watched, whose heart he has not searched, long and carefully. Did not the archbishop's message bid me have full confidence in Loriot? And now the man lies sick in Caen, worthy of pity rather than mistrust."

Pierre shook his head.

"Remember, Thomas, that the parchments you bear, if they fall into wrong hands may cost us our lives and Duke Henry his crown. Nor will I take any man's opinion of another against my own skill in reading faces, on which my life has more than once depended."

"Nay, Pierre! I have been too secret for any spy to learn our plans, or what we carry. Only the duke, Archbishop Theobald, ourselves, and Loriot know our errand; and I will vouch for Loriot. By tomorrow night you will have so much to think of that you will forget your fears."

"BECKET?"

"Aye, your Grace, and a soldier called Pierre Faidit."

The old archbishop leaned back in his great armchair, his wrinkled face lighting up with pleasure.

"Pierre Faidit? That must be he whom men call Pierre de l'Espée—Pierre of the Sword. A good man, whom honest men praise for his stanch loyalty, and whom even the evil admire for his shrewd brain and wondrous swordsmanship. Aye, I remember—Thomas Becket told me, a month hence, that he was in Duke Henry's service.—Good! Admit them! And look ye, Canon Matthew, that the door is well closed when they have entered."

Theobald of Canterbury, Primate of England, was a man far gone in age, wrinkled and yellow like old parchment, and with hands that trembled. The firelight, playing on his features, illumined a face at once shrewd and fine—the face of a saint whose holiness was well supported by a strong, masterful soul, and directed by the penetrating insight of a powerful mind.

Never, for all that he stood on the brink of the grave, had the great archbishop been as powerful as now. He and King Stephen each had a hand on the helm of England's fate; and it was hard to say whose grip most nearly directed England's course.

Strong in battalions, weak in character, the usurper Stephen faced a crisis in his unrighteous career. Unable to control his own turbulent barons; forced to retain their loyalty by giving them free license to plunder and torture the poor; haunted by his evil conscience, which constantly reminded him how wrong-fully he withheld England's throne from its rightful ruler, Duke Henry of Normandy, his last years embittered by the shameful crimes of his only son, Count Eustace, Stephen still toiled desperately to retain the throne and bequeath it to that son, unworthy as he was.

And with every fresh tiding of new deeds of violence, blood, and shame committed by Eustace's brutal men-at-arms, King Stephen forgave his son anew, saying to himself that if Eustace reaped the whirlwind, it was he, Stephen, who had sown the wind by usurping Duke Henry's crown. In his determination that his son should succeed him, Stephen was prepared to make any sacrifice—even the sacrifice of humbling his pride before the ancient priest, Theobald, Archbishop of Canterbury.

For in Theobald's hands, and his alone, both Church and State had entrusted the right to crown kings, and to sanction the choice of a king's successor. This right had been vested in the Archbishops of Canterbury since England first became Christian; neither baron nor king dared question it. Therefore Stephen now smiled on Theobald, yielded him power and influence, and prayed him repeatedly to make public proclamation that, when Stephen should die, Eustace should bear the crown.

But Theobald, wily and resolute, evaded every entreaty; and in his heart he was determined that Eustace, the wicked, should never profane the royal scepter with his bloody hands. Even now, as the archbishop waited to receive his visitors, this de-termination cast a stern shadow over the pleasure he felt at their coming.

A tall, thick-set man entered first, his square shoulders and masterful bearing a strong contrast to the humble monk's gown he wore. Swarthy, hawk-featured, with the air of one who is master over himself, he strode across the archbishop's low-ceiled workroom toward the great hearth. But even as he reached the armchair where Theobald sat, he threw himself on his knees, and kissed the hem of Theobald's robe.

"Master!" he cried.

With exceeding joy the archbishop embraced the man who for years had been his devoted servant and secretary, almost his right hand.

"Becket! Thomas Becket!" he greeted fondly. "My son!"

But now the second man knelt for his blessing: a soldier in full mail, huge of limb, darkly handsome of face; a man in whose eyes the power of command was blended with the pure fire of knightly honor. He kissed the prelate's proffered hand; and Theobald blessed him.

"You are Pierre Faidit?" he said. "Ah, I have heard of you, my son. Like the city builded on a hill, like the bright candle in the Savior's parable, your deeds are seen by all men, and give light to the feet of them who would walk the paths of honor. Aye, I know how many years you served Alphonse the Great of Toulouse, how noble a name you won by your loyalty to him.

"Now he is dead, and you serve Henry Plantagenet, Duke of Normandy, Anjou, and Brittany—who, please God, will one day be King of England. When that day comes, Pierre, I hope to see the golden spurs of knighthood on your heels, for richly have you deserved such reward."

Before Pierre Faidit could thank the archbishop for his welcome, the latter turned back to Becket.

"What brings you here so soon, Thomas?" he asked.

Becket stared in surprize.

"Your letters, holy father. Did you not send for me through your servant, Arnold Loriot?"

The archbishop's brow clouded.

"Eighteen days ago," he answered slowly, "Arnold Loriot, my servant, was found murdered in a waterside tavern in Winchelsea!"

Becket cried out in consternation.

"Then the messenger who came to me, who called himself Loriot—" he stammered. "The letters he bore, sealed with your own seal—"

"What said those letters, Thomas?" the archbishop questioned sharply.

"One contained the names, written in your own hand, of such nobles as still hesitated to pledge themselves to Duke Henry, though favorable to his cause. First among those names was the Earl of Lincoln. The second letter urged me to come to you swiftly, to report the progress of Duke Henry's preparations."

"Enough! Those were the same letters I entrusted to Loriot, to be brought to you; and they seem not to have been changed. But they have been opened, read, and resealed, doubtless by him who bore them to you; for the very day Loriot left me, my private seal was stolen. He who passed himself off for Loriot before you was—"

"A spy in Stephen's service!" Thomas cried. "Ah, Pierre, you were right! The hoofs behind us in the dark—the ship that made Winchelsea before us—"

"Then the false Loriot came not with you?" Theobald questioned.

"Nay, father; he gave himself out for sick, and tarried behind in the duke's castle at Caen. But when we were gone—"

"When we were gone," Pierre took up the word, "he crept from the castle, trailed us to the port, and took a swift ship to England! Now he has doubtless reported our arrival to Stephen, who will find a place for us in his deepest dungeons!"

Theobald sighed wearily.

"Let me examine the papers you have from the duke," he said.

Thomas handed him two parchments, which the archbishop read and returned.

"For thirteen long years," he uttered slowly, "I have watched and planned and prayed for the unworthy Stephen's overthrow. For two years, Thomas, you have gone back and forth between me and Duke Henry, or fared up and down in Henry's cause, winning over the nobles, spending my gold and his to raise a party in his favor. When I sent Loriot to you, I hoped the time had come when Henry might land in England and claim his crown. These documents you have shown me prove that I was right. But now a spy of Stephen's has put all our efforts in jeopardy; for we dare not hope that the pretended Loriot carried my messages to you without having first shown them to Stephen. Now the king knows of both our conspiracy and my own connection with Henry's cause; and his spy has surely brought him news of your arrival. Stephen has only to seize both you and me to destroy all our hopes—provided he acts before you can carry out the errand for which I sent for you. There is but one chance; Stephen is not a man who acts quickly or resolutely, and his son Eustace is away in France."

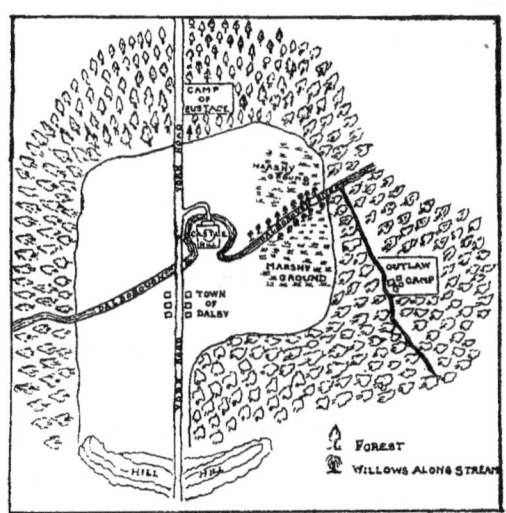

"So the pretended Loriot told me," Thomas rejoined. "It is true, then?"

"Aye, though I can not guess why the king's spy should have told you. It is public knowledge that Eustace is in Boulogne. If you can reach the more important of the men whose names I sent you; if you can win them over to take arms for Henry before Eustace returns or Stephen makes up his sluggish mind, we may yet triumph. But remember: Eustace is swift, bloody, ruthless! If he comes back before you have finished your work—"

"Then," Thomas decided quickly, "Pierre and I will ride north to the Earl of Lincoln at once. Of all who have not yet pledged themselves to Duke Henry, he is the mightiest. I have talked with him before, but he has always hesitated. If we can win him, all the North will join us; and with those who have already come over to us in the South, we shall have so strong a party that Henry's mere appearance on English soil will strike the crown from Stephen's head!"

Theobald smiled.

"You speak wisely," he commended. "Ride to Lincoln, as fast as ye may—there is not an hour to be lost. Your monk's robe and Pierre's sword may suffice—with proper caution—to protect you. But first, what answer have you brought me from the Pope?"

From under his robe Thomas brought forth a parchment scroll, with the heavy papal seal. Taking it, the archbishop broke the seal and read. His face alight with new happiness, he struck a silver bell that hung by his chair. Canon Matthew entered. To him Theobald delivered the parchment.

"Make a copy of this at once!" he commanded. "With your own hand! Let no other know what is here written!"

Turning to the two before him, he whispered cautiously:

"King Stephen has striven with all his might to wring my consent to his son Eustace's succession. But, knowing well Eustace's evil heart, I have delayed. Meantime I sent a petition to the Holy Father in Rome, praying his sanction for my real purpose—to proclaim not Eustace, but Duke Henry of Normandy, as successor to Stephen on the throne of England. And here, praise God, in this message you have brought me, his Holiness has given me full authority. Nay, more; he has himself named Henry, King of England! Wait, Thomas, till Matthew has the copy ready; show it to the Earl of Lincoln, and he may then dare to join us!"

"The earl is a timid man," Thomas answered. "But, by the rood, I think the papal sanction will convince him!"

"So think I. The earl greatly fears Count Eustace, whose name for savage cruelty is so terrible. But, Thomas—is it not possible that the murderer of Loriot, who seems to have followed you to England, may be Eustace's man, not the king's? If so, then Eustace will soon return in person. The more need for you to complete your task in haste. You must win the earl at once, and then seek safety in Normandy."

"I will," Thomas smiled. "I have a noble helper in Pierre. When I told the duke how Lincoln hesitated, he answered: 'Take Pierre with you. His shrewd head will find a way to win him.'"

"Good! See to your horses, my sons; Matthew will have the copy ready presently. Avoid the king's men; ride warily and fast, for the fate of England rides with you!"

YOUNG DUKE HENRY PLANTAGENET had dealt a master-stroke when he sent out his trusted squire, Pierre Faidit, to aid Becket in gaining the allegiance of the least vicious among the English nobles. Henry counted heavily on the justice of his cause, on his claim to the throne as the lineal descendant of William the Conqueror; he counted yet more heavily on the detestation in which Stephen and his son were held among such of the knights and barons as still held their honor dear; but most heavily of all he relied on the adroitness of his envoys.

Thomas Becket, trained under the wise archbishop, was a student of men's minds and hearts, a statesman; he knew how and what to promise, when to suggest a threat, what strings to touch lightly and what strings to strike with heavy hand. But there was something he lacked, which the equally shrewd Pierre could supply—the appeal that lay in Pierre's reputation as the foremost professional soldier between the Rhine and the Atlantic.

Soldiers themselves, the Anglo-Norman nobles would be more drawn toward Henry by the personality and the military arguments of Pierre than by any other consideration.

Straight for Lincoln the two friends rode but luck was against them. The roads were almost impassable; though it was only mid-February, a protracted thaw set in, so that their horses were again and again almost swallowed up in the mud. Moreover, King Stephen seemed to have waked to more than usual vigilance.

Whenever the roads turned out better than average, the glitter of lance-points warned the travelers that king's troops might be ahead. What with the mud, the swollen streams, and royal spearmen, it was late March before Pierre and Thomas were within a day's ride of Lincoln. Moreover, the early season meant renewed activity on the part of highwaymen, who lurked in the long stretches of forest that then covered a large part of England.

Such brigands in great numbers were created by the bitter times. Peasants fleeing from death at the hands of cruel masters; soldiers, discharged unpaid—for Stephen's funds were low— even the poorer knights, whom the great barons regarded as their natural prey—all these turned bandit, and infested the lonelier roads singly or in bands. Such men Thomas feared almost as much as he feared the royal troops; for in his saddlebags he bore large sums of gold entrusted to him by Duke Henry, to buy such aid as promises could not win.

"Yet true it is," Thomas mused aloud, "that there is more honor nowadays in being a thief than in being a baron. For the thieves are dishonest by necessity, and the barons by pure greed of gain. Many a good heart beats under a thief's homespun, but there are few such under noblemen's hauberks."

Pierre reined in, and eyed his comrade sternly.

"You have said such things as these ever since we set foot in England," he said. "And how many times, as we rode through villages burned and ravaged by greedy barons, or by king's troops, have I seen the tears come into your eyes! Thomas, you are a man of your class—better than most at heart, but with the fine gentleman's way of seeing things.

"Now I am peasant-born; and therefore I understand one thing that you, for all your wisdom, can not see: It is not for Henry's sake alone that you are toiling to gain the crown for him; it is even more for the sake of the oppressed English people. You love the folk, commons as well as gentles, and you long to deliver them from their bitter slavery. Why, then, do you look for adherents only among the nobles? Why not turn to the very people you wish to deliver, and persuade them to rise in Duke Henry's name?"

Thomas laughed.

"There speaks the Frenchman. Why, look you, the people are so crushed, so hopeless, so disunited, that no appeal would raise their courage to the point of revolt. The only men among all the common people who would dare strike a blow against Stephen are the outlaws and highwaymen."

"Why not enlist them?" Pierre retorted.

Thomas stared at him, speechless. At last he smote one hand so hard against his thigh that his horse plunged in fright.

"By the mass, Pierre, it is a noble thought! Now I, being born a London merchant's son, naturally look up instead of down; and it never crossed my mind to ask help of the poor and outcast. Why, 'tis among them that our gold would go farthest!"

"Let me carry the gold, then," Pierre advised. "I am both better armed to defend it, and better versed in the ways of common folk, so that I can spend it to better effect. Mayhap your English thieves will even join us for love of one who comes to them with peasant's talk on his lips."

As they spoke, they rode into a little town, where they learned that Earl Robert of Lincoln was even then in his castle of Dalborough, twenty miles this side of Lincoln city. The priest whose hospitality they shared added a friendly caution:

"Ride warily, sirs, through Dalby forest. To the west of the highway all is earl's land, where bandits dare not prowl; but to the east, from Dale Downs to the river, the wood is haunted by Sir Richard Paketon and his outlaws."

"I mind me of that Paketon!" Thomas exclaimed. "Is he not kinsman to the earl?"

"Aye; twenty years since, Sir Richard married the earl's sister. He dwelt in the south then, and was honored for his manly service in the Scottish wars. But five years ago his home was burned by the wild riders of Count Eustace, who shamefully slew his wife and son, and left Sir Richard for dead before his own door. But the knight recovered and came north, where he gathered round him some four hundred broken men, stout archers all. Men say that he and the earl have a secret bargain not to molest each other, so long as neither crosses the other's boundary. Be that as it may, Sir Richard has sworn to take vengeance on Count Eustace; and—help the king's son if he ever strays in the forest hereabouts!"

Pierre's eyes met Becket's.

"Where is this outlaw's camp?" he asked.

The parish priest crossed himself.

"I know not. But if you wander the quarter of a mile in the forest northeast of the Dale Downs you will find him—or he will find you. But take care, for a mailed soldier is rare prey for Paketon's men."

Early in the morning Thomas and Pierre left the village behind; and two hours later they breasted the rise of Dale Downs, whose low, swelling hills ran far out into the forest on both sides of the highway. Here Pierre halted.

"Our ways sunder here, Thomas," he said. "This Paketon is our man. Do you ride on to the earl—yonder is Dalby town, and the fortalice beyond must needs be Dalborough Castle. I will ride into the wood and have speech with Paketon's outlaws."

"But the duke's gold!" Thomas urged. "It will scarce be safe among—"

"You yourself have said that outlaws are honester than barons," Pierre laughed. "Nay, I will use the gold to buy four hundred stout archers for the duke! And bethink you, Thomas: After you have used all your arguments to win the earl, will it not prove the crowning argument if I ride into the castle, stand before you both, and say: 'Lo, Sir Earl, your kinsman, Richard Paketon, has already joined Duke Henry's banner! With them, and your stout men-at-arms, to protect you, what need have you to fear Count Eustace and his bullies?'"

Thomas laughed.

"A good plea indeed, if you ever leave the forest alive."

"Which I will," Pierre retorted. "I ride for Henry's crown and my own gold spurs!"

And he dashed into the forest.

Thomas looked long and anxiously after him; but at last he urged his own mount down the high road toward Dalborough Castle.

The earl's fortress was worthy of his greatness. A high, round tower of thick masonry within a square stone bailey, it crowned a mighty crag that dominated all the valley. On three sides the Dalborough River girdled the crag close, forming a natural moat; on the fourth, or south side, the hill fell sheer in a vertical cliff, which neither horse nor man could scale. The rear wall of the bailey terminated, at each corner, in a high turret which commanded cliff and river with battlements and menacing arrow-slots.

The highway nestled so close to river and crag that missiles hurled from the castle-walls could sweep well across it; and nowhere did the forest approach close enough to the fortress to screen an enemy's attack. The whole valley was almost tree-less for a circuit of a mile from the walls. Beyond that distance, the wood loomed dark and lowering.

To enter the fortress, Thomas must pass the entire west wall—from which helmeted heads peered down upon him—and turn into a private road that wound sharply to the right, approaching the castle from the north. This was the only entrance, guarded by the river. Thomas stopped on the bank.

"Ho!" he shouted lustily. "Open for an envoy from his Grace of Canterbury!"

After a moment's silence, there rose the screaming of iron chains on iron pulleys, and the drawbridge slowly sank till it spanned the stream. As Thomas rode across, the great gate opened.

Through it he rode into a rectangular, roofed court, with massive walls. There was no portcullis, for none was needed. This strong forecourt, or barbican, was a sure defense so long as the drawbridge was raised. Even now, in time of peace, the barbican was filled with mailed men-at-arms, who fell back on both sides to let Becket ride up the wide stone ramp into the great square bailey. A sergeant, taking his horse by the bridle, led him in.

Since the barbican gave on the stream itself, it was level with the valley; but the ramp sloped up to a terraced second level, on which the bailey walls had been erected. The hill had been so graded that a space along the west and south sides was level; and here were the stables and a narrow parade ground. Attended by the sergeant, Thomas crossed the paved court to the stables, leaving his horse in the care of a groom. Straight before him rose the massive round tower, or keep, that formed the citadel.

Once within its portal, which was as strong as the outer gate, he was taken in charge by a second officer, who led him to the earl's own chamber just beneath the battlements. He had waited but a moment when the door opened, and Thomas rose to greet the greatest man in the North.

Robert, Earl of Lincoln, was a man well into middle age, tall, strongly made, and marked with the scars of war. His face was that of a man who knows no physical fear; but the shifting glance betrayed a lack of moral fiber. Loss of life he feared little; but loss of lands or prestige he feared much. He met the archbishop's envoy courteously, but with uneasy eyes.

"Have you not done with me yet, Thomas Becket?" he asked a little wearily.

"No, my good lord, nor ever will, till you are Duke Henry's

man," Becket answered bluntly. "Twice you have given me evasive answers; now I have better hope to win you, for I bring weighty news."

The earl seated himself before a little table, on whose surface his fingers drummed nervously.

"I do not know," he said, "what news can bind King Stephen's hands, or make my walls impregnable to the assaults of his wild son Eustace."

"Eustace is in France," Thomas replied, "where he can neither see nor hear what is done in Dalborough Keep. Will it please my lord to look on these?"

From under his monk's robe he drew a number of parchment scrolls.

"This first," he began, "is an enumeration of the troops, engines, ships, and supplies with which the duke can invade England. The details are in code; but the totals are clear. Duke Henry can count on a well-equipped army of twelve thousand men. That, with the forces already pledged to him in England, will enable him to invade successfully—"

"When? How soon?"

"This Summer!"

The earl's face gleamed with sudden light.

"That is good news!" he exclaimed. "I am Henry's man at heart, as I told you when you came to me last Summer. But I must be sure of success before I march on a road from which there may be no returning."

Becket's lip curled.

"Less powerful men than you have joined us without fear."

"Aye, well they might, with less to lose—"

"And less to gain! Look you, my lord: Count Eustace, and the turbulent barons, have for thirteen years shed so much English blood that it is as if our country bled from a thousand shallow wounds. If you aid Duke Henry, your fame will bring so many other wavering nobles to our side that Stephen will not dare resort to arms, and Henry may become king peacefully.

"Then our country's wounds will be bound up, and she will become whole again. But if you hesitate longer, Henry must come with a force scarce stronger than Stephen's; there will be ruthless civil war, and our already bleeding country will suffer a wound that may strike to her heart! Be bold, and set all on the hazard for such a cause! Here—" he drew forth a larger scroll, the copy of the papal sanction—"here is something to embolden the faintest spirit!"

The earl, who had small skill in letters, went slowly over the copy, while Becket translated its priestly Latin lor him.

"Aye," the earl admitted. "I can make out *Henricus,* which is Henry, and rex, which must mean king, since it stands on all coins minted here in England. This is indeed a mighty document!"

"And one which will bring over many who now waver," Becket reminded him. "Will you, who are greatest, be the last? Small risk will you run, when your mere name will make our cause too strong for Stephen to assail!"

But, seeing hesitation still clouding Robert's brow, he added darkly:

"If you refuse your help, and Henry becomes king without it, you may lose even more than you gain by joining him. Behold!"

He enrolled the last scroll, and handed it to the troubled earl. Even Robert could read it. On the left, one below another, were the names of the principal estates and castles in England; on the right, opposite each of these, were the names and coats-of-arms of knights and noblemen.

"These are the gifts King Henry will give to those who aid him," Thomas explained. "There is your name, my lord, over against that of the most glittering fief in a king's possession— the Dukedom of Northumberland! Think well before you refuse it! Note, too, that your name is written in red—which means that you have not yet taken the step which is to earn you that splendid gift."

For a long time the earl sat in anxious thought; while Thomas, in his inmost heart, prayed that Pierre might come soon with news that Paketon, the outlaw, had brought his four hundred archers to Henry's banner. That surely would turn the scale. Earl Robert was ready to be won, if he could only be sure that he could hold off the vengeful Eustace's forces until Duke Henry came with his host. But it was too soon for Pierre.

Nor was Pierre needed, as it seemed; for the earl looked up with eyes that were resolute at last.

"I am with you!" he exclaimed. "Say to Duke Henry that he may count on me, and on every man who follows me! And it may be—"

A knock sounded at the door.

"Who calls?" the earl cried impatiently.

A hand fumbled with the latch; but, finding the door barred, he who stood without shouted through the panels—

"A messenger from King Stephen, who brooks no delay!"

Instantly Becket snatched up the papers from the table, and hid them under his gown. As he looked up, he caught the look of fear in the earl's eyes, and read the man's timid heart. All his work was lost if the message from the king had to do with the discoveries of the spy who, posing as Loriot, had learned his plans.

"The king's man must not find you here," the earl gasped. "Quick! This way! I will give you my answer later."

Thomas resisted his clutch.

"You have given your answer," he retorted. "A man of honor keeps his word."

But the earl, caught thus in the midst of conspiracy, was too disturbed to heed him. Fumbling with a section of the oaken panels that faced the wall, Robert pressed a spring, and a well-concealed door swung silently into the room, exposing a secret stair within the stonework. Before Thomas could speak again, the earl thrust him within, and closed the panel.

Thomas promptly clapped his ear to the wood. Voices murmured in the chamber beyond; but they were so subdued that he could make out no single word. Long he listened, but in vain.

He had been hurled from the height of hope into despair. Knowing the earl's timidity, his fear of the brutal vengeance of Eustace if he should be known as a friend to Henry, Thomas could not doubt that all was lost. There could be no doubt that the pretended Loriot had revealed to King Stephen the contents of the archbishop's letters—no doubt that Stephen's messenger was sent to persuade or frighten the earl into keeping aloof from Henry's party. For one of those letters had specifically mentioned the need for Thomas to win the earl.

There was only one consolation: Becket himself was safe, if he could remain in his hiding-place till the king's man was gone. Such a man as Earl Robert, confronted with the king's message, would not only refrain from giving Becket up but would deny his very presence in the castle.

Anxious to clear himself from suspicion, he would insist that he had never had any dealings with Henry's agents. And the only evidence against such a denial would be the discovery of Becket in the castle. The earl had only to keep him hidden, and the royal envoy would go back to London convinced that the earl had never harbored an enemy of Stephen's.

It was dark and cold in the secret stairway, and Thomas was not used to inaction. He resolved to explore the stair, in the hope that whatever place it led to—for it must lead somewhere—might yield him some inkling of the messenger's errand.

Cautiously, his fingers touching the wall, he groped his way down step by step. The absolute blackness told him that the stair was built in the inner wall, since otherwise the arrow-slots pierced in the outer face, and giving on the defense-platforms, would allow the daylight to enter.

He had descended perhaps two-thirds the length of the stair when once more he heard muffled voices, but this time below him. Anxiously he felt his way down, till at last he stood on a level stone surface. Now the voices were clear, and two tiny rays of light, close together, filtered in from the inner wall. Peering through the holes from which the light came, he looked into the guard-room on the ground floor of the keep.

At once he understood the meaning of the secret stair. Dalborough keep had been built in the troubled times of Henry I, when many a treacherous noble, false to the king, had been betrayed to that king by his own bribed garrison. This was one of those places of espial from which the lord of a castle, himself unobserved, could see and hear all that his men-at-arms did when they thought him safe in his chamber.

But it was not the earl's men-at-arms who interested Thomas now; it was a group of spearmen, twelve in number, who sat with them, laughing and drinking. These twelve, fully mailed and well-armed, bore on their tunics the badge of King Stephen.

O N C E   W E L L within the forest, Pierre was forced to dismount, and lead his horse. In the disturbed years of Stephen's reign these woods—once a royal forest—had gone untended. The undergrowth was thick, and the lower branches of the trees obstructed the almost obscured paths. Here, under giant oaks and beeches, the sun found scant access; patches of snow still lay here and there, and the chilly air bit through Pierre's mail and clothing.

He took no pains to go quietly. Instead he burst into lusty song, as if the gloomy forest held none but himself. Well he knew that it is not good to ride in unheard and unexpected upon desperate men.

After two hours he came to a brook, which ran roughly at right angles to his course. Here he paused; but reflecting that the brook must ultimately bring him out of the forest, he decided to cross. He had not left the stream three hundred yards behind, when a whistling hum pierced the air, and something thudded close to his right hand. Stopping, Pierre saw an arrow quivering in the bark of a huge beech. Instantly he placed his hands on his horse's neck, well away from his sword hilt.

Gliding like a shadow from the undergrowth, a russet-clad bowman seized his bridle. At almost the same moment strong hands were laid on his shoulders, and Pierre found himself between two sturdy fellows, clad like the first, and like him armed with bow and sword.

With no resistance Pierre let one of his captors unbuckle his belt, and remove sword and dagger. A calm smile rested on his lips as he watched the keen eyes of these fierce-faced men appraise his mighty limbs and the good steel rings of his armor.

"King's man?" one asked him in Norman-French.

"King's enemy," Pierre answered. "You serve Sir Richard Paketon? Good; take me to him."

The outlaw scrutinized him doubtfully.

"Shall we bind him?" he asked of his comrades; but without shifting his eyes from the prisoner.

"Not without blows," Pierre spoke up for himself. "I come as an envoy."

The outlaws exchanged a few sentences in a language Pierre could not understand—English, the tongue of the common folk. At last, with a nod, he who held the horse moved forward. The others urged Pierre to follow.

Their course turned north again, and somewhat east; so that it was half an hour before they reached the stream again, farther down than Pierre had crossed it.

"Here is Swart Beck," one told him. "You shall soon see our master."

For perhaps ten minutes they followed the right bank of Swart Beck, till they came out into a clearing, one side of which was bounded by the brook, across which loomed the primeval forest.

Half-way across the glade, and near the brook, stood a well-made house of logs and thatch, surrounded by many smaller huts of wattle and daub. As Pierre and his captors came out into the sunlight, a throng of armed men, rough, shock-headed archers, ran up to meet them, while others poured from the huts to learn the cause of the uproar.

Roused by the alarm, some one within the large house threw open the door and looked out. Seeing the mailed Frenchman with his captors, he shouted to them in English.

"Come," said one to Pierre. "There is our master."

Thus Pierre first set eyes on Sir Richard Paketon. His first impression was that of two flaming eyes, sharp as swords; and a forest of long white beard and hair. But next he noted the tall, lean body, erect and lithe, with a rippling play of muscle under the wrinkled tunic.

Last of all, as he came closer, Pierre saw how broad and high was the brow, banded with white where the helmet came down; the high, arched nose, and the long, square lines of cheek and jaw. Out of his own knowledge of men Pierre recognized one who would bear no trifling, but must be told the truth straight, swift, entire.

"I am Pierre Faidit," he announced without waiting to be questioned, "called Pierre of the Sword, and squire to Henry of Normandy."

The blazing eyes gazed straight into his own.

"Then why do you not wear his badge?"

Sir Richard's question came like a sword-thrust.

"Because it is not a safe token to wear in Stephen's England."

Paketon smiled frostily.

"What do you want with me?"

"Your aid," Pierre answered bluntly, "and the men who follow you, to help Duke Henry strike the crown from Stephen's head."

"How do I know," the outlaw countered, "that you speak truth? Where are your proofs? The name you say is yours is indeed the name of a man renowned for soldierly prowess and for loyalty; and Henry Plantagenet is a master I would fain serve; but what if you be some swaggering rascal, who has stolen the name of Pierre Faidit, and now bears lying tales to lure me to destruction?"

"I offer you two proofs," Pierre answered. "Ride with me to Dalborough Castle, where you shall find Thomas Becket, with letters to the earl from the Archbishop of Canterbury. Or give me my sword, which your men took from me; strip off my armor, and let any three of your best swordsmen assail me. If they draw a drop of my blood, if I do not disarm them all within the quarter of an hour, hang me for an impostor!"

The old knight laughed aloud.

"Nay, I believe you! Only Pierre of the Sword could stand such a test, or would dare propose it. You may ride back to your master, and tell him that Richard Paketon and his bowmen will fly to his banner so soon as it is spread to the English breeze. Nay, thank me not. I am overjoyed to have so fair a vengeance on Stephen and his accursed son. And, may God give me but one fair sword-stroke at Eustace the Devil!"

Pierre grasped the old man's hand.

"Two things remain," he said. "Your men have removed my saddle-bags, which contain Duke Henry's gold. I crave your leave to give that gold to you to be expended—"

"Not another word!"

Paketon cut him short with a look of fury.

"Have you misread me so foully as to think my sword can be bought? I fight for two things only—honor, and revenge. The very silver that enriches my followers is wrested from the oppressors of the poor, not from honest men."

Pierre's own eyes grew cold, meeting the outlaw's full and hard.

"To be expended," he resumed calmly, "in buying armor for your men, that they may stand more stanchly against Stephen's mailed spearmen. I ask you not to take reward, but to bring my master well-armed allies!"

"It shall be done," the outlaw promised. "Your other wish?"

"Some proof," Pierre answered, "for the Earl of Lincoln, your kinsman, that you are with us."

"That shall you have also. I can not write, but I can send a soldier's token. My kinsman will recognize it, for he himself gave it me long ago."

He took a richly chased dagger from his girdle, and handed it to Pierre.

"Now you had best go; for your friend Becket may have sore need of you."

Pierre stared at him.

"What mean you, sir?" he exclaimed.

"Last night," Paketon answered, "certain of my men went to Dalby Town on my errands. From the village, which lies halfway across the valley, they heard a noise as of many horsemen; and, creeping toward the tumult, they penetrated into the wood east of the town. There they saw a great force of spearmen making camp—seemingly king's men. Whether Stephen hunts me, or whether he hunts you and Becket, I know not.

"In the latter case his troopers could scarce find a better ambush than where they lie, commanding the highroad along which your friend rode toward the castle. It were well for you to reach Dalborough Keep as fast as you may, and there learn whether Becket reached its gates in safety. If not, ride back to me, and my archers will lay a counter-ambush to rescue him."

"By the five wounds!" cried Pierre. "If he is caught, the papers he bears will destroy him, and ruin all he has toiled for! My horse, quickly!"

"Ho! Peter Fox!" Paketon called.

One of the outlaws who had brought Pierre thither ran up, and the old man ordered—

"Fetch Pierre's horse, and go with him."

Mounting, Pierre turned his horse's head straight toward the castle; but Sir Richard caught his bridle.

"Not that way," he warned. "The king's men lie in wait too close to the road; and there is marshy ground all along the river.

To be safe, you must ride north till you are well past the stream, then west to the highway, and so south again to the castle. Farewell!"

Cursing the ill fortune that condemned him to a slow pace through the forest, when Becket's very life, and his master's crown, might even now be in the balance, Pierre rode down along Swart Beck toward the river. The man detailed to guide him clung to his stirrup, and so they came at last to the river and its pebbly ford.

"Here I leave you," the outlaw said. "Across the stream is the earl's land. Ride north for a bow-shot, turn as the forest turns, and strike the road within the forest. So you may keep safely out of sight till you are within two bow-shots of the castle."

With a word of thanks Pierre rode into the stream.

On the other side the wood was much more open and better cared for, as befits a nobleman's preserve. Pierre reddened his spurs and galloped down the long aisles of oak and beech, keeping just inside the shelter of the trees.

His heart was heavy, his nerves tight strung. Well he knew that it was for him and for Becket the ambush was laid. It all hung together with the murder of Loriot, the surreptitious reading of Theobald's letters by the spy who impersonated Loriot, and who must have set Stephen's spearmen on their track. Speed, speed, was essential now.

Pierre must first learn Becket's fate; and if he had not come to the castle, must get word back to Paketon in time for a rescue. If the king's men had seized Becket, they might well get away with their prisoner before rescue could come, for Paketon's unmounted archers could not overtake horsemen.

Nor would it avail anything to attack the royal troops if they had not captured Thomas. That would merely put Stephen on his guard so much the sooner, and perhaps frighten the prudent earl away from Henry's cause. Pierre's first task must be to find whether his friend had reached the castle.

The early Spring day was waning fast as he rounded the

westerly curve toward the highway. He was still about fifty yards within the forest, and meant to remain thus far from the open valley till he reached the road, which could not be far away now. He spurred his mount again, and bent low over its neck.

The horse burst into splendid speed; but suddenly, in full career, its stride faltered. Half-stumbling, it recovered and plunged on; but Pierre tugged hard at the bridle, brought its head round, and sprang from the saddle. The animal's rocking plunge had told him it was mortally hurt. Even as his feet touched ground, the horse fell, the feathered butt of an arrow protruding from its flank.

Leaping to the nearest tree, Pierre set his back against the mighty trunk and drew his sword. From the forest all around him streamed armored men-at-arms, their mail and leveled weapons gleaming faintly in the half-gloom.

The first attack came swiftly, as soon as the foremost spearmen reached him. They lunged fiercely, but their attack seemed rather an attempt to hold him in play than to kill him. Pierre had no such scruples. Eustace's badge on their breasts was enough to rouse his fury.

As one and another fell before his lightning thrusts, the rest dropped back in consternation. Well out of range of his point, they formed a wall all round him, a wall that became a complete, dense circle as more and more ran up to aid their comrades. No man spoke a word; but the savage faces and the ring of spear points spoke eloquently for them.

Pierre's eyes roved round in vain search for a weak spot in that living wall, for the slightest gap through which he might hope to fight his way. At once he saw how desperate was his plight, saw that he had no choice but to surrender or die fighting. His enemies waited for the hopelessness of the situation to sink into his heart; and at last an officer advanced one pace from the circle of steel.

"Yield, Pierre Faidit!" he commanded.

"In whose name?" the Frenchman retorted. "The king's? Ye seem Count Eustace's men, but the count is in France!"

The officer laughed, and his merriment echoed from a score of bearded lips.

"In France, ha? My master has not been out of England in six months! Well were you duped, you and the knave Becket! My master himself spread the report of his passage to Boulogne, and took good care that his ship was seen to leave Winchelsea as if he were on it. Meantime he lay hid snugly in London, till his agent—who had shown him the archbishop's letters, and then delivered them to Becket to avoid suspicion—came back from Caen with word that you were on the way to Dalborough. Aye, the very moment of your departure from Theobald's presence ye were watched and followed, till your direction was known. Now give up your sword, or you will not live to clasp its hilt again!"

Pierre had already made up his mind to yield. From death there is no return, but from captivity a shrewd man may find a way to free himself. But he played for time, hoping to win further information.

"What will Count Eustace do with me?" he asked, expecting an answer that would challenge all his courage.

"Give you your choice between death by burning and a captaincy in his service! I counsel you to choose his commission. My master rewards good men well, and proud will he be to call Pierre of the Sword his officer!"

"And what of Becket? You have taken him also?"

The officer's eye gleamed wickedly.

"Not yet; but we shall have him soon. Last night, as we lay hid in the wood west of the town, Count Eustace brewed a plan better than our first intent to take you both as you rode toward the castle. We broke camp at midnight, and came here, from whence we could watch for you to enter the castle. We knew not that you would come separately; but as soon as Becket entered Dalborough gate, and had time to come to speech with the earl, my master followed him thither, craving admission as a messenger from the king! By this time he has doubtless caught the two conspirators, Thomas the Traitor and Robert the Malcontent, in the midst of their foul plots! Had he taken Becket alone, he would have had no evidence against the earl; but now he has them both fast!"

"In that case Eustace will scarce leave the castle alive!" Pierre retorted.

"Aye, he will! In cunning he is more than a match for Duke Henry's jackals. But come, throw down your sword! Time presses!"

Silently Pierre unfastened his belt and threw it, with his dagger, at the officer's feet. His sword followed, then Paketon's poniard. The hostile men-at-arms ran in, seized him and stripped off his mail, and searched his clothing.

"He bears nothing!" one cried; but their captain merely nodded. "Then Becket has the papers," he answered. "Our lord will know how to win both them and him! Bind the prisoner!"

The spearmen obeyed. Without loss of time they lashed Pierre hand and foot, and bound him to the tree.

"You have the wit of the fiend himself, Pierre Faidit!" the officer jibed. "Men tell of the prisons from which you have escaped, the foes you have befooled; but from me you will not escape! Here, Jaques, Lenoir! Stand guard over him! And look to it that he does not so much as breathe without your seeing him, for he is cunning as Lucifer! If he gets away, ye shall burn over a slow fire!"

Two burly spearmen sat themselves down, one on either side of Pierre. As soon as they had taken their places, with their weapons leveled at the captive, their comrades melted into the wood. Only the officer tarried.

"One thing, Pierre Faidit: Often have I heard of this sword of yours, with which you have done wonderous deeds. I would fain have it for myself. If you accept my master's offer of life and a commission, I dare not keep your sword without your consent."

"Speak a good word to your master for Becket," Pierre answered heavily, "and you may have the sword!"

"I will, though it is useless. The count has sworn that Becket shall die by the torment!"

Snatching up the sword, he vanished after his men.

From the forest Pierre could hear the tramping of horses, the clatter of mail, and the buzz of voices; but nothing could be seen. Only by turning his head—and that was painful, so tight was he bound—could he see the men who watched him. One of them turned upon him angrily.

"A fine night's sport you have robbed us of!" he grumbled. "It is ill biding here with you, while our fellows have the taking and the loot of a rich castle!"

Pierre's heart beat violently. So this was Eustace's plan! Eustace himself was in the castle to surprize Becket and the earl together—doubtless in the hope that by laying accusation against the earl he could win from his royal father a grant to the rich fief of Lincoln; or perhaps he meant to use the castle to drive a ———'s bargain with the earl. When the spurious Loriot showed Eustace the archbishop's letters, the count had for a moment held in his hands precious proof of the plot between Duke Henry and the archbishop; but he had been forced to let his proof go, in order that those very letters might lure Becket to England and into his toils.

Now, if Eustace could seize the castle and the earl's person as well as Becket, he could force the earl himself to turn Crown's evidence against both Becket and the archbishop. To convict the mighty prelate of treason mighty proof was needed; and Eustace might well hope to buy the earl's testimony by offering to pardon him and restore his castle. And now, by some foul trick, the count's troopers were to make matters certain by seizing castle, Becket, earl, and all! But how Eustace could prevent the earl's men from taking his life when his trick became apparent, Pierre could not understand; nor did he dare ask the two who guarded him. Their suspicions must not be roused, for something might yet be done with them.

Long and despairingly he pondered, without finding any way out either for himself or for Becket. All seemed hopelessly lost. With Becket and the earl in the hands of Eustace's butchers, and Becket's papers captured, Duke Henry's cause was ruined. Not only the Earl of Lincoln, but every knight and noble whose name was on his lists would lose lands or life; and the party in England that favored Henry would be broken. And for Becket, and Pierre himself, nothing would remain but a shameful death.

Not for an instant did Pierre consider saving himself by taking service with Eustace. He had grown to manhood under the banner of a man who held honor above all things on earth; and the ideals of Alphonse of Toulouse had become his own. He would die a thousand deaths rather than stain his honor with treason to Duke Henry, rather than doom himself to a life of sin and shame such as Count Eustace demanded of his followers. But worse than death for himself was the fate that overhung his friend, the loss of England's crown to his master. And all this must come; there was no help.

"THERE WILL be wine and gold in Dalborough Keep," the soldier Jaques muttered.

"Be silent, pig!" Lenoir snarled at him. "Why speak of that which is not for us? If we get the licking of the empty pot we shall be lucky!"

A sudden ray of hope shone in on the black gloom that oppressed Pierre's heart. With tense eagerness he ventured a question.

"Your master will not be so mad as to let you assail now, while he is in the earl's hands?"

Jaques snorted.

"Aye, he will! The assault will begin when all is properly dark. But he runs no risk; be sure of that."

"When all is dark!"

It was almost dark now. Allowing for an hour or two more, so that the deeper blackness of advanced night might conceal the treacherous approach of the attacking force, there was still all too little time for Pierre to venture anything, even if he were not helpless. The hour of doom was drawing on fast, when any help, when the shrewdest plan, would come too late.

But the word "gold," as it had fallen from Jaques' lips, had brought a glimmer of hope. Pierre's nimble brain worked on that hint, till at last a scheme developed full-rounded in his mind. But it must be put into instant effect; it must work with absolute smoothness, if it were to succeed. Yet in it alone was any hope.

"If you are the prudent, ready lads you look to be," he muttered softly, so that his voice barely reached his guards, "you may have rarer sport and richer loot this night than any castle can bring you!"

Lenoir got up, and kicked him heavily in the side.

"You can not make fools of us!" he growled. "Did not Captain Alain warn us against your tricks?"

Pierre forced a low laugh.

"So be it, if you wish to lose your fortune," he whispered. "But you need not strike a man bound whom you would not dare face free."

Lenoir raised his fist, but the other guard held him back.

"Let him alone," he protested. "Did you not hear Alain say that Count Eustace will give him a chance to join us, and a commission? You would be finely served, if Faidit should come to be captain over you!"

"I see well," Pierre chuckled, "that one of you has sense. Be assured, Lenoir, that I shall ask to have you in my troop when I accept the count's commission!"

"I knew it," Jaques muttered. "What man would not prefer a merry life to a bitter death? When you have your captaincy, good sir, remember Jaques, who would not see you mishandled."

"I will not forget you," Pierre assured him. "Moreover, I will forgive your comrade, if he and you will do a service for me."

"No service," Jaques himself broke in suspiciously. "We will not let you go. Count Eustace would destroy us!"

"I do not ask you to let me go," Pierre retorted. "Have you not yourself said that a merry life is better than death? You have seen the common armor I wear, and can judge that Duke Henry's service is a lean one. And I have seen the jewels your Captain Alain wears. Truly Count Eustace is a kind master! Nay, do not let me go, for I do not wish it!"

"What then?" Lenoir broke in. "You spoke of loot?"

"Aye did I! The service I ask is one you can do easily; but the reward is great. It will mean that you must leave me unguarded; but you need not fear to leave a bound man; and your officer is busy marshaling his men for the assault. Moreover, I will remember your good offices when I have the count's commission."

"What is this service that means loot?" the two men asked together.

"This," Pierre explained: "On my way hither I heard that you lay in ambush about the castle; and to be sure against loss I left a great sum of the duke's gold—"

"Gold!" the ruffians gasped. "Where?"

"In safe keeping," Pierre resumed. "Now, being bound here, I can not get it again. If your master bids you ride away as soon as the castle is taken, I may never see it more. Or if he, or your comrades, hear of it, the share they will give you will be small. But if two good fellows would slip off through the dark, go to the hiding-place, and fetch the gold, I would share it equally with them."

"Where is it?" the two asked with feverish greed. "How much? Is it near enough to fetch back here before our captain returns from taking the castle?"

"Enough to make the three of us rich for life. You can fetch it, and return, in two hours. It will take longer than that to storm the castle."

"Where? Where?"

"I left it in a house in the forest, southeast of the river," Pierre answered, "in the care of an old man. Surely you two stout carles can overpower an old dotard, and fetch the gold here before your captain returns!"

For a moment there was silence, broken only by the covetous mutterings of the two spearmen, Pierre waited in the tensest anxiety. Yet he need not have doubted the outcome. Such men, without scruple or virtue, held to their master by fear and greed rather than loyalty, could not resist the golden bait. Lenoir rose swiftly, disappeared with cautious steps among the trees, and returned.

"All is well," he reported. "Alain indeed marshals the companies for the assault. No one will see or know."

If Pierre had been able to read their minds, he would have seen how they wavered between two courses; to go for the gold, fetch it back, and divide with Pierre when he should have been taken into their lord's favor and service; or to take all the gold for themselves, desert, and flee far away where neither Pierre not Eustace could ever find them. And they decided, each in his own dark heart, for the second course. For a little while they whispered together; then Lenoir spoke up—

"We will fetch it for you; but we need better directions."

Swiftly Pierre expounded to the two rascals the way to—Sir Richard Paketon's camp. So clear were his directions that even a child could not have missed the way. Nor did he fail to caution them against a short cut through the marsh. He wanted them to reach Sir Richard, and he did not care if they never came back.

And every word he said to them was true. The trap they entered so eagerly was set without falsehood, baited with their own greed.

"We go!" Jaques told him; and the two faded into the wood.

IN THE same moment Alain, who was in command of the assault, received the report of two scouts who had crept up, in the darkness, to the castle moat.

"The drawbridge is not yet lowered," they reported. "We were not seen, nor is there any trace that we are suspected; but the time has not come."

A hum of disappointment rippled over the waiting men-at-arms, as they stood gathered in companies at the edge of the forest.

"Then we must wait," Alain answered. "Count Eustace hoped to have all ready for us by an hour after dark; so the way should be clear now. But we can not strike till the moat is bridged for us. Go back, lads; creep close, and watch well. As soon as the drawbridge falls, speed hither, and we will storm."

But the waiting columns stood long in their places, fretting with impatience; and for two full hours no further word came from their scouts.

CONVINCED THAT he himself was safe, Thomas Becket had only one fear—that Pierre Faidit would arrive before the king's envoy left the castle. In his dark hiding-place he could not tell how the time passed, but day must be waning. Pierre's coming would ruin all. As soon as the gate was opened to him, Stephen's spearmen would seize him, and the royal envoy would guess that Becket too was in the castle. Their safety depended on the messenger's leaving before Pierre came in sight. As this thought grew upon him, Becket became alarmed.

As he pondered the situation, he groped his way back up the stair, resolved to listen once more behind the earl's panels. But the murmur of voices went on and on, too low to be understood. If only the messenger would go!

As if in answer to his wish, Thomas heard a chair scrape on the stone floor, and right after it the clank of mailed feet. Then came the sound of the heavy door, closing hard. Shaking with excitement, Thomas made his way down again as fast as he could in the dark, hoping to get a glimpse of the royal envoy through the peepholes, as he departed.

He had hardly taken up his position when the mailed feet clanged on the threshold of the guard-room, and Earl Robert, accompanied by a man in full armor, entered from the main stairway. Eagerly Thomas peeped in upon them, his eyes seeking the envoy's face. But the man's features were so concealed by the nasal of his helmet, and the cheek-pieces of ring mail, that he was unrecognizable across the wide guard-room.

As he came in, however, the twelve soldiers of his escort rose, shoving back their ale-mugs; and they seemed to glance at the envoy, and at each other, as if something was expected of them. But it was the earl who made the mystery clear.

"I tell you before your men, my lord, that I take this ill of you," he said querulously. "You enter my gates not openly and frankly, but under a false badge and playing a false part. Not till you are alone with me do you unwrap your cloak from your face and reveal yourself; and then your first words are an accusation of disloyalty!"

The envoy's answer was mild enough, his voice meek and courteous:

"I pray your forgiveness, Robert. You have convinced me of your good faith. I take your word that the men I seek are not under your roof."

Becket's heart beat so loud that it seemed the whole guard-room must hear it. No need now to see the pretended envoy's face—he had heard that voice many a time at Stephen's court, when he had visited there with the archbishop. The king's messenger was the king's son, Eustace, whom he had believed absent in France! Now, if Pierre came, all was lost indeed—unless Eustace went speedily. But that hope died soon.

"If you will permit me, Robert," Count Eustace resumed, "I will sup with you before taking the road again; and while your cook is preparing, I will make a survey of your castle, that I may report to my father how well you hold it for him."

As he spoke, his eyes ran restlessly about the room, as if to spy out some secret.

Somewhat confusedly the earl assented. He could scarce refuse without revealing too openly his anxiety to be rid of his perilous guest.

And now Becket was torn by fresh pangs of fear; Pierre must certainly come before Eustace was ready to go. Even if he did not, Eustace had not finished with Dalborough Castle. His wish to survey the place was a poorly concealed pretext; he still believed that Pierre and Thomas were hidden somewhere within its walls, and meant to find them.

What would he do when he failed to find them? He could not bluntly accuse the earl of hiding them, in the face of the earl's denial. Robert of Lincoln was not too proud to lie to save himself, but he would be forced to resent a charge of falsehood. And Eustace had too few men with him to use force.

But Thomas was convinced that the matter would not end so easily; he knew Eustace too well. He had studied his enemies carefully, both King Stephen and his son; had met them often both at London and at the palace in Winchester. He knew their methods, their characters.

Eustace, for all his almost insane cruelty, was cool, cunning and persistent. Whatever object he had in view he pursued with unrelenting determination. No, Eustace would not give up his hunt for the men his spy had betrayed to him, even if the closest search proved vain. If Thomas knew his man Eustace would not leave Dalborough till he had won his purpose—till both Becket and Pierre were in his hands.

Reading through the man's motives to his probable actions, Thomas felt a sure premonition that, failing to find his prey, Eustace would attempt some startling coup—would perhaps even attempt to take the castle, that he might search it at leisure, even if he had to tear down stone from stone. That was Eustace's way.

If it came to that, Thomas was caught, and Pierre would be caught too. Safe in his hiding-place, so long as the earl kept his head, Thomas was caught like a rat in a trap if Eustace found some way to make himself master of Dalborough. Such things had happened—happened more than once, in that stormy age. Treacherous cunning might well succeed where more honest methods failed. If Thomas were caught, and his papers found on him—

Something must be done, and quickly—something that would give Thomas a chance to watch, to detect, to forestall his enemy's plots. Eustace would hardly have come on so important an errand with but twelve men, especially if he meditated force as a last resort.

Shut up where he was, and in his present garb, Thomas could do nothing. Swiftly he came to a resolve. He stole up the stair, and pushed at the panel that shut him off from the earl's chamber. Having been in that room already, and seen no Becket there, the count would scarce look there again.

The panel would not move; and Thomas ran his hands all round its frame in patient, systematic search. At last it gave, and opened wide.

Two candles burned low in the earl's chamber. This was ominous; it must have been dark long for the lights to burn so far down. But the room was empty; and Thomas, tiptoeing to the door, shot the bar. He now searched through the room for what he sought, and knew would be there—a chest of arms.

At length he came upon it in the recess which held the earl's high bed. Throwing up the cover, he searched through the chest till he found a plain suit of mail, a helmet, and a heavy sword. Stripping off his robe, he donned the mail quickly, stuffed his monk's gown into the chest, and closed the lid.

Now he was as well masked as Eustace; his features hidden by nasal and mail, he could pass—especially in poor light—for one of the garrison. The earl's men numbered fully three hundred, so it was not likely that the earl himself would pick him out from all his men-at-arms. And the spot where he planned to watch was one where he might masquerade with little fear—the battlements, where he could keep out of the torchlight a good part of the time.

Unbarring the door, he stole out into the corridor. Eustace and the earl might be anywhere about the castle; he would do well to reach the tower top swiftly. The corridor was empty, save for a single spearman who stood under a torch at the entrance to a side passage. With a nod, Thomas went by him into the passage, which led to one of the defense-platforms for the third story. From this platform, with its loopholes, its piles of stones, its sheaves of arrows, and its half dozen men-at-arms, a stair in the wall led to the battlements.

As Thomas mounted the steps, a sergeant hailed him:

"What now? The guard does not shift for half an hour!"

"Earl's order," Thomas answered; and none challenged him further.

All was dark out on the plain, save for a few twinkling lights to the south, in Dalby Town. A few scattered torches burned in their cressets along the merlons; but Thomas avoided these, though even in their light only his eyes and cheek-bones could be seen.

Only a few sentinels paced along the parapet. The earl was at peace with all his neighbors, and strict discipline and vigilance were not needed. There was a strong guard in the barbican, but most of the garrison were in the keep guard-room or in the bailey.

Thomas greeted the sentries curtly, muttered, "Earl's orders," to each, and at once devoted himself to a keen, close scrutiny of the dark plain beyond the river. But the distance and the dark were enough to hide an army.

That was just what Thomas feared—that they did hide an army—or at least several hundred of the wild riders—half-banditti—that followed Eustace's banner. Slowly he made the circuit of the walls, again and again, watching for the least movement out beyond the gate, or on the plain around. But no sign could he see, either of hostile troops or of Pierre. What could have happened to Pierre?

Becket's uneasiness was by no means allayed. It was good that Pierre had not come, to fall into his enemy's hands; but it were very ill indeed if Paketon's outlaws had slain him. The hours passed; and Thomas kept up his vigil ceaselessly.

The guard had changed long since. Midnight came, and nothing happened. At last torches flickered down in the bailey; and by their light Thomas saw horses being led from the stables that lined the court. Twelve—thirteen horses. Eustace was going, then! But would he go without a shrewd, bold stroke to win his ends?

Swiftly Thomas strode to the stair, and hurried down to the guard-room. If the count did meditate some treachery, there must be at least one watchful pair of eyes on him. In the guard-room, among the earl's men-at-arms, Becket knew himself safe from detection. He was one of many, all armed alike.

The keep gate opened. On each side of it stood a spearman with a torch. Between them walked Eustace and the earl; and Eustace's men followed. A wild fear seized Thomas that the earl would be seized at the barbican, carried off in a wild gallop, and forced to reveal his dealings with Stephen's enemies. But the earl seemed suspicious also, for he accompanied his guest only as far as the arch between bailey and barbican, and there bade him farewell.

Eustace's horses were already at the open gate, and the drawbridge was slowly lowering. Four sturdy soldiers labored at the winches, to keep the heavy bridge from falling too swiftly for the good of its chains.

Mingling with the throng of men-at-arms that pressed about to see the count's departure, Thomas crossed the bailey soon after the count himself; but he did not stop when the earl stopped. With bold assurance he took a torch from a soldier, and advanced into the barbican as if to give Eustace better light to mount by; but he kept his face turned aside.

With a final hand-clasp the king's son turned from his host, found his stirrup, and mounted. His twelve spearmen mounted after him, their horses filling the space between the drawbridge winches and the gate. Fearing an attempt to damage the winches, Thomas looked back toward them; but one by one the count's riders clattered over the threshold on to the drawbridge, and disappeared into the night. Eustace was gone, and no treachery attempted.

Drawing a deep breath of relief, Thomas left the gate and approached the earl. Removing his helmet, he smiled confidently at Robert of Lincoln.

"Becket!" the earl gasped. "What—"

"My lord!" A man-at-arms ran up, his face white with alarm. "Some one has tampered with the winches! They will not turn! The drawbridge!"

The earl hurried into the barbican, Thomas by his side. Two men were straining at each winch in vain efforts to turn the great drums on which the drawbridge chains were wound. The drums did not move; the drawbridge still spanned the river, inviting assault.

"Bar the gates!" the earl commanded.

But Thomas thrust in between the spearmen who sprang forward to carry out the command, crying:

"One moment, my lord. There is no fault with the winches. I myself saw them turn to lower the bridge. The trouble lies outside!"

He rushed through the gate, a dozen men-at-arms at his heels. Running his eyes along the chains, Thomas saw that a massive bar of steel had been thrust through the links of each, at the point where the chains ran through their slots over the pulleys. Till those bars were removed the bridge was hopelessly down. The torches carried by his companions showed the disaster clearly.

There was but one way to remedy it; and that way was at hand. Two tree-trunks, hewn and stripped of their branches, lay one on each side of the gate. By these, unseen in the dark, Eustace's men had reached the chains as soon as the bridge was lowered. By these also Thomas and his assistants must mount to remove the bars. He lifted up one of the trunks, wondering why it should have been left there.

The next instant he learned. No need to take the trunks away; it was hopeless for the garrison to try to remove them. Three of his companions fell to the ground, and a storm of arrows thudded all about the portal. One, glancing off Becket's shoulder-plate, rebounded and buried itself in the neck of the man nearest him. Then the arrows ceased, and there rose the thunder of many charging hoofs.

"In!" cried Becket. "Make fast the gate!"

The men flung themselves inside the barbican; the gate clanged to behind them; and the heavy bars were shot.

Eustace had dealt his stroke swiftly and well. With the draw-bridge down and the moat spanned, he could advance his troops to the very gate, and so swiftly that they would be hammering upon it before the earl could despatch enough men to the battlements to train and man the engines. Nor could the engines be used in the dark upon a swiftly moving force; they required slow, patient adjustment and a fixed target.

A brief defense could be made, with arrows and stones, from the walls; but before such missiles could do much damage to the assailants, the gate must yield to the blows that would be rained upon it. Once in possession of the barbican, Eustace could force the bailey under cover of the barbican walls, and from the bailey assail the keep itself. It was a shrewd, daring plan, well executed.

But when Thomas entered the barbican again he found the earl another man from the timid, shrinking intriguer of the afternoon. In warfare Robert of Lincoln was at home. Already he was buckling on the hauberk that a page had brought him; his commands had been rushed to bailey, guard-room and battlements. Fully six-score men had already assembled in the bailey, and were being rushed to the barbican walls as fast as their sergeants could count out the supplies of arrows for them. Others were running up, clapping on their helmets, trailing spears, adjusting their shield-straps. Eighty men in all were assembled for the first defense of the barbican gate, and swiftly the earl marshaled them before it.

Even as they fell in there came a crash that filled the barbican with its thunder. The great gate quivered and cracked.

"They use the tree-trunks for battering-rams!" Thomas cried; and the earl's command followed swiftly:

"Stand fast, all! Wat, to the walls, and bid them clear those rams away!"

An officer ran up the stair. Again and again the great trunks, impelled by many strong arms, beat upon the gate. A bar burst; two planks shivered. Silent and grim, the ranks within waited for the gate to go, and for the grim flood of points to roll in upon them.

Down the stair rushed Wat again, pale and frightened.

"My lord!" he cried. "Eustace's archers stand off in the dark, and overwhelm the battlements with volley after volley! Our men can not approach the merlons close enough to cast stones upon them who assault the gate!"

With an oath, Earl Robert hastened up the stair. Thomas, who had himself been a soldier, saw well how futile resistance must be. The earl's men would hold their ground, though the gate fell; but the barbican could not hold out against the charge of horse that would pour in over the drawbridge as soon as the gate was down. And the gate must go, since the earl's men could not show their heads above the battlements to cast stones and javelins upon those who wielded the battering-rams. Eustace's bowmen loosed their shafts unseen in the night; the very torches which must be used on the battlements to distinguish the piles of weapons, made a rare target for the hostile arrows.

The earl came down again, his eyes aglow with the flame of battle.

"I have had the torches extinguished," he said. "It will be slow work, fumbling about for missiles in the dark; but better that than to have my walls stripped bare."

A rending crash drowned the last word. Through the weakened gate ripped the butt of a tree, and a wild yell of triumph from without reechoed through the barbican. With a wrenching twist the ram disappeared again; there was a faint sound of running feet; and again the crash of wood on wood. Another plank broke from its iron bands.

"Now!" cried the earl. "Points level; shields lapped!"

The tight-lipped men-at-arms made ready for the falling of the gate, and the storm that must follow.

Something rang loud and hollow on the drawbridge; the blows of the ram ceased.

"Well cast!" Thomas cried. "Your men hold the battlements well!"

But now other arms outside snatched up the broken tree-trunk, and bore its longer section pounding down upon the gate. More stones crashed down from the wall; and somewhere near at hand a full, clear peal rang upon the night.

"Whose horn is that?" the earl cried.

The horn pealed again. Its echoes had not died when the air was filled with a sound like the buzzing of a thousand maddened bees. A yell of mingled rage and pain rose from a score of throats; outside the gate men shouted and cursed; the drawbridge rang hollow under plunging hoofs; and the voice of Eustace bellowed angry commands.

DARK AS it was, Jaques and Lenoir made shift to follow Pierre's directions. They had only to follow the forest's edge to the river, cross at the ford above Swart Beck, and keep on along the brook. But following the brook was not so easy. The trees came to the very brink of the water, and in the thick darkness they could not pick their footing.

"What if 'tis but a fool's errand?" grumbled Lenoir. "A jest of Faidit's?"

"I'll warrant it no jest!" Jaques retorted. "What would he gain by a lie? We shall soon be the richer for a great treasure. Think of that, my lad."

Stumbling over stumps, lashed in the face by undergrowth, plunging into trees, falling now and again into the water in their anxiety not to lose the brook, the two men held doggedly on. But ever and again, as they stumbled over rocks or brought up headlong against some mighty bole, their mail clashed loud; and they quivered with fear lest the sound reach their own officers and so betray their desertion.

"It can not be far now," Jaques muttered. "If—"

"Nay, 'tis not far!" a mighty voice roared in their ears. "Strike a light, Sweyn, and let us look on these prowlers."

Strong hands gripped the two gold-seekers, disarmed them before they could draw and held them fast. Flint clicked on steel; a spark grew to a glow, and was fanned into flame athwart the blackness. The two, palsied by the sudden attack, stared bedazzled into the torchlight, against which heads and shoulders of armed men stood out. Lenoir became aware of a face that stared into his—a fierce face, with menacing eyes, and a bristling white beard. Then the light fell on the badge he wore.

"St. George," the bearded lips rasped. "Eustace's men! Gather fagots, lads, and make a fire!"

The forest rang with a wild hulloo; more torches were kindled, till the forest was spangled with fire. The sound of many men breaking and piling wood crackled through the night. At last a great heap of fagots stood close by the prisoners, and the terrible old man commanded:

"Spread them. Make a bed of coals!"

The torches threw their flaring light on a scene wild and fearful. A score of hands rapidly spread the wood into a long, low platform, at the corners of which little fires grew rapidly to a roaring blaze. At a fresh command the prisoners were stripped and held close to the blaze till the heat singed their skin. Vainly they struggled; vainly they cried for mercy.

"Mercy you shall have on one condition," the bearded man answered; and his voice was vibrant with menace. "Tell me what you seek here and where your master is. Speak truth, and all the truth; or when those flames sink down to coals you shall roast to ashes!"

Jaques and Lenoir sought futile counsel in each other's pallid face. The voice that menaced them was so pregnant with doom, so pitiless, that there was no hope of its owner's relenting. Nor had they the spirit to resist such a threat. Too often had they themselves inflicted the torture by fire not to know its horrors to the full. The cries of their own victims rang again in their ears. In their extremity of terror, they saw once more the writhings of helpless men and women on whom they had helped to execute the vengeance of Eustace. And just such torment awaited them unless they obeyed their captor to the uttermost.

"Mercy, mercy!" they wailed. "We will tell all!"

And they told all, with skilful prompting: first their own quest for gold, at Pierre's instigation; and now it was borne in on them with horrible certainty that the helpless old man they had expected to plunder was the very tyrant who now held them in his hands. The clatter of their stumbling progress had betrayed them to his sentinels; and, suspecting an attack from some source, he himself had come out to seize them. Their captor also understood, for he flung back his head and laughed a terrible, silent laugh.

"A rare trick, by the rood!" he cried. "Faidit is worthy his reputation! But what more, fellows? Your master's business here!"

The sight of the glowing coals forced an answer. Much as they feared to betray the pitiless Eustace, they feared torture more. Eustace was at a distance; the bed of flame was at their very feet.

Swiftly and fully they told how the king's son, learning from a spy in his pay that two of Duke Henry's agents were on their way to the earl, had reached Dalby before Faidit and Becket, and planned to capture them in the castle. How Pierre had ridden into their ambush; and Becket would soon be seized in the assault that was doubtless even now under way against the castle.

"——'s blood!" cried Sir Richard. "And we idle here, while the earl suffers treacherous attack! To the glade, lads!"

"And these?" an outlaw questioned.

The old man turned on the two men-at-arms.

"Were you at the burning of Paketon Tower five years since?" he questioned fiercely.

His glaring eyes forced them to speak truth; nor indeed did they know the name of him who questioned them.

"Aye, dread lord," Jaques answered. "We were. Our master there punished Richard Paketon for refusing him moneys—"

"Thank —— for this day!" the old man cried. "I am Richard Paketon! As I take vengeance now on you, I hope ere long to take deeper vengeance on your master!"

His sword gleamed in the firelight, once, twice; and they who sought gold found death.

H A L F A N hour later long lines of bowmen crept from the shelter of the forest into Dalby plain just below the marshy land south of the river. Their russet garb, the black night, and the fringe of willows along the stream screened them, so that they were invisible from the castle.

"You have your orders," Sir Richard admonished them. "Each man take his place as fast as he reaches the ground; but do not loose till ye hear my horn."

The lines of bowmen stretched out, tailed off, and scattered in the darkness. Other lines, formed in the wood, took another direction.

As soon as he had gathered his four hundred outlaws about the great fire in his camp Paketon had divided them into two companies, and given each company precise orders. With no mail to weigh them down, to catch the glimmer of the faint starlight, or to betray them with its clanking, they hastened silently to the posts their master had assigned.

One company crossed the valley between town and castle, and a little beyond the road turned north. Its orders were to take its position just west of the point where the castle road turned off the main highway, and lie flat in the dark till the signal was given them to rise. The second company, led by Sir Richard in person, sped north through the wood by the same route Pierre had taken that afternoon, and so aimed to creep up on the rear of Eustace's camp and line of attack.

"Thank Heaven, we are not too late," Paketon panted as he sprang into the trampled glade where Eustace had encamped. "Ha! Their trumpet even now sounds the attack!"

So it was; expecting to find Pierre and Becket in consultation with the earl when he entered the castle, Eustace had hoped to bully the earl into surrendering them at once; or otherwise, he had planned to leave soon after dark. In that case, scouts from his following were to creep up at dark, spike the drawbridge as soon as it was lowered for his departure, and so pave the way for his assault.

But failing to find his quarry, Eustace had delayed to hunt for them through the castle, and still further delayed to give a friendly color to his search by becoming the earl's guest at supper. Thus the efficacy of Becket's hiding-place had both forced him to assail the castle, and delayed the assault long enough for the outlaws to come up and lay a counter-ambush.

A moment after the count's trumpet came the clank of mail and the pound of hoofs swiftly eating up the distance between the plain and the drawbridge. With deeper night his horsemen had advanced to the open, formed in column under cover of dark, and made ready for the swift gallop which should bring them to the gate before the garrison could prepare adequate defense. Behind his horse came a small body of his archers, on foot. Now rang the shouts of Eustace's sergeants, relaying his commands.

"Now we must strike quickly," Paketon cried, "or my kinsman will surrender Becket to save himself! Advance, lads, and steal up to close range!"

"First set me free," a voice sounded close at hand. "And thanks for swift help!"

"Faidit!" the old man exclaimed. "Where are you? Ah!"

His groping hand found Pierre's shoulder; quickly he cut the Frenchman's bonds. Pierre strove to rise, but his limbs were cramped, and he fell to chafing them. Nor did Paketon heed him further. Slipping away, he ran after his men, who had crept so close that they could see the loom of Eustace's rear guard against the dark. His horn blared out in a wild peal.

The twanging of four hundred bows gave answer. From rear and right flank Eustace's cavalry was torn with a storm of shafts at the very moment when the castle gate reeled under the blows of the ram. His unmounted bowmen received the first fury, and melted away before the pelting arrows, leaving him no means to return volley for volley.

Then, at point-blank range—for the outlaws had been forced to come fairly upon their enemy to see the target at all—the barbed shafts tore through the rearmost horsemen, piercing mail, flesh and bone. It was Eustace's misfortune that, to cover his advance and clear the garrison from the battlements, he had had to place his bowmen where they were exposed to so un-dreamed-of an attack from the rear.

Himself in the van, Eustace was not even aware at first of the storm behind him. Simultaneously had come a fierce hail of arrows from the right, apparently from the road. Caught by surprize, assailed where he thought himself secure, he was for a moment seized with consternation. But the cries of his stricken men, the great gaps torn in his ranks, the plunging of wounded horses, called for action. There was but one thing to do—detach enough men to ride down the unknown bowmen who struck from the dark.

"Alain!" he cried. "Take forty men and crush the rascals!"

With splendid courage Alain obeyed. In the face of a deadly hail he brought his detachment out of column, wheeling it toward the danger that struck death into his ranks even as he executed the maneuver. Then, in a wild charge, he swept against the unseen bowmen.

But even this Paketon had foreseen, and had left orders to meet it. Scattering before the onslaught, his outlaws left a broad path for the horsemen to gallop through. Dark-clad, light-footed, they evaded the charge, reformed on both sides and poured another volley into the riders as they drove past. Mean-time Paketon himself directed arrow-flight after arrow-flight into the count's disorganized rear; and now, from the panic and the outcries behind him, Eustace learned how hopelessly he was caught between the castle and his hidden foes behind.

But knowledge came too late. Now the outlaws were shoot-ing high, so that their arrows descended in an arc and smote the troopers farther forward. The rearmost ranks were broken, striving to turn and defend themselves, smitten even as they turned; and the panic was spreading. A brisk rally, a swift attack would have cleared the outlaws away, for the moment at least; but it was no light matter to turn such a body of horse in the dark, in the face of the garrison. But this must be done, or all would be lost.

The horsemen responded desperately to Eustace's order. The rear wheeled to the left, and left again to face the storm of arrows; but so shaken were they that the next volley drove them in flight.

From the van Eustace brought the remaining ranks to left face; and on the instant Paketon ordered an advance. Running forward a few paces, his archers poured in three volleys in rapid succession just as Eustace got his men from column into line, to offer less of a target to the unseen foe.

It was a fatal maneuver, but Eustace had no choice. So long as he faced the gate, with his back to the hostile archers, his men were a helpless prey for the shafts that riddled them. Only by a swift, desperate charge could he crush those pestiferous archers; and till they were crushed, he could not hope to reduce the castle.

The cries of pain, the shouts of confusion, the tramping of the panic-stricken horses, made themselves heard through the battered gate. Just as Alain rode back with half his detachment slain, and blundered against the rear of his own pivoting comrades, the earl caught the meaning of the turmoil.

"A rescue!" he cried. "They break! Open the gate for a sally!"

Quickly the bars were raised, and the shattered gate flung wide. Already formed to resist storm, the garrison poured out from the barbican on to the bridge, swept across, and struck their foe on what had been his front, but was now his flank. Plying their weapons with all the zeal of men who strike for life and for vengeance, they rolled up the frightened horsemen, enveloped their lines for a third their length, and struck them from their horses.

Now the outlaws whom Alain had pursued rallied, and drove a fresh volley into Eustace's rear. Paketon too kept his company at their work, so that the milling horsemen of Eustace were fighting a hopeless fight on three sides. Only the front was free, for Eustace could not get his ranks to finish their evolution in the teeth of the garrison's sally. The end had come, and Eustace was forced to recognize defeat.

"*Sauve qui peut!*" he cried. "Flee! Flee!"

Eastward across the plain his horsemen fled, desperately plying the spur. But their torment had not ceased; for in the black night they came suddenly full into a maze of mud and reeds and water.

Their wild gallop carried them deep into the marsh before they could rein in; and when the bog stopped them, men and beasts floundered, sank, or were stuck fast. And to the very edge of the marsh the pitiless bowmen pursued them, though now the fewer numbers of the horsemen offered a poor target in the night.

But one man did not think of seeking safety so soon. The Captain Alain, frenzied with defeat and thinking only of how he might in some measure retrieve a little from the disaster, rode straight south from the castle into the wood. A few shafts sped after him; but most of Paketon's men were harassing the main retreat, and a single horseman at night is hard to hit. Past them Alain tore, through the forest fringe and the glade where he had encamped earlier, to the spot where he had left Pierre.

But Pierre no longer lay there bound. He was not to be seen. Alain broke into wild curses, lashing out with his sword in the dark. Or rather, with Pierre's sword; for the splendid weapon had seemed so sure a talisman of success that he had cast his own aside.

Suddenly a great weight seemed to fall upon his head; his senses reeled, and he slithered from the saddle. Over his body stooped Pierre, an oaken fagot in his hand. Casting the rough weapon aside, Pierre tore the sword from Alain's hand, felt the jewels in its hilt, and laughed aloud.

"My sword, my sword!" he cried exultantly. "And I have struck one blow at least this night!"

Leaving the officer where he lay, Pierre ran toward the castle.

THE EARL'S men trooped back into the castle, laughing and shouting for joy of victory. With the last came the earl, by no means so exultant. He had won, had saved castle and life; but he had made a lasting enemy of Eustace. And Eustace, mounted on a splendid horse, had escaped. Slowly and thoughtfully Earl Robert crossed the drawbridge, and entered the torch-lit barbican.

Becket strode after him, helmetless and flushed, with bloody sword. He was about to speak; but a voice from the drawbridge hailed him:

"Ho! Thomas!"

"Pierre!" cried Becket. "Where have you been? What—"

"With Eustace's men, bound," Pierre answered. "More shame to me, I have been within arrow-flight of a good fight, and my sword has not drawn blood."

A rough laugh sounded behind them. There, in the very gateway, stood Sir Richard Paketon with a handful of russet-clad archers. But the earl had turned too, and at sight of his outlawed kinsman he started in astonishment.

"So it is you, you and your outcasts, Richard, who have saved me!" he cried.

Paketon's eyes glowed.

"Some little work we have done tonight," he answered. "But he who saved you is Pierre Faidit there. The count's captive, he contrived to send the count's own men to bring me news of your plight. He has not merely saved your walls and your life, brother; he saved your honor. After this night's work you can no longer hold aloof from England's cause, no longer hesitate between Stephen, the Fox, and Henry, the Lion—Pierre Faidit has driven you into Henry's arms. But for him, I should not have come, and you would have been Stephen's captive. Now you are Henry's man!"

Paketon spoke the very thought that had been vexing the earl.

"Aye," Robert admitted. "I was at peace, untroubled, and now I must be plagued with Henry's battles!"

Becket broke in eagerly:

"But now, my lord, you will win Henry's favor, and a noble name. You will bring all the North to Duke Henry, and with the North he will win his crown!"

The earl stared from one to another of the three men who had forced his hand and at last he smiled wryly.

"So be it," he said. "Since I am now Henry's man perforce, why—long live Henry, King of England!"

And his men-at-arms, who had watched in half-comprehending wonder, cried aloud after him—

"Long live Henry, England's king!"

"**A**ND NOW—RAGS!"

The vagabond made a drunkenly eloquent gesture—and his outflung elbow knocked his pint of sour wine into shards and spatterings on the clay floor. Overwhelmed by this last calamity, he buried his face in his hands and fell to whimpering.

Bernolt the taverner scowled at him.

"You get no more drink today, Orso!" he scolded. "He who quaffs the wine of charity should value it better. But 'tis always so, as soon as the grape reminds you of your sorrows."

"Nay, give him one more, Bernolt!" A young man, short and wide-shouldered, rose from his seat in a dark corner, under a swollen wine-skin. "But one more! If a little of your thin drink makes him remember the old tale, more will make him forget, and that much is to be desired. I am as sick of it as you."

"Well may you be!" sneered the taverner. "If I have heard it ten times, you have heard it a hundred, and been at the making of it also. Rags, quotha? Rags indeed! Both of you look more like scarecrows than men. Why will a brisk lad like you not take to decent work, instead of following a worn-out minstrel about all Aquitaine? You and Orso have eaten away your welcome at every pot-house in the country, and you never pay, save in broken-winded songs and hard words!"

The young man rose and in one swift stride confronted the angry taverner. His tattered cloak fell open, revealing a long sword that had long since poked through the heel of its scabbard; his hose—once of fine, parti-colored silk—showed his white skin through many a rent and ravel and were littered with the foul straw of the stable where he had slept. But he held his dark head high, and his blue-green eyes blazed with angry pride.

"Minstrel!" he echoed bitterly. "What name is that for him who was once the noblest of troubadours, the first of swordsmen? And why should I not follow him, beg and starve with him—aye, die for him if need be? Did he not pick me out of the gutter, a beaten and unwanted urchin? Did he not share his all with me, when he was still rich and the companion of princes? Did he not teach me the glorious arts of poesy and swordsmanship?"

The drunken Orso lay slumped over a rough-hewn table, his disreputable gray locks over his eyes. But at the young man's last words he raised himself, blinked and struck a pitiful attitude of pride.

"Po-poesy and s-s-swordsmanship!" he hiccupped. "Aye, noblest of troubadours, such was I! You say truth, Cercamon! And now—what am I? Rags, dirt! All through women, lad! Ah, shun women! God made wine, steel, and man; the devil made gold, women and—landlords. Faugh!"

He got to his feet uncertainly, and Cercamon flung a strong arm about him. The fat taverner, purple with rage, shook his fist in the drunkard's face.

"Eat my bread, drink my wine, and then abuse me!" he bellowed. "Out, ye cadging dogs! Out of my honest inn!"

The lad Cercamon drew up his sturdy figure with a gesture that, for all his rags, was superb. Bernolt's eyes fell before the green fire of his gaze. The young man, turning his back insolently, half-led, half-carried his shattered idol to the door. He thrust out his free hand to open it, but the maudlin Orso chose that moment to break free, and flung his almost helpless body against the panels. The door flew open, letting a flood of sunlight into the musty room, but a crash and a curse from outside bore witness that its sudden opening had taken one of Bernolt's customers in the face.

"Wounds and nails! Can ye not heed your going, ye drunken louts? Ye have broken my head! Ha, 'tis the cast ballad-monger and his Gascon gutter-whelp! Out of my way, churls."

One hand to his smarting brow, the speaker bent to pick a velvet cap out of the dust, the steel rings of his coat of mail jingling as he stooped. He was a strongly made, sinewy man of perhaps five and thirty, and the gold fleur-de-lys and silver tower embroidered on his surcoat proclaimed him an officer of the garrison of Niort.

Cercamon's handsome face flushed scarlet at the stream of insults, but by ill luck his wretched master was between him and the soldier. Orso brought his sword out of sheath with a drunken flourish. It was ill for him then that bad wine paralyzed his arm and clouded his wits; for, old as he was, not many men could parry his thrusts when he was sober. Before Cercamon could come to the rescue, the officer's blade leaped out and licked in, and Orso fell, twitching in the dust, a miserable monument to that which drink can make of golden song and muscles of steel.

With a wild cry of grief and fury young Cercamon bestrode his master's body. His sword clashed with the murderer's and for a dozen passes he fought with the wild abandon of an angry boy in his first duel. But a grazed temple calmed him, the cunning skill learned from Orso while the troubadour was still the joy and terror of the southern courts returned, and his point played like a living thing. Lunge, parry, hack, and thrust—and the lad's blade, driven with all the force of his great shoulders and unnaturally long arms, tore through mail and flesh. His mouth open in a ridiculous expression of astonishment, the officer dropped his weapon and fell crashing across the dead Orso.

Cercamon, a little pale about the lips, stood over him with dripping point. He had killed his first man, though he had seen Orso kill many. Bernolt the taverner, propped against the frame of his own door, was yet whiter. He wrung his hands, and a low moaning breathed through his lips. At last he pulled himself together and tottered over to the stricken men.

"Dead—both dead!" he gasped. "My lord the castellan will hang me for this. A captain of his, killed before my house!"

His little eyes roved about like a hunted beast's, till at length his terror of the noose overcame his fear of the fierce young swordsman he had taken for a harmless beggar. He crept behind the lad, flung both fat arms about his neck and shrieked.

"Murder! Ho, the watch! Murder!"

Cercamon flung him off with a heave of his big shoulders and bent over the dead body of his only friend.

"Aye, dead," he murmured. "And so shall I be, if my legs do not save me!"

He caressed Orso's stubbly cheeks, wiped his sword on the slain captain's surcoat, sheathed it and ran. Across the sunlit squares, through the narrow, tortuous alleys of the town, he took his flight, followed by Bernolt's cries and the frightened glances of the citizens. The small, round cobbles—called by the folk in bad years "apples of hunger"—hurt his feet; yet on he dashed with flying heels, turning, twisting, and ever making for the bottom of that lower of the two hills on which the town was built. Ever and anon his eyes sought the higher summit, crowned with the great, square tower of Niort Castle, from which mounted men must soon set forth in quest of him.

Before he had gone fifty paces the hue and cry was after him. Roused by that baleful cry of "Murder!" men dashed out of shops and houses, armed with whatever they had in hand— cudgels, knives, hammers, weavers' blades, hemp-heckles. A gigantic butcher joined the chase, brandishing a leg of mutton. Disheveled women leaned out of upper windows, screaming. Officers of the watch appeared from the arched mouths of dark lanes and bawled to the fugitive to stop. But his heels vanished in an unpaved by-way, and with a shout of joy the watch ran in to close its entrance.

One glance at the refuge he had sought and Cercamon knew he was in a trap. He turned, hand on sword, but seeing seven armored soldiers close in on him from the only exit, he ran on again. He was in an empty court, high-walled, and the few doors leading from it were barred. His feet slipped on heaps of stable refuse.

A SERGEANT was close on him, naked sword raised for the stroke, left hand extended and clutching. In that last second of grace Cercamon saw a chance for safety. In one corner of the enclosure was a low shed or pent-house with a sloping, tiled roof. In half a dozen bounds he gained a single precious yard, leaped, caught the roof-ridge with the fingers of one hand and pulled himself up. Even as he gripped it, his foremost pursuer seized the corner of his cloak. But the rotten cloth gave way and tore off in the sergeant's hand.

The eaves of an upper story ran down almost to the pent-house ridge. Catching at the iron rain-gutter, Cercamon drew himself up and followed it hand over hand. Below him, out of reach, the watch hacked vainly at his heels with upraised swords. Now he was just above the rear wall of the court. Dropping to the coping, he lowered himself over the wall. The watch burst into howls of rage, beating at the wall for a moment with their fists; then they raced back out of the court as they had come.

There was nothing then for it but to go round the end of the long, unbroken row of houses and follow the fugitive down the street on the other side of the wall.

This was the Street of the Iron-Workers, which straggled half-way down the hill. Long before the first pursuer appeared at its mouth, Cercamon saw and seized his opportunity. Straight across from him lay a swordsmith's shop, open to the street. Before it, a silk-clad, well-combed page held a fine horse. Within the shop a gay gentleman in fur-trimmed mantle and plumed cap was arguing with the master-smith over the price of a jeweled dagger.

Cercamon thrust the scented page to one side with a sweep of his hand, vaulted to the saddle and smacked the horse stingingly on the shoulder. Down the street the beast sprang, snorting, while the page wailed his terror and smith and knight called loudly for the watch. The watch came too late, breathless with running and shouting. Galloping over the rough cobbles at risk of his neck, Cercamon pelted down the thinly settled foot of the hill, into the last countrylike outposts of the town and out upon a grass-grown lane. He was on the open plain now, with only green distance between him and safety.

The Spring wind blew fresh on his cheek, the hue and cry grew faint and dim behind. On he rode, pell-mell, the nearest pursuer scarce visible, a running dot. France lay before him—but behind, the grim, square tower of Niort Castle loomed, its alarm-bell clanging brazenly, and in its court men were mounting to follow him.

How he wished for spurs on his heels! He wanted to live— wanted it more than ever before in his motley life. Till now, Cercamon had taken the bitter with the sweet, with the ready philosophy of youth.

He was only twenty, in this year 1138, and his world was one which might smile softly on the young and strong. That had always been the first thought in his mind, all those six years he had begged and hungered with his broken-down master. Some day luck would turn, as it had turned before, and when it did, he was ready for it. But he had never grieved at his poverty, any more than he had been spoiled by the brief prosperity which had preceded it.

The only fault he had ever found with his beloved benefactor, Orso, was the ruined man's readiness to whimper when in drink. Orso had been great, rich, admired; through wine—and as he himself asserted, through women—he had become a penniless outcast.

When sober, he bore all with a cynical humor which won a copper or a meal from all he met. But as soon as wine mastered him Orso would begin to brag of his departed glory, of the prizes his songs had won from applauding princes, of the favors of noble ladies, and the enemies he had slain. And he would whine of his fall till all save Cercamon were sick to death of him.

Orso had been in the midst of his grandeur when he picked up Cercamon, literally from the gutter of a dirty town in Gascony. No one knew the boy's birth, least of all Cercamon himself. He had the gamin's gift for theft, lies and repartee, but with these he had a voice in which the old troubadour foresay genius. He had also a quick pride and a hand swift to strike, which pleased Orso the more.

Playing on that pride, the old man soon cured him of that dishonesty of hand and word which—merely the fruit of environment—had not yet stained his soul. Orso clothed him in fine garments, made much of him, taught him to make songs and to use his voice properly in the singing of them, and trained him to use weapons. Cercamon proved a pupil after his master's heart, learning with marvelous aptness and giving in return the rare gift of a boy's love.

It was natural that he should love his master, aye, that his love should outlast their prosperity and grow greater under trial. Trials enough they had; hunger and thirst, cold, when the Winter blew sharp, dirt and hard lodging under the sky. It was natural too, that the boy should absorb his master's hatred of women, which expressed itself in biting words and venomous stories. And so hard had been his childhood that, when their luck ceased, Cercamon never complained. That was life; luck lay just around the corner.

But now—for the first time Cercamon knew how good life really was. He had killed an officer of the constable of Niort; he had stolen a knight's horse; he a beggar. If he were caught— hanging, or worse. He had seen bodies broken on the wheel for less than that; he had passed the castle walls and heard the shrieks of men tortured in the dungeons. So, if he were overtaken, he could not hope for mercy. But if he could get away, out of Aquitaine, his voice and his sword might make his fortune in some distant court. Nothing was too good in that day for the troubadour. And with Orso's training he must succeed. But first he must escape, and Aquitaine lay long before him.

The road suddenly dipped down a little hill and then through a wood. Straight on he galloped, glad of the thick trunks and new-leaved boughs that hid him from those who followed far behind. The spicy odors of the forest stung his nostrils sweetly; the feel and fragrance of Spring were all about him. Though he did not fully understand its message, the soft wind whispered to him of the joy and pride, the greatness, the love, the fortune, that all young men dream of.

On and on he rode, thinking partly of these things, but more of the peril behind. He had a long start, but he had far to go to escape the jurisdiction of Aquitaine, his horse was weary, and the garrison of Niort was well mounted. And now his horse began to limp a little more, and it was flagging badly. At the next turn of the road he would stop and make a hasty examination of the beast's foot.

N O W   H E rounded the turn—and pulled up scarce a spear-length short of a horseman who sat his saddle full in the middle of the narrow road, on a big roan that stood as if cast in bronze. Cercamon swerved to pass, but the rider pulled straight across the fairway and eased down the point of his lance. He was a heavy-set man, mailed from neck to knee, with a heavy kite-shaped shield borne easily on one strong arm. His features—all but a smiling mouth—were hid by the cheek-mail and nasal of his helmet. Cercamon eyed him uneasily, then glanced back over his shoulder.

The other laughed deep in his throat.

"A runaway, ha? A thief? Nay, the horse is not yours; never did a low-born tatterdemalion own so clean-limbed a beast!"

Cercamon's fingers closed on his hilt.

"Let me pass!" he cried.

The knight's lips closed in a firm line.

"Times are ill," he retorted, "when such as you dare give orders to a gentleman. Nay, you pass not! When I heard your hoofs, I thought some man of birth approached, with whom I might chance an honorable encounter. But I will yet have profit from you, for I will take you back to justice and receive thanks from him you robbed. You will look well on a gibbet!"

In one glance Cercamon measured his chances, and they

looked small. His exhausted horse would go down at the first impact of the big roan's shoulder; and if the knight chose to use his long lance—sword to sword would be well enough, but sword to lance is long odds, and Cercamon had neither shield nor armor. Quickly he made the only possible decision. As the mailed man wheeled and lowered his spear-point, Cercamon slipped from the saddle and snatched out his sword.

Seeing him prepared to resist, the knight shifted his aim from shoulder to breast. His spurs just touched the flanks of the roan; which leaped forward in a mighty bound. Just in time to escape that awful point Cercamon sprang aside, with a whirl of his blade that sheared the tough lance haft in two. Then he ran after his enemy, who had shot past the lad's horse and was struggling to bring the roan's head around while its hoofs plowed the gravel.

The knight had just checked his horse and half-wheeled when Cercamon reached him. Dropping the useless lance, he clutched at his sword-hilt. But the advantage lay now with the unarmored man, who had only to strike while the knight must first free his blade from its leather scabbard. Cercamon lashed in with a terrible backhand stroke that hacked through the mail rings and bit deep into his foe's thigh.

Gallantly the stricken man strove to counter, but he had no time. With death pursuing him and this man trying to head him back into its clutches Cercamon had no choice but to kill quickly. He killed, with his second stroke.

With frantic fingers he stripped off the dead man's mail, boots, hose and leather *jupon*. One second he hesitated over the golden spurs and then placed them on the knight's breast. He himself had no right to them, being no knight; besides if he wore them, those who met him would take him for a gentleman and ask his name. Then there were folk in Poitiers who knew the names and titles of every gentleman in the country; he might make a wrong answer and be discovered.

Leaving his own rags and useless beast, he put on his enemy's

garments, mail and helmet, snatched up the great shield, leaped
on the roan's back and was off like a storm-wind through the
wood. His new mount was fresh; Cercamon himself was com-
pletely disguised in the long, bifurcated mail cloak, green mantle
and nasaled helmet.

"Gamin, jongleur and beggar have I been," he thought as he
galloped, "but never a soldier. But now I have killed—twice in
one day—and a soldier I must be."

Already he had made such plans as he could—but they were
perilous plans at best. The castellan of Niort would leave nothing
undone to reach the beggar-lad who had killed an officer of
his. Niort was a fief of Guilhem X, Count of Poitiers, Duke of
Aquitaine, and overlord of half the south of France. Not only
must Cercamon keep ahead of the pursuers from Niort, he must
keep ahead of the news of his deed till he got out of Guilhem's
domains. That was not easy, seeing that he must eat and sleep,
while those who bore warrants for his seizure would find relays
a fast as men hungered or horses tired. And the way was long;
Guilhem's fiefs stretched from Anjou to the Pyrenees, from the
Bay of Biscay to the borders of Toulouse.

At first Cercamon had thought of riding straight for Toulouse. That was the safest refuge—though two long days' ride
to the southeast. But he gave that up as soon as he remembered
the guard at the border. There was hostility between Guilhem
and Count Alphonse-Jourdain of Toulouse; and Guilhem
watched the boundary closely. It would be impossible to get
through. He must either reach Anjou, to the north—and there
too was a vigilant border guard—or Burgundy, farther to the
northeast. In either case he must ride for days through Guilhem's country, pass through town after town and city after city,
and run the almost certain risk that—while he tarried to rest
or eat—the order to seize him would go around and before
him. The corpse of the man whose mail he wore was perhaps
discovered even now; he would be held and questioned, the
truth would be learned, he would be cast into prison till the
men of Niort came up to take him back to death.

Fortunately he knew the roads well. He had been over them with Orso, in the days of their prosperity, and he forgot nothing. He resolved to ride for Burgundy. There was peace between Burgundy and Aquitaine, and the border guards would be few and complaisant—if he ever reached the border. But of that there was small hope. Guilhem of Aquitaine, a capable soldier, had his wide lands well-organized and patroled. It was Burgundy or nothing, however; so Cercamon resolved. By dark he would be in Poitiers.

He did not like to think of Poitiers. It was Guilhem's capital, and would be full of soldiers. The rent above his thigh, where his own sword had torn and bloodied the mail he wore, would rouse comment. But he could not avoid the city. He would rest his horse there and then hasten on, northeast, through the friendly night. Once in Burgundy he would have some days of grace, for it would take his pursuers time to negotiate, for his surrender. In those days he would reach the marches between Burgundy and Toulouse. In Toulouse he would be safe, free to think of his dreams. Alphonse-Jourdain would never hand him over to Guilhem; Alphonse-Jourdain loved stalwart men-at-arms. Fame and fortune before—the wheel or the gallows behind!

As far as Poitiers all would be simple—twenty-odd miles farther now. He had a fair start and a fresh horse; his pursuers could not get their first relays till they entered the capital. But he must escape question in the city—and he must leave it as soon as his beast's condition allowed. And then he must have luck—tremendous luck.

One moment the road lay in the deep, cool shadow of the wood; the next it turned sharply and ran full into blazing sunshine. Cercamon rode out into the sun-washed plain; for a moment, his eyes were dazzled with the light. A few paces farther on, his road joined the highway from Bordeaux to Poitiers; and he had almost reached it before his pupils had sufficiently adjusted themselves to the glare to see that which must overwhelm all his plans.

Poitiers lay to the northeast, Bordeaux to the southwest. Reining in, Cercamon gazed down the road in both directions. Far to the southwestward, scarce discernible, a faint cloud like yellow smoke blotched the horizon; and from the cloud shot bright flashes like tongues of flame. As he watched, the cloud grew greater and greater, looser, and the points of fire twinkled ever more brightly. It was the dust of many riders, and the sun glittering on their mail and the points of their lances! A host of horsemen on the way to Poitiers!

JERKING HIS horse's head to the left, Cercamon faced toward the capital. But ahead of him, much closer than the advancing host, rose another dust-cloud, the vanguard of that host. The dazzling flash from its armor, and the almost imperceptible jingle of mail, told that it was a small troop—perhaps bearing important tidings—riding hard, but not yet far away. It must have passed but a few moments before he came out of the wood.

He was caught between two perils. The two bodies of horse could only be Guilhem's men, either from Bordeaux or returning to the Poitiers garrison. In their own country, near their own chief city, the smaller troop had no need to keep in close touch with their slower fellows of the main body. But those few riders lay between Cercamon and Poitiers, the main host prevented a change of plans and cut off his possible flight to the north or east.

Full in the sunlight, the oncoming host must have seen him as he had seen them, and if he should ride between or away from the two forces he would be pursued and challenged. It was too long a chance to invite pursuit all the long way to Anjou.

If he retreated to the wood, he must lie hid till the last soldier passed. That would consume more than an hour, and by that time those who followed him from Niort would overtake him. There was but one chance—to ride, as he had planned, straight and hard for Poitiers. He would invite least suspicion by following that small troop ahead, overtaking it if he could, and boldly asking leave to ride into the city with it. Then he would at least reach Poitiers ahead of the hue and cry for his blood. Once inside the city gate, he would disappear down some dark street and lose little time in renewing his flight toward Burgundy.

Deciding swiftly, he struck his unspurred heels into the roan's flanks. The vanguard rode fast; they must bear news. It was more than an hour before he overtook them. No fear that they had heard of his deed! No danger in joining them, except that the sword-cut over his thigh might breed question. He must chance that.

The pound of his horse's hoofs announced him as he drew in upon them. The rear rank glanced over their shoulders, and a hoarse voice called out. The cavalcade came to a halt. As Cercamon drew abreast the rearmost riders, an officer rode from the front rank to hail him. It was a tall, lean man, full-armed, but wearing a black velvet cap instead of a helmet. His hair was iron-gray, and his features fine and sharp-cut. Cercamon knew him, as all Gascons did. This was Bertrand, the great Count of Armagnac, a veteran soldier high in the favor of Guilhem of Aquitaine. But Bertrand would not know one so humble as Cercamon.

The count's eyes flickered over the newcomer questioningly; but for a moment he did not speak. At last he nodded, as if confirming some secret judgment and asked:

"Orders? Nay, I have not seen you among the duke's riders."

"Nay, my lord count. I have ridden from Niort and crave permission to ride in your troop to Poitiers."

Cercamon wisely did not conceal the place whence he had come, since, with the main highway behind him blocked by the oncoming cavalry, there was no road save that from Niort by which he could have come.

"You are of the garrison of Niort? Why do you not wear its colors?"

"Nay, my lord, I am a man-at-arms out of service."

"Whose pay did you last take?"

Inwardly Cercamon cursed the great man's curiosity which was costing valuable time; but he must render a convincing account of himself, or fare badly. Poitiers was not a kindly land for an unattached wanderer.

"I am a Gascon, my lord, from Auch," he evaded.

"Then you have been in the service of the Countess of Fezensac," the Count inferred. "And you are out of service. We are both Gascons; will you join my banner? You look like a strong and ready man."

It was kindly meant, but to join the household of any man whose service would keep him in Poitiers longer than that night was the last thing the young man wished. Before midnight the city would be ablaze with the news that he, a beggar, an outcast, had murdered first an officer of one of the duke's cities, then a knight. No nobleman would or could refuse to give up to justice one who had committed such an offense. Seeing his hesitation, Armagnac smiled and motioned Cercamon to ride beside him.

Cercamon did not like that smile, but he could only obey. The cavalcade broke into a trot, which soon grew to that drumming, swinging pace that goes farther and faster than the gallop in the long run, nor did the count speak another word to him till they were under the walls of Poitiers. By that time it was dark and somewhat chilly.

THE CITY was not great, but it was vastly strong. High on a plateau above the plain, it was girded, on three sides by the juncture of the rivers Boivre and Clain. Roman and Frank had labored at its fortifications; generations of independent Poitivin princes had crowned it with frowning towers. In the great arch of its gate the guard stood aside to admit the horsemen, their weapons clashing bravely in honor of the great soldier who was their ducal master's bravest vassal. Under the hollow archway the torches flared red against the blackness and danced reflected on every polished helmet.

Bertrand of Armagnac dismissed his troop, and they cantered

off through the city toward their quarters. Once inside the massive portal, Cercamon prepared to lash his horse into instant flight; and it was with vast relief that he saw the horsemen ride off into the darkness. He and the count were alone—it would be easy now. But even as his fingers tightened on the bridle, Bertrand laid hold of his arm.

"Ride with me!" he commanded.

The lad's heart sank, but he dared not disobey. Had he done so, a shout from the count would bring up a dozen men-at-arms from the gate and set the whole town buzzing after him. He must make up his mind to lose some time—and time was life to him. Surely he could outwit this troublesome nobleman somehow—but now to violate his order and run for it were to make Poitiers a hornet's nest for himself.

Behind him, vague and vast, loomed the walls; ahead stretched a great square, the buildings that lined it mere blacker shadows against the deep blackness of the Southern night. The streets were for the most part pitch dark; only here and there a thin, bobbing spangle of flame indicated a torch or two, borne by the clinking escort of some noble. They were like giant fire-flies, only red and wavering. Under the flickering lights gleamed the faces of their bearers, ghostly; all else was blackness.

Footsteps sounded on the cobbles, mail jangled; but those who made these sounds could be seen only when they passed a torch-bearer or came under the glow of the cressets on the city walls. From the ramparts drifted the voices of sentinels, back and forth; far off a horse's hoofs rang on the pavement, and a dog howled.

On and on Cercamon rode behind the man he dared not run from. Where in a city shall one hide from its masters? He raged at the luck that had thrown him in with just this man. Every sense, every nerve in brain and body was strained for the least chance of evasion. He must get out of Poitiers ahead of the pursuers from Niort!

At the end of a broad street opened another square, that

hummed with life and pulsed with light. Armed men hastened to and fro, as on imperative errands. Courtiers flashing in colors and jewels rode on horseback or in litters to take the air, attended by men-at-arms and torchbearers. Slow-paced priests and monks went with downcast heads and fingers busy with their beads. All these figures stood out plain as under the noonday sun, for from all the splendid buildings on all sides flowed the light, from cressets, single torches, candle-lighted windows. This was the heart of the city, which itself was the heart of the richest province in France.

The center, to or from which all these folk radiated, was a vast, splendid structure at the farther end of the square, blazing light from every portal and window. The soldiers at its entranceways were bathed in a lurid radiance that set their armor flashing. To Cercamon's dismay his mighty companion rode straight for this mighty building, the Palace of the Dukes-Counts, the social and military focus of Aquitaine's grandeur.

"I have an errand to the dyke," Armagnac announced. "My quarters are in the Palace, and you will await me there."

In sinking hopelessness Cercamon followed him to a carved stone gateway, past men-at-arms with presented pikes, to the foot of the stair of the forecourt. Grooms ran up to take their horses. As he slipped from the saddle, the fugitive felt the noose tighten about his neck. He climbed the stair with leaden feet; not all the beauty of lacy stonework and sculptured effigies of saints and warriors could stir his numbed heart. He was like a fly that, knowing the peril of the spider's web, and having no way out of destruction but to brush past it, blunders instead into the web's very center. How should he ever escape now—and escape in time?

In the great ante-chamber, where pretty pages in silks and velvets stifled yawns of weariness, where black-robed clerks sat at carved desks and lords-in-waiting gossiped in intervals of duty, Bertrand of Armagnac called to him one of a group of soldiers in his own livery.

"Take this man to my guard-room, Olivier!" he ordered, and added a few low words that Cercamon did not hear.

Ignoring the pages, secretaries and men-at-arms, the great count then crossed the ante-chamber between rows of bowing courtiers. A bronze door opened to admit him, and the laugh of women and the buzz of many people talking together swept out and was smothered by the door's closing.

In a daze Cercamon followed the soldier down a side corridor, across an inner court and into a wing that was as stern as the central structure had been splendid. Here, too, all was brightly lighted; but the torches glimmered on plain stone and unpolished wood. This was the most ancient portion of the palace, new given over to the military business of the court. Mailed men clanged up and down its staircases and flagged passages; a hawk screamed from somewhere above.

His guide led him to a bleak suite of chambers on the second floor. Here were no dainty pages and shaved secretaries, but only hard-bitten troopers in battered mail and dinted helmets—keen-eyed men, who flashed a glance at the stranger as they passed, but neither asked questions nor gave greeting beyond a curt nod. It was in a large, drafty hall that Cercamon was halted at last. A score of men-at-arms off duty loitered about, dicing, swapping jests. But even in their mirth and idleness they were alert, and there was about them a hard quietness that spoke of perfect discipline. Now and then one drank or offered drink to his fellow; but they drank sparingly, unlike the general wont of the laughter-loving, easy South.

Beyond looking up at him, none paid attention to Cercamon. This, too, was strange, for soldiers are hospitable the world over, and Gascons—as these were—are as a rule merry and boisterous. The chill in Cercamon's heart began to spread to his limbs. Despair seized his heart when his guide closed the door and leaned his back against it.

IT SEEMED a thousand years that he waited, and the invisible noose about his neck tightened as the long minutes dragged. Yet it was but half an hour before one knocked at the door, and he who leaned against it opened it to speak a few words with some one outside. Straightway he beckoned to Cercamon, who followed him again, feeling the eyes of the men-at-arms in the guard-room boring into his back.

He found Bertrand of Armagnac in a small chamber, sparsely furnished. The count was unarmored now, in plain black tunic and hose. He was playing with a favorite hawk, that nipped at his fingers. At his gesture the soldier departed, leaving Cercamon alone with the man who had lured him into the spider's web.

Armagnac looked up at his unwilling guest with a cold little smile.

"You have not answered the question I asked you this afternoon," he said. "Will you take service under my banner?"

Cercamon looked about him with hunted eyes. There were but two doors to the little room: one led to the guard-room, crowded with men-at-arms; the other was blocked by the lean figure of the Count, and the great oak chair in which he sat—no escape either way. The riders from Niort could not be far away now. In a few minutes, perhaps, they would be crying out their errand in the city gate.

"I crave my lord's pardon," he answered with as much composure as he could command. "I am on business that brooks no delay."

The count's eyes fixed themselves on his.

"Tell me the truth," he said.

Cercamon stood staring at his tormentor. Bertrand could have heard nothing so soon. What did he mean?

"I know you have told me no lies," Armagnac was speaking again, "but when I questioned you today you did not answer frankly. You are too young a man to deceive an old war-wolf like me. I give you now a chance—a last chance—to speak the full truth about yourself. This chance I grant you because you have the face and bearing of a man, and because you are a Gascon. From whom did you plunder that mail you wear?"

It was the suddenness of the question that broke down Cercamon's guard. One instant of confused alarm, another of quick reflection, and he resolved to tell this man his story. Somehow, the count knew enough to be dangerous; if Cercamon kept silent, much evil would be suspected, and his justification not known. If the count should order him held, even for an hour— the news would be here from Niort.

The young man knew he was trapped, helpless; and with despair something of his pride came back to him. Tossing his head a little, he looked the nobleman straight in the face and told his tale from beginning to end. Armagnac listened in silence, his features unchanging.

"So," he said, when all was told. "So you are a beggar, and you have slain two gentleman—one of them an officer of a vassal of the duke. The penalty is death, and I fear in no pleasant form. I am sorry, for you have borne yourself like a man. If you had been of good births the law would not touch you, for you slew both times in a good cause. But a peasant—"

"Is it nothing, my lord," Cercamon began hoarsely, "that I put myself under your protection?"

"Suppose I should let you go," the count retorted. "So much time has been lost that within the half-hour, at most, the pursuit would be on your heels. Every cranny of the city would be searched, while fresh-mounted men from the barracks scoured every road. You would be seized almost before you could begin your flight!"

"Not while I could lift my sword-arm!" the young man retorted. "I should at least have made a brave man's end, instead of dangling from a halter!"

To his astonishment, the count burst out laughing.

"That I can believe!" he cried. "You are just such a game-cock from Gascony as I should have loved to see under my banner! Oh, if you had but said yes to my offer of service! Man, I should never have given you up—then! Aye, any other man would have surrendered you, but Armagnac protects his own!"

For a while there was silence, then—

"You have destroyed me, my lord," said Cercamon.

"Have I not said I am sorry? It is shameful that so brave a lad should die so miserable a death. To think that an unarmored boy should kill two armed veterans! Ah, one day you would have made a great soldier! It was bravely done to avenge that old man's murder—Orso, you called him? A troubadour?"

Cercamon nodded listlessly. The count's questions held ho further interest for him; they came to his ears as to the ears of one about to die. About to die! That was all that mattered. He was young—and he must die!

"I remember him," Bertrand resumed gently. "Who would not, who had ever heard him sing? He was great in his time, greater perhaps than any other in his art—excepting only my dead lord, Guilhem IX, father of the present duke—I mind now that, the last time I heard Orso sing, he had a young lad with him. Was it thou?"

"It was I, my lord. He taught me his art."

Bertrand's calm fell from him like a discarded garment. "Did he so?" he asked, springing to his feet. "Can you make verses? And sing them? By Saint Radegonde! A troubadour and a swordsman! Thou art a jewel!"

The eagerness in his tones brought a thrill of hope to Cercamon.

"Is there—" he began. "Will my lord—"

A gesture silenced him.

"My poor lad," the count answered. "I was just leaving the duke's presence when Aimon de Branh and ten spearmen from Niort came up, breathless and spent from hard riding, to report your deed. I am seneschal of Aquitaine—it is my duty to give you up."

Cercamon turned pale, but his eyes and his voice were steady.

"I may have a priest?" he asked.

But the count's thoughts were wandering.

"Aye," he uttered slowly. "I must give you up; but—but—it will do no hurt to wait a little. The mail you wear is not your own; you have no right to it. I will bid more seemly clothes be brought for you."

He struck his dagger-hilt thrice against his great shield, which hung from a peg beside him. At the signal, a soldier appeared in the door. To him Armagnac gave an order.

When the man returned with the garments Cercamon was to wear, the lad stared first at them and then at the count.

"Not these?" he cried.

Bertrand nodded.

"Take them into the guard-room and put them on," he commanded. "You will hardly escape, with so many stout fellows around you. When it is time, I will have you brought before the duke. When that time comes, see to it that you obey the orders brought you!"

THE SPRING night had turned cool beyond comfort, and the great hearth in the center of the hall roared with blazing fagots. The tables had been pulled close about the fire, and the wine warmed. Leaping and dancing, the flames threw their golden light on the gorgeous vaulting of the ceiling and flashed from a hundred jewels that nestled in glowing velvet.

Guilhem, tenth of his name, Count of Poitiers and Duke of Aquitaine, pulled his furred cloak closer about his meager frame. In the prime of life as years go, his blood was thinned by hard living and the exposure of twenty campaigns. His handsome face was deep-lined, his brown locks graying and thinned by the pressure of his helmet.

On his left sat Bertrand of Armagnac; on his right the Countess Aliénor, Guilhem's child and heir. From her grandsire, Guilhem the Troubadour, she had inherited all that wondrous beauty that had made him the admiration of the age; but in her it was made exquisite and celestial.

Her radiant young loveliness was still unmarked by the selfishness and cruelty of her heart; no one yet knew her as Aliénor the Faithless. She was tall, slender, with great blue eyes and loose silken hair like a cataract of spun gold. Yet where other women were celebrated for beautiful hair or sparkling eyes, or soft red mouths, or glowing cheeks, so perfect was she in all things that the beholder could not choose one feature that surpassed the others. Her loveliness was a surpassing harmony, that blinded all who saw it.

All this Aliénor knew, having been told of it by a hundred despairing admirers, having heard it sung by a score of troubadours. Nay, he who had just sung had even invented a new measure in which to celebrate her praises. When the tall, sweet-voiced young man had finished, she smiled upon him graciously and yawned. Courtiers and ladies carefully modulated their applause to express the same degree of mild approval and of weariness; but Guilhem shook his head impatiently.

"Well enough," he muttered, "but I have heard my father chant a canzo which, to this, was like the song of angels compared to the cheeping of young frogs. What think you, Aimon?"

A young knight three seats down from Count Bertrand set down his empty goblet and signed to have it refilled.

"Faith, my lord duke," he answered. "I think more of your grace's tingling Medoc than of your troubadours. It was otherwise in your noble father's days. We have had no true singers since then, save that unlucky Orso, whose beggar-brat I pursued hither."

The discredited singer stood flushing, shifting from toe to toe, and in pity Guilhem tossed him a jewel. Bertrand of Armagnac had sat silent, smiling sardonically to himself, but now he turned courteously to Aimon de Branh.

"I came down too late," he said, "to learn what fortune you have had. Has the fellow you followed been caught?"

The young knight of Niort shook his head.

"Nay, but he has no chance to escape. My lord duke has sent out riders in every direction, on swift horses; and the watch is searching the city. I shall not ride back till the murderer is taken."

"Then," Armagnac returned, "since Vauton's singing has failed to please you, I may offer you better entertainment, if my lord duke is pleased to permit."

"What is that, Bertrand?" Duke Guilhem asked curiously.

"There is a fellow in my train," the count answered, "who has a pretty note. He is a Gascon like myself. If 'twere not presumptuous, I should rate him a better troubadour than Orso at his best. Will your grace hear him?"

Guilhem sat up straight, his eyes gleaming.

"If he is as sweet-voiced as Orso, I would keep St. Peter waiting at the door of Paradise to hear him! Send for him straightway!"

BETWEEN THE sculptured pillars of the entrance stepped a young man, richly clad, his locks curling over his shoulders. He was short, but prodigiously wide of shoulder; his clean-shaven face might have been fair or foul for all one could see, for he wore a broad mask of velvet that came half-down the nose. But his step was light, his carriage strong and graceful, and his blue-green eyes gleamed bright through the holes of the mask. He wore hose of scarlet silk, a close, black tunic laced with gold cords, and a blue velvet mantle embroidered with the arms of Armagnac. He bowed low to the duke, to the Princess Aliénor, and to Count Bertrand.

Guilhem turned to his vassal with a smile.

"Do your troubadours go masked in Gascony?" he asked.

"If he pleases you, my lord, he will show his face," the count replied. "But he has sworn to go hence unknown if he fails to win your applause."

"He will drink, at least," Aliénor laughed. "Here, troubadour!"

And she held out her own cup, new-filled with rich Toulousan. Kneeling, the masked man drank and placed the cup in his bosom.

"Well done!" Aliénor commended. "They breed courtiers at least in Gascony!"

The troubadour's eyes met hers as she spoke, and for a long minute could not look away. A wave of color flooded his cheeks, receding under the mask. Then, backing off some paces from the tables, he threw up his head and sang. It was a canzo, five short stanzas; but every line perfectly turned, every cadence full and throbbing. When he had done, the silence was deep. At last the company roused as from a spell and burst into tumultuous cheering.

"A new song!" Guilhem cried. "Your own, troubadour?"

The young man bowed.

"My own," he answered, "and never sung before. But if ye will hear one that is old, and perfect like old wine?"

He sang again, a pastorella by that great, dead Duke of Aquitaine whose son and grand-daughter listened, enthralled, before its singer. Its golden pathos sunk into its hearers' hearts; for it was borne on a voice of purest, deepest beauty.

The duke sprang to his feet, snatched the chain of massive gold from his own neck and would have fastened it round the troubadour's; but Bertrand of Armagnac caught his arm.

"Not yet, my lord, if it please you!" he urged. "My servant asks a special gift. Judge you, if he be worthy of it!"

Guilhem of Aquitaine, shaking him off, flung the chain over the singer's shoulder.

"What he asks he shall have, and this too!" he cried. "Never has my father been so honored; never has a song of his been so wondrously sung, even by himself!"

The troubadour smiled.

"Have I your word, lord duke, that what I ask will be granted me, so that it touch not your power or honor?"

The duke nodded, impatient to hear his request.

"Why, then," the troubadour rejoined, "I ask no more than to live in peace, to be pardoned for any faults I may have committed, and to continue in my lord of Armagnac's service!"

Guilhem stared at him.

"Why, this is nothing!" he exclaimed. "You might have asked for gold, jewels, a castle!"

"I claim what I have asked, no more."

"The more fool you," the Duke retorted crustily. "What you—"

"In the duke's name!"

The cry from the door brought all the company to their feet. Rudely elbowing his way past the chamberlain, a soldier in full mail burst into the hall.

"What does this mean, fellow?" the duke asked angrily.

The soldier fell to his knees.

"My lord, I am captain of the guard at the Bordeaux gate. I was on watch when the Count of Armagnac returned tonight. The torches burned clear in the archway; and when his troop rode through, I saw there was one with him not of his company. I have reason to believe that this man was the murderer, Cercamon!"

"Splendor of heaven! Why did you not report this before?" cried Aimon de Branh.

"May it please my lord," the captain answered. "I knew not who the man was. I noted only that his face was strange, and that he had a great cut over one thigh, so that the mail rings gaped open. I suspected nothing—the news of his crime not having reached us then—until I came off watch, and went to drink a beaker of wine with a comrade in the Count of Armagnac's troop. This man told me that the stranger had joined their troop at the juncture of the highway with the road from Niort. Then came Sir Aimon de Branh, demanding the murderer's person."

Duke Guilhem rounded on Bertrand with blazing eyes.

"You, Bertrand of Armagnac! You, my most trusted vassal, give shelter to one who has slain my subjects!" he cried. "What loyalty may I expect from lesser men, when you conspire against me?"

Bertrand shrugged his shoulders. " 'Conspire' is a hard word, my lord. I did indeed give shelter to this man, not knowing of his deed till Sir Aimon rode in. Cercamon himself confessed fully to me and convinced me that he had good cause for his acts. But I knew that he, a man of low birth, would get no justice. One does not grant a hearing to churls charged with the murder of men of rank. By your leave, and with all loyalty, I will not give the man up."

The troubadour had watched the excited company in silence, noting the flashing eyes of the furious duke, and the anger of the officer from Niort. Clearly he saw that Guilhem would not pardon Armagnac's rebellion, chivalrous and just though its motive was. With a swift gesture he stripped the mask from his face, and stepped between the duke and de Branh.

"But the man will give himself up," he said. "I am Cercamon; and I have your promise of pardon for my offenses, my lord!"

Every eye was turned on him. After one short gasp of astonishment, Aimon de Branh strode forward and laid his hand on the troubadour's shoulder.

"And I have your promise, lord duke," he exclaimed, "that Cercamon the murderer shall be surrendered to my master, the seneschal of Niort, if he can be found in Aquitaine. I claim the fulfillment of your word!"

Baffled and angry, the duke's eyes roved from knight to troubadour, and then sought Bertrand's.

"You have brought me to a brave choice, my lord count," he spoke scathingly. "Because you choose to protect a criminal, I am forced to break my plighted oath to one man or another. Nor is this all—either I must pardon the murderer, and so offend my loyal castellan at Niort; or I must hand over to the gallows a troubadour whose like is not to be found in France!"

"The troubadours cause is just," Bertrand reminded him. "He slew once to avenge his murdered master, and again in self-defense."

The Princess Aliénor had been standing behind her father,

her gaze fixed on the face of Cercamon. Her own face was pale, but angry and resolute; yet when she spoke, her voice was calm and soft.

"Surely this is an easy choice," she said. "You have a hundred men of birth and valor, my father, who would make good seneschals of Niort; but such another singer is not to be bought for all the wealth of Aquitaine! It is the troubadour more than the soldier, who makes the fame of princes."

This was true; and Guilhem wavered. He recalled that more than once the verses of troubadours had wrecked the good name of those who had offended them; and that one prince who slew a troubadour had been put to death by his sovereign for his crime. No poet would sing the praises of a lord who surrendered a troubadour to death. So Guilhem turned, uncertain, to de Branh.

"Sir Aimon," he asked, "will you give me back my word? I am minded to forgive this man his offense."

Aimon's eyes blazed.

"Never, my lord! I am vassal to the seneschal of Niort, who is in turn your vassal. You can command my master to countermand his orders to me, and in such case I have no more to say; but your word to me is sacred, and I will not yield an inch of my right!"

The duke stood baffled. There was no way out of his dilemma save through breaking his word and so soiling his honor. With every moment his rage against Bertrand mounted; yet he would still have saved Cercamon if he could. For his daughter was right; the possession of such a troubadour in his court would glorify his fame more than ten campaigns.

It was Bertrand who found the one way out. His lined features began to twitch with sudden mirth, and he laughed aloud.

"A troubadour," he said, "has the same right to trial by combat as a knight. Your word, my lord, is passed one way to a knight, and contrariwise to a troubadour. Let each of these men take sword and lance, and fight the matter out. You are then absolved of your promise to him who dies, and can keep it to him who survives."

"Well said!" the Duke cried in vast relief. "Will you fight, Cercamon?"

Cercamon was smiling now, but his breath came quick and fast, and his eyes were defiant.

"I will!" he answered.

"And you, Sir Aimon?"

De Branh's cheeks were pale.

"My lord knows," he replied, "that I am no coward. I have received your praises thrice for my conduct in your service. But Jehan, the captain in Niort whom this man slew, was thrice the swordsman that I am; and Sir Auberi de Nogaro, whom he killed in the forest, had overthrown me twice with the lance. I will fight if my lord demands it; but—no man likes to throw his life away!"

"Then you release me from my promise?"

Aimon drew a deep breath.

"I do, my lord, if you will command my master to take back his order to me."

"Then all is well settled!" the Duke rejoiced. "And I am glad! You must ride back empty-handed, Aimon! Not for a hundred dead captains would I lose this pearl of troubadours!"

"Your grace must not forget that he is my man!" Count Bertrand laughed.

Aliénor smiled to herself.

"Nay," she whispered, "but I think he is my servant!"

THE KING'S CHOICE

"**THEY FOLLOW!**"

Cercamon reined in on the crest of a low hill and gazed back over the road that paralleled the blue Loire across the plain, like a white stripe and a blue one across a richly broidered garment.

"All the way from the town have they followed me!" he muttered. "But the hunter that shows himself to his quarry has little chance of a kill."

And he waved a scornful hand at the distant figures in gleaming mail, who had kept ever at his heels since dawn, without once gaining on him, without once losing sight of him.

Till now he had not been sure it was he they sought. It was no rare thing for armed men to take the high road from Tours to Paris. The riders of Anjou, who held Touraine for Duke Geoffrey le Bel, patroled it ceaselessly; merchants or pilgrims with their escorts, or men-at-arms seeking service, traveled that road often.

But Cercamon had reason to be wary of mailed men; and after leaving the Loire and the distant spires of Tours behind him he had become troubled. He had first caught sight of those riders at sunrise, half an hour after he had ridden out from the gate of the city. Their constant trailing at his heels fretted him more and more, till he resolved to test their purpose. Therefore, an hour ago, he had turned aside from the highway, down a little-used road lined with trees, where armed men could have no honest business.

If they kept to the main road, well and good; but if they turned off after him, he would know they sought but a favorable chance to overtake and assail him. And so, when he trotted out of the byway on to the high road again, having seen the shimmer of their mail thrice behind him, he was sure. And now he could glimpse the sunlight flashing full and bright on their harness as they rode out of the byway on his trail.

The certainty that he was pursued did not astonish him. Cercamon rode on a weighty errand, one fraught with vast significance for all of France. On his success hung the issues of peace or war between great princes, the fortunes of rival houses, perhaps the fate of two kingdoms.

It was early April of 1137, that year so fateful for the young realm of France. The Abbot Suger, ruling in the name of the boy King Louis VII, was soon to hand over his authority to his royal ward. It was a dangerous burden for so fiery and untrained a lad, for the kingdom of France was but a little triangle with Paris, Sens, and Orléans for its corners, claiming a shadowy and perilous sovereignty over the mighty principalities that surrounded it on all sides.

Of all those principalities the mightiest was Aquitaine, its vast area rolling from Loire to Pyrenees, from the Gascon Gulf to the borders of Toulouse. Hated by his neighbors, feared by the Regent Suger, Duke Guilhem X of Aquitaine had just gone to an unmourned grave. Only the iron hand of his great seneschal, Bertrand d'Armagnac, warded the rich lands and the beautiful young daughter Guilhem had left from the greedy hands of rival barons.

"These letters to the Abbot Suger!" Armagnac had commanded. "Let them not go from your hands till they pass into his in Paris. And ride warily, Cercamon; keep your eyes open and your hand on your sword, for I fear your errand is known to our enemies. My late lord the duke was not discreet in this matter, and his court has swarmed with the spies of Champagne."

"Why send me, my lord?" Cercamon had asked his master. "I am both too humble a man and too weak for such an errand."

"Any messenger will be exposed to attack as soon as he leaves Poitou and our garrisons behind him," Armagnac had answered. "If we send a strong force, it will be ambushed by a stronger. Touraine belongs to Anjou; and Anjou loves us little. The road lies too near the borders of Blois to be safe, even for a small army; for Thibault of Champagne has a strong garrison in Blois. A single man has more chance of slipping through than a troop; and of all men you are our best hope. You are brave, cunning, resourceful; you are a troubadour, and even the most lawless man in France scarce dares lay a hand on the sacred person of a troubadour, Castel-Roussillon's fate is fresh in men's memories; even kings fear to commit his crime, lest they perish as he perished."

So Cercamon rode northeast, leaving Poitiers in the dead of night and bearing to the mighty Abbot Suger a proposal, signed by Aliénor, Duchess of Aquitaine, for a royal marriage between herself and the young King Louis. Even as the troubadour left the dark walls behind him, two scarce dead figures dangled from the walls of Poitiers' northern tower—Champenois merchants, who had been caught that afternoon in unlawful conversation with the guard at the North Gate. In their lodgings had been found parchments which—skilfully decoded by the duchess' secretary—had been discovered to contain a full report of the task entrusted to Cercamon.

The young troubadour—a Gascon, of low birth and rare genius—had been in Armagnac's service barely a year. In Poitiers he had first sung before a courtly audience, and now his name was known over all France for the sweetness of his song and the rich perfection of his verses. In Aquitaine he had equal repute as a swordsman, and Bertrand d'Armagnac, whom he served with deep devotion, knew him for as shrewd and cool a head as any in the south. He was well equipped even for so great a task as that which now rested on his broad shoulders.

He rode now, as always, in the rich garments of his calling; for if the sacredness of that vocation were to save him from attack, he must appear at first glance for what he was. But he wore his long, double-edged sword, and under his scarlet tunic he bore a shirt of fine-meshed, impenetrable Moorish mail. His long, black hair floated unbound beneath a flat cap of blue velvet, and his green-hosed legs clasped the sides of the swiftest horse in the stables of Poitiers.

He felt assured that Count Thibault of Champagne would seek to stop him, regardless of the inviolability which surrounded one of his calling. Thibault was a hard-handed, hardheaded tyrant, who feared not men's judgments. And Thibault was most ambitious of all the French barons; he hated Aquitaine and—he had a daughter of marriageable age. The dead Duke Guilhem was not the only feudal prince in the realm who stood to profit from a marriage between his daughter and the young king. The troubadour was not yet so highly honored in the north as in the south, and if men of birth feared to assail him there were rough-handed spearmen who would undertake the task for protection and a price.

As he rode down the hill from which he had spied back upon his pursuers, Cercamon felt small fear of them. So far they had been well able to keep him in sight, for he had carefully spared his horse's strength. Whenever he chose he could leave them far behind. But he did fear lest other enemies might lurk in ambush ahead of him, for he knew Count Thibault's repute for remorseless determination and was certain that the Champenois would not pin his sole hope of heading off the Aquitanian messenger to the questionable chance of overtaking a well-mounted man from behind.

Moreover, cunning had shown itself in the first moment of the pursuit. Cercamon had not been followed until he had left Poitou; his followers had first shown themselves after he had ridden out from Tours. He had had no chance but to pass through Tours, above which there were no fords across the Loire till one came to Blois. And Blois, Thibault's strongest fortalice, lay but a day's ride from Tours.

Cercamon had planned to ride north in a wide circuit around Blois, lest he be seen from its walls. But the very fact that pursuit started from Tours proved that his enemies understood his intentions. It also proved that some of Thibault's spies had left Poitiers and arrived in Tours before him and watched for the precise moment of his setting forth along the river road. And in that case it was probable that the spies had ridden on ahead of him, to warn Thibault of his coming.

There would be ambush ahead as well as pursuers behind. And that ambush would doubtless be laid, not on the highroad near Blois, but on the northerly roads by which he planned to make his circuit.

THE AFTERNOON was half-gone when Cercamon heard a swiftly rising drum of hoofs behind him. The pursuit was drawing suddenly closer; plainly they were ready to close in and settle the matter. Smiling, he reined in and counted them. Twelve men, mailed from top to toe, on good horses. He pricked his beast with the spur, and the splendid animal shot forward like an arrow.

The pursuit was sharp for a while; but at last he drew so far ahead of them that they seemed to realize the hopelessness of riding him down, and checked their pace. Cercamon followed their example. Two or three times this was repeated, at intervals. Then Cercamon began to understand.

That handful of men-at-arms that tagged his heels had no expectation of catching him, with his swifter horse and lighter weight, for he was almost unencumbered by armor. Their task was to make him uneasy, to keep him in sight, keep him galloping. So long as their eyes could follow him, he dared not stop for food or sleep; and their sporadic spurts compelled him to wear down his mount with bursts of speed.

When his fleet roan was weary, and he himself grown desperate and careless with hunger and fatigue, they would have done their work. Somewhere ahead lay other riders, possibly hidden, who would either cut him off or take up the chase with fresh horses, when his own was no longer capable of its glorious swiftness.

There was only one way to defeat this stratagem, and Cercamon resolved to take it. On the chance that the road ahead concealed an ambush, he must leave that road—before it grew dark. If he would escape the pursuit behind, he must outdistance them now, must leave them so far behind that they could not gain sight or trace of him again. Once out of touch with him, they could not signal their relays to take up the pursuit; and he rejoiced that he had spared his horse's strength. He thrust home the spurs, and felt the long-limbed roan burst into beautiful speed beneath him.

The sun was sinking now and dusk filtering into the cool air. Cercamon knew the country well; the river lay still to the right, but to the left there was a network of roads leading off into the rich plain. At one of these—but not the first—he would turn off; and he would not return to the highway till he was well past Blois. Out of sight behind him, the hunters would not know which way he had taken.

It was at the third road he turned, to the north; and by that time the highway lay empty for so far behind him as he could see or hear. Slackening his pace, he let the horse idle for a few moments and shifted about on the saddle to ease his limbs. He was well-concealed from the main road by clumps of willow, behind which a little stream sang in the gathering darkness.

He smiled at the thought that he had confounded his enemies. That his journey was still beset with peril he did not doubt; but he would find an escape from each difficulty as he met it.

The roan nickered at the smell of water, and he let it drink from the brook. The night drew in soft and dark about him. In the shelter of the trees that grew ever thicker on both sides the road was black as a tomb. He was now riding through a wood; the air was damp, and the earth so soft under his horse's hoofs that they made no sound. For perhaps an hour he rode on, till he came to a bridle-path and paused to think.

That path led to a monastery of Cistercians, La Ferté-en-Bois, which lay on the edge of the forest, with its own fat fields spreading north and west of low, wide stone buildings. There he could find food, a refuge from his pursuers and rest—of all of which he stood in dire need. Most of all his horse needed rest. The monks would give him sanctuary, and none would dare assail him within their walls.

But—if his foes should learn that he was there, they would camp before it till he was forced to surrender. And to spend the night there would give them time to quarter the country for him or to cut him off from every road leading toward Paris. With a pang of regret he resolved to ride on all night, and in a little while he trotted past the few faint lights of the cloister, thinking ruefully of the good food and peaceful harborage within.

Half an hour more passed, a mere morsel bitten out of the long night through which he must ride, on and on, till dawn should find him close to the walls of Orléans—a royal city, far beyond Blois, and a haven where the king's law would protect him. But there were hours of the saddle, hours of ceaseless vigilance, before he could reach the city nestled in the clasp of the Loire.

A thin, clear sound tinkled through the night. A moment he listened; then he pulled in the weary roan. From far down the road to the north—in his very path—came the faint jingle of mail, and under it the staccato pound of many hoofs. It was far ahead, but he was out in the open now—between him and those unseen lay no hiding-place, no shred of cover, only the great, flat plain with its young gardens and new crops.

The troop ahead must be hostile, for he was now within the very heart of that country over which Thibault of Champagne ruled from his eyrie of Blois. He must ride back and shelter either in the monastery or in the wood; eke they who rode toward him would overwhelm him. The dozes that followed he had put off the scent.

He swung about, and the brave roan burst into a gallant spurt, which for a little seemed to have all the swiftness of fresh strength. And that little was just enough. For, as he glimpsed the first lights of the monastery again, his ears caught the drum of hoofs from the south, riding down the very bridle-path by which he had come so short a time before.

He had not thrown them off the scent after all—they had picked the very spot where they would force him from the highway; their occasional spurts had been so timed as to drive him either to take shelter with the monks or to ride straight into the ambush laid for him just past the cloister.

They had outguessed him, outmaneuvered him, driven him to earth as dogs drive a fox! And there was but one thing he could do—take to earth in the refuge they had chosen for him, out of which they could dig him at their leisure.

Having no choice, he took the one course open; it would at least give him a little time, since his foes would not dare drag him from a house of God. He turned into the road that led to the wide stone portal of La Ferté, with the tumult of pursuit so close that, but for their own noise, those who had followed all day must have heard him.

His knock roused the porter, an old gray monk yawning with sleep, and he was admitted instantly, though with a frown at his gay garb. Only the clergy scowled at troubadours. His horse was led to the stables, but he would not have it unsaddled.

"But you are weary, and your beast near exhaustion!" the hospitable porter protested.

"The abbot!" Cercamon interrupted. "For Heaven's sweet grace, I must speak with your abbot at once! There are enemies on my heels!"

The startled monk crossed himself with trembling fingers and broke into a hobbling run. As fast as his stiff legs would carry him he hastened down the corridor, into the cloistered court and to the abbot's cell. In an agony of impatience Cercamon waited, imagining his two-fold foe surrounding the monastery while he bided the coming of the father superior.

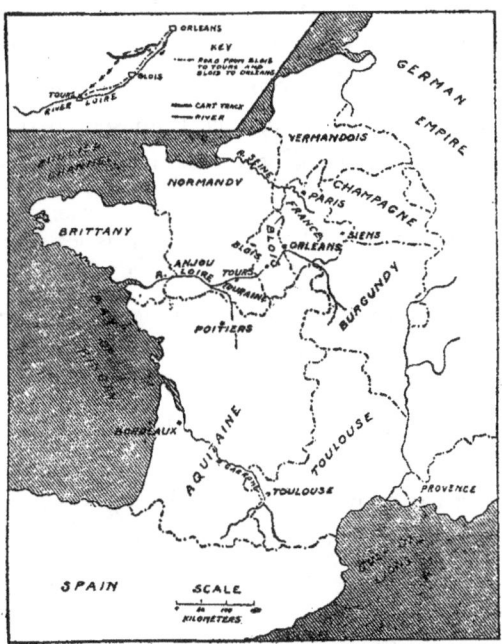

But it was scarce three minutes before the abbot's tall, emaciated form appeared in the doorway.

He was a commanding old man, in gray gown and black apron, with features sharp with fasting and eyes that glowed with the indomitable spirit of Christ's warrior.

Cercamon fell on one knee and drew from his bosom the letter sealed with the great seal of Aquitaine.

"My father," he began anxiously, "I am ambassador from the Duchess of Aquitaine to his holiness the Abbot Suger, Regent of France. Armed men, unrighteously violating the peace of this province, seek to intercept me and seize my despatches. It matters little what becomes of me, but it will be ill for France and for the Church if these letters do not reach the regent. I pray you, help me!"

The abbot took the letter from Cercamon's hand, examined the seal and read the superscription.

"It were ill indeed," he commented, "if messages of weight for the noble Suger fell into the hands of evil men. But how am I to know that such an event would injure Holy Church and not rather your mistress, the Duchess of Aquitaine, alone?"

So eager was the troubadour to insure the safety of his despatches that he resolved to entrust their secret to the monk, knowing well that a man of his calling and sanctity would not betray them.

"Because, holy father," he answered, "this letter concerns a marriage between the duchess and the King of France; and Thibault of Champagne, wishing to arrange a marriage between the young prince and his daughter, desires to prevent Aquitaine's offer from reaching the regent's ears. Your holiness knows how disastrous for the Cistercian order would be an alliance between Champagne and the Crown. Your houses are all within Thibault's territories; he would levy a heavy tax on every monastery to raise the dowry which the king would demand, and your pious order would be shaken to its foundations by the demand on its resources."

The abbot eyed him sternly.

"The Count of Champagne has always been our order's benefactor," he retorted. "This very house is within his territory. And your late duke, Guilhem X, was a heretic and an enemy of the true faith!"

Cercamon was prepared for this.

"The late Duke Guilhem reconciled himself with the Church,

and under the guidance of your order's pillar, the holy Bernard, renounced his heresy. He died in the odor of sanctity, on a pilgrimage to Compostella. Your holiness surely would not take the responsibility for preventing a letter of greatest weight to the State from reaching Abbot Suger, the truest friend in France to both Church and throne?"

This shot told. Grateful as all Cistercians were to Thibault of Champagne for lands and money, they were even more devoted to the Crown. No pious churchman would suppress a letter to the regent, whose holiness and incorruptibility made him the Church's shield against the barons.

"What shall I do to help you?"the Abbot asked.

"Send this letter, by a safe hand, to the regent!" Cercamon answered. "A monk of your order—which has never meddled with the rivalries of princes—can pass unmolested even through embattled camps. But send the bearer secretly, by night, so that those who follow me shall not see him. And further, I pray you send a message to my master also, the Count of Armagnac, who is now in Poitiers. Tell him that I have been pursued, perhaps seized; and that his letters have gone on to Abbot Suger by one of the monks under your rule."

"It were well," the abbot reflected, "for the messengers to depart at once."

But this was not what Cercamon desired.

"They who lie in wait for me," he objected, "are even now close to your walls, whose thickness alone has prevented the clatter of their mail from reaching your ears. It were well to wait till they have passed, or—"

His words were smothered in a sudden shout from the darkness without, by the thunder of hoofs and a challenging cry.

"THEY ARE here!" Cercamon gasped, clutching the wide sleeve of the abbot's gown. "They expected to seize me before this, but I eluded them. Now those who followed me have met with the troop which lurked ahead. They drove me to take shelter here, and will demand me at—"

A lance-butt thundered on the door. Seizing the troubadour's shoulder, the abbot dragged him off into the darkness of the cloistered court.

"We will hide you," he whispered, "till they have gone!"

"They will not go!" Cercamon protested. "They know I am here, and need only wait till I am forced to come out. I must surrender to them; do you get my messages through—to the regent, and to Armagnac!"

The iron-bound door quivered beneath the impact of beating spears. At a sign from the abbot, the trembling porter tottered to the archway, fumbling with his great keys. The iron lock screeched, and the door flew open. Mailed men, their armor gleaming in the faint flare of the porter's rushlight, swarmed into the corridor.

The abbot came forward from the darkness of the cloister within which Cercamon still stood concealed.

"What seek ye, men of violence?" he upbraided them. "This is God's house!"

A thick-set officer thrust himself forward from the knot of men-at-arms, concealing his uneasiness under a swagger.

"We be king's men!" he answered. "We seek a strolling jongleur, who bears treasonable letters! Deliver him to us, or it will go ill with your house!"

The abbot raised his wooden crucifix, which dangled from a long chain of carven beads.

"It is rather you who are traitors!" he rebuked them. "If ye were honest soldiers of France, ye would bear its colors, instead of prowling through the night with no device upon your breasts, like thieves and outlaws. And if ye disturb this house, I will cast upon you the Church's ban, the curse of the unextinguishable flame and the worm that is not appeased! Go hence, and respect Christ's altar!"

The officer flinched. Bloody and ruthless as the times were, few men were so bold as to defy excommunication, with its threat of eternal torture. But, frightened to the core of his superstitious soul, he still clung to his purpose. His men were less daring; they crowded together as if seeking courage from contact with one another, and their eyes were downcast.

"It matters not to you whether we ride with or without badge of service," the officer resumed doggedly, "whether we be king's men or outlaws. Yet I spoke in haste, and will not molest your roof. But we demand the body of him who we know has taken refuge here; and if you refuse him to us, we will quarter ourselves upon you till ye surrender him!"

This was a threat that would be fulfilled; and both the abbot and the listening Cercamon knew it. Once the unruly soldiers had free run of the monastery, Cercamon could not escape, nor could the monks who bore his messages pass through their lines. Therefore the troubadour, who had already formed his decision, advanced from his shelter into the dimly lighted corridor. So swift was his approach that the officer started back at sight of him. But straightway every soldier laid hand on sword, and the mass of them moved forward to seize their prisoner.

Cercamon raised both hands as a sign that he meditated no resistance. His fingers itched for his sword-hilt, and he knew his skill with his weapon was great enough to take more than one or two with him into darkness. But his deeply religious soul shrank from bloodshed in a holy place.

"I can not escape," he said bluntly, "therefore I yield. But beware how ye lay hands on me, for I am a troubadour, whose blood not even kings dare shed!"

The soldiers, straining like hounds in leash, looked to their leader. Smiling his satisfaction, the officer answered:

"You have chosen wisely and saved us much mischief. Our orders are to take you, not to harm you, and we are glad indeed not to have your blood on our hands. To him, lads!"

The next instant Cercamon was seized, spun about, disarmed, pawed over by a dozen hands. His cloak, tunic, mail shirt, undertunic and hose were stripped from him, till he stood mother-naked between the jubilant troopers and the indignant abbot.

"Ha!" cried the officer, who had been rummaging through his captive's garments. "The clever fox thought to hide his booty, but a cunning old hound smelled it out!"

And he waved in one hand a folded and creased parchment, which he had rifled from Cercamon's hose. This parchment was an exact duplicate of the letter which Cercamon had given the abbot and which he had kept hidden between hose and foot-sole. An expression of consternation flitted over the abbot's face; but Cercamon turned his head ever so slightly and made a grimace of reassurance. Then he let his eyes meet the officer's, and his face was the picture of utter dismay. At sight of his long visage the soldiers burst into mocking laughter.

"We have what we came for, lads!" the leader exulted. "Truss him up now, and be swift!"

In a few moments Cercamon was clothed again—the rough hands of the spearmen forcing his garments on in utmost disorder—his hands were bound behind his back, he was gagged and his head muffled in a bag whose meshes were just coarse enough to let him breathe, but shut out the light. Two stalwart troopers dragged him to the door, flung him out, lifted him up into a saddle and lashed his feet fast under a horse's belly.

It was not his own horse; but he soon realized that his beloved roan had not been left in the cloister stables. The commander of the troop was on its back, as his loud oaths of satisfaction proclaimed. Cercamon would have gritted his teeth if the gag had permitted, for the beast was the apple of his eye.

A COMMAND rang out; the horses began to move, and fourscore hoofs pounded away into the fresh spring night. His senses darkened more by the bag over his face than by the darkness, Cercamon knew not which direction they took. He only knew that he was in the rearmost rank and that his beast trotted with the often broken gait of the led horse. Yet his wits told him that he rode toward Blois and the dungeons of Count Thibault of Champagne.

The pace was swift, for his captors were anxious to have the

business done with. Cercamon knew that the reason they did
not wear their master's colors was that Thibault hoped to conceal
from public knowledge his double crime—interference with
an embassy to the Regent, and violation of the sacred person
of a troubadour. If it should be discovered, he would have both
the Regent and the troops of Aquitaine to reckon with; and his
assault on a troubadour would set France—the south at least—
on fire against him.

He played a desperate game, and Cercamon gave him un-
grudging admiration for the skill with which he had played it.
Thibault's men had plainly been carefully instructed not to hunt
down their quarry on the soil of Touraine—which would have
meant a quarrel with Anjou—but to chase him into the territory of Blois and lure him into the monastery of La Ferté.

The monks, who depended for protection on Thibault, might
be presumed to say nothing. But to be sure that they said
nothing Thibault's men gave themselves out as royal troops and
wore no device.

And if they met others on the road, the fact that they wore
no device would prevent their deed from being imputed to
Thibault. Once their prisoner was safe in Blois, Thibault could

deny all knowledge of his existence, and no one would dare accuse him without proof. To the eye these troopers were no man's men, probably marauders. To the casual glance—and nothing else was possible in the dark—Cercamon, whose face was hidden and over whose gay garments a coarse fustian robe had been lashed, was a mere captive about whose fate no one cared.

The troop had ridden perhaps an hour when Cercamon was aware of a faint red glow through the meshes of the bag and of a ringing challenge in a broad, thick-tongued French. With a shout of joy the troop answered it as one man. Weapons clattered, horses neighed, voices talked back and forth. The red glow grew till Cercamon could catch the shine of metal against it when he faced it directly. It was a huge fire high above the ground, a watch-fire on one of those squat, outlying towers that are the vedettes of fortified cities.

The voices died down, the troop rode on, the glow faded. On and on they trotted. The dawn breeze was in the air, and cocks crowing, when again the riders reined in, new challenges floated clear from some far height. The hoarse voice of the captain answered. There was a loud laugh from that height whence the challenge had rung; a horrible screech of iron rent the air.

Then, moving forward at a walk up a steep slope, the caval-cade advanced across a wooden bridge that rang hollow under their hoofs. The fresh air was shut out by thick walls; again the screech of metal announced the raising of the drawbridge they had just crossed. Fingers fumbled at Cercamon's neck, the coarse bag slid across his features, the light rushed in upon his dazzled eyes.

It was only the half-light of a great archway at early morning, but after his double darkness he felt it strike him like a whiplash across the eyes. It was some moments before his sight adjusted itself, and then he saw that the archway was the main gate of a large castle, whose outer bailey opened directly off the gate.

The wall was a good eighteen feet thick of squared masonry,

and in the center of the court beyond he saw the massive base of a square tower, with rectangular turrets jutting out from each corner. Then the ropes that bound his feet were cut, he was dragged from his horse and fell, saddle-worn and unable to stand, in a heap on the flagstones.

A knot of men-at-arms surrounded him, some wearing no badges—and these were the men who had brought him—others flaunting the arms of Champagne. One fell to chafing the prisoner's ankles, till the blood began to sting unbearably in his constricted veins. After a time they raised him, and forced him to walk up and down, all the while railing at him. When he could keep his feet without help, a soldier grasped him by the shoulder and led him across the court toward the tower.

It was chilly in the court, for the sun had not yet risen above the crenellated walls. In the wooden stalls built around two sides of the bailey, horses nickered, smelling the hay being borne to them by bare-armed grooms. Red-cheeked maid-servants chattered and laughed about the well or swung lithely away with buckets balanced on their heads. A smell of cooking drifted from the soldiers' quarters. An unseen cow lowed, and chickens cackled. On the battlements a soldier sang.

Exhausted, Cercamon stumbled to the inner portal, the entrance to the tower or keep. The iron-bound door of massive oak was flung open, and his guide shoved him roughly into a guard-room, bare, bleak, lighted only by two high arrow-slits in the walls. A dozen men-at-arms in unbraced tunics were washing the sleep from their eyes or yawning as they waited their turn at the tub of well-water that stood on a crude bench.

Their beds—mere mats of straw laid over other benches—lay along two walls; beside the door stood a chest of arms, with a recruit squatting by it burnishing the mail of his older comrades. A pointed archway in the rear wall led to an inner room, which Cercamon guessed to be the great hall, with its long tables and its stairway leading to the upper stories.

But he was not to enter that room yet. His guide's hand

impelled him to a dark opening that yawned, without railing, in the guard-room floor. A shout of laughter rang from the lolling men-at-arms.

"Another bird for the cage, eh, Simon?" one cried, and the soldier nodded.

"There is room, I trust?" he asked with assumed solicitude. "This bird is of fine plumage, as ye see, and his feathers must not be ruffled." Grinning, he dragged Cercamon down a dark stair into a musty vault that reeked with damp and bad air.

A murky torch advanced from the blackness to meet them, and metal clinked dully. He who bore the light was a squat, thick-set fellow in stained leather, with a bunch of keys dangling from his belt and a short, broad sword by his side.

"Look to him well," the soldier cautioned. "If he escapes, the old Bear will set up a new gallows on the wall. Thou hast not smelt fresh air for so long that it would choke thee—especially from a rope's end."

And he sprang up the stairs, leaving Cercamon to the warder's care.

The latter led the troubadour to a row of cells in the solid wall of the keep. A key whined in a rusty lock; a heavy door grated open, and he was thrust within. The warder's hand guided him to a corner; strong fingers clutched his ankles and locked them in massy fetters.

"You will be fed in an hour," the warder muttered, and disappeared.

The door clanged shut after him, and the key turned in the lock.

Though he was desperately hungry, panting for drink, and sore in every bone, Cercamon grinned to himself in the blackness of his cell. He had reason to grin; for he had tricked the men who had tricked him, outwitted those who had made him prisoner. When he surrendered himself at the monastery, and his hose had been despoiled of the letter he had hidden, he had pretended consternation. But the captured letter had gone far to insure the success of his mission.

IT HAD been at Cercamon's request that the Duchess Aliénor had let her clerk draw up two copies of the despatches to Suger and had signed both with her seal. If he had borne but one, and that one had not been found on his person, his captors would have searched every man and every corner in the monastery. But having found one copy on him, in a hiding-place which looked to have been chosen with a view to keeping it secret, Thibault's troopers had assumed that they had found that which they sought.

With these papers in his hands and their bearer safely under lock and key, the Count of Champagne would have no idea that the message, borne by a monk, was already on its way to Paris. Provided he were set free before prison broke his strength, Cercamon cared not how long he might lie in Thibault's cells. He cared only for the success of his mission; and he had already seen to that.

Nor did he fear greatly for his own life or comfort. He was a troubadour, known throughout France as its finest singer. What baron of that song-loving nation would let such a voice molder in his dungeons?

Cercamon's thoughts were so merry that he scarce heeded how time passed, till the great door screeched again and the warder's torch flared in its opening.

"Food!" the keeper muttered and, shoving a plate and a stone bottle within reach of his prisoner's corner, he stepped behind him.

The next moment Cercamon felt a steel point prick the base of his neck and understood that he was to sit motionless while the warder cut the bonds from his hands. He did so and soon was able to move his arms. With a nimble backward spring the jailer leaped out of his reach and slammed the door. But he need not have feared, for the prisoner's arms were still numb from their lashings.

When they pricked and tingled with new life, Cercamon examined his breakfast, a loaf of bread and a crock of water. The water was stale, the bread moldy.

"Pah!" he cried, and flung the food from him.

The blithe mood left him all at once, for he had not eaten in six-and-twenty hours, and the disappointment sickened him. He sat motionless, gritting his teeth.

In this attitude he was found when, about noon, the door opened again; but this time it was not the jailer who entered. It was a brace of spearmen with brightly glowing torches that lighted up the bare, damp cell, with the water trickling down its walls, the rotten straw on its stone floor and the disheveled prisoner with his despondent face and fettered ankles.

After the men-at-arms entered a big-boned man in middle age, clad in black velvet hose and tight-fitting tunic. The torch-light fell on his rugged, square face, florid with good living and scarred with battle, on a short, curling white beard and on the rich golden embroidery of his black surcoat. With obvious intent he stood so that the light illumined the golden device— the coronetted arms of Champagne, quartered with those of Blois.

Though he had never seen the man before, Cercamon knew him from his dress, his fierce, majestic features and the arrogance of his carriage. This was indeed Thibault of Champagne, the greatest baron of the North. Brother to King Stephen of England, he now cherished the ambition to become father-in-law to the King of France and so to make himself the mightiest uncrowned prince in Europe.

For a long time the two eyed each other in silence, and it was Cercamon who spoke first.

"Your grace will forgive me that I do not rise," he said, with courtesy so deep as almost to be insulting. "I am prevented by these adornments with which your grace had honored my legs."

And he pointed to his chains.

Count Thibault laughed, a rolling, good-natured laugh which thundered back from the stone vaulting of the dungeon.

"One sees that you are indeed Cercamon the Troubadour!" he answered.

His eyes examined his captive, noting the mighty shoulders, the unnaturally long arms, whose sinews showed through his rumpled, tight-fitting sleeves, and the handsome face with its blue-green eyes, that glowed like coals in the torchlight.

"I am sorry," the count spoke again, with courtesy to match Cercamon's own, "that my men were forced to handle you so. My spies reported you a perilous man, shrewd of wit and a master with the sword. It would not have been wise to give you an equal chance. Moreover, I had to take you alive and uninjured. It goes ill with him who slays one of your calling."

Cercamon nodded.

"Your grace will do me the justice to admit that I gave little trouble. I did not even draw weapon."

Thibault's eyes clouded.

"So my men reported," he mused. "It is that which disturbs me. It is unlike your reputation. You are said to be a man who fights for the love of fighting, kills when the odds are even and never gives up a task unfinished. Therefore I suspect that you have not begun to fight me yet."

"Perhaps your grace is right," Cercamon admitted demurely. "But it was not hospitable of you to feed me on foul bread and lodge me in a stinking pit."

"That was only that you might the more appreciate the kindness I still hope to show you. But I can not treat like a guest a man who may meditate some dangerous plot against me. It rests with you, troubadour, whether you lie on slimy stone and gnaw foul crusts or sleep in a fair bed and share my table."

He paused, searching Cercamon's face the while.

Now Cercamon, confident that his message would go through to Abbot Suger, and being raw with famine and ill treatment, saw no cause for prolonging his own discomfort. He had done all in his power; the rest lay with the regent and Bertrand d'Armagnac.

"Your conditions?" he asked.

Thibault smiled.

"Merely those which I can enforce with or without your consent," he replied. "You shall have the freedom of my castle and be treated with all honor—if you will but give me your parole of honor."

"And that means?"

"That you will not try to escape, nor communicate to any man those things which have happened to you at my order, nor speak a word of the errand that brought you from Poitiers, until I let you leave my castle."

Cercamon reflected a moment, but could not see that these terms could do any harm. Already a monk was on his way to Paris with the all-important despatches, and another had set out for Poitou to bring word of Cercamon's probable plight to his master. And it was true that, if he refused, Thibault could insure his obedience by keeping him a miserable captive in this noisome cell. He looked up suddenly, grinning.

"I accept, my lord," he said, "and I give you my word."

"Strike the chains from his limbs!" the Count commanded. "You, Gilles, take him to the north chamber and give him fine garments. You, Watrequin, hie to the servants' offices and bring him good meat and drink! And now, troubadour, remember your promise well—for tonight King Louis of France sups with me!"

THE KING came at nightfall, his approach heralded by the thunder of galloping hoofs and the sudden swoop of horsemen, who checked their fiery mounts in mid-career, flinging them back on their haunches at the very brink of the moat. Then rang the challenge from the walls and a fanfare of royal trumpets. It was half an hour afterward before the young monarch, with his escort of three hundred spears, rode with slow majesty across the lowered drawbridge. Louis of France loved to be well prepared for and always sent his avant-garde well ahead, that his welcome might be worthy his acceptance.

The great gate was open, the drawbridge down. The royal procession rode over splendid carpets from the looms of Arras, between lines of full-mailed men-at-arms. Thibault himself stood in the archway, bareheaded, bowing low. From the battlemented crest of the wall maidens dropped flowers upon the heads of the king and his knights. Beside the count stood his master of the garrison, Raymond de Montivre, armored from top to toe, but with his nasaled helmet in his hand.

Louis was a tall, slender lad of scarce twenty, with short, dark hair and dark eyes that blazed out of a pale face. His features had not yet assumed that austere reserve which, in later years, grief and misfortune stamped upon them; now, in his fiery youth, he had learned to conceal neither his swift, sensitive emotions nor his overbearing pride. A slight smile curled his thin lips as he acknowledged Thibault's obeisance; it pleased him to see the haughty Count of Champagne humbling himself. And he embraced Thibault with a graciousness born of that pleasure.

The two, attended by Montivre, crossed the bailey toward the tower, while the king's men rode slowly into the court and gave over their beasts to the bustling grooms who were in despair to find room for so many horses in the castle stables.

Conducted thus ceremoniously to his chamber on the third floor of the keep, Louis the King was left to the ministrations of the cringing castle servants; and Thibault, with a smile of triumph lighting his florid face, sought out Cercamon in the north turret. Cercamon was washed, fresh-shaven and habited in gay garments of Thibault's furnishing. The count entered without announcing himself.

"You are mindful of your parole?" he asked.

"My lord!" Cercamon exclaimed. "They call you the Bear of the North, but there is as much fox as bear in you. Had you told me of the king's coming before you offered me parole, I

would never have promised to keep silent before him. But
having given my word, I will keep it."

Thibault laughed.

"That is well! Tonight, at supper, you are to sing before the
King!"

The troubadour raised his eyebrows.

"You can not command song, my lord."

Thibault shrugged his shoulders.

"I can outwit you, but I can not argue with you," he answered.
"I pray you to sing before the king, if that pleases you better."

Cercamon bowed.

"What songs?" he asked. "The north does not know much
of our southern poesy. I would not choose verses that the king
will not approve."

Once more the count laughed.

"See what an advantage I have, in that I know the king!" he
exulted. "When Aquitaine wished to contract a royal marriage,
it sent its offer, by a minstrel, to a monk. Truly that monk is
Regent of France, but for all that he is a shaveling. If your letters
had reached Suger, the king would have been enraged that his
marriage should have been arranged over his head. Now I,
knowing his pride, his ceaseless chafing against the tutelage of
Suger, sent my proposal for a marriage between the king and
my daughter to Louis himself—and he is here tonight to see
the lass! Ah, you southerners are brave soldiers and rare singers,
but ye are no statesmen!

"Likewise the foremost troubadour of France, being a southerner, has to ask me—a northern soldier—what to sing before
the King. Knowing him, I can tell you. He is young, proud,
hot-headed. Sing him songs of war and brave deeds—songs of
chivalry in arms! Your whining love-ballads will not touch him,
nor your dainty pastorelles of shepherds and shepherdesses.
What are peasants, sheep and light-o'-loves to the son of Louis
the Strong? Nay, pour out your fiercest notes and sing him of
the clash of sword on shield!"

Cercamon's eyes were flashing, but less with the kindling words of the man who had beaten him than with anger at his own helplessness to strike back. He had given his word to say nothing to the king, either of his own capture or of the Duchess Aliénor's letters. And while he must sit silent, bound by his honor, Thibault would be using every art, every persuasion, to knit up a marriage between his daughter and the king. And to crown all, he, Cercamon, ambassador of Aquitaine, must sing to make them merry—must sing over the funeral of Aquitaine's proud hopes!

A sudden suspicion crossed the count's cunning mind.

"Ye troubadours are cunning fellows!" he said. "See to it that your songs contain no suggestion, no single hint, against the spirit of your parole!"

"My lord!" Cercamon cried proudly. "If we were both on the open plain, my sword would avenge that insult to my honor, baron though you are!"

The nobleman's rough-hewn face softened into contrition.

"Your pardon!" he replied. "I had forgotten the courtesy that becomes a host. You will sing for us?"

"I will," Cercamon agreed.

But when he was left alone, he pondered long on Thibault's request, turning it over and over to find what hidden meaning, what cunning scheme, might lie beneath it. 'I can outwit you,' Thibault had said; and so far he was justified in his boast.

The troubadour had countered his first clever stroke—the ambush—by a cleverer parry, which the count did not yet suspect; but it had been shrewd of Thibault to lure him into that ambush. And Thibault had indeed outwitted him in the matter of his parole. But in this last request Cercamon could see nothing, save that the count wished to put the petulant Louis in a good mood, a mood that would make him more receptive to Thibault's proposals.

And a great flame of anger swept over Cercamon, that, in spite of all his caution, for all that he could do, the Bear of Champagne had beaten him and made a plaything of him.

If he could only tell the king all—that he, an ambassador on business of state from Aquitaine to France, had been ambushed by Thibault's men; that Thibault had intercepted, by force, a messenger who came with proposals that concerned the king, and even now sought to inveigle Louis into a pledge of marriage before Aquitaine's proposal could reach the royal ears—if he could only tell Louis this, the proud young prince would flame into righteous indignation, sweep Thibault and all Thibault's designs from his path and avenge a deed that was as much an insult to his royal dignity as to the pride of Aquitaine.

But cunning Thibault had sealed Cercamon's lips till he should be permitted to leave the castle of Blois. And then it would be too late, for Thibault would not let him go till the marriage between Champagne and the Crown should have been agreed upon.

But Cercamon was not the man to give all for lost while life still surged through his veins and his shrewd wits yet had something to feed on. There was always some way out of every trap, some weak link in every chain. As he pondered, it suddenly came to him that the weak link in Thibault's chain was the proposal that Cercamon, whom Thibault had hindered from fulfilling an errand that concerned the king, should now sing before the King.

True, he could not weave into his song anything that would violate his promise; but at some future time, Louis would know how Thibault had intrigued to keep the Aquitanian offer from his ears and then the king would remember that Cercamon had sung for him at Blois. Yes, it would be too late then—but something might happen in the mean time, if the monk of La Ferté had safely reached Paris and the regent.

This was as far as Cercamon could think the situation out, and he gave his mind to the choice of songs he would sing. Shortly after, a white-clad usher came to summon him to supper.

H E F O U N D the bailey bright with torchlight and thronged with officers of the garrison and the knights who had come with the king. The great castle was crowded. Every chamber was filled, and from every turret men were flocking toward the keep. They walked by twos and threes, or in groups, talking animatedly, so that the courtyard rang with the strident hum of their voices.

Entering the tower, Cercamon followed the throng through the guard-room into the great hall, which occupied three-fourths the space of the first floor. It was a huge, high-ceiled room; its cold stone walls hung with Flemish tapestries that billowed in the draft from the arrow-slits. A score of banners, tattered and bloodstained, hung from the rafters; wood and broidered silk alike were dark with the accumulated smoke of the Winter fires that had risen from the hearth in the south corner; soot lay thick on the finely carven woodwork of the galleries which ran high up along each wall, for the archers posted to serve the arrow-slits.

Long tables—mere rectangles of deal laid on trestles—were ranged one beyond the other across the hall; one stood high on a dais at the western end of the apartment, under the crossed standards of Champagne and France. Servants had already covered the bare boards with the finest napery of the province; splendidly molded flagons of silver stood, brimful with the rarest wines, at each table's end.

The busy sewers and ushers picked their way through the gathering crowd, the former shouting orders to the harassed servants, the latter striving valiantly to direct each guest to his appointed place. Their task was no light one; wo to them if, however many the guests, they failed to seat each in his due order of precedence, taking into account his birth, title and years of service.

Now Thibault of Champagne had done a bold thing; he had ordered Cercamon assigned to a place at that highest table on the dais, the master's table, where he himself, his household and the king would sit. In the south the troubadour, as a matter of right, could claim a seat at the master's board; but here in the ruder north, where his art was still new, it was perilous for a low-born man, though he were a troubadour, to mingle on familiar terms with men of gentle blood.

But both Thibault and the young king knew by repute the fame of Cercamon, and Thibault knew he could keep his own proud vassals in order.

The great ones were already seated while yet their followers poured in, and as each entered and made obeisance to the dais king and count bowed acknowledgment. With some trepidation Cercamon took his place at one end of that high table, after his low bow had been returned and the count had signed to him to sit.

Thibault himself had given up his own place of honor—in the middle of the western side, overlooking the entire company—to Louis the King. On the king's right was Thibault; on his left, Thibault's daughter, the young Countess Alys. Beyond her sat de Montivre, master of the garrison, and the foremost of the king's and of Thibault's knights filled up the remaining places.

When all were seated, the servants came down between the tables in solemn procession, each bearing his appointed dish. Peacocks, roasted whole, their feathers carefully replaced as in life, rested on platters of silver; suckling pigs crisp and sleek; rich stews of mutton in deep bowls, spiced with every known delicacy; great mounds of grilled beef in thick slabs—all these followed, in the order of importance assigned them by fashion. The guests were already drinking, as they would all through the meal.

Accustomed to the refined luxury of the south, Cercamon paid scant attention to all these preparations and less to his wine, sipping only when the king drank, as was proper. All his attention was focused on the girl who sat at Louis' left, through whom her father had destined to unite the fortunes of Champagne with those of France.

She was a tall young woman, strongly made, yet graceful,

perhaps a little older than the king. Her hair was brown, her eyes blue. It would have been flattery to call her beautiful. Yet her gaze was clear, frank and innocent, and both her features and her bearing bore the fine, subtle stamp of goodness. She seemed a little melancholy; though her lips and chin were firm, her smile was wistful.

"It were a good thing for this young prince," Cercamon meditated, "and for the peace of France, if Thibault should win his game."

For it was plain to any that had seen them both that Alys of Blois surpassed Aliénor of Aquitaine in beauty of soul as much as Aliénor surpassed her in beauty of face and body. In the year past, the troubadour had seen much of his duchess and knew that, far as she stood above other women in loveliness, her heart was filled with pride and cruelty and love of pleasure.

The company ate like men who had fasted for a week. Well might the king's men do so, for they had ridden far in the Spring air; but there was no moderation in their manners. As they ate, so they drank. Cercamon wondered, as he watched them, that these gourmands and the dainty folk of his own land could both be Frenchmen.

So fast they reached their fingers into the stew-bowls, so eagerly they grasped the slabs of meat in their sinewy hands, that the servants had scarce time to bring them towels and ewers of water between courses. Each man seized his food firmly in his left hand, hacked at it with his dagger, and carried it to his mouth in his fingers, washing down the mouthfuls with great gulps of wine. Of all that company only Cercamon, with his fine Gascon manners, the countess and the king, ate daintily or moderately; and Louis drank as sparsely as he ate.

At last the feast was cleared away and the cloths removed, but the flagons, constantly replenished, passed up and down incessantly. Thibault of Champagne rose from his place; a trumpeter behind him blew a blast on a silver horn, and the deep drone of conversation was cut off as by a sword-thrust. The count waved a hand toward Cercamon, who rose and bowed to the king, and with a sardonic smile on his lips, Thibault presented him.

"Many of you," he said, "have exchanged blows with our countrymen of Provence or Aquitaine; a few have perchance heard their singers in their own courts. But who of us all has heard the voice of Cercamon? It is a high honor I have prepared for my king."

CERCAMON FELT every eye fasten upon him; the hot, impatient eye of Louis, full of a boy's curiosity and a boy's restlessness; the gentle, brooding eyes of Countess Alys; the hard, cynical eyes of Thibault; and the unbroken stare of five hundred war-hardened knights of France. These men, untrained to value the polished verse of his southland and flushed with wine—these men he must please. But more than all he must please King Louis; and it was well for him the king was of finer stuff than his nobles.

Remembering his captor's advice, he wasted no time on the gentler, finer forms which most delighted the southern courts, but plunged forthwith into one of those fierce, wild-paced war-songs that had come down to his countryfolk from the battles of their grandsires.

It rang with the clash of sword on shield, the clang of steel, the breathless, thundering rhythm of charging horsemen. So furiously rolled its cadences that, before the company had time to realize, it had come to an end in one fierce, shouted syllable of triumph.

The warriors of France, leaning far over the tables, looked at the singer with eyes that burned with the passion of conflict; then, as at a signal, all caught their breath together, and all burst into wild shouts of applause:

"Ai! Ai! Ohé!"

It was the old battle-shout, the cry of martial spirits when the ranks are joined in the reeling ecstasy of onslaught. With these soldier-nobles the troubadour had triumphed.

He stole a glance at the king. Louis sat with tight-locked arms, clenched hands and smoldering eyes.

Now Cercamon had heard, and remembered, a chant of ancient days—a song of Charlemagne and Roland, and the last, lost fight of Roncevaux. It began with slow, measured cadences—the march of the gallant little Frankish army into the black and monstrous pass, a march overhung with the terror of monstrous mountains and with the black clouds of storm and fate.

Into this chant he swept, the rich tones throbbing like tolling bells; then, changing time and volume, he burst into the full fury of the Saracen attack, his voice ringing like finely tempered steel. As the fortune of battle waned and waxed and waned again, so his tones swelled, diminished and rose to the fullness of tempest; at last to die down to a deep, soft death-march, filled with the passion of mourning. Roland was dead, and Oliver, the glory of France, departed.

When he had done, the silence was long and profound; yet in that silence was a tribute greater than the clamor of shouting throats or beating hands. The spell broken at last, there came from somewhere in the hall the sound of a man sobbing; and between the sobs came broken cries:

"The dogs of Saracens! The murdering hounds! Wo, wo over the traitor Ganelon!"

The pent-up emotion of the company burst forth in a mighty peal of laughter. The naïve, half-drunken warrior who had spoken turned suddenly on his table-mates, fierce-eyed; then, as his glance fell on a wine flagon, it blurred again. He reached for the drink with shaking fingers.

The young king seized Cercamon's hand.

"Sung like a man and a soldier!" he cried. "But you, who are of the south, have sung us nothing that is the south's own—nothing that we also have not. I have heard often of the well-turned verses made in Aquitaine—them I would hear!"

For a moment the troubadour was strongly minded to sing one of his own songs; but he determined in favor of one written by a man long dead, a song that he loved above all songs. It was the brave, ironical lament composed by Guilhem IX of Aquitaine, prince, lover, soldier, when he returned beaten and shattered from his inglorious crusade. Lament though it was, there was no open grief expressed in its delicate measures—rather a gentle melancholy that dares to laugh at itself. And this he sang, with its perfect form and subdued, half-cynical passion.

This time the multitude did not applaud. The mood was too fine for their northern perceptions. But the king, scholar and gentleman for all his boyishness, was lifted out of himself into ecstatic admiration.

"So should a brave man bear his sorrow!" he cried. "And well for the prince who has such a troubadour to sing him! Ah, Cercamon, I must have you in Paris!"

And, filling his cup to the brim, he drank Cercamon's health.

DURING THE next three days Cercamon derived a grim satisfaction from the subtle game played between Thibault and the king; the count trying by every device to bring his royal guest to a serious discussion of the proposed marriage, and at the same time making every opportunity for him to see and talk with the Countess Alys; while Louis as watchfully avoided all talk of the alliance and sought, by keeping Thibault anxious, to make him increase the sums he had offered as the girl's dowry.

For Louis, however young and hotheaded, had inherited his father's love of a bargain, and it was his duty to replenish the exhausted revenues of France. Moreover, the proud boy took a mischievous delight in his vassal's impatience.

Cercamon had great need of such comfort as he could get, for his anxiety over his own position grew more painful every day. Had his messages got through? Had the monk who bore the duchess's letter reached Abbot Suger? And had Armagnac heard of his danger? The time must soon come when Thibault and the king would reach an agreement, and then the cause of Aquitaine would be lost.

Such a result would be most perilous for Aquitaine: Thibault, her ancient enemy, would become the most powerful man in France next to the king; and the king's power to check his ambition would be overbalanced by his loyalty to a father-in-law. And to make Cercamon's trouble the greater, he could not hide from himself the fact that France would be much the better for just such an alliance with Champagne; and his allegiance to Aliénor was sorely tried by his growing admiration for the frank face and the noble heart of Countess Alys.

But his own pride upheld him. He could not endure being overreached; the trick Thibault had played on him irked his Gascon soul. He must win this game for Aquitaine, if he never played another. And he resolved that if, by any miracle, Thibault's schemes should fail, he would ask his master Armagnac to release him from his vassalage. For if Aliénor of Aquitaine became Queen of France, her ruthless ambition would involve her servants in intrigues that a man of honor could not stomach.

Those three days were spent chiefly in hunting, feasting, and dancing; for so the king willed. To fill his time with merriment was the surest way to prevent Thibault from coming to the point, and thus to whet his eagerness till he offered a greater dowry. The nobles of France were delighted with their entertainment; Louis went about with a thin, strained smile; Thibault grew more, and more morose. And Cercamon waited, singing, thinking, fearing.

The evening of the third day the tide seemed to turn in Thibault's favor. That afternoon the royal hunting-party had roused a huge boar, at which Louis rode with his reckless courage. His horse had stumbled just as the boar turned at bay. His horse killed under him, the king had lain a moment helpless, pinned to the ground, with the pig's yellow fangs leering in his face. In that moment Thibault's spear entered the monster's side, and the king was saved.

Louis returned silent, but after supper he was exceptionally gracious to his host. When the women had left the hall and while the wine yet circulated, the king signed to Thibault, who rose with a smile of triumph.

But before they had passed through the door for that private discussion which might settle the kingdom's destiny, the blare of many horns sounding at once brought them back to their seats. An officer from the gate ran into the hall and announced—

"The Count Raoul de Vermandois, Grand Seneschal of France!"

Thibault scowled, and Louis flung himself back in his oaken chair with a gesture of impatience. But a wild thrill of hope shot through Cercamon's heart. A few moments later, Thibault's usher entered backward, bowing low at every other step, his white wand of office waving airily in one hand. Three paces from the king he turned, knelt and cried—

"His mightiness the grand seneschal!"

Raoul de Vermandois, who had entered at his very heels, thrust the usher aside and kissed the king's hand. His back was rudely turned to Thibault, whom he did not love, though they were kinsmen by marriage. With an exclamation of anger, Louis bade his seneschal show deference for their host.

Vermandois, a big-bodied, hot-tempered warrior, turned his hot young eyes on the count's.

"Deference?" cried he. "Deference? To one who intercepts messengers to the Crown and mishandles the ambassadors of princes?"

But as the last words fell from his lips, he caught sight of Cercamon, sitting at the table's end—Cercamon, richly clothed, well-fed, apparently at liberty and in high favor.

Louis was on his feet, looking angrily from Vermandois to Thibault and back.

"What does this mean, Raoul?" he cried. "Has hatred made you mad, or have you indeed some charge to press against the Count of Champagne?"

The grand seneschal's eyes dropped, and he muttered incoherently. The sight of the troubadour had blunted the keen edge of his fury. At length he composed himself and spoke, though with some uncertainty.

"His excellence the regent, Abbot Suger," he said, "has sent me with four hundred spears to escort your Majesty back to Paris. A messenger has come with tidings that cast grave doubts on Count Thibault's loyalty!"

Every man in the company sprang to his feet, the knights of France with exclamations of wonder; the warriors of Champagne with shouts of defiance, pressing round about the seneschal with threatening scowls and hands plucking at their sword-hilts. For a little it seemed as if they would draw steel and hack the daring accuser in pieces.

But Thibault was also on his feet, his cheeks flaming.

"Does that man live," he roared, "who dares accuse Thibault of Champagne of disloyalty to his king? Raoul, Raoul, if it were not for the royal presence I would cram your lie down your throat with six inches of steel!"

Striding forward, the king caught his angry vassal's arm. His voice silenced every other; his cold, clear words drenched their passions as with water.

"Raoul," he said, "ride back to Paris and say to the regent that he presumes too much on our patience! I will not go back till I am ready. You, Thibault, have this day rendered me a service which of itself confutes this charge."

The grand seneschal blushed purple.

"Your Majesty's will is the will of God!" he answered in a choked voice. "I will go. But first I crave five minutes' private speech with your Majesty, in the interest of France. If I fail to satisfy your Majesty, I will go down on my knees before the Count of Champagne and ask his pardon for my words!"

Thibault strove in vain to catch the King's eye. Louis pondered, his face still angry; but at last he nodded.

"So be it!" he said. "Follow me to my apartments!"

IT WAS nearer half an hour than five minutes before the king returned. In that long, tense interval Thibault waited in angry bewilderment, his eyes turning questioningly from the puzzled knights of Paris to the troubadour. At last, as if making up his mind that the seneschal's charge of disloyalty must have some connection with his captive, he signed to Cercamon, who elbowed through the crowding, whispering throng to the count's side.

"Remember your promise!" Thibault whispered.

Cercamon whispered back:

"I will keep my promise; I will say no word to any man concerning your actions till I have left your roof."

Thibault nodded, as if satisfied. If Cercamon said nothing, he should be safe; for the men who had captured the troubadour had worn no badges and had observed every caution. Yet Thibault was mightily troubled to know what lay behind Raoul's charge that he had intercepted a messenger to the Court.

At last Louis reentered the hall, Vermandois at his side. By the smoldering rage in the king's white face, by the unconcealed grin of triumph on Raoul's, the excited knights could see that Thibault had fared badly in that secret conversation. Louis strode swiftly up to the count, his eyes blazing, and shot one swift question—

"How dare you stop a messenger between Aquitaine and France?"

Thibault recoiled, but his bluff features, long practised in dissimulation, assumed an expression of injury and astonishment. With every air of innocence he asked:

"What means your gracious Majesty? Have I not always been faithful?"

Vermandois sneered openly. Louis, drawing from his breast a rolled parchment, struck it, rather than gave it, into Thibault's hand.

"Read!" he commanded.

The seal was already broken. Unrolling the parchment with fingers that trembled a little for all his forced composure, Thibault read. In spite of his efforts at self-control, the flush ebbed from his cheeks, and his teeth gritted. The paper was a proposal, from the Duchess Aliénor to the Regent Suger, for a marriage between herself and the king.

"My lord!" Thibault stammered. "This paper—I do not understand. I am accused of intercepting a message, which—" he paused, and gathering firmness, concluded with an air of virtue—"which has not been intercepted at all! For lo, I saw it first in your Majesty's hand!"

The king could not repress his fury.

"You dare to bandy words with me!" he exclaimed. "This letter was brought to the regent by a monk of the Cistercian abbey at La Ferté-en-Bois, who declared that its bearer, the troubadour Cercamon, had entrusted it to his prior but a few minutes before Cercamon was dragged from the abbey by soldiers who wore no badge. And here"—he pointed to Cercamon—"here I find this troubadour in your own castle! What better proof could I ask?"

Thibault raised his eyes to Cercamon's.

"You find him in my castle," he repeated, "but as an honored guest—not as a captive!"

Louis turned to the troubadour.

"How came you hither?" he asked.

His tongue bound by his parole, Cercamon sought for an answer which would not break his word of honor.

"I rode north on an errand of my master, the Duke of Armagnac," he answered slowly. "Meeting with men of Count Thibault's, I yielded to his invitation to pass some time at his court."

Louis stamped his foot.

"What was the nature of your errand?" he demanded.

"Your pardon, my lord! I can not reveal my master's secrets!"

"Do you deny that you bore this letter from the Duchess of Aquitaine as far as La Ferté, and that it was there taken from you?"

"I neither affirm nor deny anything, my lord the king!"

Thibault drew a sigh of relief; but Louis was not satisfied.

"Your case, Raoul," he said to his seneschal, "falls to the ground because the chief witness will not speak. Nevertheless there is sufficient evidence for me to acquit you of your promise to ask the count's pardon. Ride back to Paris and say to the regent that I will return in five days. The Count of Champagne has honored me with a proposal which demands my consideration, and I would consider it under his roof. Take also this troubadour to Paris and find means to make him tell all that he knows!"

Thibault looked most uncomfortable. It did not soothe him to see the king take back the letter from Aquitaine and replace it carefully in his tunic. But he was in no position to protest against the suspicion which rested upon him. The evidence against him was strong, even in the face of Cercamon's silence.

It was certain now—and he cursed himself for failing to foresee such a chance—that Cercamon had outplayed him in that swift scene of ambush and capture at the monastery. Now Cercamon was to be taken to Paris, by the king's order, which Thibault could not countermand. The worst was that as soon as Cercamon left Blois Castle he was free from his parole and would doubtless tell the whole story.

The only comfort was that the king still meant to tarry at Blois; and even that was no longer an unmixed blessing. For Louis would use Aquitaine's offer—now that he knew of it—as a bid against that of Champagne; and Thibault would be forced to increase his own offer. Louis held against him not only Aliénor's terms, which Thibault knew from the duplicate he had captured to offer greater advantage than his own, but also the fact that Thibault had sought to prevent the king from knowing of the Aquitanian proposals.

He was outbid, and he had committed a crime; for immunity and victory he must pay a high price. He must greatly increase the amount he offered as his daughter's dowry, and he resolved to do so as soon as Vermandois and the troubadour should depart.

That night, by royal order, Cercamon slept under guard; and at daybreak the next morning he was roused by one of the seneschal's spearmen. Raoul had no desire to wait one hour longer than the condition of his horses demanded; and after a cold breakfast on the remains of last night's banquet, he led his men out under the great gate and toward Paris.

CERCAMON TOOK the road in no happy mood. His message had reached the regent, and he was free from his parole and out of reach of Thibault's vengeance; but he was as yet neither at liberty nor victorious. The king had ordered him to Paris, whither he had no desire to go. He could see no advantage for Aquitaine in his telling his tale to the regent: the king's willingness to remain under Thibault's roof after he knew of the count's treachery was proof that Louis meant to balance the offer of Aquitaine against that of Champagne.

Thus forced to the wall, Thibault could hardly do anything but make so high a bid that Louis would be tempted. Nor was Aquitaine in a position to raise its own bid, seeing that Cercamon, alone of those who favored Aquitaine, knew what had just taken place at Blois. It might well be that, in the absence of a second and larger offer from Aliénor, the king would contract the alliance with Thibault's daughter. In Paris Cercamon would be helpless to inform either his master Armagnac or the duchess of what had happened.

He was still a prisoner, though in honorable captivity. Raoul meant to carry out the king's order and take him to the capital, and had therefore placed him between two keen-eyed young knights, with whom it was a point of honor to watch him with ceaseless vigilance. They rode close by his side, and before and behind them were hundreds of men-at-arms to lend authority to their watchfulness. Yet Cercamon did not despair of eluding them if the slightest chance offered itself. And he was determined to make the chance if none came of itself, for the only hope for Aquitaine lay in his escaping to bring word to the duchess of that which was going on at Blois.

His own horse had been returned to him, and he trusted to its swiftness—if he could only win past his guards. He stole constant sidelong glances at the horses on either side of him, measuring as well as he could their probable speed and endurance. And thus the huge cavalcade cantered down the high road to Paris, in the chilly morning, through the bright noon, and in the cold twilight.

But with twilight a soft, persistent rain began to fall. The seneschal cursed furiously. At night so large a company must ride slowly, and there would be three hours more of drenching, chilling wet and of gradually worsening roads before they reached the shelter of Orléans, the first stopping-point of their three-day journey. Vermandois let his trumpets sound, and the horsemen made the most of the last light for a gallop that would take them as far toward the shelter of Orléans as possible before night shut down in earnest.

The gathering darkness brought new hope to the troubadour. He rode stirrup for stirrup beside his guards, to lull their suspicions. On his left were two men—one of the knights set to watch him, and another; on his right but the one guard, for they rode in column of fours. But on the right was also the river Loire, not easily forded in the dark and the rain. Yet it was on the right that Cercamon watched for his opportunity; it would be impossible to break past the two on his other side. Let his man but lag behind a little, let his horse stumble on the softened, slippery road, and Cercamon was ready to spur past him.

But, as if reading his thoughts, the young noble on his right caught at Cercamon's rein and held it. It was plain that strict orders had been given to prevent his escape. And once they reached Orléans, escape would be impossible. During the night he would be guarded closely, within walls whereon sentries would be posted; and the ride from Orléans to Paris would be through royal domain all the way, with king's troopers patrolling the roads.

They were still half a league from Orléans when the opportunity came. Cercamon was waiting for it with bated breath and did not let it slip. In the black darkness, the man on his right rode full into a deep crevice in the road, filled with rain-water. His horse stumbled, slithered and went down. Taken wholly unaware, the knight let Cercamon's bridle drop from his fingers as he clutched madly at his own; Cercamon tugged his beast's head sharply to the right, thrust home the spurs and shot past the fallen man into the night.

Hearing him dash by, his warder set up a shout, which was instantly echoed by those on the other side. Confused cries rang out; trumpets blew; the whole cavalcade drew raggedly to a halt. Officers rode down the line, demanding what had happened; those who first learned of the escape rode forward to report. A score of men gave tongue at once; none could see a yard ahead of him in the rain and the blackness; the officers began to curse and strike out.

The tumult lasted long enough so that, when it ceased, Cercamon's hoof-beats were no longer audible on the rain-softened earth. None could see him; it was only known that he had ridden to the right.

Calling his sergeants together, Vermandois bade them ride off hotspur toward the river, swim it and quarter the fields beyond on a front of more than a hundred yards. It was a desperate task, for the river was rising, and none could see his way to the broken bank. Only the urgency of the king's orders held them to it.

To the river they rode, some crashing over their horses' heads as they failed to take off well at the river's brim; others sinking in unexpected depths, and yet others carried down-stream in the muddy water before they could make a landing on the other side. Yet most of them won across; and then began the blind hunt through soaked meadows and plowed fields, slipping, stumbling, some going down in ditches or deep furrows.

The night bewildered their sense of direction; their mounts, afraid of the wicked footing and excited almost to frenzy by the pricking spurs and the shouting, bolted off to all sides. At last, some thrown and limping, all mired and weary, the troopers returned to report neither sight nor sound of the runaway.

Cercamon had had his own share of perils in his wild dash, but he kept his head, he was not weighted down by armor, and he had the advantage of being the pursued instead of the pursuer. In the murk night that pressed in all about him, he, too, had stumbled; but his horse, recovering on the very margin of the river, had taken off with a splendid leap into the stream.

The roan began to swim at once; and thanks to its rider's lack of mail, it had forty pounds handicap over its followers. Straight across the river it headed, made the opposite shore, floundered awhile in the fields; and the certainty of Cercamon's purpose kept the fine beast's muzzle pointed straight for refuge.

It was a precarious refuge he sought, uncomfortable and fraught with danger; but it was the best at hand. Turning southwest on the farther side of the Loire, he pressed on surely, cautiously, for the Sologne marshes. He scarcely feared being overhauled, knowing that an error of a single foot in estimating his direction from the road would widen to an error of a hundred yards in the first mile, what with darkness, rain, and excitement. But he greatly feared lest Vermandois take the back track, send men over the river at wide intervals and thus set ambushes for him at a score of points. In the Sologne he would have perfect shelter till the pursuit was lost.

The Sologne stretches along the south bank of the river in a vast chain of pools and marshes, with no roads and few and perilous footpaths between. He rode into the reeds after an hour of steady, careful going, and thereafter he let the roan pick its way, taking care only to keep it moving. The horse's sharper sense of danger kept them out of the deep pools and treacherous morasses, though more than once its feet sank deep. Only when he had ridden in so far into this land of hidden death that he felt sure none would dare follow, did Cercamon turn again toward the river.

And now began the worst stage of his adventure. Weary now,

his horse lost its first alertness, and again and again Cercamon was forced to dismount and lead it for fear that it would carry him straight into a bottomless quag. A dozen times his feet sank to the knees, and he had to pull himself out as best he could; once he sank suddenly into deep standing water and was nearly drowned before he could find firm ground. But doggedly he worked on, unable to see, yet striving always toward the river.

He came on it at last, just as despair laid hold on him. Mounting to rest his weary legs, he rode straight into a pool, which proved to be an arm of the Loire. But here the ground was mixed clay and sand, fairly firm; and after a few minutes of swimming, the roan bore him to the stream, and to shallow water formed by rising ground, where the beast could wade. A moment later he rode out on to the bank.

He still had to get across the river again, for there was no road along the south bank, and the lurking tentacles of the Sologne thrust out to break the river's edge at a hundred points. Cercamon waited to rest his beast, and then, picking his ford as well as he could in the dark, he half-rode, half-swam to the north bank.

But he did not follow the high road, for to the northeast, somewhere in the night, rode the seneschal and his men, and to the southwest lay Blois. Instead, he rode across the plowed fields, slowly and with the utmost care, hoping to strike one of the roads that lead back into the rich country of the Orléanais. He had thrown the pursuit off the track, hopelessly; but of this he could not be sure. Yet he knew that they would look for him on the other side, or else believe him drowned in river or marsh.

The first cockcrow shrilled through the chill night before he found a cart-track leading west; and this he took, following it between plowed fields till it wound into a grove. Riding deep into the shelter of the trees, he picketed and blanketed his horse. He himself was young, had often experienced wet and chilly nights in the open, and was soon asleep on the sodden ground, wrapped in his cloak.

HE WAS up at sunrise, hungry and stiff; but the roan was somewhat refreshed. Creeping to the road, Cercamon spied up and down it for a time, but saw no one. There were few hoof-prints in the mud, and such as there were were the broad tracks of peasant's nags. The chase was over, and the quarry saved.

Yet he still rode cautiously, the more so since his way led through Thibault's domain. Straight west he pounded, till he was far enough from Blois to venture on a circuit that would take him safely past. The bend in the Loire between Orléans and Tours was so marked that he could at last take a cross-country short-cut, following, as it were, the bowstring while the river and the highroad formed the bent bow.

Tours was his objective: if his message to Bertrand d'Armagnac had been as successful as that to the Regent, his master would be on the road north to inquire after him; and through Tours Armagnac must pass.

For two days he rode on, no man stopping him; finding food and shelter with the peasants. On the second day, at evening, he rode through the gate of Tours, learning from the sentinels that none from Aquitaine had come that way. But the next morning, less than a league south of the city, he beheld a great cavalcade shining against the Spring sun. By their direction, they could only come from Poitou. And as they drew nearer, he saw the great banner of Aquitaine floating in the van. With a shout of joy he spurred to meet them.

The outriders recognized him with cries of astonishment, and from behind their ranks a horseman rode out to meet him. The nasaled helmet hid his features; but his lean, war-hardened body and centaur's carriage were those of Bertrand d'Armagnac, Seneschal of Aquitaine.

The great man wrung the hand of his friend and servant in an iron grip of fellowship. Then, smiling but asking no questions, Armagnac led him to the front rank of the mainguard. Cercamon gave a gasp of surprise. There, in the midst of mail-clad soldiers, sitting the saddle with the ease of the perfect horseman, sat—his princess, Aliénor herself!

Slipping from the saddle, he kissed her hand. Aliénor laughed, and the sound was like the rippling of a brook. She rode astride, as was women's custom then; her wide cloak was of blue velvet, which well set off her bright cheeks and glowing golden hair, caught up in a net of twisted silver. Cercamon, himself and his beast plastered with the mud of the Sologne, made a sorry sight.

"When Cercamon is hard pressed, his duchess herself can not sit idle at home!" she smiled at him.

Bertrand d'Armagnac grinned wryly.

"Do not believe her grace!" he scoffed. "She followed not out of favor to thee, but from sheer mischief and love of peril!"

Aliénor motioned the troubadour to ride by her side.

"Now tell me!" she commanded; and as they rode on toward Tours, he told of all that had befallen him.

"Why, thou art fit to be one of the twelve peers of Charlemagne!" she applauded, but Armagnac only laughed.

"It was well done to choose Cistercians for your messengers," he approved. "None dares stop the Gray Monks; no, not Thibault himself, who has befriended them till their grant abbot has grown mightier than he. Word of your plight reached us two days ago, and we rode north as fast as we could collect two hundred spears. The duchess would not remain behind; there is some devilry brooding behind that angel's smile of hers."

Aliénor laughed again.

"In truth," she explained, "we ride for Paris, to lay complaint before the king concerning Thibault's treatment of you, and to demand justice. But since the king is in Blois—"

"Since the king is in Blois," Armagnac interrupted, "he will doubtless marry Thibault's daughter, and our project will be lost. Thibault will see to that. But you are weary, my lady, and well-nigh starved. Yonder looms the gate of Tours. We will talk more of this matter over the meat and wine."

WHEN THIBAULT OF CHAMPAGNE, behind the locked door of his treasure-room, counted over his gold and silver, he was a rueful man; but when he reflected on all the advantages of state he stood to reap from the king's presence he was more than comforted. Louis had indeed dealt strictly with him, during the five days since Vermandois had ridden away with the troubadour. Though the king had not once given utterance to his suspicions concerning Thibault's offense, since Raoul's departure, he had taken care, by hints and scowls, to let his host see that he had not forgotten it.

And now the king had Aquitaine's offer, in black and white, as Vermandois had brought it from Paris—the six thousand gold marks that Aliénor promised in dowry, the five castles she ceded to the Crown, her thrice-welcome consent to the union of all her provinces with the royal demain. She held out on only one point—the lands of Poitou and Aquitaine must be reckoned as part of her dowry; in case of her divorce, or the king's death before her, they should revert to her.

This was a mighty offer. For generations the Crown had vainly striven to wrest from the Dukes of Aquitaine a recognition of the king's suzerainty over them; now Aquitaine itself made the proffer, if the king would marry Aliénor—and the Duchess Aliénor was reputed the most beautiful woman in France.

Thibault could not furnish such a tempting bait. He had already recognized Louis as his liege lord; he could not give up more than two castles. Therefore he must bid all the higher in gold, and it was fortunate for him that France needed gold more than anything else. The Countess Alys was not so fair as her rival, but the king had never seen Aliénor. Thibault had not scrupled to break the seal of the letter he had taken from Cercamon and knew Aquitaine's offer as well as the king, but since Louis also knew it, the count must empty his treasure-chest to tempt the king's fancy to his daughter. This thought tore at his frugal soul, and the close smile on the king's lips maddened him.

But—once the king should sign the marriage contract, Thibault would be the first baron of France. His royal son-in-law would be obliged, by the tie of kindred, to wink at Thibault's ambitions. His enemies would be as dirt under his feet. No longer checked by the envy of the Crown, he could stretch out his greedy hands to seize Burgundy; Flanders, too, should fall before him. Then he and his brother, King Stephen of England, would squeeze Normandy between them as in a vise.

He would be mightier than the king, mightier than Aquitaine. These his glittering dreams reconciled him to the loss of his gold, which he could recover many times in the loot of neighbor provinces. To secure this boundless advantage he must press Louis to a settlement before Vermandois should bribe or force Cercamon to tell his story, and before the regent could persuade the king to break with Champagne. Aye, all this must be done before morning, for in the morning the king planned to set forth for Paris.

So each of the two antagonists in this game of state played astutely during those five days, while the sweet young countess who was no more to either of them than a pawn was pushed about the broad gaming-board of France with no regard for her shy unhappiness. She knew, now, the rôle destined for her, and took no joy in it; but she had no choice but to obey her father. Well she knew that the players both cared more for gold and broad lands than for her happiness; and she was afraid of the fierce-eyed young king, with his gusts of rage and his cold cunning.

But Louis was well-content. The menace which he held over Thibault's head, in the still unheard testimony of Cercamon, gave him a high advantage in the bargaining. So, too, did the fact that he was in no hurry; while Thibault must win or lose all before Aquitaine learned of his intervention and raised its offer. The two gamesters seemed to change natures; the shrewd old count lost patience and self-control, while the young hot-head became cool, confident and overbearing.

Neither knew that Aquitaine had already heard, thanks to

the troubadour's escape; but on the third day a messenger came galloping in on a blown horse to report that Cercamon had fled and could not be found. The King flew into a consuming passion, vowing death and torture to the fugitive so soon as he should be taken; but he retained enough prudence to hide the disaster from Thibault's ears, and so held his advantage.

Evening of the fifth day found the contract still unsigned, the two cunning adversaries still playing out their game of barter. Thibault had slowly raised his offer of dowry, till it now stood at eighteen thousand marks in gold—an enormous sum, to pay which he must pledge a sixth of his estates. He was trembling with suspense, well-nigh beyond himself at thought of parting with so much wealth.

Louis could scarce contain his satisfaction. Whichever won—Champagne or Aquitaine—he stood to win more by a marriage contract than his great father had been able to win by sword and statesmanship combined. If he allied with Aquitaine, he won half the south; if with Champagne, half the north would be pledged to support him in his impending war with Anjou, and his coffers, now nearly empty, would be crammed with gold.

Thibault drank heavily at supper, and his heart was emboldened by the heady wine. He raised his offer to twenty thousand marks. The young king, smiling sardonically, gestured as if to put the bid aside; but his spirits leaped. He knew Thibault had well-nigh reached his utmost, and the sum was indeed princely. What could he not do with twenty thousand marks? It would buy him many soldiers, professional fighting-men. He could easily overpower Geoffrey of Anjou—why not Brittany also, and even Normandy? Aye, he would seize Normandy from Anjou and hold it for himself.

So intent was Louis on his thoughts that the trumpet which blared without the walls scarce roused him, nor did Thibault regard it either. The prospect of interruption was like the buzzing of a troublesome insect. Thibault raised his shaggy brows inquiringly, and the king nodded. The count gestured to his master of the garrison.

"Admit whoso it may be, Raymond!" he muttered. "But let them not disturb us till I summon you. His Majesty and I must be untroubled."

And, bowing, he led the way to his private chamber.

In preparation for this moment, when the King's defense should weaken, he had laid out on the table in his chamber a sheet of parchment, fairly engrossed by his clerk; his seal was already appended, and tapers and wax were ready for the king's use. He had but to strike the bell that hung by the table, and his clerk would summon his daughter and two knights, to sign the contract as party and witnesses.

It was on this parchment that Louis' eyes fell as soon as he entered the chamber. He sat down on the carven bench before the table and read, for he was as learned as any monk. His long, thin fingers pointed at the words; his lank hair, blown into his face by a draft from an arrow-slit, he shook impatiently back into place.

"The amount of the dowry is not set down," he said, turning his keen eyes on the older man.

Thibault summoned his clerk, a lean fellow in rusty black.

"Write 'twenty thousand marks in gold,' Ambrose!" he said.

Louis glanced at him sardonically.

"Nay," he contradicted. "Write 'twenty-one thousand'!"

But though his lips smiled, his glance was hot, and his heart beat furiously.

The clerk caught his master's eye. Thibault hesitated, licking his dry lips. Then—

"Do as the king bids!" he cried.

The clerk wrote.

Louis caught the pen from his hand, dipped it in the oak-gall and caught the parchment to him. Thibault's hands, gripping the griffon's heads on his chair-arms, were white. The king would sign! All was won!

Louis' fingers poised over the parchment. For an instant he hesitated, then touched the pen to the sheet. At that instant a knock, thundering, impatient, beat on the door.

The king sprang back as if struck, the space for his signature still empty save for a round blot. Thibault was on his feet; but the door was flung violently open, and his master of the garrison came in with staring eyes.

"My lord!" he gasped. "You must go down to the hall—at once!"

Thibault clutched de Montivre's shoulder fiercely.

"Did I not say that I would not be interrupted?" he snarled.

"Aye, but, gracious lord—they who come—"

"Who is it?" Louis asked; and his tones endured no denial.

"It is—the Duchess of Aquitaine!"

Louis flung himself back in his chair, his mouth twitching in voiceless laughter. Thibault was staggered, white with rage and consternation. How had it happened? Who had brought word of his designs to Aquitaine? How dared the woman come here, to Blois, to his own castle?

But the king, risen, offered the old man his arm, with a courtesy just touched with mockery.

"Let us go down," he said. "I would fain see this duchess, who is said to be so beautiful. Brave she must be as well as fair, to risk herself here at such a time!"

The king's wish was a command, and Thibault dared not disobey. As he passed through the door, Montivre whispered in his ear—

"Armagnac is with her, with a hundred spears, and—Cercamon!"

THIBAULT OF CHAMPAGNE took fire slowly, but his rage, once kindled, never died. In after years Louis often regretted that soundless laugh at the great baron's discomfiture; but at the moment Thibault stifled his emotions and prepared for the struggle that lay before him.

Twenty-one thousand marks! He had made the highest bid he dared; he had scarce enough left to pay his men-at-arms their wage. He could borrow of the Jews, but they would take his fattest lands in pledge and demand a frightful interest. And now that the Duchess of Aquitaine was here, with that accursed troubadour, Louis would seize the occasion to make her bid against him.

The sordidness of the thing—that a baron of France and a young princess should bargain one against the other for an advantageous marriage—troubled him no more than it would trouble Aliénor. He had never seen Aliénor, but he knew Aquitaine was richer than Champagne. If she was set on marrying Louis, she could offer more than he.

But one thing he knew and calculated on—she was a lady of birth and breeding and must have the grace to refrain from barter against him under his own roof—at least in his presence. If he used all his cunning, all his persuasion, he might yet close his deal with the king before Louis departed. And to that end he must keep Louis with him after Aliénor could be induced to leave.

Therefore he accepted the situation with what poise he could. The two princes entered the hall together, Louis assured and smiling, Thibault outwardly calm, but on fire within. But Aliénor was not there.

Surrounded by a crowd of knights—they of France, who had come in the king's suite, rubbing shoulders affably with Thibault's vassals and a knot of new-come lords from Aquitaine—stood Bertrand of Armagnac; and at his side was Cercamon. Armagnac was talking briskly, and the company listened breathlessly. Thibault's ears caught a few words here and there—vivid phrases of battle, to which the soldiers of France ever listen avidly. And Armagnac was a soldier whom every glory-loving soldier worshiped, whose skill to paint a *mêlée* was as great as his sword was trenchant.

At the threshold Thibault stepped back one pace, to give

precedence to the king. It was Armagnac who first saw the young monarch's tall form and signed to the crowd about him to fall back. All bowed, and Bertrand stepped forward to kiss the king's hand. But Louis' eyes traveled past him to the troubadour, and anger sparkled in them.

"That man is yours, Bertrand," he said, his finger pointing out Cercamon. "Five days hence I sent him to Paris, under escort. He escaped, ignoring my orders. I pray you give him to me, that I may deal with him!"

Armagnac glanced over his shoulder at Cercamon.

"He was on my service, your Majesty," he replied. "I take his guilt on my shoulders."

Louis bit his lips. There was nothing he could say or do. Cercamon was vassal to Bertrand, Bertrand to Aliénor; and Aliénor of Aquitaine was a sovereign princess, who owed no vassalage to France. But in that moment Thibault tasted a shred of triumph: Armagnac's defiance of the king's will was a bad way to introduce Aquitaine's suit for a marriage with the king. Thibault almost forgave the troubadour for that tiny, precious advantage. And while he chewed that crumb of consolation, Armagnac, who was no courtier, made matters worse by turning from Louis and greeting his unwilling host.

"Your Grace will pardon the duchess that she has not waited your coming," Bertrand said. "She has gone to Countess Alys' apartments to rest from the fatigues of her journey."

But in that moment the voice of an usher rang from the door—

"Her Grace the Duchess of Aquitaine, Countess of Poitou and Suzeraine of Auvergne!"

Every voice was hushed, every eye lifted to the doorway. The king faced about, his eyes lighting with curiosity; Thibault stood stiff, gnawing his lip. The assembled knights fell apart to left and right, those of Aquitaine falling to one knee. Aliénor entered, on the arm of Alys; and at sight of her Thibault's heart sank.

Not for nothing had rumor heralded her the loveliest woman in France. She was tall and exquisitely graceful; not a dark beauty of that Roman kind for which the South is famous, but all gold and roses, with the perfect features which had been bred in her ancestry for three generations.

But more than mere perfection of line and color was the spirit within, that flooded all her being with a resplendent vitality. She seemed a princess of romance, descended from the gods of pagan story.

Yet there was not too much of the goddess in her to disdain human prudence, for she was clad not in the dusty robes of her journey, but in a fresh, close-fitting bodice of pale-blue silk, and a flowing gown of the same color, broidered in gold by the cunning Moors of Andalusia. Her fine arms were bare from the elbow, her wondrous golden hair was a crown upon her head. She wore no jewels, nor needed any.

Louis was nearest her, and first saw her full splendor. He uttered a soft gasp, and in the complete silence the sound was heard to the farthest corner of the room. He bent to kiss her hand, then, retaining her fingers, led her to Thibault. The count's reluctant back bent in as gracious a bow as he could manage. Though Aliénor caught the glint of anger in his eyes, her expression never altered from that meek graciousness which made her seem an angel from heaven.

And almost as such the knights of France regarded her in that moment. Adoration of beauty was in their blood; the worship of lovely women, born in the south, had already found its shrines in Paris. Never before had those soldiers seen such loveliness; never again would they see it in any other woman. Emulating her own vassals, they sank to their knees before her. Even Thibault's more stolid easterners felt her spell.

The old Count of Champagne was seized with panic. Beside this woman any other was as nothing; not a man in that hall had eyes for his daughter, hostess though she was in her father's house. She stood unseen, unregarded, her own eyes turned in rapturous admiration on Aliénor. Oh, that his master of the garrison had had the wit, the daring, to keep his drawbridge raised and his gates closed to these accursed folk of the south!

Yet Thibault knew in his heart that even he would not have dared to shut Aliénor out from his castle and bid defiance to a sovereign princess, while the King of France, with three hundred of his bravest knights, was within its walls.

IT WAS Bertrand of Armagnac who broke the tension. Striding past the king, he bowed one knee before the Countess Alys and raised her fingers to his lips. Her words of welcome lifted the spell. A huge chair, padded with the skins of beasts and silken cushions, was placed near the hearth for Aliénor; the king sat on her right, Thibault on her left and Alys behind her chair. The knights gathered round; the magic of Armagnac's martial tales vied with that of the duchess' beauty. So they sat till the tables were spread.

Aliénor knew when to be indiscreet and how to take the sting from indiscretion with her smiles. Over the wine she gave her loveliest glance to Thibault and laid her left hand on his arm.

"I have a quarrel to pick with you, my lord count!" she began. "It was ill done of you to seize my messenger!"

Thibault caught his breath and glanced at the king. The charge brought against him by Vermandois was proved now; surely all was lost! Louis was already under her spell; this would rouse him to fury. But Louis only shrugged his shoulders and returned Thibault's gaze sardonically. Thibault felt baffled and afraid; therefore he was silent.

"Fortunately that messenger was Cercamon," the duchess's flute-like voice resumed. "He found others to take his letter to Paris and to warn me. I rode north at once, thinking to lay my complaint before the regent in Paris; and so I should have done, had Cercamon not met us."

Cercamon! This was the first Thibault had heard of the trou-

badour's escape from Vermandois. Once more the count glanced
at Louis, who laughed shortly.

"Aye!" the king exclaimed, with a hard look at Cercamon,
who sat on Armagnac's left. "I would have had the truth from
him, and then taken him into my service; but he was too slippery to hold. Will you make me such a song as never before
was heard, troubadour, if I forgive you?"

Cercamon rose and bowed.

"Perchance," he said, "but it will take time to make such a
song. And in the mean time I may forfeit the pardon."

Thibault felt as if the solid earth had opened under his feet,
to plunge him into some topsy-turvy land of faerie. This woman
had spoken out such truths as should blast his good repute and
make every man of birth in France look askance at him—yet
none of all that company seemed to sense their meaning. The
king, who had every right to be furious with him for intercepting a messenger to the Court, merely shrugged and smiled.
Cercamon, fresh from an escapade that had roused all the king's
anger, even now was scarce civil in responding to an offer of
pardon. That woman from the south had so bewitched them
all that they neither saw nor heard but as she wished; and for
the moment she seemed not to wish for discord.

But there were others who glanced at her with uneasy eyes,
for they knew her—Armagnac and the troubadour. They had
seen her in her own court, in all her rainbow moods; and they
felt how heavy with peril the atmosphere had become. Cercamon, more than the old soldier his master, felt the tension.
With all his poet's sensitiveness he responded to the undertones
of Aliénor's voice, her quick, graceful gestures, the subtle note
of pride and mischief that rose in her tones as she drank more
wine.

Cercamon knew that beneath her lustrous beauty there dwelt
a hidden demon, that fed on ambition, on greed, on lust of
possessing and of using power. He watched her eyes, noting
how they roved now and again, in little, catlike flashes, toward

Thibault's daughter. The demon was stirring in Aliénor, laughing as she played with Thibault's fears, but able at any moment to leap into tempestuous, devastating life.

His eyes left her and sought the gentle, ingenuous girl on the king's left. Countess Alys would never kindle the tongues of singers to rapturous praise; she would not set princes to quarreling over her beauty. But she would bless with quiet happiness and with wise, honest counsel, the man who should know how to cherish her.

Thibault regained his tongue at last.

"You are very gracious," he muttered. "I shall remember your kindness."

In all honesty—for the disaster which he saw overwhelming his schemes had subdued both his cunning and his spirit for the moment—the old man was seeking to bury the memory of his offense; but Aliénor chose to misinterpret those ambiguous words, "I shall remember your kindness." Her eyes flashed, and into her too-sweet voice there crept an undertone of sheer malice that made Cercamon, listening, feel sick at heart.

"Cercamon met us beyond Tours," she said. "He and Armagnac advised me to ride straight on to Paris and demand of the regent that he summon you to a royal council, at which the king would have been compelled to be present also; and the charge would have been raised against you so that you could not have evaded it. But I thought otherwise. It is Louis who is king in France, not the regent; and I determined to place my case in the king's own hands. Therefore I ordered that we ride hither. I have you to thank for the thought, my lord of Champagne. Did not you choose to lay your suit before the king, rather than the regent?"

Her words were softly uttered, but they stung. Thibault recognized, as she meant him to, that his very cleverness in trapping Cercamon had been twisted against him by the troubadour's intelligence. Cercamon's message, sent just before his capture, had brought Vermandois from Paris, to give the king the means to extort a high offer and to furnish Cercamon a chance to escape and freedom from his parole.

Cercamon's report to the duchess concerning Thibault's direct suit to the king had inspired Aliénor to bring her offer, her accusation and her fatal beauty to Blois.

And Thibault glared at Cercamon with a concentrated fury, the threat of which he could not veil before the king had seen it. But Louis only laughed—a laugh which Thibault liked none the better because he could not understand it. He felt that Louis practised on him and had some trick in store; and no man likes less to be tricked than he who has himself intrigued.

BUT ALIÉNOR had more in store for him, and worse. So far, what she had said had at least been so veiled that his daughter, who knew nothing of his dealings with Cercamon, did not understand what was at stake. Alys knew that her father had offered her hand to the king, but not that Aliénor was her rival; nor did she suspect it. But Thibault understood the covert thrust in the duchess' words, and he was still reddening at it when she dealt an open stab that revealed how conscious she was of her advantage.

"I was sure," she said—and her bewitching eyes sought Louis, who gazed into them with open admiration—"I was sure I could trust his Majesty's good taste."

Unable to endure the torture longer, Thibault rose, trembling with rage. Once more he glared at Cercamon, the instrument that had made his humiliation possible. But it was a bitterly unhappy face that the troubadour turned toward him. Cercamon had few illusions about his duchess, but he had never before seen the soul of Jezebel so revoltingly plain behind her beauty.

And now Alys herself began to understand. The poor girl was aflame with affronted pride. The tension which held those in the secret spread through the company; though most of the knights knew only part of the negotiations on one side or the other, Aliénor's jeering words gave them material to guess the rest.

All were silent, scowling, or casting uneasy glances at one another. Champenois glowered at Aquitanian, while the Parisians strove to conceal an embarrassment which, for them, was unrelieved by the satisfaction of ancient hatreds.

Thibault, on his feet, bowed low to the king, stiffly to Aliénor. His pride, cut to the raw, was stronger now than greed or ambition. With an access of superb dignity, he confronted young Louis as he might have faced a haggling merchant.

"Your Majesty has received my last offer," he began. "All too much have I chaffered over that which is above price. Your Majesty must choose as may seem best for the honor of France."

Offering his arm to his daughter, he turned to leave the hall. At this, the whole company rose; but Louis flung out an arm to command attention. His prudence was flung to the winds; from the first moment of Aliénor's queenly entrance, her beauty had set his brain on fire. He had drunk more than his wont and was not his own master.

"Then hear!" he cried so that all turned in astonishment at the passion in his voice. He seized Aliénor's hand, drew her to him, and raised his wine-cup. "Then hear, Thibault, and all ye men of France! I have chosen, and now I offer you a health to Aliénor of Aquitaine, the fairest woman in the world, and soon to be queen of France!"

To Cercamon, watching with pitiful eyes, the astounded knights seemed to fade away from his vision, leaving nothing but the dark background of the walls, the glare of the torches, and between those two, standing out with terrible distinctness, the triumphant, jeering Aliénor and the humbled Countess Alys.

Why should not Louis choose Aliénor, loveliest of women even in her most evil moods, so lovely that her bodily perfection veiled the ugliness of her heart? What was a dowry of more than twenty thousand marks of finest gold beside a beauty which the world could not buy again with all its wealth, if she were no more?

No wonder the boy who bore the crown of France had no eyes for the girl who clung to Thibault's arm, red and white by turns, brutally humiliated, pointed at by Aliénor's scorn. A great pity for Alys welled in the troubadour's heart, and a fierce rage against Aliénor, whom he had served faithfully, but who was unworthy an honest man's regard.

He stood still beside his chair, his hand trembling on its carven back. Then, for an instant, the Countess Alys met his gaze and seemed to draw strength from it. Her firm chin went up, her eyes blazed; she faced Aliénor with a pride that dominated the other woman's triumph.

"I congratulate the Duchess of Aquitaine," she said in low, clear tones. "France could have no fairer queen!"

Cercamon thrilled with response to her pride, that would not let her return scorn for scorn. But his anger was greater than before, that the king could be so blind, and Aliénor so cruel.

At the countess' words, the men of Aquitaine burst into applause; but they of Champagne muttered in their beards. The knights of the king's suite, as in duty bound, cheered loudly. As the tumult died down, one who had drunk more than was good spoke his mind, and his words pierced through the subsiding murmur with terrible clearness:

"The king has chosen well! She of Aquitaine is worth a thousand of the other!"

The silence that followed was quick with menace. Thibault of Champagne swung about as if he had been struck; his knights reached for their hilts. The Aquitanians, seeing the hostile glances and gestures, grouped about Bertrand of Armagnac as if to form battle-array. Then Cercamon's endurance broke. His whole soul was outraged at the insult; his fiery love of combat and his sensitive honor forced from his lips a reply that he scarce realized before it crossed his lips. But it rang through the hall like a peal of trumpets:

"Nay, the king has chosen like a fool! He has scorned the pure gold, and has chosen the gilded lead!"

He caught one glimpse of Thibault's astounded face before the tempest burst about him. Then, with hot cries of rage, the king's knights flung themselves upon him, their swords flashing from the scabbard. The Aquitanians would have been first in avenging the slight to their duchess, had they not known Cercamon better. For a year he had been among them, and they knew his terrible skill with his weapon. Only a moment they hesitated, but that moment sufficed. Bertrand d'Armagnac, who had led them a hundred times in the storm of battle, cast himself between them and the troubadour.

"Back!" he cried. "The first man of the south to draw sword against Cercamon dies by my blade! My lady duchess, your grace can afford to ignore such words from one who has served you well in the past, and who now is mad! Bethink you well what a crime it is to slay a troubadour!"

His last words had an effect which nothing else could have wrought. The Aquitanians indeed knew the shame and peril of drawing weapon on one of Cercamon's profession. He whose point drew Cercamon's blood would never again be safe south of Garonne, though he surrounded himself with armed men every moment of his life.

In single combat, in the cleared lists, or on the field of battle one might kill a troubadour without scruple, for that is fair fight; but to massacre a singer—One prince had done that, long ago; and nobles and kings had vied for the honor of slaying him.

But the Parisians pressed on. Not yet had the north learned the singer's sanctity; and even priests have died for angering kings. Cercamon, standing at the table's end, had its poor shelter for so long as his point might keep their weight at bay. He stood poised on the balls of his feet, his point raised, waiting.

But those about him were not all king's men; Thibault's vassals also were there. At a gesture from their lord they flung themselves in front of the troubadour. They came between him and the hungry French steel barely in time; already swords gleamed in the torchlight, and here and there the blades of Paris clashed with those of Blois.

"Call off your cutthroats, my lord!" cried Thibault to the king. "Dares even the King of France do murder in my house?"

Louis, pale with fury, was forced to call his men back. They withdrew reluctant, quivering with unleashed anger. But the outraged monarch was not ready to forego his vengeance for the slight to his chosen queen. Nor would she let him forget; she stood beside him, plucking at his velvet sleeve; and her beautiful features were twisted with fury.

"Kill him!" she whispered, and Louis, nodding, turned to Thibault.

"You hear?" he cried. "This pot-minstrel is the duchess' man, and she demands his death. He has affronted your king within your walls. Will you stand between him and his just punishment? By my father's soul, Thibault! If you protect him, you answer for it to me! Give me his life!"

Cercamon stood waiting with unsheathed sword, his eyes on Thibault. The old count measured his royal master with a gaze like a roused lion's. At last he spoke, slowly, his words loud and full of majesty:

"When you, my lord, insulted me over my own board; when this woman you have chosen to reign over us heaped her scorn on me and mine, did I demand your life or hers? Of all who have broken bread with me this day, only one dared speak in my defense—and he was my enemy, by whose wit alone the Duchess of Aquitaine has won her triumph. He, whom I would have slain had I had the chance, has risked his life to say that which I, your host, was bound not to say—but which was in my heart. You shall not have his life, nor shall any man lay hand on him within my territories!"

Turning his back on the fuming monarch, Thibault of Champagne strode to Cercamon and took his hand. Then, calling his master of the garrison, he issued his orders so that they were heard by all:

"Double the guard at the gate, and let no man of the king's, or of Aquitaine, issue forth for three hours! Bid a groom bring Cercamon's horse and grant him free passage. Make haste!"

Cercamon glanced at Bertrand d'Armagnac, the master and friend whose favor at court and comradeship in the field had been so dear to him; and Armagnac nodded in approval of Thibault's words. But Armagnac said nothing, for he knew that the demon roused in Aliénor's breast would never be assuaged with less than the troubadour's death.

Then Cercamon glanced at the king and saw him gnawing his fingers in helpless anger. Sheathing his sword, the troubadour strode between the ranks of men that fell back to give him passage, the Champenois grinning at him, the rest glaring their hate. At the door he paused, and swept a low bow to the Countess Alys.

His horse was waiting at the drawbridge. The great gate was thronged with mailed men-at-arms, and as he passed between them, their friendly glances told him they had heard the news. Montivre, the master of the garrison and a man of noble birth, ran forward to hold the stirrup. But Cercamon put him gently aside, and shook his hand.

"Now ride as if fiends were after you!" Montivre urged. "There will be no pursuit for three hours, that I promise you! The king dares not make war on my master, lest France shatter in his grasp!"

Masterless, with half of France thirsting for his blood, Cercamon rode. Nor was he afraid, but rather glad, with the lure of new lands and new adventures calling him. Night, and three hours' grace—enough to bring him safely into Burgundy. Then south—far south, to Barcelona—that last, far-flung island of French life on Spanish soil. There he would find new glory and carve out a new career.

He tossed his black locks back over his shoulders, and burst into song.

JUDGMENT BY STEEL

CERCAMON'S SWIFT, sensitive instinct drew his eyes, in the midst of his singing, from the Count of Barcelona to the white-faced woman on the count's right hand. The notes faltered on his lips at sight of her ashy, frightened face; the next instant her scream cut short his song.

Then none had any list for song. Some leaped to their feet, startled and pale; others sat staring. But Count Raymond-Bérenger the Great rose slowly; his dark eyes rested, with terrible intentness, on the central figures in the sudden tragedy. And as he rose, all, men and women alike, turned toward him— all, save Cercamon the Troubadour, who could not take his eyes from the horror-stricken features of the Lady Maria de Moncada.

Beside her, hunched in his chair, sat Gomez of Moncal; and it was plain to all that Gomez was dead. His hand still clutched his thin-stemmed wine-glass, from which the blood-red wine had spilled upon the tablecover; his face was distorted in a horrible grimace of pain. His friend and lord, Perez de l'Arba, had reached across the dead man to seize Lady Maria's arm, which he still held in a cruel grip; and he was livid with anger.

"What is this?" the voice of Count Raymond, quiet and sinister, broke the silence.

It was then that Perez de l'Arba sprang up, his fury almost choking speech, and hurled his accusation full in the face of the count his host:

"It is murder, no less! And you shall answer for it to my lord the king, as this treacherous woman shall answer to me! I call all men of honor to witness the hospitality which Barcelona shows to the envoys of Navarre!"

Cercamon, still watching Lady Maria, saw no change in the rigid horror that held her bound. But across the table from her a man raised his cup, and flung its contents full in de l'Arba's face.

"You lie, you dog of Navarre!" he cried. "And if you crave further answer, I will give it!"

De l'Arba clutched at his sword; but before he could draw, the Count of Barcelona was at his side.

"Be silent, Moncada!" he commanded. "This is too great a matter for a brawl. My lord de l'Arba, I fail to understand you. I see only that Gomez is dead, and that you impute the guilt to us. If you have accusation to make, make it plainly, and justice shall be done you."

The Navarrese ambassador, with a gesture of fury, cast down the napkin with which he had wiped the wine from his beard.

"Ay, that I will!" he shouted. "But now, while yonder troubadour was singing, my vassal Gomez drained his wine. This false woman"—he raised his hand, still clutching the arm of Lady Maria, whose fingers were tight-clenched—"filled his cup again; he drank, and straightway, with a groan, fell back as you see him now—dead. None other was near him save myself, his friend and master. I accuse Donna Maria de Moncada of his murder, by some subtle poison! See, how she holds her hand!"

He seized the woman's unresisting fingers and tore them apart, but there was nothing in them. For a moment he stared blankly; then, with a cry of savage triumph, he snatched something from the folds of her dress, and held it up. It was a small vial of Moorish glass.

The knights and ladies of the court gasped all at once, with a sound like the hiss of a wave on shingle; looks of horror were cast at the pale-faced woman, and many drew away from her, as if to escape some foul contagion. But he who had flung the wine in de l'Arba's face ran suddenly around the table's end, passed the count with little ceremony and snatched the vial from the ambassador's hand.

"If this was found on my wife's person," he cried through clenched teeth, "then it is harmless. I will pledge my honor for her innocence! See!"

He pulled the stopper from the flask, and raised it to his lips; but Count Raymond-Bérenger wrenched down his arm.

"Why risk a good soldier's life, when there are dogs?" he asked.

He whistled; and one of the great boar-hounds that crouched by his chair lurched slowly to its feet. A servant brought a collop of meat, on to which Bérenger emptied the vial. The huge dog leaped to gulp down the meat in midair; but the next moment he quivered and stiffened, his eyes rolling and the hair on his neck bristling. A few seconds he stood so, growling in his throat; then he sank dead at his master's feet.

The count's eyes rested sorrowfully on the stricken face of the man he had saved.

"There can be no doubt now, I fear, Moncada. Faithful subject you have ever been to me, and I have held your lady as a pearl among women; but can you ask for clearer proof? She poured the wine that brought Gomez his death; the poison was found on her person. I fear there is nothing to be done save to hold her for trial."

"Trial!" De l'Arba laughed bitterly. "Does any man suppose that such a trial will do justice to us of Navarre? Will the Count of Barcelona inflict the penalty for murder on the wife of his foremost commander, because a Navarrese squire has been poisoned? Nay, that were too much indeed!"

The count turned on him with cold eyes.

"You have been our guest for two months," he answered. "In that time, have you seen any criminal escape our justice? Have you had any slight at our hands, that you should accuse us of condoning such an offense as this?"

Moncada, his gaze fixed balefully on de l'Arba, his hand on his sword, spoke before the Navarrese could answer:

"My lord count, my faith in my wife is as my faith in God. I have already given her accuser cause for quarrel; I now challenge him to put his cause to the trial by combat. It is an ancient and holy practise that, when a woman is accused of crime, he who brings accusation may be forced to fight, in the open lists, with any who will defend her. As her husband, I claim the right to prove my wife's innocence by combat. I will be her champion, and God will show the right!"

Cercamon the Troubadour, who had not moved nor spoken since the interruption of his song, gazed with admiration at the man who, in spite of overwhelming proof, thus took his wife's quarrel on his shoulders. Not only was their cause seemingly hopeless, in that the woman's guilt was clear; but Andreu de Moncada was no match for the Navarrese envoy. A general of consummate skill and courage, Moncada was small of stature and weak of frame. Skilled as he was with weapons, he was not by half so famous a swordsman as de l'Arba, who had learned his craft against the Moors.

And the battle would begin with the lance—it could scarce reach the drawing of swords. One spear-thrust, with de l'Arba's giant weight behind the point—and all would be finished. Moncada would be slain in the lists; his wife's guilt would be considered proved, and she would be burned at the stake as a common poisoner.

"What say you, Viscount de l'Arba?" Raymond-Bérenger demanded. "Will you accept this challenge, and put your charge to trial by combat?"

The envoy hesitated.

"It would perhaps be best," he answered doubtfully, "to put her to the question. One turn of the thumbscrews—"

Count Raymond flushed scarlet.

"For shame!" he cried. "If your cause is just, you should not fear to defend it. I torture no women, my lord!"

Moncada, who had thrust himself between his wife and her accuser, bent down and whispered in her ear. Her pale face relaxed a little, and she answered—softly, but so that those nearest her could hear:

"As I hope for mercy in heaven, I know nothing of all this! I am innocent!"

Moncada looked up, his eyes full of calm confidence.

"My lord count," he said, "I am satisfied that my wife speaks truth. If this fellow does not accept my challenge, I will proclaim him a coward in every court in France and Spain!"

De l'Arba's features were impassive; yet the watching troubadour seemed to detect a faint smile just curling his lip.

"They who know me," the Navarrese retorted, "scarce call me coward. I accept your challenge, Viscount de Moncada. But I must ask for two months' respite before we meet in the lists. I have much to do, both to order my own estate, and in the service of my king, before I risk my body even in a just cause. My lord count, will you inter my friend's body in consecrated ground?"

Raymond-Bérenger assented; the dead man was carried reverently out. But de l'Arba was not satisfied.

"And this woman?" he asked. "I can not consent that she go free and unwatched. She might escape before the combat."

"I will myself vouch for her!" Moncada broke in angrily; but the count shook his head.

"In this we must do justice to Navarre," he said. "You must

remember, Moncada, that her crime is proved in men's eyes already. I fear God's judgment also will go against you, and that I must lose my most trusted servant. Ho, Canfranc! Lead my Lady of Moncada to Montjuich Keep, and confine her in the tower! See that she lacks no comfort—and your life be forfeit if she escapes!"

TWO HOURS later the troubadour, from the rampart of the outer wall, watched the ambassador of Navarre emerge from the westward city gate and take his way toward the distant heights of Tibidabo.

The captain of the tower edged up to Cercamon, and pointed to the gallant figure of de l'Arba, mounted on a magnificent charger and topped by a scarlet plume.

"He took swift leave," the soldier muttered.

"Too swift," answered Cercamon. "There are fivescore men in his train, and eight baggage-wagons. It almost seems as if he had been ready for his departure before the feast."

The captain nodded.

"I am an old soldier," he said, "and often have I set off on sudden errands; and never could I have sped a hundred men away so fast as this without preparation. Yet how could he have foreseen his friend's murder?"

Cercamon was silent; and after a moment the captain answered his own question.

"Magic, perhaps," he conjectured. "Men say that this de l'Arba is no good Christian. He has been much among the heathen Moors, who are great sorcerers, and have foreknowledge of the future."

"Mayhap," the troubadour replied. "But if he could have foreseen Gomez' death by magic, he could have prevented it by magic. And none could have been more overwhelmed by rage and grief at the murder than he."

He turned away and climbed slowly down from the wall, pondering.

Cercamon was not quartered in the palace, for he was yet a stranger to Barcelona. A fortnight since, early in June of 1137, he had ridden in to claim refuge from persecution, a hearing for his unequaled voice and polished songs, and a chance to win the favor of a new master.

Born a Gascon, a vassal of Aquitaine, he had been high in the good graces of the Duchess Aliénor, until that all-too lovely mistress of Aquitaine, Poitou, and half the South had become betrothed to Louis VII, King of France. Her golden fetters had irked him, for she was a woman of base heart; and when she had turned his faithful service into a means for the dishonorable advancement of her ambition, he had spoken his mind of her, in her own presence and publicly.

Hence he was now masterless, exiled from France, with a price upon his head. His golden voice being his passport to the good will of princes, he had crossed the Pyrenees to the court of Raymond-Bérenger, where men of his calling had ever found welcome and riches.

Bérenger and his courtly Catalans had heard Cercamon's songs with favor; gold had already begun to flow into the troubadour's lap. But though he was welcomed, he was not yet trusted; for had he not been a servant of Aquitaine, that most dreaded enemy of Barcelona? Therefore he had not yet been taken formally into the count's service, but still dwelt outside the palace, in an ancient side-street that led off the spacious, flower-bordered Rambla. Toward this he now made his way, disturbed at heart and troubled in mind.

Of all who had witnessed the death of Gomez, Cercamon had been perhaps the calmest. The rest—de l'Arba excepted—were Barcelonans, deeply concerned in the fate of Maria de Moncada and her husband by reason of ancient friendship. Moreover, Moncada was the shield and sword of the land: his military genius had twice saved the city from siege, and many times adorned her walls with conquered banners. But Cercamon was still a stranger to the actors in the tragedy; he still knew little of their feuds and interests.

Yet he was young, and a Gascon, with the hot heart and the cool head of his race. He had grown to manhood in a land that, above all else, cherished the spirit of chivalry and a reverence for women that was almost worship. In the courts of southern France he had drunk the very quintessence of that chivalry, whose doctrines imposed on the strong and noble, as their first duty, the protection of the weak. And if many a knight or baron forgot that duty to serve his own greed or passion, the troubadour, as the high priest of chivalry, could never forget it.

Cercamon's imagination held ever before his eyes the ghastly scene in the hall of the palace: the murdered Gomez, slumped in his chair with twisted features; the frightened woman on his right, her angry accuser towering on his left; across the table, the slight, but heroic Andreu de Moncada, hurling his wine in the huge de l'Arba's face. And, Gascon as he was, the troubadour felt the woman's terror tug at his heart, no less than her husband's brave defiance and noble trust in her.

Nor was it merely his heart that was convinced of Lady Maria's innocence. In those few poignant minutes he had watched the scene with eyes undimmed by prejudice or suspicion. Those knights and ladies of Catalonia who had drawn aside from her in loathing—to them, this cold-blooded murder was an insult to Barcelona's honor, a hideous violation of hospitality, which brought disgrace on them all. It needed only an accusation to turn their scorn and disgust against the accused. To them, nobles, touched on the raw of their honor, the evidence of the vial was overwhelming proof of guilt.

So would it have been to Cercamon, but for two things: first, his eyes had seen the horror on Lady Maria's face when her scream tore through his song; and none who looked on murder with such a face could have plotted it. More than any other in the hall, she had been overwhelmed by the crime. And the other consideration was this: though de l'Arba himself had proposed that a confession be wrung from her by torture, yet Cercamon had seen a tiny smile twitch on de l'Arba's lips when the count refused.

This was not much, but it was enough for Cercamon, who could not see a woman in distress without condemning, almost unheard, him who had distressed her. And now—de l'Arba had gone, completing his preparations for departure with suspicious swiftness.

In a hard school of intrigue and blows Cercamon had learned to think without losing sight of that which went on about him; and the throng that filled the Rambla as he walked along its upper end were worth his notice. The Catalans are a social folk, brisk and eager in talk, fond of company. Every day, two hours before sunset, it was their wont to drop their labor and walk the streets, where friend would chat with friend and neighbor barter gossip and banter with neighbor. For one brief hour, men and women alike put on their gayest garments for the gladdest portion of the day.

But few were the nobles who strolled thus down the white street and between the lofty brick houses; it was beneath the dignity of men of blood to dodge between prancing horses and creaking fruit-carts, or to rub elbows with the rabble. Nay, this daily promenade was a custom of the bourgeois, from solid merchants in furred velvet to free artisans in fustian.

Today the streets were as thickly thronged as usual; but there was no gay clatter of brisk tongues, no bright kerchiefs, no thrust and riposte of quip and sally. All walked soberly, with grim faces and silent tongues; and every man and woman was dressed in black, or wore at least a scrap of cheap crape.

The news of the calamity which had befallen the Viscountess of Moncada had turned their joy into mourning; this Cercamon understood, having heard much of the people's love for her, and their admiration for her husband. And though he was still too new in Barcelona to realize the adoration with which the common folk of the city worshiped Andreu de Moncada, their "little captain-general," Cercamon was quick to feel the resentment with which all drew aside when he passed, in his gay mantle of blue velvet and his scarlet hose.

Sensing the macabre contrast of his fine raiment with their mourning, Cercamon was glad when he turned aside at the mouth of his own street; and he hastened to his lodgings as fast as his feet would bear him.

The narrow, twisting lane was dark even at midday, and now no ray of light pierced its gloom. He dwelt in an old house built centuries before, during the Moorish domination: it was flat-roofed, with a narrow entrance like the black mouth of a well, a massive, iron-studded door, and latticed windows. Cercamon turned into the dark entrance and reached for the ring of the door; but a sinewy hand caught him by the shoulder and spun him about.

"Cercamon the Troubadour?" a gruff voice questioned.

Cercamon flung the hand aside. "Aye," he answered, "but you need not paw me."

Ignoring his answer, the other announced bruskly:

"The count commands your presence. Follow me!"

As he stepped into the street, the troubadour saw that his companion was a man-at-arms in full mail. There was no ignoring such a summons, no matter how Cercamon disliked the manner of its delivery.

They passed swiftly and silently through the streets, the folk giving them room with sullen glances at Cercamon's finery. But the way to the palace was not long; it lay in a wide square a little way down the Rambla, north of the promenade. There was little life in that square, for—since the tragedy of the early afternoon—the people avoided it. There were none but soldiers stirring about the palace gate.

Under the archway they passed, into a Moorish court bright with flowers and evergreen shrubs. Here they were halted as the guard was changed; then they were permitted to cross to another gate and a huge, square staircase. The count's apartments lay in the east wing, high above the old city, overlooking its flat roofs and the port beyond.

At the soldier's knock, the door opened, and a spearman

stood aside to let them enter. A page, lounging against a pillar, sprang to attention, and then disappeared into an inner room. After a moment he returned, to bid them come before the count. They followed into an apartment that had once been Romanesque, but which was now garnished with captured Moorish columns from Cordova.

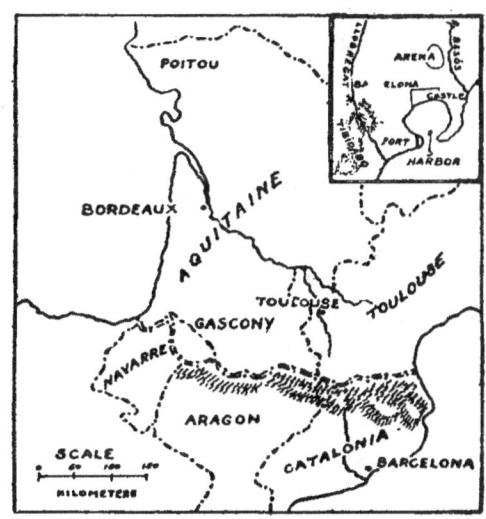

RAYMOND-BÉRENGER SAT at a massive table, facing the door. He was a young man, scarce five years older than the troubadour, huge-limbed, and with features which, for all their fineness, were hard and stern. Descended from the heavy-handed duke who had once held Barcelona for Charlemagne, he had inherited all that great bodily and mental strength which had distinguished his ancestor's heroic conflicts with Basque and Moor.

Beside him stood an officer in lizard-mail and scarlet cloak, listening in silence as the count pointed out positions on a parchment chart. As Cercamon entered, Bérenger looked up, handed the chart to his companion and dismissed him. The count turned directly to Cercamon; his face was stern, and his eyes troubled.

"You must leave the city at once!" he said abruptly.

Cercamon stared at him in dismay.

"But I can not, your grace!" he protested. "Whither should I go? All France is full of my enemies. Moreover, you have promised me protection."

"Aye, so I did," the count rejoined, "and for that very reason I now bid you go. The populace is in fury over the charge brought against the Lady Maria, and no foreigner is safe."

"But what have I—"

"Neither you nor any other foreigner, so far as I know, had anything to do with the murder of Gomez. I say, *so far as I know.* But the mob does not think when its favorites are imperiled— it strikes. My officers report that the people lay Gomez' death and the charge against Lady Maria to a foreign plot; therefore they are clamoring against all foreigners. You know what rumors fly in the city streets at the first whisper of calamity. Today the people only talk of killing; tomorrow they may kill. You are not only a stranger, but—what is worse—an Aquitanian subject, the vassal of Barcelona's worst enemy. If the mob takes the law into its hands, your head will be the first to fall."

Cercamon shrugged his shoulders.

"If your grace permits me to stay," he said, "I will run the risk."

The count looked at him searchingly.

"I do not wish you to stay. What if my people are right? What if that which has befallen is the fruit of a foreign plot? I know no more of you than you told me when you came hither, and your reputation as singer, swordsman, and schemer. It is common report that, in Aquitaine's service, your shrewdness was of more value to the Duchess Aliénor than a thousand spears. I grant that you have told me, and rumor also has it, that the queen-duchess has banished you for daring to speak the truth of her; but how am I to know that you and rumor are honest?"

Cercamon's handsome face flushed scarlet, and his blue-green eyes blazed.

"I have some little repute," he retorted proudly, "for speaking truth, and for convincing doubters with my sword!"

Bérenger smiled faintly.

"You have indeed that reputation; and as a troubadour, you have the right to challenge any peer of France. But I do not fear you, nor can you hold me blameworthy for my doubts. The Duchess of Aquitaine, always my enemy, is now twice as powerful to harm me because she is Queen of France. You have been in her service. It is her trickery that I fear: how can I be sure that your exile is not a pretense, to place in my court a spy and a mischief-monger? And you could be a dangerous spy, from what men say of you. When you came to me, I took your word and welcomed you; but now murder and dissension have flared up in my very palace. Whom should I more naturally suspect than you?"

Cercamon was wellnigh choking with rage.

"My lord," he answered, "you can thrust me out of your realm, but you have no right to insult me!"

"A fortnight after your coming," the count resumed calmly, without heeding his outburst, "a servant of the Navarrese envoy is poisoned in my very presence, and the wife of my most trusted subject is accused of the murder. So strong is the evidence against her that I was forced to choose between handing her over for a trial that would have been a condemnation, and risking her husband's life in a trial by combat. Think you that I believe her guilty? Lady Maria is incapable of such a deed. It is a vile, cunning trick, designed by my enemies to bring about a new war between Barcelona and Navarre. Navarre is too weak to oppose me alone; but what if she is assured of the help of—Aquitaine? Deprived of the genius of my first commander—for Moncada can not overcome de l'Arba in the lists—my armies drawn away to resist a possible invasion from Navarre, I should find my borders menaced by ten thousand seasoned

Aquitanian spears. Caught between two hostile forces, Barcelona could be stripped of her fairest provinces!"

"Your grace!" Cercamon broke in in consternation. "Mean you that I—that I am Aquitaine's instrument for murder and conspiracy? Did you not see that I was a full dozen paces from Gomez when he perished?"

"Aye," Bérenger retorted, "and who was near him? Only the Lady of Moncada, who is incapable of the crime imputed to her, and de l'Arba, his friend! Whom should I suspect, if not the one man present who was .neither a friend to Gomez nor a Barcelonan?"

Cercamon ground his teeth.

"All my life I have lived in honor!" he cried. "No word has ever been breathed against my good name, and now—If your grace holds me a spy and a murderer, why bid me leave the city? Why not burn me at the stake?"

"Because," Bérenger replied, "there is no evidence against you, and I am a fair man."

"Then, if you are fair, I have an offer; send me not away, but *forbid* me to depart, and see to it that every man on guard at the gates has orders to prevent my escape from Barcelona; but let me go where I will within the city, unwatched. Then I, who likewise believe Lady Maria guiltless, will strive to learn the truth in this matter, and to find the murderer. If I succeed, before the trial by combat, then you shall make me public amends for the insults you have heaped upon me, and take me into your service; if I fail, seize me and slay me!"

Bérenger's eyes gleamed curiously.

"Leave you unwatched within the city?" he repeated. "Well, I will agree. But you must prove your case to the full. I will not listen to mere suspicions, or to the testimony of interested witnesses."

"When I come to you, I will come with complete proofs!"

"Good!" the count assented. "May you have success!"

Cercamon left the palace with tingling ears and clenched

fists. His proposal, desperately made to clear his honor of the charge against it, had been accepted so swiftly that he scarce knew what to think. As his brain cooled, two things acquired new importance in his thoughts; not only was Bérenger willing to let him—suspected of conspiracy as he was—wander freely within the city walls; but the count, at the very moment when his insults were most intolerable, had trusted himself alone with Cercamon, who bore the repute of being one of the most perilous swordsmen in France. The troubadour began to suspect that Bérenger had meant from the first to use him—had insulted him only to force him into using his well-known shrewdness in Barcelona's cause.

This impression gained intensity as Cercamon strode toward his lodgings. The folk, still in mourning, thronged the streets; as he passed, they glared at him savagely, and drew together, muttering. They, at least, loved the house of Moncada, and believed its lady innocent; if events went against her, they would show their teeth. Even the count himself might find himself in mortal danger if Moncada were killed in the lists by the terrible adversary he must meet. Already inflamed, passionately devoted to the Moncadas, their idol's death would snap the bonds of law and vassalage, and they would rise in their thousands to rescue his lady from the flames. A mob that tastes blood is the most terrible thing on earth. Most prudently, as soon as he returned to his lodgings, Cercamon cast off his fur-trimmed robes and put on a close tunic and hose of black velvet. He would show mourning with the folk, and so escape their hostility and, if possible, move unnoticed among them. Then he sat down to think out his problem.

His position was one of deadly peril. He had but two months to prove Lady Maria innocent, despite the strongest evidence, and to find the murderer; else he must die. Nor had he the fragment of an idea where or how to begin his task. All the known facts were against Lady Maria; he had only his own and the count's conviction of her innocence to go on, apart from those two tiny points of de l'Arba's over-hasty departure and his unmeant proposal of the torture. And none could give more light.

The court, he knew, was divided in its opinion; but most of the nobles were bitter against the Moncadas. In their attitude, envy for the glory Moncada had won, jealousy for his favor with the count played no little part; but these only disposed them to accept the evidence of the poison-vial, damning in itself. With court on one side and people on the other, Barcelona might well find itself in the throes of a revolution. If so, would the soldiers be true to the count, whose pay they took, or go over to the people? For the army loved Moncada, who had led them to many victories. Cercamon's first task was clearly to learn the attitude of the troops.

AT NIGHT, therefore, when the watch was changed, he went to the fort on Montjuich, and was admitted to the guard-room. The great, square enclosure was lighted by flaring torches stuck in cressets, and a good half-hundred men lounged about, polishing mail, talking, and drinking.

Had they all been Catalans, Cercamon's task would have been a hard one: for Catalans are ugly and suspicious in time of tension, however merry on all ordinary occasions. But Ray-mond-Bérenger's high ambitions, his ceaseless feuds and bick-erings with his neighbors in both France and Spain, required a larger army than Catalonia could support; wherefore the ranks, and even some few high places in his service, were swelled out with professional soldiers from Provence, Languedoc, Auvergne, and even that part of Gascony—namely Auch—which had not yet submitted itself to Aquitaine's dominion. Bérenger ran no risk in this, for he paid his mercenaries so well that his enemies could scarce tempt any considerable number away from their loyalty. Even the garrison of his citadel, Montjuich, was but half-Catalan.

Cercamon's entry into the guardroom was hailed with cheers from the Gascon members of the new-relieved watch. His own Gascon birth, and his fame as a troubadour, ensured him a welcome among them. All but the Catalans soon responded; a sergeant rose to broach a cask of wine; more lights were fetched; a dozen hands plucked Cercamon into the centre of the great room.

"A song, a song!" they cried; and he sang to the rough men-at-arms as if they had been nobles in silks and jewels. Thereafter they talked freely with him; and it was not long before they reached the subject closest to all their hearts.

"You were there, troubadour!" a Catalan called to him. "Tell us what you saw with your own eyes, that we may know the truth! We do not believe, we soldiers, that any of the name of Moncada would murder!"

As he spoke, the man's eyes dwelt on Cercamon's black garb, and the troubadour was glad that he had clothed himself in accord with the general feeling. He told the tale of Gomez' death and Moncada's brave defense of his wife; and the soldiers responded with growls of rage or cheers of approval.

Nor could Cercamon hide his own sympathies; as he depicted Moncada throwing the wine into de l'Arba's face, the company burst into prolonged applause. Though they could tell him little in return, Cercamon learned from their frank emotion one thing of which he had known little: the true greatness of Andreu de Moncada, and the great love which they who followed his banner bore for him.

"He is a gallant cock, our little Andreu!" a burly Provencal declared. "Often have I seen him throw himself into the press of fight beside the humblest of us."

"Small good that does," retorted a Catalan. "His brain is worth a thousand pairs of hands, but his arms are worth nothing. So long as he sits in his tent and plans work for us, all goes well; but when his high spirit overmasters him, then we must rescue his puny body from the strokes of stronger men."

A master of engines—fugitive from Toulouse, whose cunning hand with his catapults earned him a place of honor among the garrison—bawled to be heard, and the others gave him respectful attention.

"Look you," he said thoughtfully, "our little Andreu's high spirit has led him at last into a trap from which no man's hand can save him. De l'Arba will hack him into gobbets. And it is in my mind that the King of Navarre will be very grateful to de l'Arba. Nothing could help Navarre so much as just this 'trial by combat,' as they call it. Trial, forsooth? It is rank butchery! Where will Barcelona be without her captain-general? When next we meet the spears of Navarre—led, mind you, by this very de l'Arba, who is a great soldier—it will go ill with us that our little Andreu is not there to plan our attack and to marshal our ranks!"

"You think war will break out again?" Cercamon asked.

"I smell war!" the engineer answered. "It is the chance Navarre has prayed for. Not that we can not drub Navarre even without Moncada; but Navarre will find allies. All the world is jealous of Barcelona. Aye, we shall have more fighting than we can stomach. King Garcia of Navarre would give mountains of gold for Andreu's head, and de l'Arba is the man to get it for him. Do ye know what they call Garcia in Navarre, eh? 'The Restorer!' Restorer of what? Why, the border castles we won from him a year since!"

"You do not think," Cercamon exclaimed, "that there is a Navarrese plot behind the murder of Gomez? He was de l'Arba's friend!"

"Plot?" the engineer echoed. "What know I of plots? I am a soldier, no more. As a soldier, I know that, when Moncada maintained his wife's innocence in de l'Arba's teeth, and challenged de l'Arba to combat, he gave Navarre the chance she has longed for. Moncada is Barcelona's shield and sword, and he must be wrenched from our count's hands, if Navarre is to win back the lands and glory we have taken from her. Mark my words, troubadour: brave little Andreu has walked into a cunningly laid trap!"

"You call a fair duel a trap?" Cercamon countered. "You do not believe, then, that trial by combat results in the triumph of the right? Why, it is a direct appeal to God's judgment!"

His words were childlike in their assumption of innocence, and not only the master of engines, but all his comrades, burst into sullen laughter.

"And Cercamon the Swordsman asks that!" a Catalan scoffed. "We are fighting men, and know something of the fortunes of war. When Guilhem of Aquitaine seized Toulouse, he was successful, but was he right? Did not the Moors once conquer this land, though they, as heathen dogs, were in the wrong? Do you think that a few pious words muttered at the beginning of a duel can alter the outcome? Pah! It is always the cunning and the strong who win! I tell you, de l'Arba will tear Moncada in pieces, Lady Maria will be burnt for murder, and right and wrong will have little to do with it!"

"Right you are, Pedralbes!" the engineer approved. "But do not let our chaplain hear you say such words. As good Christians, we are bound to pretend that trial by combat is ruled by God's will, though we know it to be murder."

Cercamon sprang to his feet.

"Look ye, lads!" he cried. "Were it not well if something happened to prevent Moncada from meeting so perilous a foe? Perchance Lady Maria's innocence can be proved before the combat, and a meeting in the lists avoided?"

The engineer shook his head.

"Nothing but death can prevent our Andreu from meeting de l'Arba now. That which has passed between them must be washed out in blood. That you know better than I, troubadour, for you have the name of being touchy in matters of honor. But before God! If I and my comrades could prevent that meeting, and still save Lady Maria, we would do it though we died for it! Would we not, lads?"

The shout that answered him left no doubt of the love Moncada's spearmen felt for him. Cercamon rose, reaching a hand to the Toulousan.

"I for one," he said, "make no doubt that she is innocent, and I have never seen a braver man than Andreu de Moncada. To save them from death I would do as much as you. But this is the way the matter lies:

"If Moncada fails to meet de l'Arba in the lists on the day set, de l'Arba wins by default. If they meet, de l'Arba will win in any case. Both court and church will regard either outcome as proof of the lady's guilt, and she will be burnt. Moncada's death in the duel will imperil Barcelona; and it is to Navarre's interest that he be killed outright. There is only one escape, and that is by de l'Arba's defeat—which would require a miracle."

"Miracles do not happen to those who need them!" the engineer scoffed.

"Perchance not," Cercamon conceded, "but I am prepared to do all that a man can to work a miracle in this case. I know not how; but I ask you to give me your name, so that if you can help me with the miracle, I may find you without delay."

"I am Jehan Bigot," the engineer answered, his dark eyes boring into the troubadour's blue-green ones. "If you can find a way to save our Andreu and his lady, my life is yours to command; and there are others here who say the same. A health, lads, to Cercamon!"

The toast was drunk with ringing cheers; and after it Cercamon climbed the stairs of the fort's tower to seek the chaplain. The soldiers sat silent, their enthusiasm slowly sinking before their fears. At last Pedralbes the Catalan spoke heavily:

"I have heard that Cercamon is the shrewdest man in France; and we know his fame as a swordsman. But I fear miracles are beyond his skill!"

"Aye," Bigot answered. "But grind your blade sharp, for my nose tells me this troubadour will lead some of us into perilous hazards!"

MARIA DE MONCADA rose from her knees, and saw, with some astonishment, the dark figure of a priest standing in the doorway. He was clad in the black gown of the Benedictines; his cowl was drawn over his face.

"What brings me the honor of this second visit, father?" she asked.

The black-robed figure flung back the cowl that masked his features, and carefully closing the door, moved so that the light from the single window fell upon his face. Lady Maria would have cried out; but he silenced her with a gesture.

"Fear not," he said. "I have come to help you, if I can. I am Cercamon the Troubadour."

"Only God can help me now," she answered.

"Yet it may be that God will make me His instrument. The Count of Barcelona, who is convinced of your blamelessness, has commissioned me to prove your innocence and to discover the murderer of Gomez."

The woman started; a smile of joy made her pale features radiant.

"Our lord believes me innocent!" she repeated.

"Aye. But if I am to help you, I must know many things that are now hidden from me; and from your lips I must learn all that you can tell me concerning de l'Arba. Does he in truth think you guilty? Was his accusation made in good faith? Or is he—as I have heard whispered—the agent of some secret plot, the furtherance of which requires your and your husband's destruction? If you can not tell me these things, no one can. To learn them, I went first to the chaplain of the fort, who is now your confessor. He refused to reveal anything that you had told him, being forbidden to speak the secrets of the confessional. But when I had convinced him that I came for a good purpose and on the count's authority, he lent me his gown, that I might gain access to you. For it is forbidden for any to see you during your imprisonment save Father Gervasius and the governor of the fort, lest you should escape. I gave my solemn promise not to misuse the good priest's kindness, and shall surrender his robe to him so soon as I win past the guard again."

For some moments Lady Maria pondered, her eyes seeking Cercamon's as if to read them.

"You are a foreigner," she said at last, "a Gascon. Why should you take interest in us, who are Barcelonans? Nay, I will believe you; for if the count and good Father Gervasius trust you, I were both foolish and ungrateful not to do so. Yet I fear I can tell you little. I know nothing of the murder; I know neither by whom nor for what end it was committed. It is true that de l'Arba wishes ill to my husband, and now his hatred will ruin us both—since my husband is no match for him in the lists. But I can not think that de l'Arba had aught to do with Gomez' death, for Gomez was his faithful friend. And if de l'Arba had naught to do with the murder, then he can not be suspected of causing the misfortune that has befallen me."

"Then de l'Arba is your enemy?" Cercamon cried, his eyes brightening. "Because of your husband's victories over Navarre, or for private reasons?"

"Both," Maria answered, plainly with reluctance. "He is a ruthless man, treacherous and evil, who would have used my husband to ruin Barcelona. His hatred against us began when I refused to help his designs."

"Ah! How would he have used you?"

Maria de Moncada's eyes glowed a little with pride.

"My husband," she explained, "led Barcelona to victory over Navarre a year ago. No other man in Spain is so skilled in the ordering of battles. Knowing that Navarre could never hope to regain her losses while Andreu de Moncada captained the troops of Barcelona, King Garcia sent de l'Arba hither—on the pretense of a political mission, but with the hidden purpose of buying my husband over to Navarre. De l'Arba knows how to read men, and soon recognized that to approach my husband with such an offer would be to invite discovery of his base purpose. Therefore, instead of speaking to Andreu, he came to me."

"But why to you? Is not your loyalty known?"

"Because I was born in Navarre. Hoping that my love for the land of my birth might prove stronger than my faith to my husband, knowing how my husband trusts me and confides in my judgment, de l'Arba promised me wealth and high honor if I would persuade Andreu to flee to Navarre, and become commander of the Navarrese army. I dared not reveal his treachery or betray his plans to my husband; for he swore that, if I betrayed his confidence, he would deny my accusations and challenge my husband to combat. Well he knew that I would not dare expose my husband to such a peril. For a meeting between de l'Arba and Andreu in the lists means my husband's death; and would not only bring wretchedness to me, but would deprive Barcelona of her finest soldier."

"And now," mused Cercamon, "he has gained his purpose. For your husband must fight him to prove your innocence. But why, if he needed only your husband's death to help Navarre, did he not hire an assassin to stab Don Andreu?"

"Because he desires not merely to rob Barcelona of my husband's services, but to win them for Navarre; and to the last he hoped to persuade or compel me to help his design. When promises of gold and titles failed, he would have made love to me, to win my husband through my heart. Only when that, too, failed did he let me know the deadliness of his hate. I can not think that he himself caused Gomez' death, for a man does not poison his friends; but so soon as Gomez died he seized the opportunity to destroy me and force a quarrel with my husband."

"Gomez—or so I have heard—was de l'Arba's vassal as well as his friend," Cercamon mused. "As a Navarrese by birth, you should know something of the noble families of the land. Has Gomez heirs?"

"He was unmarried," Maria answered.

"Ha!" Cercamon exclaimed. "Then you may rest assured that none but de l'Arba murdered him! He must have dropped the poison in Gomez' cup while all—Gomez, yourself, the count, and all—were intent on my song; then he dropped the vial in the folds of your gown. His friend, forsooth? Aye, many a man has been untrue to his friend, and de l'Arba's baseness toward you proves him vile enough to murder one who trusted him. You know the feudal law—when a vassal dies, leaving no heirs, his possessions revert to his lord! De l'Arba found his friend's possessions and your husband's death more valuable than his friend, by whose murder he could not only enrich himself, but also compel your husband to risk his life to clear you. He trusts his own ability to slay Don Andreu, and thereby both serve Navarre and win a rich revenge on you. And I fear that he will succeed—unless his treachery can be proved to the count's satisfaction."

Lady Maria was pale and trembling.

"But you will go to the count and tell him?" she pleaded. "He will believe you, since he has commanded you to help us!"

Cercamon put aside her fluttering hands.

"It is not so easy," he answered sadly. "The count has commanded me to prove you innocent, and to find complete proofs against the murderer, before I come to him. 'Neither suspicions, nor the testimony of interested witnesses,' were his words to me. If I should go to him with your story, he would believe it, but he would not be justified in acting on it. The evidence against you was such that, in justice to Navarre, he can not take your statement against it. It is your word against de l'Arba's; and in the eyes of all men it seems fair that the truth be settled by an appeal to God's decision, through trial by combat. To avert that combat, which means death to your husband and condemnation for you, I must not only find a strong case against de l'Arba, but catch him with the proofs of his villainy upon him. That is my task; though it is not light, I trust that what you have told me will make it easier. Keep a high heart, for I shall succeed!"

He turned to go, glancing back in pity at the unhappy woman. Lifted to hope by her confidence in the power of her revelations to save herself and her husband, strengthened by her trust in Cercamon's influence with the count, she had been dashed back into despair by his last words.

"I shall succeed!" he repeated. "My own life is pledged upon it!"

He hid his features in his cowl, opened the door, and stepped out. A soldier shot the bolt after him.

"Is it well with her, father?" he asked anxiously.

"It is well," Cercamon answered, striving to imitate the voice of the chaplain.

Wrapping his disguise closely about him, he descended to Father Gervasius' cell.

CERCAMON KNEW better than to report to Raymond-Bérenger what Lady Maria had told him. As he had assured her, the count would have believed, but—in his capacity of just judge between accuser and accused—could not have given more weight to it than to the damning fact that the vial of poison was actually found on Maria's person. Nor, once the trial by combat had been arranged, could Bérenger interfere with it. Church and state both upheld the sanctity of this absurd method of justice. If Cercamon were to help at all, he must find complete and damning proofs against de l'Arba.

But the combat was still two months away, and he soon learned that there was little he could do for the present. De l'Arba was in Navarre, ordering his affairs; and if he had left behind him any loose threads of his evil-doing, he had concealed them well. Therefore Cercamon spent his days in the unsatisfying task of gathering opinions, and of making such friends at court as he could. For he knew not how deep his task might lead him into peril or into need of help; and he had long since learned the value of honest friends.

The next ten days Cercamon devoted assiduously to the court, where his position had become that of a partisan. Raymond-Bérenger, anxious to leave him a free hand, neither interfered with nor rebuffed him; the count had set Cercamon his task, and if the troubadour chose to spend his two months of grace among the ladies and the fine gentlemen of the palace, that was his affair.

But among the nobles themselves Cercamon had already won the favor that the South accorded a skilful courtier and a polished singer; and this favor he now deliberately compromised with the faction which opposed the Moncadas. His black garb proclaimed him in sympathy with the folk, and an adherent of Lady Maria.

A large minority of the nobles, jealous of the Moncadas and embittered against them by an honest belief in Lady Maria's guilt, at once turned a cold shoulder on Cercamon—the colder because he, a foreigner, dared to show a preference in their quarrels. But the pro-Moncada faction, which fed and grew on its intense patriotism, eagerly welcomed him as an ally.

In spite of their prejudice against his birth, it was easy for Cercamon to win their confidence. The half-French, half-Spanish culture of Barcelona was a brilliant polish on the surface of their wild Catalan nature; France was the source and inspiration of all that they admired; and Cercamon was a courtly Frenchman. His repute as a swordsman appealed to their martial fire; his gift of song won them through their sensitiveness to beauty and grace. His songs won from the Moncada faction more applause than ever; great lords listened eagerly to his tales of love and martial adventure, and their ladies smiled on his graceful handsomeness. If Moncada's enemies shunned him, the captain-general's friends heaped him with gold and honors.

They also talked freely to him, both of the murder of Gomez and of its probable consequences for Barcelona. All were agreed that, if de l'Arba slew Moncada, Navarre would seize the opportunity to assail its ancient enemy; and that Barcelona, thus deprived of its great commander, would be hard put to it for defense.

Moncada's foes were by no means foes to the state: the nobles were all devoted to their land and their count. But they envied Moncada his position in the count's esteem; and with all their fiery souls they resented the blot on their honor which they ascribed to Lady Maria's crime. Their belief in her guilt was fed both by their envy and by their pride in the good name of their land; and they had seen with their own eyes the discovery of the poison. Between this faction and Moncada's partisans quarrels were frequent; challenges passed, and a dozen deaths resulted. Therefore Bérenger forbade all quarrels under pain of death.

On the tenth day the court was plunged into consternation by a rumor that Aragon had broken its treaty of alliance with Barcelona. Three years before, King Alphonso the Battler had died, leaving no heir to reign over Aragon save his brother Ramiro, a weak man, already in holy orders. Rather than expose his kingdom to the rule of an incapable king, Alphonso bequeathed it as a trust to the mighty military orders, the Knights of the Temple and the Hospital.

But his barons, jealous of these mighty brotherhoods, violated Alphonso's will, called Ramiro from his cloister, and forced the scepter into his unwilling hands. Against his will Ramiro took a queen; and so soon as a daughter was born to him, in 1132, he betrothed her—infant though she was—to Raymond-Bérenger of Barcelona. Then he returned to his cloister; and five years later—the Spring of this same year in which Cercamon came to Barcelona—Raymond-Bérenger was recognized as Prince of Aragon. But he took no measures to secure his power there, lest he arouse the enmity of the Templars and Hospitallers, who resented their own loss of the realm. Raymond du Puy, grand master of the Knights of the Hospital, sold Bérenger his claim for a round sum in gold; and the count held Aragon as good as his.

But now came the news that du Puy had broken his promises, and that the Temple and the Hospital had declared Aragon theirs by the terms of Alphonso's bequest. It was rumored that they had bought over the Aragonese barons, and purposed to maintain the independence of their land against Barcelona. None knew whence the rumor had come, but it spread through the court like a pestilent disease, spreading consternation, seizing on minds already disturbed by the tragedy of Gomez.

From the court it spread to the city; within three days all had heard it, all were speculating wildly on its direful meaning. Here was an ally for Navarre! So soon as Moncada fell in the combat with de l'Arba, Navarre would declare war, join forces with Aragon, and their united armies would advance to the siege of Barcelona. Such was the talk in the palace, in hall and antechamber, in the wine-shops, on the Rambla during the daily promenade.

And at this unpropitious time Andreu de Moncada resigned his office as captain-general into the count's hands, announcing his intention to proceed at once on a pilgrimage to the shrine of St. James of Compostella, there to implore the saint's help in his approaching combat with the envoy of Navarre. He departed at once; and his going plunged the shaken city into consternation.

It was on Moncada's recommendation that city and army were placed under the command of his subordinate, Amat de Cascadour. Cascadour, like Cercamon, was a Gascon, exiled from Aquitaine; but he had come to Barcelona many years before, and had proved his loyalty by serving in Raymond-Bérenger's wars with heroic courage and unsparing devotion. Now that suspicion was directed away from Aquitaine toward Aragon, none saw any peril in entrusting the city to him; the rather because Amat de Cascadour, driven from his home by Guilhem X of Aquitaine, had received no pardon from Guilhem's daughter Aliénor, the Queen-Duchess. He had risen rapidly in the count's service, distinguishing himself for both valor and energy.

Cascadour's first act after taking over Moncada's responsibilities was to send a force of a thousand men to guard the Aragonese border; and all praised his prompt energy. But Barcelona herself could not be weakened; every available Catalan was already beneath her banners; and therefore the new captain-general sent agents into France to hire mercenaries. The plain of the Besós, where the city's garrison exercised, was bright with flashing armor and the rippling of banners.

The peril of war, and the excellence of the new commander, became the common talk of folk and court. Leaving the count's presence with two young Catalan knights, Cercamon's ears were ringing with the exciting news. But the two young men, friends and rivals for the next vacant captaincy, had of late become estranged over the unhappy affair of Gomez; and not even their common admiration for the indefatigable Cascadour could re-unite them. Thoma la Barca, believing in Lady Maria's guilt, praised the Gascon commander as a better man than Moncada; while Luc de Sobre Ter was confident that God would vindicate Maria's innocence, overthrow de l'Arba with Don Andreu's spear, and prove Moncada the first soldier of Barcelona.

"Bah!" cried young Thoma, with all the fledgling warrior's contempt for a man inferior in the lists. "Andreu? Cascadour would have eclipsed him within the year, even if we had never heard of de l'Arba! And now his wife must needs poison the Navarrese, de l'Arba will make her a widow by this day six weeks!"

Luc de Sobre Ter scowled blackly, and plucked at his soft mustache.

"If 'twere not for the count's order, Thoma, I would cut your comb for that!" he cried. "Andreu de Moncada has more worth in his little finger than all your ancestors had in all their carcasses together!"

Thoma's hand flew to his hilt.

"Order or no," he retorted, "you shall pay for this!"

Cercamon thrust his broad shoulders between them.

"One moment, *messires!*" he said with a cold smile. "I trust your disregard of the count's command conveys no want of respect for him, no lack of loyalty to your master?"

The shocked, angry faces of the youths convinced him that they were indeed loyal enough to Bérenger, however they might stand in the great quarrel that divided the sympathies of the court.

"Then," the troubadour added softly, "you may have heard

that I have some small skill with my weapon. If one of you kills or wounds the other in this mad quarrel, I will kill the victor!"

Both knights turned on him hotly, but he gave them no time to speak.

"It is said," he resumed, "that there will be war with Navarre and Aragon. If that war comes, the count will need you both. At such a time it is treason to deprive your lord of loyal followers. Which of you is so faithless as to weaken his ranks by even a single arm, merely to satisfy a private spite?"

He watched the young men narrowly, and their looks satisfied him. He left them reconciled, and complimented himself with the certainty that he could rely on their help in the event that the plans seething in his brain called for execution.

THE EXCITEMENT of the populace rose to fever heat during the week that followed. Ever unquiet, the common folk of Barcelona were now restless as dogs in August, and as ready to run wild. It was said openly in the wine-shops that King Garcia of Navarre had hired de l'Arba to compass the murder of Gomez, and by casting the blame on Lady Maria, to deprive the city of its great general.

No carter, no butcher's apprentice was too humble to assert full knowledge of the political peril, and to swear that it was Navarre which had bribed the Templars and Hospitallers to break with Barcelona. And hearing such words over and over again, Cercamon was amazed at the quick instinct of the mob-mind, which out of its loves and hates leaped to the conclusion concerning the murder which he had not reached until after his talk with Lady Maria.

But he did not agree with the folk that Navarre had hired the spears of the two great knightly orders. He knew well the tradition of stainless honor which the Temple and Hospital still proudly maintained; and he knew as well that Navarre was too poor to buy men whose vows set them above earthly wealth. Ambitious the Templars might be, the Hospitallers greedy for fame; but neither could be bought for gold.

Yet right or wrong, the people were dangerous. Convinced that Navarre was to blame for both the misfortune of their beloved Moncadas and the new peril from Aragon, they had set their wills on taking vengeance if Moncada perished. Day after day brought closer the date set for the trial by combat; and with each passing night their nerves grew rawer, tauter with the strain.

When the fateful day came, they would be near the breaking-point, ready for revolt. If Moncada fell, they would rise in blind fury, and slay all that was noble, unless the authority of the count and the spears of the soldiers could hold them in check.

If Cercamon's profession of singer drew him to the palace, his soldier's instinct drew him by a stronger lodestone to the city walls. He soon saw that Raymond-Bérenger, through his new general, was taking every precaution against the impending war. Every day the engineers were overhauling siege-engines, directing the storage of pitch, oil, and fagots on the battlements. Sheaves of arrows and javelins and heaps of stones were stacked behind the merlons.

Every day and all day, from the crenellated towers, Cercamon could see divisions of foot or squadrons of horse maneuvering on the plain beyond the town. Great wains creaked up to the gates on their solid wooden wheels, laden with grain and wine; sheep and cattle were driven in, so that there might be plenty of meat in case Moncada's fall should hearten Navarre to renew the war.

And one day, in his survey of the walls, Cercamon met Amat de Cascadour face to face. They had not met before, save on that day of Gomez' death, when Cercamon had seen the red-cloaked officer in lizard mail taking orders from the count.

The soldiers were exultant at the hope of action. Weary to death of garrison duty, still keenly mindful of the booty won in the war with Navarre a year ago, they longed for a second brush with the enemy. But their eagerness was dashed by the knowledge that war would come only if their beloved Andreu fell before de l'Arba's lance.

The news had flown from the garrison of Montjuich to the city walls that Cercamon was a friend to their captain-general, that he was eager to save Moncada if he could; and wondrous tales were told of the cunning he had shown in the service of Aquitaine. The soldiers came to look upon him as the only possible deliverer, Moncada's and Barcelona's hope. Wherever he went among them, Cercamon was sure of a cordial hand-clasp, a pot of wine, and much wild speculation and idle gossip.

"I have heard," a captain of archers said one day, "in the wineshops, that the folk will rebel if de l'Arba wins. They purpose to seize him after the combat, hack him to pieces, march to the palace, and demand instant war with Navarre. I, for one, will not order my company to loose a string against them!"

"So I have heard from others," Cercamon replied. "It is bad talk. If Moncada dies, the count will need every man's loyalty. What will happen to Barcelona, if both people and troops mutiny?"

"Why, the count will be forced to obey people and troops!" the officer replied. "Think you we will let our Andreu perish unavenged?"

"My counsel is," Cercamon answered him, "that ye cease to think of rebellion, and see to it that every arm is ready, every point sharp, when Barcelona needs them. But it would do no hurt if you let me hear all talk on this matter that reaches your ears; and if ye know of any brave fellows who would risk a stroke or two for me—"

"Every man who wears steel in Barcelona—" the captain began.

"Not so. Where there are many men, there are many hearts, and some of them false. Watch your men carefully; note down the most faithful. I may find use for some of them before swords clash in the lists."

"You shall have the best!" the captain promised.

CERCAMON HAD scarce reached his lodging when he

heard the clang of mailed feet on the stair. A soldier entered, looked cautiously over his shoulder, closed the door softly behind him. It was Jehan Bigot, the Toulousan engineer from Montjuich.

"There is treachery in the wind," he announced darkly.

Cercamon stared at him. "How?"

"Half of the garrison of the fort is ordered to the Aragonese border!"

"Well?"

"They are replaced with mercenaries from Auvergne, Burgundy, Gascony, and Poitou."

"All this I have heard. War threatens with Aragon, and the border must be protected. But since the city must not be exposed, new troops must be brought in to defend it. The count has found, in the past, that he can trust mercenaries if he pays them enough."

"What if some other pays more than he?" the engineer retorted.

"You mean?"

"That it is dangerous to strip Montjuich—the citadel of Barcelona—of so many seasoned men, and to replace them with troops of untried loyalty. Moreover—wellnigh every *Catalan* has been sent to the border. The garrison is now nine-tenths foreigners—most of them subjects of Aquitaine!"

"You are foreigner—so am I—and we are both loyal to the count. May not these newcomers prove as good as we?"

Bigot smiled mysteriously.

"What think you of this, then? This morning I found a purse of gold in my arms-chest!"

Cercamon pondered.

"Have you noticed," he asked, "what these new levies look like?"

"Think you I have asses ears?" the Toulousan answered. "They are stout lads all, but there is a gleam in their eyes that I like not. They have come hither on mischief. And what means the purse in my chest, eh? Some one would buy me!"

"Aye," Cercamon meditated. "You come from a land that has long been at feud with Barcelona, and it is thought you may be willing to serve her enemies—for a price."

"So you are awake at last? Aye, I have my price, but not to bite the hand that feeds me! No gold will buy my faith to Andreu de Moncada!"

"If you are wise," the troubadour smiled, "you will keep the gold and say nothing. If more appears, or if any whisper treason in your ears, pretend to be ready for any offers—and tell me straightway!"

"But I am no traitor!"

"Assuredly not, good Jehan. But you are a prudent man, who would dissemble a little to learn the plans of him who would bribe you."

The engineer bit his lip. "I like not dirty gold, but you are wiser than I. I will do as you say, if it will help our little Andreu."

"I am not sure of that," the troubadour replied, "but I hope it may. What you tell me is indeed suspicious. It would have been more natural to send half as many Catalans away, with as many mercenaries, so that the new troops, both here and on the border, might be seasoned with loyalty by the old. Watch your companions closely, and seek to discover their thoughts. If any treachery is planned, I must know of it. I rely on you to discover it; to that end you must keep your ears open and your tongue smooth. Seem to assent to any treason—even the worst—and then bring me word. I promise that no harm shall come of it. And—let me see—seek me not here, lest you be watched, and our counsels discovered. I have ordered a suit of mail made at Anselmo the Weaponsmith's. He is an honest man, and lives in the Street of the Armorers, by the Long Quay. Seek me there, if you have news. I have taken quarters there, to mature my plans undisturbed; but I keep this lodging to deceive any who would spy on me. Any soldier can go to an armorer's without being suspected, therefore you can meet me safely. Ask for me under the name of Gualter the Apprentice, for such is my character at Anselmo's."

"You have a plan, then?" the soldier whispered eagerly. "You can save Andreu? There are still enough loyal hearts in Barcelona—"

"My plans are unformed yet," Cercamon replied, "for I know neither the enemy's plans nor whether there indeed be an enemy. But if I need an honest heart and a strong arm, I shall remember you, Jehan Bigot!"

The next morning Cercamon revisited the battlements to speak with the friendly captain of archers. The man was not there.

"Where is Captain Salvier?" he asked the nearest soldier.

"Ordered to the border at midnight last night," the man answered with a scowl. "All is not well in Barcelona, troubadour! A third of the troops have been sent from the walls, and foreigners have taken their places."

"Who gave the orders?"

"Who would give them? Amat de Cascadour, our new general!"

Cercamon came closer to him.

"Say naught of your suspicions," he whispered. "Whatever happens, take care that ye neither murmur nor talk too much among yourselves—but get word to me! This may mean treason; or it may only be the recklessness of a man unused to such high command."

And he gave the soldier the same instructions as to finding him that he had given to Bigot.

The question Cercamon had first asked himself concerning Gomez' murder was: to whose advantage was it that Gomez should die? To this question there had been no answer, till he had spoken with Lady Maria. His talk with the soldiers in Montjuich, and Maria's statement, had convinced him that the murder was merely the first step in a cunning game, designed to strike through Gomez at Moncada, through Moncada at Barcelona itself. And to whose advantage was it that Barcelona should be weakened by the death, at de l'Arba's hands, of Moncada? Plainly, the advantage of Navarre; which feared the little leader's generalship more than a thousand spears.

But now Cercamon was puzzled. It would surely also help Navarre that so many stanch Catalans had been withdrawn from the city to the border, so that the city was now protected very largely by mercenaries of doubtful loyalty. But that was only a transposition of forces; it was believed that Aragon was instigated to war by Navarre; and if the two hostile lands should strike together against Barcelona, it seemed folly to weaken Barcelona while strengthening the border. The enemy must pass the border before he could strike at the city.

Unless—unless Aragon was only Navarre's cats-paw, and Garcia intended to let his allies shatter their strength against a solid Catalan army, while his own Navarrese came through the passes of the Pyrenees to assail the city. Or—and this thought came to Cercamon as a thing too good for reason— unless the report of Aragon's hostility were false, designed by a cunning, hidden enemy to draw away the most faithful troops from the city, and replace them with hirelings in an enemy's pay.

But the news from Aragon had been confirmed by a breathless messenger to the count, who had straightway sent an embassy to the Grand Masters of the two great orders to inquire into the truth.

Moncada was gone on his pilgrimage; else Cercamon might have reported the situation to him. It would avail little to speak with Cascadour, the new commander; for it was he who had ordered the withdrawal. Cercamon was too proud to mention the matter to Raymond-Bérenger: for the count had forbidden him to report mere suspicions. He resolved to wait a little longer, to be vigilant. There were still five weeks to the day set for the trial by combat—time enough for the mysterious threads to unravel.

ANSELMO THE WEAPONSMITH had his shop
on a twisting lane named for his craft; and men who wanted
the best Milanese mail went to him. His wares were so precious
that only a hauberk of his dainty mesh cost more than full
panoply elsewhere; but the men-at-arms of Barcelona, being
better paid than most, visited him as often as the dice had run
luckily. Cercamon had chosen wisely in making Anselmo's his
secret rendezvous; as he said to Bigot, any soldier could come
to the Italian armorer's without attracting suspicion; and
Anselmo was devoted to Raymond-Bérenger.

To get to the dingy room Cercamon had hired of the Italian,
one passed first through the stall—a booth open on to the street,
flashing with polished mail and sharp-ground swords by day,
shuttered with massy iron by night—and into a long shop with
helms and hauberks on pegs along the walls and lance-heads
littering the benches. An inner door—bolted against the
public—led into an open court with a forge, and a second hearth
under a wooden lean-to against the brick wall.

This court was backed by a higher wall with a gate, behind
which was Anselmo's low, flat-roofed house. In one of its four
rooms Cercamon passed each night from the first darkness till
the end of the third watch. An armful of straw and a sheep's
fell served as bed in case he chose to pass the night; there was
no other furniture save a wide, rough bench, and an iron cresset
for a torch.

Anselmo, a little, stooped man with scraggy, grizzled beard,
was glad to serve Cercamon, who had paid him well for the
mail he had ordered, and now offered the noble sum of ten gold
marks for the use of his room. He was a shrewd, silent man,
this Lombard smith; he understood that he must not talk of
his guest, who was accessible only to those who asked for
Gualter the Apprentice.

In determining on this secrecy, Cercamon had been moved
not only by a desire to keep his own doings under cover, but by
the certainty that—if there were indeed any treason afoot in
the garrison—any soldiers who were seen talking with him

might well be among the next contingent sent to the border. For Cercamon was known by his black garb as a friend to the Moncadas, and hence to Barcelona; and he had been seen too often on the battlements not to have attracted observation.

If there were indeed any connection between Navarre, the murder of Gomez, and the shifting of troops from the city, then there were doubtless men, even of high position, within the walls whose business it was to prevent just such inquiries as Cercamon had been making. In his new retreat he was confident of seeing Bigot, and such others as he need see, without discovery.

Anselmo's shop rang with the jingle of mail and the clank of armored feet all day long; but at sundown he closed his doors to business. From that hour on he played doorkeeper to Cercamon, who had no visitor, however, till midnight of the second day after his arrival. Two hours after the second watch at the fort came off duty, a knock at the door of Cercamon's hiding-place announced Jehan Bigot.

The engineer's eyes were bright with excitement. After making sure that none was eavesdropping, he whispered—

"The garrison has been reenforced again!"

"How many?"

"Two hundred men more. The fort now has its full complement of four hundred and fifty, of whom but fifty are of the original force, and only three Catalans. I paused for a moment by the north wall to ask of a comrade how matters passed there, and learned that more than half the forces in the city are new-come mercenaries from France. Two thousand men have been sent to Aragon!"

Cercamon was startled. The new captain-general was indeed taking the fate of the city in his hands.

"These latest comers—what are they like?" he asked.

"Stalwart fellows, scarred with war. They bear themselves well; but they stick too close together for my liking." He paused, but it was plain that he had more to tell. After a pause well calculated for its dramatic effect, he resumed:

"Roger de Canfranc, Governor of Montjuich, has been placed under arrest. We are now commanded by a Breton captain of mercenaries."

"What make you of that?"

"Accusation was brought against Canfranc—who is Aragonese by birth—that he was plotting for Lady Maria's escape. Amat de Cascadour signed the order for his arrest. *Peste!* We of the fort have served under Canfranc for twenty years, and he is faithful as steel. Our new governor's first act was to degrade the last four sergeants left of the original garrison and fill their places with new men—Poitevins. I tell you, Barcelona is rank with treachery!"

Cercamon seemed to pay little heed, but he was indeed much stirred by this news. To put the last of the old garrison under men from Poitou—the heart of Aquitaine—was either madness or treason.

"Have you received any more gold?" he asked, with seeming indifference.

Bigot drew from under his cloak a heavy purse, and flung it into Cercamon's lap.

"This morning," he replied, "I found this in my chest. And tonight, just as I was setting out for this place, one brushed past me in the gate, and plucked at my sleeve. Remembering your counsel to keep ears open and mouth shut, I followed him. He led me this way, stopping at a tavern by the fishers' quarter. The wineshop was empty—doubtless designedly, for none disturbed us while we were there.

" 'Do you want more gold?' he whispered. His cloak was drawn over his face, and hid all that the nasal of his helmet left visible. I snatched the cloak from him, and pulled off his helmet before he could draw weapon. His knife was out the next moment, but I calmed him.

" 'You know my face, so I must know yours,' I told him. He

was one of the new Poitevin officers. 'Yes,' I went on, 'I want more gold, and care not how 'tis earned, so it be full weight.'

"He stared at me, as if to read my thoughts. At length he resolved to venture. 'You are a Toulousan,' he began.

" 'Aye,' said I, 'but under outlawry. If you can work out my pardon from the Count of Toulouse, as well as get me money, I will cut any throat in Barcelona for you.'

" 'You languish for home?' he leered at me. 'I grow old apace,' I answered, 'and the old always long to spend their last years in peace at home.'

"He ordered drink; we emptied the cups before he spoke further. Yet all the time he watched me, and I watched him.

" 'It might be done,' he says at last. 'I will speak to my master about it. In the mean time you shall have enough gold to buy a freehold in Toulouse, or to live in comfort in Barcelona for all your days.'

" 'What must I do?'

" 'Obey order,' he answers, 'whatever they may be. Remember, for a pardon and gold you will cut any throat in Barcelona—those were your words. Gold you shall have, and I think my master can get you the pardon. Obey orders—whatever you are told to do, do it like a soldier. That is all.'

" 'But I obey orders now,' I told him.

"He grinned at that. 'The orders that will come—very soon—' he says, 'are such as you never had before. They will come from your own officers. And now farewell; I must not be seen with you.'"

"And you came straight to me?" Cercamon asked.

"Not I—though you are well hidden here. I made a circuit, stopping at two more taverns; then dodged back hither through side-streets. If any were following me, they are lost by now."

"The game is plain," Cercamon mused aloud. "A large part of the faithful garrison has been drawn off; new and unknown men—good soldiers, but with no loyalty to Barcelona—are sent to replace them. Stanch officers are discredited, foreigners and mercenaries put in their stead. Any man who, like yourself, is too useful to send away, is bought. This will be done till the garrison is at least half-disloyal, including most of the officers. But that all this can be done under the very eye of Amat de Cascadour, aye, so openly that the count can not but hear of it—that baffles me. It is Navarre, of course; or Aquitaine—since so many of the new troops are Aquitanian mercenaries."

"Bah!" the engineer retorted. "It is none so baffling. The count leaves all to Cascadour, as he was wont to leave all to Moncada. Cascadour is a good enough soldier, but no commander. Whatever foes to Barcelona are at the bottom of this thing, they can easily befool him. But hold! I mind me that Cascadour is himself a Gascon! It is he who was entrusted with the defense of the city, and 'twas he who brought in the new men. What if he brought them—knowingly?"

"I have thought of that," Cercamon answered. "But I am not sure. He is not in favor in Aquitaine, and men say that his service here has ever been honorable. He may be a blind tool—I think him no knave."

"You are doubtless right," the engineer conceded. "But hark you! Go you to the count, and tell him all! Urge him to recall the faithful troops from the border, put back our old officers, and spurn the newcomers out of the gates!"

Cercamon shook his head.

"That is a good way to smash the plot, but not to catch the plotters. It leaves our main task unaccomplished: for if the hand of Navarre or of Aquitaine is concerned in this, that hand, will not strike home till Moncada lies dead under de l'Arba's spear. We must save, not merely the city, but Moncada and his lady. Let the fruit bide on the tree till it ripens."

"Well and good, if it does not hang too long!"

"I will see to that. Now go, or you will be late. You can always find me here at this hour, or Anselmo will know where I am."

TWELVE MORE days passed. Each day Cercamon visited the palace, where talk of the Moncadas was now overshadowed by the new threat from the Great Orders in Aragon, The count's messengers had not returned; some said that they must have been intercepted. Most men declared openly that Garcia of Navarre had egged on the Templars and Hospitallers to dispute Bérenger's claim to the throne of Ramiro.

The young nobles, whose zeal for war made them see its lightnings near, were confident that Barcelona would have to stand a combined assault from the two western kingdoms at once.

The might and wealth of the Orders would swell Garcia's power to formidable proportions, and in Raymond du Puy, grand master of the Hospital, they would have a leader worthy of Moncada himself. And now, when Moncada's life hung on the issue of the approaching duel in the lists—

"The count himself is no mean soldier," Cercamon observed.

"He is strong as a bull, and a champion!" Thoma la Barca answered proudly. "But he has never yet marshaled his own host in battle, and how know we that he can pluck victory from the clouds like Moncada?"

Day by day the palace buzzed with excitement and hummed with energy. In every corridor men grouped together, whispering, with faces high with warlike hope or dark with foreboding. In the bowers, the ladies grew pale and anxious; glory was well enough for their golden-spurred husbands, but it was they who tasted the bitterness of war with none of its fiery joys.

Twice each day Raymond-Bérenger showed himself before his court, serene of face, apparently undisturbed by the clouds that threatened his ambition and his very coronet. But he spent most of the time in his chamber, receiving reports from the walls, hearing messengers, or closetted with Amat de Cascadour, Moncada's Gascon successor.

Every night Cercamon returned to his lodgings, just at sunset; well after dark he slipped out through the night-black byways to the house of Anselmo the Armorer. Every night Jehan Bigot came to him; on the fourth night the old soldier was swelling with importance.

"The walls have been reenforced again," he said abruptly. "Frenchmen all, I hear; mostly from Poitou!"

"Like him who gave you gold!" Cercamon exclaimed. "Now it is sure that Aliénor of Aquitaine strikes at Barcelona! That the new garrison is chiefly from Poitou or Gascony is a sure sign of her hand."

"Aye," growled the engineer, "and so is Amat de Cascadour a vassal of hers!"

"Not so—he is a vassal of our lord the count, and has been for twelve years. He has more to gain from loyalty than from treacherous service to the queen-duchess."

"I like not these Aquitanians," Bigot grumbled, "saving your presence, troubadour, for you are an honest man!"

"Mayhap I am," Cercamon answered, half to himself. "I have ever striven to act honorably and faithfully; but now it is an ill plight in which I find myself. Aliénor of Aquitaine is indeed sending these men, through some traitor in the count's confidence; and so I must play a strange part. For I myself was born her vassal, yet now I strive to the best of my might to defeat her purposes and aid her enemy. But, as I hope to save my soul, I can do no otherwise! For Raymond-Bérenger is as noble in heart as in birth; while Aliénor, duchess and queen though she be, is a tyrant and a Jezebel!"

"And your enemy," Bigot reminded him, "who has sworn your destruction. I, born a Toulousan, serve the greatest enemy Toulouse has. And one man out of every four in France today— if he follow the profession of arms—is in the service of some prince other than his own. 'Tis topsey-turvy, but 'tis the fashion—and a good one, for it saves some of us from a hempen collar."

Cercamon rose.

"Time you were going back," he said. "I think I will speak with Amat de Cascadour tomorrow."

Shortly after Bigot's departure, Cercamon put on his cloak and set out for his lodgings. He was weary, and the bed there was more tempting than the straw and sheepskin at Anselmo's. He had advanced perhaps a hundred yards up the Street of Armorers, and was about to turn into a by-lane leading west toward the Rambla, when his ear caught the faint *chink-chink* of steel on stone. Instantly he stopped, hand on sword; and the next second three men sprang upon him from the shadow of the corner house-wall.

His sudden stop saved his life. As they leaped in he stepped back, and their blades stabbed the air. Cercamon drew and thrust in one smooth motion, swifter than light. Not for nothing was he known for one of the first swordsmen in France. His blade licked in twice, and came back red. The foremost bravo fell sprawling, his throat spouting blood; the second gave back just in time to avoid the troubadour's point.

"Cut him down!" cried the third, and flung himself into the fight.

His weapon grating against two, Cercamon fought for life; his sword played fiercely back and forth with all his great strength centered in his supple wrist. A hot pain seared his temple; but his next thrust stretched a second adversary on the cobblestones. The third turned and ran, but Cercamon followed hard on his heels, and launched a mighty stroke at the fellow's head. The descending blade lost much of its force from the man's speed; but it fell true on the steel helmet, and the would-be murderer fell.

Cercamon thought at first that the man was dead; but feeling his head, discovered that the blow, having split the helmet, had been turned by a steel coif underneath. Sheathing his blade, Cercamon picked the stunned man up, threw him over his shoulder, and carried him back the short distance to Anselmo's shop.

In his dingy quarters back of the court, the troubadour laid the man out on his own couch, stripped off the coif, and bathed his head. The ruffian was a sturdy fellow of forty, scarred and dark-visaged. For a few moments he gave no sign of life, but at last he opened his eyes. By the light of the half-consumed torch he stared at Cercamon, as if uncertain of his sight; but his dazed senses gathered themselves, and he gasped in dismay.

"Cercamon!" he cried.

"And whom did you take me for, since you sought to murder me?" the troubadour answered grimly. "And who are you? Ha, now I remember! You are Gui le Balafré, captain of the guard in Poitiers!"

"You remember well," the soldier answered, with a wry smile. *"Peste,* but you deal hard blows! A good helmet spoiled, and a dint through plate and mail! Had I known it was you we were sent against, I should have bided at home rather than risk my skin in Barcelona."

Cercamon said nothing; but bolting the door on his captive, he crossed the court into Anselmo's shop. Soon he returned with a brace of new-made fetters, and clamped them on le Balafré's wrists and feet. Then, sitting down on the floor, he drew from the pouch at his girdle a thin roll of parchment, a reed pen, and a tiny vial of ink. While his captive craned his neck to watch, Cercamon slowly and carefully wrote out a dozen lines.

"What is that?" asked Balafré, his voice edged with fear.

In that day men who knew not the art of writing still saw something awful and magical in written characters.

"I am writing," Cercamon answered coolly, "a report to the Count of Barcelona. It says that you, with two others, sought to murder me, who am engaged on an important task at the count's orders; and it requests that you be tortured and broken on the wheel!"

Gui le Balafré went white.

"Before God, write no more!" he pleaded. "Destroy it! Have not you and I been comrades in arms, served together under the banner of Aquitaine? Have I not said that I would have lifted no hand against you had I known you? I guessed indeed that he whom I was to slay was a man of importance, else I, a

Captain of Poitiers, would not have been set upon him; but how should I guess that it was your life my master sought?"

"Who is your master?" Cercamon countered. "You would best tell me the truth, or this paper shall go to the Count at daybreak."

"I will tell you all, only do not send that paper! You have ever been a gallant man, troubadour—you would not have a soldier tortured! I have faced death a hundred times, and could face it if it came swift and sure—but crushed limbs and shrieking nerves—have pity!"

"Why should I not send you to the rack and the wheel, you who would have murdered me by treachery?"

Gui's dark eyes watched his captor's face with a strange commingling of terror, admiration, and submission; but he saw no sign of mercy there. Love of life was strong within the soldier's powerful body.

"I will do as you bid," he repeated. "I will do all—serve you, obey you, follow you till death!"

Cercamon held the man's eyes with his own cold, blue-green stare.

"If I spare you," he answered slowly, "you will obey all my commands—all! Though riches, greatness, everything should be promised you by my enemies, you will obey me alone; else I will hunt you down and bring a bitter death upon you!"

"I know your sword, and I know your cunning," Balafré replied. "Not alone because I fear you, but also because—because it is better to stand by your side than to bear the banner of a prince! But you must protect me, for if I change masters and serve you, Aquitaine will hunt me!"

MANY OF the rough spearmen of Poitou had given their admiration to Cercamon the Troubadour. The French, whether rogues or heroes, ever honor gallantry. And Cercamon had proved, in battle, in the lists, in the snares of intrigue, that he was as brave as cunning, as honest as invincible. Therefore the men who once had served with him regarded him with half-frightened worship, as one who could not fail.

"Who is your master?" Cercamon asked again.

"Amat de Cascadour!"

Cercamon smiled grimly.

"Bigot was right, then. Go on."

"Cascadour sent orders to me, through the new governor of the fort, to kill the man with whom Bigot was in secret communication. It seems that Bigot, for all he has taken our gold, has been under suspicion. Spies dogged his tracks and followed him hither twice; each time, his confidant was seen to leave this place a little after him and to turn west. I was told that this man knew too much for the good of our cause, and therefore I was to take two men and slay him. Bigot is to be sent to the border in two days."

"A dainty game," Cercamon commented. "So Amat de Cascadour, who commands the forces of Barcelona, is in the pay of Aquitaine?"

"Aye. He has received secret couriers from the queen-duchess. I myself came hither with a message to him, which ordered me to place myself at his service. He detailed me to Montjuich. Thrice have I been sent to him from the fort for gold to be distributed among those who, like Bigot, seemed too useful to be sent away. It will hurt Cascadour to send off the best engineer in the garrison."

Cercamon pondered long. "So Aquitaine," he said at last, "having often sought to humble Barcelona, is to strike at last. Navarre is concerned in the game as well; but how? And what of Aragon?"

At the last word Balafré laughed.

"Your count is all too credulous. The threatened rebellion of the Great Orders against him is pure illusion—a cunning rumor spread by Aquitaine's agents, to draw off your best men to the border. Since the first messenger that reached Aragon from Bérenger would have learned the truth, Cascadour has laid ambushes to cut off and seize all messengers. It is not from Aragon that danger threatens—'tis from Barcelona itself! I am but a little pawn in the game, and know little of kings and castles; but I know that nine out of every ten men in Montjuich, and one out of every two on the walls, are Aquitainians, or mercenaries in Aquitaine's pay. I was among the first to come, and have been used as agent in getting others."

"But, *Mordieu!*" cried Cercamon. "Even with the city under the command of a traitor, how could two thousand spears be brought within the gates without arousing attention?"

"The threat of war—the fear of Aragon. Have you not heard yourself how Cascadour is praised for his energy in holding both city and border, and finding the necessary men in the shortest time? And how did he get those men? Why, they were waiting in the passes of the Pyrenees, ready to filter into the city by companies so soon as the fear of the bogy Aragon should have wrought upon the nerves of Barcelona. And every man of them hired to cut Barcelonan throats! The Queen-Duchess Aliénor detached most of them from her own forces in Poitou and Gascony. Cascadour had only to send away all Catalans, the most of the faithful mercenaries, and fill his garrison with the foes of Barcelona."

"But this is madness!" Cercamon objected. "You can not hold the city for a fortnight, once you have taken it. All Catalonia will rise against you! You do not know the richness, in men and money, of this land!"

"Navarre will take care of that!"

"Ha! What is Navarre's part?"

"Of that I know little, save that at one and the same moment her troops will invade your northwest border and Cascadour will strike in the city."

"When is that moment? Who gives the signal?"

Balafré shook his head.

"I know not. Navarre and Aquitaine plan to divide Catalonia

between them; but when they will strike only Cascadour knows."

"And the murder of Gomez? The charge against Lady Maria?"

"I can not say. I had not so much as heard of it until I came hither."

Cercamon fixed him with his keen eyes, now smiling with cold menace.

"If you wish to live," he said, "if you wish a reward so great that nothing Aquitaine can give you will equal it, do as I bid you. If you fail me, may God have mercy on your wretched soul!"

Gui le Balafré held up his fettered hands.

"As I hope for divine grace," he swore, "I will obey your every wish!"

Cercamon unchained his wrists and feet.

"Go back to the fort," he ordered. "Report to Cascadour that you took up your post as he commanded, and fell upon me in the street. But say that I came sooner than you expected—on the very heels of Bigot. Say that I slew your two comrades, and that Bigot, hearing the alarm, came running back and helped you. Say that a stroke from my sword split your helmet just as Bigot ran his sword through my heart; that then you recognized me for Cercamon the Troubadour, and were frightened, knowing how perilous it is to kill one of my calling. You therefore tarried to cast my body into the river, while Bigot hastened back to the fort to be in time for his watch. That will account for your late return. But before you report, warn Bigot, that he may swear to your story. Do you understand? I wish it to be thought that I am dead. You can also spread the rumor in the town that I have been killed in a brawl."

"I will obey," Gui assured him. He thrust his two hands between Cercamon's. "I am your man till death! I know your cunning; I know how you can turn calamity into victory. Through you I will flourish, or through you perish!"

"That is true!" said Cercamon.

THAT NIGHT Cercamon spent at Anselmo's; the next morning early he roused the armorer.

"Get shears," he commanded, "and clip off my hair!"

Anselmo gaped at him.

"That beautiful hair!" he cried, "soft and long as a woman's!"

"Cut it off, and make haste!" the troubadour repeated. "And fetch the armor you have made for me."

Shrugging, the armorer obeyed; and Cercamon was shorn of the black locks that had been his pride. He made Anselmo crop him to the scalp; then, putting on undertunic and hose of fine, soft leather, he waited for the Italian to help him into his mail. Anselmo had done justice to his reputation: never was so fine a hauberk seen in Catalonia.

The meshes were tiny and soft, but so close-linked and highly tempered that they could defy the keenest blade. The helmet was ridged, and furnished with wide nasal and long cheek-curtains of close mesh. From Anselmo's stock the troubadour selected a shield that suited the strength of his left arm. Full-mailed, no one would have taken him for the courtly singer in silks; his figure was a soldier's, his features hidden by plate and mail over cheeks and nose.

The final payment for the mail—paid in gold marks of France, so eagerly sought in Barcelona for their good, full weight—almost emptied his purse of all that his songs had won for him. That which was left he counted out into Anselmo's palm.

"Now," he directed, "go out and buy me a pair of Spanish boots at the cordwainer's, and a surcoat with the badge of Barcelona. Also—if you have recently made a pair of gold spurs for some knight, lend them to me for a space."

"Gold spurs!" cried Anselmo in consternation. "But they are the badge of knighthood, and your excellence is not a knight! I entreat your forgiveness, but it will cost me my trade if men learn that I have lent a knight's gold spurs to a man of low birth!"

"Do as I bid, and I will see that you profit by it. And stay—
you may hear on the streets that I am dead. If so, say nothing,
but—show fear!"

The Italian took himself off; and bolting the door of his
quarters, Cercamon sat down to wait. With parchment and pen
he occupied his time till Anselmo returned, and knocked at his
door. The armorer was frightened indeed. With shaking hands
he delivered two parcels: a pair of soft, high-heeled Cordovan
boots, fit for a prince to wear, and a surcoat of white wool
embroidered with the arms of Barcelona. Then he fumbled in
a wide drawer in his shop, his trembling fingers rousing echoes
of tinkling metal, and returned with a pair of gold spurs, which
he clasped upon the boots.

Cercamon laughed at his terror.

"What news?"

"The town seethes with the news of your murder," Anselmo
replied unsteadily. "It is said you were slain in a brawl with
certain soldiers, whose corpses were found but an arrow-flight
from my shop. The watch are patrolling the streets. I was stopped
and questioned thrice, and had to confess that you had lodged
with me. It would not be well for your Excellence to venture
forth till night."

"Yet that I shall, and right speedily," Cercamon answered.
"For now that the watch know that I have been here, they will
search the place."

He drew on the boots over his hose, put on the surcoat, and
strode across the court.

The Italian stared after him in amazement. Used, in the way
of trade, to measuring men's figures with his eye, he was startled
to see that the Troubadour looked a good head taller than he
had known him; then he realized that this was the effect of the
high-heeled boots and the tall ridge on the helmet.

This was exactly the effect Cercamon had counted on. He
had devised the ridge as a better protection against swordstrokes
than that afforded by the ordinary uncrested helmet; and now

it helped to disguise his stature. His shortness and the unusu-
ally wide spread of his shoulders made disguise difficult for
him; but the additional six inches lent by heels and helmet not
only made him seem a tall man, but even restored his huge
shoulders and long arms to seemingly normal proportions. This,
and the completeness with which nasal and cheek-pieces hid
his features, made him unrecognizable. His blue-green eyes, so
rare in one with hair so dark, he could not disguise; but the
gold spurs, marking him for the knight he was not, might serve
to distract attention from them.

The Watch being merely garrison troops detailed to keep
order, Cercamon knew they were well leavened with traitors.
As he came out into the sunshine of the street, he ran full into
a squad of spearmen. At sight of a knight in fine armor, wearing
the badge of the service, they checked; this was surely some
officer, perhaps not of their faction. But Cercamon, blinking
his eyes as if to keep out the sun, hailed them bluffly:

"There is none within but the armorer, lads!" he said. "And
he knows no more than he told a few moments since. I will
wager Gui told a true tale."

He spoke not in the refined Provencal which, as a poet, he
used at court, but in the broadest Gascon—his native dialect,
which he had not used since boyhood. As Gascony was a fief
of Aquitaine, its tongue would serve to avert the suspicion of
men smuggled into Barcelona's service by the queen-duchess.
The result justified his expectation. The men raised their
weapons in salute, and turned away from the shop. When they
had disappeared, he went in again, and greeted the frightened
Anselmo.

"Take these letters," he directed, "one to Thoma la Barca, and
one to Luc de Sobre Ter, knights in attendance at the palace!"

And out to the street he strode once more.

AMAT DE CASCADOUR left the count's presence
with a thin smile of satisfaction. All was flowing smoothly: the
messengers sent to Aragon had not returned, and it was rumored

that they were slain or held captive by the Great Orders. More than half the original garrison of Barcelona was on the Aragonese border, holding the castles against possible invasion. Of the force now within the city, nearly two thousand men were mercenaries, paid with Bérenger's gold, but twice bought by his enemies. Only a trifle more than fourteen hundred men of Moncada's old command were left within the wall. The count had no suspicion: he had but now sought Cascadour's advice concerning the wisdom of sending yet more men to the border. The Knights of the Temple and the Hospital were renowned fighters, and it would not be easy to resist them without a great host.

Cascadour had seemed unwilling to weaken the garrison further—too many men already were new and unused to their positions. He had cannily let the count press the point, and then promised to consider further. He was playing his game carefully, for he had much to win. Exiled from Aquitaine twelve years before, he had found in Barcelona asylum and favor, had risen rapidly by his soldierly courage, and won Raymond-Bérenger's confidence. But among the jealous Catalans, who liked not to see favors conferred on foreign adventurers, he had no hope of further advancement.

As deputy-general of the city during Moncada's absence—and as Moncada's successor if the latter perished at de l'Arba's hands—he stood at the crest of his career, beyond which crest lay nothing better in store. He was still a simple knight, with no holdings of his own.

He had nursed his balked ambition till it had grown to a sore grievance—a grievance against the proud, envious Barcelonan nobles who blocked his advancement, and even against the count himself. To Cascadour, in this mood, had come the sudden offer of riches and power, of a future such as he had not dared dream of.

It at once tempted his greed and tickled his craving for revenge upon these Catalans, who would not let a man thrive by his sword unless he were of their own stock.

Aliénor of Aquitaine, the queen-duchess, in letters signed with her seal and delivered by a squire of her household, had offered him a free pardon of his ancient offense, large revenues, and a castle in Poitou if he would follow the instructions given him verbally by her messenger. Acting on these orders, he had used his high trust as temporary Captain-General of Barcelona to surround the city and its count with craftily-woven, invisible nets of intrigue. The queen's messenger had returned with his pledge to obey her instructions to the letter. And so far he had done so, adding nothing of his own—except to take measures against the life of Cercamon. Cercamon had already shown his partiality for the Moncadas both in his dress and in his conversation, and Cascadour's spies had reported him as perilously familiar with certain soldiers of the garrison.

Cascadour himself had scarcely seen Cercamon, but he knew his repute for cunning, and cared little to have so dangerous an antagonist alive. Besides, it was said that the queen-duchess would pay well for Cercamon's destruction.

One of the officers with whom the troubadour had been friendly had been sent to the border; another, Jehan Bigot, was retained only when his readiness to take gold and his reported share in Cercamon's murder were assured. Now Cascadour's spies declared that no man in the city had the least suspicion of their master. There was but three weeks left before his task should be complete, and the moment come to strike.

Returning to his own quarters in the north wing of the palace, Sir Amat opened a huge cabinet sunk in the wall, and took out a sheaf of records. Swordsman and intriguer, he was something yet more perilous—a scholar. In his cunning youth he had perceived the advantage of being his own clerk, and had hired a learned priest to teach him.

His exile from Aquitaine had come about through the treachery of a squire who also could read, and who spied on his master's manuscripts. From that time on, Cascadour had permitted none about him who could decipher a single letter—and he kept the key of his cabinet in his own pouch.

On the wide table of polished olivewood he laid out a roll of parchment, spreading it with his strong, fine hands. It was written in his own small, clerkly style: a full inventory of the garrison—men-at-arms' names in black, officers' in red. Wall by wall, tower by tower they were listed, Montjuich fort separately. Thirty-four hundred names, of which fourteen hundred were pricked out with little blue dots.

"We have enough," he muttered, glancing up to make certain that he had not forgotten to bolt the door. "We have enough; yet it might be well to send away a few hundred more. Surprize, and the capture of the count's person, should save the spilling of overmuch blood—but it can do no hurt to make sure. And the count—"

A knock at the door startled him. He thrust the manuscript under a plan of the fortifications; then, skilfully composing his features, he rose swiftly and flung back the bolt.

A man-at-arms—a life-long follower of Cascadour's fortunes—stood in the entrance.

"A knight, Sir Amat, who will not disclose his name. He has important matters for your Excellency's knowledge."

Amat made a gesture of assent, and the soldier ushered in a strongly made man of middle height, clad in mail from top to toe. The stranger seemed, by his finely-textured armor, to be of wealth and position; his gold spurs assured his knighthood. In a voice thick with blurred Gascon consonants, he uttered a polite greeting, and cast a wary glance over his shoulder.

His dialect alone was somewhat of a reassurance to the newly startled deputy-general. The glance of caution showed that his business must be delicate. A master-swordsman himself, utterly fearless, Cascadour did not hesitate to admit his visitor and bolt the door behind him.

As soon as he had done so, the stranger—who stood well out of the narrow stream of sunlight from the solitary arrow-slit in the thick wall—drew from his mantle a roll of parchment, and handed it to Cascadour with a bow.

Amat glanced at the seal, then he hesitated.

"I have not seen your face," he hinted, "and do not know your name."

"I am from Aquitaine," the other answered. "My name and face are too well-known to be shown in this city—even to you—with safety. My master is he whose seal lies in your hand."

A conspirator himself, Cascadour hated secrecy. He was about to answer angrily, when a second glance at the seal checked him. It was that of Bertrand d'Armagnac, grand seneschal of Aquitaine, and most trusted officer of the Queen-Duchess Aliénor.

"You come from her Majesty?" he asked.

"When I left Poitou, I came straight from her Majesty's presence," the stranger answered. "And I have full authority to act in Barcelona according to my discretion. But—though her Majesty trusts you—it has seemed well that you should know neither my face nor name. If any heard of me, your plans might be ruined through the need for premature action."

"You wear the badge of Barcelona," Cascadour commented.

"Of necessity. What armed man, in these anxious days, would be permitted to enter Barcelona without its badge?"

Convinced that he was speaking with a man of eminence in the queen-duchess' service, Cascadour drew up for him a deep, round-backed chair, then bit his lip as the man turned the chair so that the light did not fall on his eyes and mouth—which were all that his helmet left visible. Amat himself drew close to the embrasure, to get the light on the letter, which he unrolled and read carefully. His cheeks flushed with satisfaction, but he was not too exultant to cast a second glance at the date of the letter.

"To judge," he said coldly, "from the day on which my lord of Armagnac signed this letter, you have ridden hither all too slowly for one who bears me such important news."

The Gascon drew himself up proudly, and his retort was haughty. "Let me remind your excellence that the Count of

Armagnac is the queen-duchess's grand seneschal, and that I, his friend and messenger, have other errands quite as weighty as bearing despatches to you!"

Cascadour hastened to apologize.

"I might have known," he said humbly, "that no small man would ride on such business." And to himself he added, "Surely a noble high in her Majesty's grace, else he would not be so insolent."

"I have been in Barcelona for some time," the stranger resumed. "It was part of my instructions to observe the measures you have taken, that I might assure my master of their sufficiency. It is for this reason I have not come to you sooner."

Amat concealed his anger. So those who had bought him did not trust him, but set spies on him! So far he had revealed nothing to this arrogant messenger; but now he must justify himself.

"I trust," he replied silkily, "that you have been pleased?"

The stranger nodded slowly.

"There is but one thing I find amiss," he said. "The queen-duchess has lent you many of her own good men-at-arms, and it were well that as few of them as possible should perish in this business. You have not sent away enough of the count's men."

Cascadour gulped in relief. Since the stranger knew so much, he was certainly in the very heart of the conspiracy, and could be trusted.

"I have thought of that myself," Amat rejoined, "and but now I have lured the count into giving me authorization to do so."

"That is well," the other commended. "But one thing more: you were too credulous in the matter of Cercamon's death. How do you know that he was slain?"

"I have the word of Gui le Balafré that the troubadour perished by the hand of a Toulousan named—"

"Named Jehan Bigot. Aye, I know all, and more than you

suppose. But how know you that Balafré and Bigot speak the truth?"

"You must know, my lord—" Amat answered, giving the title because the messenger's tone was such as only a noble would dare assume—"you must know, being yourself in the Count of Armagnac's household, that Balafré is a trusty man. He had been—"

"Has been captain of the guard in Poitiers for many years? Aye, true. But the tale he tells has its weaknesses. Your spies tracked Cercamon from his lodgings to a shop in the Street of the Armorers, and followed Bigot to that street. You commissioned Balafré and two others to kill Cercamon as he left after consulting with Bigot. Now I ask leave to point out two suspicious details. Since Bigot was in Cercamon's confidence, is it likely he would kill the troubadour? I foresee you will reply that you had bought Bigot with your gold. Aye, but it was Balafré that dispensed that gold, as it was Balafré who swears that Bigot killed Cercamon. Now for the second point; if Cercamon was slain, why did not his slayers bring you his head, instead of reporting that they threw his body in the river? What if Bigot and Balafré are in league with Cercamon?"

Cascadour twisted uncomfortably in his chair. He had not often made mistakes, and did not like to be caught in one. And this messenger, who had confessedly been watching him, knew too much. Moreover, that the stranger knew Cascadour's part in Cercamon's murder troubled him greatly. Cascadour had carefully spread the report that the troubadour had died in a street brawl. In France, and not less in Barcelona, it was a grievous crime to slay a troubadour. If Cercamon were indeed dead, and it should come out that Cascadour had ordered his murder, then Cascadour would be cut to pieces by the infuriated nobles, or broken on the wheel by the count's order.

The messenger understood his fears.

"I shall say no word," he hastened to make assurance, "of your part in this matter. But between ourselves I would remind you that the queen-duchess will add materially to your reward if it turn out that Cercamon is slain. There is ancient enmity between them. But you should have taken more pains to make sure. If Cercamon lives, he may make grave trouble for us. I have learned that he knew more of our enterprise than is safe for the queen-duchess' plans—or for you."

"What would you have me do?" Cascadour asked uneasily.

"First, send away five hundred more of the Barcelonan troops who still remain in the city. Put them under the command of Balafré and Bigot—who, if untrustworthy, will then be out of your way—and send them to reenforce the garrisons on the Aragonese border. That will leave but a handful to oppose your host of mercenaries—perhaps nine hundred?"

"Nine hundred and forty," Amat corrected, happy at last to find a detail of his plans that the Gascon did not know.

"Give command over the last nine hundred and forty to Thoma la Barca—"

"But," protested Cascadour, "la Barca is not one of us!"

"True. He is known to be faithful to the count. So much the better; if all the loyal forces are sent off, and no troops remain under officers known to be devoted to Barcelona, suspicion will arise. This handful, under la Barca, can easily be enveloped by your greater numbers. Now let me see your dispositions for the final stroke."

"I have no orders to confide—" Amat began; but the messenger cut him short impatiently.

"If you had read well the letter which I brought you, you would know better than to dispute me!" he cried.

Cascadour once more glanced at the message. Opening with warm praise for his efforts on Aquitaine's behalf, it went on to introduce the bearer:

> A man high in our confidence, who must be nameless until our triumph. You are to follow such instructions as he may give you. Rest assured of her Majesty's gratitude, and of high reward.

B. de A.

The signature and seal were those of Bertrand d'Armagnac.

Had Cascadour known d'Armagnac better, he might have hesitated; but having no honor himself, he could not know that such intrigues as his had never seen countenanced by Armagnac, and that the queen-duchess had always to choose other instruments for her less honorable designs.

"I will obey, my lord," Cascadour agreed. "You shall see my dispositions, which are carefully mapped. I am sure of your approval."

He unlocked the wardrobe again, took down a beautifully drawn plan and spread it flat on the table.

"Here," he explained, "are the lists; yonder will be Moncada's pavilion; from this tent will de l'Arba enter for the trial by combat. Here is the count's seat, with such and such guards about him."

He pointed out various troop-positions, while the Gascon knight watched closely.

The latter cut into his explanations.

"You are safeguarding our interests?" he asked. "It is not wise to trust Navarre too far."

Cascadour smiled, "These," he said, drawing from under his papers a plan of Barcelona's fortifications, "go to de l'Arba before he leaves Navarre. He will be followed, at two days' interval, by the Navarrese army. I stipulated for the two days.

"We shall have the count in our hands, and will hold Montjuich and the gates in the teeth of the populace till the Navarrese arrive; then, with Raymond-Bérenger in chains, we sail for Bordeaux. De l'Arba will then take possession of the city; but with the count as a hostage, we can force the nobles of Catalonia and Bérenger himself to cede Aragon to Aquitaine. If Navarre cheats us, we have all France behind us—seeing that the duchess is now queen."

"It is well arranged," the messenger complimented him. "I

foresee a vicomte's title for you. And now farewell; delay not in sending Bigot and Balafré, with five hundred of the Catalans, to the border. And keep a vigilant eye on the city; I would not have that meddler Cercamon appear alive. He knows too much—he knows you are in our pay!"

TWO HOURS before midnight that same day, the west gate of Barcelona opened to pass out a little army—five hundred of the last true men in the garrison of Barcelona. It was very dark, and sultry; the torches of the guard shone hot on their mail as they passed through the vaulted gateway. The guard saluted with clanging weapons; the ranks replied, the movement of their arms sending little runlets of sweat a-trickling under their armor. Then they were gone, into the dark plain; one hundred mounted spearmen, as many archers, and three hundred foot.

The officer of the guard signed for the closing of the gate; but a last pair of riders checked him.

"Hold!" cried one of them. "I tarry but to receive last orders from Sir Amat de Cascadour!" The gate remained open for him; and he continued to talk to his companion, in tones too low for the guard to hear.

"And I make no doubt they will listen," he concluded. "Verily, you are a devil for cunning."

"I am devil enough to take your life if you fail!" the other answered. "If you do not convince them, Barcelona falls! Farewell, and—God help you, Gui le Balafré!"

ANSELMO THE ARMORER had promptly set off to the palace, as Cercamon had bidden him. But being a prudent and timid man, he had contented himself with entrusting to a page the troubadour's letters to la Barca and Sobre Ter, and had then run back to his shop as fast as he could. Had he not been questioned thrice by the watch? And should he risk calling public attention to himself now by tarrying at the gates of the court? Better men than he had died for interfering in the quarrels of the great.

But he had not been an hour at his forge when the clatter of hoofs rang in the narrow Street of the Armorers, and stopped at his very door. Loud voices sounded in his shop, calling his name impatiently. Before he could take off his leather apron two young men ran into the court, their fine garments disheveled with fast riding, their faces red with exertion and excitement.

"Where is he?" they cried with one voice.

Anselmo gaped at them, too frightened to answer. One seized him by the arm, while another produced a crumpled parchment and held it under his nose. But Anselmo, though he stared fascinated at the parchment, could not read.

"If my lords will deign to explain—" he stammered.

One of the young courtiers, catching sight of the gate in the rear wall of the court, pointed it out to his companion, who straightway dragged the trembling Lombard toward it. Anselmo did not dare cry out nor resist, but suffered himself to be dragged to the door of his house and thrust within, whither his captors followed him. Once the door was shut, they turned on him, and asked together, breathlessly—

"Where is Cercamon?"

The armorer glanced from one to the other in desperation. He did not know these men, nor whether they were friends or enemies to the troubadour; and he remembered that Cercamon wished all Barcelona to believe him dead.

"Indeed, my lords, he is slain!" Anselmo gasped out.

"Liar!" cried one of his persecutors. "Did he not send me this letter, signed with his own hand, but this very morning? And does he not say here that he sent it by your hand?"

Anselmo began to understand.

"Ye are my lords la Barca and Sobre Ter?" he gasped.

"We are! Now speak—where is he?"

"Alas, my lords, I know not! He went away three hours since, leaving these letters for you. Nay, how should I know whether he will come back?"

Thoma la Barca and Luc de Sobre Ter gazed at each other in dismay. Sobre Ter was the first to speak.

"We must wait, then, as he bids us," he said. "But, by St. Andreu de Palomar! It is ill waiting at such a time!"

"Aye," la Barca answered. "But we know nothing more than Cercamon has told us, and can do nothing till he tells us more. He says in these letters that he will meet us here when he has need of us."

Sobre Ter, quicker to take heat than his friend, was also quicker to cool.

"Think you it can indeed be so ill as he says?" he asked.

La Barca nodded thoughtfully.

"Cercamon is known for the shrewdest of men, and is not one to be frightened by trifles. Likewise I am sure that he is to be trusted, for the count was furious at the report of his death."

"Then we will do as he bids us. Hark you, Anselmo! Every day, at noon and at sunset, one of us will send his squire or his groom to you. If Cercamon comes, and desires our presence, you have but to say to our messenger, 'The hour has come.' No more, do you understand? Do not speak Cercamon's name save to us, for he has too many foes in Barcelona."

"That was well said," a voice sounded behind them. All turned on the instant. The door had been softly opened, and in its archway stood a man in full armor.

Sobre Ter's sword flashed from its sheath; but the newcomer, removing his helmet, laughed at him. It was Cercamon.

"You have done well, Anselmo," the troubadour smiled. "You may get back to your forge, while these lords and I speak together. Follow me, sirs."

And he led the way to his room, where he stripped off his mail with a sigh of relief.

"*Pardieu, messires!* It is hot, and I am like to faint with all this iron on my back! I have just come from sweet converse with the arch-traitor, Amat de Cascadour."

"Cascadour!" the youths exclaimed.

"That astonishes you? Did I not say in my letters to you that the safety of Barcelona was threatened by traitors in high place? Aye, it was Cascadour who plotted my murder, and it is Cascadour who takes bribes from Aquitaine to seize the count's person and divide his lands with Navarre."

"Splendor of God!" swore la Barca. "And you have been to him, and come back alive?"

"Cascadour! A traitor!" repeated the confounded Sobre Ter, unable to comprehend such a monstrous thing.

"Aye," Cercamon assured them. "It is even as I tell you; I have it from his own lips."

"Nay, this passes belief!" cried Sobre Ter. "You say that Cascadour, the most trusted man in Barcelona, after Moncada, plots to sell the count to his enemies; you tell us that Cascadour hired assassins to slay you; and yet you tell us that he confessed his guilt to you! Why, if he were indeed the devil you paint him, he would have bidden his men-at-arms cut you to ribbons, rather than confide in you!"

Smiling at their amazed unbelief, Cercamon placed his helmet once more on his head, and faced them.

"Would ye two know me, with my face thus masked, armor on my body, and six inches added to my stature?" he asked. "Moreover, I went to him with the best of passports—a letter from Aquitaine!"

"From Aquitaine!"

"Aye, writ with my own hand, signed with the initials of Bertrand d'Armagnac—also in my hand—and sealed with his seal. You know that I was once in Armagnac's service. Many a letter have I sealed for him, and it was easy to make a lifelike drawing of his crest. A Jew in the Moorish quarter, who traffics in cut gems, made the seal for me. Behold it!"

He threw down on the table a beautifully cut jasper seal.

"Thus," he resumed, "I came before the traitor, in the person of a messenger from Aquitaine. I knew just enough—from one of his underlings whom I won over—to deceive him, and to lure him into telling me more. On a day already fixed the garrison of Barcelona will revolt, seize the count's person, and overthrow the liberties of all Catalonia. Two days later, a Navarrese army will occupy the city, while the count is carried in chains to Aquitaine!"

"Cascadour, whom the count has heaped with honors!" murmured Sobre Ter, his honest young soul shaken to its depths by such treachery.

But the more practical la Barca turned to Cercamon with the question—

"When is this day?"

"The day," Cercamon replied slowly, "when de l'Arba overthrows Moncada in the lists!"

"Ha!" cried Sobre Ter. "I knew that snake from Navarre would sting! Then this plot is his contrivance?"

"So I guess," the troubadour replied. "It was he who poisoned Gomez, partly to secure his estates, but chiefly to ruin the Moncadas. If he is permitted to meet Moncada in the trial by combat, he will win; and I know that the time of the combat is also the time fixed for the attempt against the count. I told you in my letters that all the faithful troops of the garrison had been replaced—save a mere handful—by hirelings. It is by these foreigners, in the pay of Aquitaine, that the count will be surrounded when he takes his place in the seat of honor, to preside over the combat between de l'Arba and Moncada. He believes them faithful to him; yet they but wait for the signal to seize him. Their comrades on the walls will hold the city for Aquitaine, while those in the fort hold open a way of retreat for the traitors in case the plot does not fully succeed."

"And the signal?"

Cercamon glanced approvingly at la Barca.

"Wisely asked," he answered. "I do not know—I dared not ask Cascadour. But I think the signal for the outbreak will be given by de l'Arba's lance, when it tears through Moncada's breast."

"But if Moncada wins? There is a just God in heaven!" Sobre Ter cried out.

"The fate of Barcelona must not depend on one man's hand!" the troubadour retorted.

La Barca nodded.

"Then we must report this to the count!" he said.

"Not so. It is too late. What can the count do, but order Cascadour's arrest? And who will arrest him? The traitors in the army outnumber the true men three to one. The moment the count tries to act, the plot will come to a premature head, and he will be taken prisoner—perhaps slain!"

"Ah, troubadour!" exclaimed Sobre Ter. "You should have warned our lord in time!"

"I had not proof enough till now; and now the time has passed. But, as I learned more and more of the traitors' plans, I contrived a counter-plot. It can not fail—if ye two will help me."

Overwhelmed by the revelation of the odds against them, Luc de Sobre Ter covered his face with his hands.

"Too late!" he groaned. "What can we do—three, against thousands of veteran soldiers, the whole city in the hands of a cunning and desperate traitor?"

Once more Cercamon smiled, and turned to la Barca.

"We are not three," he said, "but more than nine hundred. I have secured from Cascadour the command of the last remaining faithful troops for you, my friend. With these nine hundred and forty spears we can do much, if they are well used—"

"Well done!" la Barca answered. "Give me your orders, and I will obey!"

As Cercamon had foreseen, Sobre Ter's high spirit revived at this appeal to his companion, and his pride stirred.

"What have you for me to do?" he asked.

"You," Cercamon replied, "are from the country north of Ter, where the peasants are said to be hardy folk, loyal, and brave. Can you raise four hundred spears?"

Luc's eyes gleamed.

"I will set out for my home this day!" he promised. "My father commands sixty men-at-arms; his elder brother will lend me two hundred. From among our vassals I can find two hundred more—men who can ride and use lance and sword, men trained in the wars with Seville and Navarre. The time is short, but I can promise you close on five hundred fighting men in time to strike a blow for Barcelona!"

"Then we shall win!" Cercamon exulted. "I have already made provision for the return of our faithful troops from the border. While you, Sobre Ter, are recruiting your forces, la Barca shall be provided with means to get them into the city. The trial by combat is fixed for the Day of the Magdalen: you and your five hundred must be on the further slope of Tibidabo—where they will be hidden by the mountain from the city—by midnight of the day before. Remain there till a messenger from la Barca brings you orders. When does Moncada return from his pilgrimage to St. James' shrine?"

"He should be here within a fortnight," la Barca answered.

"Good. I will see to it that de l'Arba does not slay him. Is all understood?"

"I am to get orders to Luc," la Barca repeated. "But how shall I know what orders to send?"

"You are subject to Cascadour's commands," Cercamon replied. "In my rôle of secret messenger from Aquitaine I can persuade him to give you orders that will help our cause. When the time comes, I will tell you what to do. But come hither no more—I will get word to you."

"In Heaven's name, do not fail!" urged Sobre Ter.

"I will not—if you will lend me ten gold marks to live on till the Magdalen's day. And the count must still think me dead!"

THE DAY OF THE MAGDALEN dawned hot and sultry, and a brazen sun rose in a windless sky. For two days and nights the clatter of hammers had rung from the plain of the Besós; now that they were stilled, an ill-boding structure loomed between river and town. A huge oval of wooden stakes formed a stout palisade, within which rose deal stands like those of an amphitheatre: at one inner end of the oval stood a flattened pyramid of fagots. Above the amphitheatre a canopy of sailcloth was stretched, to keep out the direct rays of the sun; but it only shut in and intensified their heat.

There was a wide gate in the palisade; and to this gate, even with the dawn, a multitude of folk streamed. Some rode, in gay clothes and preceded and followed by men-at-arms; but by far the most thronged up on foot in clothes of black. And every black-garbed man, in spite of the awful heat, wore coat or cape, as if to conceal something unlawful under its folds. Women were there too, from the dainty ladies of the court on their mincing Moorish palfries to grim-lipped burgesses' wives and hard-faced fisherwomen from the port. Like their men, the women-folk of the people came with bitter looks and clenched hands; and now and again, as the cloak of one fell apart, something bulked beneath like a bag of stones.

They scowled and muttered as the fine folk from the palace rode by them; and many a man-at-arms, forcing a way through the crowd with his lance-butt, received a look that chilled the blood in his veins. Yet no hand was raised, however roughly the mailed men elbowed the mob aside to make room for knights and ladies. All, as with one purpose, streamed steadily toward the gate in the palisade—silently, menacing with their set purpose, but as yet peaceful. The smell of trampled grass and sweating bodies rose in the still heat.

Now the forefront of the procession reached the gate, and stopped. For the last hundred yards they had been crowding forward between straight ranks of massed men-at-arms, whose pikes were lowered. At sight of the menacing steel, the common folk growled deep, like angry dogs; yet they pressed on. But the gateway was filled with archers, arrow on string; and behind the archers were mounted spearmen.

"Back, ye scum!" shouted an officer. "None enters here save well-born folk!"

His accent was that of Poitou; and as they heard the hated dialect, the Barcelonans' bitter calm broke. Their growls became shouts of rage; hands came out from under cloaks, brandishing stones, clubs, knives.

"We will see our Andreu fight!" a voice cried from among them. "And, by the mass! If he falls, we will avenge his blood!"

A roar of approval followed the words, and the tight-packed crowd surged, swayed, and strove to push forward.

"Draw string!" cried the officer; and every bowman, advancing one foot, drew back his shaft.

The mob paused, irresolute; and in that moment the massed foot on one side of them extended their lances—gently, so that the points just pricked through to the skin. Simultaneously the opposite rank opened, leaving a wide breach; and, driven by the menace of the lowered spears, the folk, muttering, turned instinctively toward the breach. Again the ranks behind them thrust, gently, barely drawing blood; and the mob came to its senses. There was death in front, death behind; and before them an open way to safety.

"Through, good folk!" cried a voice by the breach. "I will vouch for our little Andreu's safety! Ye do him no good by periling your own lives. Better avenge him afterward, if need be, than die vainly now!"

Every eye was turned to the speaker, a tall officer on a gray horse. His helmet masked his features, but his voice was Catalan; and on his shield was the device of Sobre Ter. Half-convinced, half-afraid, the mob began to trickle through the breach. Those behind strained forward; and the terrific pressure and the heat together drained from them the last of their spirit. At last they were through; the soldiers closed ranks behind them again. The mob was baffled, revolution stayed.

And now the fine folk had a free way to the lists. On they came, shielded from the mob by the screen of soldiers—knights and ladies riding together in festal dress as to a feast. Yet they, too, rode silently; there was no festival in their hearts. Maria de Moncada might be guilty or no; but it would be a grim sight to see her burn on yonder pyramid of wood, if her husband should fail to prove her innocent with his sword. And brave as would be the spectacle of two champions clashing together in the lists, the champion of Barcelona was foredoomed. But festal dress all of the court must wear, to honor the solemnity of the event. It was an ordeal, in which God was expected to grant triumph to the right.

Two hours before noon the great gates were closed. Every seat of the wooden amphitheater was filled, its sides gay with massed color. In the middle of the south side, close to the lists, was a raised platform, its seats provided with comfortable backs and piled with soft cushions. Here, among his greatest nobles, sat Raymond-Bérenger.

On either side of him stood heralds, their mailed breasts covered with satin surcoats blazoned with his crest, their trumpets of silver in their gloved hands. Just below him on the trampled grass, a bodyguard of fivescore soldiers was drawn up. To his right, between the royal dais and the gate, four hundred spearmen waited at attention. These were the only soldiers within the palisade; but as many more waited without, supported by two hundred archers, to discourage further insolence from the mob.

Just in front of the pyramid of fagots, at one end of the tilting course, was a wide tent; and another stood at the opposite end. Between these two stretched a wide expanse of bare, hard ground, thinly covered with sand. Each tent gave on this earthen course through a doorway with a flap of silk, before which stood a mailed squire. The spectators, knights and ladies all, gazed intently at these silken screens, which would soon be withdrawn to let the champions ride into the lists.

Raymond-Bérenger sat silent and bitter in his chair of state. For him, more than for any other, this was a day of grim foreboding. He had visited Lady Maria in her prison, the day before, and had found her filled with a lofty spirit which he could not understand. Some vision seemed to have been vouchsafed her, for the prospect of her husband's fall and a dreadful death had lost its terrors.

She appeared sustained by a certainty of victory, of vindication. He had gone to Moncada's villa, and had found the little soldier upborne by the comfort he had found in prayer at the holy sanctuary of St. James, confident in the righteousness of his cause, and joyously eager for the combat.

These hopes, this exaltation, the count could not share. He loved Moncada, and honored Lady Maria; and he could scarce bear the thought that de l'Arba's terrible sword should compass their ruin. His was not the faith that works or receives miracles. He could but foresee the death of his two most beloved subjects, and the peril that Moncada's fall must bring upon his realm.

It made Bérenger's cup more bitter to reflect that he could have avoided all this ruin, if he had had the courage to prevent the trial by combat. He might have refused, might have insisted on Maria's innocence. Yet he knew well that such a course would not only have brought on him the charge of injustice, but would have earned both for him and for Moncada the charge of cowardice, the scorn and detestation of Church and nobles.

He had relied on Cercamon's renowned cunning to find some escape; but Cercamon was dead, slain in a brawl. All the troubadour's shrewdness had not availed to save himself. It had been madness to count so heavily on him.

Unable to endure the suspense longer the count signed to his heralds. These raised their silver trumpets, and blew a long, clear note. Two men-at-arms appeared, leading between them a tall, slender woman, robed in a single loose, white garment. Her hair was unbound, her feet bare, as the law prescribed. In her white hands she clasped a crucifix. Behind her walked a priest, his eyes downcast. Slowly they led her to the dais, into the very presence of the count. All turned to gaze upon her, and a deep, prolonged sigh rose from the multitude.

Raymond-Bérenger rose.

"Read the charge!" he commanded his heralds.

One of them unrolled a scroll, and read in a voice that echoed through the arena like the voice of judgment:

"Whereas, accusation having been laid against the Lady Maria de Moncada, subject of this realm, that she did falsely and traitorously murder by the ministration of poison the squire Hilario Gomez of Navarre, vassal to the noble knight and Viscount Perez de l'Arba, also of Navarre, the said accusation hath been upborne by the said Perez de l'Arba.

"And, whereas the noble knight and Viscount Andreu de Moncada, vassal and captain-general of Moncada, and husband to the aforenamed Lady Maria, hath brought charge of falsehood against the said Perez de l'Arba, and denies his accusation.

"And, both these good knights having declared their readiness to maintain their contentions on peril of their bodies.

"It is hereby commanded that they shall fight together in the lists till one of them be overcome, that thereby the judgment of God, to which they have appealed, may be manifested between them.

"If Almighty God shall grant victory to the accuser, Don Perez de l'Arba, then shall the aforenamed Lady Maria de Moncada be forthwith burned at the stake, in punishment for the foul crime of which such victory shall be deemed to have proved her guilty;

"But if God send victory to the defender, Viscount Andreu de Moncada, then shall the accuser, the forenamed Perez de l'Arba, be burned at the stake in her stead, for having upborne a false and vile accusation.

"In the Name of God."

When the herald had spoken, Raymond-Bérenger beckoned to the woman who stood before him.

"Lady Maria de Moncada," he began, in a trembling voice, "you have heard the charge. What is your reply!"

Lady Maria met his gaze unfalteringly; her face was radiant.

"As God sees me," she answered firmly, "I am innocent!"

"Administer the oath!" the count commanded.

The priest stepped forward, laid one hand on the crucifix which Maria held, and said in solemn tones:

"Do you swear by Christ's holy passion on the cross that the words you have uttered are true?"

"I swear!" she answered, and kissed the cross.

Once more the heralds blew their trumpets, Lady Maria was led to the foot of that grim pile of fagots, and each of her guards laid hold on her. The squires attendant on the tents drew aside the silken curtains. From that tent nearest the pyre rode forth a tall, powerfully made warrior in full mail, on a magnificent Andalusian charger. His head was bare; his helmet rested on his saddlebow. Spurring his mount, and so reining him that the beast caracolled fierily, Perez de l'Arba rode to the foot of the dais and dipped his lance in reverence to the count.

The multitude of onlookers was silent: no hand clapped, no voice acclaimed him. Yet he sat his horse confidently; a smile of triumph curled his proud lips.

"Sir Viscount," Raymond-Bérenger addressed him, "are you indeed ready to maintain the terrible charge you have laid against this lady?"

"Ready to the death, my lord!"

Bérenger bowed; de l'Arba, putting on his helmet, rode back, and took up his position at one end of the tilting course. From the second tent a second horseman rode, likewise fully mailed, but helmeted, so that his eyes and lips alone were seen. The crowd, which had burst into wild applause as he flashed into the arena, fell suddenly silent; and as the defender pulled up his white charger before the dais, some one cried from the benches—

"That is not Moncada!"

The count, already risen to receive his greeting, turned on him a glance furious with outraged majesty.

"Who are you, sirrah?" he cried. "Who are you, who thus dare to come before us with covered head, and who presume to substitute yourself for the rightful defender? And where is Andreu de Moncada?"

The unknown warrior, without removing his helmet, answered calmly:

"If it please your Mightiness, I have taken a vow to hide my face until this lying dog of a de l'Arba has fallen before me. Hold it not against my lord de Moncada that I appear in his stead; reasons more powerful than the fear of death have prevented his coming. It is written in the law that, if a combatant fail to appear to maintain his challenge, his place may be taken by any whom the accused may accept. I dare to believe that my lady of Moncada will accept me as her defender in her husband's stead."

The spectators held their breath, uncertain whether this man's daring would win their master's approval or draw down his wrath; but the count was so startled, and so shaken by his fears for Moncada, that it was long before he could answer. At last he replied irresolutely:

"It indeed stands in the law as you have said. But how know I that you are a man whose rank entitles him to maintain such a cause against a noble adversary?"

"I have stood in your presence," the would-be defender retorted, "I have kissed your hand, and been assured of your favor. I pledge my word that my rank is such as entitles me to break lances with any man of blood; and I appeal to your justice."

Bérenger turned to Lady Maria.

"Do you accept this man as your champion?" he asked.

Lady Maria turned grateful eyes on the unknown warrior.

"I do," she responded. "I know him, and he is worthy!"

"Take your place!" the count curtly commanded; and the

masked defender rode to his end of the lists, facing the astounded de l'Arba.

But the Navarrese had little time to digest the surprize prepared for him, the appearance of an unknown, strongly-made
champion in place of the weak Moncada. For scarce had the
two opponents faced each other, when the trumpet sounded,
and Raymond-Bérenger signaled for the conflict.

But de l'Arba was skilled in a hundred encounters, and he
leveled his lance with steady, practised hand. The spurs shot
home; the sand flew in spurts from the hoofs of two charging
horses; and with a shock the combatants came together. The
head-on force of their impact proved both superb horsemen;
but de l'Arba wielded his lance with more skill. It drove full
through the center of his adversary's shield, and splintered there.
The defender also struck de l'Arba's shield, but his point was
dashed aside by the metal boss. The Navarrese recovered instantly, but the crash of meeting almost forced Maria's champion from his saddle. Regaining his seat with difficulty, he
snatched out his sword barely in time to ward the other's point.

Now began the perilous second half of the conflict, when
sword met sword in blow on blow. The unknown had cast his
shield aside, for de l'Arba's lance had made it useless; while the
Navarrese had both shield and blade to defend himself. The
spectators stared in an agony of suspense; for their hearts were
with the defender of Barcelona's honor, and the conflict was
going ill with him. Yet at least one of Barcelona's enemies
watched the strife with terror: Amat de Cascadour, commanding the count's bodyguard, had recognized Maria's champion
by the high ridge on his helmet, and remembered in panic what
he had told this man. De l'Arba must win!

But Cascadour was too shrewd to leave anything to fate. He
turned to one of his officers.

"If yonder interloper wins, see to it that he dies before he
can speak!" he said.

The soldier nodded, and whispered to his comrades.

But now the conflict had taken another turn. De l'Arba, holding the advantage of his good shield, had parried blow after blow, and had not shed a drop of blood; his own point had thrust home again and again. But his opponent's mail held, resisting every thrust. In sudden anger the Navarrese had launched a mighty backhand stroke for the head. Past his foe's guard it drove, and rang on the high ridge of his helmet.

Good cause had the defender then to praise that stout steel crest. His ears sang with the blow, but the helmet held. Again and again de l'Arba rained in blows, most of which the other parried; but blood was dripping now from his left shoulder. Confident of victory, the Navarrese struck harder, wider, laying himself open. One instant he lowered his shield; the next, he must fling himself back in his saddle to escape a lightning thrust. Slowed by his violent backward cast, de l'Arba felt a second thrust prick through his mail and scratch his chest. He was on the defensive now, and the spectators burst into cheer on cheer.

Then the defender launched a terrible backstroke. In vain de l'Arba strove to meet it; it cleft his shield almost to the band that held it to his wrist. He flung the useless thing aside, and strove to meet his enemy on equal terms. But his advantage was gone: sword to sword, his renowned skill was all too little to meet the play of steel that danced before his eyes, threatening throat, shoulder, breast. A cut to the shoulder forced him to slip from the saddle to avoid being cut in half. On the instant his foe also had dismounted, and in a flurry of swift thrusts drove him to the barrier, almost at the count's feet.

In despair, de l'Arba, parrying with outthrust blade, waved his left hand in a wild signal.

"Strike!" he shouted. "Strike, and save me!"

He who had fought so well for Barcelona pressed home the attack with stroke on stroke, unheeding de l'Arba's cry. His point ripped through de l'Arba's mail, tearing the flesh from the right shoulder. Crippled, his arm helpless, the Navarrese flung down his sword, and fell on his knees.

"Mercy!" he cried.

But his enemy dashed him into the dust, placed a heavy foot on his breast, and held him there. Then, his right hand guiding his point to the fallen man's throat, he raised his left to his helmet and threw it at Bérenger's feet. The beaten de l'Arba gazed up at him with giddy eyes.

"Cercamon!" he cried.

But none had eyes for them now; for the arena was full of struggling men and flashing swords. At de l'Arba's signal, Amat de Cascadour had flung himself at the head of the count's bodyguard, and with brandished blade cried on his hirelings to the attack.

"Seize the count!" he shouted. "And kill yonder dog!"

But the officer whom he had ordered to slay Cercamon turned on him, and drove his point through Cascadour's breast. Then, with a sharp order, he marshaled the guard in a phalanx around the count.

His promptness saved the day; for at Cascadour's command a hundred men had leaped forward to seize Raymond-Bérenger and hold him captive. Even as their swords clashed with those of the guard, they realized with consternation how few they were. Every soldier in the amphitheater should have been a man of Aquitaine; yet but one out of five had obeyed Cascadour's order, and a force as great as their own barred their way. They fought one moment desperately; then a great wave of men-at-arms smote them in the rear, overwhelmed them, struck them to the earth. Within ten minutes every Aquitanian was bound or stretched bleeding on the earth.

FROM THE gate outside came the clash and clang of steel, wild shouts, and cries of terror. The startled spectators were on their feet, women shrieking, knights tugging at their swords and pressing forward to climb over the seats and into the fray. But the struggle was over before they could help.

Beckoning to a guardsman to take charge of de l'Arba, Cercamon ran to the gate to take part in the combat there. But there, also, the traitors were outnumbered, overpowered, or driven in flight. Not daring to run to the city, panic-stricken by so sudden and complete a rout where they had expected an easy victory, the survivors dashed toward the river. In full flight they were whelmed from behind by a sudden charge of horse, and driven into the swift stream.

"Well done, Sobre Ter!" cried Cercamon to the leader of the horsemen. "How fares it with the city?"

Luc slid from his horse. "All went as you planned," he panted. "We moved up from Tibidabo last night, under cover of darkness, and found the west gate open for us. La Barca was on duty there; Cascadour must have been mad to let you persuade him to place Thoma there. We poured in, as silently as we could. But when we got on the walls, there was none to oppose us. How had you arranged it? We expected a battle."

Cercamon smiled. "A traitor always suspects treason," he said simply. "Cascadour believed me an agent sent to supervise his work for Aquitaine. I convinced him that there was a counter-plot on foot among the people to overwhelm the fort in case Moncada fell; and so, at my suggestion, he moved most of the garrison from the walls down to Montjuich."

"To resist a mere mob?" Sobre Ter asked incredulously.

"Nay, not only that. I made Cascadour believe that you had learned something of his plans and fled southwest to bring back our Catalans; I showed him how clear it was that the faithful troops would return not overland to the city, but march across the narrow neck of southern Catalonia to the sea, take ship, and try to seize the fort from the water at the moment when the mob attacked. Naturally he exposed the city—which he thought safely his—to hold the fort, which was the only spot where he expected attack. When you did not come that way, he left half the garrison in Montjuich and moved the rest to the arena here to carry out his plot."

To Cercamon's bewilderment, Sobre Ter, without another word, fell to his knees. Then a hand was laid on the troubadour's shoulder, and he turned to face the count. Bérenger's face was a picture of consternation and uncomprehending surprize.

"What does this mean, Cercamon?" he cried. "You, alive and fighting in Moncada's stead? My men-at-arms suddenly in arms against each other, and shedding each other's blood? Where is Moncada? And you, Sobre Ter—three weeks gone you disappeared, and now you return with mounted men at your back, and cast yourself upon my soldiers! I command, and none listens to me—all is riot, bloodshed, rebellion!"

"It means this, my lord," Cercamon explained. "There has been treason among your officers; Cascadour would have sold your person, perhaps your life, to Aquitaine. A Navarrese army is even now marching against Barcelona; Navarre and Aquitaine have bartered together for your realm. But now, praise to God, the plot is crushed, and your enemies defeated."

"And thanks to Cercamon," broke in Sobre Ter, "who alone discovered the treachery and found means to foil it! Last night three-fourths of your troops were traitors; now the true men have returned from Aragon to save you."

"But Moncada?" the count repeated.

Sobre Ter laughed.

"Locked in his own villa, guarded by Gui le Balafré. Knowing that Moncada could not stand against de l'Arba, Cercamon gave orders that he be imprisoned in his own house, and took his place."

"I promised your Highness that I would not come to you with anything less than absolute proofs," Cercamon took up the tale. "Learning that de l'Arba had himself murdered Gomez, to force Moncada into a duel that would remove him from Navarre's road to victory, I traced the threads of conspiracy from de l'Arba to Aquitaine. Cascadour was Aquitaine's agent, and had filled the city with Poitevin and Gascon mercenaries. Therefore I spread the report of my own death—which Cascadour had indeed hired assassins to accomplish—and won Cascadour's confidence under an assumed rôle. Finding that he planned to have his troops arrest you today, I sent word to your faithful Catalans on the border of your danger. On my representations Cascadour put la Barca in charge of the west gate; and last night your border troops marched in through that gate. Sobre Ter had joined them west of Tibidabo, and came in with them. Their faces hidden by their cheek-mail, they took the places of all but a few of those who had been set to seize you today. When Cascadour bade them lay hands on you, the traitors obeyed— thus furnishing the evidence I promised you; but they were outnumbered and disarmed by the faithful."

"But how did you substitute Catalans for Aquitanians among my guard?" asked the astounded Bérenger.

"It was indeed a picked band of rascals set to guard you," Cercamon answered. "But I whispered in Cascadour's ear that Sobre Ter—whose flight had made your enemies suspect that he knew too much—had bribed many of their officers, and I persuaded the arch-traitor to let me substitute men that I knew to be true to Aquitaine. But those men whom I put in the Aquitanians' place were honest men under la Barca, who himself slew Cascadour in the moment when the handful of rascals attacked you."

He stopped, interrupted by the clatter of hoofs. A single soldier rode up, reined in, and saluted. It was Jehan Bigot.

"Well done, Bigot!" Cercamon greeted him. "You and Balafré had no trouble in getting the border garrison to return?"

"Never a whit!" Bigot assured him. "You have seen today how well they fought. I feared they might not believe us, in spite of the message we brought from you that the city was in peril; but luck was with us. Just before we reached the border, word came from the grand master of the Hospitallers. He was frightened and perplexed that we should send so many men to Aragon and keep them there so long; so he hastened to assure the border garrisons of his faithfulness to the count. His message showed our men there that the rumor of war with Aragon had been false; so as soon as we came with our tale, they understood the treachery, and marched back at once. But now the remaining traitors are shut up in Montjuich fort, with our men hammering at the gates. My lord count, I pray you send what men you have here to reinforce us, or we shall not take the fort!"

Raymond-Bérenger looked from Bigot to Sobre Ter, and from him to Cercamon.

"You have proved yourselves men, all of you!" he said warmly. "To you, Cercamon, I owe my throne and my life. Truly shall I keep the promise I made you two months gone. Nay, Bigot, I will not send you reinforcements; too much blood has been spilt. Send envoys to the Aquitanians in the fort, promising them free departure and ships to take them back to Bordeaux if they will go at once."

Bigot rode off as Thoma la Barca came through the gate of the arena, wiping his sword.

"My lord," he retorted, "de l'Arba is dead. Held by two guards, waiting for your command that he be led to the pyre and burnt, he wrenched himself free, snatched a sword from a trooper, and cut down one of his guards. But he was weak from wounds, and when I crossed blades with him, I had but little ado to slay him."

"And Lady Maria?" the count asked. "In my perplexity I had forgot her."

"Behold her!" la Barca answered, pointing to the gate.

The Catalans on guard there, having quenched the last spark of revolt, had stood aside; and the spectators were streaming out. Borne in triumph on the shoulders of two nobles, Maria de Moncada headed a jubilant procession. To the count's presence they bore her, and set her down before him. She was pale, but smiling.

"Ah, my lady, much grief have I had for your sake!" Bérenger exclaimed. "But now all is well. Tell me, did you know that your champion was Cercamon? I think you accepted his services too quickly to have been wholly ignorant."

"Indeed I knew," she answered, "and was glad to have so true a heart and so invincible a sword to protect me. Two days ago he came to me, having won access in the robe of my chaplain, and promised to take my quarrel on his shoulders. I feared that my husband would forbid it; but Cercamon swore to prevent Andreu from taking part in the combat."

Bérenger clapped his hands.

"And so he had Andreu locked up this morning," he said. "'Tis a serious conspiracy against the rules of trial by combat, but God has set His seal upon it by giving victory to the right. Ha, here is Moncada now!"

The little captain-general rode up fuming, his garb awry and his eyes blazing with anger.

"My lord!" he cried, dismounting so hastily that he stumbled, and flaming doubly crimson at his mishap. "A grievous wrong has been done me—my honor is stained! When I woke this morning, and called for my servants to arm me, a dog of a spearman marched into my chamber and forbade me to leave my own house! In vain I struggled—he called four men to hold me. I pray you, do not give judgment against me, but let me meet de l'Arba now!"

"De l'Arba is dead," the count answered gravely, "overcome by the man who kept you from meeting him."

"Show me that man!" Moncada roared. "I will cut him in pieces! He has heaped shame upon me; he has—"

"He has saved your life, your wife's, and mine!" Bérenger reproved the angry little warrior. "Where your arm would have failed, his has triumphed; Barcelona owes her very liberties to him. Now, Cercamon, have I kept my promise? Have I atoned for my insults?"

"Nobly, my lord," Cercamon replied.

But Moncada was not so to be pacified.

"So it was you?" he cried, turning on the troubadour. "You have shamed me in all men's eyes, and you shall pay for it! There lie the lists; come and cross swords with me if you are a man!"

Lady Maria laid a hand on her husband's arm. "You are ungrateful, Andreu," she whispered. "Is it nothing to you that he has saved me from calumny and death?"

Moncada faltered; and perceiving his hesitation, the count placed Cercamon's hand in his.

"If you are the faithful subject I have always deemed you," he commanded, "you will shake hands with the man who has done you the greatest of services, and who hereafter shall be, second only to you, the most honored of my subjects!"

A belated blush of shame tinged Moncada's cheeks. "Your pardon, troubadour!" he muttered.

Cercamon pressed his hand warmly.

"Now to the palace!" the count cried gaily. "You shall make us a song on this day's doings, Cercamon. Order our horses, la Barca!"

"Your Mightiness will not need them," the Catalan answered. "See yonder!"

From the hills beyond the amphitheater, where they had gathered to wait the outcome of the combat, came a mass of folk, flooding down into the valley like a river. They had seen the conflict between their own troops and the Aquitanians outside the gate, but fear of flying arrows had kept them at a respectful distance. Only now had a trooper found time to ride to them with the glad news of de l'Arba's death and Cercamon's triumph. Still in their black garments of mourning, their faces radiant with joy, they swept toward the gate, casting aside as they came the sticks and stones they had brought to avenge the expected death of Moncada.

La Barca's men would have held them off, but the count forbade it.

"Let them have their joy!" he said; and the troops stood aside.

Gathered up by the oncoming wave like chips before a spate, the count, Moncada, Lady Maria and Cercamon were lifted to their shoulders. Thus enthroned, they were borne amid wild rejoicing to the city. Not till the palace was reached did the folk set down its breathless, jolted favorites.

"Viva Bérenger!" they shouted. "Viva Moncada! Viva Cercamon!"

The count faced them, his hand on Cercamon's bleeding left shoulder.

"Behold him who has saved us all!" he cried.

Of this the folk comprehended little; but they cheered again, till they could no more than whisper hoarse jubilation.

THE BLACK THIEF

"**A**UCH IS a noble city, fair sir, with seven inns; but in none of them will you taste such wine as this!"

The fat taverner filled his guest's cup for the third time, abating no whit of the almost holy pride with which he had first brought forth the bottle, caressing it with reverent affection.

" 'Twas pressed in the year of divine mercy 1132—twenty years gone!" he sighed. "Even so great a lord as yourself has never set lip to better. 'Tis called the 'Marguerite,' after the Demoiselle Marguerite de Belle Gard, who was born in the same season. Poor lady!"

He fell silent, hand pressed to lips, and glanced quickly over his shoulder.

The patron of the Sun of Paradise shoved aside his empty platter, surprizing his host with swift, shrewd eyes.

"Why 'poor lady,' good master Girault? 'Tis indeed wine for an emperor's palate, and she should be held fortunate to be made famous by such a vintage."

The taverner shook his head, his honest face turned furtive.

"You ride hence tomorrow, my Lord, and in armor. 'Tis a tale you may hear without peril, but a deadly one for me to tell. I may lose house and life if you learn it from me, and repeat it in this land of Fezensac."

The guest smiled; Girault was so anxious to speak, and yet so much afraid. Never had a more garrulous man been born, nor one so fond of a good listener. Strong must be the dread that sealed his lips, seeing that since the guest's arrival the innkeeper had kept him constant company, entertaining him most freely with tale on tale of the brave deeds and desperate loves of Gascony.

"I am no less eager to hear than you to tell, good host," the guest encouraged. "Come now! We are alone. On the honor of a man who has never broken faith, I will not betray your confidence."

Girault turned and met the stranger's glance. He gazed long into the smooth, handsome features—almost womanish, save for the stern set of the mouth—searching his guest's blue-green eyes. Heaven had made Girault loose-tongued as it had made him true-hearted; and despite his terror, he knew he would tell this bold-faced lord the tale that burned on his lips, if only he might find honesty in those strange, glowing eyes.

"I know not your name," he faltered. "How know I your word is good?"

The guest stiffened.

"That question would have brought death to one of better birth," he answered softly. "Yet you do well to ask. I am a Gascon like yourself, born in this very Fezensac, not far from Auch. My name is Cercamon; I am no noble, but a troubadour. If you have heard of me, you know what my word is worth."

The effect on the taverner was magical. He dropped on his knees, clasping both hands, his ruddy face kindling with pride and joy.

"O glorious name!" he cried. "O name renowned for song and chivalry! Blessed be Heaven, that hath brought one so famous to my house! Who in Fezensac, who in all Aquitaine, has not heard—"

He broke off, suspicion blotting the ecstasy from his eyes.

"What proof have I that you are Cercamon, the illustrious troubadour? Would Cercamon set foot in this land, which belongs to the Duchess of Aquitaine? All the world knows that her lands are forbidden to Cercamon, her garrisons under command to seize him wherever found. Nay—were you Cercamon, you had not dared come hither!"

The stranger tossed his long locks back and laughed.

"Do you hear no news in Auch, then? The Duchess Aliénor truly set a price upon my head, years ago, for some hard words I said of her; but now she has given me a free pardon, having lately married my great master, Henry Plantagenet, lord of Normandy, Brittany, Maine and Anjou. Being now free, after many years, to revisit the land of my birth, I have come with a high heart, happy to live over old memories. Ay, trust me; I am Cercamon; and to prove it I will sing for you. They say—" he spoke with a certain proud embarrassment—"that men do not take my voice for another's."

Girault held out a trembling hand.

"Too much honor for me!" he protested humbly. "The generous offer proves your good faith. I accept—"

He broke off short, terrified, at the scrape of a foot on the flags outside. A staff beat loudly on the door, and from the kitchen a brisk maid hurried to open. A tall, burly figure took shape out of the soft summer night and paused with upraised band.

"The blessing of God upon this house!" the newcomer spoke, in deep, bell-like tones.

"And upon you, Father Laurence!" the innkeeper stammered. "Be welcome!"

CERCAMON TURNED on the intruder with a scowl, anger to have lost the tale for which he had angled so patiently. Girault would not dare speak now. But as the torchlight fell on Father Laurence, the troubadour's wrath melted; for the face that peered from the monk's cowl was one to admire and reverence. The features were strong and serene, the brow majestic, the whole expression gentle and good. The figure, even under the shapeless black cassock, was sinewy, splendidly proportioned. Such a man as this might St. John have been, Cercamon mused; or, more like, St. Paul, since the sad, kind eyes were set above a stern jaw, dominant nose, and firm-set lips.

Girault paused between bows of welcome to bid the serving-maid set a place for the monk, and himself began to clear a portion of the one table. The monk strode straight toward the two men, pointed to Cercamon's platter—on which the picked bones still lay in a film of grease—and cried with sudden fierceness:

"Mutton! Are you a pagan, a servant of Mahound, to eat flesh on Friday? And you, Girault—what mean you by serving foods forbidden on such a day?"

The taverner, all aflutter, pointed to a cobwebbed hour glass.

"It is but half an hour turned Friday!" he babbled.

Cercamon took the explanation out of his mouth.

" 'Tis just after midnight, good father, and so Friday is but half an hour old. 'Twas still Thursday when I finished eating. We are good Christians, mine host and I."

"Ay, so we be!" Girault protested. "And there is a fine sole on the coals for you, father!"

The monk shook his broad shoulders and smiled.

"The less of purgatory for you then, my sons. But I interrupt—you were speaking together when I came in."

To Cercamon's astonishment—for he remembered keenly the man's fear to tell the tale—Girault answered readily:

"I was but telling of Lady Marguerite, of Belle Gard."

Father Laurence caught the taverner's shoulder in a grip that sent him to his knees.

"Wretch!" he cried. "It is death to tell that tale!"

Cercamon, puzzled and somewhat angry, reached out a prodigiously long arm and caught the monk's wrist; and for all his strength Father Laurence was fain to loose his victim.

"If the same charm that opened his lips has power over you," the troubadour said lightly, "I will tell you that I am Cercamon the Troubadour, a man who betrays no secrets—least of all those which concern a woman."

The monk spun around with quickness that would have done credit to a swordsman. His dark eyes probed Cercamon's, then swept him from head to foot, noting with plain approval the clean lines of the face, the uncanny width of shoulder and reach of arm and the supple carriage of the fine body under the small, bright meshes of his Spanish hauberk.

"I have heard that Cercamon is such a man as you," he conceded. "Your hand!"

Ere Cercamon could stir, Father Laurence snatched at his wrist and held it, looking the while straight at him.

"A steady pulse and honest eyes," he commented, "if the voice matches."

"He would have sung for me, father!" Girault offered.

"For me he must sing!" the monk retorted. "Lady Marguerite's story must not be told to a man who can not prove himself!"

So Cercamon sang; and, to prove himself a troubadour indeed, he sang an aubade of the Languedoc, asking pardon humbly at the end for defiling the ears of a holy man with a song of love. But the monk sat still his fine eyes glowing, his corded hand still beating time to the dead cadence of the music. At last he roused himself, made the sign of the cross, and muttered—

"I have sung worse in my youth—God forgive me!"

"And wielded a sword perchance," Cercamon ventured.

"Aye, and wielded a sword; for which I have done bitter penance. But tell on, Girault; this man is worthy our trust."

SO, WHILE Cercamon listened in silence, and Father Laurence punctuated the tale with nods and muttered confirmation, the taverner told his tale:

"Twenty years since, the lord Jaufre de Belle Gard, vassal of the Countess of Fezensac, and lord of a fine castle, became father to the Lady Marguerite. In the same season came the miraculous vintage, named for her. Father Laurence here, then captain of men-at-arms to Messire Jaufre, stood godfather to the girl. Two years after, he abandoned the world and, becoming an Augustine canon, in due time was made chaplain to his former master.

"The maid grew apace, most marvelous fair, so that young knights from many provinces sought her hand. Then her father fell sick, entrusting castle and maid to Father Laurence—"

"And basely I betrayed my trust!" the monk groaned, smiting his breast.

"Not so, good father!" the taverner gently contradicted. " 'Twas no fault of yours. Gaston de Fermac, a knight of Auch, was among her suitors. Father Laurence bade him begone, for he was a man of evil life. Wherefore this Gaston devised a black villainy. Sending a false message to Father Laurence summoning him to attend the Bishop of Auch, he bribed the porter of Belle Gard in the chaplain's absence. Through the treacherously abandoned postern the accursed Fermac stole with his men-at-arms, and—may he burn forever!—took the castle by storm, putting to sword the unwary garrison. The Lord Jaufre, sick as he was, they slew in his bed. Only two knights, who had sat late over the dice, heard the clash of arms in time to don mail, rush to the lady's bower and let her down with ropes. They could get no horses, the stables being in Gaston's hands; wherefore all three must needs foot it, by night, over rock and ravine, for Auch. They did not reach its shelter; and since then no man has laid eyes on the Lady Marguerite."

He paused, and Cercamon spoke:

"Truly a pitiful tale—but why so perilous to tell? Surely the wrong has been avenged?"

Girault shook his head and glanced at Father Laurence. Looking from one to the other, the troubadour saw the taverner's face wet with tears and the monk's set like flint. A moment's heavy silence; then Father Laurence took up the tale:

"The next day I came back from Audi, riding hard; for I looked for something amiss, once I knew the bishop had not sent for me. Indeed, he could not, having departed two days before for Avignon. So I came back, with but two riders, swiftly, but watching the road with care. At a ford of the Gers I came on Girault, then a vine-tender on the lands of Belle Gard. He ran before my horse, crying—

" 'They have taken the castle, and my lady has fled!'

"So I sent one of my riders ahead, while I questioned Girault. When the man came back, having dismounted and crept through the standing grain of the castle fields, he reported Fermac's banner on the wall, and ten good men of my lady's hanging from the merlons. So, giving Girault a cloak to mantle his peasant's gear, I took him back with me to Auch, where I laid complaint with the Countess of Fezensac, who was then ruler of this province. But Gaston had bought himself into her favor; and at his suggestion Marguerite was declared dead, and her lands given over to Fermac. Since then I—consecrated to God's service though I be—am in constant dread of his anger. He has made himself mighty in Auch. Though the countess is dead, and all Fezensac now ruled by the Count of Armagnac in the name of the Duchess Aliénor, Fermac holds his own in the favor of them who rule us. In Belle Gard he maintains more than a hundred savage troopers, who work his will without remorse; his spies in Auch report all that is whispered against him; and his swordsmen raven through the city like wolves, murdering all who deny his will."

Cercamon's eyes glowed like living coals.

"And the lady has disappeared?" he breathed. "Fermac has sought for her?"

"Ay, has he not!" the monk rejoined. "He has sought her everywhere. His men-at-arms have hunted her in the forest; his spies have pried through all Auch for her. That she has not been found argues her dead indeed; but Fermac is not one to give up such a quest. If he should find her living, he would either force her to marry him, that her right to her father's estate should pass to him, or slay her, lest she get in his way. Nor has he left anything undone to hide his crime, and none who know of it dare speak. If he guessed that Girault had once toiled on the lands of Belle Gard, Girault would be tortured to reveal the little he knows, or hanged, lest that little reach the ears of the Count of Armagnac, who is now our liege lord and Fermac's."

Cercamon scowled, his hands clenched.

"It was a vile deed," he muttered. "Never shall ye repent telling it to me. I will keep it as secret as you would keep the confessional."

"Meantime," said Girault gloomily, "Fermac squeezes us dry to fill his coffers, and ravages like a beast of prey. He is worse than the Black Thief!"

Cercamon started.

"What of this Black Thief, sirs?" he questioned.

The two eyed him strangely.

"Ay, what of him?" the monk echoed. "You do not know him?"

"Not I," Cercamon answered. "Confidence for confidence— my tale for yours. I am not here for my pleasure only. This city of Auch has sent an appeal to the Count of Armagnac, asking for help against the Black Thief's cutthroats. The count, having his hands full with his lady the duchess's affairs, has sent on the petition to my master, Duke Henry, who by marriage with the duchess is now lord of all this land. The duke, unable to spare

men, has sent me, with his letters authorizing me to impress
into service such men as I choose from his faithful vassals here.
My orders are to gather troops, proceed against the Black Thief
and take or destroy him. It would help me much if ye would
tell me what ye know of the rascal."

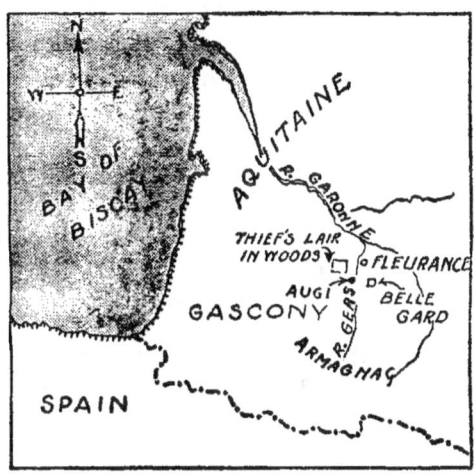

The footsteps of the maid broke in upon them. Neatly she
set the monk's place, served his fish and would have poured
him wine, which he refused. He fell to at once, eating rapidly,
speaking with a full mouth:

"Aye, the Black Thief! But that one does not plunder the
poor. It goes ill with all who walk at night, bearing gold or
silver; yet he has never harmed a peasant. The rich merchant is
his prey, the overbearing knight. He has often robbed Fermac's
baggage-trains. It is his daring that makes men fear him so. He
has thrice raided to the very gates of Auch."

"A strange thing, this," Cercamon mused. "Why does not
Fermac, with his disciplined troopers, make short work of the
Thief? It should not be so hard. And if the Thief has robbed
him—"

Girault rose, his manner restless.

"The Thief is too cunning. If it were only strength against

strength, Fermac would bag him. But the Black Thief is of less account to honest men than Fermac, who can neither keep his own hands off other men's goods nor put down those who plunder him. Your pardon, sir; I must see to your bed."

"In my youth men-at-arms knew how to deal with bandits," Cercamon observed to the monk. "Yet this Thief fears them not."

Glancing warily round the room, Father Laurence turned toward his fellow-guest with the air of a conspirator. It sorted ill with his naturally kind, frank face.

"Nay, he fears them not—fears not Fermac, at least. There may be some grudge between them. Many times has Fermac hunted him; but the Black Thief rides only by night and is very shrewd. It is rumored that he has cut down Fermac's stragglers even while they hunted him, and has vanished without leaving a track. Fermac has set a price on his head. Few dare try to win it. The peasants may or may not know where he hides, but they will breathe no word against him. This is a land of fear!"

He paused; then, leaning close, he whispered—

"A strange and evil marriage, this between Duke Henry and our Duchess Aliénor!"

Cercamon shrugged.

"Men say ill of her, but it is not for me to judge. It has this much good, that it makes my master stronger than the King of France and frees me from the ban Aliénor placed on my life. Henry Plantagenet is master in his own house."

Father Laurence nodded, thoughtfully.

"You are reputed high in his favor. Now that Aliénor has brought him all Poitou and the South in dowry, you will be one of the most influential men in France. It is said the duke harkens to your counsel."

"He does," Cercamon agreed, "but he follows his own."

"Then—" Father Laurence spoke with sudden eagerness— "you can right a great wrong! When you return to Normandy, speak to the duke of the injury Fermac has done Lady Marguerite and beg him to punish the dog!"

Cercamon considered, frowning.

"It can scarce be done," he answered reluctantly. "Duke Henry can not spare a single man—else he would have sent a troop of spears with me, instead of bidding me raise men in his name here. England is in arms against him; the King of France conspires with Thibault of Champagne and Eustace of Boulogne to wrest Brittany from him. Till he has settled with his foes, my lord can undertake no enterprises so far from home— even though Fermac is now his vassal."

"But now that you are here, with power to raise men, you can attack Fermac yourself!" the monk pleaded. "There are many who hate him, and will gladly serve under your banner. They want only a leader."

"And doubtless there are as many more to befriend him. It would plunge the province into civil war. My commission is good only against the Black Thief."

"Then you alone—your cunning—"

"It may not be," Cercamon cut him short. "My lord has given me a task to do; I may not undertake others—even to avenge murdered knights and their injured daughters—till I have carried out his commands."

The monk rose sadly.

"I had hoped for better things from you. I rejoiced when I found you here, knowing your fame as a champion of the weak. Forget what I have told you."

"A hard speech, father. To urge my lord to send troops thus far, when he needs every spear at home, were treason; and to abuse his commission in a private quarrel were disloyalty. If I were free, I would gladly risk my life in your cause."

Father Laurence stood with knitted brows; but at last, as on a sudden impulse, he thrust out his hand.

"Forgive me, my son; not I, but my disappointment reproached you. There is still something you may do for me if you will—something that requires only your single arm, and will not conflict with your commission."

"Name it—it shall be done!"

"Do you fear odds?"

Cercamon laughed merrily, touching his hilt.

"This sword has dealt with odds before! Say on!"

The monk thumped with his staff on the floor, and Girault ran to answer the summons.

"Saddle my mare, friend!" And when the taverner bustled out, Father Laurence bent to Cercamon's ear.

"When Fermac slew my good lord and friend, Sir Jaufre, I obtained consent from my Superior to dwell as a hermit in the forest. Often friends in the town, whose affairs will not let them visit my cell, give me gold to spend in charity and on masses for the souls of the dead. But I must leave my solitude and come for the gold. I have much with me now. The Black Thief has his informants everywhere. It is needful that I go to my cell tonight; but I fear the Thief. He will certainly set an ambush for me somewhere between the city gate and the forest, but will scarce think it necessary to send more than two or three riders against a poor monk. Will you ride with me, and give me the protection of your sword?"

Cercamon's eyes danced.

"If it were any other thing you asked of me, I should regret the soft bed that Girault has made me in yonder chamber. It gives forth a brave smell of lavender. But I am here to find the Black Thief, and you bid me protect you from him! Who knows but we may capture one of his knaves tonight and so get sure news of the Thief himself?"

"Who knows?" the monk echoed, and his tone made Cercamon stare.

But Father Laurence, with the most expressionless of faces, handed Cercamon his helmet; then, bending humbly, helped him lace his mail jambeaux. His fingers had the deftness of a soldier's.

Girault came back, bringing a reek of horseflesh into the room.

"All is ready, father," he announced.

Then he saw Cercamon armed to depart, and his face fell.

Cercamon flung him a piece of gold.

"I ride," he said. "Here is pay for the night."

Weighing the generous fee in his fingers, Girault poured forth eager thanks.

"God go with you, my masters! I will fetch your beast, my lord."

But the troubadour was before him. Stroking his tired gray's muzzle, he saddled it, led it forth and joined the waiting monk in the cobbled court.

"Ready!" he spoke, and vaulted to the saddle.

FATHER LAURENCE led on down a steep, narrow street that ran to the suburb at the foot of the hill. There he drew to a walk, reining up at the city gate, which guarded the bridge over the Gers. The watchman drew aside at sight of his cassock. When Cercamon would have followed, they crossed spears in his path.

"No armed man comes in or out after dark!" growled one.

Father Laurence turned, protesting.

"He is my escort, good sirs!"

"God's blessing on you, father," the warders returned, "but how long have poor monks had escorts?"

Cercamon leaned over in the saddle to speak softly to the guards:

"Your city is a fief of the Duchess of Aquitaine—and I serve the duchess! If you stop me, it will cost you your necks later— or perchance now, for my sword is swift!"

The men peered at him, astounded at his assurance; and he dropped a purse between them.

They let fall their pikes to scramble for it, and grasped it together. It was heavy.

"Pass, *seignior!*" they cried.

Cercamon thrust home the spurs, lest they change their minds; and monk and troubadour thundered over the bridge to the dusty road beyond. Here Father Laurence wheeled to the south.

For the next half hour Cercamon had ado to keep up with him, the mare being fleet and his own fine charger weary. Between fields of grain they passed, that rustled in the frosty wind from the Pyrenees; through a grove of beech, where the horses' hoofs were silenced by deep mast; and so came to the edge of a stream that cut the road. Urging the mare in, the monk rode with the current, westward.

"A poor way this!" Cercamon called, feeling his gray slip on the pebbles.

"Safer!" the other answered briefly.

The stream was a bad road indeed. It plunged through ever-deepening banks, swifter and swifter each moment, till the horses had to set themselves against its surge. Again and again they stumbled on rounded stones, floundering dangerously. Just as Cercamon protested, they came out on a wide pool, where the horses must swim.

"The right bank is low," the monk spoke softly.

They scrambled up the bank—a stretch of sheer, bare rock; a freak of formation that ran far back between dense trees and denser undergrowth, forming a narrow natural path. It stopped abruptly, and they rode into a tangle of briars. The beasts flinched; but from the swishing sound ahead Cercamon knew his companion had found a path. He forced the gray after and, passing the hedge, came into a narrow but fairly open path. Here they rode slowly, Father Laurence easily as one who knows the way, Cercamon fending off drooping branches.

"The Black Thief must be cunning to follow us!" he said. "And you choose a strange place for your cell!"

"Are you afraid?" the monk shot back.

Stung, Cercamon rode on in silence, anger mastering his caution.

Suddenly the undergrowth slipped behind them, and they emerged in a little glen, set with great trees that were no more than blacker wraiths in the night. Somewhere to their right a stream plashed—whether the same they had left, or another, Cercamon could not tell. Following its course, they passed once more into shaggy forest, listening to the unseen waters singing in tones that swelled louder and louder, till at last its roar was deafening.

"Careful here!" the monk warned. "Go not too near the bank!"

Listening, Cercamon made out that the stream, though swift and close on their right hand, was very far below, having cut itself a channel deep down in the living rock. A step too close, and horse and rider would plunge to death in the ravine.

"Here is my cell!" the monk announced. "Dismount!"

He set the example himself; the next moment the hoofs of his led horse clattered over a bridge of thick planks. Cercamon followed, keeping close to the mare's heels. Ignorant of the width of the bridge—for all was black with night and overhanging trees—he felt out before him before he dared set down a foot. It was uncanny work in the dark, the very beams beneath their feet invisible for the thick foliage that dripped in their faces, shutting out the stars. But the peril was short; soon they had their feet on rock again.

The sudden mustiness of the air told Cercamon they had entered a cavern, whose lip, on the brink of the ravine, was unapproachable save for the short bridge. He hesitated, unwilling to go farther into such a place; but the monk's hand reached out for his.

"Do you fear a priest?" he asked reproachfully. "If I did not still need you, I would bid you go back."

"Forward!" Cercamon made answer.

Still clinging to his hand, Father Laurence led him about a sheer right angle in the rock.

"A well-hid cell, this!" Cercamon reflected.

Once again they turned, and came out into the pallid rays of a torch, that showed clean-swept rock beneath them and a natural vault above their heads. Into the dim light glided a dark figure, and a hoarse voice challenged—

"You, father?"

"Father Laurence, with a friend. Let a place be made for us!"

He who had hailed them—a stout, shock-headed country-man—was just disappearing into the only lighted offset. Father Laurence took Cercamon's horse by the bridle, led both beasts into a side tunnel and came back for a torch.

"I will feed and water them," he said. "You would best accept my hospitality for the night."

Cercamon shrugged. He realized that he must stay where he was till day came. Without a guide, one unused to the country could never risk that wild ride along the ravine and through broken, forested ground by night.

A distant, grating sound disturbed him, but he could not guess what it was. Moments passed; and Cercamon, alone in the light of torch and fire, gazed about him with strange per-turbation. A strange cell, this, even for a recluse: hidden so well that even men who knew the forest might search for it in vain. Ay, and a strange monk, with the eyes of a saint and the thews of a soldier—a monk who rode fine horseflesh, hid from outlaw and baron and brooded over wrongs done years ago.

Father Laurence returned, his firm lips curved in a thin, ironic smile.

"Welcome, Troubadour!" he cried, his voice ringing like a peal of bells. "Welcome—to the lair of the Black Thief!"

As if the words were a signal, a flock of armed men tumbled from every lateral tunnel-mouth into the main cavern. Taken by surprize, Cercamon flashed out his sword and backed up against the rock wall; but none raised steel or came near him. The whole company—there were at least forty of them—stood off, eying him, and glancing now and again at the monk, as if for orders. They were a rough crew, shaggy and bearded, clad some in hardened leather, some in mail, under coarse, black surcoats. Every man bore sword or pike, and bow. Two who stood out from the mass wore fine baldrics and gold spurs that flashed in the firelight.

Cercamon faced them angrily.

"What means this, monk?" he cried. "If you have lured me hither for my horse and armor, you and your knaves shall pay for them in blood!"

Father Laurence edged back among his men, grasping his stout oak staff; but his eyes gleamed with triumph.

"Wait!" he answered. "You shall be satisfied—when the Black Thief comes!"

From the black surcoats of the men Cercamon glanced at the monk's black cassock.

"Why this mockery?" he sneered. "You are the thief! Thus far you have outtricked me; but you have but opened the game. I am here to bring you to justice—and justice you shall have if I live!"

"I hold you to that promise!" the monk answered calmly.

Cercamon knew he stood in evil case. If none could get at his back, he was nonetheless doomed at the first passage of arms. The odds against him were heavy. Twoscore pairs of eyes gazed greedily at his splendid mail; twoscore hands itched to draw bowstring. He resolved that, rather than die helplessly at the first arrow-flight, he would leap among them as soon as the first bow bent, and go down striking. But the monk had his men well under control; not one bent bow or raised blade.

A shrill whistle sounded; and the monk raised one hand.

"The Black Thief comes!" he announced.

Mail-shod feet rang on the rock floor; and from the lighted lateral, preceded by an armed guard, came a slender figure, clad all in black mail. In silence it strode among the weaponed men, and came to a halt beside the monk, its eyes resting on Cercamon.

THE TROUBADOUR returned the stare, having no longer any doubt that this, and not the monk, was the Black Thief. The all-enveloping mail and loose black cloak concealed the lines of the figure, yet not enough to hide its slimness; the features were hidden by the nasal and cheek-armor of the helmet. Yet, though this man was far from the burly ruffian Cercamon had imagined, there was something purposeful, deadly, in the slow, fixed gaze that burned upon the captive's face.

At last the bandit spoke:

"What man is this, father? Why have you brought him?"

Cercamon started. The voice was soft and rich, like that of one gently born; but it was not the voice of a man.

Father Laurence cast a mocking glance at his prisoner.

"It is Cercamon the Troubadour, my lady!" he replied. "I have brought him because he would not have come had I not laid a snare for him. And I held him of great value to us."

Cercamon sheathed his blade with an angry clang and faced the helmeted form.

"What game is this?" he demanded. "I do not fight women, nor do I forgive men who seek to play with me!"

Father Laurence stepped forward, his manner turned courtly.

"Good sir," he said, "you are the guest of the Black Thief—Lady Marguerite de Belle Gard, whom I let you think dead, as most men do. You refused to avenge her on her enemy; wherefore, knowing that none could help her so well as you, I tricked you into accompanying me to her. I was certain you would gladly serve her once you heard her plight from her own lips. Be so good as to follow us!"

Beckoning to the two officers in baldrics, he led the way into the lighted tunnel; and Cercamon had no choice but to follow. The woman in armor strode silently by his side; four black-coats brought up the rear. As they entered this natural chamber in the rock, Cercamon stared in incredulous surprize.

The tunnel, which ran at right angles to the main cavern,

was lofty and spacious, but ended abruptly not twenty feet from its entrance. Its contrast with the bare vault he had left was startling. Every inch of its walls was hung with rich tapestries; the floor was heaped with them; silken cushions were piled in the corners, and a rough-fashioned cupboard at the far end was filled with fine vessels of gold, silver, and burnished copper. On a rude table, set about with crudely wrought chairs, lay a sword in a jeweled belt, a well-worn hone beside it.

Lady Marguerite waved Cercamon to a seat on the piled-up cushions and herself took place beside him. Father Laurence stood before them, sandaled feet wide apart, the mockery gone from his grave eyes. Behind him, silent and motionless, stood the two in baldrics and gold spurs, like statues in steel.

Casting aside her helmet, the girl shook out masses of fine black hair, glancing with cold indifference at her involuntary guest. He marveled at the strangeness of her suddenly revealed beauty. For beautiful she was, with fine, small features, a skin soft and dark, a little red mouth and a carriage of the head that would have been dainty, had it not been so proud. Her eyes, large and lustrous black, were cold and bitter.

"You have refused to help me, then?" she spoke; and once more the troubadour thrilled at the melody of her voice. "Truly I knew not that you were in this province, but I have heard much of you—and never till tonight have I heard that you denied aid to a woman!"

Cercamon's thoughts, still whirling with his strange adventure, grew clear at the touch of scorn in her words.

"I denied you no help, lady. I but refused to use, in a private quarrel, the commission given me by my lord, Duke Henry; or to urge him to send against your personal foe those troops he needs to save his own lands. Is it not proof of my readiness to aid the weak that I gave up my warm bed to escort your monk hither, on his plea that he feared the Black Thief? Now I find that the Black Thief and the distressed lady of Belle Gard are one. Surely you, who command so many stout fellows and are feared by a whole countryside, can profit little from the help of one poor sword such as mine?"

Father Laurence laughed.

"It is said that you are not only the most perilous swordsman but also the shrewdest head in all France! Your sword may serve us little—it is your cunning we want!"

Lady Marguerite nodded, her cold eyes still scanning Cercamon.

"It seems Father Laurence has told you of my wrongs. I will not repeat them, then. You are no mere singer, but a soldier as well. Therefore I will not complain to you that I, a woman, have been robbed of home and lands and driven to herd with thieves—in truth, that matters little, for these thieves are the most honest men I have found in this world. But it matters much that my father, sick and helpless, was butchered in his bed, and to this day is unavenged! Help me avenge him, and I care not for lands or life!"

"This land," he said, "is now a field of Armagnac, which itself belongs to the Duchess of Aquitaine. Why have you not appealed, either to the Count of Armagnac—a just man—or to the Duchess Aliénor?"

Marguerite laughed bitterly.

"Once, ere Fezensac was merged in Armagnac, Father Laurence asked justice of the countess. Fermac was her vassal; she refused to believe aught against him. Since Armagnac took the province over, Fermac had kept the roads so well patrolled that I, and the few faithful men who have clung to me, dared not risk capture to pass them."

"But now—" Cercamon began.

"Now that twoscore thieves follow me, you would say? Ay, now I could cut my way past all patrols, if I rode by night; but now who would believe my tale? I have been declared dead. If I won through to Armagnac, I must first prove that I am Marguerite de Belle Gard, and thereby reveal to Fermac that I live. Having heard nothing of me in four years, he has lulled himself into the belief that I am dead indeed. If I appealed, and lost my case against him, he would not rest till he had taken me.

"Moreover, I cannot make myself known now without revealing to all France that I—I who come asking for justice—am that Black Thief for whom the gibbets of Auch have so long waited. Nothing can save me now but to kill Fermac and fortify myself behind the walls of the castle of which he robbed me!"

Father Laurence nodded.

"That is why," he explained, "I asked you to appeal for us to Duke Henry of Normandy. Now that he is liege lord of all this land, he could enforce his decision on the Count of Armagnac; and you, whom he loves, could so set forth the matter to him that this Black Thief business would not be held against my lady."

"But why did you, a woman gently born, take to the life of a bandit?" Cercamon objected. "Surely it does not become you; and you yourself see how it now stands against you."

Marguerite made a gesture of impatience.

"For one reputed so shrewd, you are passing dull! Without a strong following, I should have fallen a prey to Fermac, as soon as he could smell out my hiding place. Without money to buy food, I should have starved. Where should I—a landless fugitive—get men or money? Without both, how should I avenge my father?

"Through Father Laurence and his brethren of the Augustine order, all those men whom Fermac, and others like him, have driven into outlawry were gathered round me. To hold them to me, to feed them and myself, I was forced to rob—ever in the hope that the treasure I took might buy me enough spears to take the field against my enemy. The hope has been vain. Even in the strength of my longing for vengeance, I have never robbed the poor. Only the rich, who oppress the poor, have felt the edge of my wrath. Them I have pillaged; and most of all I have beset the baggage-trains bearing food, arms, and goods to Belle Gard for Fermac. Were they not rightly mine? Was it not my estates from which he has drawn the gold that bought them? And the prosperous merchants of Auch, who advance him the money to maintain his spears—are they not my foes? I have but taken my own; and so well have I planned my raids that I have never been beaten, surprized or tracked to this place!"

Cercamon's look betrayed both pity and admiration.

"Of a truth, Lady Marguerite, you need no help of me! One who could devise such deeds and carry them out has done more than I dare dream of!"

She shrugged her shoulders. The monk, his thin lips set, spoke for her:

"Now you know the matter. Will you help us, or will you have it said that the first troubadour and swordsman of France turned his back on a woman in distress?"

"I was tricked hither," Cercamon answered softly, "and I was threatened with armed men. It seems that, if I refuse your plea, I may be killed or held a prisoner."

The monk nodded.

"Here you are, and here you bide till you do as my lady bids. Forty stout fellows bar your retreat—and the bridge over the gorge has been withdrawn."

Cercamon rose and whipped out his sword.

"Whistle up your hounds and bid them make an end!" he said.

Father Laurence signed to one of the two officers, who wheeled toward the entrance; but Marguerite, springing to her feet, checked him.

"Not so!" she spoke; and there was admiration in her eyes. "If you will not help me, you are free to go! Gentleman you may not be, but you are too brave to die like a cornered rat!"

Cercamon laughed, a ringing, happy laugh.

"Then, so please your ladyship, I will help you, so far as my poor strength and wit may reach! Do you know me better now, monk?"

"I might have known threats could not move such as you," Father Laurence conceded; and his brawny fist shot out to clasp the troubadour's hand.

Marguerite beckoned to the officers.

"It is well, Cercamon," she said, "that you who have thrown in your lot with me should know two cavaliers such as these, who have given up name, fame and fortune to serve me. Here are Sir Guitard and Sir Simon, who saved me from Fermac on that night of slaughter, four years gone. They, and Father Laurence, are in my counsels."

CERCAMON CLASPED hands with the two knights—both tall, sinewy men, straight-backed, bowed of leg from years in the saddle. They were men such as the lower nobility often bred—loyal, free from the twisted ambition that made the higher baronage unscrupulous and cruel. All five seated themselves.

"Now for our task," said the monk. "Heaven sharpen your wits, Troubadour!"

"What is this castle like?" Cercamon questioned.

Father Laurence drew quill, ink-vial, and parchment from his scrip, and setting the parchment flat against the floor, began to draw with a cunning hand. As his fingers moved, the ground-plan of a fortress took shape. One of the knights held a torch, and both thrust in quick, shrewd comments as the monk drew. But he, who saw with a soldier's eye as keen as their own, was rarely forestalled.

"Thus sits the keep—here are the demi-towers. Note how the walls command the way. So runs the bailey, walls twelve feet through. Here are the stairs that lead to the parapet—and here. The gates? Ay, two—one here, in the keep; and the postern—so."

He swiftly sketched in the positions of the catapults, the turrets, stables, wells, commenting the while so vividly that the place took palpable shape before Cercamon's eyes. Following both sketch and description closely, Cercamon yet had thought to spare in wonder at the transformation of the man. Tonsure and cassock, girdle and medal, were all that now proclaimed him monk; speech and bearing were those of the old soldier, the one-time captain of men-at-arms.

"And the road thither?" Cercamon asked.

"I will show you tomorrow, by full light of day. You shall see then how well this place is hid, and how we go back and forth between forest and road without being tracked. In Auch men almost doubt whether we lurk in the forest indeed, or come down from the far foothills of the Pyrenees."

"How many men has Fermac?"

"A hundred and thirty—were not Belle Gard so strongly built, his force were all too few to garrison it. My old lord Jaufre devised it so well that few can hold it against many. Fermac is too greedy of his gold to pay the wages of a full garrison."

"He has enemies, you say? Any who might join with us?"

Father Laurence shook his head sadly.

"Enemies he has—some who would join us; but all too few to storm the walls. None who would dare march against Belle Gard. When I spoke to you of his foes who would aid us, I thought of an ambush. Many men there be—poor folk from Auch and the villages—who would gladly waylay him from the thickets, if you could lure him hither—"

"One sees," Cercamon broke in, "that you have been a captain. I have been a leader of captains. You can not beat down men-at-arms with faint-hearted, ill-armed folk, who dare not face walls. Nay, even in ambush such will not stand fast. My plan—for I have the beginnings of a plan—deals with the castle itself."

The monk stared at him, and Sir Guitard looked up with quick protest:

"But you can not storm—"

"Leave that to me," Cercamon interrupted. "Have you the courage to storm the place, if I show you the way?"

Sir Simon thundered out an oath.

"Lead on, Troubadour! Make a breach for us, and we will follow you to Satan's throne!"

Cercamon looked from one to another. The monk's face was puzzled, but resolute; the two knights sat with eager eyes, hands clasping and unclasping about their hilts. As for Marguerite, her fine, keen features were alight with restless enthusiasm. They did not know, these four, what thoughts went on in the troubadour's brain; but all had heard of his deeds, and looked to him for some miraculous wisdom that would gain the almost hopeless end they sought.

"My plan," he resumed slowly, "is venturesome, perilous; yet it is the only way. We must use only your men, my lady, whom you know and trust. Is there any among them who would flinch?"

She shook her head.

"They would die for me," she answered simply.

"Then it is needful only that you trust me—all of you. Trust me fully, no matter what appearances be. If ye promise this, and follow my commands to the letter, I will pledge my word to bring you within the walls of Belle Gard."

Leaping to her feet, Marguerite snatched the belted sword from the table and girt it about her. Then, clasping the troubadour's hand, she gave her promise, her eyes gleaming like twin fires. After her, each of the others echoed her pledge—to trust and to obey.

"How soon shall we ride?" the girl questioned, her impatience unleashed.

"I ride tomorrow, when it is fully light," Cercamon answered, "with Father Laurence as guide to the edge of the wood. The rest may not move till ye hear from me—it may be three days, or even more. To strike too soon were to court disaster. But you, my lady, must tarry here, even when the others ride forth. Nay, protest not! My plan is ruined unless you obey."

"But I can use a sword!" she blazed at him. "Am I to have no hand in the avenging of my own father?"

"You shall play the most vital part of all," he assured her; and his promise quieted her. "But all will fail if you leave this place till you get word from Father Laurence that the time has come."

"The signal?" the monk reminded him.

"That I will tell you tomorrow. Now I pray you, let me sleep. I shall need my wits with me tomorrow."

F R O M   T H E shelter of a wooded hill two men looked out over the rolling country to the east, where the villages lay amid the ripening grain, commanded at far intervals by grim, gray towers. A light breeze raffled the wheatfields, where the sun lay soft and warm.

"There lies the Auch-Fleurance road, Troubadour," said the monk. "Beyond—see yonder, on the second hill—stands Belle Gard."

Cercamon peered into the morning sun, shading his eyes with his hand.

"I see a gray mass against trees," he muttered.

"Ay; that is it. There is a wood beyond."

"The chambers are on this side of the keep?"

"As I have said."

"And your lady—the Black Thief—has never raided east of the road?"

"Never. To do so would have exposed her too much to Fermac's spears, and to the city forces from Auch and Fleurance. She has snatched up convoys almost under the walls of Auch— but on this side the city."

"Good. There is hope for our plan, then."

The monk watched him with anxious eyes.

"It is a shrewd plan, Troubadour; but the risk is great. If you fail—"

"If I fail, there is still a way out. Watch for my signal—a light from one of the chambers, well after dark. See to it that your lady obeys my order. I fear for her—she is headstrong, and fierce for Fermac's blood. A chance arrow—"

"She shall obey, though I have to bind her!" the monk assured him. "The Saints be with you, and with us!"

Mounting, Cercamon urged the gray down the forested slope to the waving grain. With all the heedlessness of the aristocrat, he trampled through the unripe harvest, at an angle that bore him east and slightly south, casting for the byroad that would lead from Auch to Belle Gard. An hour's ride through the uneven fields brought him upon it.

The castle road was rough and ill-kept, as if its owner were too sure of its safety to heed its repair, or preferred to use his peasants in the fields. Cercamon smiled grimly.

"A bad vassal this. My lord of Armagnac would think the less of him, did he know how Fermac neglects his road-building. A greedy man, I think."

The gray pulled down to a walk as he felt the slope; and under the frowning wall wound horse and rider, catching the sheen of spears from the toothed parapets. As each fresh turn opened out a new view of the stronghold, Cercamon scanned it with trained, appraising eye.

Belle Gard was a grim, square tower, standing as it were astride the roughly oval wall of the bailey, which followed the contours of the hill, the crest of which had been cut down to form a base for the fortress. Too high and too far from a stream for a moat, the place needed none, for its lofty walls held the entire hill and commanded the plain beneath. Making the last circuit—for the road wound like a spiral stair—Cercamon saw, in the rear, a narrow postern, flanked by two stout demi-towers; and he remembered that it was through this rear gate Gaston de Fermac had made his treacherous assault. On this side, too, a good mile east of the hill, lay the wood Father Laurence had pointed out to him. The last rise of the road brought him to the arched gate of the keep.

This, too, was flanked with lesser towers and dominated by the out-jut of the machicolated tower. Cercamon nodded approvingly at the lowered portcullis and the twinkle of points at the arrow-slots.

"A good soldier," he mused.

"Who comes?"

The voice from the wall was harsh and arrogant; and arrogantly Cercamon answered:

"Cercamon the Troubadour, whom all men know! Shall I enter, or seek a nobler host?"

There was no answer. Either the challenger desired no guests or he had gone to report to some higher authority. Helmeted heads peered down from the wall, eager to see him who bore so well-known a name. For many minutes Cercamon waited, conscious of the eyes that watched him, the weapons that glinted above his head, uncertain of the outcome. At last the portcullis rose with a screech and the massive double gates swung open.

The mouth of the tower was filled with men-at-arms. For a moment Cercamon feared lest even a troubadour—eagerly received in every feudal castle—might find a hostile greeting in Belle Gard. But the man-at-arms smiled at him, and a tall officer came forward to clasp hands with him.

"Welcome, in my master's name!" the officer cried with boyish enthusiasm. Naught could be seen of his face under the steel save a stubborn chin and a pair of merry, ardent eyes. "I am Marc de Lot, knight vassal of Fermac and captain of archers. We are rustic folk here, whom such as you rarely deign to visit. Ho, grooms! Look to his horse!"

The spearmen clustered thickly to see the distinguished guest, of whose golden voice all men had heard. Through them Sir Marc shouldered his way, across the guardroom, up a winding stair in the thickness of the wall. Cercamon followed, his quick eyes taking note of the arrow-slots at each landing, the doors that opened off, even the number of steps.

At the third landing Marc stopped and, flinging open a heavy door, led the way into a narrow corridor. From this other doors opened: one on the left, and many—though it was hard to see how many, the light that filtered in from the arrow-slots being dim—on the right. Entering one of these, the knight showed Cercamon into a small but richly appointed chamber.

I T WA S poorly lighted by two narrow windows, furnished with iron shutters; and between these an arrow-slot. Thick candles, stuck in sconces, stood in each corner of the room. Every opening, save the door, was in the outside wall; against the cross-wall stood a massive but narrow oaken bed, splendidly carved. Across from it was a deep clothes-chest, and three low-backed chairs, black with age and rich with gilded carving. Furs and embroidered stuffs, fine in workmanship, but worn ragged, covered the floor. Over the bed was laid a coverlet of Moorish silk.

"The chamber of honor!" laughed Marc de Lot. "My lord bids you forgive such meager hospitality, he being but poor and you the favored singer of the noblest lord in France. Bide but a moment; I will fetch water and wine."

While he was gone, Cercamon stood at the window, gazing out past the slope of the hill and the fields beyond. As Father Laurence had said, the chambers faced west. Far in the distance he could see the green loom of the forest that sheltered the Black Thief.

He turned quickly, as the door was thrown open and Marc de Lot entered. Behind him staggered a menial, bearing a huge hooped tub, followed by four others with vessels full of water. Behind these came a sixth, bearing towels, basin, cups, and a flagon of wine. When they had set down their burdens, and the contents of the vessels poured into the tub, Sir Marc bade them begone. Though he spoke gently, they shrunk away like whipped curs. He closed the door.

"By your leave, Troubadour, I will wait on you myself."

"It is not fitting for a knight—" Cercamon began; but the other interrupted with bluff good nature:

"It is an honor. I will not have it said that we of the South lack courtesy."

He laid aside his helmet, doffed his mail, and stood there in rusty leather, a fine figure of a soldier. Cercamon marveled inwardly that one who followed a man of Fermac's repute should have so gallant and wholesome a face, and eyes wherein shone the very spirit of chivalry.

When Cercamon had stripped and climbed into the tub, Sir Marc stood by with towel in hand.

"Splendor of heaven, but you have shoulders!" he cried. "And arms! No wonder you are renowned as a swordsman!"

Cercamon laughed, reaching for the towel; but the knight drew back.

"Come out, and I will dry you. So! I should not care to meet you point to point!"

"It is in the feet, eyes and wrist no less than in the arms," Cercamon explained. "A good swordsman is more than a blacksmith in mail. But I warrant you wield a good blade yourself—you have a fine reach."

"You should see Gaston de Fermac, my uncle and master!" Marc replied. "He would make a match for you, if any man may!"

Cercamon smiled, glad that he was to be pitted against a strong antagonist; yet he felt a sudden pang that this young man was of the blood of Fermac. There was no guile in Marc de Lot, if Cercamon read his eyes aright. He was of the age when men adore brave deeds, and worship—with all too little discrimination—those who are strong enough to do them.

When his guest was glowing from the towel, Marc drew from the wardrobe tunic and hose of velvet, rich and fine, though of an antique cut, and a scarlet mantle.

"Wear these, till your own can be cleansed of dust," he said. "Mine would pinch you, and my lord's would be overlong. These belonged to him who held this place before Fermac. He was just such as you in stature."

Cercamon winced at this outspoken offer of a murdered man's clothes, but he smiled a little grimly and put them on. After all, there was a certain ironic justice in the situation. He, who meant to avenge Jaufre, would first appear before the murderer in the outward guise of the victim. It was a good omen.

Pouring the wine, Sir Marc offered him a cup, and then—with that age-old courtesy that had its roots in the wish to show good faith, and to prove the wine free from poison, drank first. As they emptied their beakers, there was a stir in the corridor—the sound of many feet, rough voices and much laughter. A great voice boomed out, and all others fell silent. An excited chattering followed.

"You are in good time for undern-meal," de Lot observed. "My lord announces your visit. Come!"

Cercamon left his mail behind, but buckled on his sword-belt, and followed the impatient de Lot. An excellent young man, he thought; prompt to courtesy, with a fine appetite for food as well as glory.

They entered the corridor on the heels of a considerable company, who turned to stare frankly and nudged each other. There was nothing hostile, nothing rude, in their manner, but a plainly expressed delight and admiration.

All were making for the single doorway in the left wall, a huge entrance with double leaves, capable of defense if the rest of the keep should be taken. Entering in his turn, Cercamon found himself in the great hall—a spacious room strewn with rushes, and furnished with tables of deal laid across trestles. The two long tables that ran along the walls were bare boards, though set with many steaming dishes; but on a dais at the far end stood a lesser *table dormant,* a fine piece of well-carved oak, gleaming with fine damask and a service of silver bowls and flagons. It was set for fifteen. At the place of honor, in the middle of the farther side, stood the massive chair of the lord of the castle.

The men-at-arms off duty, and their sergeants, trooped to

the lower tables and stood waiting at their places, while their betters advanced leisurely toward the dais. At the head of the household—a little group of knights and higher officers, steward, and chaplain—strutted a huge man in fine but threadbare garments. Ostentatiously, with proud glances from arrogantly lowered lids, he took his place in the seat of honor. At a curt nod from him, the household seated themselves about him; and only then, with an unconcealed sigh of relief, the soldiers sat, reaching out for the smoking dishes. They were checked at once by their lord, who rose with an impressive gesture.

"My uncle loves to do all things in fair order," de Lot smiled, and led Cercamon forward.

As they approached the dais, every man stood to honor the guest.

"My lord Gaston, knight of Fermac, Castellan of Belle Gard!" Sir Marc announced. His voice and face were serious, but one elbow nudged the troubadour's ribs. "I present Cercamon, greatest of troubadours, vassal to Henry, Duke of Normandy, Brittany and Anjou!"

Fermac came down from the dais, his hand outstretched.

"I greet you as I would greet your master," he spoke pompously. "My house is yours. Command, and you shall be obeyed. Great is the honor you confer upon us!"

Cercamon took his hand; indeed, he could scarce do otherwise.

"Noble sir," he answered, "I thank you for your welcome, in the name of the duke, my master—and yours."

He emphasized the last two words, feeling certain that France knew how Henry's marriage with the Duchess of Aquitaine had made all the South change lords.

Fermac's broad face flushed, and his eyes kindled. With something of an effort he swallowed his pride.

"My lord and yours," he admitted. "Do you come, then, with commands from the duke?"

"I do," Cercamon replied. "But we can speak of them later,

if it be your pleasure. I would not disturb your revelry with affairs of state."

Fermac bowed, and motioned him to the vacant seat on his own right hand. Sir Marc took his place at the baron's left. Instantly a flock of domestics poured in from the kitchens at the rear, bearing flagons of wine and hot trenchers. All fell to, helping themselves with their fingers from great pots of stew and platters of roast meat, cutting the larger pieces with their daggers, and licking the grease from their hands. The hot food and the wine for a time absorbed their full attention; but as hunger was satisfied, tongues were loosed. A great clatter of talk arose.

AT LAST Fermac beat with his huge fist on the table, and the servants trooped in to remove the dishes and fetch the richer wines. There was a general hush, which Cercamon understood; but before doing his part as guest he wished to study the company into which he had thrust himself. He kept up a steady flow of talk with Fermac and de Lot, watching their faces as closely as courtesy permitted.

He scarce knew what to make of his host. In his apparel, and in the furnishing of his hall, Fermac was plainly a niggard. The ragged remnants of the splendor that apparently had been due to Jaufre of Belle Gard still decked the walls; but nothing new in tapestry or furniture seemed to have replaced them. So far, then, Fermac was close-fisted; yet his entertainment was good. Vanity was openly revealed in his every pose, in his pompous dignity and his slowness to admit vassalage to Duke Henry.

He was clearly an arrogant, tight-fisted, self-sufficient man; but there was about him no trace of that brutality Cercamon had expected to see. His features were heavy, his mouth set and grim; but even in his hard, black eyes there was nothing that could be called malevolence. Indeed, his look was frank, bold and honest. In figure he was huge, as broad as Cercamon and more than a head taller.

As for young de Lot, he was neither swaggerer nor popinjay;

but just such a clear-eyed, open-hearted young soldier as could be found about the courts of the first princes of France. The more Cercamon saw of him, the more he liked him; and his knowledge of men told him that this clean-souled youth could have no guilty knowledge of the deed with which Fermac stood accused.

Nor was the company the hard-faced set of ruffians the troubadour had thought to find. Stout fellows they were, neither better nor worse than most of their mercenary class. The half-dozen officers were hawk-featured fighting men, just such as thronged that Norman court itself. Cercamon became uneasy, wondering how such men as these could be the murderous bullies that had butchered a sick man in his bed, hanged his good knights and dispossessed a harmless girl.

The company, too, eyed Cercamon, still marveling at the chance that had brought so famous a singer among them. There was a touch of impatience in Fermac's eye. Understanding, Cercamon turned to him.

"My lord, you will be waiting for the latest song—if there be anything in poesy that the North can teach the South."

Fermac's red face beamed.

"Sing on! We shall be in your debt. Though you come from the North, the South bore you, and is proud to welcome her own again!"

So Cercamon sang, and sang his best; lest any in after days should say that he had dealt unfairly with the master of Belle Gard. He sang a stately canzo, celebrating his good lord the Duke of Normandy; a lilting aubade, to which Fermac kept time with his big, hard hands; and a chant of war that rang and thundered till the men-at-arms drowned its last echoes in cheers.

"Faith of my body!" Fermac bellowed, clapping him on the shoulder. "The roof is blest that harbors you! I pray you, bide with me as long as ever you can."

"That I will do," Cercamon agreed, "on one condition: That my master's commands find you prompt to obey."

At the word "obey" Fermac scowled.

"Repeat them, and I will judge!" he barked.

In his manner Cercamon at last perceived the kind of man with whom he had to deal; and he reproached himself that he had forgotten what manner of folk the South bred. Fermac's passion was independence; his weakness, impatience of feudal loyalty. He could not hope—as the Norman barons could and often did—to undermine and at last usurp their ruler's power; but he meant to rule his little domain as a petty king. With this end in view he could intrigue and murder, without acknowledging that he had done wrong; for the end, to such as he, justified the means.

He had gone far toward realizing his ambition, having been but a vassal knight till the possession of Belle Gard. The merging of Fezensac in Armagnac had left him without a feudal superior near enough to interfere with his acts. Nor would he ever dream himself guilty of wrong-doing; whatever pleased him, and served his ends, must be right. Though Cercamon had forgot this trait of his countrymen, he was ready for it. Drawing a folded parchment from his belt, he thrust it into his host's hands.

Breaking the seal, Fermac opened it and stared at the impress of the Plantagenet leopards on the wax.

"Ay, from the duke," he growled. "But I can not read."

And he passed it to his chaplain.

The priest, a round little man and clean-shaven, rolled his eyes in astonishment.

"This is an order," he announced in a shrill voice, "for all who read to give the bearer, Cercamon the Troubadour, such aid as he may ask, in men, arms and gold, against—the Black Thief!"

Fermac's jaw dropped.

"The Black Thief? The duke has heard of him?"

"There have been complaints from Auch," Cercamon explained.

Fermac's eyes glittered.

"I am glad!" he said. "It was time the rascal was hanged. What forces have you brought, and where are they lodged? In Auch?"

Cercamon smiled.

"They are under your roof, my lord!"

"Under my—ha! You mean that I am to supply them? If it were in any other cause, I should ask by what right your master makes free with my spears—but I would give you my right hand if it would serve to catch the Black Thief! But how can you succeed, when I have gone out against him five times and have not so much as laid eyes on him or found his lair?"

"As to the duke's right," Cercamon replied, "he is your liege lord. It can not have escaped him that you—the strongest castellan in these parts—have failed to bring the Thief to justice. I fear my lord may be angered with you, deeming you slack in keeping the peace. Yet I can assure him of your efforts—and by aiding me now, you can win back his confidence. Though it were hard for me to accomplish that which has baffled you, I have some hopes. I have already seen something of this country—which is the land of my birth. I think I have learned how to bring you eye to eye with the Black Thief. If you will do as I ask, I will pledge myself to deliver him into your hands. But I will not be so insolent as to bid you give over your troops to me. Rather will I ride with you, and show you whither I think it wisest to lead them."

He had gaged his man aright; Fermac's face beamed at this concession to his vanity.

"We will go forth tomorrow!"

Cercamon shook his head.

"Too soon, my lord. My plans need careful preparation. We must wait for a dark night."

Marc de Lot laid a hand on Cercamon's arm.

"Do not leave me out of this venture!" he implored.

"By my honor, no! You shall have a place of glory!"

Cercamon spoke heartily, but his mind misgave him. In the plot he had contrived there had been no place for Marc, nor could he yet see how to use him. It would have been easier had he liked the man less.

FERMAC HIMSELF showed his guest over the castle. Having—as he deemed—asserted his independence without refusing the will of the duke his suzerain, he felt bound to show the duke's emissary how well he defended his fief. If the troubadour carried back a good report of him, he could remain the longer unmolested by troublesome inquiries from his liege lord.

Everything he saw assured Cercamon of the strength and readiness of the defense. There was a well in the thickness of the keep wall, and another in the bailey, from which garrison as well as beasts could be easily and plenteously watered. The stables were mere stalls—easy of access—set into the eastern and southern walls, breaking off in the east wall, where the postern stood. Here paced at all times a sturdy man-at-arms, ceaselessly on guard; and within call of the guardroom. Servants and grooms scurried about the courtyard, drawing water and fetching food for the horses that stamped and nickered in the stalls.

From the busy court to the farther battlements Cercamon looked; and he saw that Fermac was not one to be lightly sur-prized. Along the parapet strode sentinels, armed with bow or crossbow, pacing their stations smartly, ever keeping an eye on the plain below. Here and there were catapults, piles of javelins, open chests of arrows, pots of oil, and fixes ready laid.

"Had Jaufre de Belle Gard maintained such vigilance, he would not have lost lands and life!" the troubadour reflected. "And I, who have been sent to catch a thief, would not now be defending the thief. But when the thief is a woman wrongly oppressed—"

Long he lay awake that night in his soft bed, weighing the chances of his plan. If he could but keep Fermac's confidence—

and he had gained it easily enough—he would win. But there was chance of accident; chance that Fermac would prove hard to manage. Moreover, Cercamon was proud of his honor; and he had passed his word to do two conflicting things: To restore Marguerite to her castle, and to deliver the Black Thief into Fermac's power. The second promise was part of his scheme for accomplishing the first; he meant to do both, and to make the result a victory for the girl. But if either she or Fermac disregarded his instructions, he would be hard put to it to keep his word to one or both.

In the morning he rose fresh and gay, for all he had slept but little. He found his host merry with the prospect of a manhunt. Cercamon's reputation for cunning was well-known to Fermac—the fame of his deeds had rung throughout France. So it was that the baron felt more confidence of success with such an ally than he had yet had cause to feel in his own unaided strength, even though he had the advantage of a knowledge of the country much more accurate than the troubadour's.

"Come to the battlements!" he cried eagerly. "I have a fair sight for your eyes!"

Following him, Cercamon felt his impression of the day before confirmed. The place was big enough for a much larger garrison than Fermac's hundred and thirty men-at-arms; yet it was so stout, so well-arranged, that half that number could hold it against heavy odds. No wonder Fermac had coveted it, aye, and played foully for it.

As they approached the parapets, Cercamon heard hammers ringing and turned inquiring eyes on his host.

"A welcome for the Black Thief," Fermac chuckled. "You shall see."

And Cercamon saw. At the edge of the rampart, in full view from the plain, rose the ugly, menacing arm of a gallows.

The hair rose at the base of Cercamon's scalp. For all his bluff good humor, Fermac was indeed the kind of man he was reported—cruel, delighting in grim deeds.

"This is unwise, my lord," Cercamon reproved him. "The Thief will see and understand that we mean to move against him."

Fermac ran one hand along his beard and gazed ruefully at his nearly finished gibbet.

"By the Mass! You are right; but 'tis too late now to take it down. If he has spies out, they have seen already. And 'twere a pity to leave so fair a scaffold unfleshed—Stay, I have it! There is a peasant in my dungeon who refused his daughter to me. I will hang him, and trick the Thief with a false scent!"

If Cercamon had felt some slight remorse at the thought of beguiling a man—however villainous—who trusted him, it vanished now. Fermac was brave, and a good host; but like many of the worse spirits of his class, he was a beast, unashamed of his brutishness.

They stood in the very shadow of the gallows, the hammers clanging above them, and looked out over the waving wheat to the forest beyond, where the Black Thief lay hidden.

"The fox is in his earth," laughed the baron, "but we shall have him out! Shall we start tonight, Troubadour?"

"Nay; there will be a moon. Wait for a cloudy night. One glint of moonlight on your mail as you cross the fields, and he would take cover."

Fermac nodded.

"And if he is truly there, and not in the Pyrenees, as some say—"

"In the Pyrenees!" Cercamon scoffed. "A poor guess, inspired by failure to find him where he hides! As well think him in the Alps. 'Tis too far to the Spanish hills for him to use them for a refuge. Trust me, he is in yonder forest. We shall hunt him as men hunt the boar in Normandy—a rare trick, that I will show you. But all in good time—in good time!"

"Plague on it, how you curb my ardor! But you are right— men say truly that you have no match for shrewdness."

Cercamon turned.

"There are woods on the east of the castle," he ventured. "Do you not fear surprize from that side?"

Fermac laughed.

"On that side I have no foes; and if I had, Belle Gard commands the road. There is no advantage in felling the forest; 'tis thriftier to thin the trees for fuel, sparing the rest."

Cercamon had the answer he wanted. If Fermac feared no foe to the eastward, he would watch there none too carefully.

Three days passed, with no abatement of the clear, dry weather and bright nights. On the fourth, clouds hung heavy in the sky. Fermac was jubilant.

"The wind has changed," he announced. "These clouds will gather thicker through the night. It will rain tomorrow. The time has come!"

All through the afternoon his officers went about among the men-at-arms, seeing that swords were sharp, spear-points freshly ground, mail mended and polished. The horses were given all they would eat. Fermac and Marc de Lot sat together in the baron's chamber, discussing their plan of action. At a word from Cercamon, the cooks and kitchen-knaves were set to such toil as they had seldom known.

"Each man," the troubadour said, "should carry two days' provisions. 'Twill be a hard task, at best, to hunt down the Thief; and we must not give over till his band is crushed."

"I will take fourscore spears," Fermac decided.

"How many has the Thief?"

Fermac shook his head.

"I know not—but scarce that many; and my lads are trained soldiers."

"Trained," Cercamon ventured, "to bear the shock of mass attack on the open plain—scarce trained to play at a murderous hide-and-seek with men who know every brake, every tree, in the forest. Stout though they be, they are not at home there. The Thief is on his own ground; and that he knows it as he knows his own hand is proved by the ease with which he has already evaded you there. You will have to beware ambush in every thicket; every trunk or leafy crown may hide an archer; and there may be marshes and broken ground where a desperate few can stand off many."

"That there are!" Sir Marc interjected. "It is evil country. Take more men, my uncle."

"This is your venture, Troubadour," Fermac conceded. "How many men do you advise?"

Cercamon seemed to ponder.

"I should take full sixscore," he spoke judicially. "We can not hope to hunt the Black Thief down in his own forest unless we draw a cordon round him, and so close in the circle slowly, beating as for game. Otherwise he will merely dodge us back and forth till our men are weary. Sixscore will be none too many—unless you fear to expose Belle Gard."

Fermac's red cheeks puffed out.

"Fear? I fear! Look you, Troubadour: I fear no man, but make men fear me! There are none who dare strike at me, save the Thief; and with my lads driving him in on his lair, he can not harm Belle Gard. Why, man! My walls are stout enough for ten to hold them against a troop of spears!"

So it was determined that they should sally forth two hours before dawn, in full force, leaving but a dozen men—including the chaplain and a sergeant—to hold the castle. It was few enough; but, as Fermac said, he had nothing to fear. And he was stung by Cercamon's shrewd hint that he was afraid. Vanity was indeed his weakness.

At dusk the castle hummed with activity. Lights bobbed and flickered in the bailey, while grooms sacked oats and trussed hay for two days' supply—for the stall-fed horses of the garrison would not thrive on grass alone—and food for the men was packed in saddle-bags. A subdued, excited buzz from the guardroom betrayed the keenness of the men-at-arms for a venture that would break the dullness of garrison routine. One would have said that the very beasts sensed what was in the wind; the lights and bustle kept them on edge. Horses pawed and fretted; cattle lowed unquietly; the cocks crowed as if it were daybreak.

The household sat late at supper. Fermac's mood was so blithe that he drank and boasted for three; and his officers followed his example. Cercamon drank little, pleading a head grown weak among the abstinent Normans. The others railed him; but Fermac bade them be still.

"Fools! That head of his is the sharpest in France; would ye have him dull it? His wits work for us this night!"

So the baron made no objection when Cercamon rose from table early, to get some sleep ere they must ride. Once in his chamber, he shut the door carefully, struck flint on steel and went close to the window with a lighted torch. Then, retreating a little, he passed thrice with the torch before the opening and stood listening.

From somewhere across the fields a dog howled, thrice. Once more he gave his signal, and again the dog answered. Satisfied, he stuck the torch in its cresset, removed his sword-belt and set to work—quietly—with a small hone that he carried in his pouch.

IN THE darkest hour of the night the garrison rode forth, moving slowly down the sandy road, lest the jingle of their mail carry across the plain. They wound about the hill like an enormous snake, uncoiling at the foot to launch itself across the fields. There the pace was increased to a trot, which brought them to the forest edge well before dawn.

Cercamon tugged at Fermac's rein.

"Now we must work swiftly!" he advised. "Send twoscore men along the northern edge, and twoscore along the southern, with orders to spread out thin. When the two detachments establish contact, they shall work toward the center, narrowing the circle as they go. Meantime the rest shall strike straight through the wood from where we stand and so serve as a corps to which all may rally."

"Is it wise to divide our force?" de Lot questioned.

"Were it not foolish to drive sixscore men in a wedge through the center of the forest, while the Thief and his *rascaille* escaped by the edges?"

Fermac nodded.

"Right, Troubadour! We must drive them like deer. Ho, knights!"

As the officers rode in, he gave orders as Cercamon had advised.

Marc was still dissatisfied.

"Evil may come of this!" he protested.

"Not for my lord," Cercamon urged. "We shall ride with him, at the head of your twoscore archers. We must lead the advance through the center. It will go hard with any who oppose so strong a force. If we are hard-pressed, the blast of a trumpet will bring help."

De Lot on his left, Cercamon on his right, the master of Belle Gard advanced. Their way led up a steep, forested slope, in the first gray of dawn. Branches slapped them smartly, drenching them with dew; sleepy birds roused before them; their horses' hoofs beat a dull diapason to the creak of leather and the clink of mail. Now and then some rider, smitten across the face by a thorn-branch, cursed under his breath. On and on they toiled, through the silvering daybreak and the late-coming woodland day; till the mounting sun, penetrating the screen of foliage, started the sweat beneath their armor.

Their work was no more than begun when they topped the ridge. On the higher, rolling ground the wood was denser, broken by streams they must often ride along for irritating distances, by rockgirt gulches or boiling pools. After many hours they brought up against a brake that they could not force a way through, and must needs ride round it. The going was hard, so that they made poor speed. But ever and again came faint, thin hails from the far distance, growing gradually louder as the day advanced, marking the progress of their comrades beating the coverts.

"They draw in to us!" Cercamon exclaimed. "But 'twill be long ere they can work so wide a circuit. Ours is the easier task."

"Some may find this ease!" Fermac grunted. "Here have we ridden half the day, and found nothing. But for my nasal, my eyes had been scratched out long since. *Peste!* Now we can no longer ride even two abreast, and this is a rare spot for an ambush!"

Cercamon laughed gaily, to hide his mounting anxiety, The complexity of his schemes—necessary for their success—kept him fearful for their outcome; and the worst was that the decisive factor depended on others. Yet, as he had told the monk, there was a way out in case of failure.

THE DOG that had howled the night before fell silent as soon as Cercamon had removed his torch from the window. Soon after came the pound of galloping hoofs from somewhere amid the wheat—dying away to the westward. By midnight a horseman slid like a ghost into the wood just above the Auch-Fleurance road, and there dismounted.

All about him the undergrowth rustled, though there was no wind. Some one whistled, a series of four ascending notes; and the rider answered. Twigs cracked; mail rang softly; dim forms suddenly surrounded him in the cloud-veiled gloom. Only those closest—close enough to touch him—could be seen, and they only as shadows. The others could be guessed only by the faint sounds of their approach.

"Father Laurence?"

"Ay, lady." The horseman scarce spoke above a whisper. "The signal has come. Is all ready?"

"All are here. Will the way be clear?"

"For that we must trust the troubadour. I have confidence in him. His repute—"

"I know," Marguerite broke in. "I trust him also. But I see no purpose in his order that I wait in the cavern till you have done the work. This is my quarrel."

"He is right, my lady. If he has prepared the way for us, the work ahead will be short but bloody. If you went with us, a chance-sped arrow, a single sword-stroke, might end your life. What then of the plan, or of us? Fermac would remain master of Belle Gard, and we should be outlaws forever. But if you live, yet, though we all die, Cercamon will find a way to make you mistress of Belle Gard once more. His plan is best; you must lie close in the cavern, with four men, while we strike for you."

"But if they find me—" the girl protested.

"There, too, we must trust Cercamon. Remember, they have never yet found your lair; nor are they likely to now. The troubadour will mislead them."

"If aught goes wrong—"

"If we do not as he bids us, all will go wrong. How can he help us, if he counts on our doing that which we do not do? Now arm me, some of you."

Unseen hands brought the monk mail and helped him strip off his cassock. A shield was hung about his neck, a sword at his waist. Horses were led up, snorting.

"Ride!" Father Laurence commanded. "Back to the cavern, my lady!"

Hidden by the blackness of the overcast night, six and thirty men scrambled down to the road, and trotted some two miles in the direction of Fleurance. Then, at a word from their leader, they wheeled to the right, dashing through the fields on a line that would bring them out another two miles north of Belle Gard. Used to night work, the outlaws rode without straggling, keeping in touch by the sounds of hoof and harness.

"Pray God we pass not too close to them as they ride west!" spoke one who rode close to the monk.

"That is the troubadour's business, Guitard. He is no fool. He means to lead them as far southwest of the castle as we are north of it. They should pass without hearing us."

Nor did they meet a soul as they trampled through the ripening grain. At last, north and a little east of the castle, well out of hail from its walls, they rode into the wood from whence Fermac feared no foes.

"The first time we have crossed his line!" the monk muttered. "By God's grace, it will be the last!"

He crossed himself and led the way south through the forest. Now the hoofbeats were muffled by the leaf-fall of years, and they were forced to keep in touch by whistling. Again and again the signal, not too loud, ran up and down the column. After a time they drew to a walk, and then the work was easier.

Suddenly they were out among the last trees, with their faces toward the castle, though they could not see it.

"Dismount, lads!" the monk ordered. "We shall approach more safely on foot. The road is close."

They tethered their horses at the edge of the wood, then, on foot, stole softly across the open space between its edge and the hill. In the utter darkness their black surcoats were as invisible as if they had been so many ghosts. West, and above them, lights twinkled faintly from the tower, which otherwise was hidden.

"The watch, in the keep," Father Laurence commented. "Cercamon agreed to see to it that there would be few enough for us to deal with. Forward—up the road!"

They followed the winding way, climbing at a steady pace, till the castle lights twinkled almost above their heads. Then—

"To the left!" spoke the monk. "Straight up! Climb warily and keep touch!"

The hill was steep, but not badly broken. Its bareness would have been fatal to them by day, but now they were invisible. On and on they clambered, each reaching out every few steps to touch the man ahead. Arriving on the crest, they halted to fetch breath; then they gathered close.

"The postern—just ahead!" whispered Father Laurence to Guitard. "Pass the word along to walk softly, lest your mail make too much noise."

They moved on, so slowly that the meshes of their armor

scarce whispered. Now and then a displaced pebble rattled down the slope; but the only warders were in the keep, distant from them by the entire length of the bailey. Minutes that seemed hours dragged by ere they halted under the loom of the wall.

Father Laurence whistled softly—so softly that none could have heard him through the solid oaken leaves of the postern gate. Instantly—but slowly, lest steel rattle against leather—each man drew sword, save for a dozen in the forefront. These tightened their grips on the staves of their pikes.

Reversing his sword, Father Laurence beat loudly on the gate with the pommel.

"Open, open!" he roared, all the music gone from his voice, which he strove to make resemble that of Fermac. "Open, in the name of the Five Wounds!"

"Who comes?" challenged the muffled voice of the warder.

"Son of a dog!" howled the monk, following up the epithet with a mouthfilling oath—and crossing himself the while, lest his soul take harm. "Offspring of toads! Do you not know your lord's voice? Open, lest I quarter you? We have the Black Thief!"

"Straightway, straightway, lord!" quavered the warder. "But I am alone here, and must be sure—"

A bar creaked back; another, and the gate swung open.

Instantly the monk leaped within, crashing his hilt into the warder's face. Before the man could cry out, his throat was seized in iron fingers and squeezed till his eyeballs started. Two men bound him neatly with his own belt, gagged him with strips from his tunic and dropped him by the door.

"Bar the gate!" Father Laurence panted. "So!"

Pikes lowered, swords ready, the six and thirty advanced. Their mail gleamed dully in the scanty light of the single cresset at the gate, then vanished in the pool of blackness that was the bailey. But ahead, where the tower loomed, a second cresset flung a broad lane of light. Toward this they made.

They had almost reached it, when the arriere-port of the keep was flung open and a man-at-arms reeled out into the torchlight. From behind him came the loud voices of men who had feasted more merrily than wisely. The man-at-arms made a weaving way toward the stables, as if to look to what few beasts remained there. He had reached the center of the patch of light—widened by the opening of the port—when one of the outlaws moved restlessly and his armor rattled.

The man-at-arms brought up short, peering owlishly into the dark bailey.

"Who is there?" he called, his voice thick with wine.

Out of the dark a bowstring hummed, and an arrow feathered itself in the man's breast. He dropped full in the ring of light with a crash of mail, and sprawled on his face in a pool of his own blood.

THE TWANG of string and thud of the shaft would have been enough to warn the handful in the keep. They ran to the door, but stopped in their tracks at the clang of the steelclad body on the stones. Some dragged their comrades back, while others hurled themselves at the door, hoping to close and bar it. Three or four drew sword or ran for their spears.

In three bounds Father Laurence reached the port and hurled his broad shoulders against it just as it swung to. His impact forced it open a little way; then, while he struggled to keep the men-at-arms from closing it enough to drop the bar, his men crashed after him. Just in time they flung their weight against the heavy wood. It burst wide open. Through the archway hurtled the advance-guard of the outlaws. Father Laurence was thrown so far by the sudden give of the port that he crashed full into a cluster of men-at-arms.

Two of them he bowled over; a third fetched a swing at him with shortened sword. Fortunately the wine in the man's veins made his eyesight poor; the steel missed the monk's neck and, turning, drew blood lightly from his left arm. Then the guard-room became a shambles.

The ten who remained of those Fermac had left on guard were in no posture for defense. Father Laurence turned his point on those he had flung to the floor; of the rest, four had been hurled against one wall by the rebound of the door; the others clustered in a forlorn heap, backs to the stair. The outlaws flooded the guardroom, beating the luckless soldiers back against the walls by sheer weight and tearing the lives out of them in the first onslaught.

Only two escaped—scrambling up the stair in frantic terror, seeking some hiding-place. Behind them raced Guitard and the black-clad men of the forest, pitiless. If the fugitives had the advantage of knowing the castle, their pursuers had the numbers and ferocity of the wolf-pack. The wine dying in their veins, loss of blood sapping their strength, the two hunted cover in the chambers above. There they were brought to bay, cowering in corners, and despatched.

"Clean up the blood, some of you!" Father Laurence commanded. "Guitard, see to the clearing away of the corpses. No time to bury them—take them to the battlements, and cover them up. Leave not a trace of struggle—see that all is as it was. You, Blaise, take four men and ransack the mail-chests. Eight of you run to the wood and fetch in the horses. Make haste!"

Having spoken, he bent to the mangled bodies of the men-at-arms, intent on offering spiritual consolation; but only three still breathed. To these he ministered as tenderly as if they had been his brethren.

His orders were carried out quickly and well. The warder was brought in from the postern and hidden away in the cells beneath the keep; the blood in bailey and guardroom was wiped up and fresh sand strewn on the floor. Mail was broken out and distributed to eleven men, selected as well as possible for their resemblance in build and stature to the slain defenders. The rest, still clad in the black livery of their outlawry, were taken to the living quarters. A search of the chambers revealed the muddy surcoat which Cercamon had worn when he first came to Belle Gard; and in this, his room, the black-mailed majority of the invaders were hidden.

Descending to the guardroom, Father Laurence set the eleven he had furnished with castle mail to overhaul the gear of gate and portcullis, that they might operate the winches promptly and without slip when the time came. When they had mastered the simple mechanism, he nodded curtly.

"We are ready now. Stay—we should have a warden at the postern. You go, Guillaume. Now, lads, here is wine, and food. Eat what you will; but if ye drink one drop, ye will have the blood of all of us—our lady's, too—on your heads! Leave the cups about—spill some on the floor. When the time comes, act as if ye were drunk—but leave wine alone!"

Guillaume, who had departed for the postern, raised a shout in the bailey. Running out, Father Laurence found him with his long arms about a tubby, cassocked figure. Close by stood a horse, its reins trailing.

"The chaplain!" exclaimed the monk. "I had forgot him. If he had won free, we should have been dead men ere another day. Bring him within!"

The little priest hung back, struggling gallantly, though his fat face was white with terror. When they had him within the keep, Father Laurence doffed his helmet, and thrust his own shaven poll in the chaplain's face.

"Monk slays not priest," he said shortly. "You are safe, butter-tub. Clap him in a cell, give him good food and wine, and set him to saying masses for the slain!"

TOWARD DUSK Fermac wearied of the chase.

"By the halter of Judas!" he swore. "Never have I sweat so much since I fought in Syria. Where is the Black Thief, Troubadour? You promised me his whole band, and we have not seen so much as a single gallowsbird."

"Patience, good my lord," Cercamon answered. "I told you it would be a long hunt. The rascals are cunning, and on their own ground."

"By this time they have likely fled the county!" Fermac growled.

"How should they do that? You have the wood surrounded. They but lie close in some ravine or cave. We have only beaten the coverts. When you have drawn blank there, you will find the fox in his earth."

"Ay, but where, in the fiend's name, is his earth? Here we be, sixscore good men, and have not roused one bandit."

Cercamon had taken the lead, and took good care to direct the hunt as he thought best. As the baron's protests died down, he reined in, studied the thickets about them and pointed.

"There—to the left!"

"What?" snorted Fermac.

"A gap in the undergrowth—broken twigs."

He urged his gray into the opening.

"A deer-path!" Fermac grunted as they saw a narrow, deep-grooved way wind through a little glade.

"Not so—a man-path!"

Cercamon pointed again, and this time Fermac drew a deep breath.

"You are right. Hoof-marks. Lead on!"

Cercamon had knowingly swung back toward the point where they had entered the forest, and so cunningly had he confused the direction with back-casts and the search of side-openings that Fermac was not sure which way they headed. Taking his course from certain markings the monk had shown him as they came from the cavern the morning after he had left the Black Thief's lair—a tree with broken, hanging branch; a heap of stones, disposed apparently by accident—he had led the chase deliberately and surely toward the stream-pierced glen. Now he drew the man-hunters along the brink of its deepening channel till he knew the cave was not far distant.

"See how the way narrows!" he exclaimed. "It is bad work for horses here. The scroggy cliff there would make a rare lurking-place for archers. By your leave, my lord, I will go on alone and make sure the way is safe."

Weary, bathed in sweat beneath his mail, Fermac asked nothing better than a chance to rest.

"As you will," he agreed. "Be wary. If you meet danger, a call will bring us up."

Cercamon pressed on ahead, while Fermac and his archers dismounted in the glade and sprawled out on the soft grass. The horses began to crop contentedly. Only half a dozen pickets, posted on each side and in the path, kept careful watch.

Riding at an even, wary pace, Cercamon followed the narrowing path till he came out on the bridge. It lay in place, with the dark awning of the cavern barely showing beyond it through the screen of trees. Halting, Cercamon whistled softly.

A helmeted head thrust out.

"Ready, Sir Simon!" the troubadour called; and the outlaw knight vanished into the cave.

Almost at once he came forth again, leading his horse across the bridge. Three others followed him; and last of all, clad still in her black armor, came the lady Marguerite. Here eyes were tired, for excitement had not let her sleep.

"Is all well, Cercamon?" she asked.

"It should be, my lady, if Father Laurence has not forgot how to lead men since he turned monk. Fermac and his fellows are in this wood, running to and fro and sniffing like hounds at fault. Now is the time to steal away, but it will be hard to pass them. Follow me!"

The girl mounted and followed, the four of her bodyguard trailing behind. They rode on cautiously, in utter silence, lest the searching men-at-arms hear them. As they neared the little glade, Cercamon reined in, signing the others to stop, and peered through the screen of foliage.

Voices came to them, half drowned by the din of the stream. A distant horse winded their animals and neighed. Marguerite's mount answered. One of Fermac's outposts rode out, his horse's head thrusting into the path.

Turning a startled face over his shoulder, Cercamon cried:

"Flee! They are close! To the cave!"

The outlaws wheeled and dashed back as they had come, Marguerite and the troubadour bringing up the rear. Cercamon's sword was out. As the four bandits galloped around a turn of the trail, past which they could neither see nor be seen, Cercamon suddenly snatched at Marguerite's rein and forced her to a halt. Before she could comprehend, much less struggle, he swung her from the saddle and set her in front of him. His strong hands holding her there, he galloped back toward the glade. Shouts and the clang of arms rang before them.

Marguerite, astounded and in despair, strove to beat at him with her hands, to snatch the reins. But Cercamon held her in an iron grip.

"Trust me!" he cried in her ear. "Trust me, though I seem to betray you! And speak no word, however they may revile you."

They burst into the mouth of the glade and almost ran into the bunched column of archers that had sprung to the saddle at the alarm raised by their outpost. At sight of the sudden apparition—the mailed rider, clasping a struggling figure in black armor—Fermac pressed forward with a shout.

"The Black Thief!" Cercamon cried. "I bring you the Black Thief, Fermac!"

The baron's red face grinned with ferocious triumph.

"The Thief indeed!" he rejoiced. "Or one of his chief officers at least."

"Nay, the Thief himself," Cercamon insisted, holding the girl close in both his great arms. She was struggling like a wildcat. "See the quality of his mail!"

In her shapeless hauberk and swathing cloak, her hair and features hidden by the nasaled and curtained helmet, Marguerite easily passed for a slender man. Fermac drew back a huge palm to strike her; but Cercamon waved him back.

"The Thief is my prisoner, Sir Gaston," he protested. "It were ill done to lay hands on him till we get him safely within Belle

Gard. There we can determine what to do with him. I found him lying close among the trees."

"Alone?" questioned the baron.

"There was none other there when I seized him," Cercamon answered, hoping that the four outlaws had been screened from the outpost's sight by the turn of the path. "Now we had best get him back quickly, lest his men find some means of effecting a rescue."

The outpost held his peace, and Cercamon sighed with relief. Fermac nodded assent, merely drawing Marguerite's sword from its scabbard. There was no need to bind her, for she had collapsed, exhausted, in her captor's arms. He wound her arms close in her surcoat, lest she regain strength to struggle. Though she lay limp, her eyes glared at him, and he knew the bitterness in her heart. Well she understood the hopelessness of escape; the man who held her had muscles of iron; before and behind, the riders of Fermac had closed in. She knew, if Fermac did not, that of all her men only the four who had escaped were now in the forest. Those four would not have known of her betrayal till they reached the cave and missed her; then it would be too late. There would be nothing for them to do but hide and drag the bridge in after them. They, at least, were safe.

Cercamon called out directions to Fermac and Sir Marc, just ahead; and the word was passed on to the archers. Straight for the forest-edge and the highroad they made, and shortly after dark they scrambled down to it. There Cercamon called a halt.

"It were unwise to give up the hunt for the band so soon," he advised. "We have the leader, but there must be desperate fellows among them who will keep together and plot revenge. When we have crossed the fields, my lord, it were best to send back the archers, to renew the search."

"But the Thief—" Fermac began.

"You and Sir Marc and I are men enough to get the Thief safely into Belle Gard. All your men will be needed here in the forest, if you are to hunt down and crush these outlaws forever.

I would not be discourteous, my lord; but I bid you remember you are acting under commission from your master and mine, the Duke of Normandy. It is his will that the Black Thief's brigandage be ended. If your slackness lets his rascals escape, you must answer for it to the duke. I desire to see the affair ended in such a way that I may bring back a good report of you to him."

Fermac cursed; but for all his bluster and pride he was not anxious to draw down the duke's wrath.

"Splendor of heaven!" he growled. "Is it not as much to my interest as to the duke's that these *pouraille* should all dance on a rope? Be it as you will—but let us first ride to the foot of Belle Gard, lest by some cursed trick the dogs slip out and fall on us!"

So the troop urged their weary beasts across the fields and to the base of the castle hill. It was dark; and though the clank of their armor rang loud to the rise and fall of the horses, they were lost in a sea of night, out of which the lights of the keep shone as shore-beacons.

"Now send the men back, my lord," Cercamon insisted. "They have provisions. By night the outlaws have twice the chance to escape that they have by day. Having lost their chief, whose cunning enabled them to evade you, they should fall an easy prey if your officers press the search."

Weary as Fermac was, it suited his mood to let his men finish the work; and the capture of the Thief had given him fresh confidence of the outcome.

"Your advice is good," he grunted. "You have done well by me thus far. Praise the Saints, but you are a shrewd man, thus to take, without help, him who is worth all the rest!"

He ordered the archers back to the forest. Unwillingly they obeyed, with the ease and comfort of Belle Gard so close; but they knew their master too well to protest. Once out of earshot, they took out their discontent in railing against the troubadour.

As they ascended the castle road, Cercamon bent down in the dark to whisper in his captive's ear:

"Trust me now more than ever, lady. The men in the castle are your own. You must contrive to make some sign to them; for otherwise the sight of you, a prisoner, will rouse them to fury. It will wreck my schemes, and imperil you, if they strike too soon!"

His anxiety had mounted to the point where all his self-command was needed to compose his features. Playing for more than the mere defeat of Fermac, he greatly feared what might happen if the monk had taken the castle as they had planned and misunderstood that part of the plan which Cercamon had not confided to him.

The three men with their prisoner halted at the great gate, exhausted, stiff-limbed, while Fermac sounded his horn.

"Who comes?" rang the challenge.

"I—Fermac, ye pigs!" the baron growled. "Open—I am weary!"

THE GATE screamed on its hinges, in sorry tune with the screech of the portcullis in its wooden slides. The three horses clattered across the flags; gate and portcullis closed. Fermac scarce glanced at the handful of men-at-arms in the guardroom; though they started forward, muttering fiercely, at sight of the captive. Cercamon felt their eyes boring into him, and saw smouldering fire in their glances.

"Now, lady!" he breathed to Marguerite. "They are your men—and Fermac in their power. Give them a sign!"

As he dismounted with his prisoner, one or two of the garrison advanced, hands edging toward their hilts. Fermac heard and saw, but took their emotion as a demonstration against the captured Thief, who had often slain his stragglers. Bending over Marguerite the better to hide his hands, Cercamon made swift gestures at them. He pointed up once; then, with two rapid motions, he indicated Fermac and Marc. A shrug of his shoulders toward the gate tried to convey the understanding that all Fermac's men were left behind; then, with both hands, he motioned the seeming men-at-arms to stand aside. Meantime—

praying that Father Laurence had indeed taken the castle and that these were his men, for their armor hid their features—he felt danger and failure very close.

Fermac caught his last gesture.

"What now?" he grumbled.

"Your lads would have laid rough hands on our prisoner," he answered. "I warned them off."

Marguerite turned her head wearily, to stare Cercamon full in the eyes; then she turned to scan the men-at-arms. Recognizing that in Cercamon's truthfulness lay her one chance of life, she took that chance. She nodded once, almost imperceptibly, to the men in mail and, freeing one hand, laid it on Cercamon's arm. The men's eyes flashed recognition; one of them raised a hand and passed it along his steel-masked nose. Cercamon drew a deep breath as he saw the signal; for it meant that the men, too, understood—at least enough to let him carry his game a little further toward its end.

Fermac, as if he felt the men's grim glances at his broad back, wheeled about.

"Well?" he barked from the stair. "Bring him up, Troubadour. Follow, Gui—you too, Reinard. Why in Lucifer's name do ye tarry?"

Picking the girl up bodily, Cercamon mounted the stair. Two of the men, starting tardily as they realized the rôles they must play, followed. Cercamon's back still prickled; he was not yet sure the men understood enough to know that he had not played falsely with them. He was somewhat consoled, however, at the assurance that these were truly Marguerite's men. This was plain, though they wore castle mail—plain from their start toward him when they recognized the captive; plainer from their response to her signs. But if they mistook his purpose now, his first warning of their error would be a foot of steel in the back.

But he reached the stairhead safely and entered the hall behind Fermac and de Lot. The two mailed men halted at the door, standing guard one on each side.

Fermac stalked on to the dais and flung himself down in his great chair as one who means to deal out justice; yet he sprawled in a weariness that lacked all dignity. He turned his great head toward the kitchens.

"Ho, there!" he bawled. "Hot meat! Wine!"

A sleepy varlet thrust his tousled head through the door.

"Eh?" he yawned; and then, his face blanching, "My lord! What—food and wine? Of a surety, my lord!"

He vanished, trembling, and there rose the protests of wakened servants. A great bustling followed; the crackle of fires, and the smell of meat.

Fermac sprawled back in his seat, yawning cavernously. De Lot and Cercamon waited, as they must needs do, for the master of the castle to act. But Fermac had no thought of anything but food; and he was determined to eat before dealing with his prisoner. So all abided his will; Cercamon and Sir Marc impassive, Marguerite with white, set face and questioning eyes, and the men on guard at the door with a grimness of posture and a thrust of the jaw that boded ill for some one.

At last, as the servants scurried in with food, Cercamon rose.

"Give me leave but for a moment, my lord," he spoke. "And pray you, proceed not against the prisoner till I return."

Fermac nodded. Cercamon made his way to the door, where the two on guard stiffened suddenly, eyes doubtful, hands creeping toward hilts.

"Steady!" Cercamon whispered. "I go to inform the monk."

"He knows," one muttered back. "Play no tricks on us, Troubadour!"

"Tricks, fool?" Cercamon answered softly. "They are but two, and ye many. Be wise—stir not till I give the signal. There is more to this than ye guess."

They fell back to let him pass. Crossing to his chamber, he entered, closing the door behind him.

The room was packed with black-mailed men, who closed

in about him, silently. Father Laurence, stalwart above the rest, faced him with suspicious eyes.

"What treachery is this?" he demanded. "You bid my lady stay behind till we have won the place for her; then you bring her here a captive. Men ride behind you—we heard them approach—then ride away again. If you have plotted to betray us to Fermac's spears, you shall not live to see them enter!"

Cercamon regarded him calmly.

"I could not tell you all," he replied, "else you would not have consented to my plan. Nor can I tell you yet. I pledge you my word that she is safe. When I go out, do you and your men steal into the corridor and wait at the hall door. There are none of Fermac's men nearer than the forest; you hold the castle, and only Fermac and de Lot are here to oppose you. When I call, or you hear the clash of steel, enter—but do not interfere with any save as I bid."

Father Laurence eyed him steadily.

"I do not understand," he said; "but what you say is true. We do hold the place. I see not how you can betray us. Eight men are below, holding the gate; there are five on the parapet."

Cercamon turned his back and went to the hall.

Fermac and de Lot were eating; but Marguerite sat where she had been placed, and there was no food before her. Cercamon turned to his host with a courteous gesture; but there was an angry glint in his gray-green eyes.

"Does not a thief eat, my lord?" he asked.

Fermac laughed gustily.

"This one does not. What use? He will grace my gallows tomorrow."

"Then let him eat, that the birds may have fatter pickings," he retorted.

The idea amused Fermac, and he bade the servants set food before the captive. As the troubadour hoped, she had wit enough not to remove the disguising helmet, though it impeded her eating somewhat. She took little food, glancing at Cercamon between listless bites. He fell to with lusty appetite.

When all had finished, and the cups were refilled, Fermac rose, raising his beaker.

"To you, Troubadour!" he spoke, his voice full and merry again. "To you, who have given my enemy into my hands! You are indeed cunning, as men call you. Ha, Black Thief! No more shall you rob my baggage-trains! A day or two, and all your band shall swing from my merlons, as you shall swing tomorrow!"

Cercamon moved toward the prisoner and laid one hand on her shoulder.

"By your leave, Sir Gaston," he said, and there was a new ring of authority in his voice, "the Black Thief is not yours to hang. I was sent by Duke Henry to kill or capture him; you but acted under my orders. You have seen my commission, and know that I speak truth."

Marguerite raised her eyes to the troubadour; they were bitter again, and so scornful that he would have turned aside. Her lips, moving softly, barely framed the words:

"You bade me trust you! Now you confess you were sent against me. You have betrayed me from the first!"

"Peace!" he whispered back. "Your own men guard you."

Their speech did not escape Fermac.

"What means this?" he cried suspiciously. "You will not let me hang him? You whisper with him? By St. Peter's sword, you plot to save him!"

Cercamon reached out and snatched off Marguerite's helmet. Her long hair, loosely coiled, fell about her face; her fair features, were revealed.

"A woman!" Fermac cried.

He sprang from the dais, seized a torch and strode to her.

"Death of my life! Marguerite de Belle Gard!"

HE STOOD like one turned to stone, staring at her, helpless to speak. The girl's eyes blazed hate at him. Cercamon watched them a moment, then let his glance drift to Marc de Lot. The young knight hunched forward in his chair, his strong face rigid with astonished emotion.

"Will you hang the Black Thief now, Fermac?" Cercamon asked silkily.

Mastering his confusion, the baron answered:

"Since the Thief is none other than Dame Marguerite—and you know of it, though I understand not how—I will spare her life on one condition. She shall either marry me, as I once asked her to, or grace my gibbet!"

Marc de Lot sprang to his feet.

"No!" he cried. "This is unknightly! Thief or no thief, she is a woman, and of gentle blood. You can not hang her—it were the deed of a devil! Nor can any man of honor force a girl to wed him under threat of death!"

Cercamon, leaning against the table by the girl's side, smiled at him.

"You are the man I hoped to find you, Marc," he said. "He is right, Fermac. Having no right of high, low, and middle justice, you can not doom to death one of gentle blood, nor one not subject to you. You and she are both vassals to the Duke of Normandy, who alone can judge between you. You shall neither hang her nor marry her."

Fermac wheeled on him with blazing eyes.

"You are in league with her!" he shouted. "In league with a bandit! Though the duke were twenty times my liege lord, neither you nor he shall interfere with my will! Her lands are mine, my lawful grant. She shall either confirm my right to them by giving me her hand, or she shall die, and be henceforth out of my way!"

The two guards at the door moved forward tensely; but Cercamon shook his head. Understanding at last the rôle he played, they obeyed his signal.

"Her lands are yours by right of murder, Fermac!" he spoke

softly, and though he moved not, his muscles set for a swift spring. "You slew her father, an old man and sick, in his bed; you took his castle by the foulest treachery!"

Fermac, beside himself with rage, cast aside all caution.

"However I took it, I hold it!" he bellowed. "You have played me false, Troubadour, and you shall pay. Guards! Seize him!"

The two at the door laughed mockingly. Their defiance told Fermac that he was outwitted, though he mistook the manner.

"You have bribed my men!" he roared. "Hold them off, Marc!" Whipping out his sword, he rushed at Cercamon.

De Lot threw himself between them, even as Cercamon's hand shot to his hilt.

"My uncle!" the young man cried, his face ghastly. "Is it truth he speaks? Did you murder Jaufre de Belle Gard? When I came to you two years since I heard this tale and flogged a peasant for spreading it. You told me Jaufre died in fair fight, sword in hand. Was it false? Have I given my service and love to a dastard?"

Fermac struck at him with clenched fist.

"Out of my way, squeamish fool! What matters it to you what means I took, so that I won to power? Are you a woman, to blanch at a man's deeds? Curse you, get hence, and let me deal with this rascally minstrel!"

"Ay, do you get hence, Marc," Cercamon urged. "He had insulted me, threatened me—and I must answer him. Clear the way, lad!"

With a full-arm heave he shot the young man crashing against the dais. Leaping back from Fermac's instant thrust, he flashed out his blade and struck in one swift motion. Steel clanged on steel, as the two men hacked and lunged, both shieldless, both resolute to kill.

Fermac's rush had brought his back to the door and the two on guard there. They had drawn steel, and strained like hounds on the leash.

"In, ye two!" Marguerite cried at them. "Seize him!"

The disguised outlaws leaped to do her bidding; but on their very heels the door burst open, vomiting black-mailed men. Marc de Lot, his own sword drawn, faced the two who ran against Fermac.

"Hands off!" he ordered.

His mind was awhirl with consternation that these two, whom he took for his uncle's men, should obey the girl's bidding; but, though the inrush of the outlaws enlightened him in terrible fashion, surprize did not blunt his wits nor stay his hand. A second more, and he would have been at blows with them.

"Down arms, lads!" rang the bell-like voice of Father Laurence. "Ye fools, this is a private quarrel! Your lady is safe!" Leaping past de Lot's weapon, he sprang with buffeting hands at the two pretended men-at-arms. They whirled; but recognizing him, they sheathed weapons.

With a few sharp commands, he brought his men to heel, marshalled them about Marguerite, and waited, his fine eyes following the duel with unfeigned ardor. Marc, gasping at sight of the black surcoats, stood helpless to one side. Uncertain what to do against so many, his sense of right and justice wounded by the sudden knowledge of his uncle's baseness, he could fight on neither side. Nor was there any fight to join just then, save for the lashing duel between Fermac and the troubadour.

Those two were now at the very dais, exchanging blows so fast that the steel flashed like incessant lightning, and the clangor of steel on steel almost deafened the ears. His whole soul bent on killing the man who had thwarted him, Fermac had neither eyes nor ears for the inrush of the outlaws. If he heard them at all, he took them for his own men from the guardroom. His blazing eyes were fixed on Cercamon's; his mind and arm were given wholly to his sword.

Cercamon fought coolly, but with every ounce of strength and nerve. Fermac was not a foe to be played with. A giant in strength, he was also a born swordsman, trained in many battles. The pair were well-matched: Fermac's greater height was balanced by the troubadour's amazing length of arm; what Cercamon lacked in weight he gained in the power of his huge shoulders; such advantage as lay in his thrice-polished skill he lost to Fermac's desperate fury.

Slowly Cercamon gave ground, setting his feet daintily, like a cat's; and Marguerite bit her lip deep as she saw him retreat. His parries seemed to lack force, and they who watched were certain that the strength ebbed from his arms. Yet his thrusts were as fierce as ever when his edge descended, Fermac's upflung blade took them with a grinding clash that portrayed the fury of the strokes. The baron followed his advantage hard, taking every inch of ground his adversary yielded, leaping in with stroke and stab that Cercamon seemed scarce to evade.

Yet, even as he gave way, Cercamon began to smile. Fermac's slashes slithered from his sloping guard as surely as if he had wasted more strength in meeting them; Fermac's breast was beginning to heave. A sudden snake-like thrust opened the mail above the baron's thigh and drew a thin stream of red.

Maddened by the pain, Fermac flailed in with a backstroke so terrible that the staring beholders thought to see Cercamon cut half in two and Marguerite gave a piercing shriek of fear. But Cercamon had leaped from under the descending blade, which bit the edge of the dais, and he recovered even as Fermac wrenched his point from the wood. In and out, out and in licked the troubadour's point, swifter than eye could follow; and Fermac was forced to give ground in his turn.

A little patch above his breast was reddening; his breath came in sobs. Cercamon, his lips humming a song, pressed the giant back and back, his blade weaving a flickering circle before the baron's eyes. He feinted with the point, drew Fermac's guard and leaped in with a swift cross-slash from the elbow. Fermac crashed to the floor, his throat torn half in two.

Marguerite gave a deep sigh and fell forward over the table. De Lot stood rigid, horror in his eyes. Even as the outlaws raised a hoarse cheer, the monk turned on them.

"To the battlements, you! No man knows how soon the avengers will be here!"

They fled; and he bent over Marguerite. She had not fainted, as he thought; but her shoulders heaved with sobs. She looked up at the monk's touch.

"I thought him a traitor!" she groaned. "Mercy of Heaven, I thought him a traitor!"

"So did I, for a moment," Father Laurence answered. "I do not understand him now. He is a man, that troubadour."

SIR GUITARD, down from the tower, reported the plain empty in the gray light of dawn.

"Fermac's hounds still hunt the coverts, then," Father Laurence muttered. "We are safe for a little longer."

None had gone to bed that night; the thrill and horror of what had befallen, and the peril from Fermac's absent garrison, forbade thought of sleep.

Cercamon had drawn Sir Marc into one corner of the hall, and was speaking to him earnestly.

"It would have come to this, or worse," the troubadour urged. "He was an evil man; you would have come to dishonor in his service. Look you: You can not fight me, for I killed him in fair combat. It was a base thing he meant to do with the girl."

De Lot faced him at last.

"You are right," he said dully. "He deserved his fate, and you have righted a great wrong. But—he was my mother's brother!"

"I knew it, lad," Cercamon answered kindly. "For your sake, and for naught else, I gave him his chance. When I asked him if he would hang a woman, I hoped he would say no. Had he given way then, I would have held off yonder black-coats, and taken him with Lady Marguerite to Duke Henry, who would have judged fairly between them. I meant even to ask the duke to pardon him, on condition that he restore her lands. But he showed himself vile, so that there was naught to do save slay him."

He had turned as he spoke, so that his words reached Marguerite.

"It was for this," she exclaimed, "that you feigned to deliver me into Fermac's hands? That he might have his chance to show mercy?"

Cercamon shot her an amused glance.

"Nay, not that. That was to satisfy my honor. I promised you to win back your castle for you; and I have done it. But to help you I had first to gain Fermac's confidence; and to that end I was forced to promise him that I would deliver the Black Thief into his hands. Also I had bound myself to Duke Henry to capture or slay the Black Thief. I have now fulfilled all three promises.

"But under Fermac's roof I met young Marc here, who is a man and a cavalier. So, hoping to spare him sorrow, I resolved to let Fermac show his chivalry, if he had any. For this reason I revealed your face to him. He disappointed me."

Sir Marc raised his unhappy eyes.

"You have acted like the gentleman all men take you for," he said. "It can not even be said that you betrayed my uncle's hospitality; for the very food and wine he gave you, the roof that sheltered you, he had falsely stolen from Lady Marguerite. To me you have been generous indeed. But—"

"But the earth has crumbled beneath your feet," Cercamon interposed not unkindly. "You have found your kinsman wanting in honor, have seen him slain, and your service bloodily ended. You know not what to do with your life. Come, I—"

Marguerite, on impulse, interrupted.

"There is still a home for you at Belle Gard, Sir Marc!" she cried warmly. "I have no quarrel with you, who have done me no wrong. Take service under my pennon!"

"Lady!" cried Marc, his eyes blazing. "After all, yon dead dog was of my blood!"

Marguerite flushed, stammering regrets.

His own back turned full on the embarrassed girl, Cercamon drew de Lot aside.

"Lad," he pleaded, "can you take my hand, for all the blood on it?"

"Why not?" Marc answered. "You are such a man as I have prayed to be!"

His hand gripped Cercamon's hard.

"Then ride with me to Caen!" the other urged. "Take service with my master the duke, who loves men with strong arms and clean hearts. Is he not your overlord? Proud will I be to ride with such a comrade!"

For a space Marc answered not; then, with dragging steps, he walked to the covered corpse of Fermac. Long he looked down on it, tears gathering in his eyes.

"I will empty my purse in masses for his soul!" he said at length. "And—aye—I will go with you!"

Mailed feet clanged suddenly on the stair and hammered on the landing. As all turned toward the door, Guitard rushed in.

"Horsemen on the plain!" he shouted. "Fermac's men!"

"To the wall!" Father Laurence ordered. "Troubadour, will you hold the gate?"

Cercamon laughed.

"No need!" he answered. "Trust to me—and to Marc de Lot. Come, comrade!"

He led the way down the stair, and sent two men from the guardroom for horses. Once mounted, with de Lot in the saddle beside him, he bade the gate be opened.

"You will confirm what I say?" he asked; and as the grind of the portcullis drowned all words, de Lot nodded.

The outlaws in the guardroom stared after them and would have left the gate open against their return; but Cercamon shouted back that they must close up swiftly. Afraid for him, but more for themselves and their lady, they obeyed.

Cercamon pointed down across the plain. Jogging forward

through the sea of wheat came a weary procession. Spearmen, archers, worn to the bone with two nights and a day of sleepless toil, rode weary nags back from their fruitless search for the Black Thief's band. Horses and riders came on in disarray, heads down, spear-points weaving drunkenly in the morning light.

"There is no fight left in them!" laughed Cercamon.

He pricked the gray forward, down the twisting castle road, and Marc held even with him. They met the riders well out in the fields. Halting his men at sight of them, one of the knight-officers advanced, scarce able to hold his crest aloft.

"We have found—nothing!" he croaked.

"We have found much!" Cercamon answered. "To make all short, we have found you masterless. Fermac is dead."

"Dead!" gasped the knight; and "Dead?" echoed up and down the startled column.

All eyes stared at the herald of misfortune who but twelve hours since had ridden forth with them and their lord.

"Aye, dead. The Lady Marguerite rules in Belle Gard. In the name of Henry, Duke of Normandy, Brittany and Anjou, lord of Maine, Touraine, Poitou and Gascony, I command you to keep the duke's peace and ride hence without disturbance!"

The officer stared at him in dull anger, while the men-at-arms exchanged startled looks and questions.

"What jest is this?" the knight blazed.

"No jest, but grim earnest, if you disobey! Here is my warrant from the duke—read it if you will. Ye are his subjects, and a gallows waits the man who disregards the commands I lay on you in his name. Sir Marc—whom ye know, and whose orders ye have taken—will vouch for my word."

"It is as he says," de Lot assented. "Your master is dead, and ye will do well to heed Cercamon's word. Otherwise I myself will give you your dismissal, and the duke's hand will rest heavy on your heads. Go—Belle Gard has no more need of you!"

A murmur rose among the men—mercenaries all.

"Our pay! Who gives us our wages?"

"Take the mail on your backs, and your horses, for pay!" Marc answered. "They are worth more than a year's wages!"

Only a moment they hesitated; then, as with one accord, the men-at-arms wheeled about and rode wearily toward the highway. They were indeed overpaid; nor was there any other course open.

The knight alone stood his ground.

"How did my master die?" he asked hotly. "How come ye safe from the fate that destroyed him, ye two?"

De Lot frowned, but Cercamon found speech before him.

"If you think that your concern," he answered smoothly, "I, who slew your master, will do as much for you!"

The knight looked once into the glowing blue-green eyes, whirled his charger and spurred the beast into a reeling gallop.

"Now, lad!" Cercamon cried gaily, "for Normandy!"

"But—but—" de Lot protested. "They wait us in the castle— we have not said farewell!"

He pointed back to the keep, where a slender figure in black stood upon the battlements, against the golden background of the new day.

"Bah!" cried Cercamon. "I like not to be thanked. Forward!"

BROTHERS-IN-ARMS

I T H A S been told how Henry Plantagenet, lord of northern France from Seine of the sea, wedded Aliénor of Aquitaine, and with her won the better part of the south, with its fine towns and fiery fighting men. But how the thing came about makes a better tale, in which Cercamon the troubadour and Pierre Faidit, his friend, played perilous parts.

The two comrades sat in Pierre's chamber, high in the keep of Chinon West Castle, just under the fat bulge of the battlements. Pierre gazed moodily down upon the steep red roofs of the town and the sun-washed plain beyond, through which the broad Vienne wound in gracious contours. Through the one embrasure the April light filtered scantily in past his broad shoulders, and struck fire from the angry eyes of the troubadour.

"It is a graceless thing," Cercamon cried, "with no good in it!"

Pierre shrugged, and was silent, chewing his bitter thoughts. For some time neither spoke again, their thoughts grappling with the strange things that had happened this fortnight past.

It was 1152, in an early, lush spring; and Henry Plantagenet had moved his court from Caen in the north to Chinon in mellow Touraine. No sooner were his orders given than messengers—swift, secret messengers—stole off by night to take the news where it would be most valued: to London and to Paris. Stephen of England, whose crown Henry claimed, was surprized and joyous at the tidings, having expected his foe to use the fine spring weather for a swift stroke at the Channel ports; but Louis of France ceased to sleep of nights.

Count of Anjou and lord of Maine, Duke of Normandy and Brittany, master of Touraine, Henry Plantagenet coveted a yet wider realm. Being well served, and possessed of the huge frame and dominating temper of his race, he stood every chance of getting what he wanted. It was the full knowledge of these things that made King Stephen bless the Saints when Henry's spears were removed far south of the Channel—and the same knowledge made Louis VII curse the day he had wasted the strength of France in a futile crusade.

In Henry's own court there were those who guessed much, and shrewdly, concerning this journey to Chinon. For not only princes, but barons, had their spies out, knowing that this year was big with the fate of Europe. Every man who boasted noble blood and had swords to fight for him waited on events to fling himself into the mad scramble for lands and power; every prince watched his barons, fearing to read the treachery he suspected in their hearts.

But though some guessed why Henry left the coast across from England just when all was ripe for a second conquest of the island, few were right. For all his youth, his wild Plantagenet temper and his boisterous ways, Henry kept his plans close in his own red head, letting the world whisper itself hoarse.

His brother Geoffrey—a precocious, handsome lad, whom men liked as much as he liked women—was by turns sullen and feverishly excited, ripe for rebellion. He had asked Henry for Touraine and Anjou, and had received only three castles, including the double stronghold of Chinon. Now Henry was his guest in Chinon, and Geoffrey found himself unable to give commands even in his own house. But he, too, was a Plantagenet, ready to take what was refused him. Only Henry had brought three times as many men as Geoffrey could muster. So Geoffrey went about, very softly, making friends of dangerous men. By the time the beeches had opened their vivid leaves the soft April air was sultry with conspiracy. The ladies were discontent, for their lovers deserted them to mutter together in corners, or to grind their swords.

All this was bad enough, but to Cercamon the troubadour it was not the worst. Pierre, his dearest friend, his brother-in-arms, had lost the duke's favor. Cercamon himself still kept his place of honor at Henry's table, received generous largesse whenever it pleased him to lift his perfect voice in song and was courted by all who desired the ducal smile; but all this was less than nothing beside the injustice that had been done his friend. Pierre took it well, which but made Cercamon the bitterer.

"Why? Why?" he cried for the fiftieth time. "What have you done to displease him?"

Pierre twisted his big shoulders.

"Nothing. But it is his will."

"Bah! He is a petulant boy, this duke!" Cercamon was angry, his blue-green eyes blazing in his hot, handsome face.

"Has he forgotten all you have done to serve him? Does he not know it is to you, no less than to Thomas Becket, that he owes his strength in England? Have you not risked your life for him a thousand times, ay, and saved his?"

Pierre got up from his uncomfortable seat in the embrasure and stretched himself to his full height. He towered above his friend, a man in the prime of life, immensely tall, with the strength and grace of a gladiator. His dark, lean face, clear-cut and hawk-like as any Roman Cæsar's, was bitten deep with the lines of care and fatigue; his great dark eyes were heavy with pain. None would have guessed him a year younger than the light-hearted troubadour.

"Look you, lad," he said quietly, "Henry is our master, and it is a man's duty to serve his master well. I take that to mean without complaining. Think you it will help either of us to rail at him?"

He turned, took down from the wall his baldric and un-sheathed his great sword. Squatting on the floor, he laid the beautiful weapon across his knees, and began to rub its perfect edge with a fine hone. The stone whispered against the blue, damascened steel; the sun, slanting in a thick beam, struck fire from the jeweled hilt. As he caressed the blade, the sorrow vanished from his eyes and his thin lips relaxed in a faint smile.

Cercamon watched him with understanding. Pierre de l'Espée—Pierre of the Sword—ay, he was well named. By the sword he lived; he loved his sword; no man in France was his equal in duel or *mêlée*. His sword was to him what wife and children are to other men: there was comfort in the mere touch of it.

"I ride to Angers within the hour," Cercamon broke the silence, "on the duke's errand. I am to escort his mother, the Lady Mathilde, to Chinon. That means there is something afoot. He always seeks her counsel when he plans some bold stroke."

Pierre looked up with interest.

"You do not know? He has not confided in you?"

The troubadour shook his long locks.

"No. And that is strange, too. Till lately you and I both shared his secrets; but for this fortnight past he has taken neither of us into his counsels. I must ride now. Remember this, Pierre:

If he wrongs you further, he wrongs me, and I will hold him to account. We are brothers-in-arms."

Pierre sheathed his sword with a clang.

"Ay, we are brothers-in-arms," he answered fondly. "For that reason my loyalty is your loyalty, and you shall not act, speak or think against the duke till I do."

Cercamon laughed dryly.

"That will be never! Well, so be it; I have some name for loyalty myself."

He departed, his gay crimson-and-blue mantle flaunting behind him.

Pierre hung up sword and baldric and slowly went down the stair. He reached the inner bailey just in time to see his friend spur over the drawbridge, velvet cap ablaze in the sun. A group of Henry's Norman nobles stood gazing after him.

"OUR PRETTY bird goes to sing in some lady's bower!" sneered one, a tall, lean man in a rich silken robe. "A fine thing, truly, that men of birth must bow to such as he!"

"Ay!" growled a thick-barreled knight in rusty mail. "And our nightingale is but a cuckoo after all. I have heard it said he knows not his own father!"

He who had spoken first turned at the crunch of Pierre's mailed feet on the flags; and at sight of Pierre's eyes his swarthy face paled. He plucked at his companion's sleeve. But Pierre was on them in one long stride. Grasping the big man's shoulder with fingers that stung through the mail, he whirled him about.

"Sir Ormeric D'Orbec," he said quite softly, "it ill beseems a gentleman to say in another's absence what he dares not say to his face. If Cercamon were here, you would be the first to fawn on him. Since he is not here, I, his friend, tell you you lie!"

D'Orbec started back, his eyes wide with fear. Then, seeing that Pierre wore no weapon, he drew his hard features into a sneer.

"Fine words!" he mocked. "If a gentleman had spoken them, I would make him eat steel. But one does not fight with such as you—the son of a fisherman!" He pinched his nose with his fingers, as if to shut out the stench of rotten herring. The lean man beside him laughed and imitated the gesture.

Pierre understood. Knowing he had lost the duke's favor, the proud Norman nobles, long jealous of his influence at court, now made the most of their chance to humiliate him. The duke would not protect Pierre from insult now—and men who feared to cross swords with him could refuse to give him satisfaction on the ground of his low birth.

"You will insult me—and not fight?" he spoke gently.

D'Orbec drew back a little from the flame in his eyes, but answered insolently.

"I fight only with my equals!"

"Then go bicker with the dogs for bones!" roared Pierre, and drove his fist into D'Orbec's face. The thick Norman crashed to the pavement, and lay still.

The lean man half-drew his sword, but dropped his hands as Pierre advanced on him.

"You shall pay for this!" he snarled, backing away. "Ay, with the last drop of your blood!"

"Strike in the dark, then, Sir Hugo D'Orbec!" Pierre retorted grimly.

THE TORCHES made the great hall stifling, and from every arrow-slot the tapestries were drawn back to let in the cooler outside air. A nightingale sang somewhere in the dark; but the knights and ladies of Henry's court, preoccupied with food and drink and laughter, scarce heard. The merriment was forced. All felt a tension in the air, for the duke was angry.

Henry Plantagenet sat at the head of the table on the dais, as beseemed a man master wherever he lodged. On his right sat his brother Geoffrey; but few had eyes for the lithe, blond boy. Henry, flushed of face, big-limbed, sat with his elbows on the table, chin cupped in his great hands, his eyes glaring like a wounded lion's.

A man appeared in the doorway, and straightway all fell silent. Men paused with tankards halfway to their bearded lips; white-necked women peered over the shoulders of their table-mates to see the better. Geoffrey Plantagenet leaned back in his chair, watching through half-closed eyes. His cheeks grew flushed as his brother's; his hands shook with excitement.

Slowly the man came forward toward the dais, halted and bowed low.

The duke leveled an accusing finger at him.

"Pierre Faidit!" he cried—and his voice was a maddened bellow—"Pierre Faidit! You have struck a Norman knight—you, a man of no birth! By the splendor of heaven, I will make an example of you!"

Pierre's head went up, and his eyes met the angry duke's full.

"There was a time, my lord," he said with quiet dignity, "when you would have forgiven me more than this. I trust you may forgive me now, when you know the provocation."

Henry rose, struggling for self-control. His big features worked with passion. At last, every muscle rigid, he spoke; and every face in the hall, save Pierre's, was white and frightened. The duke had seldom been so moved. When men had seen him so before, he had wreaked his wrath with a fury not to be forgotten; nor did innocent onlookers always escape.

But now he was calm—calm as a sultry day, just before lightning strikes.

"We have done you too much honor," he said, with a gentleness that stung. "You have grown to regard yourself as the equal of better men. We must teach you humility. From this night on you are no longer captain of our guard. Lay no hand on a Norman gentleman again, lest that which befall you be a terror to all France. Go to your chamber, and bide there till I send for you!"

Pierre withdrew, his head higher than ever; but his eyes stung with restrained tears of rage and humiliation. Deus! How he had served this tempestuous boy, ay, loved him! What a reward for his labor, his sacrifice, the blood he had gladly given! Shamed before all the court! When he reached the corridor his proud, firm step faltered; he stumbled up the stair to his chamber.

Ormeric D'Orbec, his face swathed in bandages, glared after him. His brother's eyes met his across the table. Hugo raised his black eyebrows; Ormeric nodded and grinned wickedly. The knights and ladies, seeing the cloud lift from their lord's brow, heaved a great sigh of relief, and fell to food and laughter.

Pierre sat for many hours in his dark chamber, staring out at the stars and the lights of the town mirrored in the dark bosom of the Vienne. He had never known such wretched- ness—nay, not since that bitter night, five years since, when he had stumbled over the dead body of his first lord, Alphonse- Jourdain of Toulouse. But there was a bitterness in this. The injustice of it, the cruelty!

His door creaked open, but he scarce heard it, and did not stir. Then a voice—

"Pierre!"

Pierre started to his feet. The voice was stern and hoarse. The door closed, and an unseen hand shot the bolts home.

"Ay, lord!" Pierre answered, the words scarce audible.

"Where are you, Pierre?"

Then, as his eyes grew accustomed to the dark, he saw Pierre by the window. Swiftly Henry Plantagenet strode to his officer's side, and flung one thick arm about his shoulders.

"Pierre! Forgive me!"

"My—my lord! You are not angry with me?"

The duke would have knelt at his feet, but Pierre prevented him. He did not understand, but a great gladness flooded his heart. For a moment the duke fought for words, like the awkward boy he was; then they came surging:

"My knights—even my barons——were jealous of the favors I have shown you. They murmur that I take you, a peasant's son, into my secrets, and pay no heed to them, the gentlefolk. They hate you, Pierre. The time draws near when I must strike for England. God knows it is you—you and Becket—who have won me friends there, that your valor and your cunning have gained me adherents without whose aid I should not dare to strike. But from the moment my ships anchor in an English port, it is my barons and their men-at-arms who will win the throne for me. Without their loyal support I can do nothing. To hold them to me, I must sacrifice you. For this reason I have lately denied you my confidence, shamed you, taken away your commission—and it may be that I must wrong you yet more. Can you bear this, Pierre, for me? Knowing that it is only for a little while, and that, as soon as I dare, I will more than atone? Knowing that your lord loves you, Pierre?"

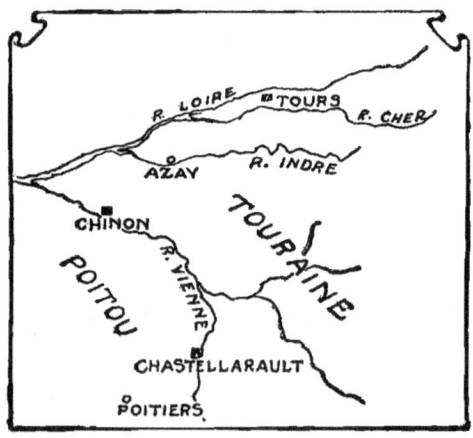

The swordsman groped in the dark for his master's hand.

"All this, and more, will I bear, if it may help my lord."

"It will not be for long," Henry resumed. "By midsummer, at least, I shall send you to England again, to make ready for my coming. Now there are other matters which require me to leave England alone for a little. Remember this, Pierre: Whatever I may say to you, whatever I may do, you have my love and trust. Endure, and you shall be rewarded. I have stolen from my bed to tell you this. I dared not let any one see me at your door."

"As you trust me, my lord, so I trust you," Pierre responded. "But—it were better that you tell Cercamon what you have told me."

Henry laughed softly.

"Right! He loves me, I think, but he loves you more. He is as true to you as hilt to hand—Sleep well!"

BARSAND THE armorer held the heavy hauberk at arm's length.

"He is a man who can wear this!" he laughed. "Were its workmanship less fine, 'twould burden even you, Pierre! I have pieced it here, where the arbalest bolt went through; but though I take pride in my work, I cannot match the rings. Its maker was a master of craft!"

Pierre Faidit donned the hauberk and told over two gold crowns.

"Your work will turn arrows, Barsand, and that means much. A Cordovan Moor forged those rings. My thanks!"

Leaving the armorer's, where bare blades and shirts of mail hung ghostly in the flare of the forge, he passed out into the narrow street. It was dark as a cavern after the red glow of the smithy; the tall houses, with their projecting eaves, shut out what little light the stars afforded. Peering about him, Pierre took the middle of the cobbled way, which writhed like a snake through the foulest part of the old town. The stink of the marshes stung his nostrils.

His mail made din enough as he strode along; but the town was still as death, save for the faint *tink-tink* of hammer on steel that pursued him, ever fainter, from Barsand's shop. The armorer worked late on the duke's business, and so was granted leave to labor and burn lights even this late after curfew. All else was dark and silent, for the duke enforced the law with a hard hand.

Of a sudden Pierre, with his soldier's ear, caught the thin

grate of steel on stone. Stopping instantly, he clapped hand to hilt and listened. It was nothing to him that other armored men—who might have leave, as he himself had—walked the streets after curfew; but it was much that they walked stealthily. Stretch his ears as he might, he heard nothing more. Treading so softly that his mail scarce rustled, he resumed his way toward the castle.

A casement opened just to the left of him, pouring forth a flood of light that threw him into full relief against the opposite whitewashed wall. This was ill, at an hour when none might lawfully unbar shutter or kindle torch or candle. Acting swiftly as suspicion awoke in him, Pierre leaped back into the protecting darkness, sword out. Even as he did so, a squat figure sprang into the patch of light, ran swiftly after him and was likewise swallowed by the gloom. Something hissed through the air, and a point thudded against Pierre's breast.

Its force weakened by his retreat, the blow glanced off his mail. Pierre drove his sword forward in one swift thrust, felt it tear home through steel and flesh and wrenched it out. Some one fell with a clang of steel and a groan.

The casement slammed shut, blotting out the light; a shutter crashed, and bolts flew home. Plainly he who had opened the window had heard, not seen, and had been satisfied with the groan that bore witness of a man's death. Pierre glided across the lane, flattened himself against the wall of the house opposite and waited.

For a long moment nothing happened; then a hoarse whisper came from somewhere in the shadows—

"Is he dead?"

"There are two, then!" Pierre reflected grimly, his fingers tightening about his hilt.

Then the whisper again, frightened at the silence—

"Ormeric!"

Smiling, Pierre stole forward. Silence again—then the *clang-clang-clang* of running steel-shod feet. Dashing forward in pursuit, Pierre struck once with his heavy blade, felt it tear through cloth, and brought up crashing against a projecting cornice. The feet ran on, turned a corner and were lost in the long, straight Rue du Grand Carroi that leads straight to the castle.

It was useless to follow farther. The fellow had a fair start, and Pierre was still dazed by his collision with the house wall. He stepped back, and slipped in a pool of blood. Striking flint on steel, he caught a brief glimpse of a distorted face staring up from the pavement.

"Ormeric D'Orbec!" he muttered. "Then he who fled was his brother Hugo. And the duke bade me keep my hands off Norman knights!" With a shrug he resumed his way.

I T W A S very late when he climbed to his room in the western tower, but he spent half an hour putting a fine edge on his sword where it had gone through D'Orbec's hauberk. He sat long reflecting on the night's work. Just after second cock-crow his door swung open, and the duke entered. Henry's face was troubled, but not angry.

"The watch have found Sir Ormeric's corpse in the town," he said, eyeing Pierre nervously.

Pierre nodded.

"They found it where I left it," he answered. "Ormeric and one other—Hugo—aided by the folk of the nearest house, laid an ambush for me. Hugo escaped."

Henry frowned.

"You can prove it was Hugo?"

"Hardly. But the folk of that house can be made to confess."

The duke shook his head.

"The body was found far from any house, by the quay. Could you tell the house by day? No? Then where is your proof? I bade the watch hold their tongues; but if that other was Hugo, there will be trouble over this. He will swear you slew his brother treacherously."

"The wound was in front," Pierre pointed out, "and Ormeric's sword in his hand."

"Not when the watch discovered him—he was weaponless. You have had to do with cunning men, lad, and they have outmatched you. Even if we find the house, its people will swear to what Hugo says, and how can I prove they lie? Nay, Pierre, for your own sake and mine this must not come to trial. I could and would protect you; but then my barons would turn on me. My position is perilous. The Normans, jealous of you already, will cry for your blood. When I refuse, they will rebel. I could deal with them bloodily, but I need their loyalty, as I have told you. And I suspect that Geoffrey conspires against me to wrest Anjou from me."

"Why not give it to him, and so win his support?" Pierre urged.

"Give a province to that boy, who has never learned to rule himself?"

Henry spoke scornfully, and Pierre knew he was right. Young Geoffrey was a spoiled child, whose tyrannous caprice would do more harm in Anjou than a wise ruler could undo. He chafed at the tight rein his older brother held him on, and his resentment was dangerous; but it would be worse to give him his head.

"I am playing a sharp game for high stakes, Pierre," Henry resumed. "I cannot tell even you what hangs on the turn of the dice. But to win I must be stronger than my foes. If my barons desert me because you, whom they hate, have slain one of them, I shall lose. I shall lose England, Normandy perhaps, Anjou and Touraine certainly. It means the end of all my high hopes, which you have labored so faithfully to fulfill."

"What must I do, master?" Pierre asked simply.

Henry laid a hand on his arm.

"Go into exile—this night. When Sir Hugo comes to me to demand revenge for his brother, I will say that I have banished you. In June or July I will send you word to go, secretly, to

England. When I join you there, after my triumph over Stephen, then, by ——'s glory, I will see to it that my barons have no more power to weaken me!"

"How?" Pierre asked, his eyes gleaming.

"As soon as England is mine, I will fill my armies with common men—men from the City Guard of London, Oxford, Winchester, and other towns; professional soldiers like yourself, who owe fealty to no baron; and I will raze to the earth every castle not held by a man I can trust!"

"It is good!" Pierre approved. "But in the meantime, where shall I go? Exile means death to me. King Louis has forbidden me to set foot in his realm; Aliénor, his divorced queen, would have me slain if I entered her domain. Between them, those two and you, you hold all France save Champagne and the Languedoc. To reach either I must pass through Louis' lands or through Aliénor's duchies of Poitou and Aquitaine."

Henry smiled slyly.

"You will never leave Touraine," he answered. "I shall send you to Tours, with a messenger for the governor, who is faithful to me. He will keep you safe hidden till I send you safe-conduct to England. Thus you shall escape all danger, and at the same time serve me. In the letter to the governor I shall place another, which he will give to one who dwells within the city. This is a most important errand, which must not fail—lest it cost me more than Normandy."

Pierre began to gather his belongings.

"None will know of this?" he asked.

"None—save my clerk, whom I can trust. He is even now inditing the letters. You cannot send to the stables for your horse, lest your going be known; I will have a swift courser brought to the postern from my own stalls. The guard at the gate is one of your own men. You must leave within the hour."

Henry vanished into the dark corridor, and made his way swiftly to his own chambers. In the first of his three rooms, his clerk—a lean, pinch-faced man in the gown of a minor canon—

was seated at a high desk, writing in a fine hand. Henry watched him a moment; then:

"One left my chamber as I came up, Gerald," he said. "His face was in the shadow. Who was it?"

The clerk started, his eyes blinking.

"It was Sir Hugo D'Orbec," he replied, in a dry whisper. "He came to lay a complaint before Your Grace."

Henry scowled.

"But he passed me by. Why did he not wait?"

Gerald had recovered his self-possession.

"Your Grace has said it was dark. Doubtless he did not know you."

"Belike," Henry growled. "You take long to finish a simple letter."

"Please, your Grace, there were two letters; and Sir Hugo delayed me."

It was the duke's turn to start.

"He did not see your writing?"

Gerald smiled wryly.

"That he did not, my lord."

Henry nodded, and summoned his squire from the inner room.

"Fetch me the sergeant Le Balafré from the postern!" he commanded. Bowing, the squire departed, staggering with sleep, and returned shortly with a tall, stocky soldier.

"Fetch the black stallion from my own stable, Balafré!" Henry ordered. "Bring him to the gate. Then resume guard. Deliver the black to him who comes to you with my name on his lips. You will know the man. Say nothing of this, or your head pays for it!"

As Balafré went off, the clerk finished his letters, and gave them to the duke to sign. Taking the pen from him, Henry scrawled his name and titles in an awkward hand, and himself sealed them. Then, placing them in a wrapper of oiled parchment, he sealed this also.

"Go with these to the postern, Gerald, and give them to Pierre Faidit. You shall hang if they go astray!"

Gerald drew a sharp breath, and his face seemed more pinched than ever. Bowing low, he slipped from the room.

I T WA S time for the dawn when Pierre rode down the castle hill with the duke's black courser between his knees; but the sky was black as a pall. An April storm had come up, bringing the soft, steady rain of spring. The roads would be heavy in an hour's time, too heavy for him to make swift work of the ride to Tours. He knew the duke wanted as much distance as possible between him and the court before it should be light enough for any to recognize him.

He dashed through the town guard at the outer port of Chinon with a shout:

"Duke's messenger! Delay me not, at your peril!"

But the duke's orders had been before him, and the gate swung open to pass him through ere he could check his pace. The black bounded out on the straight white road that runs like a bow-shot to Azay-le-Rideau on the way to Tours.

He had left Chinon well nigh an hour behind when the cloud-wrapped sky grew gray, and his beast, tossing its head in the teeth of a rising breeze, neighed shrilly. Pierre loosened his sword in the sheath, and felt of the saddle-bag on his shield-side, where the duke's letters lay. Slackening his pace, he rode on more carefully.

The minutes passed, and he heard nothing; nor were objects yet very clear in the half light. They grew dimmer still as he rode between the aisles of Chinon forest; but knowing the road before him was straight, he pricked the black's flanks. The stallion shot ahead, gathering speed, flinging mud from his hoofs.

Suddenly Pierre felt something smite his breast and sweep him from the saddle. He flew, whirling, over his horse's rump, and crashed full length against the road. For the briefest instant voices sounded faintly in his ears; then he lost consciousness.

It was light when he roused again. He lay by the side of the road, a cluster of armed men standing over him. All wore masks over their helmets; their shields and surcoats were bare of any device. He strove to rise, but one of his captors thrust the point of a sword against his throat.

"Unhelm him, Gui!" ordered a hoarse voice, that was plainly disguised.

One bent down and tore off Pierre's helmet, which was still held in place by the lacings of his cheek-curtains. The man was none too gentle.

"*Peste!*" growled the leader. "It is the wrong man! Your pardon, good sir; we were after other game. Mount, lads!"

Leading their horses from a screen of undergrowth, the masked men sprang to the saddle. When Pierre rose, painfully testing his bruised limbs, they were already far down the road to Tours.

"Tours!" he meditated. "They speak true, then: they stopped me by mistake. I have no foes in Tours."

He stood in the middle of the road in a drenching downpour, his head still buzzing from the force of his fall. His horse was nowhere to be seen; his sword and scabbard were gone.

"They were not above plunder, then!" he mused. "But 'twill go ill with him I find wearing my sword in Tours!"

Glancing about him, he discovered the means of his capture: a rope stretched across the road between two trees, at the height of a mounted man's chest. He cut it with his dagger.

"I must walk to Tours, then!" he reflected bitterly, "and without the duke's letters! God grant they be not in the hands of his foes!"

But it was poor comfort that in any case they would not reach the ones for whom they were intended, and that the duke, in his own words, stood to lose more than Normandy if they failed to be delivered. He strode on in the rain, whose freshness revived him; but his head ached wretchedly. The extent of his loss, and the thought of its possible consequences, made him utterly miserable.

He had gone perhaps a hundred paces when a cry of joy burst from his lips. From a clump of alders protruded the rump of his horse, its tail twitching as it munched at the rich grass. He ran forward as fast as the mud and the weight of his armor permitted, and recaptured the beast, whose bridle was tangled in its forelegs. His saddlebags were still there. With trembling fingers he fumbled at the fastenings, got them undone at last, and plunged his hands into the left-hand pouch. His letters were safe! To make utterly sure, he drew out the packet and scanned it closely. It was the same, untouched, the very seal intact.

Rejoicing, he rode on, more charitably inclined toward those who had ambushed him. Had they not left him his horse and his precious burden? Ay, and had made excuse for their mistake, as gentlemen should. But then he thought of his sword, and his heart hardened. He would never forgive, never spare, the man who had stolen that which was dearer to him than all else save friends and honor.

It was high noon when he rode over the hills where the first site of Tours had stood, before the Romans moved it across the river. The clouds were scattering before the warmth of an ardent sun, which already kindled the blue river, swollen with spring floods, and the densely massed roofs and spires of the walled city beyond. It was a glowing jewel, that city, bright and many-colored, in a setting of rich valley and budding flowers—the heart of the garden of France. With a lighter heart he urged his horse across the single bridge that led to the great gate.

The guards eyed him askance, as well they might.

"Who is this that comes garbed in mud, with blood on his face and no sword to his side?" growled the officer of the watch.

Pierre judged it unwise to speak his name, seeing that he was supposed to be in exile. He drew from his pouch the packet with the duke's seal and flourished it under his challenger's nose.

One glance at the arms of his overlord, and the soldier became all courtesy.

"Will it please your Excellence to enter!" he cried. "Verily, we are honored to receive the duke's messenger. Your letters are to the governor?"

"So it appears," Pierre conceded. "And there is some haste about them."

The officer detailed four men to escort him under the frowning arch, with its jutting turrets; and through the ill-paved streets they passed in strange procession. The soldiers, eager to show their loyalty to the duke, strutted as if accompanying some grandee; and Pierre, conscious of his battered, befouled appearance, grinned to himself. A tail of curious lookers-on attached itself to them, growing as they advanced, till with their entrance on the wide grain-market a throng ran up from all sides to stare and fling questions. The escort waved the crowd back with their spears, shouting loudly for room for the duke's envoy; and so, a magnet for all the idlers in Tours, they drew up before the square-towered citadel, surrounded by gaping citizens ere they could dismount.

Through the press the soldiers elbowed, forcing a wide path for Pierre to follow. On the stone steps lounged armored men, just relieved by the change of guard, eying the buxom bourgeoisie with more attention than they gave even the duke's messenger. Before the embattled entrance a dozen more crossed pikes.

"PLACE FOR the duke's ambassador!" howled the escort; and the pikes grounded. Passing between them, Pierre made his way to the Salle D'Armes, where a clerk took his message. In a few moments the governor appeared.

He bowed.

"Sire Marc de St. Martin," he announced himself; and, in

lieu of giving his own name Pierre handed him the sealed packet.

The governor, a tall, somewhat portly man, gazed at him with keen eyes.

"I have not yet heard your name," he said, courteously, but with emphasis.

"I know not whether my lord duke wishes it known, even to so true a vassal as the Sire Marc," Pierre countered. "If so, it will stand written in one of his letters, which concerns me. The other is for a person whose identity his Grace did not reveal to me."

Frowning, the governor scanned the superscriptions, and looked oddly at Pierre.

"It is strange," he said, "that the duke should make you his envoy without revealing to you the condition of the—the— person to whom this is addressed."

He broke the seal of his own letter, and read slowly, once and again. When he looked up, his eyes were hard.

"This does not tell your name," he spoke coldly, "but it does give strict commands concerning you. Be pleased to follow me."

He led Pierre out again to the entrance hall, and beckoned to a group of soldiers.

"Take this man," he ordered, "and put him in the dungeon of the North Tower!"

Pierre recoiled and clapped his hand to his side before he remembered that he had no sword. Before he could make a second movement, he was surrounded, seized and hurried away. He was borne swiftly to a wing of the stoutly built castle, dragged down a winding stair in a corner tower, and clapped into a filthy cell. Before leaving him, his captors stripped him of surcoat, mail, and dagger, and left him in his leather jipoun.

He thrust his face to the small, barred aperture in the solid, spike-studded open door, and called after the departing guards:

"What does this mean? Send the governor to me!"

Mocking laughter answered him, as the men-at-arms clattered up the stair.

Peering through the bars, Pierre inspected the vault that contained his cell. The place was hewn out of the solid rock on which the tower was built. It's walls, thick as they were, were damp and slimy. The paved floor was foul, and the air stale with mould. At first he thought himself alone in the dismal crypt, till he heard a groan from some cell near his own. The meaning of the sound was borne in upon him by the sight of a trough-shaped instrument longer than a man, fitted with cords, a windlass and metal wedges, and stained with blood.

His own quarters were comfortless and vile. There was not even a bench—no place to sit or lie save the stone floor, thinly covered with rotten straw. A single barred window high above his head let in a gloomy light from what must be a high-walled court. One side of the cell was hung with rusty chains, fast to the stone.

Pierre stood bewildered, trying to understand what had befallen him. Treachery? What ground was there? He had given the governor the letters entrusted to him. The duke had said that Sire Marc would find him a place of refuge, where he could lie close till he could make his way to England to renew his secret work for Henry there. And now—

He grinned wryly.

"Perchance this is the safe refuge?" he meditated. "I could wish the governor lodged his guests more cleanly!"

It was entirely possible that the duke's letter might have ordered Sir Marc to place Pierre in honorable confinement—under guard in respectable quarters—as the surest way of keeping him from the vengeance of his foes. But to treat him like a criminal, cast him into the most noisome dungeon in the city—that was unthinkable. Anger and despair struggled in his mind as he surveyed his surroundings. Such a fate as this was reserved for traitors.

Had Henry betrayed him? Was his master's friendship but

a pretense, and the shame which had been done him in Chinon the true expressions of the duke's feelings toward him? His soul revolted against the thought. During the three years he had served Henry he had never, till a few weeks back, received aught but kindness and honor at the duke's hands; and well had he earned such honor. Yet now, without reason, he was hurled from favor into ignominious captivity. And was this the end? Might there not be worse to follow? He thought of the blood-stained rack and boot he had seen in the crypt, and shuddered.

Weary from his ride, still shaken by the fall of the night before and faint with lack of food, he leaned against the wall of his prison. He wanted to lie down, but a glance at the reeking straw dissuaded him. Dizzy as he was, his thoughts would not focus on his plight. One moment he was convinced of his lord's treachery, the next his mind raced from one improbable explanation to another. But always he came against the blank wall of the letters he had been given to deliver; he had handed them over intact as they had been put into his hands, the seals unbroken. They must represent Henry's will. The governor was the duke's faithful vassal—Henry had said so.

But what if he were not faithful after all? The man's face was honest, even noble; but in the possibility of his dishonesty lay Pierre's only hope of the duke's good faith. The puzzle was insoluble. After some hours, faint and exhausted, Pierre gave it up.

Then the warder came with food, sliding it through a narrow panel in the door. Pierre heard the wooden edges grate, and looked down to see a panikin and a loaf of bread in the straw. He snatched them up, ate and drank, and felt his strength return. As he was munching the last of the bread, a face appeared in the barred aperture of the door. Pierre looked up just as it vanished, but he caught sight of the silken sheen of a woman's hood. Low voices sounded in the crypt; the door screeched on its hinges, and three men-at-arms came in, points leveled at his breast.

As the men advanced, Pierre was compelled to back away

before the threatening points till he stood at bay against the wall where the chains hung. One man slipped in, and, protected by the swords of the others, fastened the gyves about Pierre's hands and feet. They were cruel chains, so placed that they held his hands above his head and far apart, close to the stones. He could neither lie down nor stoop, nor touch one limb with another.

Then the woman came in. She was tall, slender, lithe as a cat, her big eyes blue and cold. Her gown, clinging skin-close above the broad, jeweled girdle, was of finest sky-blue silk. One moment she stared at Pierre, then threw back her hood from a glory of spun-gold hair.

"You!" she said in a voice like frozen music.

Pierre caught his breath.

"You!" he echoed. A cruel smile curled the woman's thin, red lips.

I T W A S Aliénor, Duchess of Guienne, Poitou, and Aquitaine—and, until King Louis divorced her, Queen of France. The sight of her called to Pierre's mind the death of his first lord, poisoned by her hands; his own banishment from the French kingdom, after he had exposed her guilt to the king, and so made possible the divorce that followed. And she was here, in Tours—in Duke Henry's realm!

His astonishment amused her.

"Welcome, Pierre Faidit!" she said with smooth irony. "It gives me pleasure that one so famed should be my guest."

"Your guest?" he repeated in confusion.

"Ay; why not? I have greatly longed for this honor. After all your pains to spread my fame—my ill-fame, I fear—throughout France, your skill in disembarrassing me of a husband and a kingdom, should I not cherish the wish to reward you as you deserve? And now, thanks to your master, I have the opportunity."

She smiled with dainty irony, showing small, white teeth.

Pierre glared at her.

"My master? What mean you?"

"You do not know?" She shrugged her shapely shoulders. She was still beautiful as he remembered her, the most beautiful woman in Europe; but her face had grown hard with the years.

"You do not know, when you yourself brought his commands to me? See!" She took one hand from behind her back, holding out a sheet of parchment.

"Read it! You should be the first to know, since it concerns you so nearly."

With mocking solicitude she held the parchment before his eyes, close, that he might read. His eyes widened, first incredulously, then with rage and horror. Addressed to Aliénor, with all her titles and honors set forth at formal length, the letter was a proposal of marriage. It was signed with the hand and seal of Henry of Normandy.

Pierre choked.

"Impossible!" he cried hoarsely. "My lord would never—does he not know you for—"

She clapped her firm little hand over his lips, glanced round to see that the door was shut and laughed in his face.

"For a murderess, you would say? A poisoner? Ay, he knows. Why should he not, when you blazoned my name abroad for all France to scorn and hate? But he also knows me for the mistress of all the rich South, with lands and gold and men-at-arms such as few kings can boast. He wants these things, Pierre—perhaps as much as he wants me."

"You do not love him!" Pierre stammered.

"What matter, so he loves me—or my dowry? Ah, you think that he values you too much to marry a woman you hate, perhaps? What know you of statecraft? He wants more men and money to conquer England—and perchance a wife who will give him sons as bold, as unscrupulous, as himself!"

"You would never—"

"Ah, but I will! I am but a few weeks divorced, yet already two princes have bid for my hand. They were very great, very strong; but neither of them can match Henry Plantagenet. Our marriage will unite under one rule all the land from the Channel to the Spanish March, from Bordeaux to the Languedoc. I shall be lady of two-thirds France—ay, Queen of England!"

She threw back her dainty chin and laughed, a hard, metallic, yet very lovely laugh.

"And England I shall owe in large part to you, if men say true. It will amuse me to think of that when your head rots on the gate of Tours!"

"You would not dare!" Pierre flung back at her.

Her little teeth ground.

"Would I not? Who forbids me to slay you? Not Henry! See there!" She held a second parchment before his eyes. "This is the letter you brought the governor!"

Pierre read, and turned his eyes away, lest she see his misery. Stripped of its titles and pedantic phrase, the parchment bore to the governor the order to seize the bearer, cast him into bonds, and hold him at the disposal of the Duchess Aliénor, to do with as she would. There could be no doubt of its genuineness; Pierre instantly recognized the sprawling signature of his master.

Aliénor's sweet voice broke through his bitter thoughts.

"But a little more, and I will leave you to your meditations. They will be pleasant, I trust. I shall leave you here four days, that you may taste in full the knowledge that princes value their servants less than the least advantage they may buy. Then, when your reflections have sufficiently prepared you, I will have you gently hanged. I think there could be no better way to repay you for the scorn you have brought on me."

She was silent for a little, so that he thought she had gone. When he turned his head, he found her still gazing at him mockingly.

"Tell me, Pierre, has my beauty faded with the years?"

His eyes burned on hers.

"Nay," he groaned, "you are as fair as ever. In all things you are as you always were."

She swept him a low bow and went out. The guards, returning, freed his limbs again; but in the face of their weapons he could not have broken away from them, had he been mad enough to try. Nor indeed did he greatly care, now, for his life.

Till now he had had the strong man's love of life in more than ordinary measure. Fame, the taste of power, the sharp give and take of battle, had been as wine to him. In the friendship of his comrade Cercamon, in the trust and kindness of his lord, he had known joy that to him surpassed all else on earth. Nor was it prison and the threat of death that broke him now, but the certainty that his lord was false. Ay, false. Henry had sold him for a smile from the woman whose lands he coveted. There was no more truth nor loyalty in life.

Unheeding the filth that had revolted him before, he sank down on the straw. Four days he must live in this misery, four days of solitude with his torturing thoughts, before the hangman came to bring him the release of death. Truly Aliénor was wise in the ways of vengeance!

So he sat till the afternoon sun slanted its last rays through his window, lighting his prison for a few brief moments. It was then that another face, dark, narrow, leering, was thrust close to the bars of his cell. A harsh voice broke in on his wretchedness.

"Ha! Faidit! Have I not well paid the score between us?"

Pierre looked up, but his power of surprize was exhausted. He stared dully into the eyes of Hugo D'Orbec. The Norman laughed, withdrew his head, and held up to the bars something that glowed in the sun's rays—a burning, lambent ruby.

An answering gleam kindled in Pierre's eyes, and D'Orbec laughed again. The thing he held was the hilt of Pierre's sword.

"You slew my brother, dog of a fisherman! Now he laughs at you from hell! Men call you cunning, yet I have played with you as one plays with a child, and brought you to death. Think on me when you dangle in a noose!"

Pierre turned his back on the fellow; but his apathy enraged the Norman.

"Ha! So you do not care! But when you know how I befooled you—It was I and my men who stopped you on your way, and lulled your suspicions with a pretended excuse that we had taken the wrong man! While you lay senseless, I robbed you of your letters, giving you another packet in exchange; and you knew not the difference. If you but understood how cunningly the thing was contrived—"

Pierre cut the jeering voice short.

"You lie," he said dully, "What you say is impossible."

"Think you so? Impossible to forge the duke's seal, so that you should not see the deception? To counterfeit his hand well enough to beguile you and the governor both? Impossible for me, ay; but not for—the duke's clerk!"

"Gerald?" Pierre's tone was weary, but incredulous. "He is loyal."

"LOYAL? THOU fool! No man is loyal beyond his price. The price of Gerald's honesty was fifty gold crowns—a tidy sum, eh? But it was worth as much to avenge my brother. It was Gerald from whom I learned of Aliénor's presence here, Gerald who wrote and signed the forged letter, copying the duke's hand to perfection; and Gerald has access to the great seal. He drew up false and true alike, while you were waiting to take them. I and my men had but to have half an hour's start of you on the road."

Pierre looked up quickly, a strange light in his eyes.

"You speak of one forged letter," he said, in a strained voice. "But the letters I bore were two."

"Ay; the one to the duchess was on matters of state, higher matters than I dared meddle with. We made an exact copy of it, and when I took the true packet from you, I substituted the false. The duchess received a fair copy of that which the duke intended for her; but in place of the orders bidding the governor find you safe lodging, you bore him a message in Gerald's best style, commanding that you be given up to Aliénor. Her hate of you is common knowledge. I knew the death she would contrive for you would be worse than any I could deal; and thus you will die by my cunning while I run no risk of punishment for your murder. She will hang you certainly, perhaps torture you first."

Pierre thought a moment; then, suddenly, he burst into peal on peal of laughter. D'Orbec, hate in his eyes, stared at him.

"Are you mad?" he cried. "You are to die, and you laugh? I have your precious sword, and you laugh?"

With difficulty Pierre restrained his mirth enough to speak.

"O fool, fool!" he mocked. "You would torment me, and against your will you bring me joy! Begone, that I may laugh my fill at thee!"

D'Orbec turned away, baffled and furious; but Pierre called him back.

"Hunt thyself a safe hole!" he cried. "When I am free, I will search thee out, take my sword from thee, and with it thy life!"

D'Orbec snarled at him.

"Thou canst not escape! The duchess knows she has me to thank for thy presence here, and has made me thy keeper. When thou leavest this cell, it will be on thy way to the gallows!"

Pierre began to stride up and down his cell, thinking. The letter to Aliénor was genuine: Henry had proposed marriage to her, knowing her for a woman wicked as she was beautiful. This was bad enough. But what had been worse, for Pierre, was proved false. His lord had not betrayed him; Henry had kept faith. Pierre's present plight was the work of a cunning rascal; and against such, though they had trapped him, he might find means to fight. He had won free from desperate straits before; he had uncommon strength and uncommon wit to draw on. And now—now that he knew his lord was innocent of wrong to him—life was worth fighting for. Joy flooded his heart, and with it came resourcefulness and vigor. Hugo D'Orbec had frustrated his own revenge.

But the walls of Pierre's prison were as stout, the door as staunch, as ever. And he was unarmed.

THE LADY MATHILDE sat in her bower, her wise old eyes very bright as she looked at her two tall sons. She was proud of them both, in different ways, and with a pride that was void of all illusion. She knew them for what they were. Of the two, she loved Henry best. A life full of hardship, of vain struggle, that had aged her before her time, had given her a high regard for men who were men indeed. She loved Henry's strong body, his fierce pride that brooked no rivalry nor opposition, his hot temper and his hard hand. Geoffrey she loved for his courtly manners and his fair face; but her love for him was tinged with pity. Ay, he was cunning; he was not afraid; but there was an instability about him that reminded her of his father. Henry was his mother's child; and Mathilde had been a better man than most men of her day.

Henry gestured to a servant.

"Fetch Cercamon!" he commanded.

"He is here, my lord!" The troubadour's deep voice rang from the doorway.

"My mother would hear a song, lad."

Cercamon, taking the privilege of his profession, shook his head.

"I am not in the mood for song, my lord. What have you done with Pierre? One of his men has told me that you took away his captaincy. Now he is not here, and none knows whither he has gone."

Henry hated to be questioned.

"He is on my errands," he replied shortly.

"It is said you have banished him," Cercamon pursued relentlessly. "Why? For killing an assassin who would have murdered him? And where has he taken refuge? Is he safe?"

Henry stamped his foot, and the veins swelled in his temples; but Lady Mathilde checked his wrath.

"I see this is something you would keep hidden," she said bluntly. "Which of us do you mistrust? Geoffrey? Me? Cercamon you can not doubt, for you have always taken him into your counsels."

The duke was fairly caught, forced into the open. He could not confess, to Geoffrey's face, that it was his brother he mistrusted.

"Pierre has gone to Tours, then," he admitted. "With letters to the governor. See that ye say nought of it."

"And to—some one else in Tours?" Geoffrey thrust in slyly. Henry flushed.

"Seek not to know what does not concern you. Pierre is safe—by my order."

"That is well, my lord," Cercamon said slowly. "The castle rings with the tale of Ormeric D'Orbec's death, and Ormeric's snake of a brother will plot revenge. Are you sure Pierre is safe in Tours? Hugo D'Orbec is not here in Chinon, and his spies may learn more than they should."

Mathilde turned her dark eyes on the troubadour.

"Listen to that man, Henry. He is wise—wiser than you or I. Do you know more than you have said, Cercamon?"

Cercamon shook his head.

"Not a jot, my lady. I only know that Pierre is not here, and that his enemy—who should be lurking near him to strike—is also gone. And that Pierre has been publicly rebuked by my lord, and shorn of his honors. All this looks suspicious. I know nothing more—but I smell evil. I also would go to Tours."

Henry started, and his hot eyes flashed.

"Not you, lad! Pierre is safe there, but you—you would not be!"

"It is said," Geoffrey observed blandly—but with a covert glance at his mother—"that he has an enemy who hates you also, troubadour."

Cercamon turned his blue-green eyes full on the boy, as if seeking to probe his heart.

"What mean you, lord Count?" he asked.

Mathilde cut in between them.

"He means nothing, save that he is a fool who will some day die of his folly! Play with the ladies, girl-face; men wear weapons."

Geoffrey turned scarlet, and rose with a stiff bow.

"If my lady mother, and the duke, my brother, will grant me leave, I will even do as she advises!" he said angrily. Henry nodded curtly, and Mathilde smiled. Geoffrey glided from the room, graceful as a woman. Out of the tail of one eye Cercamon saw him turn slightly at the door, and beckon.

"I crave leave to seek the ladies also," he said, with a smile; and followed the young count.

As the door closed behind him, Mathilde took Henry's hand in hers.

"Mischief is brewing there, boy!" she said. "So long as you cherish Pierre, Cercamon will follow you to the death; but if aught happens to his friend, 'ware Cercamon!"

Henry started to his feet, but his mother held tight to him.

"Nay, let them be, lest a worse thing happen! If you must question them, question them separately!"

"NOW, TOUCHING this matter of the ending of a *canzo*," Geoffrey spoke in a loud voice for the benefit of those who stood in the passage, "I hold that the last rhyme should vary, to give greater strength to the whole."

Cercamon eyed him meaningly. He knew that Geoffrey had some secret word for him; and it was for him to play his part in the game that masked that secret from curious ears.

"Strength can be attained by the wise choice of phrase in the line, my lord," he countered, "without ruining the harmony of the rhymes."

"Ruining? Nay! It is my belief—"

And so the fictitious argument ran on, while the two climbed the winding stair to the battlements. Geoffrey was too wise to feed his brother's suspicions further by a private conference with the troubadour in his own chamber. When they emerged into the clear, sweet night, Geoffrey summoned a spearman, a man of Anjou.

"We would speak apart," he said. "If you would keep my regard, Matthieu, let none come nigh us. And warn us if any man comes up the stair."

The spearman saluted.

"As my lord wills." He took his stand at some distance, between Geoffrey and the other sentinels, at a spot whence he could watch the stairhead.

"That man is devoted to me," Geoffrey whispered in the troubadour's ear. "Now we can speak plainly. Aliénor of Aquitaine is in Tours."

Cercamon started.

"It is worse than I feared, then," he said. "I was sure Hugo D'Orbec would dog Pierre's movements, waiting for a safe means to avenge his brother. But the duchess—are you sure?"

Geoffrey laughed bitterly.

"You are no fool, Cercamon. Use your wits. My brother suddenly removes his court from Caen, where he can watch England, to Chinon, where he has usually no great interests. Why?

"This happens but a week after the arrival of a swift courier from Paris, who immediately sought the duke. What had happened in Louis' kingdom to warrant the messenger's haste? Do not all men know that about that same time Aliénor was divorced from the French king? Being divorced, and being the woman she is, she would be ordered to quit France straightway after the divorce. She would then go home—to Aquitaine, or Poitou. The nearest and safest way would lead through Tours. And at this time—at this time, mark you, my lord brother drops his English intrigues and posts to Chinon—which is but four and thirty miles from Tours. Is it not plain?"

"Plain enough," Cercamon admitted. "But you do not know that she is in Tours? You but surmise it from the facts?"

Geoffrey snorted.

"I surmise it, and I know it too. I have my spies, though I can not pay them well, thanks to my brother's niggardliness." He broke off with a curse; then:

"Why can not my brother treat me like a man?" he burst out passionately. "Am I not older now than he was when he succeeded to the dukedom? Am I less wise than he? Yet, of all that he inherited from our father, he gives me but three bare castles! If I am to have honors, lands, money, I must find them for myself! And, thunder of heaven! If he will not give them me, I will find them!"

Cercamon said nothing, looking ostentatiously over the parapet; but his thoughts were busy.

Geoffrey's tone changed to one of kindly solicitude. He laid a hand fondly on the troubadour's shoulder.

"I know your affection for Pierre, my friend. He is a brave man, worthy your regard. I would give much to save him from harm. Now it is in my mind that he is in deadly peril at this moment. Henry knows of the hate Aliénor bears him—yet he sends him to Tours, where she is. What if she discovers his presence there?"

"He is doubtless under the duke's safe-conduct," Cercamon murmured.

"What avails a safe-conduct against poison, or a knife in the dark?" Geoffrey sneered. "May it not be that Hugo D'Orbec has followed him thither to wield that knife? Or to betray him to Aliénor at the least?"

Cercamon stirred uneasily. Geoffrey's dark hints tallied all too closely with his own fears.

"My lord," he said slowly, "you can never mean—or think—

that the duke sent Pierre to Tours because he knew Aliénor
was there—to be rid of him?"

Geoffrey cried out in shocked protest. "Never! Though it is
true that the duke hath been most unkind to him of late. Yet I
do not believe—"

Cercamon understood the cunning insinuation.

"Nay!" he objected. "It can not be. The duke is a hard man,
but honest. I think he trusted to Pierre's shrewdness to keep
him out of danger. Yet that there is danger if Aliénor learns of
his coming, I can not deny. It is very bad that Hugo also has
gone—perhaps to Tours."

Geoffrey, after a moment's hesitation, ventured a bold stroke.

"You are wise, Cercamon. You know Henry's ways. It is not
his way to betray his servants. But it is ever his wont to seize
what power he can. Do you not see why he has come here,
where he can be so near Aliénor?"

Cercamon stared at him.

"You mean?"

"He means to ask Aliénor to marry him!"

"Ah!" Cercamon drew in his breath with a quick hiss. "You
are right. It is clear. Evil woman though she is, she would bring
him the richest dowry ever woman had. He would do it. Any
wise prince would do it. It will more than double his power."

"But it will imperil his friends—such of them as Aliénor
hates," Geoffrey hinted.

"Perhaps. But I think my lord believes himself man enough
to master even such a wife, and compel her to leave his friends
alone. I should have no fears for myself—after the marriage.
But Pierre, in Tours, now—I see I must ride to Tours."

"Bide a little," Geoffrey interposed, "and I will ride with you."

"You? But my lord—"

Geoffrey nodded thoughtfully.

"I will tell you something, Cercamon. I need friends, and you
will keep my secret. If Henry marries Aliénor, he will be the

strongest man in France—stronger than the king. But if—if that should happen which would prevent such a marriage—"

"Stop, my lord!" Cercamon interrupted. "I can hear no more. What you have said I will not disclose to your brother; but I am his vassal, bound to him by the strongest ties of loyalty and regard. I will ride to Tours alone."

Geoffrey sighed.

"As you will. I am sorry, for you could have helped me—and I you. I fear greatly that your refusal will prevent me from saving Pierre in his dire peril."

"Peril—" Cercamon began; but the sentinel, grounding his pike with a loud clang, warned him to be silent. Hard on the man's signal Henry appeared at the stair top, his wide shoulders outlined against the light of a torch behind him.

"It grows late, lads!" he growled. "Best go to bed, brother. You are over young to watch so late."

The mockery in his words jarred on Geoffrey. Smothering a curse, he bowed low, and obeyed the scarcely veiled order. When he had gone, Henry took his place at the troubadour's side.

"What had he to say to you?" Henry demanded. "Nay, good Matthieu! Keep your distance! Overlong ears can be cropped, knave!" The spearman strolled off.

"Half the Angevins in the castle are Geoffrey's spies!" the duke complained. "And I am their ruler! A pretty pass, when a man's own brother plots against him!"

"You keep too tight a rein on him," Cercamon retorted. "Had you given him more power, he would be your loyal vassal."

Henry shrugged.

"Mayhap. I have been over-stingy with him. I will make amends, if it be not too late. But I did not think you would conspire with him against me."

Cercamon removed his belted sword, and handed it, hilt first, to Henry.

"I have not conspired, my lord, nor will I; but if your Grace doubts me, take my sword, and have me put in chains."

Henry's voice boomed in a hearty laugh.

"Nay, lad, I trust you, but I am out of humor over this affair of Pierre's. I sent him to Tours, as I said, with a letter to the governor, which should ensure his safety. It had to be done. I gave out that he was banished; partly because my barons would deny me their homage if I failed to act after Ormeric's death, and partly because Pierre's own life was in danger from them. If I had more money, I could buy their loyalty. They are all for sale. But I have spent all I have buying the support of the English lords in preparation for the coming invasion."

"And so," Cercamon put in boldly, "you plan to raise more money by marrying the Duchess Aliénor?"

Henry stared at him.

"You got that from Geoffrey!" he growled.

"It is plain from the facts themselves," Cercamon answered lightly. "Here are you in Chinon; there is she in Tours. And—Pierre—is—in—Tours! I mean to go thither myself, my lord!"

"No harm can come to him," Henry persisted stubbornly. "The governor—"

"Where is Hugo D'Orbec?" Cercamon countered.

"Ha! I understand! But how—"

"My lord, Pierre is my brother-in-arms. His danger demands my aid. Give me a letter to the governor, bidding that he obey me in all things as your deputy. If D'Orbec should get word to the duchess concerning Pierre, she is cunning enough to find ways of destroying a man she hates so bitterly. Knowing her, and armed with your letter, I can defeat any plans she may have against him."

Henry thought hard, rubbing his fox-mane with stubby fingers.

"If D'Orbec betrays him to her," he pondered, "and she strikes against him; if then you present my order for his safety—she will be angered against me—and my plans for a marriage—"

"Would you sell your friends for political advantage?" Cercamon shot at him.

"By the mass! You take too much on yourself, troubadour! Do you dare—"

"For my friends I dare anything, my lord, even as in the past I have dared many things in your service. If I were not true to him, how could I be true to you?"

The duke's anger melted, swiftly as it had arisen.

"I will give you the letter," he decided. "In the last extremity it will save Pierre. But you are a man of shrewd parts. If you can save him without imperiling my suit for the duchess's hand—and that means without using my letter—you will save me from a ruin as great as ever befell a prince! Her temper is such that she would never forgive me if I forced her to give up her vengeance!"

"I will try," Cercamon promised. "I pray you, let me have the letter soon, for I would ride tonight."

"H E   W H O   rides fast rides to a fall," muttered Cercamon to himself, as the watch-fires on the crest of Chinon Castle died to yellow patches against the night. The town was well behind him, the highroad before, and a good—but not a handsome—horse between his knees. He had stolen away as secretly as possible; yet, though his anxiety for Pierre tugged at his nerves, he reined his mount in to a dog-trot, his ear inclined down-wind to catch the least sound.

"The road is empty," he decided, and dismounted. By the wayside he tethered his horse, doffed mantle and spurs, and weighting them with a stone, flung them far into the undergrowth. From a bundle at his saddle-bow he took a shapeless garment, the cowled gown of a canon of St. Martin de Tours which he had purloined from the duke's chaplain, and put it on over his armor. He stood thus in the dark, fumbling at his scabbard to make sure that his short, broad, two-edged sword was wholly hidden by the skirts of his cassock, and smiled to himself. Adjusting the cowl so that it concealed his long locks and almost masked his eyes, he gathered the long gown and carefully mounted.

The morning sun bathed Tours in crimson fire as he rode into the city, troubled at heart, but eyes afire with the joy of action. His ready brain worked best against odds, and here was promise of odds enough. Pierre might be safe, but the chances were against him in a city that held Aliénor of Aquitaine for guest.

Cercamon did not mean to use Henry's all-powerful letter in any way that would compromise his lord's plans. It would suffice to free Pierre from anything but a coffin, but only at great cost to the duke. Having incurred Aliénor's hate himself, the troubadour knew she would sacrifice even a most advantageous marriage to satisfy her vengeance against one who had offended her as bitterly as Pierre. Therefore Cercamon resolved to have full resort to his letter only if all else failed, and first to try the full resources of his own crafty mind.

His religious habit won him entrance past the guard, who were just opening the city gates. At his request a soldier guided him to the citadel, where he cooled his heels for an hour before the governor rose. Once announced, however, he was admitted without difficulty into the governor's presence.

He at once delivered his letter.

"If I mistake not, my son," he began, speaking in character with his religious garb, "a message has already reached you from the duke our lord."

The governor nodded.

"But three days ago, holy father. I obeyed the orders it contained."

"Then you behold here the authority by which I question you concerning them. I have leave to speak?"

"Assuredly, father. This letter commands me to obey its bearer in all things, as the accredited representative of the duke."

Cercamon's heart was considerably lightened. The governor had obeyed Henry's first letter, which had commanded that Pierre be placed in safety.

"The man who came to you is out of harm's way?" he asked.

Sir Marc smiled grimly.

"As safe as a man can be behind stone walls. Whatever he has done to offend the duke, he will sin no more."

Cercamon started.

"To offend? Stone walls? What mean you?"

It was the governor's turn to be surprized.

"I received orders," he explained, "by the letters which the fellow carried, to cast him into prison. I did so. My dungeons will keep any man harmless. To make all sure, he hangs tomorrow morning!"

His previous words had warned the troubadour that all was not well; nevertheless it was with difficulty that Cercamon concealed his consternation.

"I think," he said uneasily, "I think, my son, that you have not fully comprehended the duke's will concerning this man. May I ask you to show his letter to me?"

Over-sensitive on the point of honor, the governor rose stiffly.

"I regret that I have given the letter to the Duchess of Aquitaine, whose affair it seemed to be," he answered. "But I assure you there was no mistake. I make no mistakes of that sort. The letter clearly bade me cast its bearer into prison, subject to the duchess's will. I did so."

Cercamon's worst fears were realized. Nonetheless, warned by his mistake of the moment before, he bowed.

"I crave your pardon, my son. The mistake was not yours, but her Grace's."

"That is a matter for you to discuss with her Grace. I will inform her of your coming."

Cercamon held up one hand.

"That you must not! I give you my word, my son, that it would peril the duke's interests on which I have come. He has entrusted me with a task so delicate that the smallest misstep would cost him dear. If you would serve him, let me come before the duchess unexpected and unannounced."

The governor was impressed.

"A strange pother this, over a single soldier," he mused. "Yet I marked that he wore fine mail, as if he were one in authority. May I ask his name?"

"Surely, if you will not repeat it. He is Pierre Faidit, whom men call Pierre of the Sword."

Sir Marc's face for the first time betrayed uncertainty. He tugged nervously at his mustaches.

"I trust," he said anxiously, "that my zeal to obey my lord's commands—"

"Be at ease, my son. I shall report to the duke that you have in all things punctually obeyed the orders you had from him."

The governor bowed.

"My thanks, good father. If you would see the duchess, she lodges in the north tower."

"And the prisoner?"

"In a cell of that same tower, all of which is assigned to her Grace."

"In what force did the duchess come to Tours?"

"Four knights and twenty men-at-arms."

Cercamon reflected.

"Then, with your permission, I will see the prisoner first. After which—if I may have a chamber as close as possible to the north tower, and a trusty man to attend me, who will not speak of what he sees?"

Sir Marc smiled a puzzled smile.

"You shall have my own squire. He can neither read nor write, and he is by nature a silent man. Ho! Bruyn!"

A short, stocky soldier entered, very quietly. He was mailed, but bare-headed, and a shock of black hair framed his square, swarthy face.

"THIS PRIEST," the governor explained, "has come on an errand for the duke. He is to come and go as he likes, and to command your services at all times, in all things. Understood?"

The soldier fixed his keen eyes on Cercamon and nodded. The troubadour, with a gesture of benediction, commanded to be led to the dungeons of the tower. But in the doorway he turned.

"It may chance, Sir Marc," he said meaningly, "that I shall need to issue certain commands which it would be best you did not know of, that you may disavow them if any question you. I shall issue them in your name, and expect to be obeyed; but, being ignorant of them, you may deny them afterward with a clear conscience."

The governor stared after his broad back in uncomprehending astonishment.

"A strange priest, that!" he muttered. "Yet his letters—"

Cercamon's own thoughts raced as he followed the squire Bruyn across the wide, rough-paved bailey. Pierre's letter to Sir Marc—there was foul play there! But how? The governor was clearly innocent. It was unthinkable that the duke had betrayed Pierre. Had he given him a *lettre de cachet*, it would account for Pierre's fate—but Henry would never have done such a deed. Nor, had he done so, would the duke have given Cercamon such plenary power to investigate. Somehow, after the letter had left the duke's hands, it must have been tampered with. But by whom? Gerald, the clerk, was surely honest. Cercamon gave the problem up, yet he praised the Saints that he had written with his own hand the authorization Henry had given him, seen the duke sign and seal it and taken it at once from his master's hands. Cercamon suspected no one; but he let no third hand mingle in his affairs if he could help it.

He had not expected to find Pierre lightly enough guarded to warrant a bold attempt at rescue. Descending to the crypt in Bruyn's wake, he was confronted, at the foot of the stair, by a half-dozen soldiers, armed to the teeth. Behind, and a little to one side, stood Hugo D'Orbec.

Cercamon was not surprized. He had been sure, before leaving Chinon, that any harm which might have overtaken Pierre was of this man's contriving. Nor did he flatter himself that D'Orbec would be easy to outwit. He could not show the Norman his letter from the duke—such a course would at once result in an open breach between Aliénor and his master.

He was glad that the semi-darkness of the crypt aided his disguise. Adjusting his cowl the better to conceal his eyes, he asked in a deep voice:

"Your leave to see the prisoner, my son!"

The Norman pointed to the row of cells.

"He is there, father," he smiled, "but I do not think you will see him. The duchess has ordered that he be allowed to speak with none."

"But surely spiritual consolation—"

D'Orbec shook his head, with unconcealed delight.

"He is to die without absolution and without the sacrament."

Cercamon gasped, in consternation at the brutality that would condemn a man to perish with all his sins on his head. D'Orbec naturally interpreted his emotion as that natural to a priest outraged in his most sacred feelings.

"It is not by my order, father," he explained, "but by her Grace's. Not that I—"

Cercamon nodded, and withdrew up the stair, the governor's squire keeping pace with him in utter silence. The troubadour had noted one thing that meant much: Four of D'Orbec's men were his own vassals, men Cercamon had seen in Chinon. The other two wore the livery of Aquitaine. D'Orbec was, then, definitely in Aliénor's service and doubtless high in her favor. The situation was bad indeed; even if a plan could be contrived, the Norman would die rather than let his enemy slip from his hands. What must be done could be done only through Aliénor herself; and knowing her, Cercamon had scant hope.

"Where is my chamber?" he questioned.

The silent Bruyn halted him at the landing, which gave on

a corridor running west from the tower, and pointed to the left; then held up three fingers.

"The third room west of the tower?" Cercamon asked, and the other nodded.

"And where does the duchess lodge?"

The squire turned as if to lead him up the second flight of the winding stair; but Cercamon held him back.

"Nay, it is as well you should not be seen with me near her quarters. As guide to a priest you are not an object of suspicion, but as guide to—Take these!"

He whipped off his cassock, and stood there in full mail; then, stripping away belt and sword, he placed the whole in the squire's hands.

"Hide them under your cloak!" he commanded. "Take them to my chamber, and hide them there. It will be enough to tell me how I may reach her Grace."

Bruyn rolled astonished eyes at him, and spoke in the swift, curt manner of a taciturn man:

"The next landing. To your right—the second door."

"Good. Now go—and wait in my chamber till I come."

The man went swiftly, and as swiftly Cercamon climbed the stair. Emerging on a broad corridor, he found himself halted by three men-at-arms on duty at the landing.

"Governor's orders!" he barked at them, praying that none of them had been in Aliénor's service long enough to remember the days when he had sung in her court.

They passed him through, and he strode to the second door, at which stood a brace of sharp-featured Gascons, none too busy with their watch to bandy jests with a pretty maid-of-honor. They sprang to bar his way just as an officer clattered up the stair and demanded entrance. The men-at-arms parted to let the officer by, and Cercamon leaped in at his heels.

He closed the door behind him, set his back against it, and smiled into the astonished officer's face. He trusted his cast-off disguise was still a secret. A monk had stood on the landing below; and now a courtier in armor, weaponless and so not dangerous, stood, debonair and self-reliant, in the midst of an angry group.

The officer fronted him, hand on sword, while the Gascon guards pushed at the door. A red-faced clerk bustled up, protesting:

"You must knock! None enters her Grace's lodging unknown and unannounced! Such insolence—"

Cercamon, ignoring the knight, turned his blue-green eyes on the clerk. Cold and arrogant, he carried an air of authority that brooked no denial. The clerk cowered, used as he was to be bullied by men of rank; but he stood his ground, and the knight eased out his sword. The clerk edged over to a door giving on an inner room, and set his back against it. Two ladies-in-waiting directed shocked and curious glances at the intruder.

C E R C A M O N B O W E D ironically, his long locks brushing the officer's face.

"I am a guest," he said with a ripple of laughter, "whom her Grace will receive with joy. Say to her that Cercamon the troubadour craves an audience."

At the name of one whom all France knew for the duchess's enemy, the clerk paled, and one of the ladies uttered a little scream. The officer gently set his point to Cercamon's breast and stood waiting. But the younger of the two women, readier of wit, darted to the clerk's side.

"Open the door, Master Estienne!" she cried. "Nay, open, fool! And do you, Sire Golfier, sheath your weapon. Her Grace will indeed bless the day that brings her such a guest!"

The clerk turned to fumble at the latch; but the sprightly lady thrust him aside and flung the door open wide. Then, turning to let her dark eyes rest mockingly on Cercamon, she curtsied to the very floor, and cried in a ringing voice:

"My lady! An audience—for Cercamon!"

A cry came from the inner room. With a clank of steel, two

armed guards burst into the antechamber and laid hands on the troubadour's shoulders, while the knight Golfier slipped nimbly behind him. Between them he advanced, helpless, but very much at his ease, into the presence of the woman who had once put a price on his head.

He bowed before her as gallantly as the clutch of his captors permitted.

"My eyes have been denied the sight of perfect beauty since I left your service, my lady," he said, with a conviction that drove the anger from Aliénor's eyes. "Now they are blessed again. You inspire me to a song that men will sing when I have become dust."

The duchess swept him a low courtesy.

"Loose him, *messires!*" she commanded. "There is neither purpose nor wisdom in holding captive a man unarmed—whose master's anger is more perilous than many swords."

"Your Grace is magnanimous as ever," the troubadour smiled. She felt the mockery, and swept him with a swift, challenging glance.

"Why not? I know full well it were dangerous to lay hands on you. You are Henry Plantagenet's man; I am in his territories. There is no man in his realm whom he values as highly as he does you. You knew I should not dare harm you, or you would not have placed yourself in my power. Is it not so?"

"Even so, your Grace. It is true that my master knows I am here, and expects me back—soon. Moreover, I have taken certain precautions with respect to the governor, who would be likely to search for me if I do not return to him within the hour. I do not trust myself rashly in my enemies' hands."

Aliénor bit her lip.

"Have you come merely to remind me that we are enemies, sir?"

Cercamon smiled winningly.

"Not so, madame. The enmity between us has been my misfortune, not yours. I come to atone for my old offense against you—to give your Grace a great gift."

Aliénor's fine blue eyes widened to the full.

"What gift can you give me—and—on what terms?"

Cercamon laughed aloud. It was pleasant to fence with this woman, now that his favor with Duke Henry made the pleasure a safe one. Had she not feared the duke and desired to please him, Cercamon would as soon have trusted himself with a viper as with Aliénor.

"You have a prisoner," he answered easily, "whom I would ransom."

Aliénor turned one shapely shoulder on him, and spoke with the guards.

"Leave us alone!" she commanded. "Do ye also depart, ye women!"

One of the soldiers protested:

"Your Grace is not safe with this man—"

Aliénor stamped one tiny, satin-shod foot.

"Be off!" she cried. "Think you I stand in any danger from a troubadour and gallant gentleman?"

Sullenly the guards withdrew, the women after them; and long were the glances the ladies-in-waiting cast in Cercamon's direction as they left the room.

"I thank your Grace," Cercamon said softly, "for that title of gentleman, which my birth scarce deserves."

The duchess smiled enchantingly.

"You are a gentleman by nature, which is better than the nobility of birth. Being a queen has taught me much, and not all of it pleasant—But you say I have a prisoner?"

"So I am told, your Grace. One who is my friend." He did not smile now; his eyes were grave, but full of confidence.

Aliénor nodded, tapping thoughtfully with her slipper.

"You mean?" she parried.

"Pierre Faidit. You mean to have him hanged tomorrow."

Aliénor turned her eyes to his, but he could read nothing in them.

"You are come, then," she spoke with forced calmness, "to say to me that Henry of Normandy, your master and Pierre's, demands his release? Yet the duke, in a letter signed with his own hand, gave Pierre to me!"

Cercamon noted the thin line of her lips, and understood that she would never give Pierre up alive. He had scarce hoped a more favorable outcome of his interview. He must seem to yield to her, if he would find a way to outwit her purpose.

"I think that letter was forged," he said calmly, "and I think you know it. But in any case my lord does not demand his release. Indeed, he bade me do nothing that would hazard his—friendship for you."

Startled out of her calm, Aliénor confirmed his suspicions of the letter.

"He knows I have Pierre, then?" she exclaimed. "And he will not force me to surrender him?"

"He suspects you have him, and prefers to do nothing that will displease your Grace. For my part, Pierre is my friend—-but the duke is my lord. Even to save my friend I would hesitate to use the duke's name for a purpose that would cost him your—"

Aliénor laughed, a most musical laugh, like the song of a bird.

"My friendship, I believe you said. Ah well, troubadour, there is no need of concealment between us. We have been foes too long for that. Henry would save his servant from me if he could, but prefers not to risk my displeasure by demanding him, lest I refuse his offer of marriage. Is not that it?

"That is my meaning."

"And you—you are shrewd, Cercamon, but you do not deceive me. I warrant you have come with full power from the duke to do whatever may be necessary for Pierre's freedom, even at the cost of my—friendship; but you and Henry are both resolved to keep both your friend Pierre and my consent to this marriage. Bah! I can read you. You are not the man to betray a friend; nor is Henry that kind of master. I should care little for him if he were. You have come here with a plan—a clever trick. Tell me—what is it?"

"What trick would avail against one who can so shrewdly read men's minds?" Cercamon evaded. "Have I not said that I come with a gift—a great gift—to give in ransom for Pierre?"

This time Aliénor laughed scornfully.

"What gift have you that can buy my revenge? What can you, a troubadour, offer the mistress of the richest provinces in France?"

"Something that not all your wealth can buy, lady. Safety!"

THE DUCHESS sprang to her feet, her chiseled nostrils dilated.

"Safety? Ah, I understand! I had scarce left Paris, but three days freed from him who had been my husband, when Thibault of Champagne sent horsemen to seize me. Now that I am free to marry again, every noble in France covets my lands—ay, my lands, not my beauty! I escaped from Thibault and sought refuge here. Who seeks me now? Am I not safe in Tours, surrounded by Henry's garrisons?"

"You are not safe here, nor anywhere but in your own lands," Cercamon replied meaningly. "As you say, every great lord in France desires your lands and your beauty, and will hazard all to win them. It chances that I know—and for a price, will tell—the danger that threatens you. Unless you yield what I ask, you will be carried off—ay, from Tours itself—to become the wife of a man without lands, almost without title. Your Grace knows—"

Aliénor eyes blazed.

"Ay, I know! All France will laugh if I, who have been Queen of France, am forced into a marriage with one who can bring me neither lands nor coronet! Tell me—who threatens me? How may I escape? How know I that you speak truth?"

"Your Grace has called me a gentleman," Cercamon re-torted. "On the honor of a gentleman, I speak truth. Now, touching your prisoner—"

She cut him off with an imperious gesture.

"Not that! Tell me, and I will give you your weight in gold; but for no price on earth—no, not to save my life, would I give up my vengeance on Pierre of the Sword! Your own offense is as nothing beside his. It was he whose accusations cost me the crown, cost me the respect of men, made me a byword for hissing throughout France! By my soul, he shall hang for it!"

"His accusations—" Cercamon began.

"Were true? Ay, what if they were? Did he injure me the less for that? Ask not for his life—I would not give it for my hope of heaven!"

Cercamon's head bowed, his face dark with despair.

"I have done what I could," he said heavily. "You will bear witness to that. The knowledge I possess may still be yours for a lesser price. If you will not forego your revenge, at least mit-igate it. I have been told you have denied Pierre a priest. Is it not enough to hang him, without sending him to—with all his sins unshriven on his head? Grant him the last ministrations of the church, and I will tell you the danger in which you stand. It is not yet too late to avert it, though time presses."

Aliénor pondered, her lips twitching with her emotion. At last she smiled, a hard, bitter smile.

"He shall have a priest," she agreed. "But you are a shrewd man, famous for your skill in snatching your desire from the very jaws of death. I will trust no priest you furnish. Pierre shall be shriven by my own chaplain; and I think you will find him no easier to move than me."

"It is enough, your Grace. I have your word?"

"Not my word only, which I have been known to break." She said this frankly, with a dazzling flash of her blue eyes. "Not my word only, but my oath by the Five Wounds, which I dare not break. But lest you hope to effect a rescue, the priest shall not go to him till one hour before he dies."

Cercamon bowed.

"Now for my part of the bargain, my lady. If you do not leave this city very soon, you will fall into the hands of Geoffrey of Anjou!"

The duchess started.

"Geoffrey? That boy? The duke's brother?"

"Ay, that boy. He is desperate with the harsh treatment—well deserved though it be—that Henry has given him. Neither lands nor men—not even money—can he get from the duke. But there are those who follow him, in the hope that they can overthrow Henry and make Geoffrey duke in his stead. Our turbulent barons know well that the boy would make an easier ruler than his stern brother. Therefore I bid you flee from Tours as fast as you may. Geoffrey has told me just enough to make me sure he plans to seize you, and make himself great with your inheritance. How would you fare then, the enforced bride of a penniless, landless lad? How greatly would you regret the folly that deprived you of all marriage to Henry would bring you. For Henry is not only lord of all the Northwest—he will one day be King of England!"

Aliénor's little hands were clenched; but the calculating lines of her forehead showed she was thinking desperately.

"You know he will come soon?" she questioned. "Surely he can not find men enough to storm Tours?"

"I do not know how swiftly he will come—but, having betrayed his plan to me without winning my help, he will strike very soon, for fear I will reveal his secret. He dares not wait long, lest Henry learn of it. If he does as I should do in his place, he will slip quietly out of Chinon with such men as he can trust, gather his garrisons from Loudun and Mirebeau and ride at once for Tours. There are many in Touraine who will join him once his banner is raised. He may be on his way hither now— and with a force that the city can not resist; and he has certainly friends within the walls. Unless he is a fool, he has every chance to win. I myself could devise a dozen plans for snatching you from the very presence of the governor."

He meant this to frighten her; and he saw that he had succeeded.

"Then—I must go tonight!"

"I think so, my lady. And go warily, lest he ambush you on the road to Poitiers."

Aliénor's eyes were troubled.

"For this great service I thank you, troubadour. You have given me much, and have received little in return. Your friend shall have his priest. Now go, for I have much to do if I am to ride tonight!"

But Cercamon stood motionless, till Aliénor turned on him impatiently.

"Pardon, my lady. I would feel safer if I heard you command your chaplain to attend Pierre."

"Ha! True! If I ride tonight, Pierre must hang tonight, lest I be cheated of my revenge."

She clapped her hands, and her women hurried into the room.

"Fetch Father Ambrose!"

Cercamon waited stolidly till the priest appeared: a short, pursy man, black-gowned, with a square, hard-lined face. In his eyes burned the flame of the zealot, pure of heart, inflexible of purpose. To him Aliénor gave her signet ring, with the command that he shrive the prisoner within the hour, and transmit her order that he be hanged as soon as shriven.

"I commend your altered purpose, my daughter!"

The priest spoke in pure Gascon, and Cercamon's heart warmed to him, remembering his own ragged boyhood in Gascony. Hastening to his chamber, he found the taciturn Bruyn waiting with curious eyes. From him Cercamon took his short sword, and girded it on.

"Now, my lad, I have orders for you!" he spoke briskly. "You know me for Henry's man; perchance you know not I am Cercamon the troubadour."

Bruyn's face lighted. He had heard of Cercamon—as who in France had not?—and was ready enough to serve one so famous.

"WHAT I bid you do will peril your soul and mine, yet not so much but that we may have absolution. If you disobey, I will see to it that your head parts company with your shoulders. Do you understand?"

It needed not the fire in Cercamon's blue-green eyes to win the squire's eager nod. He knew the repute of the troubadour's sword-arm.

"It will comfort you to know that you stand to win the duke's favor and my friendship—and mayhap much gold. You are to lie in wait in the passage just above the door to the crypt, and seize the duchess's confessor. Take him swiftly, lest he cry out. Bind and gag him if you will; it will make less trouble. Hide him so securely that none can find him, and do not set him free till I have left Tours. Bring me his gown and the ring he wears. If you fail—"

The squire's reticence melted under stress of fear and admiration.

"By the mass, good sir! I shall not fail!" he stammered.

"Then, my lad, I shall see to it that you have a brilliant future," Cercamon smiled meaningly. "But be sure he does not cry out!"

The squire vanished, and Cercamon sat down to wait the outcome of his plot. The minutes dragged interminably, till he could bide still no longer, and paced the floor with nervous strides. He reckoned it close to the allotted hour at the end of which Pierre must die, before his door stealthily opened and Bruyn glided in. Under his cloak was wadded the priest's black gown; between thumb and forefinger he held the carved ruby that was the duchess's signet.

"He is safely bestowed," he whispered, "in the chamber next this. I have the key. He made no noise. Saints, but I am afraid!"

"No need, now I have these." Cercamon compared the priest's gown with that of the monk of St. Martin in which he had come to Tours, and smiled faintly. The gray habit of St. Martin would not serve him now. He put on the cassock of Father Ambrose and strode to the door.

"Follow me. When I descend into the crypt, do you stand by the door. If you hear sounds of fight, stand fast, and refuse to pass any who would go down to interfere. Kill if you must, but pass no one—not even the duchess. Say the governor forbids it."

"But if the governor himself—"

"He lodges at the other end of the castle, and can not come till I have done what I came to do. But tell no man Cercamon is here. The duchess knows, but she will scarce speak of it. I will take the responsibility on my own head."

The two hastened down the corridor to the massive door of the crypt, Cercamon with his cowl pulled far down over his forehead. At the entrance he thrust Bruyn back, laid a finger to his lip, and descended the damp stone steps.

Sir Hugo D'Orbec and his six men-at-arms waited at the foot of the stair. Cercamon held up the duchess's signet, and D'Orbec nodded sullenly.

"It is her Grace's will that he be shriven," Cercamon spoke, in a tone as like the priest's as he could counterfeit. "When I have done with him, take him out and hang him."

Hugo hung back, muttering.

"He was to die without the sacrament," he protested. "Why trouble with such a dog?"

"Would you peril a mortal soul?" Cercamon asked sternly. "Her Grace has relented. Open swiftly now, for the duchess rides tonight, and her going must not be delayed. Already her horses wait at the gate."

The guards darted surprised glances at one another. Unwillingly D'Orbec fitted a heavy key in the clumsy lock and the door opened with a whine of rusty hinges. Then Cercamon had cause to rejoice at the feeble, flickering light cast by the two torches of the guard; for outside their radiance the huge crypt was a black well of darkness, and his own figure, between the Norman and his followers, threw D'Orbec into deep shadow. Letting the wide sleeve of his gown touch D'Orbec's arm, even as the door moved, Cercamon slid his fingers cunningly over the Norman's hilt—the hilt of the great sword stolen from Pierre. Then, thrusting hard with his free left hand, the troubadour flung his foe backward with all his strength, jerking at the hilt with his right. D'Orbec crashed back among his men, who raised a shout of alarm; but ere they could act, Cercamon was inside the cell, and thrust Pierre's sword into his hand.

"Out, comrade!" he cried. "Out, and strike for freedom!"

"Cercamon!" Pierre's voice rang trumpet-clear with joy and ardor. He leaped through the door even as the soldiers rushed to close it; and on the instant Cercamon, short sword out, was at his side with whirling blade.

D'Orbec, disarmed, hung back behind his men; and these were in no wise eager for fight. They were still confused; and strong habit made them slow to strike at a priest's gown. But Hugo, wresting a sword from one of his followers, flung himself forward.

"Fools!" he bellowed. "Did ye not hear? It is no priest, but Cercamon the troubadour! He has betrayed us! Cut him down!"

Still they hung back; for they knew it was not good to exchange blows with two such splendid swordsmen. Pierre and Cercamon took advantage of their hesitance to leap for the stair. They might have made it, had not Pierre had a debt to pay. He turned at the lowest step, his eyes on Hugo.

The Norman snarled at his men, who moved forward uncertainly.

"It is not good to slay a troubadour!" one shrilled. "They are under the protection of princes! The duke—"

One of the Aquitanians rushed forward with an oath.

"The duchess has put a price on this one!" he roared. "She will assure our safety. Slay!"

Under this urge the spearmen charged, and the two comrades awaited them, calm and confident. Pierre struck first, his great sword flashing in the torchlight like a monstrous gem. His first blow drove the helmet from D'Orbec's head. The Norman stepped back in sudden fear, but Pierre thrust home under the chin, and stretched his foe dead on the stones.

Four of the spearmen drove in doggedly, their long weapons at disadvantage between the columns of the crypt; while their two comrades held the torches for them to fight by. Pierre, bestriding the dead Hugo, made his whirling blade serve as weapon and shield both. While he fought for his life, Cercamon skipped, passed a plunging point and knocked the torch spinning from the hand of one of the light-bearers. As he did so, an Aquitanian drove his point full against the troubadour's breast. The fine mail checked its force, but the keen steel tore a gash over his breast-bone. Swinging short, Cercamon cut away the point of the spear. The soldier, raising his lopped shaft like a quarter staff, struck down at his adversary's chin; but Cercamon warded and countered with a slash that shore away the mail's arm. In that moment Pierre, having felled his second opponent, lashed at the second torchbearer. Darkness swallowed them.

"Pierre! The stair!" cried Cercamon, lunging out to keep his foemen clear. He sprang up three steps and waited, while the crash of wildly swinging blades, now against steel, now grating on the stone pillars, ground in his ears. There came the ring of blade on blade, a groan; and a great figure hurtled against him, bowling him over. He struggled up, shortening his sword for a thrust; but a voice rasped—

"It is I, comrade!"

The two stumbled up the stair together, the blind chase blundering after them, mail clanking as men slipped on the damp stone. Angry shouts lifted in wild cries for the guard. Then the fugitives struck the door and flung it outward, landing full sprawl in the lighted corridor.

As they picked themselves up, a third figure stood beside them. It was Bruyn.

"None came!" he growled. "Ye struck too fast. But—ha!"

As he cried out, the squire stepped nimbly round them and lashed out with his point at the stair-head. One of D'Orbec's men, caught in full stride, clattered headlong down the stair with his breast pierced through. The three who remained, Normans all, saw themselves matched and held back; but their yells echoed deafeningly down the corridor.

Other cries answered them from the inner court, where Aliénor's men-at-arms were housed. Swiftly Cercamon, catching his comrades each by an arm, hustled them up the second flight of stairs that led to the duchess's quarters. Seeing them apparently in flight again, the three Normans ventured forth and made a half-hearted move to follow. A dozen men-at-arms in the livery of Aquitaine, an officer at their head, rushed in from the court. The Normans burst into full cry, but Cercamon forestalled them. Raising his resonant singer's voice in a mighty shout that drowned their cries, he pointed straight at the astonished Normans.

"Ho, duchess's men!" he roared. "Slay these dogs! They plot treason against her Grace!"

The officer, already bewildered by the sight of the three weird figures on the stair—a priest with blood-stained sword, a huge man in leather jipoun who flourished a long, dripping blade, and the governor's squire—stood open-mouthed, waiting explanation.

"Father Ambrose!" he gasped, recognizing Cercamon's robes. Moreover, the troubadour had spoken in the Gascon tongue, in which he had heard the priest acknowledge Aliénor orders; and his southern accent lulled suspicion.

"These dogs would have murdered me because I heard their

plots!" he cried again. "They meant to carry off the duchess. Slay them! Take no prisoners!"

HE COUNTED shrewdly on the officer's having heard of Aliénor's purpose to ride forth that night, lest she be taken by Geoffrey. He knew her orders must already have gone forth that her men prepare for the march. Nor did he reckon amiss. With a howl of rage, the Aquitanians sprang on the astounded Normans. These, seeing no way to explain themselves ere the long spears should rend out their lives, burst into headlong flight down the corridor. After them raced the duchess's guard; and after the guard—but much more slowly—Cercamon led his comrades. When the chase had passed the door of his chamber, he drew the other two swiftly in.

"We are safe—for the moment!" he gasped. "Go you, Bruyn, and bid the governor, in the duke's name, admit none to this room. Let him place a guard over it—but say nothing to him of what you have seen!"

Bruyn vanished into the passage, heading swiftly for the Salle D'Armes. Cercamon sank onto his bed.

"By the mass, that was brisk!" he panted; and straightway he rolled upon his side and broke into silent laughter.

Pierre, casting down his bloody sword, reached for his friend's hand.

"I know not how you did it, lad, but I have you to thank that I am not this moment dangling in a noose!" he said earnestly.

Cercamon sat up, wiping his streaming eyes, still struggling with his laughter.

"When I think how the duchess—" he began; then he grew suddenly serious.

"When she learns how we have outwitted her," he said, "she may think I lied to her about Geoffrey, and remain here after all! Ay, and she may yet cajole the governor into searching every corner of the castle for you, Pierre!"

"Geoffrey?" echoed the bewildered Pierre.

"Ay—ask me not now." He tore off the robe of Father Ambrose, stuffed it under the bed and forced on Pierre the gray habit in which he himself had come to Tours.

"Wear that! You are sore in need of garments, and I have hose and mail. So! Now, if any comes, you are a blessed monk—if you can make yourself look smaller, and clothe your face in piety. And I am Cercamon again."

The tramp of mailed feet rang down the corridor; a heavy hand beat on the door.

"Who comes?" Cercamon challenged.

"I—Marc de St. Martin. My squire brought your message, father. Are you in peril? Here has been bloodshed and murder."

Cercamon winked at Pierre.

"Bruyn is a wise youth," he whispered. "He brought my commands as from the duke's messenger, and said nought of the troubadour."

He flung the door open. The governor, backed by a knot of mailed men, turned his eyes to the figure clad in the monk's robe, and stared in astonishment to see how its wearer had grown. Then he gazed at Cercamon, full-mailed and splashed with blood.

"Which of you is you, father?" he gasped; and Cercamon smiled.

"I am Cercamon the troubadour, Sir Marc," he answered. "I was the monk who came to you with the duke's letter. It were unwise for you to ask the name of this holy brother beside me. If you knew, you might deem yourself forced to act in a way that would displease either the duchess or the duke. But you spoke of bloodshed?"

"Three men have been slain under my roof by the duchess's guards," Sir Marc said anxiously. "The alarm was given too late to prevent the deed, and her Grace's officer spoke of a plot against her. Do you know of this?"

Cercamon nodded soberly.

"I know—but here again is a matter which I dare not speak

of now. It is most important that the duchess should not know where I and this pious brother lie hidden; but I have an urgent message for her, which I pray that you will take her in person."

He paused, and eyed the governor. It were hard to say whether Sir Marc or Pierre was the more perplexed.

"Say to her," he resumed, "that the warning I gave her is a true one, and that she will do well to flee for Poitiers with all speed. And tell her that the duke knows nothing of what has happened this night, but that I have no doubt of his approval. Assure her that Cercamon the troubadour swears all this upon his honor as a gentleman. And in the meantime—I think you said the duchess has four and twenty men with her?"

"Even so. But—"

"Good. Then, before you go to her, have two score of your staunchest men mounted on the swiftest horses in your stables, and hold them for me at the great gate."

"But—"

"This is the last order which I shall give you in the duke's name!" Cercamon spoke sternly. "As you fulfill it, so will I report on your loyalty to him!"

The governor drew himself up stiffly.

"It shall be done! My squire will bring you word." He marched off, angry, puzzled, but obedient.

Pierre looked at his friend with a whimsical smile.

"What means all this mystery?" he asked.

Swiftly Cercamon explained to him all that had happened since his arrival in Tours; explained, too, how he judged from Geoffrey's half made confession that the young count meant to seize Aliénor's person and lands for himself.

Pierre sat in deep thought for a space; then.

"If Geoffrey is not a fool," he said, "he will not seek her in Tours. You say that you told him you meant to ride hither on my account. Well, by this time—and before—he has learned that you are not in Chinon. He will have guessed that you might use his confidence to force Aliénor to give me up. He will assume, then, that the city is prepared for his coming, and will not dare attack it. He will also suspect that the duchess, frightened by your warning, will flee for her own city of Poitiers. Therefore he will ride, not hither, but straight for the Tours-Poitiers road, and set an ambush for her there."

Cercamon nodded.

"If he is not a fool, yes. I count on his doing so. Your head is clear as ever, my Pierre."

"And for this," Pierre hazarded, "you ordered the two score horse?"

"Even so. Will you ride with me?"

Pierre took his head in his hands.

"I have no love for this duchess," he spoke slowly, "nor do I think it will make for our lord's happiness to marry her. But his will is his will; and who am I to interfere with it? Since he wants her for himself, it is not meet that he should be cozened out of her by his own brother. I will ride with you."

They clasped hands. As they stood thus, they heard footsteps again in the corridor, and the governor's voice craved admission. Entering, he stood before them, the torches borne by his men-at-arms blown backward by the draught. He was smiling. Taking a light from a soldier, he closed the door, shutting the guards out.

"Your men are ready," he announced. "They know they are to ride under Cercamon. Before you go you will do me the honor to dine with me."

"If we may eat swiftly," Cercamon ventured.

"And thoroughly," Pierre amended. "My stomach has had little encouragement for a long ride."

"As it pleases you. The duchess is in a rage. She desires to depart swiftly, but has spent overmuch time searching the tower for her prisoner, Pierre Faidit, who it seems has escaped. She asked also—very angrily, I thought—about yourself, Cercamon. I informed her that you are my guest, and that, to my knowledge, I have not seen this Pierre since I had him cast into prison for her some days gone. Do you perchance know him, good father?"

"He is a friend of my own, and a worthy fellow," Pierre answered, suppressing his laughter. "I trust he is safe."

"That may be. I see you bear a sword, father. A strange weapon for a monk, and somewhat like this Pierre's. It may be you would care to see his armor, which is in my care?"

Pierre's eyes twinkled.

"I should like it of all things. I will even wear it a little, in his memory."

The Governor chuckled.

"Sometimes it is good not to know too much!" he said. "Come now and eat, ere your spearmen grow impatient."

WITH THE governor's aid the two comrades made their start well ahead of Aliénor, and for the greater part of the night pushed on with all speed to maintain their lead. This they had every hope of doing, for their horses were the pick of Tours. It was an hour past midnight ere they felt safe in taking a softer pace.

The white road, ghostly in the light of a faint moon, stretched straight ahead on its way to Poitiers, the first great city of Aliénor's realm. Faint smells of flowers and moist earth, borne on a light breeze, rose from the night-mantled valley of the Vienne, far southeast of its broader waters by Chinon. The night was still, save for the rattle of the riders' mail and the steady beat of their horses' hoofs.

"If Geoffrey means to set an ambush for her," hazarded Pierre, " 'twill be close to the border of Poitou, north of Poitiers. That is the nearest place to his own castle of Mirebeau, which is doubtless his base."

"So I think," Cercamon agreed. "Mirebeau is the only point where he could concentrate his men without Henry's knowledge. From now on we must go warily. Now I do not wish to seem too much against Geoffrey in this matter, seeing that what

I suspect of his purpose came to me from his own lips. It were best if you took over command."

He summoned his sergeants, and bade them take orders from Pierre, who at once picked out two of the best-mounted.

"Do ye ride ahead very vigilantly," he commanded, "and make sure that the way is clear. Spur back if ye see or hear men on the road between here and the border."

Certain now that they were well ahead of Aliénor, they resumed the march; but more slowly, that her cavalcade might draw sufficiently close for the purpose Cercamon and Pierre had contrived. The night waned, and the little breeze that blows just before dawn began to shred the fog from the river.

"What town is that which lies ahead?" asked Pierre, pointing to a few bunched lights to the south.

"No town, messire!" a trooper answered. " 'Tis the watch-fires on the keep at Chastellarault. We draw close to the Poitou march."

"And dawn is in the sky. Either we have made fools of ourselves, or Geoffrey will be somewhere close at hand. Halt!"

The horses stood, snorting and stamping in the gray chill. Impatient troopers swore under their breath, using the pause to tighten girths and see that their swords were loose in the scabbards.

"It will be soon, or not at all," Cercamon muttered.

The scouts came tearing back.

"There is a wood a mile ahead," they reported. "We heard the neigh of horses and the voices of men."

Pierre glanced at Cercamon.

"Had we ridden farther, they would have heard us also," he spoke. "Now do you two lads reconnoitre the rear!"

They waited again, restless and nervous, till word came that a troop of horse, riding fast, was approaching from the direction of Tours.

"Aliénor!" Pierre exclaimed. "Ride, lads, and make what noise ye can!"

They went on at a canter, calling back and forth loudly, rising high in the saddle to make their armor clash. The sky turned from gray to white, from white to pink. A little ahead lifted the dark tops of massed trees.

The edges of the wood winked suddenly with the glint of steel; and Pierre, pointing, lifted his voice in a great shout:

" 'Ware ambush! *À droite à l'épéron!*"

His column swung to the right, faced west, and sunk their spurs in their horses' sides. Even as they turned, the whole rim of the forest spouted horsemen. Cries rang out, lances dipped; and the rim of the sun, throbbing above the eastern horizon, set the mail-clad ranks ablaze.

The men of Tours had no more than a half-mile lead, and their mounts were weary with the night's work; yet their burst of speed gave proof of the wisdom with which Sir Marc had picked them. They broke across the fields at a splendid pace, red nostrils aflame, clean limbs lifting fleetly. Turning in the saddle, Pierre glanced at their shouting, galloping pursuers, whose ragged front swept on, men crouched over their horses' necks. They rode without formation, still pelting hit-or-miss after their emergence from the broken ground of the forest.

"Nobles—noisy, and too proud to drill!" he mused. "With a boy for leader!"

A clear voice cried after the fugitives; but distance and the clank of mail drowned it to a thin wail. The chase drummed on over the dew-wet grass, swerving to avoid the marshy river-brink, melting into groves, sweeping out again into broad meadows. For a time the men of Tours gained; then, as the long night ride told on their weary beasts, they caught the flash of spears nearer, and heard the beat of hoofs closer behind. At last the pursuers slowly, steadily began to overhaul them.

Pierre pointed to a low hill just ahead, and gave a burst of sharp orders. His men checked their pace to a trot, a canter, a walk, and drew to a halt on its crest. There they shifted from column into line.

A joyful howl rose from the throats of their hunters. In a final flurry of speed the pursuit drew up at the foot of the hill, its stragglers streaming up in disorderly fringes. The morning sun, warm now and bright, touched the bunched horsemen into flame.

"To the rear!" Pierre hissed at Cercamon. "Yon is Geoffrey—you are helmetless, and he will know you!" Cercamon obeyed, and Pierre waited what was to come.

A slender figure in fine mail advanced from the clump of spears at the foot of the hill, while the two forces rested immobile, spears couched, waiting on a word to charge. Pierre, watching the single rider approach, estimated the hostile force at no less than three hundred.

The slender leader halted, and made an impatient gesture.

"Yield!" he shouted. "Surrender the duchess, or we grind you to pieces!"

Pierre smiled. The other's face was hidden in his helmet, but his voice was Geoffrey Plantagenet's.

"In whose name?" he demanded.

Geoffrey hesitated; then—

"Plantagenet!" he cried.

"You are Duke Henry's men?" Pierre asked calmly; and the other, furious to be thus questioned, flung back at him:

"Whose else? Do ye yield, or die?"

Pierre held up his naked sword—that sword like no other in France—so that the sun set the great ruby in its pommel burning.

"We also are Duke Henry's," he made answer. "You can have no quarrel with us!"

The young count's eyes fastened for a moment on the glowing jewel, then roved to Pierre's great height; and recognition shone in them.

"Pierre!" he gasped. "But you—you were—in Tours! And where is—"

He faltered, aware that his errand was one he could scarce confess to his brother's trusted servant.

"I was in Tours," Pierre answered easily, "but now you see me here, on the duke's business. How can I serve you, my lord? And who is this duchess of whom you speak?"

But Geoffrey was only a boy; his patience broke.

"*Peste!* Do you mock me, Pierre? Before ——, I could stamp you to dust, if it pleased me!"

Pierre coaxed his horse forward, step by step, and halted within arm's reach of Geoffrey. He flashed a glance past the angry lad, to the massed spears that waited within the space of a javelin-cast. He slid his sword into its scabbard.

"My sword is now sheathed," he said. "I am a peaceful man. But I can draw fast, my lord. It is not for you to interfere with the duke's affairs. Have I your word to let us go unscathed?"

Geoffrey's men swayed a little forward behind him, and gripped their spears so that the points quivered. But Geoffrey knew Pierre. One look into the hard, dark eyes that were all he could see of the steel-circled face; one glance at the sinewy hand that rested lightly on the jeweled hilt, and he cried angrily over his shoulder—

"Fall back, men of Anjou!"

As they retired, he answered, sullenly—

"You have my word, Pierre."

"That is good, lord count. Now I think your business here is brought to an end. For while ye have chased us so far from the highway, the Duchess Aliénor has safely passed the border into her own land. We have saved you from a deed that would have done you great harm."

Geoffrey turned his back.

"About!" he cried, in a voice thick with rage. As his men wheeled, he pointed a trembling hand toward the distant Poitiers road.

"Ride, while there may be time!"

So the knights of Anjou and their men-at-arms galloped back, in a last, hopeless attempt to overtake their quarry. But they of Tours laughed, knowing the chase vain.

Cercamon returned to his friend.

"And now?" he asked.

"Back to Tours," Pierre answered gravely, "with these borrowed spears. And there our ways part for a while. You must go to Henry, and account for these two days. They have been good days, lad, and I shall not forget them. I must bide in Tours, where I shall be safe—now. But there will be another spring, when the wind blows fair for England; and there we shall meet again."

Cercamon seized his hand.

"Ay, we shall meet, under the duke's banner!"

"Nay!" Pierre cried, his eyes shining. "Under the king's!"

CORRESPONDENCE

Now here is a letter from one of our writers' brigade, setting forth his troubles, and mine, and maybe yours. I persuaded him to change his decision and let me pass the problem on to you. Meanwhile I've made two suggestions—that he use the woman-element, though in minor degree, in his tales of medieval France and that he also give us some more stories of the vikings, among whom the love-element played no such vital part.

Berkeley, California.

It's two years and a half since my first story of old France went to you. During that time I have sent you—if my count is right—eight stories with that setting—five clustering about Faidit and three about Cercamon. I don't believe you guess how much downright labor went to the making of those stories; and most of the labor was expended on a single question—how on earth to contrive a plot for a story which, though set in medieval France, should contain no love-element.

I'M NOT asking, and don't want, any preferential treatment. The readers of *Adventure* have expressed themselves clearly to the effect that they don't want love-stories, and the magazine has quite properly shaped its policy to suit what its readers want. That's good business and good judgment. Your attitude on that matter is quite just, and none would endorse it more cordially than I. As a fair man, you can't permit one author more latitude than another, and a decent author wouldn't ask it. You have, to be sure, stated in Camp-Fire that occasionally, when a story is exceptionally interesting and well done, you may publish it even though it has a love-element; and I am with you strongly both on your attitude there and on the manner in which it is carried out in actual practise. Nor would I ask any extension—least of all on my own behalf—of the latitude already shown.

But in view of your question concerning my stories, I want to let you know just what my difficulties are, and what I propose to do about them. It's the most difficult thing I ever tackled to write a story set in medieval France without a love-element. I've done it in eight stories, and almost busted myself doing it. But though I've tried again and again to work out plots for stories of old France during this year, both for the *Faidit* novel and for shorts, I've not been able to dope out a single acceptable plot. I don't believe the *Faidit* novel as I've at last shaped it would suit you. Stories of *this kind* simply won't be written without some love-element—not necessarily much, but some. I might be able to hammer out a few in the course of a long time, but the eight already published seem to have exhausted my ingenuity so far.

THE REASON is this: I'm somewhat saturated with the history of medieval Europe, and naturally it's hard for me to get away from historic fact when I write stories. Now as a matter of cold, sober history, the Frenchman living at any time between 1080 and 1500 gave most of his waking thoughts to the subject of love. Medieval France made a cult of love; the troubadours and trouvères were its high priests, and every man of any social status outside of the priesthood was a worshiper. Every aspect of love was discussed, formulated, put into practise. France set the pace, and all the world followed. The reason Aliénor of Aquitaine exercised such a tremendous influence on history was that all the western world knew of her as the woman whom troubadours everywhere had hailed as Queen of Love; at one time or another almost every great noble of France aspired to her hand and shaped his policy according. Every medieval court was a court of love; the whole conception and institution of chivalry had its roots in the doctrine of courtly love. Almost all medieval non-religious literature was a literature of love: even the Nibelun-genlied is drenched with ideas of courtly love derived from the French troubadours. It was the love-poets who came to England in Aliénor's train who, more than any other single force, changed the character of England's civilization from a rough and semi-barbaric feudalism to the courtly, polished thing it had become by Chaucer's time. The Crusades themselves were the outgrowth of an idealism determined by the ideas of courtly love quite as much as by religious fervor. This isn't just my view; it's historic fact. Every medieval gentleman—however much of his time he spent in hunting or war— was occupied in his thoughts more with love than with any other one thing. Froissart himself, in his own lifetime, was known not as the chronicler of wars and statecraft but as a poet of love. The middle ages simply couldn't get away from love, and didn't want to.

I'VE SHAVED historic truth pretty fine—come mighty near to misrepresenting it—in my *Faidit* and *Cercamon* stories, just because I've left out the love-element. Imagine any real troubadour knocking about without any love-affairs, as I've made *Cercamon* do. Imagine such a soldier as *Pierre Faidit* fighting his way through life, in contact with courts, without falling in love. And when the poet or soldier of the middle ages fell in love (and they always did) they made love the mainspring of their acts; in the thick of battle their courage was sustained by it. The unity of France in the reign of Louis VII was disrupted by the quarrels of two princes over the love of a woman; it was in the first instance a love-affair that set Richard against Iris father, Henry II; England became an empire with French possessions that led up to the Hundred Years' War—simply because Henry Plantagenet fell in love with the divorced wife of Louis VII.

Now the point of all this is that one can't leave love out of stories of medieval France without distorting history past all recognition. "Hamlet" without *Hamlet* isn't a patch on the middle ages without love. And when I sit down to work out a story of medieval France that shall be devoid of a love-interest, I simply can't get away from the fact that cutting out love cuts out the motivation for almost any conceivable plot a story of this period could have. To be sure, there were events and situations in the middle ages in which women did not figure; but they were mighty few in comparison with those which women and love played a big part; and when one tries to use loveless situations as the basis for a medieval tale, he runs the great risk of turning out what is merely a cross-section of history—a fact-article—instead of a story. "Complication" meant *love* in the middle ages.

NOW WHAT am I going to do about this? I had thought of asking you to print this letter in Camp-Fire, and to ask for an expression of opinion from the readers about the advisability of permitting a moderate use of the love-element in medieval stories—about as much use of it as Doyle makes in "The White Company"; but I've decided against any such request. It wouldn't be fair to the men who write modern stories, and it would also reopen the whole question of the love-element, against which the readers have already decided. That issue is settled, and I haven't any right to reopen it.

So far as I can see, my only possible course is to recognize frankly that the veto on the love-clement must curtail my production. I'll try my best to write stories—as good ones as I can—on medieval France without that element. I probably sha'n't succeed very often; the, number of stories I shall be able to send you will probably therefore be few and somewhat far between. I'll send them to you whenever I can write them, and shall simply have to apologize for their fewness. I'll try to make them extra good.—ARTHUR G. BRODEUR.

Fair enough, isn't it? And even the most hardened wretches among us probably can, for the sake of his stories as a whole, manage to stand what woman-interest Mr. Brodeur is compelled to put into them for the sake of trueness to the times and their conditions.

www.ingramcontent.com/pod-product-compliance
Lightning Source LLC
Chambersburg PA
CBHW051054030726
47504CB00006B/1626